WHITNEY

RUSSELL C. CONNOR

Visit us online at
DARKFILAMENT.COM

Contact the author at
facebook.com/russellcconnor
Or follow on Twitter @russellcconnor

Cover Art by SaberCore23 Artwork Studio
For commissions, visit sabercore23art.com

ISBN:
978-1-952968-09-9

Third Edition: 2021

PRAISE FOR RUSSELL C. CONNOR'S WORK:

GOOD NEIGHBORS

"Connor's ability to richly develop each character and plot thread is fascinating even when the horror is reserved... the constricting pressure as the dread piles on makes this book hard to put down and even harder to go to sleep after reading. This is a great novel..."
-David J. Sharp, *Horror Underground*

SECOND UNIT

"Intricately plotted and vividly layered with suspense, emotional intensity and strategic violence."
-Michael Price, *Fort Worth Business Press*

"Drips with eeriness...an enjoyable book by a promising author."
-Kyle White, *The Harrow Fantasy and Horror Journal*

FINDING MISERY

"Major-league action, car chases, subterfuge, plot twists, with a smear of rough sex on top. Sublime."
-Arianne "Tex" Thompson, author of *Medicine for the Dead* and *One Night in Sixes*

THE JACKAL MAN

"Connor delivers a brisk, action-packed tale that explores the dark forests of the human--and inhuman--heart. Sure to thrill creature fans everywhere."
-Scott Nicholson, author of *They Hunger* and *The Red Church*

Also by Russell C. Connor

Novels
Race the Night*
The Jackal Man
Whitney
Finding Misery*
Sargasso*
Good Neighbors
Between
Predator

Collections
Howling Days*
Killing Time*

The Box Office of Terror Trilogy
Second Unit*
Director's Cut

The Dark Filament Ephemeris
Volume I: Through the Deep Forest
Volume II: On the Shores of Tay-ho
Volume III: Sands of the Prophet
Volume IV: The Halls of Moambati

eBook Format
Outside the Lines*
Dark World
Talent Scout
Endless
Mr. Buggins

*Indicates Dark Filament Ephemeris supplementary connection

For the DFWWW, Abbie, and all that jazz.

For the people of New Orleans, whose hardships in the wake of Katrina inspired so much of this book.

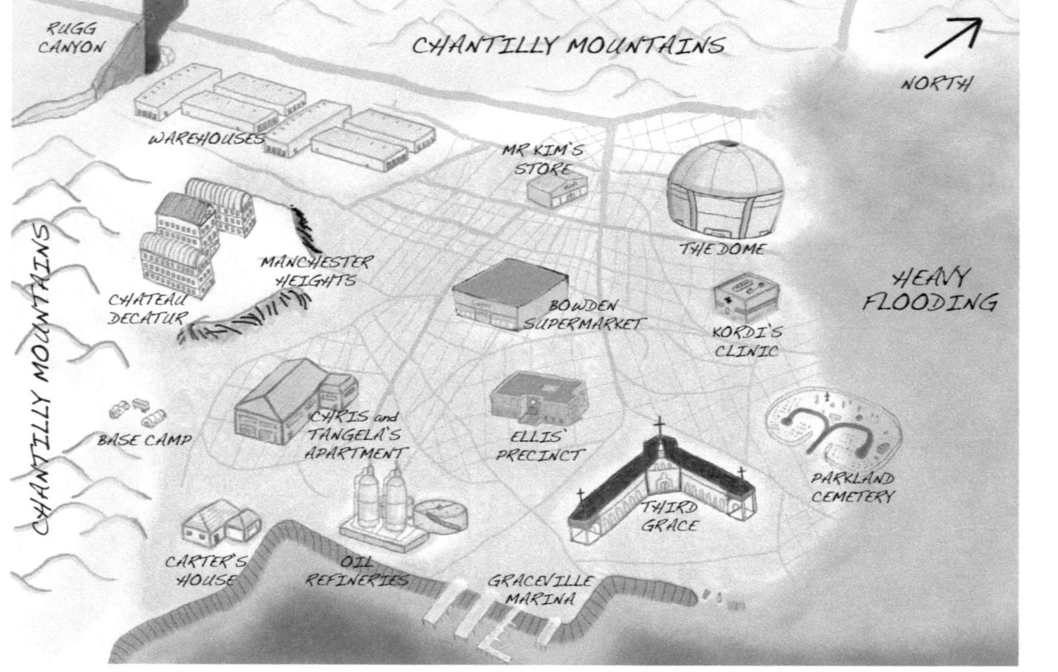

RUGG CANYON
CHANTILLY MOUNTAINS
NORTH
WAREHOUSES
MR KIM'S STORE
THE DOME
HEAVY FLOODING
CHANTILLY MOUNTAINS
MANCHESTER HEIGHTS
CHATEAU DECATUR
BOWDEN SUPERMARKET
KORDI'S CLINIC
BASE CAMP
CHRIS and TANGELA'S APARTMENT
ELLIS' PRECINCT
THIRD GRACE
PARKLAND CEMETERY
CARTER'S HOUSE
OIL REFINERIES
GRACEVILLE MARINA

TABLE OF CONTENTS

The creature swam.

It pushed into the warm currents of the Gulf, gliding on webbed feet that churned as mechanically as a metronome. The speed reduced it to no more than a green glimmer in the water.

Little in its head besides thoughts of feeding, feeding, always feeding. Even now, it swooped and dove, snatching fish from teeming schools and tearing them apart in a mouth overflowing with razor-sharp incisors. The claw-tipped appendages it used for this were close enough to hands to send any marine biologist into conniptions.

Each kill released a cloud of blood and viscera into the murky waters that every shark for a hundred miles could detect, but even the hungriest of them was deterred by the scent of the thing performing the slaughter. Their kind had faced this species again and again since the dawn of time, and they invariably came out on the losing end.

The creature's usual hunting ground lay deep in the abyssal belly of the Atlantic, beyond the last of the eastern seaboard's shipping lanes, but its current condition had outstripped its regular food sources. Hunger had forced it to creep closer—with timidity at first, and then with the assurance of the unopposed predator—to the dull wall of noise eternally reverberating from what it thought of only as Water's End.

Sated, the creature turned back, preparing to migrate home and sleep with its fellows.

That was where it ran into trouble.

It encountered resistance at the opening of the Gulf, a churning disturbance that lit up its array of delicate senses like flashing neon signs. It recognized the source: one of the destructive wind circles that scattered fish in droves.

The creature kicked hard and fast, a torpedo in the water, and attempted to slide by the pressure of the impending storm on the northern side of Cuba. Rough seas and shallow waters made the route dangerous. Normally it would ride out the violence beneath the surface…but there was more than just its life to consider.

Panic swept through its brain like brushfire.

No place to hide, no place to run.

No place…except shoreward, toward the land-dwelling beings with all their endless hammering and yammering. Perhaps it could find shelter in one of the bays or coves along Water's End. If the waves drove it out of the ocean, it could breathe air quite comfortably for short periods.

But it would have to feed.

Its belly would remain quiet only so long before driving it to berserker frenzy.

A sudden thought occurred to the creature: perhaps the land-dwellers themselves might serve in a pinch. It had never tasted their flesh before, but as long as it was meaty and filled with blood, they would suffice.

Humor, or as close as it could get to the concept, flashed briefly in its alien mind as it continued swimming.

PORT ALLEN

VERTIGO

"Are you seeing this storm potential?" Kirby asked, balancing the phone on his shoulder as he took his popcorn out of the microwave.

"Yes, doofus, we've been tracking that rotation since day before yesterday," Nielsen answered. Kirby could imagine him with the faux snakeskin heels of his wannabe-cowboy boots up on his desk in the fancy control room of the National Weather Service's Center for Environmental Prediction down in Miami. Kirby had met the man only once, at a convention in Anaheim, and he could say with certainty that Erik Nielsen was about as much a cowboy as he was an astronaut. "It's your move, by the way."

"And you guys aren't worried about it? I mean, this thing is shaping up to be an asskicking of biblical proportions." Kirby rechecked the data on Whitney it had taken the rickety printer in his office nearly twenty minutes to spit out, then sat down at the chessboard on his desk.

He, on the other hand, was at the Atlantic Meteorological Advisory in Brunswick, Massachusetts. The station, which routinely gave little more than local projections of winter storms for the northeastern states, was about the size of a spacious closet, manned by one person at any given time (said person paid by government stipend that made employment at McDonald's a viable career move), and outfitted with equipment that would've been obsolete during Carter's presidency. *Your tax dollars at work,* Kirby thought, as the last of the paper rattled off the printer. On the three-color monitor in front of him, the bright blue, rotating eye of Whitney glared forth.

"Fer chrissake, Kirby." Shuffling papers and a creaking chair as

Nielsen swung those so-green-they-were-almost-iridescent boots off the top of his desk in agitation. "Who cares, as long as that asskicking is being administered to our friendly neighbors in the good nation of Cuba, and whatever dolphins are stupid enough to get in Tropical Storm Whitney's way. Now, are you gonna play, or do you wanna get an early start worrying about next year's storms too?

"Oh…this is rich." Dawning pleasure spread across Kirby's face. The moment was savory enough to taste. "Knight to B7."

"What's rich? Bishop to E9."

"Queen to F2. You, uh…you haven't updated the world Doppler model in the last couple hours, have you?"

"Noooo." Hesitation in his smarmy voice for the first time. At this time of night, there was usually no need, not when they were all so sure Whitney would fade away into meteorological history. The depression had started out southeast of Cuba, turned into a mother-of-a-storm just before making landfall, and was already losing strength when predicted it would limp northward and die quietly over the mid-Atlantic. Just one of the many alphabetized storms every year most Americans paid no more attention to on the evening news than they did to the local PTA bake sale. "Queen to A7. Why?"

"Why don't you do that now? I'll wait. And rook to A1."

Nielsen didn't answer, didn't even comment on the devastating checkmate Kirby had just performed, but there was the click of keys as he followed the suggestion.

Wait for it, wait for it…

"Holy *shit*," Nielsen muttered, and Kirby thought he could've died happy right then and there. Imagine *him* getting the drop on the NWS all out here by his lonesome, and on what was sure to be one of the most destructive storms in U.S. history. "Where the hell did that come from?"

Kirby assumed he meant the new visitor from the north. "Sprang up from that pressure system in the Arctic and gained strength from the winds out of Canada. That little depression you see moving south is going to bounce this girl back our way as neat as a cue ball."

"But…but…when Whitney hits the system coming in behind it…"

"When that happens, my man, Tropical Storm Whitney is going

to become *Hurricane* Whitney in a big hurry. Based on my current trajectory models, it'll pick up about 20 times current wind velocity, gain mass like a pregnant woman, then head back north again, this time right up the middle of the Gulf. It'll be one massive ball of fury when it washes up somewhere along the Texas-Louisiana border. Sound familiar?"

"Katrina." He whispered the dreaded name of another meteorological bitch.

"That's right! Gimme an 'F,' gimme an 'I,' gimme a 'V,' gimme an 'E!' What's that spell? Category Five, baby!"

"Jesus…Jesus H Christ," Nielsen wheezed. "I mean, *fuck* Katrina. If those warm currents from the south don't let up, this thing is gonna make Katrina look like a goddamned drizzle. At this rate, it'll make landfall in…"

"Just under four days." The glee was gone from Kirby's voice. He suddenly felt ashamed at his flippancy. Not because people were almost surely going to die, but because this hurricane was going to be one mean SOB, it *was* going to make Katrina look like a drizzle, and he felt as disrespectful as if he'd just blasphemed in a quiet church.

"I have to go." Kirby could hear other voices calling out in the background, other meteorologists on the late shift just alerted by Nielsen. "I have to call FEMA, the President has to be notified immediately."

"Checkmate," Kirby said softly as the line disconnected in his ear. The baleful eye of Whitney stared at him without blinking.

WHITNEY -80:05

When the desk intercom buzzed in the Oval Office, the President of the United States brought an impatient fist down on it. "Is he here, Sherry?"

"Yes sir, but—"

"Don't 'but,' just send him in so I can get this over with." He cut off the conversation with another smack to the device and then swiveled in his chair, not bothering to smooth his hair or straighten his tie because, frankly, he had far more important things to do than meet with the weasely little Director of FEMA. But here it was a goddamn *election year*, and, with a timing that half made him believe the unholy Democrats were behind it, Mother Nature decided to see what a monster hurricane would do to his approval rating.

All anybody would remember when they stepped up to the polls in a few months was whether he had clothed and fed every last victim of Whitney with his own two hands. He didn't have the luxury of lame-duck-itis like Bush after Katrina, visiting the disaster site when convenient and smiling vacantly around at the destruction.

He had to be proactive, dammit, had to prepare himself, and unfortunately this meant sitting through a pre-briefing from that worm David Sinclair, before he and the Joint Chiefs got the full dog-and-pony show.

A knock came on the Oval Office door before it opened just enough for the head of FEMA to slouch through. The President suppressed a shudder at the sight of him. Short and froggish, eyes hidden behind lenses thick enough to see Mars, usually slick with nervous sweat. He came into the room dressed in a ragged tweed suit carrying a sheaf of papers, beady eyes darting right and left, leaving the door open behind him.

The President started to yell for him to close it, until it opened wider and another man entered the room behind Sinclair.

He had no idea who this one was. Mid-forties, tall and lean, packed with rolling muscle. His eyes were cool and confident, and a small scar corkscrewed left of his jaw in a rudimentary sideways question mark. He wore a black dress shirt, open at the throat to reveal a swatch of hairy chest, with the sleeves rolled up. The President's nostrils flared. This man looked ready to go club hopping rather than meeting with the leader of the free world in his own office, but that was the sort of disarray the President expected from any member of Sinclair's organization.

"Sinclair," he greeted, without standing. Mr. GQ gave no introduction, and the President shot him an eyebrow. "Have a seat."

"Th-thank you, sir." Sinclair glanced back at Black Shirt as though expecting him to come forward as well. When that didn't happen, he plopped into one of the chairs in front of the desk. The mystery man gave a knowing little smile, then turned his back and began to examine books on the far side of the room.

The President laced his fingers on the desk. "All right, just how the hell bad is this thing gonna be?"

Sinclair's eyes rolled in their sockets as he shuffled papers. He leaned forward to place a few graphs and satellite photos on the desktop, all of which meant squat to the President. "Well, it…uh… they're telling me it's definitely a Category Five, sir. It'll make landfall sometime around 7:30 on Thursday evening. Winds will, um, probably reach 150 miles an hour, which means we can expect significant structural damage. The storm surge alone is likely to be in excess of fifteen feet, which should cause flooding at sea level or below. It'll be…catastrophic."

"And just where is this heaping ball of catastrophe going to land? New Orleans? Galveston?"

Sinclair's brow wrinkled. "Well…b-both of them, sir. And everything in between. That entire section of the Gulf coast needs to be, um, evacuated. Which is impossible with the resources available and the time we have left."

"Good God." The President leaned back in his chair. Sinclair's unpleasantness as well as Black Shirt's presence (now leaning to watch the President's angelfish—Burr and Hamilton—in their aquarium) were all forgotten in the face of this news. What the director of FEMA was describing, in a nutshell, was the complete and total destruction of the southern seaboard on his watch. "Okay, we'll talk to the Joint Chiefs in an hour as planned, but I'll go ahead and get the National Guard scrambled and ready to deploy as soon we come up with target areas."

For the second time, Sinclair turned and glanced uncomfortably at Black Shirt. "Sir, I, uh, I was told, uh, that is, I don't know if that's…"

"You'll have to excuse Sinclair," Black Shirt spoke at last, sauntering over to the desk with a grin so shiny, it could only come from a politician. "I'm afraid I kept him mostly in the dark as to why I was accompanying him to this meeting. I just thought it might raise less suspicion if I rode in on his *desperately* out-of-fashion coattails."

"What are you talking about?" the President snapped. "Sinclair, who the hell is this man?"

Black Shirt reached the front of the desk beside the chair Sinclair sat in, and here something happened so fast the President could barely follow it. The man with the question mark scar flashed a hand in front of Sinclair, like a magician getting ready to yank a quarter from his nostril, and a puff of something white billowed into his chubby face. The director didn't even have time to protest; his eyeballs rolled back, the lids fluttered, closed, and then he slumped in his seat, the rear of his head thumping against the high chair back.

"Jesus!" The President scooted away from the desk before remembering security button was on its underside.

"Relax, he's just sleeping," Black Shirt said. Sinclair's chest rose and fell visibly. "We need to have some private time, you and me. Which reminds me, would you mind turning off the Presidential Archive in the bottom right drawer of your desk?" He grinned again, only now it wasn't so political; it was a shark-like expression that never touched his eyes and stretched that scar on his chin almost straight. "Oh, and feel free to press the squawker all you want if it makes you feel any better; it was turned off long before I ever set foot in here."

The President glared up at him, ran through a list of possible scenarios in his head including assassination and kidnapping, and rejected them. A piece to the puzzle was missing, and as he tried to figure out what it might be, he rolled forward and slid open the indicated drawer. The device that recorded all conversation in the Oval Office was active. He reached inside and switched it off, exercising his 'presidential prerogative.' "I don't need a button for the likes of you, son. I used to box in my younger days. Now tell me who you are before I come over there and take care of you myself."

Black Shirt waggled a finger at him. "A direct man. I like that. I guess that's why Aurora put you in office."

"A-Aurora?" The single word melted his demeanor. The President suddenly felt as pale and jittery as Sinclair usually looked.

"That's right." Black Shirt sank into the chair beside the now drooling FEMA director. "The name's Kyler, by the way. And don't look so serious. I'm not here to kill you. We play for the same team, your goals are my goals, blah blah blah. I'm just more of a first string player."

"What do you want?" the President asked again, only this time it was reverent.

'Kyler,' apparently deciding he was properly softened, finally got to the point. "One of the cities that Whitney is about to wash off the map is called Port Allen, Texas. You know it?"

"Can't say I do."

"Not surprised. There's not really much to it. About seventy miles northeast of Galveston, population of near 300,000, lots of oil refineries, fishing, modest economy, people run the usual gamut from rich to poor you find in coastal hubs. Pretty average, mostly invisible."

The President waited for Kyler to continue. He didn't resemble what he figured someone from Aurora would look like, but, hell, he'd never even been entirely convinced the agency existed.

He really only knew enough about them to be very, very scared.

"The thing about Port Allen is, it's going to be hit hard by this hurricane. *Real* hard. It's in a valley depression, most of it between seven and fifteen feet below sea level. A bowl, in other words. It has a rudimentary seawall that will fail under this kind of strain. The place is going to be hell on earth during and after Whitney. I need as many people as possible out before that happens, but the whole city is surrounded by shallow hill country and a fucking canyon, with two land routes in and out, which is going to make evacuation a real bitch."

"Why? What's going on there?"

Kyler let out a giggle. It was short and soft—almost under his breath—but it conjured gooseflesh across the President's arms and neck. "Tell me Mr. President, do the words Project Mercury ring any bells for you?"

"No. Should they?"

"Not if I've done my job."

"Plausible deniability?"

"More like a need-to-know basis."

"And do I need to know now?"

"Not really. The only thing you need to do is make sure the National Guard, or whoever you send to keep order in Port Allen, stays *out* of the city. Once they've established posts, they're to let people leave, but not enter. And once the storm begins, all access either way is revoked. At that point, anyone inside the city, be they civilian, Guard or otherwise, is…let's say, off limits. You are to withdraw your forces and turn complete control of the situation over to my team."

The President snorted. "Oh really? And just what am I supposed to tell the press and the refugees and the family members and anyone else that asks what's going on, huh? I'm up for reelection this year, I can't just—"

Kyler moved, gliding from his chair with ghostly speed and leaning across the desk to grab his collar. He hauled the President of the United States forward until their faces were inches apart.

"That doesn't concern you." Kyler giggled again, the crazed grin on his lips in direct contrast to the emptiness in his eyes. Looking into those murky pools, the President understood one very important fact: this man was insane. "If Aurora wants you in this office for another term, you'll be here. If they want you in a grave up at Arlington National…you'll be *there*. Most of the attention will be on the big cities, so when the truth needs to be told about what's going on in Port Allen, we'll decide what it is and give it to you."

Kyler released him and stood up, running a hand down his shirt, passing for normal once more. He headed for the door. "We'll be in touch," he said over his shoulder. "Just remember, when the wind starts blowing, not a single soul leaves that city. I have a few creative ideas in mind to assist with that."

He reached the door, stopped with his hand on the knob, then turned back and pointed at Sinclair slumped in his chair. "When he wakes up, he's gonna have one helluva headache. Tell him to eat a banana. You might want one yourself. You look pale."

With that, Kyler opened the door to the Oval Office and disappeared from the President's life.

WHITNEY -29:53

That dick UPS driver left the package by the mailbox.

This was the only thought in Carter Vance's head as he paced by the huge, double-paned bay window at the front of his house, repeating like a brainwashed cult mantra, edging out all other mental traffic. He stopped halfway through another trip to look outside, to see if this fact had somehow changed on its own since he last checked. Nope, thar she blew: a brown parcel sitting in the strip of grass outside the gate, too big to fit inside the mailbox. As tantalizing through the iron bars as a raw steak held in front of a starving lion.

Less than twenty yards from the front door of his home.

Might as well be the moon.

That prick, Carter thought, before realizing he was actually muttering aloud. "That...*asshole*. I don't know what circle of hell Dante reserved for negligent deliverymen, but I'm gonna make sure he ends up there."

He resumed pacing, this time craning his neck to keep the source of his agitation in constant view. If only Terrance, the old route driver, hadn't retired and paved the way for this little...this little...*cockbite* to begin delivering Carter's daily packages, this never would've happened. Terrance, God bless his patient, understanding soul, had known the routine—call at the gate, wait for it to trundle open, bring the boxes up the drive and into the glass alcove at the side of the house, then place them behind the airlock door until pressure equalized so Carter could get them. And he never griped, never complained, and never seemed as generally put-out and unfriendly as this intolerant...twenty-something...*nerf herder*, if you could excuse a Star-Warsian insult, because he was just too frustrated to think of any more on his own.

Or if Rosa hadn't taken the day off for her cousin's roommate's uncle's funeral, she would've been here to get it, and this crisis would be over. Or if he could only fool himself into believing the package in question was just the fifth season of "The Simpsons" on DVD he ordered from Amazon last week—instead of the latest specs on the Southerland project from the Houston office he knew it to truly be—he could at least get back to work and stop obsessing.

C'mon, cut the whiny bullshit, Cart. He recognized this sarcasm. It was the non-deluded part of his psyche that had been banished to a back corner of his brain sometime after college. He'd taken to calling it the Lucid. *You're not so far gone that you really, deep-in-your-heart believe there's any physical reason you can't go out there and get that package.*

"That's not the point," he argued aloud with himself. "I shouldn't *have* to."

Something about that sounded like a five-year-old stamping their foot in defiance of parental logic. He tore his eyes away from that package and stared to the left, down the road his house overlooked, to where Teague Street ended at the western section of the Port Allen city wharf. A snatch of the boardwalk was visible from here, then a stretch of sand, and the cool, emerald green Gulf beyond. He could still see the army of volunteers there, stacking sandbags to form a barrier against the coming fury of Whitney.

If anything, *this* should be eclipsing his delivery dilemma. He could hear the TV in the other room, preaching the same doom since Whitney's announcement three days ago, the brutal violence of the hurricane ripping across the ocean and the massive destruction, flooding and power outages predicted in its wake. It was a little hard to swallow, with the sun shining now and not a cloud in the sky, but he had no illusions about it staying that way. Evacuation of the city began two days ago at Mayor Edward's decree. Carter's neighbors, none of whom he'd ever met, had skedaddled already, leaving behind condos and beach houses like shed snake skins, windows boarded over, gates locked tight against looters.

Meaning that only he and yon witless volunteers were still stupid enough to stick around here...and even those brave souls would be gone by the time the storm made landfall at 7:30 PM tomorrow night.

A twinge of fear rattled somewhere deep in his guts like a shaken maraca.

No, he refused to rehash this. He'd made up his mind that he wasn't leaving (*couldn't leave*, he defended, *let's use the proper terminology, I* can't *leave*) so why spend the remaining time before the bitch blew into town stressing about her?

Because this is stupid, the Lucid argued in its languid tone. *You can leave, just like you can walk out there right now and get that package.*

That is...if you really wanted to.

Carter looked back at the delivery, sitting by itself next to the mailbox where it would stay until tomorrow morning, when Rosa promised she would return to bring him some supplies. Besides the fact that it would start raining long before then and ruin the contents, he needed those specs in hand today if he hoped to make his deadline before the hurricane.

He sighed and wiped a hand across his eyes. Might as well face it: he couldn't rest with that package sitting out there. The only thing worse than his extreme agora/germophobic complex was his obsessive-compulsive disorder, and his mind had clamped down around this with the tenacity of a pit bull.

He let his eyes wander the length of the driveway.

Twenty yards.

Front door to gate, and back again.

A sixty second trip, if he ran.

Carter's stomach performed a tightly executed barrel roll.

He crossed the room, past his massive computer center in the sunken living room and his 80-inch widescreen TV, to the house's only door. He keyed the code for opening the gate on an entry pad set into the wall.

On the opposite side of the door from the keypad hung two compact rebreather oxygen masks on steel pegs. These little gadgets consisted of a clear plastic cup with rubber seal that fit across both nose and mouth, a heavy-duty strap to hold it in place, and a thin, metal cylinder attached to the left side that lay across the cheek during operation. They looked rather cheap upon first inspection (Rosa, that Spanish comedienne extraordinaire, called them 'jock straps for the face') but they were, in fact, state-of-the-art and not easy to come by, requiring government permits to own and each costing somewhere in the neighborhood of three thousand dollars for their miniaturized filter technology. He picked up the one on the left, stretched the strap over his head, and positioned the cup over the lower half of his face. He flipped the tiny switch on the small unit under his left eye. The air tasted fresh and slightly metallic as he began to breathe.

He paced a little more, now with the mask on. He turned on one of his three iPods that housed his massive music collection, found some mood music—Green Hornet theme, thank you very much—and cranked it through his house-wide stereo system.

Finally, Carter reached out and put a hand on the pad that opened the inner airlock door and noticed the appendage was vibrating. He almost stopped there, but something steely inside him took over, relegating him to a bystander in his own body, and he watched as the hand pushed against the pad. The thick glass door swung open.

He knocked exactly four times on the jamb, as he did with any door—a superstition picked up sometime in the last six months, when he became certain that failure to do so would result in a cataclysmic separation of all the molecules in his body—and stepped through.

It swished shut behind him and sealed against the frame with a pneumatic *whoosh*. The air changer in the ceiling cycled. The entire house was built to his specifications. He often wondered how he would've indulged his growing phobias if not for his lucrative job that allowed him to not only work from home, but to turn that home into a clinically sterile fortress. Dr. Pellner, the psychiatrist he saw by video conference once a week, presented it a different way: Carter's dementias developed *because* he had the means to sustain them.

A soft chime sounded above him, indicating the airlock was now open to outside air. Disgusting air, air full of putrid infections and diseases by the thousands.

And he was now ready to step outside in it for the first time in more than eight years.

He hummed along to the muted music coming from inside the house, the rebreather distorting his already quavery voice. Carter pushed on the outer door and stepped onto his driveway.

A wave of vertigo hit him almost immediately, hard enough to make him swoon. Agoraphobia: the fear of open spaces. He'd once heard someone on TV call it 'a kind cousin to seasickness,' but there was nothing kind about his version. He was safe as long as he was inside, even windows didn't bother him, and he loved being able to see the ocean, which was the whole reason he'd moved here. But everything was so frakkin *big* out here, with no walls to hold it in, and a sky that stretched into cool, blue infinity. He glanced up only once and was stung by the surety he would fall into it, spinning forever without any point of reference, and then looked away so he didn't fill his mask with his still-digesting lunch.

The sun beat down on him in crushing waves, the air compressed. Carter stumbled a few steps up the driveway, realizing he must look like a mime doing an impression of an astronaut, or maybe an Antarctic explorer in jeans and a Blue October t-shirt, struggling to walk against an invisible wind. He fixed his eyes on the end of the driveway, but that twenty yards had multiplied into forty, a hundred, a thousand.

His chest hitched once. His breath disappeared. He clawed at the mask, helpless, frantic, not concerned with germs and filtered air now but desperate only for air of any sort. He was dizzy, so dizzy his eyes must be spinning in their sockets, and the first black motes spun across his vision. Nothing was obstructing him except his own stubborn brain, which had shut down his lungs as a way of dealing with the fear consuming him from the inside out.

He had, quite literally, forgotten how to breathe.

He couldn't make it. *Couldn't*; not wouldn't or shouldn't or any of the other contractions the Lucid wanted to heap on him.

There was just too much world out here.

Carter turned back, and was shocked to find the door of his house looked just as unattainable, though he'd gone only a handful of steps. He staggered forward, but as the black motes played connect-the-dots in front of his pulsing eyes, he fell to his knees on the driveway and crawled. His memory of reaching the airlock would be completely erased by oxygen deprivation, but when he passed through the first door—even forgoing his obsessive knock— he curled up into a ball and closed his eyes as the air changer did its work and his lungs finally did theirs.

Whitney could blow as hard as she wanted.

Carter Vance was simply unable to get out of her way.

RIDERS ON THE STORM

WHITNEY -7:34

"Mister Vance?" Rosa Sanchez rolled the words in her thick Mexican accent. The inner airlock door tried to close on her as she wrestled her armful of groceries through, and she elbowed it roughly back open with a muttered Spanish curse. "Mister Vance, I come all the way here to bring you this, now you get that skinny white ass of yours in here to help me!"

No answer, but she could hear music playing, something mellowish and 70's. Of course there was music, there was *always* music going in this house, and TV and video games and a thousand other distractions competing for attention. It was a wonder the man ever got any work done.

She put down the bags to remove her tennis shoes and rain slicker and tossed them into the airlock. Any water tracked in would be teeming with bacteria according to her employer. She pulled on rubber gloves—latex free—from the box beside the door, pushed her stockinged feet into paper slippers, wrapped a paper surgical mask over her mouth and nose, then gathered up the bags and crossed the living room to find his computer desk empty. The man lived at that computer, sometimes working but mostly on the internet or playing his games. He took his meals at it, and, though she'd never proven it, she half-suspected he slept in the light of its nauseating glow. Whatever he was missing by not being out in the world, he was content to replace it with all these other things.

Rosa turned the corner into the sparkling white kitchen (spotless thanks to her own vigorous daily cleaning) and found Carter Vance sitting at the table in the middle of the room under the glaring fluorescents. He stared down at the table's marble top in his pajamas with the vacant gaze of a doped mental patient.

"Mister Vance?" A bag of groceries dangling from her right hand nearly slipped from her grasp. She heaved it onto the nearest counter and found the button to turn off his music. "Are you all right?"

"What?" He looked up. She saw his eyes were red-rimmed, unfocused, his usually sallow cheeks flushed, the underside of his nose raw from repeated tissue-rubbing. On anyone else, they might be signs of the world's most vicious flu, but Rosa could only roll her eyes as she set down the rest of the groceries.

"Oh Lord, Mister Vance, what now? Mad cow disease? Black plague? Enola?"

He frowned. "That's E*bola*, you cynical cow. It's a disease, not the bombing of Hiroshima."

She flapped a hand at this and then placed it on her ample hip. "Well, whatever. Is it rotting what little brain you have left, or shutting down your heart, or what?"

This put a grudging smile on his boyish face. With all his comic books and cartoons, it was sometimes easy to forget he was thirty-one. "For your information, I just have a cold."

She decided to let that go. She knew from experience it was useless to tell him you had to be around someone with germs already in their system before you could get sick. The only person that came and went from this house was her, and she was permitted only because his germophobia was selective enough to put some kind of shield around her in his head. After all, his carefully constructed world needed someone to do all the things he couldn't. Instead, she dug into a grocery sack and pulled out a sodden and dripping UPS package and placed it on the counter. "This was outside the front gate. The rain almost washed it away."

"Might as well have. Nothing but garbage now." He followed this up with a hearty—and probably forced—sneeze. She watched him for a second as she unpacked the grocery sack. This whole act seemed a bit heavy-handed, even for him. His germophobia episodes always needed a trigger: a seal broken on a food item, the inner airlock door left open just a bit too long, or, her favorite, the time a bird followed her inside and flew around the high ceiling of the living room, driving him into a hysterical ball under his desk. She'd laughed until her sides hurt as she tried to shoo it out, but he'd been on his deathbed for a week.

"How bad is it out there?" he asked.

"Bad. The wind is already awful, and the rain is so cold and hard it feels like little needles. They wouldn't even let me back in the city. They have a barricade set up at the bridge."

"What? Why?"

"Because the evacuation order was *mandatory!* They aren't just politely asking people to leave, you know. I had to come up the western trail, so be glad I drive a truck!" She pointed a finger at him. "I hope you appreciate the things I do for you, young man."

"I never said I didn't." He stood up with a moan and shambled over to the counter. "You're doing that wrong." He began to unload the groceries in alphabetical order, actually repacking some items after removing them to get to others. She'd stopped trying to keep up with all his eccentricities a long time ago. Carter turned the music back on, now some punk rock she didn't recognize.

"I got you as much as I could." She pulled out a case of D batteries and two spare flashlights. "Even the stores outside the city are picked clean."

"This is great, Rosa. Between this and what I have stored up, I'll be fine until you get back."

She stopped unpacking with a box of his damn marshmallow kid's cereal in each hand and sighed. "And what if you're not, Mister Vance? There's more to surviving a hurricane than having enough food to eat, you know."

"Oh yeah, like what?" Sick or not, he smirked at her. "Tell me about it, Miss Survival Expert."

"*I'm not joking with you.*" She turned off the music again. "This is serious. I'm worried about you, and your poor mother is nearly sick over it. You could be flooded out. Blown away. You're a hundred yards from the shoreline, for sweet Lord's sake!"

"Yeah, well…I can't help that."

"Yes, you can. Come with me. My sister will let us both stay with her in Fort Worth until we can get back into the city—"

"I can't." His eyes flitted away, and he coughed against his fist. "I already told you, I'm not leaving."

"But why?"

"You know why, Rosa. I can't go out, I can't leave this house."

"Because you don't try." She emphasized the last word by banging a fist on the counter. "This is all in your head, the doctor says so, you even say so, so why can't you just step through that door?"

"I tried."

It took several seconds to understand what he meant, and even then she was too stunned to speak for several more. "When?"

"Yesterday. I tried to go out. I couldn't breathe, even with one of the masks on. I nearly passed out. I don't even remember how I got back inside."

She blinked at him. Now it made sense, his sudden illness, just because he'd gone out into the world. Hope lifted her. "But don't you see, that's great! Not the passing out, but that you *tried!* You can't stop now, you have to try again, and this time I'll—"

"No, I'm not going. I'm not ready. It's not something I can rush just because of a hurricane." He turned on the music. "And as long as I'm in this house, I don't have to."

"This isn't one of your fantasy movies. This isn't one of your computer games, where you can just turn off the power when you get bored. A hurricane doesn't care if this house was built to keep out every germ in the world. But if you won't leave, *I* will." She spun and marched back toward the airlock.

"What, now?" He raced ahead—stopping to knock four times on the door from the kitchen into the living room, of course—and then attempted to block the way to the airlock door. "You're going *now?*"

"Did you think I wanted to have lunch first?" She sidestepped him without a pause. "You may be willing to gamble with your life Mister Vance, but I am not. I told you I would bring you supplies, and I have done so."

"But Rosa, the place is a mess, and…I'm sick!"

"You're only sick because you made yourself that way. If you're—" This time a shriek of violent wind from outside cut her off. The lights dimmed, the music sputtered. From the living room came the sound of tiny whirring motors as his computer restarted after the brief power loss. She turned back to face him, pulled the mask down around her neck, and placed one hand against his stubbled cheek. He flinched from the contact. "Mister Vance…Carter…

I think of you as my own child. But I can't support you in this. If you…If you are still here when this is all over, I will come back. In the meantime, I will pray for you, all alone in this big city."

With that, she pushed through the airlock door, waited for it to cycle while putting on her shoes and raincoat, and went out into the dark, rain-swept morning.

WHITNEY -7:18

"All alone." Carter considered this for a moment before shaking his head. "No way."

He shuffled up the spiral staircase to the loft overlooking his living room on one side of the house, into the area where he kept shelves upon shelves of alphabetized books, CD's, and DVD's. In the middle of the library-like stacks was a northward facing window, with an excellent view of Port Allen, sloping downward into its little valley. He could see the huddle of buildings and short-stacked skyscrapers that made up downtown, the lay of the suburbs around them, the super-wealthy neighborhood of Manchester Heights up the road from him on the left, and the curve of the Allen Civic Center dome far to the east. He could barely catch a glimpse of I-85 as it elevated just before the Rugg Canyon Bridge on the west side of town, visible only as an endless trail of car headlights against the backdrop of the Chantilly Mountains that encircled Port Allen on its curved section of coastline.

The rest of the city was dark and silent. Abandoned.

"There must be *someone* else." Whether he was stating a fact or trying to convince himself, he didn't know. "This isn't *Night of the Comet*, for Christ's sake. And even if it was, there would still be other people out there somewhere. There's *always* someone else."

Of course there was, right? There had been thousands of people still in New Orleans after Katrina, and logic was screaming at him there had to be some here, as well. He wondered, in a wistful, distant way, who they were, and what their excuses were for staying.

Behind him, System of a Down cut out in mid-screech. The lights flickered off.

This time, they didn't come back on.

WHITNEY -6:21

"I'll get it, I'll get it!" Tangela Kittrick tore through the apartment toward the ringing phone. The windows had all been boarded over on the outside by the apartment maintenance crew, creating a gloom like something in a Halloween spook house. The candlelight caused her shadow to jump from wall to wall.

"No way, assface!" Chris shoved his eight-year-old stepsister aside as he dashed out from his bedroom. He timed this maneuver with eerie precision; Tangela avoided serious injury by bouncing off the couch and sliding into the floor on her butt. "It might be *my* dad!"

"That's not fair, Chris!" Tangela scrambled to rejoin the race. "And you cussed too, I'm telling!"

"Go ahead, but tattling never got anyone what they wanted." He picked up the receiver to illustrate this clever advice, then said cheerfully into the handset, "Hello, Sloan residence!"

"Chris, is…you? Thank Go…afraid the phone lines would… down!"

"Dad?" Daryl Sloan's voice sounded as if it came from the far end of a cardboard tube, with a little television static thrown in for good measure. Chris had tried to push thoughts of the impending storm out of his head, but something about the loss of phone service was worse than the rain or the power outage.

This made him feel isolated. Cut off. Alone.

"Dad, where are you?"

When his father answered, the static was gone. "I just crossed the state line back into Texas from New Mexico. This is the first phone I've seen in the last hundred miles!"

"Did you—" A clap of sharp, rolling thunder came from outside, and the phone in his ear gave a short burst of static like a snake hiss. "Did you get the job?"

"We'll talk about that later, sport. What was that? Is everything okay?"

"Just thunder," Chris said, sounding much braver than he felt. "It's been raining here all day and the lights are off. When are you going to get home?"

"Let me talk, let me talk!" Tangela bounced around him like an excited puppy and grabbed for the phone. Chris frowned and held it out of her reach.

"I'm doing my best to get there. Do me a favor and get your mother on the phone. Quick as possible, please."

Chris furrowed his brow, anger and stubbornness etched in his young features. His father's use of that word always brought out a black mood in him he never knew existed before the man's re-marriage seven months ago. *Don't say it, don't say it*, part of him pleaded.

So he did the only sensible thing any angry 14-year-old would do: he said it.

"My mother's not here, Dad. She's buried at Parkland Cemetery, remember?"

He braced for a lecture, but his father just gave a dangerous few seconds of silence before saying, "Get *Nichelle* on the phone, please."

Chris held the phone even higher out of the girl's reach. "Nichelle, Dad wants to talk to you!"

"Thank you, Chris." Nichelle Kittrick-Sloan left the dark kitchen where she'd been listening. She looked at her stepson, took a deep breath, and said, in the most diplomatic manner possible, "But I didn't appreciate you pushing your sister."

"He cussed, too!" Tangela added eagerly.

"Or cursing in front of her. She's a little girl, Chris. You have to treat her like one."

"Who cares what you appreciate?" the boy muttered as he surrendered the phone.

"Hey," Nichelle said, more sharply than she intended. This is how it went, the two of them pushed one another back and forth, back and forth, just a big, frustrated teeter-totter. "Go to your room! There's only so much of that smart mouth that's gonna be tolerated around here, young man!"

Chris shot her a venomous look, but retreated without further comment.

She sighed, knowing the confrontation had cost her a week of the silent treatment, but perhaps that was better than the alternative. Before she could lift the phone, her daughter grabbed her arm and pulled.

"I wanna talk to Daddy!" Tangela had taken to their new familial nametags with much greater ease.

"I know sweetie, and I'll let you if there's time. But right now, Mommy needs you to be a big girl and go to your room so I can talk to Daddy in peace, okay?"

The girl crossed her arms in an adorable display of defiance. "Okay, Mommy." She followed after her stepbrother.

When her daughter was out of sight, Nichelle pressed the receiver to her ear. Her hand gripped the plastic casing hard enough to turn her brown fingers ghostly pale, but it was either that or shake uncontrollably. She put on a show all day for the kids, tucked her fear neatly away, but now she needed someone to be strong for her. "Daryl, please tell me you're almost here."

"Not quite baby, but I'm doing my best."

She bit her lower lip and allowed a tear to spill onto her cheek. "You're not gonna make it before the hurricane hits, are you?"

A second's worth of hesitation told her everything her heart dreaded. "No. Probably not."

Nichelle gave a long, shuddering sigh. "Why did this have to happen now? Why did you have to be gone with the car halfway across the country?"

"That's not fair, don't make it sound like I abandoned you!"

"I know that Daryl, in my heart I know that, but that's exactly how it feels, like Tanj and I have been left all over again. And Chris hates me no matter what I do, no matter how nice I am to him."

"It's going to be okay, baby, it's—"

"Don't say that just to calm me down, because you *don't know!*" She shouted this before she could stop herself. She wanted to say this was all just nerves, a case of pre-storm jitters, but it wasn't, it was cold, electric, and justified fear. She lowered her voice to a whisper and said, *"They're evacuating the city, Daryl!* The freeway is jammed, and it's pandemonium outside! I heard gunshots this morning! I can't get any help on the phone, the lines are busy through that number they had on TV! I'm scared to take the kids out to try and catch one of the National Guard transports, but I'm even more scared of what'll happen if we stay here! And we're running out of time!"

"Listen, just…don't go anywhere!" Daryl sounded frantic for the first time. In a way that was what she wanted, to know he was taking this seriously, for him not to sound like his usual, cool self—that cocky, confident man she'd fallen in love with a year ago—but now that it had happened, it didn't make her feel any better. "Stay there! The apartment's on the third floor and there's no way the flooding will reach you! I will come for all of you! Do you hear me? *I will come for you!* I don't care if I have to paddle in there on a canoe!"

"Okay." She wiped away the other tears. "After all this, at least tell me you got the job."

"I got the job. We're moving to California babe, where a hurricane is just something you order at the bar. We just have this one last little bump in our road and then it's sunny skies and a house of our own."

She pulled open the front door, which looked out on the landing they shared with the other third floor apartment and then the zig-zagging staircase down to ground level. A gust of wind almost blew it out of her hand before she could close it. "I don't how 'little' that bump is gonna be."

"You just stay safe, and tell Chris I'm gonna wallop him if he doesn't show you some respect."

"Okay. But the first thing we're buying with the money are cell phones for all of us."

He laughed and then told her, with a sincerity that still made her knees buckle, "I love you."

"I love you, too, Daryl." There were more words, so many words that wanted to come, but before she could get them out, the phone in her hand went dead.

WHITNEY -4:45

Bryce Decatur ducked, and the glass vase Maryland had intended to take off his head—a 'gift' to her from his pretentious mother (the vase, not the head, although she was sure the woman thought they both were)—shattered against the wall instead.

"*Fuck!*" He straightened up and stared around him at the shrapnel. He was a squat man, hefty in the middle, brutish face. Not the kind of guy that, all things being equal, anyone would picture with a younger woman like her, but money had a way of tipping even the most weighted scales. At the moment, his puffy cheeks were red with anger, nose and upper lip wrinkled in a snarl. "*Would you calm down, you stupid bitch?*"

"'Stupid bitch?'" Her hand quested along the mantle of the massive fireplace next to her for another marital missile. This time she found something of his; a small but hefty crystal globe he'd bought at a Tiffany's auction.

This got the bastard's full attention. She could tell; when something affected the great, the rich, the powerful Bryce Decatur's world, the charm came out, the engaging act that won him so many cases in the courtroom.

And so many ladies in the bedroom, apparently.

"Maryland," he said evenly, all traces of rage extinguished. He held out a hand to her. "Mary, sweetheart, put that down, that's worth eight-thousand dollars. Let's talk about this."

She might've been willing...*if* he hadn't mentioned the price. Instead she raised the object above her head and brought it crashing down on the tiles of the hearth at her sneakered feet. The action sent an electric spark coursing through her, like the first tickles of an impending orgasm. "Talk about *that*, Bryce!"

"*You goddamned CUNT!*" he roared, the red on his cheeks rising again to blend with an unpleasant shade of purple creeping up his neck. It made him look old, and reminded her of the near decade-and-a-half he had on her.

"Yep, that's me, that's the woman you swore to love and honor, just another cunt." She wiped locks of curled brown hair out of her eyes. "And that's you, more concerned with the things you bought than you are with our marriage."

"Oh, don't be so fucking melodramatic. You're just pissed because I cheated on you."

"*Again.*" She was surprised to find she really wasn't mad; how could she be, when she'd taken him back after the last two times? What was she expecting, a transformation into husband of the year? Hell, it was just positive reinforcement. This time the moron accidentally forwarded an email to her detailing every sordid little act he'd been up to on his office desk.

Still, not upset.

Not about *that*, anyway.

"Bryce, the fact that you can't keep your shriveled dick in your pants is not top of my priority list right now. I know it might be hard to believe some things in the world don't revolve around you, but it's true."

He rolled his eyes. "I told you, *there's no reason to leave!* We live in the highest elevated and most remote neighborhood in the city! This house is rock-solid and we have our own generator, and enough food and water to last us a year! If you think I'm going to leave now just so some looter can come in here and steal everything, then you better goddamned think again!"

"But I don't care about any of that!" She tilted her head back in exasperation. "Nothing in here, not a single thing, is worth our lives. I mean, Christ Bryce, don't you see that? It's simple: I'm scared, and I want to leave. I trusted you this far, and I stayed this long, and what did I get for my trouble? A detailed autobiography of the sexual positions you've performed with the temp pool!"

"Oh, *that's* the only reason you stayed? Really, Mary? Not because this is where your designer clothes are, and your gourmet food, your maids, yours cars, and all that money you spend? You see, you can pretend all you want that none of this matters, but this is *your* life too. I would be surprised if I even figured in the equation."

Maryland Decatur—once Maryland Williams, in a past life she sometimes would give anything to relive—felt something break inside her. She'd suspected this break might be on its way for a while, had envisioned it as the support beam of a rickety house finally giving way and allowing the structure to collapse, but now that it was here, she was surprised to find it was actually more like a dam bursting, and what it had been holding back was a flood of resolve.

"I'm leaving you."

"Oh, sure, I've heard that one before."

"Maybe," she admitted. She moved toward the front door of the house—always a house and never a home, just some place, as George Carlin had once said, to keep her stuff—and took her goosedown parka down to put on over the green, short-sleeve blouse and Capri-cut jeans she was wearing. Somewhere inside her, a nasty little voice screamed for her not to do this, and for all the same reasons he'd just named.

She hated herself for that.

"This is different. I want a divorce." How clean those words sounded, how pure.

"You're gonna leave all this?" He started to cross the room—but warily so, she saw, with some satisfaction. "You know what, Mary? I don't think you can. I don't think you can leave all this behind. You've gotten too used to it, and thirty-five is way too old to be starting over."

She grabbed her purse and cell phone and opened the door. In the driveway sat Bryce's Bentley, not yet pulled into the cavernous garage. The other abandoned homes of Manchester Heights were obscured by curtains of pouring rain. The sky was a seething cauldron of lightning-streaked clouds.

It looked terrifying out there.

It also looked like freedom.

"We'll see," she told him.

"Maryland." That same reasonable courtroom tone. "If you walk out that door, we *are* through. I'll make sure of it. And don't think you're gonna take half of me either. You can wave all the proof of infidelity you want in front of a judge, but it won't matter. I won't *let* it matter. You won't get a goddamned dime in a settlement."

She turned back and grinned viciously at him. "Then I better take what I can now." And she grabbed the keys to his precious Bentley from their peg before racing out into the storm.

Maryland could hear him screaming her name, even over the sound of the grumbling thunder. She was drenched by the time she reached his car, but also exhilarated. Bryce pounded down the driveway after her, the paunch he'd been developing the last few years jiggling with each step. He waved his arms and roared soundlessly. Maryland laughed.

She threw the car into reverse and squealed down the driveway before he could close the King-Kong-esque gate, still giggling.

When she glanced in the rearview mirror and spotted the ridiculous sign over the entrance—Château Decatur—she began to outright roar with laughter.

A minute later, she'd left Manchester Heights behind.

WHITNEY -3:31

The next thunderclap was so loud, it drowned out Captain Lewis' words, even inside the dark foyer of the precinct with the doors closed. Ellis Wright and several of the other assembled officers glanced uncomfortably at the front windows. It was just shy of four o'clock in the afternoon, but the day beyond the glass was pitch black, the sky overrun with purple and green clouds the color of rotten fruit. Jagged forks of lightning wove through them, illuminating their ugliness.

"Say again, Cap?" Charles Van Ness, Ellis' partner, asked.

"I said, I think we're it, buckos. Ninth precinct just closed its doors per Mayor Edwards' orders. I got the call from Chief Tyler over the radio just a few minutes ago."

A general murmur went through the small group of cops crowded into the lobby. Their precinct, good ol' number six, was on the south side of the city, twenty minutes from the waterfront and the last scheduled to lock its doors. It was the biggest in the city, the only one with a vehicle repair bay and long-term holding cells. The mayor insisted police presence be maintained throughout Port Allen's evacuation, but now...

Now it was time to get the hell out of Dodge.

"So they gonna leave us here till Whitney's blowin up our asses or whut?"

Ellis didn't need to turn around to know who had asked that cheerful question—the molasses-thick country accent was enough— but he did anyway. Officer George Sturney had positioned himself halfway to the front doors, and stood with his thick arms crossed over his broad chest. He was surrounded by his usual crew; officers JD Myers, Harold McNamara, and Mike "Drano" Jenkins, the three of them reminding Ellis of scrawny hyenas hiding behind their pack leader.

Most of the other men also turned to look at the speaker, but Sturney targeted a sneer at only Ellis. He swallowed a sudden lump in his throat and looked away.

"We're out of here right now," Captain Lewis told them all. "We've been asked to take one more spin around the city on an extended patrol, round up anyone still on the streets—"

"Fuck that. If they're still stupid enough to be here, let 'em drown," McNamara muttered, drawing a chuckle from Sturney. Myers—a young, angry-looking kid who had been on the force two years—grinned toothily. Drano Jenkins maintained his usual implacable expression.

"—and then head out of the city," Lewis finished, pretending not to hear them. "Let me remind you, body armor is optional today just in case, God forbid, you find yourself in a situation where you're forced to swim. But if you don't press your luck, that shouldn't be a problem. Chief Tyler was very explicit: *everyone* is to be at one of the exit barricades by 6:30 so you can help out with the evacuation. The westbound lanes will be open for your use. Is that understood?"

"Yes sir," they answered in unison. Ellis felt eyes on the back of his neck. He knew he shouldn't give the son of a bitch the satisfaction, but he turned again.

Sturney's gaze was still locked on him. His biceps flexed three times, almost rhythmically. McNamara, at his right elbow, clearly mouthed the words, '*you motherfucker.*'

Ellis whipped his head back to his captain for the second time. Charlie gave him a look of his own from Ellis's side and then shook his head reassuringly.

"Just keep in mind, boys, this is not the time for heroes." Lewis turned to each of his officers as he spoke. "There are dangerous people on those streets right now, and this isn't the time to haul them in. Save the ones that want to be saved, but be out of Port Allen by 6:30. No excuses. This is *not* worth your lives. You've done everything you can to hold this city together, but now it's time to put it in God's hands. Your families are waiting for you outside the city, so don't disappoint them."

Family; he should be so lucky. Ellis had sent Schlitterbaun, his seven-year-old tabby cat, out of the city with Charlie's ex-wife. His car, clothes, and other essentials were waiting for him at the motel room he'd rented in Huntsville two days ago. Other than that, it was just him and Chef Boyardee taking up residence at his apartment, and, though they'd had some good times together, the Chef was on his own for this one.

"I'm putting three officers to a car. I have assignments and some quick patrol routes for you. Drive them hard and fast. At last estimates, we have less than four hours till Whitney knocks on our door."

Lewis began handing out papers. Ellis and Charlie hovered near the back of the crowd, waiting their turn. After a few seconds of unbearable tension, Ellis glanced back once more. Sturney and his gang were gone, into the storm, not waiting for assignments or patrol routes.

"Goddamn Ellis, let it go." Charlie put a hand on his shoulder. Ellis had known him four years, the same length of time the man had been growing a thick gray mustache that was now his trademark around the precinct. "You're obsessing."

"I am not. I'm just scared shitless."

"Hey guys, looks like I'm with you," someone said. Billy Dunham stood behind them with an assignment sheet. The kid was a good ten years younger than Ellis, thin and gawky, barely six months into his civil servant career. The rookie still had honest-to-God pimples on his smooth little face, beneath a brown buzzcut almost short enough to see skull.

"Let's do it then." Charlie pulled on a day-glo orange rain slicker and flipped the hood over his black-and-gray peppered hair. "We're not gettin any younger, and neither is that bitch outside."

Ellis and Billy zipped up their own slickers over their uniforms and all three stepped outside, from one gloom to another. The rain was light but constant at the moment, just enough to be depressing. Ellis hunched deeper into the plastic as they headed for the parking lot at the side of the building.

"You mind if I drive?" Billy asked as they reached the patrol cars.

"I'm driving," Charlie told him.

"Aw, c'mon, I really want to!"

"Then you should've called it."

"I did call it!"

"No, you *asked* me, there's a difference."

"Can I call it now?"

"Get some hair on that ball sack of yours and then we'll talk." Charlie unlocked the driver's door of their ride.

Billy crossed behind the vehicle and up the passenger side. Ellis put out an arm to cut the boy off between the front and back doors. "I know you didn't think you were getting shotgun."

"You guys are assholes," Billy whined, and opened the rear door.

"It's called 'seniority,' rookie." Ellis grinned as he reached down to open his door...

And was slammed against it instead, smashing his chest painfully against the top of the vehicle frame.

He recovered, spun, and found Sturney leering over him, forcing Ellis to squash himself against the patrol car to keep from touching the man's broad chest. Billy froze with one leg in the car and watched them over the door with a confused frown.

"Hey Wright," Sturney said conversationally from under his slicker hood. Even in the pelting rain, Ellis could smell the sweetness of the peppermints he constantly chewed.

"George," Ellis offered.

"You and yer crew be careful now, ya hear?" A grin tugged at his hound dog cheeks. "Like the Cap said, there's a lotta bad folks on the streets right now. I'm sure some of 'em would love ta hurt a *nigger* like yerself."

"Back off him, Sturn," Charlie warned over the roof of the car. "Back off him, right fuckin now."

"I'd be careful, Van Ness." Sturney's gaze never left Ellis. "Ya never know when this piece of shit might roll over on you, too."

"I'd want him to, if I was as dirty as you. Now get off him, or I swear to Christ, I'll knock your lights out right here in the precinct parkin lot. This ain't the time for this bullshit."

"Fine." A flash of anger showed in his yellowed grin. "Just a friendly warnin anyway. You boys make sure ya get ta the barricade, all right?"

"Y-you do the same." Ellis tried to mimic the man's sarcastic tone, and immediately wished he'd just kept his mouth shut.

George Sturney retreated into the rain, heaving his bulk between the rows of squad cars and over to where Drano waited.

"What was *that* about?" Billy asked over the constant hum of the rain.

"Nothin kid, get in the car." Charlie studied Ellis silently. When Billy saw he wasn't going to get an answer, he ducked his head and sat down in the caged rear of the vehicle.

"I don't know how much more of this I can take." Ellis wiped moisture from his dark face. "Even if this job is still here after the hurricane, I don't know if I'll be coming back to it."

"Nonsense. This investigation finishes, and *you* won't be the one goin away, trust me on that."

"I hope you're right," Ellis said, and opened his door.

WHITNEY -3:09

Imogene Freeman should've expected something like the note. Especially after the fight she overheard between Janie and Eric the night before, loud enough to echo through the thin walls of the house. They'd been moving toward this inevitable conclusion all week even if no one had talked about it. It was more of a thought that simmered on the subconscious backburner as options were explored and deemed impractical.

Looking back, she was just surprised it hadn't come sooner.

She told herself all of this, and yet seeing it in black and white, clutched in her dark, shriveled, trembling hands, was still shocking. She sat by the window—a frail little black woman with gray hair hanging in limp strands down to her shoulders—and stared at it until her eyes hurt, willing the words to change, to say something different. When her wish didn't come true, she looked through the glass instead, at God's tears falling outside. Those tears came hard and fast now, washing away the dirt and muck of the city.

Don't you cry, old woman, she chastised herself when she felt the sting at the back of her throat. *Don't you dare spring a leak over this.*

She was doing an admirable job of following these instructions so far. She'd grown up in hard times after all, been forged tough as nails by depression and disaster, and she refused to go to pieces now, at what would probably be the end of her life.

It's not as if they're being unreasonable, she thought, stiffening her upper lip mentally if not physically. *It's only logical; they have more to think about than your wrinkled old bony bee-hind.*

She smiled briefly at this voice, who sounded like her but always put things just the way her own grandmother had. The smile left as quick as it came, and Imogene brought the note she'd discovered on her bedroom door this morning back up. She read the hastily scrawled message from her daughter once more.

Mom-

I love you, I'm so sorry, but we had to, we didn't know what else to do. The kids just can't be here, and we have to think of them first. One of us would've stayed, but they need their parents. There's no way that we could get you out, I'm sorry, please forgive us...
Janie

All of that was true. She'd come here to live with her daughter six years ago, after her husband passed on. Janie's husband Eric and their three children welcomed her with open arms and never made her feel like an intrusion into their lives here in Port Allen, despite her declining health, constant medical needs, and the fact that they struggled to make payments on their two-bedroom house and feed the mouths they already had. Sixteen-year-old Alice, thirteen-year-old Duncan, and eight-year-old Delia were darlings, the joys of her life, and Imogene had been in turmoil knowing they were only staying in the city—in harm's way—because of her.

"This is *right*," she whispered. And it damn sure was. Out with the old, in with the new. It just wasn't logical to put the needs of one seventy-three-old bitty, whose God-granted time, by all rights, was up long ago, in front of three children who still had their futures spread out in front of them. They couldn't stay...and she surely would've died if they attempted to move her.

She knew this was true.

Knew it.

But damned if that made it sting any less.

Imogene Freeman set the note down on the padded armrest of the wheelchair—the one she'd been confined to for the past twenty years—and turned on the oxygen machine on the stand beside her.

The ancient contraption was a huge blue box with more switches and dials than what she imagined a rocket ship would have, the size of a doghouse for a Lassie-sized dog. With the power out, it was reduced to using the remaining charge on its battery. The thing revved to life, emitting a chugging, gulping wheeze that reminded her of that heavy-breathing movie villain Mr. James Earl Jones had voiced. She wrapped the tubes around her head, over her ears, and pushed the prongs into her nose.

She could go without the air for small increments of time, a couple of hours at most, and then her Chronic Obstructive Pulmonary Disease (she was just as content to call it by its acronym, because COPD was actually how she felt about it, like it was just a cop out on life) flared up too much to take. She'd left this house little since coming to live here, because her daughter and son-in-law just didn't have the money to maintain a portable tank.

The house was her prison, and the oxygen machine her warden.

She'd become a useless thing and the world was finished with her, the same way a child casts off clothing and toys as they grow. Well…all good things must end. Death was a part of life. To everything a season.

She believed all these things…she just didn't believe it was *her* season. Not in her heart. She didn't feel used up, no matter how much life wanted her to believe so.

Rather than dwell, Imogene looked out the window at the little swatch of Oak Street in front of her daughter's house and proceeded to give God's weeping a run for its money.

WHITNEY -2:52

No one in Lincoln Briggs' crew hesitated after the plate glass shattered under the metal garbage can. This pleased him; they were soldiers, *his* soldiers, every bit as trained and disciplined as the men of the American military. They charged into the little electronics store with victorious whoops and pulled televisions and stereos off display shelves, wrapping them in scraps of tarp before running off into the rain with them.

"This some good shit, Links!" a stick-thin, wiry boy to his left screeched over the downpour. Lincoln's cousin, Tyrone Clancy—C-Tone on the street—wore only sneakers, a t-shirt, and a pair of jeans so sopping wet they probably weighed more than he did. Water rolled down his cornrows in twisted rivulets. "If even half this stuff survives the trip to the crib, we gon' be rollin!"

"You know it." Lincoln shrugged deeper into the poncho he'd stolen from the deserted JC Penney's on Frost Avenue earlier that morning. It did a pretty shitty job of keeping his own jeans and white wifebeater dry, but it was way better than nothing. The rain seemed to be getting colder by the minute. "All those other niggas gonna come out after the rain stops and find out we didn't leave them nothin to steal."

"You goddamn right!" Franklin 'Tagger' Marx, one of his sergeants, stepped out of the store window with a TV wrapped in layers of blue plastic. "Best idea you EVAH had!"

"Lootin *befo'* the disaster?" C-Tone brought his arms up in front of his chest and crossed them just below the wrists, forming their gang sign. "That's fuckin brilliant, Links! East Side X-Dawgs fo'evah!"

"Yeah, well why don't you get yo' mouth off his dick long enough to give us a hand," Tagger grunted.

Lincoln clapped him on the shoulder. "Get goin, man. Take care of base till I get back."

Tagger nodded and disappeared into the veil of rain along with the bulk of the other soldiers.

C-Tone wore a sulky frown now. "Links, why you let him talk to me like that?"

"Because he's right. You need to spend less time yappin and more time takin care of business."

"Man, I do what needs to be done! When I run this crew—!"

"Shut up with that 'when-I-run-this-crew' shit, grease stain," a rumbling voice behind them said. Lincoln turned to find Maquea Jones—homeboy since the third grade but going by the more respectable title of lieutenant these days—striding through the rain toward them, a goliath wrapped in shadow. The nineteen-year-old towered over Lincoln by at least a foot and closer to two over li'l ol' C-Tone. He wore a white poncho, the largest one he could find, but it still just reached to his knees, making him look like a short-sheet-ed ghost. "The only thing you ever gonna run is yo' girly mouth, son."

"Sup, Mac." Lincoln held up a hand, which Mac grabbed hard and squeezed. "How was the hunt?"

"Cleared out three stores after we split up. Sent the rest of the troops from my unit back to base."

'Base' meant an abandoned two-story tenement in the heart of Port Allen's only real ghetto—stretching from 15th to Dallas Row on the far southeast side—that the X-Dawgs had taken over after a drug bust by PAPD cleaned out the rightful residents. It was spacious enough for the twenty or so 'full-time soldiers' (Lincoln's term for those, like himself and Mac, without any real home to go to), but it could get crowded when the entire crew was in attendance.

The wind gusted, blowing rain directly into their faces. Mac twisted his head to the side, producing a crack of joints as sharp as the thunder overhead. "It's gettin bad out here."

"All right Mac, mine are headin back too." Lincoln looked briefly up at the sky, letting the rain wash over him, and breathed in the moist air. He closed his eyes and savored it, basking in the moment. He felt like a king today, like he owned every inch of Port Allen. His X-Dawgs had marched up the main streets of the inner city all day, taking what they wanted without so much as a single member of the Port Allen Pig Department to stop them. With the electricity out, there were no alarms, and even the few rival gangs on the west side of Seventh Street were staying indoors.

For the first time in as long as he could remember, he felt free of obligation and responsibility.

He'd left his mother when he quit school and joined the X-Dawgs at fifteen, and hadn't seen her junkie ass since. His soldiers were the only family he had now, and it was his job to make sure they survived, to provide for them the way most of their own parents didn't, against competitors, cops, or, in this case, a hurricane.

The three of them were alone on the street now; the other soldiers had taken off at a dead run with their stolen goods, and had a long head start back to base. Lincoln said, "You know we need supplies before we go back, right?"

"What we need?" The look of concentration on C-Tone's face was almost comical. "Liquor? Smokes? "

"How 'bout some food, porch monkey?" Mac barked at the sixteen-year-old.

"I may be a porch monkey, *beeyitch*, but at least I don't look like the KKK dressed me this mornin!"

"Well if the alternative is to go runnin around in the rain without some protection like a dumb little darkie, then sign me up for some burnin crosses."

"Man, whatevah," C-Tone said grudgingly. "Why we need food, Links?"

"Because, there may not be anyone out right now, but once this storm is over, *everyone's* gonna be lootin. Only they're not just gonna be after TV's and iPad's; they're gonna want all the food they can get their hands on. If we stock up now, we won't have to fight for it later."

"Oh yeah, Links, you right! Damn, you smart!"

"What'd you have in mind?" Mac asked.

"Try Kim's on the way back. Bust in, take what we need."

"You sure, man? That's shittin where we eat. You know the rule 'bout that."

"Course I know the rule; I'm the one that made it up. But it's prob'ly not gonna matter." Lincoln shrugged. "Whatever the storm don't wash away, somebody else is just gonna take. No way it points back at us."

"Besides, that Kim fuckin deserve it!" C-Tone pulled his nine-mill out of his sopping waistband and waved it around in the rain. "That muhfuckah always be hasslin me 'bout shit! If he was still there…BLAM…I'd bust a cap up in his ass so fast, he'd *nevah* see me comin!"

"Oh yeah, you a reeeeal killer," Mac told him. "Now put that piece away before you end up ruinin it, you negroid. I saw you drop the fuckin thing in a puddle earlier."

C-Tone scowled, a dangerous crossbreed of anger and embarrassment on his face. Lincoln saw his hand squeeze the weapon's handle. "Mac, why you always gotta be callin me racist names and shit?"

Mac saw it too, but he didn't back down. "Cause you ain't nothin but a stereotype. And what's worse, you *proud* of it."

They stared at one another, until Lincoln said, "All right, we got all night to crack on each other. CT, put the gun up. Let's get some supplies and head back to base."

He led the way up the street, sloshing through the growing puddles, one soldier on either side.

WHITNEY -2:47

"'Stay out of the rain, Hernie,'" the man who knew himself only as 'Hernandez' recited. He pulled the rags of his overcoat tighter around him. "That's what Momma used to say, Hatch. 'Course, that was before the government spies took her away to experiment on her brainy-brain."

Hatch raised his shaggy head from the wet corner of the boat-house and whimpered miserably.

"I know, Hatch, I know," he told the filthy brown Lab, with as much assertion as if the animal had spoken an actual protest about their surroundings. "But we had to get ourselves out of the rain like Momma said, so we came in here. No one will get mad at us about that, right?"

If the dog intended to answer, the howling gust of wind outside the leaky boathouse cut him off. They'd taken shelter here in the early afternoon, when the rain first began falling. The structure was in Graceville Marina, a large, private docking facility on the west side of the city's coastline, just down the shore from where the oil refineries sat huddled against the high seawall. The two of them had gotten used to the angry ocean sloshing under the boards at the open far end, where the long boathouse jutted out over the water, but now the wind was kicking up as well.

The dog's head turned in the direction of the noise. His hackles rose. He settled his head back on the wet floor and looked at Hernie.

"Don't you worry about that, neither." The young Hispanic man with the mop of tangled brown hair shifted on the bed of cardboard he'd made. "Everyone knows the government controls the weather. When they want all that mess to stop, it'll stop."

'Hernie' Hernandez had been spouting this and other equally ridiculous conspiracy theories to anyone that would listen for years...but since he'd been living on the streets for longer than he could remember, that audience usually consisted of the junior high kids from Manchester Heights, who called him names and threw rocks at him on their way to school. He had only the vaguest memories of a life that wasn't about scrimping and survival, ridicule and rousting, and even those felt like dreams most of the time. He tried very hard to remember the face of his mother, but what his mind conjured was more like a cartoon than a mental snapshot. Lordy, he could barely remember a time when Hatch wasn't at his side for every step, and just looking at the animal he knew he couldn't be more than three years old.

Hernie had no past, and could conceive of no future.

The present was all that existed for him, and right now that present was filled only with cruel wind and cold rain; the harbingers of Hurricane Whitney.

"We'll be okay, Hatch ol' boy." He took out the remains of a sopping wet hamburger he'd rescued from a fast food dumpster yesterday afternoon. He tore the bit of food in half and tossed one section to his dog. Hatch swallowed this without chewing and chuffed his thanks.

"Yes sirree," Hernie said around his own mouthful of burger. "We'll be just finey-fine. So long as the government doesn't use their laser satellites to shoot us."

WHITNEY -2:28

The helicopter was military, but the man flying it was far removed from such service. The hardware had been commandeered, pressed into service for a new master. It wobbled badly as it sank through the rough winds and touched down in front of a nondescript warehouse on the eastern edge of Port Allen, one of the last structures before the city petered out into sharp foothills at the inside edge of the Chantillys. A man named Tony stood just inside the glass doors at the front of this warehouse, watching his salvation as it fought to reach the ground.

When the chopper finally settled on the plot of dead grass and overgrown weeds outside, the pilot began frantically waving him out. Tony shouted at Simon, "It's here man, c'mon, let's go!"

"Almost finished." Simon sounded calm as he stood hunched over one of their workstations, typing on a keyboard.

In the helicopter, the pilot was now screaming something and sweeping an arm toward himself in broad, angry strokes. To Tony, it sure looked like the universal sign for 'get-your-fucking-ass-out-here.'

"I don't think he's gonna wait, Si! We gotta go, right now!"

"If I don't finish downloading these recombinant strains, then we start all over again wherever Kyler sets us up next. Don't know about you, but that prospect doesn't sound too appealing to me." Simon continued to type, then reached down to remove an external hard drive, which he added to a briefcase filled with more of the same beside him. "There, that's the last of 'em."

"C'mon then!" Tony pushed open the door to leave without him. The wind caught him by surprise, shoving it back closed and nearly breaking his fingers. Any cool he'd preserved up to this point was vanished, gone, ka-put, because the pilot wasn't gesturing anymore, he appeared to be fiddling with the controls now, undoubtedly in preparation to leave them. And if that happened, if they missed their only shot at getting out of the city before the hurricane hit...

"He won't leave us," Simon told him, and Tony stopped panicking just long enough to look at him. "He knows what'll happen if he does. Now, if our friend Kyler had these," he held up the briefcase, "then yeah, we might be a bit more expendable."

Tony shook his head. "I don't care if it takes us ten years to get back to this point, I just don't want to be here when Whitney gets her hands on *those*."

He pointed over Simon's shoulder, at the two monstrous tanks filling the entire warehouse from floor to ceiling behind a thick glass wall on the other side of their workstations. Two tanks filled with enormous quantities of a substance called P3, but codenamed 'Project Mercury.'

Mercury, as in the Roman messenger god with the winged shoes, the one that moved with the speed of lightning.

Simon paused at the door with Tony and looked back at eighteen months of work. Work that had been too far advanced to move to a minimum safe distance on the short notice they were afforded by the National Weather Service. Work that almost certainly wouldn't survive a hurricane of this magnitude according to the tanks' manufacturers; a fact that was buried in the reports when Kyler chose to have them built here, for reasons known only to him and the top brass who authorized it.

"Yeah," he agreed, "I feel real sorry for anybody left in this city after one of those things springs a leak."

WHITNEY -2:12

Rosa Sanchez's departure from the city wasn't nearly as smooth as she'd hoped. After leaving her employer's home early in the day, she headed west, planning to take the same mountain trail back out of Port Allen that she used to sneak in. It certainly wasn't the shortest route, but with the only two freeway exits clogged—the Rugg Canyon bridge in the northwest corner and the pass through the Chantilly Mountains in the east—it was probably the fastest. She was terrified of the impending hurricane, a near hysteria that drove her onward with single-minded determination.

She was on a back street weaving through the hills south of Manchester Heights when the front passenger tire of her truck blew. The wheel wrenched out of her hand, and suddenly she was riding a bucking bull that tried its best to toss her off. She wrangled the vehicle to the side of the road, coming to rest against the guardrail of a short bridge, then sat and contemplated her options as the rain beat down on the roof.

Options. Now *there* was a laughably short list. She had no spare and her mobile phone might as well be a paperweight at the moment; wireless communication had been the first thing to go as the weather worsened.

"Oh, you've done it now," she moaned. A sharp crack of thunder caused her to wince. "Why, oh why, did you have to come back into the city?"

But that was no mystery, she knew exactly why, and, even though she was frightened to the verge of tears and mad that the stubborn man who'd caused all her misfortune wasn't here to share in it, she knew she would do it for him again without a second thought.

She just wished she'd left him with kinder words, as it may be the last time she ever saw him.

Rosa got out of the car, not bothering with the umbrella in her back seat. The rain came from everywhere now—above, both sides, even, somehow, the *ground*—so nothing could've prevented her from being soaked within seconds. She examined the car and saw the tire was shredded to the rim. She spat a curse at it as she trudged by.

The last sign of civilization—a block of businesses she was sure contained a tire outfit—was several miles back. The hike back was cold and miserable. They were closed and boarded up, but she broke a window, found a replacement in her size that was already rim-mounted, and left a note with her address saying she would pay for both, if the storm didn't blow the whole place away.

She rolled the wheel all the way to the truck like a child of the 50's playing hoop spin. By the time she got the bad tire off, the afternoon had gone prematurely dark. She was exhausted and wheezing, her back aching. The rain only got meaner, and when she finally looked at her watch after tightening the last lug nut with hands now shaking and numb, she saw she had little more than two hours to get out of Whitney's path.

Rosa continued driving, her only concern for the ticking clock in her head, not her sopping wet clothes and hair, not the growing fever she could feel in her ears and the back of her neck, not even the dangerously wet roadways.

The 'western trail' was a small turnoff on the edge of the city few people knew about and even less actually used; it was a circuitous, inconvenient way to get to Interstate 10, which then went on to Houston. But between the last paved roadways of Port Allen and the two smooth lanes of I10 was a maze of dirt trails and rural roads, winding through dense woods and muddy fields and then up into a rough trail over the low mountain range. Most of the roads required a four-wheel drive to traverse.

The first path Rosa turned onto had become a sludge pit in the unrelenting rain. There was a moment where she thought the truck had become mired, but then she spurted forward, and the next trail led up into the rocky hardpan at the foot of the mountains.

Trees closed in on both sides, intensifying the unnatural darkness preceding the storm. Even with the headlights on, she had to squint to see more than twenty yards in front of the vehicle through the sheets of driving rain.

Which was why she almost crashed into the mound of dirt before she could halt.

Rosa sat behind the wheel as she had after the blowout and stared ahead, through the swish of the windshield wipers, into the cone of light created by her headlamps, and tried to convince herself this was a feverish hallucination.

Ahead of her, the western trail was simply gone, swallowed up by a huge pile of loose soil and rock debris twice as tall as her truck. It sprawled across the length of the road, blocking the mouth of a narrow pass bounded by steep, craggy earth. It hadn't been here when she drove through earlier in the day. It looked so natural she might've been inclined to believe *she* was the one out of place if not for the remains of the trail ending beneath it.

She wasn't even really concerned with why it was there, but rather *what to do now?* The road was wide enough to turn around, but if she did, where could she go, except back into the city?

Her thoughts became desperate, as inventive as the reasons Mr. Vance fed himself about why he couldn't leave his house. Maybe there was someone on the other side of this obstruction, someone that could help her. She didn't care about her truck, but if she could catch a ride, she would gladly take it. She opened her door, stumbling out into that downpour once more...

And then the world blazed with light, chasing away the early nightfall.

Rosa put a hand up to shield her eyes. Spotlights were carefully hidden at the sides of the mound of dirt and in the trees all around her, the bright kind used on performance stages. And that's how they made her feel, illuminating her every move. They turned each plummeting raindrop into a flashing prism.

"Hello?" Rosa called. "Hello, is someone—?"

"RETURN TO YOUR VEHICLE," a booming voice declared.

Rosa jumped at the sound of the gruff, amplified words. "RE-TURN TO YOUR VEHICLE IMMEDIATELY AND REENTER THE CITY."

"I-I can't! Please, who are you? I need help!"

"RETURN TO YOUR VEHICLE," the voice repeated. She couldn't see where it came from. "YOU HAVE TEN SECONDS TO COMPLY."

Something in Rosa screamed for her to obey that godlike voice, to heed its commands, but, once again, her fear of the coming storm was so all important, she just couldn't convince herself there was any other reason to be scared. "Are you with the National Guard? Or the Army? Please, I just need a ride away from here, I don't care where, my sister lives in—"

There was no countdown, and no second warning (and, if truth be told, only an elapsed time of nine seconds since the first was issued, instead of the promised ten). A hail of gunfire erupted from the trees on both sides of her, and Rosa Sanchez was cut down like wheat beneath a sharpened scythe, dead before she could comprehend what happened.

Four men emerged from the woods on either side of her into the glaring spotlights. They wore black rubberized body suits that conformed to each curve of their bodies. The same material covered their entire heads like a ski mask and attached at the neck, with a reflective plastic plate over the face. From the lower half of this jutted a cylinder as big around as an empty toilet paper roll, and another, smaller tube was built onto the end, forming a cross junction. The sounds of their breathing issued from these, hollow and rasping. They stopped in front of the small Mexican woman's body.

"What do you want us to do with her?" one of them asked, the voice a high-pitched squeal through the mask.

"Dump her in the car, and bury the whole thing with one of the heavy loaders. I'll contact Kyler to let him know we gave some relief to our first hurricane refugee." Though his face was hidden, the smile was evident in the words. Here was a man who enjoyed his job, despite—or perhaps because of—the killing it entailed.

He started away from the others, to the base camp just on the other side of the mountain of dirt that had stopped Rosa's car.

THE WISE MAN BUILT HIS HOUSE UPON THE ROCK

WHITNEY -2:00

The rain had become a hammering deluge by the time Mac, Lincoln, and CT turned one last street corner and spotted the dingy yellow awning of Kim's Grocery. It fell so thick and hard that the droplets had a collective weight, almost beating them into the ground, while the wind shoved around like feathers. Poncho hoods flapped in Lincoln and Mac's faces. Every storm drain they passed overflowed, water running freely in the gutters.

Whitney was almost here.

"*Links!*" CT screeched from behind him over an unearthly gust of wind. They had drifted into a single file line as the weather worsened, Mac in front and CT bringing up the rear. "*Links, man, I don't know 'bout this! Let's just get back to base!*"

"*It's just a little rain!*" Lincoln shouted back. They'd left the main hub of downtown thirty minutes before, and were now in the outskirts of Port Allen's commercial district, an area with older buildings and crammed together storefronts, where every other business had a foreign translation beneath its name, mostly Spanish but some Korean and Chinese. An ethnic neighborhood, a melting pot of cultures that separated upper society from the poor, black folks on the east side of town. A buffer so the whites could keep eating their TV dinners and watching their reruns of *Friends* without having to be reminded whose backs they did it all on. "*Remember what I told you? It's get wet now, or starve later!*" He moved forward, pushing through the relentless wind, and took up a position next to Mac.

"Pains me to say it Links, but he could be right." Mac leaned close so he could lower his voice. "This just gonna get worse, and home's still a long walk when we get done!"

A sliver of irrational anger jabbed at Lincoln. This was just Mac, the responsible lieutenant, the vocal conscious, just one big Negro boy scout. "We have to do this first, man! For the crew!"

He saw Mac's mouth open, an attempt to talk some sense into him, but the storm stopped him before he could say a word. There was a loud *shhhhrip!* from down the street and they looked up to see the yellow canvas along the front of their destination tear free in the wind and go sailing into the sky above their heads, visible against the clouds in a flash of lightning.

Mac pointed up after it. *"I don't know 'bout you son, but I don't wanna get flown like a kite if the wind gets any stronger!"*

CT squeezed in between them. *"Let's just bounce till the storm's over! Somebody'll bring us food!"*

Lincoln spun on him, eyes narrowed. *"Oh really? And just who's gonna do that, huh?"*

"Shit, I don't know! The Red Cross or the gub'ment or somebody!"

Lincoln looked from one to the other and grimaced. *"Did both of you go retarded? Did you forget what happened after Katrina? We watched it on TV! People—black people just like you and me—starvin in the streets and the government didn't do shit! You think it's gonna be any different if Port Allen gets destroyed by Whitney? When New Orleans and Galveston're gettin hit just as bad?"*

Neither of them answered. His cousin wiped water out of his eyes and stared at him sulkily, but Mac looked away, back down the street they came from.

And you know what he's thinking, a paranoid voice whispered. *He's thinking you might already have the food, if you hadn't spent so much time snatching those other 'essentials.' You know, like toasters and TV sets.*

"Shut the fuck up," he growled under his breath. But that voice was right, and the idea stung. Looting had been his bright idea, and his alone.

"What?" Mac asked.

"I said, we're on our own! We don't find somethin to eat now, we might not be here when this is over! So go if you want, run back

to base with your tail between your legs! I'm gonna get us some food!"

He crossed the street without waiting for an answer, and stepped onto the broad sidewalk in front of Kim's. After a second, the other two followed.

WHITNEY -1:56

"Jesus wept, I remember when Alicia hit back in '83. Took my neighbor's roof right off. That was back when I lived with Jan and the kids, you understand. But even the rain from that was nothin compared to this." Charlie stared out at the downpour during this musing. The silence in the car after leaving the station had gotten too thick for him. There was no chatter on the radio with the precinct closed and the dispatchers gone, just the steady skitter of rain and mechanical swish of the windshield wipers. He decided to try a different approach to conversation. "So Billy, tell us somethin juicy about that young thing you date."

"I'm not dating her, she's my fiancée." Billy peered out through the mesh separating the seats. The glow from the instrument panels turned his face shades of green and blue. "We're getting married in October."

"*October?* Who the hell gets married in October?" Charlie teased, as he maneuvered the patrol car through the water choked streets. He kept an eye on Ellis beside him, anticipating a response, a smile, some damn *movement*, any sign he might be coming out of this funk. "Anyway, tell us somethin she wouldn't want you to."

Their route through the city had been slow, as they were forced under the speed limit to compensate for the increasing rain. So far, they'd not seen a single soul. No big surprise there; anyone ignorant or poor enough to ignore the mandatory evacuation was huddled somewhere out of the rain. Whatever overpaid beancounter was in charge of figuring such things estimated there would be at least a few thousand people still within the city after Whitney blew through, people that would need food and aid, but it was hard to start relief planning until they saw what kind of damage Port Allen sustained. For now, however, they might've been the only three people for miles.

"Why do you wanna know that?" Billy asked suspiciously.

"Brothers in blue." Charlie gave him a serious look in the rear-view mirror. "You gotta prove your allegiance to us over the girl. Besides, I only wanna help you out. Some of us believe she's *waaay* too much woman for you." He nudged Ellis, trying to get his partner involved in the ribbing, but the man remained sullen.

"I'm sure you hear the same thing about your mother, Charlie."

"Whoa ho! The kid's got some spunk!"

"Besides." Billy leaned forward to hook his fingers through the iron barrier. "If you *want* some information, you gotta *give* some information."

"Oh really, junior?"

"Yeah. So tell me what that was about back there at the station."

"What?"

Billy clarified, but only after he moved sideways enough so he could watch Ellis' face in profile. "All that with Sturney. Sounded like he was threatening Ellis or something."

"No, not threatening." Ellis finally spoke for the first time since getting into the car. "More like...subtly reminding me."

"Of what?"

Ellis paused for a long moment, deciding on an answer. Charlie didn't envy him. The rookie still had innocence practically glowing from his baby face. All cops came to the startling conclusion at some point in their careers that putting on a badge didn't make you immune to the temptation to break the law, but it was awful to be the one who actually slammed the book closed on the fairy tale.

"Of how far down my throat he's going to ram his fist the first time he catches me alone."

"That's bullshit." Charlie glanced away from the road. "Don't start believin the hype on him and his little flunkies. They'd never have the balls to really come after you, not when every finger would be pointin right back at Sturney. They're two-bit crooks, not killers."

"Yeah," Ellis agreed, and said nothing more.

What are you keepin from me, partner? Charlie wondered for roughly the thousandth time in the past month. *You think I'm stupid pally-boy, but I know there's more goin on with this Sturney business. I just can't find a way to get it outta you.*

"Woah, woah, I don't understand." Billy rattled the cage. "C'mon guys, quit talking around it and tell me what happened."

A moment of silence while Charlie waited for Ellis to take the initiative. Finally he gave a permissive wave without turning. So Charlie told no more than the plain facts his partner had given him. "Ellis was a witness to one of Sturney's frequent brushes with bribery about two months ago. He went to IA with it, but there's wasn't enough evidence to pull him off active duty. They gave him a Garrity warning, and the son-of-a-bitch is still out on the streets, doin whatever he wants."

"Wow," Billy murmured. "I can't believe it. Well, I mean, I *can* believe it, Sturney is a major dick, but I can't believe you had the guts to rat him out. I gotta give you some cred, Ellis."

"Yeah, my partner can still surprise even me sometimes." Charlie grinned. "In any case, Sturney has it in for him now, but, like I said, even if that fat weasel found the courage, he couldn't make a goddamned move without bein the prime suspect himself. Might as well tattoo a fuckin confession on his forehead."

"Can we drop this?" Ellis faced him at last, his fingers drumming the armrest. "We're supposed to be looking for people still in the city."

Charlie studied his face for a moment. "Yeah, okay. Let's swing by the Asian storefronts."

"Are you sure that's a good idea?" Billy asked. "It's not on our patrol route. Captain told us to be out of the city before Whitney hits."

"We're too late for that," Charlie told him. "Whitney's *here*. We'll just tell the Cap we got caught up along the way. After all, what are they gonna do if we're late?" He tipped the kid a wink. "Keep us from leavin?"

WHITNEY -1:52

Nearly three hours had passed since Maryland sped away from Château Decatur, and she was still within the goddamn city limits.

She had no problem getting out of Manchester Heights. Their extremely upper class brethren had fled their million dollar homes at the first hint of the hurricane, flying out to secondary residences in California and New York on private jets to watch the action on CNN. The entire neighborhood was built on a steep-sided mesa springing from the western foothills, Bryce's eyesore nestled in the back where he could look over the whole valley. The sloping road out brought her to the guardhouse at the front of the mansions. This was also empty, something she'd never seen in the three years since they'd moved here. The knowledge that they were protected by a pimply-faced kid armed with a can of mace was the only thing letting some of the stuffy residents sleep at night.

Again, she felt that surge of elation at leaving it all behind. Sure, she'd enjoyed this life, taken advantage of every right and perk, but part of her had been sleepwalking through it all—the parties and events and charities Bryce pretended to care about, and the social circle that barely knew her first name—and that was the part that was awake and roaring now.

She sped through every red light on the deserted streets as she headed into the sparse fields ringing the northern edge of the city before the mountains took over. The rain cut visibility, and the car rocked with wind blasts that threatened to push her off the road, but other than that, the driving wasn't so bad. Her intent was to use the closest access road to get on I-80 and leave this city behind for good, the same way she'd left her home, her marriage, and the only life she knew. She was beginning to think she and her new 'possession-is-9/10th's-of-the-law' Bentley were in for smooth sailing until she turned left, swung around the underside of the freeway, and came up the inclined access road to find traffic at a stand still.

Both lanes on the elevated freeway contained rows of idling, honking vehicles, a line stretching all the way back and forward as far as she could see. Drivers attempted to pass on the shoulder wherever there was room, creating even greater havoc. The eastbound lanes were empty, but, if they hadn't been separated by a concrete median, she was sure this monster traffic jam would've spilled into them.

"No no no no no," she begged. She threw the car into reverse only to find two other vehicles coming up behind, blocking her in.

Maryland struggled out of her parka as she waited to merge. After a few minutes, a kind—or perhaps distracted—soul opened up a spot for her to squeeze into the sluggish traffic flow. Now that she was in the middle of it, she goggled around at the mass exodus of families and evacuees, those that had changed their minds about riding out the storm at the last minute and those held back by obligation until now. Their cars were piled to the roof with every possession they could carry. It was Bryce Syndrome, she decided, BS for short, because that was what all of their crap amounted to, a huge steaming pile of BS. She'd been one of them for so long, so obsessed with collecting the biggest pile of stuff and for what? So it could all be sold after she died and become part of someone else's pile of stuff.

It even felt liberating to know they had so much to worry about, while she had only herself.

That shallow, BS-infected side of her let out a cruel little laugh. *Yeah, we'll see how long that lasts, sweetie. This is the real world out here, and you've been insulated by a pile of money for so long you forgot just how cold it can be.*

They inched along at a snail's pace, while time flowed like water. She tapped the wheel, readjusted the seat fifty times. Car horns blasted in a continual stream until her nerves felt like frayed electrical wires. It couldn't be more than fifteen miles from the onramp to Rugg Canyon Bridge, and beyond that the freeway led through a shallow area of the semicircular mountain range before running down into Texas prairie land. The severity of the storm would be lessened with the Chantillys as a buffer, so her only real concern was getting at least that far on the packed roads before Whitney arrived. She lifted herself off the seat of the car every thirty seconds or so, trying in vain to see over the roofs of the other vehicles, hoping to see movement.

"Should've taken 35," she moaned. She didn't know if the only other way out of the city would be as bad as this, but at the moment, she would settle for anything that kept her moving. Just sitting here, with nothing else to occupy it, her mind kept offering up tainted morsels she hadn't considered before walking out. That gorgeous Jovani cocktail number she hadn't even worn yet. That one necklace with the teardrop emerald Bryce bought her after the first time he went extramarital. The outdoor jacuzzi on a cold night followed by a book next to the fire. She had told him nothing was worth their lives, but she hadn't even taken into account that lamb dish that Chef Scôtalé sometimes made…

Maryland was startled out of this by an SUV that cut into her lane. She added her own honk to the chorus and gave it the finger. Screw this. If waiting was making her this insane, she would take the next exit and double back to 35, which would lead her to the Louisiana border, and then she could find another freeway to…to…

To *where?*

For the first time, she realized she had no idea where she wanted to go. She'd been so intent on getting out of the city and away from the storm (away from *him*) that she never stopped to consider what came after. After Whitney blew through, and Bryce pushed for the divorce. Alimony was right out, thanks to those wonderfully conservative Texan legislators, but what if Bryce really did keep her from securing anything in a settlement?

She pulled out her cell phone and scrolled through the contact list. Nothing but Bryce's cronies or women that would be jumping at the dinner bell as soon as they heard about the split. Both her parents were deceased, she had no close friends Bryce hadn't alienated her from years ago, nothing to fall back on, no assets save for the fifty or so dollars in her wallet and the car she was driving, and Bryce would have all her credit and debit cards turned off by the time she could get anywhere to use them.

Panic bit into her with the speed of a rattlesnake.

Holy hell, what was she going to do?

You'll go crawling back to him. You've made your point, thrown your little tantrum, but in the end, you'll be right back where you started. Where you belong.

Just like he said you would.

No. That would *never* happen.

For just a second, she looked to her left, between the cars and out over the rain swept city south of her. She could see Manchester Heights falling behind, the collection of mansions on its plateau, like fancy cuisine served on fine china. Port Allen appeared to be sleeping or abandoned, and behind it was the gathering fury of Whitney, looking like a black, tumorous growth sweeping across the ocean.

Then she realized the bald guy in the car next to her thought she was looking at him, and, after he slid a tongue suggestively across his spotted lips, she faced forward again and pretended he didn't exist.

You'll come back, her mind insisted. *You haven't escaped from here yet.*

She fumbled in her purse for a cigarette, realized she had none. In a sudden fit of frustrated fury, she hit the seat next to her, pounded the steering wheel, punched the dashboard. When she glanced left again, it was now the bald guy who found other places for his eyes to roam.

WHITNEY -1:42

Blackouts were boring.

Carter hadn't been in one in years, at least since he lived in his parent's house before college. Everything electric was out. Except for the industrial air filters—which drew power from a backup generator in the attic so he didn't suffocate in the otherwise airtight enclosure—he was all alone in the dark, still womb of the house.

At first the silence itself was almost headache-inducing, compounding the lingering symptoms from his impromptu trip outside yesterday. As a child of the electronic-driven, mass-media, microsecond attention span generation, the lack of sensory input from television, music, computer, or video games was like someone had reached into his skull and scooped out his brains, leaving a great big hollow at the core of his consciousness.

If there was one thing he hated, it was boredom. Boredom just gave him more time to obsess, and right now its only focus was Rosa's assertion that he was the last person left in Port Allen.

Lucky for him, as six o'clock rolled around, Carter found a new game that required no power source, no internet connection, and no extra players.

It was a bit of metaphorical fun that came about after he remembered every interview he'd ever seen with hurricane survivors, and how they unerringly referred to the winds produced by the storm as sounding like a 'freight train.' Carter hadn't heard a freight train outside of the movies in close to a decade, but he thought he could safely say the unearthly shrieks preceding Whitney weren't even close to the rhythmic rumble of a locomotive. Unless Satan had taken over the B&O since he'd been away from the world.

So that left him pondering: what comparison would *he* use if a microphone was shoved in his face after this was all over?

He called this game, 'Blow-job.'

How about a nation full of fire whistles sounding at the same time? A bag of kittens ground up in a blender? The very earth splitting open in a good approximation of the end of times?

Well, maybe now he was getting carried away.

But in any case, the wind coming off the ocean—pure and unbroken by any structures—was constant, unrelenting, and absolutely *everywhere*, moaning and squalling around every corner of the house and roof, searching for the tiniest nook or crack to get in.

He realized the game could easily become an obsession itself, another file in his OCD Rolodex, and looked for something else to do.

Carter changed out of his robe in the dark of his bedroom into a sweatshirt over a Cartoon Network t-shirt, jeans, and sneakers, to prepare for when the stored heat in the house was lost. The air filters only made sure he had fresh, clean oxygen; the systems cooling and heating it were as dead as everything else. Two years back he'd priced different fuel-sourced electric generators big enough to power the entire house, but ultimately decided they would be a waste of money. And if the past version of himself responsible for this shortsightedness was present, he would stab the man with a salad fork, and paradoxes be damned.

He tried his handheld, battery-operated radio and received nothing but static. The last news broadcast he'd picked up was interrupted by an automated, tinny message advising people trapped in the city to make their way toward the Civic Center. Yeah, right; he'd seen Spike Lee's Katrina documentary, and if he wanted to live in filth like an animal for a few days, he would just book a trip to Guantanamo, thank you very much.

Finally he made a bowl of cereal with the ripening milk in the fridge, sat on the couch, and used a flashlight to read a tattered Dean Koontz novel. And when the growing screeches from outside had him rereading the same passage four times, he stuck the ear-phones to one of his iPods in and cranked up some Weezer.

Reality was almost escaped in the pages of the book when there was a loud clatter on the roof—audible even over a high-volume rendition of "My Name is Jonas"—followed by what sounded like a giant, claw-tipped hand raked down the metal siding of his house, scratching at the impenetrable shingles imported from Germany, the ones guaranteed to never spring a leak.

He snapped the book closed, turned off the iPod, and sat listening in the dark, his heart a dull thud somewhere in his throat.

It's going to get inside, the Lucid proclaimed calmly. It reminded him of that line from Romero's original *Living Dead* flick, 'They're coming to get you, Barbara…'

"I'd like to see it try," he declared to the otherwise silent house.

C'mon Cart, do you really think this house can possibly be as secure and airtight as you want to believe? For Cloister's sake, it was built by the lowest bidding contractor, who then hired a team of illegal immigrants to actually put the pieces together.

Carter covered his ears with his hands; kind of stupid, he had to admit, considering the voice he wanted to shut out was in his head. He knew the Lucid was just an internal counterbalance, the last shredded remains of his conscience trying like hell to get him to face up to the ridiculous shell he'd become, but sometimes it seemed so cruel, so ready to give him a good kick in the ribs whenever he was down. Right now, he needed to believe, to *know*, that this house was his sanctuary, as solid as a rock.

Yeah, well the wise man may have built his house upon the rock, but I bet even that thing was brought down by the first hurricane that came through.

The wind gusted even stronger as though in agreement.

And, backing it up, a groan from somewhere in the house.

He suddenly couldn't sit still another second—between the Lucid and his phobias fighting for space in his head, he was going insane; or more so than usual—so Carter jumped up from the couch and paced to the shatterproof picture window at the front of the house. It was closing in on 5:45 (which meant Whitney was still just getting start-ed, and that, absent neighbors of Teague Street, was not something everyone's favorite left behind shut-in even wanted to contemplate), and the world outside was pitch black, clouds indistinguishable from earth at the point of the horizon on either end of the street.

His front lawn had grown a lake that was swallowing up the driveway. He could dimly see the sapling trees in Mitch Connelly's yard across the street, the ones the investment banker and neighborhood misogynist planted himself several months ago, now slanted at 45 degree angles in the wind. Carter looked toward the pier, straining for a glimpse of ocean, and, during a stuttered flash of lightning, he saw two people down at the makeshift levee, two silhouettes working diligently to stack sandbags in place. Just the confirmation that he wasn't the only one in town made him feel less jumpy.

He stepped away from the window, determined to find a way to ignore the storm, ready to take a handful of valium if he had to...

Squelch.

The noise as his foot came down froze him as neatly as if he'd just caught a glimpse of Medusa. He slipped a hand in his pocket and withdrew the flashlight he'd put there, pointed it downward, and clicked on the beam.

The light fell across his sneakers, and the huge puddle of liquid around them, soaking into his living room carpet.

Water.

Water from *outside*.

From beyond his hermetically sealed home, host to God knew what scum and disease.

A horrified shriek rose in his throat, one that, had it been released, would surely sound like a cartoon woman standing on a chair to escape a mouse, but the was passage locked so tight that air no longer went *in*, much less *out*. His mind flamed with utter revulsion.

He could feel them, oozing up his sneakers and under his pants legs, millions of invisible conquerors making a beeline for his nose, his mouth, and any other ports of entry to his bloodstream. Hell, it seemed entirely plausible in that moment of unchecked hysteria that he was exposed to every disease known to man, up to and including black plague.

Carter jumped away, leaping nearly half the distance to the kitchen door, and released the scream trapped in his throat as a high, reedy whisper. An exaggerated series of half-coughs, half-sneezes gripped him, the explosions so violent he bent over in anticipation of vomiting. His head pulsed, a red light strobing behind his eyeballs, and then he forced himself to calm down and breathe before he dropped dead of an aneurysm.

The flashlight beam jittered in his hand now, but he steadied it enough to shine it back on the floor under the window.

The puddle slowly seeped and spread across his living room, undoubtedly from the flood on his front lawn.

"Oh my God, oh no, this isn't happening." His vision still wavered like heat shimmers on hot concrete, but he gave his head a good shake. He would not pass out, not here in his own home.

He crept forward again, almost crawling, the flashlight carving a path through the gloom. The water moved fast now, pouring in across the carpet in the direction of his sunken living room. From the expanding edge of the puddle, he used the flashlight to examine the windowsill, where the pane of clear plastic that served as a window was fitted to the frame.

Dry.

Which meant the water was coming from somewhere at the base of the wall, a wall supposedly impervious to outside elements.

The Lucid chuckled.

His attack surged back, and this time he was helpless to stop it. His world, the bubble of safety he'd created, was violated, and he suddenly felt more vulnerable than if he'd been stripped naked and thrown in a cage with starving jackals. He could feel that largeness out there pressing in on him, could imagine all those germs squeezing in through a million tiny holes, flaws, and imperfections.

As the world spun in front of him, Carter grabbed one of the rebreather masks from the wall and slipped it on.

WHITNEY -1:33

Just two hundred yards from where Carter Vance battled his phobias, the two shadows he'd seen from his window continued to haul sandbags back and forth across the private pier at Hayden Beach. They belonged to two large, burly men, both hunched into the strengthening wind with their loads and soaked to the bone even under their raincoats.

Danny Marsalis and John Nighbaum—neither of them actual residents of Port Allen or even the state of Texas—hadn't spoken a word to each other in the last two hours. This was partially because of the effort required to make themselves heard over the storm, but mostly because they were exhausted, close to crashing out.

They'd carried sandbag after sandbag from the pile brought by the Red Cross to the makeshift seawall stretching the length of the beach in this lower section of coastline, continued this operation long after the other volunteers bussed in with them congratulated themselves on a job well done and ran for the hills, didn't stop even when their clothes became little more than sodden rags and the afternoon was swallowed by a pitch black early twilight.

John, the older of the two, finally stopped to check his watch, pressing the button on the side to light up its face, and found it close to six. He stood at the edge of the pier and looked out over the wall of sandbags they'd helped to create, now up to shoulder height.

The beach that was here yesterday morning when they arrived from Massachusetts was gone, smothered by the storm surge Whitney pushed in front of it. Most of the city's coastline was protected by seawall or elevated coastal development, but the rich bastards in the housing development behind them had blocked the local government from doing anything to mar their view. The water level had risen seven feet in the past four hours, full of surging whitecaps getting bigger with each passing minute, and do you think any of them had come down to help save their homes?

But even with so much work still needed, it wouldn't be wise for the two of them to still be here when Whitney came ashore and turned those whitecaps into crashing waves. John turned to his partner and shouted, *"Danny! It's gettin late! We need to go!"*

"Not yet!" Danny hoisted another bag into place. *"There's still a few places where the wall's not high enough!"*

"We've done all we can! The storm's gonna be here any minute!"

"Just a few more! It might make all the difference!"

Something in the younger man's face broke John's resolve, and he smiled before leaning in to give him a gentle kiss beneath his slicker hood, the way he did the morning Danny rolled over in bed and begged him to come save a little city in Texas. *"I can't say no to you!"*

"I'm well aware!" Danny gave his lover's wet face a caress before turning around to head back to the sandbag pile.

John made to do the same, but halted when an even darker shadow whispered over him, flickering across his face in the illumination of a sudden lightning flash. He looked up, expecting to see a frightened seagull hightailing it for safer ground, but instead caught the end of something much bigger as it streaked just a few feet over him.

A loud splash came from his left as whatever it was landed in one of the deep puddles collecting all across the pier. John's head whipped in the noise's direction to see only a blur of sinuous movement. He tried to follow it in the darkness and the rain, but it disappeared into the maze of pillars supporting a raised section of boardwalk.

"What in God's name?" Each word was ripped from his mouth by the wind. It hadn't been a bird. It looked far too big to even be capable of flight, but he couldn't give a more accurate guess from the flash he'd seen.

John walked a few paces forward, peering into the murk beneath the boardwalk. The space was low, only about three feet high, but it stretched a good distance under the wooden walkway. Perhaps the animal was wounded and scared, needing his gentle hands to rescue it. This thought kept him moving until he arrived at the edge of the support pillars.

"Hello?" The sound of the rain thunking against the wood above him created a droning backbeat. *"C'mon out, so I can help you!"*

From under the boardwalk came a strange, ululating cry, warbling and unpleasant enough to make the hair of his forearms stand on end. An acrid, fishy smell, like rotted sushi, hit his nostrils. John searched the blackness for the source of both, and settled on a low clump of shadows stretched across the sand a few yards further in from where he stood.

Two sickly yellow eyes gazed out at him from its depths, regarding him with reptilian calm.

Suddenly John no longer wanted to save whatever was under there, wounded or not. He no longer wanted to save the people of Port Allen, Texas either. What he wanted was to collect his lover and go home to the Bay State as fast as his legs would take him.

A hand—or something resembling a hand—swiped out as the creature moved forward with uncanny speed, and John had time to see its scaly texture and to loose one scream before the claws on the ends of its malformed fingers sank into his chest and hauled him deep beneath the boardwalk.

WHITNEY -1:31

Danny heard the scream during a brief lull in the wind, turned, saw John's flailing legs slide out of sight. He dropped a sandbag and shouted the man's name, then pelted up the short slope.

He'd covered half the distance when a shape emerged. Danny halted in the wet sand, relieved his boyfriend was all right.

As the shape approached, crawling on four legs first and then rising upright on two, his relief dried up as he realized this was not John.

The thing was big, about his height and twice as wide, but the shadows of the storm and the shifting curtain of rain made real details impossible. Danny backed up without taking his eyes off the thing until a close burst of lightning lit up the entire pier.

It's the fuckin Creature from the Black Lagoon, was Danny's last addled thought, before the thing leapt on him.

WHITNEY -1:27

Kim's Grocery was small, really more of a glorified convenience store, but it would suit their needs. Lincoln didn't care if the crew survived on Ramen noodles, as long as they survived.

The three of them huddled in a brick alcove between Kim's and the Laundromat next door, partially protected from the wind. Together, they managed to pry off one of the boards nailed in place to protect the storefront's glass. Mac wrapped his mallet-sized fist in the sleeve of his rain slicker and punched through the window next to the door, then reached through and turned the dead bolt.

The air inside was stale and thick from lack of air conditioning, the weather outside creating a muggy, suffocating climate in here. At least it shielded them from the wind enough to talk normally, but that probably wouldn't last too much longer. After a minute, their eyes adjusted. The place was narrow, but deep. Short aisles marched away from them toward the darker back end, centered in the middle of the store with passages across both sides. The front counter sat against the wall immediately to the right of the door, so no one could leave without passing under Kim's scrutinizing glare.

It was a relief just to be inside, shielded from the rain and the noise of the storm, but Lincoln fought the urge to draw his gun from the back of his waistband, a snubnose .38 he'd bought off a desperate crack addict two years before and never even fired. This was by no means his first B and E, and he found they went a lot smoother with the confidence a gat in hand provided even if he never intended to use it. Just seemed kind of silly to go waving it around though, with the whole city virtually empty.

"Grab baskets and carry everything you can get." Lincoln pulled back the hood on his poncho. He took off the covering and threw it on the floor beside the door, happy to be dry if only for a few minutes, and Mac did the same. "I wanna be outta here in five minutes."

"This is great!" CT scratched at his neck absently while he spoke. Lincoln watched the movement carefully. He'd heard his cousin was hitting the pipe on the side. That junkie itch brought back vivid memories of his mother at the kitchen table, clawing at the vinyl top until her nails were bloody when she couldn't score. CT's last hit must be at least a few hours gone; he was probably jonesing bad. It made Lincoln sick. His cousin stopped long enough to dump boxes of cereal into a wire-handled basket dangling from his elbow. The image reminded Lincoln of Little Red Riding Hood, if that dumb blond had been a skinny brother. "I been wantin to hit this fool long as I lived in the hood!"

"He's not so bad," Mac said from an aisle further into the store.

"Whatevah! He always eyein me every time I come in, like he just 'spect me to steal shit from 'im!"

"You're stealin shit from him now." Lincoln filled his first basket with dehydrated Chinese pasta. Personally, he liked the elderly Korean gentleman. He watched members of the crew when they came in from behind his comically oversized glasses, but, shit, they *were* gangbangers. They stole, they sold some weed, but mass media these days would have everyone believe them to be stone cold killers. In any case, old Kim typically didn't bother them if they didn't bother him.

"That ol' chink deserves it," CT grumbled. The boy opened the first of the upright coolers lining the left wall and started pulling out cans of soda and bottled water.

Lincoln chose not to answer, just worked his way to the end of the aisle, filling his baskets with canned goods. He turned and started down the next aisle, where Mac appeared to be studying tins of Dinty Moore in the dark.

"You got a grievance?" he asked his lieutenant in hushed tones.

"Naw, Links. I'm solid." Which, in Mac terms, meant, *Fuck you, dawg.*

"You got somethin to say, just say it."

Mac put his basket down and straightened, checking to make sure the other soldier wasn't within earshot. "I don't know Links, you been different lately. You act like everything you do is for the crew, but…you just seem gone all the time."

"What're you talkin about? I'm here, I'm always here!"

Mac touched his temple with one thick finger. "Up here, man. Off in your own world. We could've stocked up on supplies earlier, but instead we was off stealin half the city."

Here it was, exactly the accusation he feared, and even though part of him agreed with the sentiment, he felt compelled to argue. "That's what the crew wanted, Mac! We cash that stuff in after the hurricane, and we set!"

"Yeah, but you the leader. You the one supposed to keep 'em from doin somethin that's gonna hurt 'em, like stealin shit that don't do any good if they don't live long enough to use it. But you just been spaced out…" He trailed off and shrugged.

Lincoln inspected the watery tracks their shoes had left on the tile floor. "I got a lot on my mind, Mac. This crew just keeps gettin bigger, and everyone else just keeps tryin to take shit from us. Plus, we're *nineteen*, man. That's pretty old to still be in the game and not underground or behind bars. And there's a lotta youngsters like C-Tone over there just waitin to step into my shoes. I don't know, today was the first day in a long time I didn't worry 'bout all that."

"You want my opinion, part of you wants out, Links."

"Out? Of the crew? No way, man, that ain't—"

Mac reached out and gave each of his cheeks a light slap. "Always said you were worth more than all this shit, and I think you startin to realize it. And that's fine if you do, you ain't gotta feel guilty about leavin me or them or anybody. But you gotta do one of two things, and it's a choice you gotta make soon: either leave, get the fuck out, forget about us and try to make somethin of yourself...or get your head back down to earth and start leadin us again."

There it was, laid out in no uncertain terms. Mac had just put a problem into words that Lincoln couldn't even explain to himself.

He was tired of the unending responsibility, tired of having to put everyone else before himself, tired of having to struggle just to survive. But it was the only life he knew.

Lincoln raised his gaze from the floor. "If I *were* to go...would you and I be good?"

"We always good, bitch." Mac wrapped a huge arm around his shoulders. "East Side X-Dawgs."

"East Side X-Dawgs," Lincoln agreed.

They turned around, preparing to work their way further up the aisle, but instead found themselves gazing down the black barrel of a very big shotgun.

WHITNEY -1:21

Chris would've been content to sulk in his room all night away from the 'Ill-more Girls' (another nickname for his stepfamily that had already gotten him grounded twice) if the noise from the storm hadn't reached intolerable levels outside their third floor apartment. All alone on his bed, with no electricity or even a candle, it was too easy to imagine the dark as some howling animal whose throat he was trapped inside.

He knew he was smart—even without all the gifted and talented programs they placed him in at school, or the letters his teachers sent home, always about one of two almost mythic words, APTITUDE or POTENTIAL, or the engineering and electronics classes they kept trying to get him to take—but even with his intelligence, he couldn't for the life of him understand why his father had chosen to marry that she-devil half a year ago.

It was like a "Twilight Zone" episode. *Submitted for your approval,* he thought, as he got off his bed, grabbed a flashlight from his dresser, and padded on bare feet into the hallway. *One Nichelle Kittrick, a shrewish, dull, and not terribly attractive woman, with the added baggage of a daughter who took after her in all of these traits, plus a generous dose of plain old annoying. What could a healthy, non-brain-damaged man like Daryl Sloan possibly see in her?*

Conversely, it wasn't nearly as hard to see why Nichelle married his father. The she-devil moved in, took over, and now that his father was getting this job in California, she would cash in on her marital investment.

And he didn't even know where to start the mental list of complaints about his new stepsister with the goofy name. The kid followed him around closer than his freaking shadow, tried to talk to his friends, thought she was so cute all the time with her innocent, cow-eyes routine and sickly sweet voice, and, worst of all, she was already calling his father 'Daddy.' His father was *not*, and *never* would be, her daddy. Her daddy was just some deadbeat that knocked up her mom and then left town as soon as he found out. The girl had even been given the extra bedroom in the apartment. Since his mother's death two years ago, he and his father had used this space for Nerf basketball tournaments and model airplane construction, neither of which they'd done together since the arrival of the Ill-more Girls.

Chris stood in the doorway of the darkened room next to his—now decorated in Hannah Montana posters and High School Musical memorabilia—and tried to relive those days, the last time in his life he could recall being happy. In the wake of his mother's death, he thought that would be impossible.

And what's going to happen to those memories when you move to California?

With a resigned sigh, Chris turned to go.

Then he stopped. Turned back with a frown.

Tangela had a small plastic table in the middle of the room with four chairs around it where she held dinner parties for her precious Bratz doll, Kiki. In the light from his flashlight, he could see a familiar checker-patterned swatch of cloth spread across the table under a smorgasbord of fake food.

Chris' jaw clenched and then began to move back and forth, the way it always did when his mind kicked into overdrive. He crossed the room, yanking the blanket from the table with the flair of a magician, except nothing on it stayed in place. He held the fabric at arm's length in front of his face while her crap scattered on the floor.

A blanket; a small, square, felt blanket about two feet long, in a checkered design of deep blue and black. Didn't look like anything special, but one could never tell just by looking at it that Pamela Sloan once placed it on her son's pillow each night before bed until he was eleven years old, without which the boy couldn't sleep. This was one of Chris's fondest memories of his limited time with the woman. Last he checked, the security blanket—Mr. Softy—was stowed away safely in his closet.

And that little *bitch* turned it into a tablecloth.

Chris stormed out of the room with the blanket clenched in both fists, blinking back tears of rage.

Nichelle sat on the couch in the dull glow of the candles with her daughter cradled in her lap, the latter crying in fear of the storm.

"Chris, you need to stay out here with us." She was forced to speak up to be heard over the wind, but, even so, her words were too fast, distracted. "We have to stay way from the windows, or maybe even go downstairs and see if we can get in Ms. Zwykowski's apartment."

"What is this?" He held up the blanket.

Tangela lifted her head from her mother's breast and gazed up with tear-swollen eyes. "Hey, that's my tablecloth!"

"No, that's *my* blanket. Where'd you get it?"

"Chris, I'm sorry, it's my fault," Nichelle told him, obviously trying to stop a fight by shifting blame to herself, but he didn't want to be calmed. That howling animal outside was nothing compared to the one awakening inside him. "I found it in the top of your closet and I told her she could use it."

"Yeah, well why do you think it's any more okay if *you* do it, huh? Who gave you the right to go through my shit?"

"Christopher!" His stepmom eased Tangela over on to the couch beside her and then stood up to face him. "Don't you dare talk to me like that! I said I was sorry! I don't know what the big deal is anyway, it's just an old blanket!"

"My *mother* gave me this 'old blanket,'" he snarled. His fists were wrapped so tight around the cloth he could feel the fingernails biting into his palms through the fabric. The wind outside roared before falling into a lull. "My *real* mother, not the woman that weaseled her way into marrying my dad."

Nichelle's face fell, her own anger gone. "Oh, Chris. I'm so sorry, I...I didn't know."

"Yeah, you didn't know, you *never* know!"

Tangela broke into renewed tears on the couch. "Stop it! Mommy, Chris, stop it!"

But Chris couldn't stop. He'd let the occasional sass slip before, but this was the final violation, the last indignity, and if he didn't let the volcano inside him get rid of some lava, he would explode. "You took away my dad, you took away my life, and now you're trying to take my mom, too!" He threw the blanket. It landed in a pile at her feet.

"Chris, I would never do anything—"

"Yes, you would, you already have! I hate *you*, and I hate *her*!" He leveled a finger at the little girl crying on the couch.

Now Nichelle was more than just repentant, she looked upset, close to tears. "I'm sorry you feel that way, Chris. I don't hate you, though. And neither does Tangela. Do you, Tanj?"

"Noooo," the girl wailed through her tears. "You're my friend, Chris!"

"You hear that?" she asked him, as the wind renewed its fight even louder than before. "This little girl looks up to you. You're her hero, Chris. She would do anything for you. And so would I. You just have to give us the chance."

I don't want to give you the chance, was how Christopher Sloan intended to respond.

Before he could, the roof above his head tore off and flew into the night, letting in the ungodly noise of the storm. The ground beneath his feet tilted and Chris fell backward toward the gaping hole Whitney had ripped in the side of their apartment.

WHITNEY -1:17

Around the time Carter Vance realized his house shared a pressing quality with Swiss cheese, Nichelle Kittrick-Sloan watched her stepson fall into the night, and Lincoln Briggs found himself at gunpoint, the man who had told the President his name was Kyler sat in a mobile command center just outside Austin, streaking toward Port Allen. He would've flown, but a last minute meeting with his superiors had required a communication console.

Meeting, in this case, being very loosely defined.

He didn't know the identity or faces of any of these men (or women; Kyler certainly wasn't sexist enough to believe a woman couldn't be on the other side of his orders, just that they undoubtedly wanted to sleep with him), and interfaced with them only by text on an encrypted server. Things tended to work smoother this way: if someone at his level of Aurora's management structure needed to be disavowed, there was no fear of them bringing down the entire works, because they literally didn't know who to point the finger at. They could be cut off in a heartbeat, ostracized from cash, resources, and identity, which made for employees damn careful they did their job right.

Of course, if it reached that point, you were usually dead before you knew you fucked up.

A phone call was patched through to the man with the question mark scar on his chin, now in a military ops turtleneck and night camo pants. His hand shook as he reached to accept. He paused with it held over the console, watching the tremors with a raised eyebrow and a twitching grin.

This had been happening a lot lately. He had no idea why, but he couldn't see a doctor about it. Oh no; that sort of thing shot right up the pipeline to the brass, and before you knew it you were being debriefed and packed away in a crate on its way to Siberia. Couldn't have shaky hands when the security of the nation rested in them. That's how earthquakes happened, right?

That thought made him release some of those giggles that had unnerved the President, but Kyler barely heard them. God, his head was so muddled lately. His thoughts had a way of just straying off into inanities, like a tourist hopping over the roped path in a museum. He had to get shit straight before he lapsed in front of someone that mattered.

Kyler answered the call. The person on the other end let him know Simon and Tony had been safely airlifted out of the city, and were even now uploading their notes on Project Mercury to a new computer system, after which they would be shot in the back of the head.

Good news. All on time and according to plan.

Once this call finished, Kyler had a new outgoing line sent through to two of his men already on the scene in this dipshit burg.

"Phase 1 is behind us with Whitney barely an hour from the shore," he said. "Pull all our people back to failsafe, wave bye-bye to the National Guard, and then you boys close up that city tighter than your mammas' coochies. Make me proud, now." He didn't wait for confirmations before signing off.

Since he couldn't be there to see them for himself, Kyler sat in the dark of the mobile command unit and imagined what the fireworks would look like.

WHITNEY -1:15

When Lincoln tore away from the empty gaze of the shotgun, he looked along its length to find two slanted eyes boring into him behind a pair of black-rimmed glasses so large they reached all the way to the owner's balding forehead.

"Mr. Kim!" he blurted.

The small Korean grocery store owner was in shorts and a white t-shirt with a bathrobe hanging open over them, the stock of the shotgun jammed against a bony shoulder, one hand supporting the barrel and the other firmly on the trigger. The gun itself was a single-barrel, pump-action job. Kim squinted at Lincoln and Mac with about the same amount of distaste as someone who just stepped in dog shit.

"Drop stuff and get hands up!" The shopkeeper barked in staccato bursts.

"Mr. Kim, we—"

"Now, get hands up! Do it!" He poked the shotgun in the air at them, and both boys slowly raised their hands into the air. Mr. Kim grinned victoriously. "See, I smart, I stay here through storm! Nobody rob me!"

"Mr. Kim, this ain't what it looks like," Lincoln tried again, knowing it was exactly what it looked like.

"Shut up, both of you!" Kim ordered, although Mac hadn't opened his mouth once. Kim's round moon face screwed up in anger, eyes squinted almost closed. "I catch you with red hand! You break window and take things! Now back up, stand against wall!"

Lincoln glanced at Mac, who raised an eyebrow questioningly. Lincoln knew what the question was, too. After all, they both towered over the diminutive shop owner, and both had guns within a few seconds' reach; it might be possible for them to turn this around.

"Stop looking at each other like gay boys and move!"

They did as asked, sliding their feet backward while keeping hands hoisted high. Lincoln pretended to look over his right shoulder to see where he was going, but instead scanned the dim interior of the store for CT. Things would go from bad to bloodshed if that little hothead got in the middle of this.

They exited the row where Kim got the drop on them and passed into the dark side aisle in front of the coolers. Desperation twitched beneath Lincoln's muscles.

"Please Mr. Kim, you gotta listen to us! We didn't know you were here! We just needed some food for after the storm! We can pay you whatever you want, and we'll replace the window!"

Kim scowled at him. "No, no, I know *you*. You…bad kids! You always steal from me!"

"We never stole one goddamn thing from you before today, old man," Mac growled.

"Be quiet! Don't talk again, or I shoot you!"

"Oh yeah? You willin to go to jail for that?"

"*Jail?*" Kim snorted disbelief. "You think I go to *jail* for this? You loot my store! Nobody get upset if two less thugs like you in the world!"

Lincoln's spine tightened. He was fooling himself if he thought the old man ever saw them as anything more than street trash.

There was movement at the end of the next row, and one of the shadows to the right broke away from the others and glided forward. CT had his own pistol out. He sidled up to Kim from the old man's left side and placed the barrel at his temple. "Drop that shit now, you wrinkly yellow bee-yitch."

"No!" Kim's voice was shrill, on the verge of hysteria. The shotgun shook in his hands now, his finger still curled dangerously tight around the trigger. "You drop gun, or I kill you friends!"

"*You* drop it, motherfuckah!"

"*YOU!*"

Things had spiraled out of control, and Lincoln could feel sweat popping out across his brow in the store's trapped heat. "CT, listen to me, man, don't do anything stupid. Just put that gun down. We're just talkin to Mr. Kim."

"The hell you is." CT's eyes wobbled, either from adrenaline or withdrawal; the weapon shook. "This niggah got a gun on you, and if he don't drop it in 'bout two seconds, I'm gonna put a bullet in his brain!"

"I kill you friends!" Kim's gun roamed over them in his unsteady hands, and Lincoln winced in anticipation of the shot that would surely cut him in half.

Mac broke the standoff, sweeping in from Kim's opposite side when the shotgun wavered away. He grabbed the barrel with both hands, trying to force the business end away with CT cheering him on.

Lincoln moved just in time, dropping to the floor. A hot mass roared through the air where he was standing. The glass fronts of two of the coolers along the back wall exploded in a shower of glass. He looked up to get a reading on the situation.

The blast had shaken Mac free. Kim controlled the shotgun again, and was in the process of pumping the barrel to chamber another round. CT raised his gun to the Asian's head again with a snarl.

"NO!" Lincoln shouted, a split second too late.

Kim's brains splattered against the back wall.

At least, that's what Lincoln's imagination wanted to insist.

In reality, his cousin's gun made a hollow click, and a stream of water dribbled from the tip.

Mac waved at the weapon. "I told you not to be playin with it in the rain!"

Kim took advantage of the misfire, swinging the shotgun back around on CT. The boy moved just as fast, throwing the water-logged gun at Kim and jumping out the way of a second deafening boom that lit up the interior of the store and left ghostly imprints on the backs of Lincoln's eyeballs. CT sprinted to the far end of the aisle and dove left for cover, slipping on the tile. Kim cocked the weapon again and whirled to bring the gun back around on his former captives.

Mac was already retreating, disappearing further into the store with his head ducked. Lincoln scampered on hands and knees the opposite way, toward the protection of the aisle closest to him.

"I kill you ALL!" Kim's accent reminded Lincoln of a crazed Vietcong in some old war movie. He raised the shotgun above his head and shook it, no longer the sullen shopkeeper, but turned into some kind of psychopath as if to match the insanity Whitney was unleashing outside.

Lincoln found himself crouched in the potato chip aisle. The shelves all had solid backs, so it was impossible to see through them. The store was dead silent now aside from the howl of the wind against the front glass, the tense quiet becoming thicker as the seconds ticked by.

He reached behind him, felt for the pistol in the waistband of his pants.

"Mr. Kim!" He listened for the slightest sound over the wail of the storm to betray the man's location. "Mr. Kim, just let us out of here! We don't want any trouble!"

He was closest to the door, which meant the Korean was somewhere between him and the other two members of his crew. He could probably escape, but there was no way he would ever leave a man behind.

Something struck one of the remaining coolers next to him once, again, and on the third time the object rebounded and struck his cheek. He looked down as a little round object came to rest against his foot.

A Skittle.

Lincoln duck-walked to the end of the aisle where the candy came from and peeked around the edge of the shelf.

Mac was three aisles down, his eyes like floating quarters. He held a finger to his lips, pointed at Lincoln, then into the next aisle, and then twirled his finger in a half circle.

Lincoln understood: Kim was trying to come up behind him.

He eased the rest of his body out into the cross aisle and looked around the next corner just in time to see Kim disappearing into the far end of the row he'd just vacated. He waddled forward on stealthy feet until he reached Mac, and found both soldiers huddled next to the displays of candy. Mac had his own pistol out, held against his chest. "What's the play?" he whispered.

"We make a run for the door."

"What?" CT looked offended by idea. "Fuck that, let's smoke this fool!"

"We're not smokin anybody! We're gonna get out before that lunatic shoots us all!"

"And what about that food, huh? Thought the crew needed it!"

"We'll find it somewhere else."

CT smirked. "Man, Links, if you too chickenshit to handle bidness, gimme that gun and I'll do it myself."

Mac grabbed Lincoln's cousin by the front of his sopping shirt and hauled him closer. "You mouthy little fuck—"

"Enough." Lincoln pried them apart and asked Mac, "You think this place has another way out?"

"Prob'ly lets onto the alley somewhere in back, but we'd be searchin for it blind in the dark."

"Then we go with the front." Lincoln thought about this, mind flying through scenarios. "All right, I'll fire a shot down the back aisle to draw him away. You two take off for the door and I'll be right behind you."

"Fine, except one thing," Mac said. "*I'm* firin the shot."

"Why?"

"Cause both of you are smaller and faster than me, and whoever stays behind is gonna want a clear path to that door."

Lincoln couldn't argue. Mac crawled past him and waited for Lincoln and CT to get to the opposite end of the aisle. When they were in position, he pointed his gun around the corner and fired a blind shot toward the ceiling.

Kim roared in anger. They heard him running to the far side of the store, away from the exit.

Lincoln gave CT a shove. They stood up together and took off for the door at a dead run, heads ducked. A second later, he heard Mac's clomping steps behind him.

We got this, we got this…

They were almost at the door when his foot skidded in one of the puddles they'd tracked in. The world slid sideways. His legs went in different directions. He fell against the front counter, slamming his shoulder and the side of his head painfully against the lacquered top before coming to rest on the tile in a daze.

"Get up, Links!" Mac dropped his gun to grab Lincoln's arm and lift him off the floor.

"AAAARRRRHHH!" The inhuman howl came from the aisle directly in front of them. Lincoln hung from Mac's grip by one arm, head spinning. He looked up to see Kim racing toward them like a kamikaze pilot, shotgun bearing on the bigger of his two targets.

Lincoln's revolver was still clutched in his other hand. It felt fuzzy and far away. He lifted the gun, took wobbly aim, and pulled the trigger.

The first bullet took Kim in the left shoulder, cutting off his zealous shriek. The second took him high in the chest. He staggered back a step. Blood poured from the wound to soak his robe, the color a deep black in the dark store. A confused look crossed the Korean's face as he let the shotgun slip from his hand and collapsed backward on the tile with a heavy, wet *thud*.

Outside, the storm raged, but in the store, the silence in the wake of the gunshots was even louder than their explosions.

"Oh God," Lincoln murmured. He and Mac were frozen in their figure-skater positions, Lincoln dangling backward and still holding the pistol up. It felt like it weighed a thousand pounds now. Smoke drifted from the barrel in a lazy trail. He finally let his arm drop and the weapon fell to the floor beside Mac's gun.

Mac finished pulling him to his feet and let him lean on the counter. He ran to the Asian, knelt to examine him. He looked back over, his jaw working on its hinge for a second before he could speak. "Links, man…he's dead."

Lincoln tried to step away from the counter and felt his legs give. "Well...what the fuck, man? He coulda just calmed down! Was this shit worth *dyin* for?" He spoke the words, but didn't feel them. The world slowly came back into focus, but an almost paralyzing numbness sank into his skin, into his bones. There was a hole in him somewhere, a plug pulled, and his entire identity, everything that made him Lincoln Briggs, was slowly circling that drain.

He had never killed anyone before.

"All right, Links!" CT shouted gleefully from the door. "You showed that old fool!"

"SHUT UP!" Lincoln rushed the boy before he could react. He backhanded him once across the cheek, hard enough to rock his head to the side. "You think that's *good?* If you'd done what I asked, this wouldn'ta happened! Next time I give you an order, you better goddamn listen!"

CT's head moved at turtle speed, creaking back on his neck to face him. A welt had risen across the left side of his face. In a lifeless drone, he said, "You hit me again Links...and we gonna have trouble all over."

"Oh God. I can't believe this shit happened..." Lincoln backed away as his vision blurred.

"CT, get the supplies," Mac said softly.

The younger boy gave him another baleful look, but seemed to know enough to keep his mouth shut. He went to collect their goods. Mac retrieved both guns from the floor and held the revolver out. Lincoln cringed away.

"C'mon, it's evidence, you can't leave it here."

"I don't care. I'm not touchin it. I...I didn't mean to do it, Mac."

Mac wiped the gun down with his shirt to remove the fingerprints and then set it on the counter beside the register. After a moment's thought, he did the same with his. "There's nothin for this, Lincoln. You just have to keep movin and let it go. You saved my life, and we both know it."

"Yeah? You think that's what the cops are gonna say? They throw you in a hole so deep for something like this not even the cockroaches come to visit."

"You ain't ever gonna stand before the cops for this, Lincoln,

I promise you. We gonna get this food, get back to base, and then Whitney's gonna wash away everything else. Be days before they even find the body."

Lincoln felt a tear threatening to spill. Somehow it was worse that only Mac was here, the one person he could show weakness in front of.

"Don't think about it right now," Mac insisted. "Just help us carry this and let's go home."

They never called base 'home,' but at that moment, it sounded like heaven. Lincoln wanted a hot shower, the biggest blunt he could roll, and then to crawl into bed until the insanity of the hurricane was over.

They decided to just leave the ponchos rather than be slowed down by them, and all three X-Dawgs gathered up baskets of food. When they were lined up at the front door, Lincoln said, "Go straight for base, all the way down to 10th Avenue and then cut over to Green. Don't stop moving."

He pushed opened the door, which the wind promptly grabbed and slammed against the storefront, shattering the glass and ripping it off one of the hinges. They stumbled into the night with their load, rain whipping them. Lincoln crossed the sidewalk quickly and stepped off the curb into the flooded street, then wiped at his blurry eyes to get a better view of their surroundings.

And froze in horror.

A police car glided toward them, skidding to a stop right in front of the trio.

WHITNEY -1:07

"Well, gentlemen, looks like we have some early Christmas shoppers."

Charlie braked hard when the three figures exited Kim's Grocery and raced in front of their patrol car, sending the vehicle into a skid as it rode the six inches of water on the pavement. They came to a stop diagonally, partially blocking both lanes of traffic.

Ellis peered through his window, which now faced the three looters. All black, arms full of food from the store and guilty, deerin-headlight expressions. Physically, they were a ghetto version of the Three Bears just awaiting a Goldilocks: one of them big enough to be a linebacker, one muscular but average size, and one so scrawny it was a wonder the storm didn't blow him away. The wind flapped their clothes and forced their eyes down to slits.

"Let's do this." Charlie flipped up the hood on his rain slicker.

"You serious?" Billy leaned forward against the grate. "We're in the middle of a hurricane, who cares if they're looting the place? If they don't take it today, someone else will just do it tomorrow!"

"Hey." Charlie turned in his seat, and pointed a crooked finger at the rookie. "Don't you ever let me hear you talk like that again. Crime is crime, junior, and if we look the other way, we're no better than them. Now let's take care of this before they run."

"Look like gangbangers," Ellis muttered. Port Allen's gang problems ranged mostly from the inner city to the suburbs on the east side, a lot of them three and four member groups filling neighborhood pocket niches but there were a few major players in the world of disorganized crime. He would never say it to his partner, but he leaned closer to Billy's side of the argument.

"Yeah, and we're gonna bang their gang if they give us a reason." Charlie pulled his pistol from the holster on his hip. "But be goddamn careful. None of us is wearin body armor." With that cheerful parting thought, Charlie leapt out the door.

First rule of copdom; back up your partner. Ellis climbed out of the passenger side, now facing the hoodlums. Wind sliced through the car, screeching as it tried to slam the door closed on him. Rain blew into his face under the hood, but rather than wipe at it and impede his vision, he blinked the moisture away. He braced his feet in the ankle-deep water running down the street and, using the door as a shield, rested his arms on the rim of the window frame to aim his pistol. Without turning his head from his targets, he reached with one hand to open the back door of the car for Billy to do the same.

"*Freeze, all of you!*" Flecks of water sprayed from Charlie's lips and mustache. Amazing how much the wind dampened his voice; Ellis was three feet away and his voice was barely a whisper over the roof of the car. "*Drop the baskets and put your hands where we can see them!*"

The three black boys either had better hearing than he did, or had been through the scenario enough to know what was expected. They opened their arms one at a time; average-sized first, followed by the human mountain, and then the shrimp, who seemed to give up his prizes after some hard thinking. Canned goods, bags and boxes spilled onto the wet street, some of them floating away, and the three of them raised their hands into the air.

Charlie was in motion, closing his door and then coming around the front of the car to cover all three of the boys at once. Ellis yelled, *"Call it in, Billy!"* over his shoulder, and then dashed forward as well, keeping his gun trained on the suspects.

"Down on the ground, one knee and then the other! Cross your feet at the ankles!" Charlie shouted when he got close enough to be heard. The trio complied, kneeling in the water. Only when they were in this precarious position in the middle of the street did Charlie reholster his pistol, leaving Ellis to continue coverage.

He took the opportunity to examine them more closely as they knelt in the downpour. Papa, Mama, and Baby Bear were little more than tatted-up high schoolers, two of them barely eighteen if even that, and the little guy with cornrows surely around the late end of sixteen. All three kept their hands high and faces as empty as professional poker players, betraying nothing.

"Nice night for a burglary, boys." The wind lulled enough so Charlie didn't have to yell. "You wanna tell us what's goin on here?"

Hesitation and silence. Finally, the ones on either end—Papa and Baby Bear—swiveled their heads to glance at the kid in the middle. Ah, so this one with the rose and dagger tattoos was dominant. The kid's face was serene, eyes squinted against the rain but still staring dead ahead at nothing in particular. He opened his mouth to speak, and Ellis waited for the usual stream of gutter filth.

"Officer…we're sorry. We just wanted some food, that's all. We were just takin what we needed before the storm hit."

"That so?" Charlie paused to take in the objects they'd let fall from their hands, still bobbing in the current. "Well, you're tellin the truth about that. Nothin in there that won't give you cavities and acne. You take any money, anything besides food?"

"No sir."

"Looks like you busted up the front door to the store."

"Only a little bit. The wind did the rest."

"And you know a hurricane is no excuse for looting?"

"Yes sir, we do." Still with that complacent tone, no sign of disrespect. The big one was just as meager, but Ellis noticed the little one on the far end had eyes that flashed every few second with barely concealed anger whenever his homeboy answered a question.

"Why you still here? You aware the city is under a mandatory evacuation?"

"Yes sir, but this is our home. We didn't have anywhere else to go."

Charlie sighed, shook his head, wiped rain from his face, and softened. "All right, fine. You boys carryin anything? Drugs, knives, etcetera?"

"No sir."

"Any objections to me pattin you down?"

The two bigger boys shook their heads; the little one scowled.

"All right then, stay calm, and don't move." Charlie walked behind the largest boy first, bending over to pat him down and then brought his muscled arms behind the boy's back. "I'm gonna put a zip-tie on you, son. This is just for my protection, cause you look big enough to eat me for breakfast. You aren't under arrest at this time, you understand?"

The gangbanger cracked a smile, but then grimaced as Charlie took his hands and bound them at the wrist with one of the heavy plastic cords that looked like bigger versions of garbage bags ties. Ellis gave an inward sigh of relief once he was contained. Charlie repeated the procedure with the next one, the leader, but left him with his hands in the air instead of binding them. An errant thunderbolt whipcracked overhead, echoing into a grumble.

"So what are you boys?" Ellis asked. "Beach Street Rippers? Allen Bloods?"

The answer came from the little one. "X-Dawgs," he stated proudly. This time it was the other two who shot him an angry look.

"X-Dawgs, huh? You're operating a little ways from home, aren't you?"

"Only cause yo momma didn't call me over again last night."

"Shut the fuck up, CT," the one in the middle told him.

"Listen to your friend and keep your lips closed." Charlie reached this boy last and gave him the treatment.

Ellis felt a tap on his shoulder and turned to find Billy at his side. The rookie's face was wet, but Ellis could see fear beneath the moisture.

"I couldn't raise anybody," he said in Ellis' ear. "The radio...it's completely dead. Nothing but static on every channel."

"Just the storm. No big deal."

"Yeah, but what if we need backup?"

"What, for these three?" Ellis indicated the trio with a flick of his pistol. "I think we got them handled."

Charlie told the boys to stay still again and came to join the huddle. "They're clean, just like they said."

"Great, fine, let's cut them loose and get outta here," Billy said.

"Goddammit kid, they're three gang members caught during the commission of a robbery! We need to take 'em in!"

"Take them in *where*, Charlie? They emptied out the prison and all the jails! We'll have to haul them all the way to the rally point in Houston, and the only way they'll even fit in the car is if I ride in Ellis' lap! Jesus, with the big one it'll still be a tight squeeze!"

"We have an obligation to get them out of the city—!"

"Fuck that, Charlie! It's impossible to empty an entire city! You know how many other people are probably still here that *wanted* to leave and couldn't? Why the hell should we worry about the ones that don't even wanna go?"

Charlie was quiet. Ellis glanced back at the three perps and then into his partner's shadow-shrouded face beneath the orange hood. "He's right, Charlie. We don't have to arrest these three. They were only stealing food. Let's put the fear of God into them, and...and just let them go."

The older officer nodded slowly, resigning himself to an action which went against every fiber of his being. "All right. But if somethin comes of this, it's my ass on the line."

"As long as we don't say anything, who's even gonna know?" Billy asked.

The three of them turned back toward the perps. Ellis holstered his pistol at last. The strength of the wind was rising again, increasing each minute they stood out here as Whitney got closer.

"Okay boys, listen up!" Charlie shouted. *"We're confiscatin this evidence, but we're lettin you go! Find some shelter and stay in it! If we come across any of you committin a crime again, you'll be prosecuted not only for those offenses, but your actions today as well! You understand?"*

The relief in their faces was actually a little heartwarming, even on the little mean one. They broke out in ear-to-ear grins.

The leader looked at Ellis for some reason and said, *"Thank you, Officer!"*

"You're welcome!" Ellis extended a hand to help the young man to his feet.

As the boy reached for it, they heard engines behind them. All six of them, those both kneeling and standing, watched as two other Port Allen patrol cars pulled to a stop on the other side of their vehicle, one in each lane of traffic.

The passenger side door of the one on the right opened, and a figure stepped out into the rain. Too far away to see the face, but Ellis would recognize the hefty form anywhere.

It had, after all, been haunting his nightmares.

"Looks like you boys could use some assistance," George Sturney said through a megaphone, the echoes of his twangy-accented voice still carrying tones of sarcasm as they bounced between buildings.

Their backup had arrived after all.

WHITNEY -1:01

To Nichelle, the destruction of the apartment didn't seem real.

For one thing, it happened at a snail's pace, time stretching out like gooey molasses as her brain struggled to process what she was seeing. But more than that, it just looked fake, like computer generated special effects from a summer blockbuster.

One second, the wall behind Chris—the wall where her and Daryl's wedding picture hung, right between the window and the china cabinet she inherited from her grandmother—was there.

The next, it was *gone.*

She was fairly certain the wall didn't collapse, the side of the structure sloughing off like a melting ice cliff, otherwise the boy would've been killed outright by falling debris. She had a vague sense of the side of the apartment and part of the ceiling peeling away in chunks and jagged pieces, and then the storm came roaring in, windy fingers scrabbling for purchase. The candles blew out, plunging them into a world of screaming black.

Before she could call out, before the boy could even register the radical change, a groaning crack drifted up from below, audible even over the wind. The floor dropped a full foot, jarring her so badly her teeth clacked together. A crack appeared across the length of floor separating her from Chris, tearing the carpet by sheer pressure. The edge of the divide on Chris's side came up, spitting out thick lengths of pipe and coils of torn wire. At the same time, the far side of the room fell, and she realized with surreal wonder that half of their living room was tilting away from her, spilling that china cabinet and the kitchen table out into the night from the third floor.

Chris fell backward toward the gaping hole behind him, eyes wide and confused.

Her paralysis broke, and time caught up with her in one giant wallop to the senses. Nichelle fell to her knees at the edge of the newly formed precipice in the middle of their living room, narrowly avoiding impaling herself on a length of pipe.

The other half of the room was now a slope down to the missing corner of the building, an angle of nearly 45 degrees. Even if their roof hadn't collapsed, then certainly the portion of building below them had, because there was *nothing* to support this section of floor, nothing down there at all except a huge chunk of missing exterior the storm had ripped right out, like a lion tearing a bite from a gazelle's hide. The warped sight made her dizzy, an out-of-proportion carnival fun house.

Chris was two yards away. The boy had managed to turn during his fall and grab a protruding board with one hand and a shred of cheap apartment carpeting with the other. His bare feet and jean-covered legs hung over the edge into empty space, his Nike t-shirt flapping around him. From this perspective she should've been able to see the ground two stories below, but the night beyond the hole was a pitch black vortex of wind and rain. Every freezing gust seemed to raise him up a few inches, as though attempting to help him fly.

"*Mommeeeee!*" she heard Tangela shriek behind her.

Nichelle's head whipped around in time to see her daughter coming to her. She held up a hand and waved the girl away as lightning blossomed overhead. "*Get back, honey, right now! Into the hallway! Not too far, so Mommy can still see you!*" She desperately wanted to make sure her daughter was safe, but if she didn't help Chris right now, the boy would surely die.

And what do you think is gonna happen if the whole building *collapses?*

She couldn't think about that now, she had to solve the most immediate problem first. Nichelle looked back down at Chris, who tried to pull himself up enough to swing a leg onto the cantered floor. He was already drenched. "*Chris!*" she screamed into the wind, and got a mouthful of rain. "*Chris, can you hear me?*"

The boy looked up at her, young face full of terror.

"*Reach for my hand, baby!*" She leaned out, holding onto a thick black pipe with one hand and stretching the other arm out as far she could. She could already see this was useless, but when he let go of the carpet to reach, the board in his other hand snapped, and for a split second, he was falling. Nichelle let out a helpless squeal, but the boy found his grip on the fabric just before sliding completely off the edge.

The motion, however, was too much for the floor. The edge under her came up even further, causing a wooden fragment to scrape across her side hard enough to tear her shirt and draw blood. The opposite end dropped, creating an even steeper grade. Chris screamed but held on. The entire surface jiggled and wobbled.

The floor wouldn't hold.

If she wanted to save her stepson, she had to do it *now*.

"*Chris, I'll be right back!*"

"*Don't leave me!*" His voice sounded small and distant with the storm raging around them.

"*I have to find something you can hold on to!*" Nichelle didn't wait for a reply. She turned and ran across the living room, into the hallway where Tangela waited. The girl was bawling, but Nichelle could only pause long enough to touch her face as she rushed by.

The utility room sat just off the hallway on the right. She looked frantically inside, finally grabbing the sturdy handle of a wooden broom.

She was terrified the boy would be gone by the time she got back, plummeted to his death, and the strength of that fear surprised her. He may hate her, may hate her daughter, but they were a family, and that was something she was desperate to preserve.

He still dangled when she returned. Relief overwhelmed her. She squinted into the rain, planted her feet in preparation to take the boy's weight, and lowered the wide sweeping end of the broom.

Nichelle could tell as the wood slid through her wet fists that even this wouldn't be enough. The end stopped two feet short of where Chris's fingers curled around the carpet. She saw the boy reach with one hand, but come nowhere close to purchase. She stepped forward and leaned, bracing one foot against the crack to try and give as much broom as possible.

And then the section of floor dropped for the third and last time from her added weight, swinging into the ruins of the apartment below, and came to rest almost vertically.

Nichelle's center of gravity shifted, and then she was falling too.

WHITNEY -0:58

A full two inches of water stood in Carter's sunken living room.

The leak from the window had grown until it reached the drop off into his hardwood floor and then spilled over, creating a serene lake with his furniture as upholstered islands.

It would've been almost pretty if it weren't, you know, in the middle of his house.

He'd already taken his shoes off and run into the freezing cold water once to pick up anything still on the floor, including the trailing cables and wires from his computer. This was not only one of the hardest actions he'd ever forced his body to do—a feat, in his head anyway, akin to those guys on reality TV that dragged airplanes around with a rope attached to their penises—but it also cost him ten minutes of near black-out hysteria once he got back to safety in the kitchen. If it weren't for the rebreather mask, he probably would've hyperventilated.

He knew he should be worried about property damage as most normal (most *Lucid*) people would. Worried about the irreplaceable files for his work that were on his soon-to-be drowned computer, all of his ruined belongings and the restoration work that would be needed. But all he could think about were the germs incubating within the walls of his sanctuary, about their violent invasion into his secure life.

Carter stood in the kitchen trying to clear away the thick cobwebs in his head, the plastic mask over his face fogging from his heavy breaths.

As muddled as his brain was, there was nothing wrong with his hearing. Even over the thunder, rain, and ungodly wind, he heard the tapping noise behind him, a *drip-drip-drip* kind of noise. He spun around, his fevered imagination preparing him for the giant, amorphous amoeba that had surely gotten into his house, a creature like something from a 1950's horror movie, where everything grew enormous from nuclear radiation.

After he got the flashlight turned on, he found, to his horror, a new puddle spreading across the spotless marble top of the cooking island, sprung from a leak in the ceiling above. No, no, forget *leak*, a leak was a drop every few minutes you just stuck a bucket under, this was a *trickle*, a urine-thick stream of water pouring down from a water spot in the plaster as big around as a basketball. Carter goggled at the steady downpour until he worked out the implications of such a leak in his kitchen.

His kitchen, which wasn't directly below the roof, but under the loft on the second floor.

Carter broke from his horrified standstill, hurtled through the living room, splashed one re-tennis-shoed foot into his new living room pool and jumped across to the spiral staircase leading to his second floor. He took the stairs on hands and knees.

Again his ears were first to bring him the bad news, this time the muted tinkle of water falling on soggy carpet, but coming from all over. He raised his head above the last tier on the staircase and shined his flashlight around the dark loft of the second floor.

More leaks sprang from the ceiling in streams similar to the one downstairs, running down his bookshelves, his original Mortal

Kombat arcade machine, onto his pool table, down the one-of-a-kind Spawn wallpaper he'd found on eBay and battled it out for a grueling 10 hours with five other bidders to procure. Todd McFarlane's creation was a bubbled smear now under the water pouring across his life-size features. He couldn't even get to his bedroom or the other rooms up here containing his sizeable comic book collection and shelves of collectable figures still mint in boxes without passing through this disease-ridden water torture-chamber.

Everything he loved and cherished, all the irreplaceable components that made up his solitary life, all waterlogged and destroyed.

Carter placed a hand against the plush upstairs carpet and pressed. Water bubbled up around his fingers like a sponge. The only way this could've happened is if the storm had simply stripped away every last bit of shingles on the roof, ate through all his defenses an inch at a time. How much of the original construction remained up there above his head, and how long till the wind ripped it away like the peel from a banana?

The wise man built his house upon the rock, the Lucid sang.

"Shut...up," Carter wheezed. His next breath dragged through his throat, catching on imaginary obstructions. Now he *was* hyperventilating, mask or no mask, and if he couldn't get it under control, he was going to pass out right in the middle of—

The wind shrieked even louder than normal—maybe like a wounded dinosaur screaming in pain, for those still playing the home version of Blow-Job—and something deep in the belly of the house groaned in protest. It was an eerie, protracted sound, like something you'd hear when a door opened in Dracula's castle, and Carter froze, eyes wild, listening for something further.

From somewhere below came a brittle *snap*, the sound of cracking wood, and then the entire upper floor of Carter Vance's house shifted a good two feet north.

Everything crashed together. Furniture shifted, his bookshelves fell into one another like dominoes, spilling their contents into the soggy floor. He heard the sound of glass breaking, either dishes in the kitchen or those supposedly-bulletproof windows. The movement of the second floor turned the spiral staircase into more of a straightened Slinky. He was thrown under the thin railing into freefall.

Carter braced for pain, but instead got shock. He landed on his back in the ocean that was once his living room, creating a miniature tidal wave. The flashlight was knocked out of his hand. He scrambled back up before the rebreather could go under, thoroughly soaked and shivering, and half-stumbled, half-crawled back toward the kitchen in the two feet of water now collected in his home.

"Holy jumping Spielberg, what was *that?*" he whined, but he didn't need the always cool and composed Lucid to answer this question. Something had broken in the fundamental structure of the house, some load-bearing element snapped like a toothpick, and for the first time, he understood the place could actually collapse on him.

He made it to the kitchen, but everything in here seemed to be at vertical degrees, the doorway shifted to skewed angles, pieces of plaster and wood ripped from the ceiling and walls and standing in miniature rubble piles across the tile floor. A layer of wet dust coated every surface. As he watched, new leaks started all across the ceiling, pouring water into the room as it soaked through the floor from above. He thought briefly of a scene in the *Money Pit*, where Tom Hanks' dream house falls apart around his ears, only Carter had laughed during that movie, and at this moment, he never felt less like laughing in his whole miserable life. Another leak opened up right above him, pouring down onto his already wet hair and into his eyes, but he hardly noticed.

The wind was still out there, trying to get in, merciless. The house shook like an autumn leaf each time a fresh gust hit.

You have to get out of here Cart, before the whole place falls down on top you.

No. No, absolutely unthinkable, it's too big out there, too open, too many germs.

It's either survive out there, or die in here.

The house groaned again and then apparently decided it had given him enough time to argue with himself.

Just as Chicken Little Lucid predicted, the sky began to fall.

GIMME SHELTER

Maryland was lost in a daydream about driving out to Los Angeles with nothing but the cloths on her back and hitting it big as a movie star (she could picture herself co-starring with her idol, Susan Campbell, who'd come from no more glamorous background than Maryland herself), when a police car, lights and siren blazing, shot past her on the left, traveling the wrong way in the empty lanes on the other side of the concrete divider. Maryland, who had squeezed over two more lanes in the stop-and-go (but mostly stop) traffic, craned her neck to follow the speeding vehicle.

"Where are they going in such a hurry?" She was crabby from lack of nicotine and trying, successfully, so far, not to let her doubts creep back. The clock told her it was close to six-thirty, which meant Whitney was practically on the city's doorstep. The blasts of wind blowing across the freeway rocked every vehicle side to side on their springs, producing a field of tottering metal gleaming in the rain.

She finally switched on the radio, looking for anything to keep her occupied, and found only static across the dial. Bryce's CD's were the only music in the car, mostly easy-listening, Phil-Collins-and-Kenny-G crap. What she wouldn't give for some female vocals with bite and beat to go along with her mood, Hole or Garbage. She elected to turn the stereo back off and sulk.

More motion to her left, and Maryland looked back over to see two camouflaged, army-type vehicles—she assumed National Guard—go streaking past in the same direction as the cop car. They were hauling ass on the slick roadway; sixty-five, seventy miles an hour, and the speed looked like a stretch for the sluggish, boxy conveyances.

One of the Guardsmen, in a camouflage uniform and matching helmet, stood in some kind of turret attached to the back, open to the elements. He was young, fresh out of high school, and stretching up on his toes to see over the top of the vehicle at the road in front of them. As they flew past, Maryland got a good look at his face through the veil of windblown water.

It was filled with absolute terror.

She pondered this for a second as she inched the car forward a whopping three feet. The freeway was on a steady, curving downslope, and ahead was a view she usually loved—Rugg Canyon spread out diagonally off to the west, with the mountains on the far side—but now the early twilight turned the chasm into a pit of murky black. The bridge began just ahead, most of its expanse visible as a thread across that dark scar in the earth. She was close enough that she could see the guide cables swaying in the wind along the top. Traffic seemed to pick up speed as it flowed across. She could be out of the city in another fifteen minutes, safe on the other side of the mountains.

So why would the police and National Guard be fleeing the city at breakneck speed, especially when they had an open traffic lane?

Anxiety mounted in her chest. God, she'd give anything for a cigarette to steady her nerves. Something was definitely wrong here. She was a big believer in the subconscious being more perceptive than the forebrain, and right now hers was setting off every alarm it could lay hands on. The air was thick with a tension she could find no source for.

And then she found it, when the world blew up in front of her.

WHITNEY -0:53

Lincoln felt sick during the interrogation by the older cop while the black one held a weapon on them (it was, after all, his second time at gunpoint tonight, and his head was still a little woozy from its slam against the store's counter), but the rain and wind helped hide it. Part of him wanted to scream a confession, but living on the streets most of his life had given him a hell of a self-preservation instinct.

He continued to debate with himself, while the older cop—Charlie, he thought he heard one of the others call him—went back to confer with the black one and the younger guy that had stayed behind in the patrol car.

"Don't you say a word, son," Mac warned him, loud enough to be heard over the thunder but low enough the cops couldn't. Their kneeling position alone would've made it hard to balance, but it took an even bigger effort with the wind shoving at them. With his hands tied behind him, Mac was even worse off. "Don't you dare. Keep your mouth shut and everything's gonna be fine."

Lincoln did, but not for himself. If he went down now, Mac and CT would go down also, as accomplices at the very least. This was *his* burden, *his* responsibility, *his* finger on the trigger, and he wouldn't let either of them pay for it. Not even so much for C-Tone's sake—his cousin was going to end up in prison sooner or later anyway—but the idea of Mac doing time for him was unbearable.

And then the officers came back and told them they were free. He blinked rain out of his eyes and addressed the black cop, whom he was sure had a big hand in convincing Charlie to let them go. "*Thank you, Officer!*"

"*You're welcome!*" The cop extended a hand.

And that was when two other patrol cars pulled up and four more of Port Allen's finest piled out, leaving their headlights blazing. One shouted out a greeting over a megaphone, and Lincoln didn't even need to see the change in demeanor that came over their three cops to know this pudgy new arrival was no officer; he was an A-class *pig*. His words dripped with those familiar asshole overtones, the kind Lincoln was used to hearing from members of the PAPD.

But this, oddly enough, seemed directed at their fellow officers.

Their liberators tensed up. The hand the black cop had offered Lincoln withdrew, forgotten, and the X-Dawgs were left kneeling while Charlie's group turned to face the newcomers across the hood of their car, still parked diagonally across the street. Lincoln put his hand back up in the air and watched the proceedings through the driving rain.

"Links!" C-Tone was jittering, either from the cold of the rain pounding them or his increasing need for a fix. "Links, let's just go, they told us we could!"

"Don't you move one goddamn muscle," Lincoln commanded through clenched teeth. His bare arms ached from being held up, but he was afraid to do anything that might start the police looking at them again. He didn't know why, but the arrival of these four started an uneasy boulder rolling around in the pit of his stomach.

"*What do you want, Sturney?*" Charlie shouted over their patrol car, holding up a hand against the glare of headlights.

"Ellis, what are they doing here?" the younger cop asked the black one. Lincoln absorbed each name as it was dropped.

Before 'Ellis' could speak, the one on the megaphone, a real redneck by the sound of him, answered both questions. "*We heard yer call go out, came by ta give ya a hand.*"

Lincoln rose up as much as he could on his knees, peering over the trunk of the patrol car in front of him. The chubby pig with the megaphone—Sturney—stood in front of the car on the right beside another figure, both silhouetted in their headlights. The two from the vehicle on the left were splitting up and coming forward, preparing to go around both the front and back of the original patrol car, which was the only barrier between the two groups.

"*Why didn't you answer us on the radio?*" Charlie called out.

"*We tried. Guess ya didn't hear us. Storm has 'em all messed up.*" Even Lincoln could tell this was a lie.

"What is this shit?" Mac asked him from the side of his mouth.

"I think these cops got a serious beef with each other."

"Yeah, but where's that leave *us?*"

Charlie yelled, "*We're fine! We have this under control! Just go on and we'll be right behind you!*"

The two cops from the new group advanced, edging their way closer and closer to the sideways patrol car, essentially boxing them all in. They were little more than shrouded orange shapes, but it was clear they made Charlie, Ellis, and the young cop nervous.

"*Would if I could Van Ness, but the Captain got through to us just a li'l while ago with a new directive. You're ta come with us, right now.*"

"*What the hell for?*"

"*Well, that's not really any of my bidness, now is it? The Cap said to find ya and bring ya in, so that's what we're doin. If you'll*" *jest let Officer Myers and Officer McNamara take care of you and yer new friends there, we can all get outta here before Whitney blows us away.*"

The ones he called Myers and McNamara reached opposite ends of the patrol car and hesitated. Lincoln could see their faces now, the one at the back end a younger guy and the one at the front middle-aged, both predatory and smirking.

"What do we do?" the young cop asked hysterically.

Charlie shouted his answer, addressing them all. "*I don't know Billy, but we ain't goin anywhere with them until I hear it from the Captain himself!*"

"*That would be resistin arrest, Van Ness. Don't make this go any harder than it has ta,*" Sturney warned them over the megaphone. "*Officer McNamara, take Officer Van Ness' sidearm from 'im, so we can get this show on the road.*"

McNamara stepped the rest of the way around the hood of the car, and Charlie didn't back down as they came almost chest to chest, close enough so the rain couldn't even get through the space between their bodies. Lincoln had to give the old guy props. Ellis and Billy watched wearily, turning their heads from Charlie and McNamara to Myers creeping up on their opposite side.

"Give it up, Charlie." McNamara flashed a Cheshire grin into the officer's face.

"Over my dead body, Harold."

The moment lingered, no one speaking, no one moving, starbursts of lightning throwing shadows into disarray. Lincoln was reminded of the old westerns, in the last seconds before two gunslingers drew their pistols and mowed each other down.

The standoff would've gone on forever, if Lincoln hadn't noticed the object McNamara fingered in his hand.

Lincoln pointed. "*Hey, watch out, he's got somethin!*"

Charlie glanced at him, understood, and might've been quick enough to do something about it (the oldtimer looked like he still had a little bounce in his step), if the sound of the Rugg Canyon Bridge exploding hadn't reached them at that exact second.

WHITNEY -0:52

Chris' arms hurt so bad, his hands numb from clutching and cold. The wind clawed at him, seeking to pull him from his perch. He couldn't hold on any longer, his fingers peeled back one at a time, and he wondered what it would feel like when he let go and plunged into the tempest.

He was too tired to be scared for himself, but when his stepmother lost her balance on the ledge above him, his heart jackhammered.

Nichelle snagged one of the pipes jutting from the crack in the floor and held on as she slammed against the now vertical floor, her feet just inches above the top of Chris' head. The broom she was using to rescue him was snatched away by the wind and went sailing into the black night.

A groan of protest came from the dangling building chunk.

"*Nichelle!*" She couldn't possibly hear him, he couldn't even hear himself, but she looked over her shoulder down at him and mouthed something. Chris shook rain out of his eyes, and saw his stepsister's head appear at the edge of the apartment floor, close to where her mother clutched the pipe. Her mouth worked as she held a bundle out to Nichelle.

He recognized Mr. Softy.

Nichelle let go of the pipe with one hand and took the blanket. She held on to one corner of the thick fabric and lowered her arm, trying to get it to him, but the wind flapped it crazily until she pinned it with one foot, and held it against the wall just above him.

At first he didn't think he would be able to do it, he would plummet if he tried to change his grip from carpet to blanket, but a new well of strength bubbled up in him, one that helped him grip the blanket and even pull himself halfway up its length, enough to dig his bare feet into the carpet and take some of the pressure off his aching arms.

Nichelle strained, pulling him up another foot, and Chris reached, grabbing her by the wrist as he let go of the blanket. He could hear her now, screaming in pain as his weight was added to her one-handed grip on the pipe above. She turned to him, face drawn and strained. "*Go Chris! Climb up me!*"

Chris didn't pause to think how he would accomplish this with the strands of cooked spaghetti that had replaced his arms, he just grabbed the back of her jeans and stretched for her left shoulder, climbing his stepmother like a ladder. Once he let go of her hand, she brought it back up to cling to the pipe. He shimmied his way up until he stood on her shoulders and then slid back onto the horizontal floor, where he could only lay in a soggy heap on his back and breathe.

"*Chris, Chris!*" Tangela jumped into his arms.

He gave his stepsister a quick embrace before holding her at arm's length. "*Get back!*"

"*But Mommy—!*"

"*I know, Tangela, I'm going to help her, now get back!*"

The girl retreated, and Chris scrambled to his knees at the edge of their ruined living room.

Nichelle's face was two feet below, looking up the length of her arms to where her hands still gripped the jutting pipe. He noticed his old security blanket twined in her fingers where they curled around the metal. A single instant of ripe, burning shame at everything he'd said just minutes before stabbed him. She pulled on the pipe, the muscles in her smooth forearms bunching as she tried to climb, but she was too weak from helping him to safety. She collapsed back against the teetering section of floor after a few seconds.

He wrapped both of his wet hands around one of her wrists and pulled.

She didn't budge an inch.

Chris hauled at her, planted his heels and pulled until it felt something in him would break, doing so more out of frustration than anything else, because it was obvious her weight was just too much, he would never be strong enough to pull her up.

He burst into tears as he leaned over to look his stepmother in the face, the one he'd just told that he hated. Those words felt so childish and stupid now, an expression teenagers always said but never really understood, and even with all those brains his teachers claimed he had, he wasn't above such petty outbursts. "*Nichelle, I'm sorry, I didn't mean it!*"

She smiled up at him. "*I know, baby! I know you didn't!*"

Chris was too busy seeking forgiveness to differentiate the sound of the explosion in the distance from that of the storm, or to tell the flash of light from the direction of Rugg Canyon apart from the lightning flickering all around them, but when the shockwave reached them a few seconds later, he registered the rumble that ripped through the apartment.

The vibration became a miniature earthquake. The vertical floor ripped away at the seam. Chris reached for Nichelle again, far too late, and watched her fall away, fading into the cauldron below, then becoming obscured by the piles of debris falling after her.

He pounded his fists against the ledge, cutting his dark hands on shards of wood and metal.

"*Chris!*"

He heard the shriek and turned. Tangela stood shivering in the hallway, eyes wide and round.

Chris got to his feet. They needed to get to safety, to be protected if something else fell on top of them. He grabbed his stepsister by the hand and tried to pull her down the hallway.

"*No, Chris, I want Mommy, where's Mommy?*"

"*Tangela, you have to come with me right now!*"

"*No, not until Mommy comes!*"

The building shook again, and he just couldn't tell her, couldn't explain now, so he simply threw his arms around the girl's waist and hoisted her onto his shoulder. He tore down the hallway to her bedroom with her kicking and screaming the entire way.

Chris fell to his knees beside her bed and laid her on the floor. He pushed her into the narrow space beneath and then crawled in after her while the world collapsed around them.

WHITNEY -0:50

A giant, invisible hand pushed Maryland back against the Bentley's leather seat.

The windows in the vehicle shattered, showering her with bits of sticky Safe-T glass. Her ears were assaulted a roar, her vision blotted out by a flash of white light so pure she figured it must be the same one clinically dead patients claimed to see on the operating table.

When her eyes cleared, Maryland raised her dizzy head and blinked at the new world around her.

Somehow, her car was now flush against the concrete divider separating east and west traffic, several feet to the left of its previous position. The divider was just high enough to smash the side mirror to smithereens in the impact; it now resembled a metal pancake hanging from the door. Rain poured in through the missing windows, soaking the interior and her clothes. The car in front of her, a bright blue SUV, now rested against her hood, just as her tail end was against the car behind her, both ends of the Bentley buckled from its sandwiching.

Bryce is gonna be so mad, she thought dreamily, with a detached mixture of dread and elation.

She rubbed her eyes, trying to clear out the bleary paint job coating her brain. When she looked to her right, she saw that every car on the freeway had shifted backward and to the side, crashing into one another like bumper cars. The other occupants also looked around in a stupor. Some of the ones with enough room to open their car doors stumbled out into the rain. If she could only get the ringing in her head to stop, then she might be able to figure out why...why...

Maryland's thoughts drifted off track as she spotted the fireball in the sky in front of her. A mushroom cloud of roiling black smoke and red fire blossomed against the turbulent clouds, the storm winds creating eddies in its surface like miniature cyclones. She followed the trail of smoke back down toward its origin, straining to see around the SUV and down the long, curved stretch of hill before Rugg Canyon.

She gasped.

The structure she would've crossed in mere minutes now ended in a sheared concrete edge jutting out over Rugg Canyon barely a half mile ahead. The steel support cables hung down around it like loose threads, dangling from the guides stretched across the narrow chasm. The cars closest to the explosion had been pitched like toys onto their sides and roofs. She could see figures scurrying about in the rain, some helping the injured, some staring over the drop at whatever carnage lay below. If she really squinted, she thought she could see the same thing happening on the far side of the canyon at the other end of the bridge.

"Holy...*hell*." The words felt like coppery stones in her mouth.

A minute ago, there were cars across every foot of that bridge, all of which were now lying at the bottom of Rugg Canyon.

People wandered by her car in the rain, other drivers weaving between the vehicles toward the ruined bridge. She heard one of them shout, "*What happened?*"

"*It...it must have been a car!*" someone answered. "*Or maybe an oil tanker or something!*"

That had to be bullshit. Rugg Canyon Bridge was nearly a mile in length, four lanes wide, constructed of solid concrete and steel, and approximately three-quarters of it was now missing out of the middle. She couldn't envision an oil tanker large enough to breed such destruction.

Besides...someone knew about this beforehand...didn't they?

She thought back to the young Guardsmen in the back of the vehicle, the terrified look on his face as he stared ahead, toward the bridge.

Was this some sort of *terrorist attack?*

She noticed a vibration in the soles of her feet. The engine of the Bentley had turned off when the shockwave pitched it against the divider, so this was nothing from under the hood. The dashboard rattled, Bryce's crappy CD's spilled out from the sun visor and pelted her purse in the passenger seat. She heard a noise growing along with the motion, a distant grumbling. It seemed to come from the air hanging over the freeway.

Maryland looked to the bridge again as the first screams reached her ears.

The rest of the structure crumbled away into the canyon as the support cables snapped one by one. She could hear them from here, a metallic cracking that cut through the drone of the rain and screech of wind. The end of the bridge dipped like warm taffy and then broke away in chunks, taking cars and people with it. She saw several of them try to flee as knowledge of the situation struck home, but they had no hope of outrunning the destruction. It was like Wile E. Coyote after he ran off the edge of a cliff, on solid footing one minute and then kicking in empty air for a few seconds before they fell away.

The collapse continued to where the bridge met solid land. Maryland expected it to stop, and it did, in a fashion. Instead of simply falling, the last remaining bridge posts *slid* into the abyss, riding the land as though it was a magic carpet.

As Maryland watched, the entire edge of the canyon sloughed off into the gorge, mountains of earth shaken loose by the explosion. This was the rumble in the air: a gigantic earthquake peeling away the land and reshaping the face of Rugg Canyon. A wave of soil and grass rushed uphill, a crest that rose briefly before plunging into that deep rut in the earth.

And it was heading right toward her.

Now the air filled with screams, and the people who had wandered by her galloped in the opposite direction as death swept over the face of Port Allen to claim them.

Move, Maryland, her head commanded.

She couldn't. The sight of that destruction rushing at her was too mesmerizing.

Goddamn it, MOVE, YOU BITCH!

Maryland jerked at the unfamiliar, unreasoning voice in her head. No way to drive the Bentley with the other vehicles hemming her in. She couldn't even open her door with it jammed against the lane divider.

She scrambled across the car seat. Her senses started to come back, allowing her to go faster, but it also poured freezing cold fear into her veins. She shoved the passenger door open and nearly fell out onto the pavement, then jumped up in time to avoid being kicked in the face by a pair of large black boots.

Rain pelted her head and back. The wind was strong enough to knock her off balance. She broke into a run, moving with the crowd as it surged through the tangle of cars sprawled across the freeway. No one seemed to care where they went as long as it was away from the landslide. People screamed, carrying children and luggage, some of the more able bodied leaping over vehicles rather than trying to find a path between. She saw one man jump onto the slick hood of a car just before a monstrous gust of wind blew him sideways. He fell, struck his head on the bumper of another vehicle and landed unmoving on the ground. No one stopped to help him.

She would never be able to recall how long she went on, but the rumble in the earth was still growing when two teenage boys shoved her aside. The wind pushed her back the other direction into a woman only a few years older than herself. This lady looked through her in abject terror and then jerked away, taking the last of Maryland's precious balance.

She went down on the wet pavement stretched full out on her stomach.

Someone did kick her this time, grazing across the top of her left shoulder as she tried to get back up. Someone else stepped on the small of her back. Pain flared through her like an electric jolt. Legs were everywhere she turned, kicking her, tripping across her, but never slowing.

A truck stood to her right, with two feet of clearance beneath. She crawled through the forest of legs to the safety it offered. She was so tired and wet and shivering, wondering how she'd gone from wealthy socialite to gutter rat in a few hours, but she wriggled straight through and stood up in a narrow space between this vehicle and the concrete lane divider.

That rumbling abated. She spared a quick look back down the freeway. The land now ended less than fifty feet from where she stood in a precipice of torn soil, but the landslide had stopped. She was on a section of suspended freeway above Johnston Avenue. A gigantic crack raced up the middle as she watched, parting the surface of the road like Moses on the Red Sea. Some of the cars slid into this hole as the suspension fell apart, crashing to the road beneath, others tumbling off the sides.

Some of the runners had hopped the lane divider into the empty eastbound lanes. Maryland did the same, swinging one leg over and then the other, and ran as hard as her legs would pump. Her breath came in short wheezes. Every muscle in her body begged for reprieve, but she pushed on, determined to run until she was worn down like an over sharpened pencil. She could feel the freeway collapsing behind her, and cut diagonally across to its edge.

A short drop off waited here, followed by a steep embankment down to a flooded median.

Maryland jumped just before the freeway surface she stood on cracked open.

WHITNEY -0:43

Ellis had no idea what the explosion in the distance was. From their position amidst the tall buildings in the middle of the city, their attention was drawn by a sudden blaze and rumble like muted thunder, and, a few seconds later, the column of fire and smoke drifting toward the muddy sky.

All the men standing in the torrential downpour that dark afternoon turned their heads to the west in unison, but it was Sturney's boys that came to their wits first. Harold McNamara brought up the object in his palm, the one the gang leader had warned them about. He held his hand in front of Charlie's eyes beneath the slicker hood, fingers curled around a small cylinder and thumb resting on a button.

A jet of something gooey and red spurted across Ellis' partner's face.

"*What the*—!" Charlie staggered a few steps back toward Ellis and Billy. He reached to wipe at the substance, and then, realizing what it was, "*Oh, you miserable sacka shit!*"

"*That's right! Pepper spray, old man!*" McNamara shouted over the wind. "*You wanna stand down now?*"

"*Aw, godDAMmit,*" Charlie's moan was a mixture of anger and pain. He used his slicker sleeve to swipe at his eyes.

"*Stop messin around and bring 'em!*" Sturney stood in front of the other cruisers with the megaphone, beside the silent lump that could only be Drano Jenkins.

To either side of them, McNamara and that little shit J.D. Myers went for their sidearms.

And, Ellis had to admit, if it were just him and Billy, they would've probably surrendered. But Charlie—now blind and feeling the burn—drew his own pistol with graceful speed and aimed it in the general direction of McNamara. He squeezed off three rounds as weak as firecrackers in the midst of the whirling storm. The shots went ridiculously wild (*Stevie Wonder at the gun range,*

Ellis thought crazily), but it scared the other officer badly enough that he cursed and leapt for cover on the far side of the patrol car.

"*Hey, HEY!*" Sturney's amplified voice yelled. "*Calm the fuck down!*"

Myers hesitated when Charlie opened fire on McNamara, hand inches away from the butt of his gun. It gave Ellis a chance to pull his own pistol and point it at the younger man's chest. "*Get back!*"

If he'd been thinking clearer, he would've had the man drop his gun first, but Myer's hasty retreat gave them some breathing room. He backed around the end of the car and joined McNamara as he scrambled against the wind toward their leader.

"*What's happenin?*" Charlie asked. "*Ellis, what's goin on?*"

"*It's okay, Charlie, they're gone!*" Which wasn't exactly true. The four of them conferred in front of their vehicles, after seeing their prey wouldn't be taken so easily. But they would get in their cars any minute now and haul ass out of here, maybe just run and keep running before he and Charlie and Billy had a chance to report this. Feeling, for the first time in his life, like a bon a fide black Dirty Harry, Ellis slipped his pistol back into its holster.

"*Charlie, man, you okay?*" Billy asked.

"*Ah, God, I forgot how much this shit hurts!*" Charlie bit his lip, reholstered his gun, and faced them.

In the glare from Sturney's headlights, they could see how red and swollen his face was, the eyes puffy globes. All of them were forced to go through pepper spray training at some point. Ellis knew only too well what the man was going through; skin on fire, eyelids glued shut, lungs burning. "*Turn your face up, the rain'll help!*"

"*I thought you said they wouldn't try something like this!*" Billy pulled back the hood of his slicker. Rain splashed against him. "*You said it was too dangerous for them!*"

"*They must've figured the hurricane would be good cover!*"

His words were punctuated by a distant popping noise Ellis only recognized when the rear driver's side window of their squad car blew into the back seat of the vehicle.

"*They're shooting!*" Billy cried.

Those muffled, tiny gunshots picked up speed. Bullets parted the turbulent air and ricocheted off the car. Billy was first to drop behind their vehicle, splashing on his knees into the running water on the street. Ellis grabbed Charlie by the shoulder and yanked him down.

The cold water nearly knocked the breath out of him. It was so deep now it nearly reached the underside of their patrol car, and his clothing—kept dry by the rain slicker up to this point—was soaked through. He pulled his hood back and scooted against the door of the patrol car.

Someone else jostled him, and he looked around to find all three of the gang members crowding into the limited space. With everything that had happened in the last (what, three minutes? Had it really only been that long?) he'd completely forgotten them. The little one was on the far side of Billy, peeking out around the rear bumper, but the other two were crowded up almost on top of Ellis, the leader trying to keep the big guy from drowning in the water.

All six of them, cops and gang members, huddling together for safety.

"*Just you boys remember, ya brought this on yerselves!*" Sturney hollered over the unrelenting barrage of gunfire. "*We tried to do this peaceable, but Van Ness opened fire on us first!*"

Everyone behind the cruiser was shouting, the younger gang member screeching in terror as he demanded to know why the pigs were shooting at them, Billy asking what they should do, the big black boy bawling for someone named Lincoln to cut his hands loose, cut his hands loose before he drowned.

"*QUIET!*" Charlie bellowed from his position at the other end. The cover of the car provided enough sanctuary from the roaring wind to allow them to hear one another without screaming. "Ellis, I still can't see! What's our situation?"

"They got us pinned down." Bullets whined overhead, at such a rate that standing up to assess their position any further was impossible. And the water was too deep to see under the car. As he spoke, the passenger window above them caught a round and exploded outward. "We have to return fire!"

"No, don't do anything yet! Let's just think our way through this!"

"*Think* your way through it? They're shootin at us!" This from the gang leader; Lincoln maybe? "What do you wanna do, solve some math problems at them? Get on your radio and call somebody!"

"We can't, the radios are down!" Charlie cupped water between his submerged legs and splashed it into his eyes. "Besides, we're safe back here as long as they're not tryin to flank us, so let them waste all the ammo they want. Let's play this smart before we start gunnin down cops!"

"But you just shot at that one!"

"That was to get them to back off! There's no way I'm killin anybody if I don't have to!"

A louder *pop!* and the car jumped on its springs; one of the tires had been punctured.

"Man, what the hell these pigs want?" the cornrowed kid on the other side of Billy squealed.

"Isn't it obvious?" Billy undid the snaps on his rain slicker, taking the garment off to give him unfettered access to his pistol, and Ellis did the same. They tossed them in the shattered window of the car above. "They want to kill us, all of us!"

"No way, man." Lincoln looked at Ellis, sitting right next to him. "That ain't it at all! They said they was here to *arrest* the three of you! What are you, crooked cops?"

"*They're* the crooked cops!" Ellis said. "They weren't gonna arrest us, they were gonna take us somewhere and shoot us in the back of the head! I've seen what that son of a bitch is capable of, all right?"

"Yeah, no shit, me too! The three of us are just caught in your bullshit, and those pigs are willin to kill us to get to you! You cops call *us* criminals, but look at you, you're no better!"

Charlie turned his blind face to Ellis. "What did you see him do? The truth, now! Cause there's now way they're takin a risk on killin six people just because you saw Sturney take a bribe, hurricane or no hurricane!"

Ellis looked away, trying not to appear guilty, but was thankful his partner couldn't see. "I didn't want you involved in it, Charlie!"

"It's a little late for that!"

The gunfire tapered off all at once. There was silence, or at least what passed for silence with the wind shrieking around them, growing louder by the second.

No one moved.

This time, the hiatus was broken by a single word growled over the megaphone.

"*Dunham.*"

Every face, even Lincoln and his crew, turned to Billy, who had the horrified look of a kid just called out by the cruelest teacher in school.

"*Dunham, truth be told, this has nuthin to do with you,*" Sturney continued. "*You, and those niggers ya'll collared neither. Wright is the only coon I want tonight. Mighta let Van Ness go too, but he's really startin ta piss me off. If all four of ya come out with yer hands up, I'll let ya'll walk right outta here. Do it quick though, 'fore I change my mind.*"

"Oh Jesus." Billy dropped his head into his hands.

"You hear that?" Cornrows asked Lincoln. "He gonna let us go! Grab Mac and let's bounce!"

"Kid." Charlie pried his eyes open to slits, "don't you so much as twitch if you wanna live to see tomorrow."

"You threatenin me, pig?"

"No, I'm *warnin* you! You're a fool if you think those men are gonna let you walk away from this after what you've seen!"

"Yeah, you would say that, you ol' coot, *you* the one they want!"

Cornrows looked back to Lincoln for the final word, who waited only a moment before saying, "He's right, CT. This smells bad. We can't go out there."

"Man, this some bullshit! We gonna get killed if we stay!"

"I'm going," Billy said with his head still down.

"Billy, you can't!" Ellis exclaimed.

The rookie raised his head, his wet face tortured. "I have to! I'm getting married in four months, I-I can't get myself killed over this!"

"Billy, think this through, even these punks are smart enough not to trust Sturney!"

"Sorry guys...but I just got assigned to the wrong car! This... this is none of my business!"

Before they could stop him, Billy stood up behind the trunk of the patrol car and started out with his hands in the air. "*Okay, I-I'm coming out!*"

"*You the only one smart enough ta take my offer?*"

Billy glanced back at the others still huddled behind the car. He looked agonized, like the guilt from his betrayal would haunt him to the end of his days.

"*Yeah, I…I guess so!*"

"*Well…all right then. C'mon over here.*"

Billy kept walking. The wind used him as a punching bag. He made it halfway across the distance before something changed his mind. He spun and tried to run back to them.

Ellis and the others could never know which one of their attackers actually fired the shots that killed William Dunham. They only watched as his body was riddled with holes, the blood blown away by the storm before it could fall. On any other day, those bullets would've been stopped by the armor under his blue uniform shirt, but, as Ellis was coming to understand, today was about as far removed from any other day as you could get.

Billy fell forward, splashing on his stomach into the flooded street.

WHITNEY -0:37

Carter dove from his kitchen.

Behind him, the entire second floor crashed down with a sound he wouldn't even attempt to put a comparative label on. He landed back in the growing lake that used to be his living room, now deep enough to swim in. Carter regained his feet just in time to hear the house give another protesting groan. He stood in his sopping wet jeans and sweater, goggling at the renovations Whitney had made to his fortress.

In the constant flicker of lightning, he could see the upstairs loft and second floor had collapsed as the support beams gave way, leaving an obscenely open area in the top corner. The ragged remains of his bedroom walls clung to drywall and ceiling, looking like a disorienting, upside-down, M.C. Escher drawing. The spiral staircase still jutted from the ruins, more of an art sculpture now. His kitchen was squashed by a pile of rubble filling the doorway, a mish-mash of plaster, wood, pipes and the various furniture and items that once graced the second floor. As he stared in numb horror, the torn cover of his coveted first issue of *Watchmen*—signed by both Moore and Gibbons—floated down and landed feather soft atop the surface of the water.

He was too dumbfounded to worry any more about germs crawling across him.

Dr. Pellner would no doubt call this 'a breakthrough.'

Great, one phobia down, about fifty to go.

Before he could decide if it was a fair trade, another of those sharp, wood-splintering snaps drew his attention. He looked to his left to see the front wall of his house bulge inward, flexing with the elasticity of a rubber band. A gigantic crack appeared through the middle of the paneling. His picture window blew out, the plastic rupturing and spraying Lego-sized pieces in all directions.

Above him, there was a tearing sound. The vaulted ceiling over his living room blew away into the night, dropping a trail of debris around him.

Wind rushed in through the hole, batted him around as if he weight no more than a shoestring. Rain smacked him, the assault like a solid blanket of cold thrown over him. The experience of the storm now being *inside* his house had all the most unreal qualities of a dream.

His head creaked on his neck, turning to face that gaping hole above him. The world was coming in, proving that nature didn't just abhor a vacuum, she wanted to destroy them.

Don't look, the Lucid pleaded, *please Carter, this will only go from bad to worse if you look.*

He wanted to heed that advice, wanted to squeeze his eyes closed and feel his way to someplace familiar and safe, to block out the horror that could only enter his polluted psyche if he let it. But he was helpless, as compelled to look as any rubbernecker.

Carter gazed up through the sheets of rain and found the entirety of the majestic, furious sky staring right back.

His breath trickled to a halt beneath the rebreather mask as a great, monstrous terror crashed in at him from all sides. Nothing but openness existed out there, an unending expanse of stygian chaos. As his oxygen-starved lungs ached, Carter felt himself drifting up into it, where he would be lost in its turbulent waters.

Another crash brought him back to earth, rattling him just

enough to jump start his breathing and break the hypnotic hold of the boiling clouds. This time the crash was caused by the back of the house falling in on itself.

The remaining walls around him quivered in the ungodly wind. It would only take one of them to fall over like a downed redwood, and he would be crushed.

Carter ran for the airlock door.

WHITNEY -0:32

Imogene huddled in the living room, staying clear of the windows and trying to get news from the outside world on a battery-operated radio from her youngest granddaughter's room. It was in the shape of some square, yellow cartoon creature wearing only a pair of brown shorts, and she tried not to think how sad it was that her life might depend on the ridiculous gadget.

She couldn't find any news, any updates. Just the same mechanical voice on several static-heavy channels, telling all Port Allen residents to head toward the Allen Civic Center.

The battery indicator on her clunky oxygen machine showed less than four hours remaining. If the electricity didn't come back or she didn't find an alternate oxygen source before then, her decrepit lungs were on their own.

Assuming the storm didn't kill her first.

A gurgling from the kitchen. The floor was covered in two inches of freezing water, seeping in under all the doors and window seals, and even up through the flooring. She'd tried to halt the worst, shoving towels and blankets into crevices until her lungs felt like lead balloons. She was forced to return to the machine before the COPD kicked in.

Imogene turned her wheelchair toward the kitchen and rolled forward to the length allowed by the respirator tubing. A clap of sharp thunder ripped through the house, accompanied by a vibrating blast she could feel all the way to her bones. The windows blew inward, firing glass through the area where she was just sitting.

Wind and rain invaded her daughter's house. Imogene turned back to face it, dropping the silly radio and throwing up a hand to keep the water out of her eyes. She trembled at how close the thunderclap must've been to do such damage.

Except it really hadn't sounded like thunder.

Imogene took a last gulp of precious air before pulling off the tubes and moving to the front door. Her wheelchair crunched over broken glass. She flung the door open and went out into the storm, down the little walkway to the flooded street, already heaving and gasping again but not caring. If this was the end, if her season had finally come, then the least the good Lord could do was to let it come quickly.

The wind rolled her backward every time she let go of the wheels to rear back for another push. The freezing water rose past her feet in their stirrups, past her ankles and up to mid-leg; it drug at the spokes of the wheelchair and threatened to carry her away in the swift current.

The front of her daughter's house faced west. It was an old suburban neighborhood, far enough north to be clear of the taller buildings of the inner city, so she had a clear view of the fireball hanging against the dark sky to the west. The houses on the other side of the street blocked her from seeing its origin, but she estimated it would have to be near Rugg Canyon, on the opposite side of the city.

That's what the commotion had felt like just now: not thunder, but an explosion.

But how in God's name had she *felt the blast?* Short of a nuclear explosion, could a shockwave be powerful enough to blow out windows on this side of town?

She struggled to spin her wheelchair around in the water—now climbing toward her knees—and gaped at what was right behind her.

A *second* fireball loomed over her daughter's house in this direction like a wrathful god, so close she could still feel the heat from it. This was the one that had blown out the windows, and she only had to look in the gap between this house and the one next door to tell where it came from.

Besides the bridge over Rugg Canyon, there was only one other place where traffic exited through the mountains. Interstate 35 led through a narrow pass just a few miles from here before heading into Louisiana, and that seemed to be the source of the turmoil spreading above her.

Two explosions, on the only routes out of the city. Coincidence or not, Port Allen was cut off from the outside world.

Imogene's chest blazed with brittle heat. She decided she wanted to live, at least for a bit longer. If something was going to snuff her out, she wanted it to be Whitney, and not the damn disease that had caused her family to abandon her. She wouldn't give it the satisfaction of suffocating her when there was plenty of water to drown in.

She turned and fought her way through the rising flood toward the house.

WHITNEY -0:28

"*TAKE 'EM!*" Lincoln heard that redneck pig squeal. This didn't come over the megaphone; it was just shouted to his cronies, and the wind was so loud he caught only a distant whisper. "*TAKE 'EM ALL, GUN 'EM DOWN LIKE FISH IN A BARRELL!*" It was too easy for Lincoln to envision white sheets and burning crosses with the man's chicken-fried accent.

Against the cruiser, no one spoke. The death of the young cop had hypnotized them all. The current pushed Billy back toward them where he lodged in the gutter, facedown amidst the drifting groceries from Kim's store.

Lincoln thought he could hear splashing footsteps on the other side of their bullet-riddled barrier. They would have company in a few seconds, company that would find them all ripe for plucking. Everyone to his left was either blind or bound, and to the right was one unarmed street soldier and a cop about whom he was having serious doubts.

Which left Lincoln, whose eyes went to the pistol still in Billy's holster just above the surface of the rushing rainwater.

Killing Kim has been awful, made him feel dirty and tainted, but this time it was cops. Wouldn't matter if they were dirty as hell, or if his newfound buddies in blue backed up his story, he'd be branded a cop killer. That was do not pass go, do not collect two-hundred dollars, but go directly to the death penalty.

"Fuck it," Lincoln muttered. "It's die now or die later."

He scrambled through water to the body and yanked the pistol out.

"What are you doing?" Ellis asked in dazed wonder.

"Saving us!" And then Lincoln Briggs stood up and opened fire.

The wind almost knocked him right back down. He didn't even try to aim at first, just let the large pistol do its thing while he took in the scene. This time McNamara, Myers and the silent fourth figure were all closing in, like hunched ghosts in the driving rain. They came in at a wide circle on either side of the car, hoping to catch the five of them in a lethal crossfire. Lincoln registered their positions, recalibrated his aim, and alternated a few shots between the two coming up on his left and the one on his right.

All three about-faced, scattering and weaving to present him with more difficult targets. He squeezed off another two rounds and then watched as they dove behind their cars for a change, along with their fat hick of a boss.

"*Yeah, how you like that?*" CT peeked over the edge of the trunk beside him and pumped a fist in the air.

"Goddamn it, stop!" Charlie waved his hands. "*Stop shooting!*"

"*Hey, listen to me!*" Lincoln's anger stunned the officer into silence. "*I know you can't see, man, so let me tell you, this ain't Disneyland out here! I forced them back, but all of us gotta make a run for it, right now! I'll cover you!*"

"*He's right!*" Ellis peered through the vehicle's shattered side windows. "*It's now or never!*"

Charlie grimaced, his jaw working back and forth. "*Go! Into the store!*"

"*Into...into Kim's?*" Lincoln saw Mac staring up at him with wide eyes.

"*Unless you got a better idea, kid!*"

Lincoln shook his head, thinking about what waited to be discovered in the floor of their proposed sanctuary. "*If you're gonna go, do it now!*"

Ellis and C-Tone were first on their feet. Ellis slipped an arm around Charlie's shoulders and helped him up, while Mac, with Lincoln's assistance, got his legs under him in the water and stood up by bracing against the side of the police car.

Lincoln saw a cautious head pop up from one of the other cop cars.

CT was already gone when he turned back, splashing through the water toward the convenience store. Lincoln gave Mac a shove. *"What're you waitin for?"*

"You come right after me!"

Lincoln shook his head. *"Somebody's gotta keep these pigs off our back!"*

Mac watched him with anguished eyes.

"Goddammit, GO!" Mac turned and took lumbering steps, leaning into the wind with hands held awkwardly behind him.

Ellis and Charlie passed by, the older man leaning heavily on the other officer. *"You only got about five or six shots left with that,"* Ellis told him, and then he was off, leading his partner around Billy's corpse without looking down.

Leaving Lincoln alone in the rainswept street.

He walked backward as fast as he dared, holding the dead man's pistol with both hands. It was only seven or eight yards from the tail end of the barrier to the door of Kim's—out of the street and across the wide sidewalk—but it felt like five minutes before he felt the curb at his heel in the flooded gutter. He glanced down to make sure he didn't trip over it.

Shots sounded. He whipped his head back up to find all four of them emerging from cover to charge with suicidal urgency. Each blast was marked by a burst of light from the muzzle of their guns.

Lincoln fired at the closest approaching shape and heard a satisfying cry of pain. He turned to run full out, throwing a few more rounds over his shoulder.

Mac reached the door and turned to check if they were following. In front of Lincoln, and still two yards from safety, Ellis and Charlie moved at their hobbled pace. Lincoln raced toward them, bent at a 45 degree angle into the stone wall of the raging wind.

Pain blazed across his right shoulder. He pitched forward, dropping the gun and splashing to his hands and knees on the wet concrete.

"Lincoln!" He heard Mac shout his name from far away.

He looked up, vision blurred by a haze of pain, and tried to make sense of the kaleidoscope of colors and images in front of him. Someone was screaming, more shots were fired, and then his head became too heavy to support.

He collapsed to the pavement.

WHITNEY -0:22

The boathouse shuddered in every windy shriek. Hernie laid his head on the bare ground and covered his ears to shut out the noise. He'd given up trying to find a place where the roof didn't leak, and instead took a blue tarp down from the wall to use as cover. Hatch shivered against him beneath the vinyl, terrified and freezing.

"We could be in bad trouble, Hatch ol' boy." Hernie could barely hear the words as they left his mouth. "Looks like the government is really after us this time!"

The boathouse gave a loud, brittle *crack* as something in the building gave. Hernie lifted one hand from his ears and raised the edge of the tarp. The wall in front of him cantered at a drunken angle, several of its boards cracked and splintered.

"What do we do, what do we do?" He drummed at his temples with his fingertips in frustration, as though trying to turn over a stalling car engine. "C'mon, *think*, brain!"

You can't stay here, a feather-light voice whispered. Sometimes, when he needed it most, this voice would talk to him, as distant as a fading echo, telling him not to cross a specific street, or not to sleep in a certain alley. It sounded neither male nor female, but he still liked to think it was his mother, speaking to him with her mind from wherever the government had her trapped.

"*What do I do? That storm is scary!*"

The refineries, the voice told him, fainter with each word. *You'll be safe in the oil refineries.*

"The oy…yul re-fine…ries." If he didn't make sure it stuck, it would leak out of his brain like water through a sieve. He didn't know how this idea was smart, but he'd never questioned the voice before. He shouted to the dog, "*C'mon boy, we gotta go!*"

Hernie stood and tossed the tarp aside. The interior of the boathouse was alive with motion and sound, everything rattling and wobbling from the voracious gusts. He moved to the door of the boathouse and looked into the marina. Dark out there. He *hated* the dark, and the rain came down at a steep angle so hard it shrouded the world in wet haze. He wrapped the ruins of his trench coat around him and stepped beyond the relative safety of the boathouse.

The wind felt like it could pick him up. He kept moving, hunched into the gale to make himself as small and heavy as possible. Hernie risked a glance toward the shoreline just around the other side of the boathouse.

His breath caught.

The sky above him was dark, but the sky over the ocean was one big roiling black cloud with twisted veins of lightning. It bore down on him, making him feel tiny and a little dizzy. The marina's seawall—which came to an edge on both sides of the tiny shack to allow nautical entrance from the water—already had monstrous waves crashing over the top, close enough to splash him with their spray.

Hernie tore his eyes from the maelstrom spreading around him. He couldn't see them in the dark and the rain, but he knew the metal towers of the oil yard were just on the other side of the marina, separated by a chain link fence. They always looked like black fingers reaching toward the sky, nightmarish and skeletal. After a few more steps, he realized Hatch wasn't at his side.

The dog cowered in the boathouse doorway, hunkered low and head down. Hernie knew how he felt. The structure wasn't much protection, but far better than being outside.

"*Hatch!*" The wind was too strong to stand out here for long, the rain too cold and heavy, but abandoning his only friend wasn't an option. "*Be a good doggy! Come, right now!*"

Hatch took a tentative step into the rain, but withdrew when thunder cracked overhead. The boathouse lurched, ready to fall sideways like a house of cards. A section of roof soared into the boiling sky.

"*HATCH! Come NOW!*"

The dog shook once and then streaked out of the boathouse at full speed.

Hernie ran, this time with Hatch matching him step for step. They wove their way down the boardwalk, past other structures—

boathouses, hot dog kiosks, equipment rental establishments—that disintegrated. The air was full of debris and stinging sand, stirring around them in a manic display. One gust threw a trash can into him hard enough to sweep him off his feet. Hernie hit the ground on his face and left hand, hurting his wrist and scraping a slice off his cheek. Hatch barked as he got back up, warning the storm away from his master, but Hernie could hear no sound from the dog's open mouth.

They reached the end of the marina. Hernie could see the spires of the oil refineries, no longer belching smoke. The ground at the base of the towers was a zigzagging network of metal pipes, and he thought he understood why the voice sent him here.

The chain link fence separating the two properties had been ripped away in the storm, eliminating the problem of how he would get the Labrador over. They pelted into the refinery yard, blinded by rain. Hernie ducked under one pipe and then another even lower, and finally crawled through the mud into a cubbyhole formed by a dense tangle of metal beside the first tower. The opening of a large, slanted culvert began here, and Hernie shimmied up inside it far enough to be out of the flood. It was by no means cozy or warm, but a sturdier shelter from the elements.

Hatch squeezed in next to him, lay a head in the crook of Hernie's arm, and whimpered.

It was going to be a long night.

WHITNEY -0:18

Ellis heard the shots behind them—the storm dampened their blasts to little more than firecrackers—and tried to get Charlie to go faster. Kim's grocery was just a few steps ahead. The big guy, Mac, hopped from foot to foot in the door.

Then Charlie jerked, and the arm around Ellis' shoulders was suddenly supporting all his weight instead of just guiding him.

The shift threatened to pull Ellis off his feet. He bent as Charlie went to his knees. The man's mouth was open and he appeared to be screaming, but Ellis couldn't hear a single syllable over the fury of Whitney. The wind screamed in cycles, each one longer and louder than the one before it.

His partner writhed on the pavement, clutching at his left leg. In the chaos of rain and flapping cloth, he couldn't get a good look at how bad Charlie was hit.

Mac shouted something, venturing from the store. Ellis looked back and saw Lincoln also on the pavement, facedown a foot away. Three of their group down. Ellis' blood thumped an anger-quickened tempo, washing the fear out of his veins.

At least the kid had retaliated before going down. The only reason they weren't dead is because three members of Sturney's gang were carrying the fourth back behind the barrier of squad cars.

Lincoln! Mac mouthed the word, coming forward and sidestepping Charlie entirely. Ellis held out a hand.

"*I need you to get him inside!*" Not a sound came from his mouth, like he'd gone deaf or mute. Whitney swallowed each word. Frustrated, Ellis pointed to Charlie as he held his leg, then at Mac, then at the store. "*Let me get your friend!*"

Mac's nostrils flared. He glanced again at Lincoln, but nodded. The big kid squatted, grasped Charlie's hand between his tied wrists, and dragged him across the pavement.

Ellis scrambled on all fours to the boy. Lightning revealed a deep graze across the outside of the shoulder, the part bared by the wifebeater tee. The bullet had sheared off half of the rose tattoo on his dark flesh. A thin ream of blood from the wound was washed away by the rain as soon as it dribbled out.

He was too weak to pull the boy to safety, so he slapped his wet cheek, then lifted his head and pried open an eye to find the cornea rolled back.

In the street, the engine of the patrol car closest to them roared to life, audible for only a second as the wind reached another peak.

"*C'mon man!*" Ellis shouted uselessly. He grabbed the teenager and shook him.

The vehicle turned until its front end aligned directly to where Lincoln lay sprawled with Ellis crouched beside him. The hood of the Crown Vic looked like the maw of a hungry beast as the headlights fell upon them. Rain pounded the front windshield, obscuring the driver.

On the ground, Lincoln's eyes fluttered open, blinking away water.

Ellis tugged. The gangbanger got the idea just as the car shot toward them. Together they tumbled out of the way just before the vehicle jumped the curb. It screeched to a halt, half on the sidewalk, blocking the way into the grocery store. Ellis caught sight of Sturney leering through the side window.

"*RUN!*" He gave the boy a push.

They threw themselves into the wind and fled down the line of storefronts. Behind them, the engine growled as Sturney backed the vehicle up. Ellis pulled his pistol, turned, and fired two shots to give the man something to think about. It didn't work; Sturney forced the squad car the rest of the way onto the sidewalk, angling it so he could run them down. Ellis wanted to put a bullet right through the front windshield and into that peppermint grin.

Instead he put his head down and barreled on, waiting to be crushed under hard tires.

Lincoln grabbed him by the arm and yanked him to the right just as Sturney rocketed past, braking so hard after missing his targets he skidded another fifty feet on the wet sidewalk.

The gangbanger had pulled him into a tight alley between stores. The wind was blocked enough that he could hear again, but his eardrums throbbed. The endless, ruthless grind of the storm was as deafening as the loudest rock concert.

Lincoln trampled through windblown trash with Ellis at his heel. The alley ended in a ninety degree turn to the left and opened up into a much wider lane that ran behind the stores all the way to Bale Avenue at the end of the block.

"*We have to keep moving!*"

Lincoln shook his head. "No *way man, if we keep going, it just takes us further away from the others!*"

"*We'll have to circle around and try to get back!*"

Sturney's patrol car appeared on the street at the open end of the alley.

Other narrow offshoots opened between the buildings in front of them. Ellis had no idea where any of them led. The older structures and warehouses in this section of the city had been built haphazardly in the early import/export days, and some of the alleys formed mazes that wove through without seeing another major street for miles.

He and Lincoln broke for the closest of these. Sturney shot down the alley after them, firing his pistol from the driver's side window.

They bolted without stopping this time, Lincoln leading them down aimless turns in the system of back streets. The storm grew around them, weighting each step. The area around them became a war zone. Roofs tore away with screeches of tortured metal from the smaller warehouses, wooden and even brick walls crumbled, and the air was filled with heavier debris, chunks of mortar and even brick blowing above—and occasionally past—them. Ellis tried to keep a sense of which direction they headed, which streets they might possibly come out on, but the storm or the stress or the fatigue or…God, take your pick…left him disoriented. It was all he could do to keep up with the fleet-footed youth in front of him as they dodged everything Whitney threw at them, with less of a goal in mind than rats in a science maze.

When his lungs burned and he didn't think he could lift his legs anymore, Ellis climbed a short concrete staircase attached to a building on their right, leading up to a wooden door set into the long wall. He tried the knob, found it locked, but saw the bolt was flimsy in its setting. He threw his shoulder against it once, then again, and on the third time it snapped, swinging inward.

Lincoln limped back to him, shielding his head with both arms. They entered the door shivering. Once it was closed again, Ellis pulled his flashlight and turned it on.

Metal racks stretched away in rows across a vast concrete floor. The roof was high above them, made of corrugated steel. It gave the howling wind a hollow, metallic quality, but at least it kept the din far enough away to make conversation possible without screaming.

"We can rest here." Ellis was soaked, teeth chattering. A chill had worked its way into his bones. "They'll never be able to find us with all the twisting and turning we did."

The gangbanger had both arms wrapped around his chest, rocking back and forth at the waist to warm up. "Maybe, but resting ain't gonna get us back to the others!"

"We can't go back out in that!"

"I sure as shit ain't stayin here! Those're my boys we left behind!"

"I don't like it any more than you do, but that's a hurricane out there, and it's only going to get worse!"

"What if those cops kill them?"

"What if they're *already* dead?" Ellis snapped. He knew he was just using anger to hide his fear, the same fear that made him quit nearly everything in his life—the way he'd been ready to run from the Port Allen PD with his tail between his legs rather than face Sturney—but he couldn't stop. "I guarantee you, whatever's gonna happen to them has already happened, and putting ourselves at risk isn't going to change that! You've already been shot; you want to die tonight?"

"That's a real chickenshit attitude!"

"No, that's a *realistic* attitude! You wanna go back, I won't stop you! But I intend to ride out the storm here tonight, and try to find some help once it's over!"

Before he could let shame convince him otherwise, Ellis sank into the concrete floor beside the door, his sopping clothes creating a puddle around him. Lincoln glared for a few seconds, headed toward the door, hesitated, and then slumped on the opposite side with a sour grunt.

Ellis meant to rest just for a minute, but exhaustion overtook him. He shone his flashlight on his wristwatch before laying his wet head in the crook of his arm.

He was amazed to find it was barely seven PM.

WHITNEY -0:14

Maryland hit the concrete embankment awkwardly with her left ankle. She pitched forward, scraping both palms bloody in an attempt to catch herself, and then rolled down to the curb below in a ball of flailing limbs.

She splashed into shockingly cold water.

Maryland struggled to get her feet planted. The water down here was much deeper than it looked in the frantic moments before she leapt from the roadside. The raging flash flood swept by her thighs along the ramp of the raised freeway and then down through the wreckage of the suspension bridge. She looked back, holding both hands up to block wind and rain out of her eyes, and saw the flood waters sweeping over the open plain on the other side of

Johnston Avenue, following gravity to the depths of Rugg Canyon. The current around her legs was strong, as liable to pull her off balance as the wind, and it would wash her off into the gorge.

The air was clogged with debris blowing out from the city. An entire bicycle sailed by, the Wicked Witch of the West conspicuously absent. Maryland needed shelter, but there wasn't much this far north except a few gas stations further down the freeway and scattered industrial parks, none in walking distance. Far ahead of her, other survivors of the landslide clambered down off the elevated highway to join her in the water, struggling eastward through the wind away from her, and she slogged through the water after them.

"Hey! Heeeey!"

Maryland barely heard the voice during the briefest of lulls in the storm. In the tight angle formed by the crumbled remains of the suspension and the steep concrete embankment she'd just tumbled down, a man waved at her from the forest of concrete support posts. From what she could see, he looked small, balding and bespectacled, wearing a sweater and gray dress pants. He motioned to her, waving her over to his little shelter.

Yeah, right, she thought. How long until the wind blew the rest of the suspension down on top of him, or the flood waters rose enough to drown him? Then again, 'any port in a storm' never sounded as applicable as now.

A chorus of screams reached her from the opposite direction. Maryland faced forward again in time to see a wave big enough to surf on rippling along the freeway, a wall of wind-propelled water that plucked those in front of her right off their feet and washed them back toward her.

Maryland leapt at the embankment in a panic, clawed at its steep side until she was high enough to be out of the wave's grasp. She flopped down on her stomach and clung to the inclined concrete. She could see the wave coming, people riding its crest like a water park attraction.

They would die, every last one of them. That thought terrified her as much as if she had a ticket to go with them.

She scooted around on the incline, turning until she lay facing the wave, and then extended a hand as the tangle of bodies swept below her.

One of them, a youngish guy, spotted her and fought the current, scraping along the embankment wall and snagging her offered wrist in a death grip. The force of his weight was too much for her tenuous position. Instead of pulling him out, she slid in after him, screaming all the way.

She felt a hand grasp her left arm just before she slipped in. The bald man sat on her other side, bracing with his heels to haul at her. With his weight as an anchor, she got her knees under her, and in a soggy, straining chain they pulled the other man out of the flash flood. Without a further word spoken, all three of them crawled up the embankment and back to the cramped space under the crumbled edge of the suspension.

The concrete over their heads kept the rain off as the storm worsened, and if they remained amid the posts, the wind was blocked, but its screech was all-encompassing. It certainly wasn't the level of comfort she'd gotten oh-so-used to, but considering she'd rejected all that today, she couldn't complain. Maybe she should just look at sleeping under a bridge as practice for her new life, once Bryce got finished ripping her to shreds in the divorce. She huddled on the sloped ground, one strange man on either side of her, and cursed two people in ascending order.

Bryce Decatur, for being the despicable shit he was.

And herself, for accepting her life at face value for far too long.

WHITNEY -0:10

Mac dragged Charlie into the grocery store, pulling him far enough inside the busted door to be out of the line of fire. For someone as big as him, the action required little effort even with his hands behind him, but the cop kicked and bucked like an angry mule. Once Mac turned him loose, he rocked back and forth on the floor in front of the counter, cradling his left leg.

But that was a problem for later down the line, if they survived that long. Members of their ragged team were still outside, one of whom was his best friend and the leader of the organization he'd committed his life to.

Lincoln and the black cop were just jumping out of the way of the murderous pig's vehicle. Mac started through the open door into the roaring wind, meaning to throw himself across the windshield to give them time to escape, but a bullet slammed into the frame beside his head, announcing its presence only as a shower of wood chips across his face. Reflex pulled him back.

The police vehicle took off again, driving down the sidewalk. Mac tried to step out again to see what was happening, but the other cops threw more fire his way from behind the other patrol car.

He grabbed the half-broken glass door and pulled it shut. The wind had already blown over the first few shelves and scattered products everywhere. He came further inside until he could hear over the wind. Charlie moaned continuously from the floor, "*Oh Jesus, my leg, my leeeeeg!*" Now that he was out of the rain, blood pooled under the appendage, but Mac couldn't do much with his hands still tied.

"CT! CT, where you at?"

"Right here." The boy stood at the end of one of the store aisles, clutching Kim's shotgun in both hands.

"Get over here and find somethin to cut my hands loose! We gotta help this guy 'fore he bleed to death!"

"Fuck that! He's one of 'em! Let that fool die!"

"He saved our lives! We ain't lettin him die!"

"You think that means anything? He tried to arrest us too! He ain't no different than those muhfuckahs out there!"

"CT," Mac said through clenched teeth. "Get the fuck over here and get me outta this. *Now.*"

C-Tone looked at him long and hard, eyes jittery, and then yanked his hand down to cock the shotgun. "And what if I don't?"

"Then your head's...gonna have...a new hole in it..." Charlie lay on his side with his own pistol pointed shakily at C-Tone's chest. He squinted through red, swollen eyelids.

"See?" C-Tone demanded, looking back at Mac. Despite his indignant tone, a wicked smile played at the corners of his mouth. "He turned on us first chance he got! Whatchoo think he gonna do...when he finds out 'bout Kim?"

"SHUT THE FUCK UP, TYRONE!"

"What about Kim?" Charlie wheezed through gritted teeth.

"It was an accident, we didn't mean to, he attacked us and…" Mac trailed, not knowing what to say, how to cast it in the right light.

"What did you bastards do to him?"

"Links shot him!" C-Tone put the icing on his treacherous cake. "His body's right over there! Now this fuckin guy knows *everything* Mac, and the only way to help Links is to waste him 'fore those other pigs get brave and come through the door! C'mon, he can't cover both of us at once!"

It was all just manipulation to get what he wanted, but it didn't matter. The milk was spilt, and the cop had all the information needed to put Lincoln—if not all of them—away for years. Besides, if they helped him, he would just be dead weight, and if they left him, the pigs outside would undoubtedly finish the job anyway.

"No," Mac said, surprising even himself.

"*No?*"

"That's what I said. I don't take orders from you; last I checked, nobody did. And until we find Lincoln and he says otherwise, this man is under my protection, cop or not. So if you gonna shoot him, you gonna have to shoot both of us."

The boy would; Mac had no doubts. CT was a vicious thug, the sort of banger that burned hot and took as many souls as possible with him before he was extinguished.

But right now they had the drop on him.

C-Tone stooped and placed the weapon on the ground. He came forward while Charlie covered him, took a pocketknife from a jar of knick-knacks on the front counter, and sawed at the plastic cord around Mac's wrists until it snapped. Mac brought his shoulders forward to their normal position, sighing at the wonderful sensation of being able to move freely again.

He put his hands on C-Tone's shoulders and squeezed enough to hurt. "You ever threaten me again, I'm gonna tear your head off. You hear me, you crackhead?"

The name caused his eyes to widen in surprise, but then they filled back up with rage. Things had changed tonight, allegiances reshuffled like a deck of cards. Mac and Lincoln would forever have to watch their backs where Tyrone Clancy was concerned.

"Stand by the door and keep watch. You so much as twitch, and you'll wish I let him shoot you."

Mac turned to Charlie. Next to the register lay his abandoned Glock and Lincoln's revolver. Mac picked these back up, meaning to tuck them in his pockets.

"What do you...think you're doin?" Charlie asked, the words coming in a great rush with each exhalation of pain-laced breath.

"I just...I thought we might need..."

"Until I decide...if I can trust you any more'n him...I'm the only one that carries a gun."

"C'mon man, we need every advantage we can get!"

Charlie pointed his pistol up at Mac. "Don't make me say it again."

"A'ight, chill man, it's cool." Mac laid the guns back on the counter. From behind him, C-Tone chuckled.

Mac knelt and examined the officer's leg. "Damn man, you really bleedin." He tore off the shredded remains of the pants leg as gently as he could to get a better look. The wound was as big around as a quarter, the flesh around it puckered inward and leaking a steady trickle of blood. Mac tore the pants leg into a strip and tied it tight around the man's leg, just above the knee. "I think the bullet's still inside, but that's the best I can do for you."

"Thanks kid, it helps a little. What are they doin out there?"

"Don't know, they ain't tried to come in yet. I think they just holdin us here till the other one comes back."

"When they come for us—and they will—we won't be able to hold them off."

"Not with you the only one holdin a piece," Mac muttered.

Charlie ignored the comment. "We gotta find a way out."

"What about Lincoln and your other cop?"

"Don't worry, Ellis'll take care of your friend. Right now, we've gotta keep ourselves alive."

"What do you suggest?"

"Gotta be an alley door, a fire exit, *somethin.* We use it, put some distance between us and them, and hole up somewhere until the storm's over. Then we'll be able to get some help."

"Oh yeah?" CT asked. "You think yo' pig friends gonna give up that easy?"

"They'll have no choice. Their whole plan depended on killin us while we were cut off by Whitney. Once there's even the slightest chance we contacted somebody on the outside, I have a feelin they're gonna hightail their keysters all the way to Mexico."

Mac turned his head sharply to the side and popped his neck. "And what happens to us?"

The officer hesitated long enough to convince Mac he would never lie to them about anything, and for that, he got respect. "Why worry about spoiled potatoes before dinner time?"

"Yeah...I don't know what the fuck that means."

"Let's just find that door before they do."

It didn't take Mac long to locate an exit in a back office of Kim's store. It led onto a dark, flooded alley. With C-Tone's reluctant help, they lifted Charlie off the floor and draped him across Mac's broad back so he could cling to his neck. Mac could maintain a brisk trot, but anything more and the injury jostled too much for Charlie to take.

After CT left for the back door, Charlie said from his perch on Mac's back, "I'm gonna tell you this while your psychotic friend is gone: when this is over, we will have a talk about *that*." He motioned with his head toward Kim's body, still in the aisle where he fell. "He had a family, for chrissake."

"The man went crazy. We offered to pay for what we took and he tried to kill us. It's not Lincoln's fault. He saved my life."

"People are throwin that phrase around a lot tonight. I hate to say it, but I don't know if any of our lives are worth savin."

"Let's go!" CT shouted from the other room.

Mac started in that direction, stopped, and came back to the counter. He picked up a plastic bottle of aspirin on display in the racks beneath the register. "Have a feelin you gonna need this."

C-Tone led the way into the tempest, holding a thick rubber trash can lid in front of him. Mac followed with Charlie hanging on for dear life, and within seconds Kim's Grocery was lost to rain behind them.

WHITNEY -0:06

McNamara was gut shot.

By the time Myers and Drano Jenkins hauled him back to cover, Sturney was gone, squealing off around the corner at the end of the block. And by the time he came back, they'd found a fire door in the alley and determined the rest of their quarry was no longer inside Kim's store. This might've been a big problem for their futures on this planet, if their boss hadn't come back equally empty-handed.

"You're not gonna believe this though!" Myers screamed after they'd gotten back into his patrol car. The storm would make landfall any minute, and communication was only marginally possible inside the confines of the shaking vehicle. *"There's already a body in there!"*

"Who?"

"That old chink that runs the place! Shot twice, it looks like!"

"Those fuckin gangbangers! Goddamn animals, all of 'em! Be doin the world a favor to gun 'em down along with that snitch Wright and his asshole pardner!"

"That still the plan?" Myers shifted uncomfortably in the back seat. *"What if they, you know, get away?"*

The usually silent Drano spoke for the first time, somehow maintaining his monotone even while shouting. *"This storm was supposed to be our only chance to get that stuff out of the city! If we don't, then all this is for nothing! I say we just leave!"*

"Don't go runnin fer the border just yet, boys!" Sturney told them. *"I'm pretty sure that explosion earlier was Rugg Canyon bridge goin up! And I think I seen another one out yonder toward the northern pass just a few minutes ago! I don't know what in blue fuckin blazes is goin on, but I'm pretty sure Port Allen just got it's only two legs cut out from under it!"*

Myers persisted. *"What if they call someone? I don't wanna go to jail, man!"*

Sturney was reaching for the door of the patrol car, but stopped. He turned a murderous glare on Myers over the seat. Whenever Sturney got that kind of look in his eye, Myers had a hard time re-membering why he'd gotten involved with the man in the first place. *"Even after the storm ends, we'll have some time till phone service is back up! And by then, we'll have hunted down all five of their sorry carcasses and fed 'em each a bullet! I ain't givin up my life till I got no other option! Nobody leaves till they're DEAD, got me?"* He punctuated the operative word by jabbing a finger into Myers' chest.

"What's the plan then?" Drano asked.

"Throw Dunham in the backa their car before he floats away! We'll stash it at the precinct garage, take shelter, and then cruise the streets tomorrow!"

At the conclusion of this sentence, the entire storefront of Kim's Grocery fell inward with a tremendous crash, pulling down half the roofs from the neighboring stores with it and making a mockery of the pitiful precautions the old man had taken to protect his establishment.

"What about McNamara?" Myers inquired.

Instead of answering, Sturney opened the door of the patrol car and jumped out into the storm, stumbling toward the back door of the second car.

Harold McNamara lay sprawled across the back seat, hands laced atop the bleeding wound in his stomach, eyes glossy with pain. He seemed to gulp at the air rather than breath it, and a dark red stain was spreading across the seat beneath him and into the floorboard.

"Harold, ol' buddy!" Sturney shouted. *"You gonna make it?"*

"N-o." McNamara turned the word into two syllables with his ragged breathing. *"Need a…need a…need a ho-hospital…"*

"That's too bad," Sturney said, so quietly the wind all but drowned him out. *"That's a real cryin shame."*

He turned to Drano, nodding solemnly, and stepped aside. Drano took his place in the open car door. As he drew his pistol, a sadistic grin twitched at the corners of his mouth.

Myers turned away before the gunshot.

WHITNEY -0:02

With the power out, the airlock door didn't open.

Carter knew there was a manual release, but he'd never read the instructions to find out how it worked. New fear mounted in him as he pressed and repressed the activation button, actual *claustrophobia*, and what a new sensation that was…

He looked at the shattered picture window, hand still jammed against the airlock door button, and wanted to slap himself.

Carter hurried over, still wearing the rebreather mask clamped over mouth and nose, knocked four times on the jamb (he'd never wondered if this compulsion applied to windows as well as doors;

now he knew), and stepped onto the swamped cobblestone patio beneath. The water was almost high enough to pour over the lip of the window and directly into the living room lake, but he didn't care anymore. Everything that could be taken from him was already gone. He cast one glance over his shoulder at the sodden computer and entertainment center before splashing away.

Whitney was in full swing around him, its drafts hard enough to abrade the skin. He leaned into the resistance. It shrieked around him until his ears throbbed, filled the air with so much water he could've drowned standing up if not for the rebreather pulling out what little bits of oxygen it could grab. The ruins of the house disappeared behind him, swallowed up by the storm's unnatural night, and he stumbled blindly in the direction he thought the gate lay, trying to decide whether to laugh or cry at the idea that he might be lost in his own front yard. Vertigo pressed down on him, but he kept his thoughts moving, always cycling away from the fear, churning his brain like a laundry machine.

He almost smashed into the gate; gray vertical lines suddenly loomed out of the murk at him. It was off the motorized track and canted over, creating a space wide enough for him to slip through.

His trailing foot caught. He fell, splashing down into the two feet of running water sluicing down the sidewalk. It was slightly salty, ocean water shoved in by the storm, mixing with rain, and moving inland to the lower parts of Port Allen. Carter pushed up on his elbows, raised his miserable head.

That was when he saw the shape.

It was in the middle of the street, just a few yards away, on the edge of visibility. Something large, distorted, and foreign enough that he couldn't make it out with the few details the storm afforded. Hunched and spiny, low to the ground but long and wide, probably just a mass of tree branches or debris blown here by the storm.

The shape shifted in a way that couldn't be the wind's effect on some flotsam, a surety of motion indicative of living creatures. And the more it moved, the more Carter was able to make out in the shifting veil of rain.

A massive head sat atop its bristly body, one that turned in his direction and then tilted in a puzzled gesture. Muted yellow orbs floated in the darkness. Carter froze, something inside him far older and more primal than the Lucid warning him that he did *not* want this thing to know he was here.

They stared at each other for a full minute.

Carter held his breath, not wanting to even risk fogging the rebreather.

And then the thing—whatever it was—moved down the street (*slithering*, was the term his mind actually used) toward a distant glow coming from the elevated neighborhood of Manchester Heights just up the road from him.

No time to puzzle. Carter struggled across the street and into Mitch Connelly's yard, dodging a chunk of masonry the size of an engine block that blew past him. The sapling trees were gone, roots and all, leaving muddy sinkholes in his neighbor's waterlogged yard. He had no way of knowing if the man's house still stood, or if it would survive the storm any better than his own.

But if not, he would die.

The house suddenly towered ahead of him, the sturdy brick facing still intact, and Carter felt a moment of irrational anger that this jackass wifebeater's kingdom should remain whole, while Carter's had fallen to ruin around his ears.

He entered this residence the same way he exited his own, by kicking glass out of a broken front window. He climbed through, shards slicing his shoulder, and imagined he could feel bacteria defiling the wound. Carter came to a staircase in the dark and, fearing a flood, made his way up.

The first bedroom he could find was on the right. Carter flopped across the bed and wrapped himself in the sheets, wet clothes and all. He couldn't go any further, couldn't push himself any more, and if Whitney was strong enough to blow this little piggy's house down, he would just go with it.

Carter left his phobias behind and fell into the land of sleep.

WHITNEY -0:00

Bryce Decatur—now changed into silk pajamas and matching robe—made his way down to the sprawling basement of his home, where the main electrical generator was installed. Beside the sections closed off for his wine cellar (only the rarest vintages) and his workout room and spa (which he visited at least once a year; probably the reason for the spare tire swelling his lower gut), the entire sub-floor was a survivalist's wet dream, stocked with enough water, canned food, and other essentials to keep him self-sustained and alive through everything from nuclear winter to his personal apocalyptic nightmare: a full-blown pandemic of queer.

And, of course, sufficient weapons were stashed throughout the house to defend the property against an army, if they even managed to get past the eight foot high, spike-tipped outer walls surrounding Château Decatur. He'd told the designer he wanted the place to look like a modern day Spanish Inquisition castle.

Once downstairs, he checked the main generator's fuel usage over the past three hours. The large machine hummed along at exactly the levels the specs claimed it should. With the supply of gasoline stored in the attached work shed, he could power every light and electrical gadget in the house for six months solid, exponentially longer if he made even the slightest attempt at conservation.

More than long enough to survive the hurricane and whatever chaos ensued afterward.

So why then, with all this good news, did he have the undying urge to put his fist through the nearest wall?

Maryland, of course. At first he seethed with rage that she'd left, but after working through the scenario and seeing the benefits to her departure—such as freedom to bang away at any of the thousand sluts that worked for his law firm without fear of a tedious drama session when she found out about the smallest percentage of them—he realized he wasn't even upset she was gone. The real source of his anger was the fact that *it hadn't happened on his terms*, that she'd worked up the audacity to leave before he could toss her out on her gold-digging ass.

If their marriage was one big game, then he'd just lost.

And Bryce Decatur did *not* lose.

Oh, she'll come back, she'll come crawling back, the only question is, will you open the door for her when she's scratching on it like a fucking dog?

He had no answer for that. It depended on many factors. As one of the best trial lawyers in the state of Texas, he wasn't one to jump to hasty conclusions.

Bryce went back upstairs, heading toward his living room—a living room that, from the outside, looked like a lighthouse, a beacon on the high plain where the neighborhood of Manchester Heights sat—and then down the hall to the kitchen to make a snack and maybe watch something from his endless film collection. Up here, Château Decatur was out of the way of whatever flooding swept the city, and the structure of the house itself was standing up well to the squall. Hurricanes were considered in the construction of his 20,000 square foot castle, incorporating steel reinforced wall and ceiling interiors into the design that would keep them standing in everything but a ballistic missile hit. A nice side effect of this was a hollow core that acted as an amazing sound baffle; coupled with the bulletproof glass in the windows, he was even insulated from the incredible roaring fury of the storm.

As Bryce slapped together a sandwich, the idea of Maryland actually on her knees and scratching at the door like a dog stayed with him. It was so appealing, he might just make it a condition for her surrender when—

The fantasy seemed so real that, for just an instant, he thought it had become a reality.

He paused in front of the refrigerator, hand on the mustard, listening to the faint, clumsy noises coming from somewhere in the house. Sounded like the back door.

One thing for sure: it goddamned well wasn't Maryland. He'd locked the grounds and gate up tight after her escape; she would need to plead at the intercom to be let in. Whoever was back there had scaled the outer wall and was now trying to find a way past the lock at the rear. As there were plenty of abandoned homes to rob in the city, he could only deduce the target was his working electricity.

Before he could close the fridge door, the burglar alarm went off. Ear-splitting klaxons blazed all round Bryce.

His nearest weapon was a large caliber Desert Eagle in a spring-loaded clip beneath the kitchen sink. Maryland would've bitched if she'd known about it, but the maid used the cupboards more than that woman ever did. He pulled the weapon, checked to make sure it was loaded, turned off the safety. He didn't intend to shout a warning at anyone stupid enough to break into his domicile.

Bryce left the kitchen and moved toward the southern wing of the house, away from the massive entrance foyer and grand staircase. The main halls formed two straight lines on either side of the kitchen down the middle of Château Decatur, connected by myriad other passages and rooms on the first floor. He strode toward the back without turning on any lights. The sirens kept wailing, and a stiff breeze blew past him now. The last dark cross hall fell behind, and he rounded the corner into the vestibule that housed the rear entrance with the large gun held out in front of him.

His jaw dropped.

The back door was just as sturdy as everything else in the house, the quaint faux-wood veneer hiding a solid steel core with two titanium, supposedly un-pickable locks. And that claim might still be true; after all, the locks hadn't been picked so much as the door itself *ripped out of the frame.*

It stood all the way open, smashing against the wall in the wind that gusted into the house. The steel was bent out of shape, enough pressure applied in the middle so that the locks had popped out of the strike plates. The storm blew rain under his porch roof and across the threshold, soaking the carpet.

Bryce pushed through the wind, to the electronic box beside the door, and input the code to turn off the burglar alarm. The sound was replaced by the wind's brutish symphony. He turned to the door and took in the torn remains of the wood veneer on the outside. It looked *clawed.* He forced it closed again and got the lock to catch on the seat after a minute of careful manipulation, closing out most of the wind.

A soft, melodic hooting came from behind him. Bryce spun, dropping to one knee and bringing the gun up. He fired two rounds without aiming, the shots booming in the confines of the room.

Nothing there.

The bullets had thunked into the plaster on the far wall, next to a portrait of him at age 12, but that didn't mean he'd imagined the noise. Whoever bashed in the door had waited in one of the rooms until he'd passed by, and now they were between him and the rest of the house. Bryce got back on his feet and crept to the corner of the hallway, then slid around in one fast motion.

The passage was blocked by a monstrous shadow a few yards away from him, something misshapen and twisted and taller than him. He let the bizarreness of it distract him for only the barest of moments before opening fire.

It moved like goddamned *lightning*. One second it filled the hallway, and the next it took flight in a series of graceful, sinuous movements carrying it around the corner and into the next cross hall before his shots could find it.

"Jesus Christ." His lungs had trouble finding their next breath. It wasn't a person that broke into his home, but some animal, either an escapee from the zoo or something the storm had blown in.

Bryce ran forward, turning the corner where it disappeared.

Empty.

At the same time, a crash resounded from the other side of the house, and another of those hooting cries came. He wove his way through the long corridors toward it. One of his weapons, a Winchester Defender shotgun, sat in a display case in the hall. Bryce swapped the pistol for it and a handful of shells, which he dropped into the breast pocket of his robe.

The door to his hunting room stood open. Inside were the preserved trophies of the animals he'd killed over the years. Bryce swung into the dark room with the shotgun held low and reached for the light switch.

Various animal heads lined every wall of the room, and the floor was packed with the intact bodies of other beasts he'd sent to the taxidermist whole, all of them gathered around in a semicircle. For his birthday one year, Maryland had given him a giant stuffed carnival bear, telling him it would fit right in with the others. Bryce, not finding the joke funny, had used it for target practice. Now his eyes played over the cluttered collection, looking for signs of tampering, two elk here, his brown bear, an upright crocodile, one mountain lion frozen forever in mid-roar, a beautiful 12-point buck...

Bryce halted.

He'd never killed a crocodile.

A flash to his left as the creature shoved over the stuffed animals in its haste to get at him. Bryce brought up the Winchester in time to see that the thing only superficially resembled a croc; its skin was scaly and reptilian but it bore about as much resemblance to a crocodile in the face as a Lamborghini did to a mini-van.

Not only that, but it walked on only two legs, dragging a broad tail behind it.

Bryce aimed at its wide, spiny chest as it closed in and pulled the trigger.

The scattershot hit it square, but the leathery hide was too tough for the shredding effect of the round. It gave a high-pitched snarl, though in pain or anger he couldn't tell.

Bryce fell back, holding up the shotgun as a shield against a swipe of one of its thick arms. Claws flashed at the end of the webbed digits on its—hand? Shit, had that been a *hand?*—and not only was the shotgun knocked out of his grasp like a rattle from a baby, but the last two fingers of his left hand went with it. His wedding ring clinked as it struck the floor.

He cried out, gripping the injury as blood spurted, and retreated back into the dark hallway. Nothing he'd hunted had ever been this aggressive. The creature followed, the yellow sheen of its eyes like sickly headlamps. It made quick, jerking motions, bobbing its head up and down like a bird and giving its questioning warble.

The end of the hallway was in sight, leading to the front of the house. All of his heavy weapons were upstairs in a vault. The only problem was, he didn't think he could make it that far. The basement door was at his back, and he retreated down the stairs, toward his precious generators and end-of-the-world supplies that didn't do dick for you when a refugee from the Discovery Channel found its way into your home.

The creature never let him get more than two feet away, its elongated jaw full of teeth gnashing. It clawed him across the chest, shredding his silk pajamas and opening up gashes on his skin.

Pain bloomed. Bryce lost his balance and went tumbling down the stairs. He crashed at the bottom, the agony in his broken left femur and shattered collarbone taking precedence over the heat from the wounds in his stomach and hand.

Last Resort, he thought desperately. *Gotta get to the Last Resort.*

Bryce crawled forward, hooking wounded and unwounded hand alike into the carpet to pull himself forward, leaving a smear of blood. He sensed when the thing crouched over him, felt hot, foul-smelling breath across his neck as it lowered.

A last moment of fury gripped him at what he'd been reduced to—*him*, the great Bryce Decatur, wriggling on his belly like he'd wanted Maryland to do and bleeding on his own floor. He pushed himself over, rolling to meet his attacker face-to-face.

"Fuck you, pal, I'm a *lawyer!*" he screamed.

The creature tilted its head curiously at this outburst, then bent and began to feed.

THE
DOME

THE MORNING AFTER

The traffic stretched as far as Daryl Sloan could see, and it hadn't moved in more than seven hours.

Most people will *say* traffic is at a standstill, but it's usually exaggeration; they're always inching or lurching forward in some measure. In this case, Daryl first put his old Civic in park after his foot cramped up from holding the brake down, and then, just past two in the morning, when the gas meter finally dipped below the quarter-tank mark, he turned the ignition off as well.

A lot of folks wanted into Port Allen. He'd prayed he was the only one stupid enough to brave the weather, but the backup started about fifty miles out from the city limits, on a nondescript stretch of highway in the middle of nothing but open flat land.

He fell asleep sitting up, despite the tension turning his muscles to stone, the screaming wind outside, and the last lingering elation from his successful job interview. His dreams were troubled. Nichelle and the kids in danger. Chris and Tangela calling for him. He awoke after one that caused him to flail, smashing his hand into the dash.

Daryl blinked and rubbed a hand over his face. He jerked when he realized where he was, scrambled for the keys, sure a chorus of honks would sound behind him at any minute.

His urgency bled out. The traffic going into the city still hadn't moved. The same green Le Baron sat parked in front of his car.

He checked his watch. Close to seven in the morning. The sky was blanketed with clouds the color of elephant's hide, and a moderate rain dotted the windshield, but it was nothing compared to the downpours throughout the night, as the shredded remains of Whitney spread out over the Texas plains.

"C'mon, c'mon, what's the problem folks?" To ease his frustration, he turned on the car's electrical system and then the radio. Lots of reports about the storm's aftermath in New Orleans—where flooding was not as severe as expected and power was already being restored—and Galveston—which had suffered severe damage and had an estimated death toll close to a hundred. Some smaller towns had been washed away entirely. Heartwarming stories of kitten rescues, harrowing tales of survival, more weather predictions, comparisons to previous storms, but not a single damned word about Port Allen. The absence of news almost seemed intentional, considering the city was big enough to rival just about any other mentioned.

The people in the other cars around him were waking up from their own uncomfortable slumbers. He saw bleary faces as they got out of their vehicles and stood in the drizzle, stretching muscles, retrieving food and blankets from their trunks, and wandering off the sides of the highway to go to the bathroom behind the low clumps of bushes that dotted the landscape.

Daryl got out himself as a low mutter of thunder sounded in the distance. The rain was chilly but didn't feel too bad; it was the only shower he was likely to get today. He walked around to the hood of his car and then climbed on top of it, staring at the metal snake that wound to the horizon in the watery morning light. The green swells of the Chantilly range were also visible, sprawled along the backdrop north and east, parallel to the freeway. A good twenty, twenty-five miles away, but somewhere just on the other side of those low peaks was the familiar skyline of Port Allen.

Or what's left of it, he thought.

As he climbed back down from his perch, he spotted a white guy in a suit one car back from him, punching numbers on a cell phone with a frustrated look on his face.

"You got any signal on that thing?" Daryl asked eagerly.

The guy eyed him for just second, probably anticipating exactly what Daryl was contemplating: that this unfamiliar black man was going to ask to borrow his phone. "Signal came back last night. I could call China if I wanted. The problem is, every number I can think to dial into the city is shut down. Same recording, 'We cannot connect your call at this time,' over and over."

Daryl sighed.

From the rustbucket van next to him, a lanky, stringy-haired John Lennon look-alike in a Che Guevara t-shirt got out, yawned and stretched. "Mornin, man," he said, sounding more like Tommy Chong than the deceased Beatle.

"Morning."

"Some 'cane last night, huh?"

"I guess so. It was my first one, so I really don't have much basis for comparison."

"Oh trust me, bro, it was *bad*. That kinda wind'll pull your hair out at the roots. We're just lucky we were on *this* side of the mountains. Only imagine what it was like in the city." The hippie pulled his greasy hair back in a ponytail and slipped what was either a homemade cigarette or a joint behind his ear. "You know what caused it too, doncha?"

"Uh...what?"

"The hurricane. You know what caused it, right?"

"Noooo."

He held up a hand on either side of Daryl's head, so that he was looking down the tunnel of the man's arms into his face. "Global. Warming. Man. This is the fault of the corporations, and all the shit they pump into the 'sphere nonstop, okay? I have awareness buttons if you want one."

Daryl grunted and stepped out of from between the hippie's hands. "No, I'm okay. Listen, have you heard anything about what's going on? Why we're stuck here?"

"Not me, dude. Looks like traffic of Woodstock proportions though, huh?"

"Yeah, unfortunately."

"Burt Weaver." The hippie offered his hand, which reeked of patchouli oil.

"Daryl Sloan."

"Nice to know you, Daryl. So what's your excuse for goin back into the city? You leave your weed garden too? I gotta get some pictures. You know, for insurance purposes." He reached into the open door of his van and held up an ancient Polaroid.

Daryl tried on a smile that didn't fit. "My...my family was—*is*—inside."

Burt shook his head. "That's a bummer, dude. Tell you what, I'll let you cut in line."

"I might take you up on that, if I could. I just wish I knew what the hell was holding us up." A wave of urgency overtook him, and he cupped his hands around his mouth and shouted to the crowd milling around on the highway blacktop, "HEY, DOES ANYBODY KNOW WHY WE'RE STOPPED HERE? ANY NEWS ABOUT THE CITY? *ANYTHING?*"

The people who acknowledged him at all just stared, some of them shrugging or shaking their heads. All as clueless as him.

He glanced back at Burt and tried not to show how desperate he was. "I just don't get it, even if they were enforcing the mandatory evacuation last night, there's no reason not to start letting people in now. We're allowed to comb through the wreckage, right? I mean, I haven't even seen any outbound traffic in the opposite lane since sometime early yesterday evening, have you?"

"Nope," Burt muttered. "Which means, as much as it pains me to say it, that the bridge is probably out."

Daryl hadn't considered the possibility, as obvious as it was. But if that was the case, then *what was he going to do?* If he left here and drove all the way around to try entering the city from the north, it would take the better part of two days. He jabbed a finger into each eye socket and rubbed.

"Hey man, don't stress. Let me make some calls and see what I can find out." Burt turned and wandered away, yelling, "Let me borrow your cell phone, dude!"

Daryl looked past his new acquaintance, to the outline of the Chantillys in the morning rain. Twenty miles; a good hike across open, soggy fields—not to mention a climb over the sheer mountains themselves—was all that separated him from his family.

The promise he made to Nichelle the day before burned in the forefront of his brain. *I will come for you.* Only two things had come out of his mouth in his life that meant as much to him as that promise, and they were his wedding vows to both his spouses, one dead and one alive, his oaths to cherish and keep them safe.

And if he couldn't find a way to get into Port Allen, he could count all three as failures.

Daryl Sloan sat down on the front bumper of his car and covered his face with his hands.

WHITNEY +11:09

Carter floated in the murky sky when he awoke.

He screamed and thrashed, throwing himself off the bed and into the floor, where he landed on his side in a tangle of blankets. The hard surface was reassuring enough to bring his wits back.

So not floating in the eternal vastness of the atmosphere after all, just privy to an unobstructed view of it. The upstairs bedroom of Mitch Connelly's house where he'd fallen asleep underwent renovations in the night that he'd somehow slept right through. The entire corner of the room was missing, leaving a gaping hole of wooden beams, shingles, and plaster, and tearing in half a poster of a mostly naked Carmen Electra. This must be Mitch's son's room.

A moment of hysteria pressed on him as bluntly as a mallet. All the panic and grief from last night tried to come roaring back, but he was too exhausted to get really worked up. Besides, an attack wasn't going to change the situation. He had to stay calm. Get his mind on something else.

He looked away from the soupy clouds, focused on the enclosed space under the bed, and started singing the first song that came to mind: AC/DC's "Big Balls." When that didn't work, he tried the mantra Doc Pellner had given him: *I'm okay, you're okay, the universe is center.* He'd always thought it was garbage, but he would take anything right now if it got him over this hump.

The distraction downshifted his racing heart, and, to still it further, he caressed the rebreather mask around the lower half of his face. The device still operated normally and would for another two weeks on its tiny battery. So that was one positive to be thankful for. Even though they were crawling all over him, those were two points of entry that didn't have to worry about germs.

Now there was just all that openness out there trying to eat him.

The small space under the younger Connelly's bed looked inviting. If he moved the cardboard box full of Playboys out of the way (geez, this kid was oversexed for a twelve-year-old), he could crawl beneath and close his eyes until the nightmare was over. Preferably until the electricity was working again and his house was in the same perfect state he'd worked so hard to get it to. He'd survived the worst, and now he just needed to concentrate on not hyperventilating to unconsciousness until someone came to rescue him.

Wake up, Cart. Superman ain't gonna fly out of the sky. Aquaman wouldn't even waste time on your pathetic ass. If there is a rescue coming, it's gonna take days to get here, and you might have the urge to eat between now and then.

"God, leave me alone." He pulled a damp pillow from the bed and pressed it over the back of his head.

The Lucid retreated. Carter got to his feet, careful to keep his eyes averted from the slice of steel-gray beyond the torn ceiling and unconsciously set about making the bed.

A football phone lay in the corner of the bedroom. He picked it up with thumb and pinky, wanting to call his mother in Oklahoma or even Rosa on her cell (he would feel like a heel asking, but maybe she could come back and get him for that road trip to Fort Worth after all), but the cord ended in a frayed edge.

The temperature was sweltering now compared to last night. He slid out of his soggy sweatshirt and—though he had trouble doing it—let the garment drop to the floor beside the useless phone. His jeans and t-shirt were moist, his sneakers squishing, but he could deal with it. After four quick raps on the doorframe and one last glance at the upper half of Miss Electra, he left the upstairs bedroom.

The stairway he'd come up the night before in the dark ended in an uneven edge about twelve feet from the ground. But the front of the house had caved in, leaving a pile of bricks and wood that, after scooting off the last splintered stair, he was able to reach and work his way down to the living room.

Most of the house now looked moth eaten, or maybe Mothra eaten: huge stretches of ceiling and the upper floor either collapsed or missing, holes in the walls, sections of sheetrock crumbled. The floor was flooded with mud and silt and strewn with a layer of detritus; branches, dirt, leaves, various household items, bits of floating paper and garbage, which he forced himself to walk through. A car tire was imbedded in the carpet of the den, which had no roof and only one wall.

"How am I even alive?" he whispered. The odds of falling asleep in one of the few parts of the second floor not to collapse, or be crushed or impaled by flying debris, was…well, he had no idea what the odds were.

It felt good though. Empowering somehow. If he could make it through something like this, then what could those old phobias possibly hold over him anymore?

Taking a deep breath, Carter stepped through the ruined wall at the front of the house and took in the rest of the street. A light shower fell from the overcast, but it was just bright enough to see that the few parts of Teague Street not flooded by a foot of water were covered in debris. And for the few houses remaining, they appeared to be the site of a bomb blast.

Like his home, for instance, visible through the missing gate across the street. There was nothing recognizable in that pile of wood and brick, half-submerged in a gloomy Scottish loch. His heart ached just looking at it. Still, he had to give thanks it wasn't the place next door. He'd never known the couple's name, but their property was now a scoured dirt lot.

Briefly he recalled crossing the street in the dark with the wind howling. The shadow he'd seen occurred to him again for the first time since regaining consciousness. He tried to picture its shape again, to capture its utter alienness and assign it some kind of rational explanation, but even now, in daylight and with a (relatively) clear head, his bucket came up empty from the logic well.

Dizziness crept in at the edges of his vision. Apparently his brush with death hadn't cured him after all. Carter retreated into the Connelly house before vertigo set in.

So that was the situation. He couldn't very well stay here, but where was he supposed to go and how was he supposed to get there when the sight of open sky turned him to Jell-o? He paced through the living room muck, but not a single solution came to his exhausted brain. And the Lucid was done giving orders for now. Not that they would've helped. He was finding the saner part of his mind was great at telling him what he *couldn't* do, but not what he *should* do.

First things first. He was hungry, but more than that, he was thirsty. He explored until he found the kitchen. Most of the room appeared to have been sucked into the night through a hole in the wall big enough to drive a tractor through. Even the refrigerator was missing, leaving a few severed connectors, and he would love to know how Whitney accomplished *that* feat. No food left besides scraps on the floor, but he found a few bottles of warm water buried in mud on the floor of the pantry. He stared at them for two minutes, gearing up to touch one. In one fast action—as if that would make it more sanitary—he unscrewed the cap on one, wiped the mouth vigorously with the tail of his filthy t-shirt, succeeded only in making it more dirty, finally got that off with a shred of towel, and brought it reluctantly to his lips.

Clink!

The rebreather.

"Crap." He'd actually forgotten about the thing for a second. The idea of taking the mask off made his empty stomach clinch, but the odds of finding a hyperbaric chamber or medical clean room anytime soon were, not to be too much of a Negative Nelly, pretty slim. He took a deep breath, pulled the mask off his face—it made the sort of pop a suction cup does when pulled from glass—took a hurried swig and then readjusted the air filter. "See, not dead yet. Cholera maybe, but not dead.'"

The bottom line was, he needed help. Some food. A phone, at the very least. And he could hyperventilate and throw as many hissy-fits as he wanted, but this was one problem he couldn't imagine or buy away.

Looked like he was headed for the Civic Center after all. If it was even still standing. And since he didn't own a car, he would have to get there the old-fashioned way.

He took the towel, tied up the two and three-quarters left of his bottled water, and poked a long branch through the knot to form a hobo traveling pack. Feeling like a Hanna-Barbera cartoon character, he made his way back to the front of the house. Carter stood in the pale light, gazing out at the rain-soaked street and the emptiness beyond.

By Crom, it looked big out there.

You can do this. You have to. I'm okay, you're okay, the universe is center. Just take it one step at a time.

This encouragement wasn't from the Lucid, only himself. Carter stepped out, measuring his breath in the mask, and stared at his feet as they carried him forward and up the street one agonizing step at a time.

WHITNEY +11:18

"Bryce, stop hogging the covers," Maryland grumbled. Without opening her eyes, she reached over to give him a shove and make a play for the blankets, but her hand landed on a fully-clothed leg too thin to belong to her husband. A throbbing pain shot through her palm from the contact.

Her eyes flew open, seeking the familiarity of her bedroom, the only space Bryce let her decorate to her taste because he hardly ever slept there. But she wasn't in her king size, four-poster bed with the silk sheets and cozy goose-down comforter. She was lying on a hard, tilted surface in damp clothes, her wet sneakers braced against a pillar leading up to a graffiti-peppered concrete ceiling a few yards above. Maryland turned her head to the left to see whose leg she was touching.

A crinkled face at least ten years older than Bryce stared back at her, blinking sleep away and squinting as its brown eyes focused on her. One bushy, red brow went up as the other person recognized— or *didn't* recognize—her in return.

She jerked her hand away with an embarrassed squeak.

"Oh. Good morning, miss." His voice was proper, some derivative of British accent floating through each word.

"Um, morning," Maryland croaked, sitting up. The images from the night before bled into her consciousness; blurred mental snapshots of the explosion, the landslide, the mass exodus, and the miserable night beneath the overpass, clinging to the pillars as the wind tore at her. It seemed like a lifetime of bad luck, all crammed into...what, the last twelve hours? Her watch was gone, torn off her arm at some point during her adventures, but guessing from the brightness of the strangled light coming through the haze, it must be around seven in the morning.

On the other side of her was the guy she'd saved from the flash flood, still passed out with a thread of drool running from his mouth. The pillar blocked most of her forward view, but she could see to the left and right that the raging waters had subsided, leaving a series of deep, scattered puddles.

"Is it...is it over?" she asked. "Whitney?"

"It would appear we survived." The older man braced himself on the incline with one hand against the pillar as he stood and stretched his back. He was a good foot shorter than Maryland, scarecrow-thin, with sparse red hair lying lank against the back of his skull. His clothes looked almost too big for him, his blue and white striped sweater so waterlogged it was almost comical. One hand slid into the pocket of his baggy dress pants and removed a pair of tiny, round-frames glasses. He slipped these over his nose with a relieved grin. "Thank God. I was sure they'd be broken."

"Guess you kind of saved my life last night." The memory of slipping into the flood herself was vivid, and this stranger risking his own life by dragging her to safety.

"Think nothing of that." He waved the words away with one hand and looked down bashfully. "Any gentleman would do the same."

"Yeah, well, not many of the 'gentlemen' I hang around with." She stood up, kicked shoulder and twisted ankle moaning in protest, but neither felt too bad. She started to wipe off the seat of her jeans before realizing it was pointless. The dirt and filth were glued to her moist outfit. "I'm Maryland...well, Williams for now."

"Thomas Winston Cruise, at your disposal."

She smiled, charmed by the accent and the introductory use of his full name, then cocked her head and blurted, "Wait, wait, Thomas Winston Cruise? As in...Tom Cruise for short?"

He smiled a tiny, exasperated grin. "Yes, yes, an unfortunate coincidence, I'm afraid."

"Really? You sure you didn't change your name after seeing *Vanilla Sky*?"

"I honestly can't say I've watched a single film the man has ever made."

"Consider yourself lucky."

"Now you see why I use my full name. You'd be surprised how many people don't even notice."

Maryland laughed, and the sound surprised her. The future had looked so dismal ever since that one shining moment where she found the courage to leave Bryce. It was nice to see the simple things could still offer humor. She stuck out a hand. "I never thought I'd say this, but...pleased to meet you Tom Cruise."

"Tom will suffice." They shook, his tiny mitt swallowed up by her comparative bear claw, and another bolt of pain shot through her arm at the pressure.

"Jesus!" She turned the hand over. Road rash, from her dive off the freeway, stretched across both palms where she'd tried to slow her fall. They were scabbed over, the normally smooth flesh replaced with dark scales. The wound must've bled during the night, but she hadn't even noticed.

"Say, that looks pretty bad," Tom told her.

"What looks pretty bad?" The third member of their hurricane slumber party sat up and rubbed sleep out of his eyes.

Tom pointed at her wounds. "It appears Miss Williams sustained an injury while trying to save you last night."

"No, it...it happened before that," she mumbled.

"Oh yeah, I appreciate that," the new guy said curtly as he got up. He was far younger than Tom, closer to her age, fit and muscular, strong jaw and black hair cut short on top and buzzed at the sides. He wore a University of Texas athletic t-shirt and track shorts with sneakers. He knelt to set about retying the laces. "You guys know what the fuck happened last night?"

Tom flapped a hand toward the destroyed freeway. "An explosion destroyed the bridge, I believe, which then triggered some sort of avalanche."

"Thanks for the newsflash Gramps, but I think everybody saw that." Their new companion was self-confident (*some of us call that, 'cocky', babe*) as well as attractive, exactly the type that usually set her heart aflutter. Oh, why pretty it up; he was the kind she wouldn't hesitate to tumble into the nearest backseat with on the first date in her younger, pre-Bryce days. "I meant, what *caused* it?"

"I was pretty close to the bridge when it happened. I didn't see..."

She trailed as the image of the fleeing Guardsman flitted across her mind. For some reason, it didn't feel nearly as important as it had last night, without that vague sense of impending doom to back it up.

"Didn't see?" Track Shorts prompted, impatience in his tone.

"Anything," she finished. He straightened up and she watched against her will. It made her feel guilty, but what did it hurt to look? She would be on the market again soon. His attitude reminded her of Bryce though, a big turnoff, but the rest of her body just wasn't getting that memo.

"What about a cell phone? Either of you got one?"

Tom shook his head. "I'm sorry to say mine is resting in my vehicle at the bottom of the gorge."

Maryland had no hopes of finding hers, but she patted the pocket of her jeans just in case. "Yeah, I think mine was in my purse." Along with her driver's license, credit cards and the little cash she'd left with. There was something gleeful in the knowledge that Bryce's Bentley must resemble a pancake at the bottom of Rugg Canyon, but she would rather have the vehicle than a petty revenge.

Without it and her purse, she really was reduced to nothing but her clothes. *Better get used to sleeping under bridges.*

Track Shorts shot them an exasperated look and started down the concrete hill under the bridge. Maryland and Tom followed, the latter being careful to keep his balance on the steep, slick grade. They halted beneath the crumbled edge of the overpass and stood side-by-side.

The ruins of the elevated portion of the freeway lay in front of them, huge chunks of concrete and crushed automobiles littering the crossroad of Johnston Avenue beneath. Thanks to the landslide, the vehicles were all empty at the time of the collapse, the owners running for their lives, but Maryland spotted a few twisted bodies amid the rubble, people sucked down when the road gave way. No blood, thankfully; the flood and rain left only bloated, pale limbs jutting from the wreckage.

"*Is anyone out there?*" Tom called out, hands cupped over his mouth. The world felt unnaturally quiet as his words rang out against the rafters above them.

"Christ old man, can you keep it down?" Track Shorts snapped. "I've got a raging headache."

She glanced at her new British friend, whose face screwed up in annoyance. "My name is Tom, not…'old man' or 'Gramps.' I don't believe we caught yours."

"Gerald Baxter."

"Well Mr. Baxter, if there is anyone alive out there, they might need our help. The same way *you* did last night when both Miss Williams and I risked our lives to pull you from that flood."

"*Risked your lives?*" Gerald rolled his eyes. "Don't exaggerate."

"No, he's right." Maryland met his gaze with all the unflinching directness she could muster. "You would've been washed out to Rugg Canyon just like…just like those other poor people…"

"Oh God, here come the waterworks. As if we haven't had enough of those."

"You insensitive asshole." She wiped at her eyes before they could spill. "I wish I'd let you drown! I could've offered my hand to someone who appreciated it!"

"I said I appreciated it, but just because I lived doesn't mean I have to stand around crying over a bunch of strangers who didn't!"

"Fighting amongst ourselves isn't going to solve anything," Tom cut in. "I don't know you people, you don't know me, and no one said we have to be friends, but we *are* in this situation together."

"Speak for yourself." Gerald walked out a few paces into the rain before facing them. "The only reason I came to this town was to batten down my brother's house since he's overseas. My stupid mistake, right? But I have to get back to UT. I have classes to teach and my girlfriend is waiting to hear from me. And since my car is somewhere up there in terminal gridlock, I'm gonna walk my happy ass right outta here. *Arrivederci*, people." He started away, weaving through the field of shattered concrete.

"Did you not hear us say the bridge is gone?" Maryland shouted after him. "Unless you can fly, you're not getting out that way."

He turned back again, grimaced and shrugged. "Gotta be some other way out of this shithole."

"Yeah, and it's the pass through the mountains on the other side of town, genius."

He sighed and threw his hands up. "Fine, I get your point. I'm stuck with you for a little while longer. What do you propose?"

Maryland didn't have an answer to that one. While she and Gerald shouted at one another, Tom had lost interest, turning to survey the open land to the south, towards the city. Now he said softly, "Something isn't right about this."

"What do you mean?"

"Think about it. The hurricane is over, and we're standing at the site of a major catastrophe. That explosion was seen for miles, thus someone must be aware of the situation." He looked at Maryland, brow drawn together above his funny little round glasses. "So where are the rescue vehicles? Police and paramedics and volunteers, sifting through the wreckage, looking for survivors in the canyon? Surely they would've had time by now to come through the alternate route you mentioned, or fly in on helicopters or…or *something*. But…just us."

Maryland swallowed. Now that he'd said it, the absence of other people—living people—was creepy. Maybe they were unaware of more pressing storm-related emergencies, but she just couldn't see the powers-that-be not sending a single squad car or ambulance to check the devastation. "What do you think it means?"

"I have no idea. But if there are no other survivors for us to help, I suggest we start back into the city to find assistance." He took in the ruins of the bridge once more, and Maryland saw his upper lip was shaking. "And an answer to that very question."

WHITNEY +11:41

Chris awoke to find his stepsister gone.

His heart sent an injection of crazed fear into his sluggish veins. She'd been sucked right out from under the bed, he just knew it, pulled away by the maelstrom of tornadic winds like a dust bunny into a vacuum cleaner.

"Tangela!" The mattress above him muffled most of the sound, trapping his cry in the confined space and making him think of all the Edgar Allen Poe buried alive stories he'd read in Advanced English. He suddenly felt claustrophobic.

He squirmed out of the tight space, shoving aside stuffed animals, a tree branch, and a chunk of ceiling plaster, and emerged into semi-bright light streaming through the broken window. Tangela's room was trashed: walls bare, furniture overturned, belongings scattered in the floor along with other garbage blown into the apartment. The room itself looked intact, with only a large crack running across the ceiling to indicate the building's severe structural damage.

Chris shouted his stepsister's name again, but received no response. The apartment seemed dead silent after the constant rumble of the storm, the soft patter of rain the only thing to break the stillness.

Where could she be? He'd kept his arms wrapped around her all night as Whitney raged and the building creaked and shook, but somewhere along the way he'd drifted into a sleep tortured with visions of Nichelle's face.

Oh God, Nichelle...

Don't think about that. Not now.

Chris flew into the hallway, stubbing his bare toe on a section of baseboard jutting from the wall. The action saved his life, causing him to slow before he plunged through a splintered hole in the hallway floor leading straight through to the apartment below. He edged around it, started to run by his bedroom, and then came to a skidding stop.

His door stood open just a sliver, and the light seeping around the edges was too bright to be from his small window. Chris gave it a push. The door creaked open to reveal...nothing.

It was no less surreal than if Wonderland or Narnia had been on the other side. The room that once contained all his belongings stopped at the door's threshold, carved off as neatly as a slab of Thanksgiving turkey. The ceiling, the roof, *the entire top of the building* was missing, revealing naked heavens. To the right, the wall he shared with Tangela's room remained, and looking down from the ledge at his feet he could see a cross section of the two apartments below, also sheared away.

Everything gone. His computer, his little TV, the used Playstation 3 he saved 75 dollars to buy, the iPod Nano his Goma gave him for Christmas, all his books, his sports memorabilia...blown to oblivion.

Of course. His room gone, Tangela's room still here. The little brat got everything handed to her. Even God was on her side.

From this vantage point, he had a pretty good view of the surrounding blocks, and though he'd been up and down their streets countless times, he recognized little. The two-story apartment building next door had collapsed inward. Where once there were stores and small houses and duplexes now existed only an endless field of wreckage and debris. He would've expected hurricane damage to look like the area surrounding Mount St. Helens after the volcano blew, everything knocked over in neat domino rows, but this looked like a giant had smashed everything. It reminded him of news stories about third world countries, where the reporters walked through shanties and slums made of scrap wood while starving locals looked on. The depth of destruction was awe inspiring, and his pathetic losses were nothing compared with that.

Sometimes he hated being so smart. All he wanted was to begrudge his stepsister a little without feeling guilty, was that so much to ask?

Chris sped down the rest of the hall, coming around the corner into their destroyed living room.

The entire building was cored out like a worm-eaten apple. Only a narrow strip of warped floor remained attached to the wall on his left. Their kitchen appeared to still be on the right, but was inaccessible due to the huge span of missing floor. Two or three feet of leftover ceiling formed an umbrella above him, keeping the raindrops away. The two outer walls had vanished all the way down to the first floor, one of which had contained their front door, the only way in or out of the apartment. Chris could see straight through the gaping hole to where their concrete landing stood, to their neighbor's door on the opposite side, and could follow the stairs as they zigzagged all the way down to ground level. He was afraid to look over the edge, afraid he might see Nichelle's body down there, but when he finally got the nerve, he found no sign of her. All of their furniture—the sofa and beaten recliner, the television, the coffee table—had fallen downward with the floor; he could see the TV shattered two stories below in the middle of old Ms. Zwykowski's flooded living room, but no trace of the rest of their stuff.

"*Tangela!*" he wailed, clinching his fists in frustration. Out here, in the open air, his voice sounded flat. The only answer was the drip of water on the exposed floorboards.

He started to check the other rooms, when he heard, "Go away."

Chris faced the missing part of the apartment again, frowning. He could swear it came from this direction, but there was nothing this way except an empty space, and, beyond that, a diorama of their destroyed neighborhood. "Tangela? Where are you?"

A short, sulky silence. Then, "Down here."

This time, instead of just looking down from the ledge, he leaned over further to check *beneath* it. And gasped.

His stepsister was two yards away. She still wore the same purple Capris and striped blouse from the day before, but she'd found her shoes. She clung to a crude, inclined ladder formed by a jumbled mess of building materials once part of their sub-flooring. Pipes and boards and a heating/cooling shaft, all nailed onto a frame that used to separate their apartment from the second floor. It was attached somewhere on the underside of where he stood, the whole contraption suspended at an angle over the long drop to the ground floor. Even as he watched, the whole makeshift scaffolding swayed in the stiff breeze blowing through the building.

"Geez Tanj, what the hell are you doing?"

She glared up at him, eyebrows pulled together in exaggerated anger. "Stop cussing at me!"

"Okay, okay, I'm sorry, but you have to come back up! I'm gonna reach down and I want you to grab my hand!" He got on his knees and leaned out, extending one arm, trying not to think about the echoes of last night. The distance was too great, but she would have to climb up to him; no way would he trust this thing to hold both their weights.

"No! Just leave me alone! I'm gonna find—" She stopped as a coughing fit seized her. Her hands squeezed the pipe until it passed, and the rudimentary ladder clanged against something below. "Find Mommy," she finished.

A pang shot through him. "Tangela, listen to me, you have to climb back up right now! It's dangerous!"

She gave him the blackest look her eight-year-old face was capable of. "So what? You don't care! You said you hated us! I'm gonna find Mommy and…and we're never gonna speak to you again!"

She climbed down further on the conglomeration, wedging her feet into new toeholds.

Her ladder didn't even go anywhere; it ended just a few feet from where she was now, hanging over open air. Perhaps she'd believed it a way down from up here, but he got the idea she only persisted now to defy him.

What was wrong with her? Why did she have to be so…*annoying?*

He could feel the fury growing, that anger animal, the impatience he always felt when dealing with this girl. He took a cleansing breath before he spoke again.

"Tangela, please come back up and we'll look for her together!"

"No Chris, I won't ever listen to you again! Mommy got hurt because you said those mean things!"

Tears welled; he squinted his eyes to stop them from spilling. His stepmother was dead. How many times had he wished for this to come true, and now, here it was, and he even got to have a hand in it. Tangela was right; he might as well have pushed her off the ledge himself.

He'd lost a second mother, one he never even bothered to get to know.

"Why are you crying?" she demanded, a note of suspicion tainting the words.

"Your mom isn't down there." He couldn't hold it in, couldn't be the only one with the awful truth in his head. "She's…she's dead."

"No." The denial was quick enough to show she had probably already toyed with the idea. "No, that's not true, she is NOT dead!"

"Tangela…I lost her. I don't want to lose you. Please come back up here before you get hurt."

"NOOOO!" she shrieked. "NO, MY MOM IS NOT DEAD!" She coughed again, her whole body wracked and shaking, and whatever held the tangle of sub-floor aloft broke.

She plunged, screaming, but her ladder wasn't completely detached. It swung inward, smashing against the wall of the apartment below. He could see her feet flying back and forth like a pendulum, in wide, sweepings arcs.

"Help me! Chris, heeeeelp!"

"Hold on!" He surely could've rigged something, actually

would've found the engineering and mechanics of such a challenge entertaining, but there was no time to let his brain do its usual problem solving. He reacted by instinct, running along the narrow strip of floor against the wall to the left, boards snapping under his weight, and hurtled into three stories of open air when he reached the end, sailing through the missing wall of the apartment.

He slammed against the outside of the metal railing along the staircase leading from their door. One hand found purchase on the banister before he dropped. He pulled himself up and over the top, grunting with effort, until he could slide over onto the steps.

Chris skipped three and four at a time, continuing past the landing for the second floor and going all the way to the bottom. Ground level sat in a foot of brackish water, but he jumped in with his bare feet. He hopped over the stump of wall down here, in the opposite direction from the leap he'd just taken. Now he was inside Miss Zwykowski's apartment, looking up at a reverse angle from the view at the top.

Tangela clung to the scaffold as it swung in the wind. Only a bit of crimped pipe kept the whole mess from dropping, and it bent a little more with each teetering swing.

"Tangela, just hold on another second!"

The drop wasn't that far, now that the scaffold was pointing down. Maybe a floor and a half. She could break a few bones, but he was more worried about what would happen if the rest came down on top of her.

"C'mon think, *think*." His jaw moved in circles.

He splashed through the water in his elderly neighbor's apartment until he found the master bedroom. Miss Z had left all her furniture when she evacuated, and that included her bed. Chris grabbed the sopping mattress from the top and hauled it off the box springs. He turned it on its side to get it through the doorway, then tugged until he got it back to the living room, and laid it in the water under where Tangela still hung.

"Okay, let go!"

His stepsister looked down. "Uh uh, no way!"

"It's safe! The water will help absorb the impact!"

"I'm scared!"

"I know, but I promise you, nothing is gonna happen! Now LET GO!"

Something in the ladder gave way with a metallic groan. She let go, screaming again as she plummeted. She hit the wet mattress on her bottom, bouncing back up and clearing a good three feet of air before coming back down.

Chris swept her up, half-carrying, half-dragging her out of the way. The rest of the construction material came down right behind her, tearing straight through the wet mattress in a tremendous crash. Once they were a safe distance away, he set her down. She started to cry, pounding at him with her small fists. He sank to his knees and hugged her, and her hands finally stopped hitting and slipped around his neck.

"Please no Chris, not my mommy," she begged.

He remembered, oh man, he remembered moaning that same thing against his father so many times, and he broke then, for her or himself or both of them, and they wept in each other's arms as the rain stopped falling on the ruins around them.

WHITNEY +11:57

A tremendous clatter catapulted Ellis from sleep. He felt disoriented, unsure of who he was, let alone where. But his body reacted to the clamor on instinct, scrabbling for his weapon and yanking it from the holster on his hip.

"It's me, it's me, don't shoot!" he heard. Ellis blinked sleep from his eyes. Dusty light floated into the warehouse from small windows up near the ceiling, enough for him to recognize the black youth in the white sleeveless T and sagging jeans a few yards away. He stood in front of an overturned metal rack full of tools, spread across the concrete floor.

Memories hit him like machine gun fire. The hurricane. The looters. Sturney and his crew. Charlie. Poor Billy.

"You scared me out of five years of life," he panted, putting the gun away. "What are you doing?"

"Just…pokin around, man. Tryin to figure out where we at."

"Yeah, well don't steal anything."

The young man scowled. "Just because I'm in a gang don't mean I'm a klepto."

"Well, it sure doesn't make you a candidate for sainthood either." Ellis' spine felt like a bent steel rod after sleeping on the concrete floor, but he was too thankful to be alive to dwell on it. He glanced at his watch, squinting to make out its face. Close to eight in the morning.

The kid watched him warily, as though afraid he might rethink the whole shooting-him thing at any second. Their angry exchange at the end of the previous night came back to Ellis. "Kind of thought you'd be gone by now."

"Oh trust me, I was plannin to leave your ass snorin first thing today."

"Then why are you still here?"

"Hm, let's think about that." The kid closed half the distance between them. In closer proximity, he looked haggard. His bare right shoulder was crusted with blood from the bullet graze. "Maybe because four armed men—and not just any men, but *cops*—are out to gun me down 'cause of some shit I don't have anything to do with. Much as I wanna get outta here and find my crew, I figure I'm better off with the man who's got a gun and a license to use it."

Ellis considered that while taking stock of himself. He'd dried in the night, but his uniform was ruined from stains and tears. A few items were missing from his belt, but his handcuffs and extra ammo clips were still in place. "You don't have to worry about them."

"Oh really, *Officer*? And just why is that?"

He sighed. "Look, I know this is how the world says we're supposed to treat each other, but let's just pretend for one minute we're not who we are. I'm not a cop, and you're not a gang member. We're just two people meeting for the first time in the middle of a FUBAR situation. My name is Ellis Wright. Yours is Lincoln, correct?"

The boy rolled his eyes and seemed to rethink his sarcasm. "Yeah. Lincoln Briggs."

"Okay, cool. Well Lincoln, you don't have to worry about those guys because as soon as I can find a phone, I'm gonna call my captain and report exactly what happened. I'll have the police, the FBI, the...the damned *Army* after them. They're not gonna get away with what they did to Billy." By the end of this, he was speaking through clenched teeth, and no longer strictly to Lincoln.

"Hey, I'm sorry about your boy, but you gotta see, my crew didn't ask for any of this. We got enough people tryin to kill us without addin the cops into it."

"I know, and I'll get you out of it, I promise. How's your shoulder?"

Lincoln winced as he touched it gently. "Not bleedin anymore, but it still hurts like a bitch. C'mon, let's stop talkin and *do* somethin!"

"I want to find my partner as much as you want to find your friends, but if we rush out, it'll be the quickest way to get ourselves killed. I'm sure that fat asshole and his cronies have already scatted right out of town—they'd be stupid not to—but just in case, we ought to find a phone, alert the authorities, and stay low until they come for us."

"That's your plan, huh? Sit back and wait to be rescued?"

"Look Lincoln, in case you haven't thought about it, Port Allen is essentially lawless right now. My precinct was the last to clear out before Whitney hit, and depending on the damage, it could be a while before they can get back in. And crooked cops might be the least of our worries."

Lincoln's brow furrowed in thought. "The explosion."

"What?"

"Remember last night, the explosion across town when ya'll were facin off against those pigs? What was that?"

In all the chaos, Ellis hadn't stopped to think about the flash and distant rumble that ended the standoff. He hadn't even thought of it as an explosion until Lincoln referred to it that way. He shrugged. "Could've been storm damage or...well, like I said, the whole city could be in anarchy by now."

Lincoln swallowed hard. He looked very much his age in that moment, a good decade and a half younger than Ellis. These gangbangers grew up fast on the streets. "All right, man, I'm with you. Let's find that phone."

They searched through the rest of the warehouse, using Ellis' flashlight to illuminate the windowless corridors. They tried any switches they came across, but either the power was still out or the switches didn't go to the lights. A few rooms on the second floor had either collapsed or been blown away, leaving them open to the rain, but other than that, damage was minimal. Finally they came across a bank of small management offices in one upstairs corner.

"This one's dead!" Lincoln shouted from the next room over.

"Same here." Not quite accurate, though. When Ellis picked up the handset on the desk in front of him, he could hear the hum of an open line but no dial tone, no matter how many buttons he pressed.

Lincoln's head poked around the corner. "What do you think? Line down or somethin?"

"Maybe." He knew little about the way phones worked, so it could be that simple…but he always thought if the lines were down, the phones were entirely silent.

"Okay, so what do we do now? You live close?"

"South side. Too far to walk." He brightened, throwing a smile at Lincoln. "How about a compromise? If we can get back to my squad car, we should be able to pick someone up on my radio to at least let them know what happened, and we can look for the others at the same time."

"Fine man, let's hit the streets. The sooner I know the coast is clear, the sooner we go our separate ways."

They made their way downstairs to a door at the front of the dark warehouse. It was unlocked, but the frame had either shifted or the wood swelled in its seat; it wouldn't so much as budge. Lincoln pulled on the knob until it came off in his hand. They grabbed a wrench from the warehouse floor, stuck it through the hole, and used it as a lever until the exit popped open.

Three feet of water rushed in at them, the current strong enough to bowl them both over. Ellis splashed down face first in the foamy green water, struggling to get his arms under him. Lincoln flopped around like a fish beside him as the water flooded the warehouse. It just kept rushing over the threshold, like an opened hydrant gushing its contents.

"Where's it coming from?" Lincoln yelled over the splashing.

Ellis regained his footing and forced his way into the current, moving through the doorway and outside the warehouse. The front

faced a broad avenue of other broken down depots and storehous-
es, some of them storm damaged. A layer of still, green water lay
across all of it as far as he could see.

"Storm surge and rain," Ellis said. "Port Allen is one big bowl,
but it's tilted to the northeast. This is where all the rain and water
that moved through the city last night collected." He looked back
at Lincoln and shook his head. "I'd hate to see what the furthest
corner of the city looks like."

WHITNEY +12:13

The pain was bitter and sharp, a raging bonfire of the nerves. It
yanked Charlie out of fitful sleep when he rolled onto his injured
leg. He came to full consciousness just in time to clamp down on a
bloodcurdling scream.

Kim's alley had led him and the two X-Dawgs to the flooded
eastern end of Willis Street, and from there they fled downhill,
deeper into the ethnic suburbs that filled out the northeast edge of
Port Allen. Nice houses and estates through here, but the swanky
construction was no indication of the inhabitants; the once stately
neighborhoods had fallen into disarray long ago and been sold to
lower class clientele as property values plummeted. Now most of
the little one and two story colonials were marked as gang territory,
abandoned, or used as crack houses, with a few decent low-income
families trapped in between.

They'd run for what felt like hours, until they put enough distance between themselves and Sturney's crew to warrant a rest. The
first house they broke into, when the wind and rain simply became
too much, disintegrated almost as soon as they entered, the roof
tearing away like a cellophane wrapper. The big gang member never
hesitated, just snatched Charlie back up and led the angry little black
youth into the fray. The sloping streets were filled with four feet of
water by this point, and they fought through the current to a tidy
two-story home just up the street. The bottom lay swamped, so they
took the stairs to the upper floor and sprawled panting on the carpet.

Charlie studied the interior of their shelter in the morning light
to take his mind off the pain. The storm had spared the dwell-

ing, but only because it probably didn't see the point in destroying it. Walls rotted and mildewed, carpet threadbare and stained with God-knew-what, and the ceiling had more leaks than he could count. This wide space started as some rich kid's bedroom, but now it was no more than an animal den in need of some heroine addicts.

His two new companions slumbered on the far side of the room, the smaller one curled in the fetal position in the farthest corner. He also appeared to be sucking his thumb, but after his threats the night before, any comedy in the sight fell flat. The boy was a stone cold killer, and had all the symptoms of a far-gone addict.

As much as they needed to be taken into custody, Charlie would've preferred to get up early and sneak away while they slept, but walking was nowhere close to possible.

Sweat popped out on his brow. Distraction wasn't working. He dug in his pocket for the bottle of aspirin the larger of the two—Mac—had snagged for him the previous night before leaving Kim's. He shook three pills into his hand, dry swallowed, and then took another two for good measure.

"Look on the bright side, old fart." He grimaced as he waited for the pain to subside. "At least your eyes ain't burnin outta their sockets anymore."

"That bad?" a gravelly voice croaked.

He jumped, causing another sharp wave of pain. Mac sat up across the room, adjusting his rumpled jersey on his wide frame.

Charlie shrugged. "Naw, not at all. Just short of excruciating."

Mac stood up and crossed the room to him. "Let's take a look."

The bruiser was surprisingly gentle for his size. He turned Charlie's leg to the side so they could see the wound under the makeshift tourniquet. Charlie tried to relax, but every muscle in his body quivered in anticipation of the youth going for his gun.

Bleeding had stopped sometime in the night. The constant rain had cleaned it, but the bullet hole looked bad. Early-stages-of-infection bad. Red and swollen and oozy.

"You need a doctor," Mac said. "And soon."

Charlie scooted up against the filthy wall, mainly just to prove to himself the pain couldn't be as bad as he thought. This theory turned out to be very wrong. "Twenty-five goddamned years on the force, all the murderers and drug dealers and scum I've faced, and I end up gettin shot by another cop. Hell, I've only fired my gun in the line of duty twice." This included last night's fiasco, but he didn't know if defending yourself against fellow officers was technically 'duty'.

"Yeah, yeah, that's what they all say." Mac grinned, and Charlie allowed himself a chuckle. "So what's the plan?"

"The plan, my friend, is to clear outta here ASAP and find a phone, cause I'm pretty sure my cell is kaput. And after we ensure the four dickheads who caused all this are toppin the Most Wanted list, then we see if we can track down my partner and your...what do you boys calls 'em? 'Dogg?' You know, the one with two G's?"

Mac grinned even wider. "Don't try for street slang, okay?"

He turned away, and Charlie reached out to grab his arm. "Hey, it's Mac, right? Listen...I wanna say thanks. For carryin me all the way here last night. And standin up to your friend."

"Ain't no thing." The kid seemed embarrassed. He tried to hide this by clearing his throat, and ended up releasing a deep, hacking cough that went on until Charlie was afraid he would choke to death.

"Jehosaphat kid, you need a doc too? Sound like you're ready to spit out a lung."

"I don't know," Mac gasped. "I just suddenly had this burnin in my throat, like a cold."

"It's from bein out in the rain so long. Be lucky if you don't catch pneumonia."

"Fuck man, you two wanna be alone or sumthin?" The wiry gangbanger yawned from the corner. "Cause if you gonna start suckin each other off, I'll go sleep in another room. Shee-it."

Mac's teeth clinked together one time, loud enough for Charlie to hear. "CT, I'm gonna take him out to find a phone. Just stay here."

The boy jumped up and swung a fist through the air. "No way, I ain't just gonna sit around here! I'm goin back to base, let the crew know what happened."

"You're not goin anywhere," Mac and Charlie said in unison.

"Why the hell not?"

Mac sighed and threw his hands up. "Do you ever think about anyone but yo'self, crackhead?"

"*I don't do no crack, muhfuckah!*"

"That ain't what I hear. And you can't leave because if those shifty pigs are still out there and you lead 'em back to base, then the whole *crew's* in danger."

"So? I ain't scared of them, and neither is any X-Dawg worth a shit."

Charlie thought about the confrontation between the two of them last night in the convenience store. He doubted these two would ever be able to occupy the same room again without finding something to fight about. Mac just shook his head.

"Listen runt." Charlie shifted, moving back so he could sit up further against the wall, and received another jolt. "Until the situation at Kim's can be investigated, neither one of you is leavin my sight. We all go together."

CT snarled, kicked the wall beside him, and then scratched at his scalp like a dog getting behind the ears. Definitely junkie. He turned to stare out the smeared window as he cursed under his breath. Mac watched Charlie for a moment, face as unreadable as a statue. "So we're supposed to aid and assist you in reportin those four from last night, just so you can throw us in jail when you're finished with us?" He wheezed again, covering his mouth with one cantaloupe-sized fist. "You can thank me for helpin you, but you can't cut me any slack? That about the size of it, Officer Charlie?"

"I don't know what you expect from me kid, but I can't change what you two and your other friend did, and I sure ain't responsible for it. The law is the law."

"This ain't 'bout the law. The law left town before Whitney hit so the poor folks could tear each other apart. Anything any of us did last night was purely 'bout survival."

"Keep tellin yourself that if it makes you feel better." Charlie pulled out his pistol and made a show of checking the clip. "The only thing I know right now though, is that we need to get movin."

CT turned back with a toothy grin. "Then I hope you got a boat, piggy, cause otherwise it's gonna be a long swim."

"What are you talkin about?" Charlie braced his good leg and pushed, inching himself up the wall. The pain was enormous, an endless wave of hot misery radiating up his hip, but after a struggle of forty-five seconds that felt like three hours, he was on his feet. He hopped over to the window and leaned on the sill. Mac steadied him with one hand on his shoulder.

The flood waters from the night before hadn't drained; in fact, they'd *risen*. The neighborhood appeared to be floating in the middle of a vast, green ocean. Only the roofs of the still-standing one-story houses peeked out, like those hotel suites in the French Polynesia that he'd seen pictures of, little huts built right on top of the water, whole floating communities. Looking down, the flood started a few feet below the level of the window, and was still climbing.

"Oh, this just keeps gettin better," Charlie whispered.

Beside him, Mac coughed.

WHITNEY +12:29

A cold, wet nose pushed against Hernie's cheek, rousing him from a dream in which the spectral form of his mother used kung-fu to fight a horde of secret government agents dressed as ninjas, all to protect him. He opened his eyes to find a muddy and shivering Hatch lying on his chest for warmth.

"O-okay, Hatch, I'm uppey-up." He shook also, teeth chattering in Morse code. The small space beneath the pipe where he'd taken shelter had become a pit of mud overnight. He had no choice but to slide down into the muck with a syrupy squelch.

He couldn't even remember going to sleep. The roar outside his cubbyhole kept him awake the majority of the night. He thought it would never end, and he screamed and screamed for help, but couldn't even hear himself.

Hatch whimpered and drug a rough tongue across his master's chin. Hernie started to smile, but was gripped by a monstrous cough that started deep in his stomach and tore at his throat. He forced his mouth closed when he felt on the verge of vomiting, one of his least favorite things in the whole world.

"Oh no, I d-don't feel so good," he said through those uncontrollably chomping teeth. And boy, did he not. He felt dizzy, like he'd spun around a few too many times on a merry-go-round, and there was still a tickle in his throat, as annoying as a hair in the mouth.

The last time he could remember being truly sick was before Hatch came to him. Frost on the ground, cold outside, and his head and chest burned. A nice lady told him he had 'New Moan-ya' (she laughed fit to bust when he told her, if this was the new kind, he hoped he never caught Old Moan-ya) and let him sleep in the back of her car and gave him soup until he felt better.

He pushed Hatch out of his lap and crawled from beneath the tangle of oil pipes. It was early morning, and a light shower fell across the refinery yard. But at least the clouds had thinned enough that the sun could struggle through; even that small blessing was enough to thrill him.

He just hoped those government men didn't send their storm back after him.

His back throbbed, and his wrist hurt where he'd landed on it during their hasty escape. He coughed a few more times, then turned his head up and caught a mouthful of rain to wash the taste of sour spit out of his mouth.

The refinery yard had survived with barely a scratch. Hernie spun in a slow circle as he tried to wipe mud out of his hair, taking in the big, black towers and their maze of pipes. The ground was a watery brown pit with deep puddles standing everywhere, but the machinery still looked as big and mean and scary as ever. He understood for sure now why the soft voice told him to come here.

Hatch gave another whimper in front of him and sat down. Not hard to figure out that message; Hernie's belly felt just as empty.

"Hold your horsey right there, young man." He placed filthy hands on hips for emphasis. "We can't go off with mud on us. They won't even let us in McDonald's lookin like this."

Hatch gave a mighty, full-body shake, flinging wet dirt from his fur in ropes, a generous amount of which landed on his master.

"Yeah, well, that might be good for you, but I feel icky."

Hernie turned in the direction of the shore and wandered through the refinery yard, coughing every few minutes, but the dizziness passed. The place wasn't nearly as scary in the daytime, especially after the night he just lived through. Might even make a good place to sleep once the weather warmed up.

He came around the wide base of a machine that looked like

a dinosaur, and the concrete barricade of the seawall stretched in front of him. The ground didn't run up to the edge like at the marina; the barrier towered five or six feet over his head here. On the other side was a short uphill climb to the ridge that led back down to the beach, where he could clean up in the surf. He walked in the direction of the marina until he came across a metal rung ladder built into the side of the seawall.

"Go play, Hatch," he told the animal, who took off in the other direction, nose to the ground. Hernie climbed up the slick rungs, forcing himself not to look down, and crawled onto the narrow walkway along the top of the wall. The wind up here was stronger, flapping his overcoat and stringy hair. He goggled around at the new landscape.

The land on the other side was gone, swallowed up by a massive amount of ocean water that came right up to the edge of the seawall, just a few inches below his feet. In the distance, forty or fifty yards out, he could see a sandbar that was the only evidence of the beach. The flooding had been pushed in by the storm and now lay trapped between the wall and the roll of the land, but he couldn't grasp this concept. In his head, he imagined a huge spigot being turned somewhere, filling up the Gulf of Mexico like bathwater about to overflow. The falling rain gave the endless surface of the water a dimpled texture.

He looked to the west. The marina was completely gone also, wiped from the face of the earth. He could see the flooded patch of ground where it had been, no more than a few boards sticking up here and there to mark the former location of a boathouse. Half a speedboat sat a good thirty yards from the water, turned on its torn end so it appeared to be sinking in the mud. The outside of the seawall down there had just as much water pressing against it.

Hernie tried to swallow the fear rising in his throat. He understood that he was standing on the only thing holding back a raging torrent that could easily tear through the refinery, washing away anything in its path.

And he couldn't swim.

Memories of childhood attempts flashed through his head, him in a pool, flailing around like a monkey with broken legs, until someone pulled him out. He wasn't afraid of water, but he was *terrified* of swimming.

Hernie no longer wanted to clean the mud off; the rain would do that anyway, given time. He just wanted to climb back down and run, to get away before this wall sprung a leak, and all the water it held back came crashing down on him like those Bible guys in the middle of that sea, after Jesus or Santa Claus or whoever parted the waters.

He dropped to his knees and reversed direction, feeling for the first rung, and halted with foot poised in midair.

Voices.

Someone was approaching through the field of refinery towers, along the seawall from the direction opposite the marina. Hernie didn't need the protective presence in his head to tell him to hide; in his experience, other people were never a good thing.

He lay down on his stomach along the top of the seawall and peered over the side.

WHITNEY +12:42

The water rose steadily throughout the night, and by 8 o'clock the morning after Whitney, it still hadn't stopped.

Imogene stayed with the oxygen machine as long as possible, covering up with blankets as the storm clawed through the shattered front windows. The entire experience was like being in a sensory deprivation chamber: the cold numbed her skin, and the wind forced her eyes closed and buffeted her ears until she might as well be deaf. The entirety of her consciousness became devoted solely to the tube pressed over her nose, unable to envision anything past the next breath, and the next, and the next.

Finally something lapped at the hand clenched in her lap. She opened her eyes to find the living room of her daughter's home flooded up to her waist in the wheelchair.

She tried to scream, but couldn't tell if any sound came out. Even as she watched, the flood mounted, pushing up toward her breasts and reaching the heavy oxygen machine on its miniature table. The device gave off a puff of smoke that the storm snatched away, then the stream of pure oxygen died.

Of course, if the water kept rising, getting *pure* oxygen into her lungs wouldn't be the problem.

Just let it happen. That advice sounded like the voice of her daughter, but there was a malicious note in it that the real Janie would never have affected. *This is the way it should be. Let that water rise up and pretty soon all your aches and worries will be over...*

NO! she railed at it, *I'm not finished yet, I'm* not *used up, no matter what you say!*

Imogene pulled the mask off and shoved at the wheels of her chair, forcing her way through the water. The thought of leaving the machine sent the same trills of unease shooting through her as usual; instances like this made her realize how *mentally* dependent she'd become too. She could think of only one refuge left to her in the tiny house, one that would provide shelter only if the wind didn't rip the roof off. Maneuvering the chair into the hallway, she stretched up as far as she could from the seat and was just able to snag the cord dangling from the door to the attic.

By the time she could get the ladder straightened out, she was practically submerged. She floated free of the chair, then had a moment of panic when one of her dead legs caught on something. She gripped the highest rung of the flimsy wooden ladder and hauled with all her might, popping free just before her head slipped below the swelling water.

Imogene struggled into the small attic. The space was cold, but at least it was dry. She sprawled across scratchy insulation, chest heaving from exhaustion. Dangerous black motes spun across her vision. It hurt so *bad* to breath. The COPD was awful enough on its own, but exertion only aggravated the symptoms.

The pain eventually died down. Imogene drew ragged breaths only by staying calm. She was lucky enough to have a stronger heart than most of the poor souls with this affliction, otherwise she'd have been dead already. The attacks normally came and went, but if she had a bad enough one now, while she was away from the machine...

Lord knows how she managed to fall asleep, but when next she woke, an unknowable amount of time later, the wind had stopped, and water gurgled at the open trapdoor of the attic.

Imogene propped herself on her palms in the insulation. What was she supposed to do now? The attic had seemed like a great option at the time, but she realized now it was only the equivalent of painting herself into a corner. The only way in or out was choked with water, and it would be a long swim down through the house and out the front door even for someone with functional lungs and legs. But up here, she had no food, no drinkable water, and already her stomach was tightening with one of the familiar asthmatic attacks.

There was a hollow slurping noise. The water rose above the lip of the horizontal attic door, spilling out onto the insulation.

"Damn it, I'm not gonna sit here and drown like a rat!"

The entire space was just one big triangle, built against the slant of the roof. It was dark, but she could make out its contents in the gloom. Nothing much up here except boxes of old clothes, the girls' toys, and…Eric's tools. Her son-in-law held a brief job as a carpenter before realizing he was about as skilled with his hands as a walrus.

Imogene crawled across the floor to the tool chest, careful to stay on the crossbeams. She was wheezing by the time she reached it, but didn't stop before rummaging through the drawers. In the third one down, she found what she was seeking.

A short, thick hatchet.

She moved back across the short space to the slanting wall. The surface had a layer of insulation she tore away with her bare hands, revealing a layer of particle board. She had no idea what lay on the other side, but hoped it wouldn't be too thick.

The hatchet was heavy. She swung it in short arcs with both hands, measuring her breaths between each chop. At any second the COPD, her most intimate dance partner, could wake up and decide to really kick up its heels, and she would be forced to stop. She had to get as far as possible through this operation before that happened.

The steel edge of the tool was sharp. It bit deep into the boards. After just a few minutes of lumberjacking, she'd carved out a rough circle about two feet across, a shallow depression in the wood surface.

Unfortunately, it just wasn't going fast enough. The water had now wetted the insulation and was filling up the spaces between the crossbeams. Good gracious, where was it all coming from? Fear caused her breathing to stutter.

Imogene renewed her chopping, and then, as suddenly as an arrow, a single beam of weak sunlight hit her square in the eye. At first she flinched away, but once she recognized it, she chopped all the harder.

The wood fell away in chunks. Whitney had actually aided her in this at least, by stripping off the outside layer of shingles. She broke the last jagged piece from her oval and stuck her head through the hole, feeling like a baby slipping out of the birth canal.

She emerged into muddled sunlight and delicate rain. The outside of the roof was a steep slant studded with a skeletal wooden frame. Imogene dropped the hatchet and gripped one of these boards. She wriggled up and out of her attic prison with little more than a rip up the back of her yellow blouse to show for it.

Of course, she wasn't too much better off up here. The entire house was surrounded by water up to the eaves, and the flood's ascent wasn't slowing. She could climb up to the tip of the roof, but what was left after that? Even if she could swim, the only place to go was one of the two-story houses she could see on the next block.

The pressure on her chest increased every second, amplified by anxiety.

She was wrong. She *was* used up. This was the world's not-so-subtle attempt to tell her it didn't want her any more than her family.

Imogene was so intent on the problem that the buzz growing in the distance didn't immediately register with her. As the sound got louder, she turned toward it, concentrating on the sputtery, high-pitched whine for the first time. She squinted down the street, or where the street lay under all this water, and saw a shape moving toward her.

A boat. Small but sleek, a tiny fishing motorboat with a black undercoat overlaid by twisted red flames. She was so shocked by its appearance, so surreal on an avenue where cars had been driving twenty-four hours before, she didn't even think to flag it down. Its driver spotted her anyway, stretched out across the roof's surface like the girl in *Christina's World*. The engine's purr slowed and then cut entirely as is drifted toward her.

Inside was a gawky, thin white man in his mid-forties, wearing filthy jeans, a white t-shirt, and a green John Deere cap on his gaunt head. He smiled, revealing a snaggled, tobacco-stained row of choppers, and raised a thin hand.

"Morn' ma'am." His accent was so thick she barely understood him. Not Texan either; too syrupy, too drawled in its rhythms, dropping all the hard consonants at the end of each word. Cajun maybe? "Look like you cou' use a han', *fo sho*."

She nodded, too grateful to conjure words and too out of breath to expel them even if she could. He maneuvered the boat up to the edge of the roof, babbling cheerfully in his mushy speech about how the flood had gobbled up his house and he was only just able to escape on his fishing 'trawl.'

He held out a hand to her, and Imogene shook her head. "I...I can't, sugar." She motioned to her legs.

"Wha's da matter? You can't walk?"

She nodded again.

He grinned wide enough so show all his crooked teeth, an expression she would've found unbelievably lowbrow in other circumstances, but was actually quite endearing at the moment. "Ain't no prob'em t'ere."

The boatman stepped onto the roof and lifted her up easily, carrying her stretched across both arms. There was something so chivalrous in the gesture, it made her feel girlish and very young. A small giggle escaped her before she could stop it. She covered her mouth in embarrassment, but her savior just kept smiling.

They stepped into the boat, and he set her gently down on a bench seat by the prow.

"Where you headin?" he asked, sounding like a cab driver.

"I...I don't know. I guess whichever way you are."

"Radio say da Dome is where ev'rbody suppose' go."

"Dome?"

"Con-ven-shun cen-ter," he said, drawing out the words for her to understand. "T'at's where I'm goin."

Imogene thought for the first time about the mechanical voice on the radio the night before. She hadn't given it much thought then, because she never expected to have a means of getting there.

She started to agree to this plan when it hit, the COPD, walloping her with the suddenness of a wrecking ball. Her airways closed, lungs deflated, and suddenly she couldn't breath. It felt like a fire in the center of her, one stoked hotter with each passing second.

"Ma'am? Ma'am?" Her new friend sounded quavery and far away. She realized she'd never even given her name, or asked for his.

Imogene collapsed in the boat, losing consciousness as the fire in her chest spread.

GO YOUR OWN WAY

Hernie thought he could hear two different voices drawing closer, but they were oddly garbled, so he couldn't be sure.

He lay still atop the thin ledge of the seawall and peered over the side, breathing only in small, quick spurts. The gurgle of rain and ocean behind him was distracting, but he could swear the newcomers' words sounded dry, smothered, and…*metallic*, is the word that sprang to mind, though it was far more descriptive than he would normally be. The new arrivals came around the base of an enormous length of refinery piping, their shadows stretched long in front of them in the morning sunlight.

Hernie was helpless to stop the moan that escaped his lips.

Black outfits covered every inch of them; tight, seemingly one-piece garments made of some shiny material. Rain beaded against the surface and rolled off in tiny streams. Both had belts with the handles of guns visible at their hips, weapons that, to Hernie—who had never so much as seen a real firearm—looked big enough to shoot cannonballs. The one on the left carried a black duffel bag by hand straps.

All of that might not be so bad, no worse than the occasional scuba divers he watched from the pier, but their faces were covered by awful masks. The kind that haunted his dreams almost every night. Dark, reflective glass over the top half of their heads, sloping down to a black cylinder like a prominent chin that split off into smaller tubes at the end.

Government agents. He was sure of it. Or maybe robots.

Either way, they'd found him at last.

He watched the sleek domes of their covered heads just a few feet below, and listened to their conversation.

"The guy's acting weird lately, I'm telling you," one of them, maybe the one with the duffel bag, said. The words rang in the air with that muted, mechanical quality, almost enough to vibrate Hernie's skull. "And I'm not the only one that's noticed."

"Not like you couldn't get reassigned, if you really wanted."

"Yeah, I'm sure Kyler will sign off on that one. Right after he makes me shoot my wife, kids, and parents to prove my allegiance."

Laughter; in their ringing voices it made his teeth buzz. At least it proved they were government agents. Hernie was pretty sure robots didn't laugh. Well, maybe the ones from the future.

They stopped below him. Hernie slunk back from the ledge. He held his breath and attempted to keep his heart from beating, but if they were tracking him by the chip in his head, it was game over. All they had to do was start up the ladder in pursuit and there would be no place for him to hide.

But they hadn't zeroed in yet. Instead he heard the whine of a zipper. Instinct told him to stay put and remain quiet, but curiosity overcame, and he took another peek.

The black-clad figures crouched in the dirt at the base of the seawall. The duffel was open in front of them, revealing stacks of silver disks an inch thick and four or five in diameter, like giant novelty quarters. As Hernie watched, one of the agent-robot-whatevers held out a disk in the palm of his gloved hand, taking no pains to keep the device out of the rain.

So that was their plan. Send a killer probe after him.

The agent raised a small rod attached to the disk, and then slid open a tiny panel on one side to perform an operation Hernie couldn't see. He attached it to the concrete of the seawall like a suction cup against glass.

"I told you not to configure them like that," the other one said.

"It'll work fine."

"No, it won't. You get the mix off or send the blast the wrong direction and you'll wash the whole fucking city away. The majority of the water has to drain into the flood system. We want to drive them *toward* the civic center, not drown them out."

A mechanical noise from the other, which Hernie guessed was a snort. "Like it matters. All gonna end the same way for those saps.

Just a question of when."

"Maybe, but this is the way Kyler wants it, so this is how we're doing it. I don't exactly relish the thought of putting a bullet in my kid's head either."

The second agent bent down toward the little silver disk clinging to the seawall and readjusted whatever the first had done. Hernie comprehended none of what they said—they used words too big and spoke too fast, like so many people he met—but it prompted that mothering voice to whisper, *Hernie, you have to be very careful; it's so important they not know you're here.*

"Annnnd there." The second agent now held a narrow wand lined with lit-up red squares close to the device. Another button on its face flashed quickly and then glowed solid. "Synced with the others."

"A few more and then comes the fun part." They stood up amid a burst of more of that nerve-rending laughter.

Hernie didn't really care what their plan was anymore, as long as they left. He didn't like feeling so trapped, with them on one side and the swollen ocean on the other. When they were gone he could climb down and run, find some food, find someplace to get out of the rain and hide—

His throat suddenly caught fire. He clamped a hand over his mouth before the cough building in there could get free. The urge was so bad his eyes watered. He swallowed rapidly, using spit to quell it.

A new sound reached him, one that immediately took his mind off the cough. He lifted his gaze from the figures below, toward the closest of the dark refinery towers.

Hatch stood just a few yards from the men, legs splayed, head lowered, tail tucked protectively under him. His muzzle wrinkled back from yellow canines in a snarl, and a steady growl issued from his throat.

The two agents turned to the Labrador in unison. Neither said anything for a span of seconds. Hatch continued to growl, watching them warily in the rain with raised hackles. Hernie bit his lip in anticipation and risked raising one arm to wave his friend away. The dog didn't betray him with even an upward glance.

Finally, one of the men motioned toward the animal. "Think he qualifies for Kyler's No-Eyes mandate?"

"Certainly is a mean ol' boy, ain't he?" The one with the glowing wand knelt again and patted his knee with his free hand. "C'mon fella, come over here."

Hatch stood his ground.

"Hey," the one still standing said in a low voice. "I got an idea. Give me one of those charges."

"What? Why?"

"I'm gonna put it on our new friend here."

"No you fucking well are not!"

"C'mon, can you imagine what it'd look like when we detonate? BOOM, a one way ticket to the big kennel in the sky, in more pieces than a jigsaw puzzle!"

Sensing the gist of this, Hernie sat up and made urgent gestures for Hatch to leave.

"That's gotta be the dumbest thing you've ever said. You want to let *primed* C4 run around the city unchecked?"

"Just an idea."

"A stupid one. Besides, we have to account for these things." This one stood, transferring his light up wand to his other hand—careful to keep his fingers away from those glowing buttons—and then reached for his gun holster. "Let's just do this the easy way and get on with it."

"Sorry little guy." The other one pulled his own pistol and aimed it at the dog. "But we can't let you live after seeing us. Them's the rules."

The only thing that frightened Hernie more than the government was the idea they might hurt his only friend. He swung around, dangling his legs in the air above the agent's heads, and then leapt off the seawall with a cry of, "Hatch, RUN!"

He plunged down on the duo, striking the one on the left directly on the shoulders with both feet, then sprawled across the one on the right, driving them both flat to the ground. The impact jolted up his legs and drove the air from his lungs, but the one he'd hit the hardest screamed in pain as his gun tumbled away, firing once.

"Run! Run away, Hatch!" he choked out, and then coughed so hard he saw stars. The one he'd landed on moaned something about his arm. Hernie scrambled over the prone bodies and into the mud while he gasped for air, crawling toward the dog on hands and knees. He was just about to stand when a hand closed around his ankle.

The other agent lay on his stomach in the mud, holding onto him with one gloved appendage that felt like rubber. Hernie could hear him snorting in anger or pain through the black cylinders sticking off his mask. He raised his other hand, bringing his gun to bear on Hernie's face.

Hatch streaked in, sinking his teeth into the slick material around the man's wrist. He snapped his head to one side, pulling the weapon away from its target. Hernie heard a whine past his ear followed by the *spang!* of the bullet as it ricocheted off the tower on the other side of him.

"Get off me, you fucking mutt!" The agent let go of Hernie so he could grab Hatch by the throat. Once the gun hand was pried out of the dog's mouth, the man turned the pistol toward his furry chest.

Hernie kicked out with one boot, smashing the heel directly into the dark glass plating across the agent's eyes. It cracked, spiderwebbing out from the point of contact, and the agent dropped the gun to clutch at it.

"Shit, SHIT!" That droning timbre made Hernie's eyes roll back in his head. "I'm breached, oh fuck Tim, I'm contaminated!"

'Tim' still rolled on the ground cradling his right arm, which was humped into a bizarre shape at the shoulder. He lurched upright. "Worry about that later and *kill those two!*"

Hernie stumbled to his feet. Hatch was still trying to bite the one with the broken mask, and Hernie grabbed him by the tail and yanked him away. "Let go, Hatch, let go right now!" The dog obeyed, then crossed the yard at his side.

They headed for the nearest refinery tower, seeking to put obstructions between them and the agents. Just as they reached the first metal base, Hernie chanced a look back.

They'd forgotten all about him for the moment. The agent with the broken mask shook as he tried to piece it back together. Tim, the one with the redesigned shoulder, stood up, wheezing in pain through his mask, and hobbled toward his gun.

A loud beep from the ground, stopped him cold. He looked down while holding his hurt arm.

The wand had been under him when he fell, and now the little red buttons were flashing again.

"Oh my God, that asshole set the charges!"

"Christ, deactivate it!"

Both men sprang into motion, forgetting their injuries. Tim fell to his knees, scrabbling for the wand in the mud, while the other dove toward the silver disk attached to the seawall behind them.

There was an explosion that made the ones from the guns sound small. Hatch yelped. Hernie slapped hands over his ears. The government agents sent to kill him disintegrated in a flash of fire and a cloud of smoke and dust. Distantly he heard other explosions, hollow booms further down the shore from the direction these two had come.

The seawall fractured, giant chunks of concrete collapsing to the dirt as far as Hernie could see, and the water it held back poured into the refinery yard in a giant, nightmarish wave.

Hernie ran. Hatch kept pace. He could hear the water behind him, crashing against the towers as it spread through the yard. He'd made it nearly to the front of the property when the wave, still higher than his head and cold enough to steal his breath, swept him off his feet.

He tumbled in the flood, gulping air whenever his head found the surface. The storm had stripped away the fence around the property, and soon he was rushing along suburban streets. He caught sight of Hatch once, treading water with his front paws. Hurricane-ravaged houses flashed by on either side, a neighborhood he thought he recognized. The water swept more debris up until Hernie floated in a sea of bobbing wood and garbage.

But the level steadily lowered as the water had more room to spread out. After a few minutes of riding the wave like a surfer without a board, he felt the concrete of the street scrape against his knees, and then he was deposited roughly on his back as the wave lost the momentum needed to keep him aloft.

Hernie jumped up and wiped water out of his eyes. He was in the middle of a street somewhere several blocks from the refinery. The surrounding houses were nothing but piles of rubble. Ankle deep water rushed past his feet, ocean shoved into the city by the flood and rushing to fill up the low areas.

"HATCH!" he screamed. The animal was nowhere in sight.

His breath hitched. He and the dog had never been apart, not since Hernie found him as a puppy. And now he might be laying somewhere in need of CPR, or whatever the dog version was. Hernie couldn't think what to do. He whacked at the sides of his head with the heels of both palms this time, bashed at them until he saw bursts of light across his vision, but, as usual, this didn't make him any smarter. He plodded through the fast moving water and turned right at the nearest intersection.

All of the streets were flooded. Hernie turned haphazardly from one destroyed road to another, shouting the dog's name. He cut across the corner of one intersection, skirting by a house with one wall mostly still standing, and charged full-body into another person as he turned the corner, hard enough to send him splashing down on his butt in the water.

Another government agent stood over him. This one wasn't dressed in black—was, in fact, wearing jeans and a t-shirt with a cartoon figure on it—but he definitely had a mask over his face.

Hernie screamed.

WHITNEY +12:56

Looking down was good.

As long as he looked down, keeping nothing but the ground in his peripheral vision, Carter could pretend there was a roof over his head. His OCD helped out, forcing him to count every left footfall. However, it only took three instances of falling into sharp rubble for Carter to see the inherent downside of staring at his feet while he walked. Lab rats had learned their lesson faster.

The last time, he bruised his shin on a chunk of oak headboard blasted out of someone's bedroom by Whitney, but kept himself from falling into a nest of broken glass. After this, he forced tentative glances up from his shoes as he strolled through the wreckage of Port Allen, just enough to pick a clear path without letting too much sky into the picture.

At first the agoraphobia came anyway. His stomach rolled, his skin crawled from bacteria (real or imagined…but probably real), and he prayed for some music—even something utterly unlistenable, like late era Britney Spears—to take his mind off it. But the rain stopped, and after a while he hummed his own music and slipped into pleasant daydreams about the next issues of his entire sub-service list at the comic book store (always picked up by Rosa as soon as the doors opened every Wednesday morning) and what he would do with the insurance money. The house could be rebuilt, better than before. Most of his collection was replaceable if the buyer was determined. If anything, he should look at the bright side and admit the hurricane helped him get rid of some of that worthless crap he'd been hanging onto, like his collection of M.A.S.K. vehicles, or his repeat set of series 1 Garbage Pail Kids cards, or that damn out-of-the-box Perceptor he'd been putting off listing on eBay for way too long…

Eventually he realized he was walking fully upright, head held high, the entire landscape in view, and he didn't so much as feel dizzy.

Carter moved his mind away from that direction, afraid the revelation itself would bring his symptoms rushing back. For some reason, this was working. He was outside for the first time in nearly a decade and, if he wanted it to continue, it was important to keep his mind on something else, just like Doc Pellner said. I'm okay, you're okay, the universe is center and all that. The Lucid chuckled smugly.

To fill his wandering thoughts, he looked more at the surroundings. He'd tried to travel in roughly a northeast direction from the end of Teague Street for the last hour, judged by the gradual downslope of elevation, but there were no landmarks. Everything was just the same shade of destruction, the equivalent of trying to navigate in a landfill. Of course, his knowledge of the city was mostly limited to what he could see from that spectacular view on his now-non-existent second floor.

Carter stopped in the middle of the broad street he'd been following since he left his refuge, hobo pack hanging limp over his shoulder. A body lay facedown in a large puddle collected next to a flooded storm drain. He could see only part of its shirtless back, and one leg flung out onto the dry concrete in jeans and a tennis shoe, but it was enough to hit a reboot in his skull that left him as empty as a DOS prompt awaiting a command.

That person was *dead*. He had to work to force this thought into his internal truth column. Here was another person, probably not so different from him (although likely without the debilitating pathological fears), whose life had ended in a muddy pool.

And what was he worried about? Comic books and insurance checks.

Carter stood a little guiltily, the urge to do something for the poor soul battled by his dread of the diseases crawling all over the corpse.

He'd yet to make a decision when a series of distant, cracking booms sounded, jerking him out of his solemn inspection of the body. He looked back toward the southwest. The last of the flat thunder rolled across the land.

PONK!

This noise came from just behind him, the sound of one big corkscrew released from a champagne bottle, followed by a jangling crash. Carter jumped, dropped his hobo pack, and spun to defend himself.

The source of the disturbance was five yards away, still rattling on the ground. A manhole cover, settling on the concrete next to the open sewer grate it had covered. The noise repeated from his left, quick as a gunshot, and now he turned in time to see the next lid, twenty yards up the street, shoot into the air and then smash back down.

He could hear those same metallic crashes all around him now, on the surrounding streets. A deep gurgling came from the depths of the open manhole closest to him. Water boiled out of the hole, filling the street from side to side in seconds.

This wasn't caused by flooding from the rain. A situation like this wasn't exactly within the realm of his job, but physics were physics, and he knew pressure powerful enough to blow off manhole lids could only be caused by some drastic and sudden change to the city's water table.

Those booming explosions.

From the direction of the shore and the seawall.

Carter picked up his hobo pack and raced back toward home. He was gripped by an irrepressible need to know exactly what this event was.

By the time he reached the end of the block, he was panting into the rebreather. Ye gods, he was out of shape; it was a wonder he'd stayed so thin from eight years of junk food and couch-riding. From every open manhole he passed, more water bubbled out, festooned with sewage, a sight that made his gorge rise. He reached the intersection of a street without a sign and looked to the left, toward the Gulf.

Any view of the ocean should've been blocked by the roll of the land, but instead a greenish flood rushed toward him, flowing over the street and curb and manicured lawns on both sides. Judging from the way it engulfed fire hydrants, it had to be hip deep.

He gaped. It might as well be a wall of menacing, anthropomorphic germs coming at him, like the cast of a disinfectant spray commercial. There was nowhere to escape, nothing to climb on to get away from it. He could only squinch up his face and prepare for impact.

By the time it reached him, the flood had subsided to his ankles. He stood stock still and winced as it rushed over his shoes and shins. The water was cool and actually looked much cleaner than any of the stagnant pools he'd seen so far.

It had to be ocean water.

The flood didn't stop. It just kept flowing past him toward the lower interior of the city, the same direction the rainwater headed last night. It wouldn't look like a miniature tidal wave when it got there, but it *would* fill up every low-lying area. The storm drainage system would catch some of it, the sewers a little more depending on how far the water penetrated, but the vast majority would end up sitting on the streets wherever it settled.

Carter splashed into it, one foot and then the other, slow at first and then—when it didn't devour his flesh—building up speed. Couldn't be but a few more blocks to the shore, and then he could see with his own eyes. This was a vacation after all, a daytrip from his self-imposed asylum; might as well throw in a stop at the beach.

The road jogged around a stately manor whose insides were now showing, how embarrassing, and as he came around the end of the only standing wall, he collided with another body in motion hard enough to snap the branch of his hobo traveling pack.

He staggered a few steps back and rubbed the spot where his forehead had struck the other person's chin. His attacker sat down in the water with a splash.

A youngish guy—well, younger than Carter anyway—maybe mid-twenties, vaguely Hispanic in skin tone and features. He had long, greasy black hair, and wore clothes long past even their Salvation Army prime. He sat in the rushing flood for a moment looking confused, then raised woefully accusatory eyes to Carter.

And proceeded to scream his lungs out.

"Whoa, whoa, hey, what the hell?"

"Government!" The younger man scrambled away from Carter on his back. Something was wrong with his speech, a slight impediment of some sort. "Help, government! Leave me alone, don't hurt me, I didn't mean to do it!"

Carter dropped the remains of his traveling pack and held up his hands. "What? I-I'm sorry, I have no idea what you're talking about."

In response, the guy raised one booted foot and kicked him in the balls. *Hard.*

The pain was like a sudden sunrise in his brain, a flash of almost sensual agony. He tried to screech, whimpered instead, and went to his knees in the water with both hands clutching his groin. "Oh Jeeeeesussss," he finally moaned. "I was still planning…on using those."

"Government, government agent! Help, someone help!" His assailant's eyes rolled in their sockets, and Carter was finally able to understand even through the haze of pain: the guy was mentally challenged. To some degree, at least. Nothing obvious in his face like with Down's, but the jittery eyes combined with the speech impediment and the irrationality added up to a solvable equation.

Carter unfolded, straightening up but keeping both hands over the Wonder Twins in case the guy decided to take another shot at turning him into a falsetto. "Hold on, man. Give me a second here. I don't know who you think I am, but I don't even believe a functioning system of government exists, so trust me, I don't work for the Oil Puppet Brigade."

"Yes, you are, you can't fool me! I see your mask right *there!*"

"Mask...?" Carter frowned, and his cheeks brushed against hard plastic. He suddenly felt like he'd gotten the punch line to this cosmic joke. "You mean this? No, this is just a rebreather. For oxygen."

The other guy watched him, still sprawled on his back and breathing heavy as the water flowed across his waist and legs. "What's that mean?"

"It...uh, well, it helps me breathe. I have a condition. Like a medical problem. I have to wear it."

The Hispanic guy cocked one eyebrow and squinted suspiciously. "You're not a government agent?"

"Only in RPG's." He smiled, and then, at the fearful look he got, added quickly, "No, I'm not a government agent."

"You *very* sure?"

"...ninety-nine percent."

"I don't know...that's what a government agent would say..."

"And it's also what a *non*-government agent would say. Look fella, you've already taken away my ability to have children, what more do you want from me?"

The guy didn't seem to understand this, but a cautious grin crept over his round face. "Oh. Okay then."

He was filthy, but seemed jovial enough if you didn't count his habit of going for the family jewels as a first resort. He was also, Carter realized, the first person besides Rosa, his mother, and Terrence the UPS guy that he'd spoken to face-to-face in eight years.

He forced himself to take one hand from his throbbing nuts—hard to do—and hold it out to this complete stranger—even harder. "C'mon, let's get you out of that water."

Now the guy grinned outright, transforming his whole face into a dopey caricature it was impossible not to like. He accepted the hand. "Okay mister, thanks."

"Listen, I'm sorry if I scared you. I don't think neutering was a suitable punishment for it, but hey, maybe that's the way things are done since I checked out of the world. Anyway, I'm Carter Vance."

"That's okay, mister. My name is Hernie."

"No reciprocal apology, huh? All right, I can live with that." The urge to wipe his hand on the leg of his jeans was too strong to deny, even if they did come away dirtier than before. His new friend didn't seem to notice. "Hernie, huh? Is that like a last name or a first name?"

He shrugged and said shyly, "It means Hernandez."

"Fair enough. Well, Hernie, I don't suppose you know where all this water came from?"

Hernie looked around at the flood as though seeing it for the first time, and then the same horrified look came over him as when he'd first caught sight of Carter. "Government mister, government! I saw them, they tried to shoot me with their lasers! Me and Hatch were at the seawall and they came, and they had masks kind of like yours but not really, and they shot it from space with a satellite, and all this water came out and Hatch and I got washed away, and then I stood up and I was yelling for him but I couldn't find him nowhere and—!"

"Slow down, slow down," Carter told him. "I don't understand, who is 'Hatch?'"

"My dog, he's missing and I don't want those government guys to get him!" He let loose a monstrous sob and whapped at his temples with his fingertips all pressed together. "Please mister, please help me find hiiiiiim!"

"Yeah, all right, calm down." Hernie continued to clear his throat and sniffle, wiping at tears that cut clean tracks through the dirt on his face. "Let's just…start at the beginning. Where do you live?"

"Don't," Hernie answered simply with a shake of his shaggy head. He emitted a hard, dry cough that made Carter take another involuntary half step back. "Don't have a home. The government stole it with a spaceship after they kidnapped my mother to take out her brainy-brain."

"So…you're homeless?"

He nodded.

Great; not just mentally challenged, but a mentally challenged street person. And with a scorching case of whooping cough to boot. What a trifecta he'd discovered. "And you saw government agents…with *lasers?*…at the seawall?"

Hernie's face screwed up in concentration for several seconds. He did that drumming on his head thing again with his mouth hanging open, as though he wanted to say more but couldn't figure out how. Finally he nodded again, more emphatically.

"And they blew it up from space with a satellite?"

"Uh huh."

"Hernie, let me ask you: who's the president of the United States?"

Hernie shook his head with certainty, like a college professor negating a student's answer. "There isn't one right now. The one on TV is a robot. He was switched with the real one by—"

"Let me guess. Government agents?"

Hernie's mouth dropped open again, this time in amazement. "You know about it too?"

Okay, so add 'deranged' and 'paranoid' to the list. *Ought to fit in real well with you.* The Lucid's voice was shrieky with laughter. *You two might as well rent out an apartment and call yourselves* The *Really* Odd Couple.

"Hatch, mister, please, you have to help me find Hatch," Hernie insisted.

Carter stared at him. The other man's arrival had broken his compulsion to see what had caused the flood. There was no time to spend looking for a dog—if said dog even existed, and wasn't another figment of his whacked imagination—not if he wanted to reach the Dome sometime today. But as much as he hated the idea of a sickly tag-a-long, he couldn't leave this guy wondering around by himself with no food or shelter.

"I'll tell you what." Carter retrieved the bag of water, the only part of his traveling pack that hadn't washed away. "I'm heading to the civic center to find some help, maybe get something to eat. Do you wanna come?"

"The…civic center?" Hernie's face scrunched up, as though the words meant something to him.

"Yeah, the Dome. Doesn't that sound good, aren't you hungry?"

Hernie gave up on whatever he was trying to pull out of his head. "Yes, real, *real* hungry."

"Okay, why don't you come with me, and…I don't know, we'll look for your dog along the way?"

Hernie cast a fearful look over his shoulder, at the direction he and the water had come from. Something back there had frightened him; that much Carter believed. He just doubted it was blaster-packing spooks. "I don't wanna stay here."

"Then let's leave."

Carter walked, going with the floodwater instead of against it, no longer so disgusted, and Hernie fell into step beside him. He took out one of the bottles of water and passed it to his new acquaintance, who drank greedily. "Mister?"

"It's 'Carter,' Hernie."

"Okay. Mister Carter?"

He sighed. "Yes, Hernie?"

"Do you think Hatch is all right?"

"I'm sure he is. Dogs can take care of themselves. Incidentally, why do you call him Hatch?"

"I named him after the bravest man in the whole world, Richard Hatch!"

Carter shot the younger guy an impressed smile beneath the mask. "You're an old-school *Battlestar Galactica* fan?"

Hernie furrowed his brow and then said quietly, "I like to watch Survivor reruns at the homeless shelter."

Carter performed a double-take worthy of any 80's sitcom, snickered a little, allowed it to build to a giggle, and before he could stop, he was shaking with laughter.

"Hernie," he said, when he could speak again, "I think you and I are gonna get along just fine."

WHITNEY +13:09

Tangela and Chris didn't move or speak for half an hour. When the girl's tears finally dried up into distracted sniffles, Chris made her sit on a damp chair he'd found in the destroyed apartment building and promise to stay still until he returned. With her safe, he'd become acutely aware of his bare feet.

He harbored no hope of finding any of his clothes, and part of him was scared to go exploring in case he came across his stepmother's body. He tried to imagine how such an encounter would make him feel, and came up with a big emotional blank spot.

He splashed back into Miss Zwykowski's apartment, stepping much more carefully than when he'd raced through before. The flood completely hid the ground floor in tepid water as black as coffee. A minefield of splintered boards and nails sat down there, just waiting to puncture the delicate skin on the underside of his foot.

In the bedroom again, he sloshed over to the closet. Miss Z's husband had died four years before, but she'd been saying for the past two that she needed to clean out his belongings. Chris had never even seen a picture of the man, but he hoped his feet were small.

The interior of the closet had collapsed, leaving a heap of wet clothes in the bottom. He found a pair of thoroughly waterlogged size 9 Keds in the back corner, under a pair of lacy lingerie that made him sick to his stomach to imagine Miss Z wearing. Mr. Z's feet had been small all right, smaller than even Chris', but he was able to squeeze his size 10's into the shoes.

As he walked back out, a snatch of blue and black caught his eye from the base of the bedside table. He stared at it, one eyebrow raised in disbelief. "Can't be."

He went over and retrieved a soggy lump of cloth from the small space beneath the table. It was snagged on something below the water, and he tore the corner in the process of freeing it.

Chris wrung out the little blanket and then held it up in front of him. Mr. Softy, all right. The incredible odds of finding it weren't lost on him. It had flown away into a *hurricane*, and yet somehow ended up right here for him to discover. With the speed the water was rising—also a fact he'd attached significant importance to, but more on a subconscious level—it would've been completely submerged if he'd come by even a few minutes later.

He stroked its material with his eyes closed. The scrap of cloth had saved his life, in more ways than one. Usually it reminded him of his mother—he slept with it cradled against his chest for two months after she died—but now he could only think of Nichelle and everything he said the night before.

A burst of coughing from outside brought him out of a vivid mental replay of his stepmother's fall into that black hole. Chris left Miss Z's bedroom, clutching the blanket with both hands behind his back.

Tangela sat in the chair where he left her, feet tucked up to keep them from the dirty water. She looked up when he emerged from the building into strained sunlight and gave another hack. "Chris, what's gonna happen to me?"

"What do you mean?"

She hesitated, wrinkling her small nose and staring down into the water. "Will…will your daddy send me away…like, to an orphanage…?"

"No. Jeez, no," he said quickly. Little Orphan Tangela; the idea was hysterical and repulsive, especially when he tried to imagine her with red hair and those blank circles for eyes. She looked like she might start crying again, so he said something he never thought would come out of his mouth. "You'll stay with us, with Dad and me. I promise. Dad would never send you away. I wouldn't let him."

"That's not true. You're just saying that."

Honestly, he didn't know if he was or not. All of this was just too…*real*. Every bit as emotionally confusing as when his own mother died. He was kind of surprised Tangela was even able to function so well; he couldn't talk for a week.

Instead of answering, he sat on the arm of the chair beside her, and held the wet blanket under her nose. She looked at it, then up at him. "Where did you get that?"

"Found it inside. Go on, take it."

"Me? How come?"

"So I can prove to you that I want you to stay. This blanket means a lot to me. Since everything I own is probably halfway to Canada by now, I guess you could say it means everything to me. And I'm giving it to you."

"Really?"

"Uh huh. But only if you promise to take care of him! He's not a tablecloth!"

Tangela cocked an eyebrow at him. "He?"

"Yeah, his name is…um, Mr. Softy. And I swear if you laugh, you'll regret it."

She was already giggling, but slapped a hand over her mouth to stifle it. "Thanks, Chris."

"No problem. He's a little gross, but we'll run him through a washing machine."

Tangela accepted the blanket. They sat in silence for a moment, during which Chris realized he had no idea what came next.

"Is someone gonna come and get us?" Tangela asked, mirroring his own train of thought.

"I hope so."

"How long will it take?"

If he was any other normal fourteen-year-old, he might've been able to indulge in fantasies that helicopters and police cars and ambulances were speeding toward them even now (with his father in the lead vehicle of course, because that was the way it always happened in the movies) but that big brain of his kept him firmly based in reality.

"I don't know. Maybe a long time."

"But I'm hungry and thirsty and I have to go to the bathroom!"

Chris didn't reply. He stood and walked away from her, through the missing wall of their building and out to the front of the complex. The stiff breeze from the south was rich with the salty tang of the ocean, and an undercurrent of something rotten. Their parking lot was empty except for a Towncar that had a tree branch as thick as his fist through the radiator grill. Beyond that, as far as he could see, was only more wreckage and water, but not a single human being.

His jaw moved in rhythmic circles, the way it always did when his mental gears started shifting. What *were* they supposed to do? The whole city had been evacuated. They were really in a lot of trouble here. He badly wanted an adult, someone to give him orders so he didn't have to think.

According to your teachers, thinking's what you do best.

Yeah, but this wasn't a clearly defined problem, with a specific goal. This wasn't building a generator from scrap parts to power a light bulb (completed in eleven minutes), or creating a basket that could keep an egg safe after it was tossed off the top of the school (his actually glided twelve yards, coasting to a feather-soft stop), this was…

He didn't know what this was.

Something next to him caught his eye. A dead cat lay belly up on the hood of the Towncar, an orange tabby, its paws tucked in by its sides. A miniscule amount of blood was crusted in the fur around its muzzle and whiskers.

"Ewww." Tangela had come up beside him, Mr. Softy tucked under one arm. "Why is it like that, Chris?"

"The storm probably killed it." But even as he said it, he wondered how, if Whitney was responsible for its death, it had gotten up here. Wouldn't the wind have blown it away? Then again, maybe it had, and the thing just landed here.

Chris shook his head. He needed to turn off his brain for awhile. He reached down and grasped the girl's hand in his. "C'mon."

"Where are we going?"

"To find my dad. To find *anybody*. We're gonna walk out of the city if we have to."

"But that's a long way! I don't wanna, Chris!"

"Tanj...do you trust me?"

"Yeeeees," she said, sounding anything but sure.

"Then come with me. We have to do this."

"Okay. Just remember to look both ways before we cross the street."

"I don't think it'll be a problem, but we'll do it."

They walked only two minutes, stopped for a bathroom break, and then continued north.

WHITNEY +13:31

Maryland, Tom, and Gerald traveled in a meandering south-eastern course for the next couple of hours after awakening under the bridge, trudging through the mushy fields sandwiched between the Chantillys and the city. From the top of a small rise, they'd spotted several other hurricane survivors far to the east also making their way out of the freeway of dead cars, but other than that, they were alone. The rain stopped soon after they set off, for which they were, at first, thankful, but in its place the sun tore wispy holes in the blanket of clouds and the summer heat melted its way through.

She learned more about Tom as they walked, through easy and pleasant conversation it felt wrong to be having in the middle of a ruined city. The tiny Brit was from Mildenhall, where he worked for a computer equipment supplier whose pointlessness, operating procedures, and management were, he claimed, not a far stretch from *The Office*. The 'Ricky Gervais version, not the recycled American bollocks.' He'd saved for three years to have enough money for his dream vacation: five days at a dude ranch outside Houston, riding horses and living like a cowboy (to which Gerald muttered he should've just watched an episode of *Bonanza*; it was all the boring and none of the dirt). Tom flew into Louisiana two days before his reservations at the ranch with the intent of renting a car and driving along the Texas coast. He knew about the hurricane, figured he had more than enough time to make it through, but weariness forced him to rent a room in the city or risk driving into the ocean instead of along it. Extreme jet-lag caught up with him, and he ended up sleeping through his alarm and waking up in the midst of the city's evacuation nearly a day later.

"And, when you couple that with the rather unfortunate name my parents saw fit to saddle me with, I think it proves, conclusively, that God hates me," he finished, and then immediately launched into a politely restrained coughing fit. He'd taken his baggy sweater off when the heat got too fierce and tied it around his waist, and now walked only in his slacks and a white undershirt.

Maryland, who giggled throughout the story, burst into full-out laughter after this final deduction. "He couldn't hate you too much. I mean, you're still alive, aren't you?"

Next to her, Tom attempted to clamber over a sprawling pile of bricks and torn concrete in the middle of the street from a nearby collapsed building, caught his foot on a piece of metal rebar, and went down on one knee, tearing his pants in the process. He looked up at Maryland with exaggeratedly forlorn eyes. "I think you only make my case further, Miss Williams."

She was laughing so hard as she helped him up she almost went down herself. Not even the pain rocketing through her palms as she grabbed him could dampen her spirit.

"For Christ's sake, do you two ever do anything but talk and giggle?" Gerald came to a stop to wait on them. On the other end of the spectrum, he'd been mostly sullen and silent as they traveled up the first empty streets, always well ahead. She knew no more about him than she'd learned this morning, except that his ass looked great from behind. "I swear to God, it's like being on a walk-a-thon with two drunk sorority chicks."

"Excuse us if we like to make the best of a bad situation." Tom leaned against Maryland's hunched back while she disengaged his pants leg.

"I do too, but for me that means drinking enough alcohol to make the problem go away. And unless you got about eight cases of Jim Beam in those MC-Hammer-proportioned pants of yours, it ain't gonna happen anytime soon."

"Then let me say what Tom is too nice to." Maryland switched to the most sugary-coated voice in her arsenal. "Take your complaining…and your opinions…and shove them directly up your—"

"Hey, babe," Gerald cut in. "You're the only one of us native to this dump, although I can't understand why you'd admit it. Does *anything* look familiar yet?"

She resisted the urge to tell him what would happen to his testicles if he ever called her 'babe' again and studied the area. They'd passed a few large corporate business parks and trucking depots on the outskirts of the city after leaving the freeway, but at some point during their walk, the outlying roads had widened into four-lane boulevards, and the sides filled up with storefronts. Some of them damaged and crumbled, many with shattered windows despite the boards across them, all of them plastered with windblown trash, but on the whole it didn't look like Whitney had taken too extreme a toll, at least on this far side of Port Allen. From where they stood, she could see a place called Larry's Used Computers, a Taco Bell that wouldn't need too much restoration before it could continue serving slop to its patrons, a fitness center with its roof caved in, and further up the block, the familiar red lettering of a Staples sign.

Obviously a bustling, well-trafficked part of the city, and yet she recognized none of it. A street sign hung from a bent light post at the next intersection, but she had a feeling it wouldn't be any further help in figuring out their location.

Maryland always told people she and Bryce lived in a quaint little seaside town in Texas, but that was only because she'd spent so much of her time hiding in Château Decatur or traveling to whatever functions he dragged her to. Now that she was lost in it, she saw Port Allen for what it really was: a gritty, sprawling port not nearly as unique or lovely as she'd made it out to be while looking down on it from their mansion.

Over two hours of steady walking to the south. They had to be somewhere east of Manchester Heights. Maryland looked in that direction now, and had the very real urge to hightail it that way, with or without her new companions.

Don't you even think about it, the new, no-nonsense Maryland snapped. *That's not your home. Never was.*

"Hello? This is Earth calling Queen Zone-Out! You reading me?"

Maryland flinched as she came out of these thoughts and shook her head. "I don't know where we are."

Gerald shrugged. "Well…shit. I need something to eat and drink, or I'm gonna crash out."

"That's the first sentiment you've expressed that I can actually second." Tom rubbed a hand across his stomach and coughed again. Maryland had been ravenous for the past hour or so, but walking had kept her mind off the worst of it.

"All right then. I'll check out a few of these places and see if I can find a working phone. You two…feel free to go on without me, if the urge strikes you." Gerald took off at a jog toward the Taco Bell, and Maryland stuck out her tongue at his back.

"God, I really don't like that guy."

"If it makes you feel any better, I don't believe he likes himself."

"Jesus, why does he have to be so hostile about everything?"

Instead of answering, Tom wondered across the street. A black Ford Taurus with three flat tires sat halfway on the curb next to the ruins of a wooden snow cone stand. All the windows in the vehicle were broken out, and most of the paint along the hood and driver's side was nearly rubbed away. *Can the wind really do that?* she wondered, before remembering what it had been like last night.

Tom leaned in the front window of the car and dug around in the seat.

"What are you doing?"

He gave up his rummaging and instead flipped down the visor. A ring of keys tumbled past him. "Humanity's insistence on stupidity never fails to amaze me," he mumbled, and began trying to fit each one into the ignition.

"Do you want to drive it?"

"No, it looks to be out of service." He turned the key and received a sickly sputtering. "I'm more interested in…" She saw him turn the switch the opposite direction, and a burst of static came from the car's stereo. "The electrical system."

Maryland was at his side in a few seconds, and watched as he fiddled with the radio's seek buttons. For several seconds all he got was more static, then half a word that he skipped past in his hasty scan.

"Go back, go back!"

He tuned to the channel and let his hand fall away. She saw from the little digital readout they were listening to Mix 104, a pop station out of Houston that claimed to play music from the last three decades but somehow only let the same thirty current top hits onto the airwaves. Reception was sometimes lousy, but this was coming in loud and clear.

A perfectly inflectionless voice issued from the car's speakers, so apathetic it would be impossible to determine a gender if not for the deep timbre.

"—Allen," it was saying, "please proceed immediately to the Civic Center on Whiteman Avenue just northeast of downtown. Food and water drops will be made only at this location. Buses will arrive shortly to transport storm survivors to shelters outside the city. This is a mandatory evacuation order." A small click, and then, "Citizens of Port Allen, please proceed immediately to the Civic Center…"

The message continued its repetition while Tom turned to Maryland and asked, "But who is broadcasting this? It never identifies itself as government sponsored."

"Yeah, not to mention they took over an entire radio station's programming to do it."

Tom frowned. "Is that odd? I just thought it was standard American disaster procedure."

"Honey, they might ask them to make an announcement, but nothing preempts the media except the media itself. And I can't see them foregoing ad dollars just to broadcast the same message over and over to a city they don't even really service when a deejay could just as easily do it every half hour or so." She leaned in the shattered window with Tom and turned the radio setting to 98.9 the Rock.

"—and water drops will be made only at this location," the same message told them.

"I don't get it. This station is local, over on the south side of town. Does that mean some sort of rescue operation is already here or not?"

"Perhaps it was too badly damaged in the storm, and they're just making use of the airspace."

Maryland said nothing. It made sense, but listening to the dead voice repeat its message again was giving her the willies.

They tuned through the rest of the dial, but only three other stations swam out of the static, all of them playing the same advisory on an endless loop. It made her think of old sci-fi movies where the heroes respond to a distress signal, only to find no one alive.

"You two miss MTV that much?"

Maryland jumped hard enough to hit her head on the roof of the Taurus. Tom reached to turn off the car's electrical system and both of them pulled away from the window. Gerald stood behind them with a plastic bag full of water bottles. He tossed one to each of them. "Found these in the ruins of a convenience store around the corner, but no food. I did, however, get you these." He threw Maryland a tube of antibiotic cream and two Ace bandages. "For your hands. Don't say I never gave you anything."

"Don't suppose you picked up any cigarettes?"

He made a gagging face. "Those'll kill you."

"Well, anyway...thanks," she said dryly, and went about dressing her wounds. If he thought one good deed was enough to get back in her graces, he was sorely mistaken.

"Did you find a phone?" Tom asked.

"Several. All of them dead. Well...not dead, exactly, but I couldn't get a line out. Just...empty air. What did the radio say?"

"Everyone in the city is supposed to head over to the Civic Center. They're bringing food and buses to start transporting everyone out."

"All right then, let's get to the Civic Center, children. Uh...do we know where that is?"

Maryland felt both their eyes on her as she secured the last bandage on her left hand. "Somewhere to the east. If we can just find downtown, I can get us to the Dome from there."

"Fantastic. I wanna be on the first thing with wheels outta this place."

They went another two blocks before the din of the riot reached their ears.

WHITNEY +13:40

The water had risen past their thighs when Lincoln and Ellis plodded out of the shelter, but as they turned south and left the warehouse district for higher elevation, it slowly subsided. By the time they could see the first sprawling urban shops and parking lots—and the taller structures of downtown in the distance—they were on dry concrete. Lincoln's sneakers felt like wet sponges.

The rain downshifted to a misty sprinkle before it cut off. The sun came out, a blurred yellow coin on the horizon, and burned away the leftover chill. It felt wonderful, but there appeared to be another bank of heavy clouds hanging in the sky above the Gulf, waiting for their chance to roll in.

They left the industrial section on a cross street Lincoln didn't recognize. From the way his law-inclined companion gazed around, Lincoln suspected he didn't either.

He badly wanted to be rid of the man; an aversion to police was so ingrained in him it was beginning to manifest physically, like a constant, itchy skin irritant. Mac used to call it the 'pork allergy.' Lincoln didn't really care about himself—he probably belonged behind bars after last night—but for the sake of Mac and CT, he was stuck. Even if all their lives were safe, he wanted to make sure none of the facts got misconstrued before they reached official ears, like a game of Telephone, and suddenly their self-defense against the quartet of crooked cops became him leading an army of X-Dawgs in an assault on precinct 13.

Lincoln's shoulder throbbed and his stomach growled audibly. He opened his mouth to ask Ellis what came next, but the scrape of a footstep made him realize they weren't alone on the sidewalk.

People drifted by them from right to left, as listless as zombies. Lincoln spotted ten people across the street, and more coming from the west in a straggling line. A black family of three shambled by on the far sidewalk, the daughter—a girl no older than five with a Barbie doll tucked in her armpit—giving them a weary look as they passed. Lincoln stepped out of the way to allow an elderly Mexican man to brush by on the sidewalk with his neck bent. It sounded like he was weeping.

"What the hell is this?" Lincoln whispered. The morning was deathly quiet now, and the words carried in the still air.

"More survivors. And from the look of it, they didn't get off as easy as we did."

"Shit man, you call that easy?" Something about the line of downtrodden refugees made Lincoln uncomfortable. His brain kept wanting to compare their sad flight to an old Bible story he could barely remember, one about people leaving those twin cities as they burned, then glancing back and turning into salt. "Where they goin?"

"I have no idea."

"The Dome," a white woman passing behind them said. She was dirty, her clothes saturated with mud, dark hair swept back in a matted ponytail. Her eyes flicked over Lincoln and then settled on Ellis, drawn to that tarnished badge pinned to his breast. "That's where the radio said to go. That *is* where we're supposed to go, right? They didn't change it, did they?"

"I...uh, I don't..." Ellis bit his lip and shrugged at her questions.

The woman didn't let up. "Look Officer, my whole house was destroyed, I barely got out alive, if there's someplace closer I can go to get some help, please tell me!"

"Ma'am, I know just as much as you do at this point!"

"Huh, less than that," Lincoln muttered.

The brief exchange drew the attention of other trekkers. They seemed to be waking up to the fact that there was a cop in their midst. People piled up, some crossing the street to form a loose crowd around Ellis. It was kind of amusing; things in Lincoln's neighborhood typically worked the opposite way.

"What are you saying?" someone from the bystanders shouted. "We're not supposed to go to the Civic Center?"

"Do they have food there? My family is starving!"

"My son is sick, can you get me some help?"

"Can you find out if anyone has seen my mother?"

"Where did the National Guard go?"

Ellis tried to back away, but they surrounded him. He looked horrified by the people clamoring for answers. Lincoln was pushed to the edge of the crowd, but fought to keep the cop in view.

"Folks, please calm down! I don't have any information to give you! If the radio said to head to the Dome, then...it's probably best to get there as soon as possible!"

"Whaddaya mean, you don't have any information?" a fat man next to Lincoln bellowed. "You're a cop, ain't ya?"

"Well, yeah, but I—!"

"But nothin, you have to do help us, it's your job!" The fat man held up a fist.

"Lay off him!" Lincoln's voice was lost in a growing chorus of pleas and demands from the crowd. People clutched at the poor guy like a crack dealer in the ghetto on pay day.

"HELP! SOMEBODY HELP!" The shriek cut through even the rabble of the crowd. Everyone stopped tearing at Ellis as a young white guy careened into the mob. He looked conservative, red polo shirt with khaki pants and loafers, the kind of dude that wouldn't survive ten minutes in Lincoln's part of town. He grabbed at shoulders and arms, giving them a taste of their own medicine, but when he spotted Ellis he leapt at him and snatched up his dark hands.

"Officer, come quick, please, my wife is trapped, she could drown!" He didn't wait for a response, but dragged Ellis away by the hand. When the cop didn't start moving on his own, he screamed, "Please, come NOW!"

Ellis broke into sluggish motion, like a steam engine gathering speed, pushing through the crowd with Lincoln tailing. Once they were in the open, the white guy ran, and both of them strove to catch up. After a few steps, Ellis turned back and shouted, "All you people, just head to the Dome! You'll be safe there!"

"You don't really know that, do you?" Lincoln asked as he jogged beside him.

"The less people out wandering the streets the better."

The white guy led them past the end of the line of shuffling survivors, throwing a glance over his shoulder every few seconds to make sure they followed. At one point, two cars passed them going the other way, honking for them to get out of the street. The three of them made an abrupt right that went down a steep grade between more rows of nondescript brick warehouses and the first hurricane-damaged urban tenements. The water began again just a few yards down, covering the land like a sheet of smoked glass. The guy didn't pause for a second, just started splashing into the mess, but Lincoln and Ellis stopped at the edge of the flood.

"Sir, wait a minute, tell us what's going on! Where is your wife?"

"She's in our car! It's right down here, Officer! We were just trying to make it to Rugg Canyon and out of the city!"

"You tried to drive through *that?*" Lincoln pointed at the dark water. "What's wrong with you, man?"

"It wasn't this high at first, I swear!" The guy was hysterical, nearly in tears. "It started rising after we went in, and the next thing I know this current shoved us over! I was able to climb out, but my wife is pinned!"

He stomped further into the new lake.

"That make any sense to you?" Lincoln asked. "How the water can still be risin when it's not rainin anymore?"

"It's probably draining in from somewhere. I've got to help him. Stay here if you want."

For a split second, Lincoln considered doing just that. Of course, he knew if he did, the temptation to just leave while Ellis was gone would be too great to ignore. "Wherever you go, I go, Mr. Policeman."

Ellis raised his eyebrows, shrugged, and then took off his belt with his gun and handcuffs and set it on the sidewalk several yards from the edge of the water. They followed after the guy again, down into the water, which this time rose up past knees, thighs, hips, and was soon at chest level. Almost easier to swim than try to run. The water was murky and disgusting, full of floating debris, and assaulted Lincoln's nostrils with a smell like spoiled eggs.

Finally they turned one last corner, and the man leading them pointed ahead. "There, she's there, I-I didn't know what to do!"

Lincoln saw the problem. The car, a little red Kia, was on its passenger side, the roof almost against one of the buildings. The undercarriage faced them, although they could only see the sliver that rose above the level of the water. The driver's door was propped open where the husband climbed out, sticking straight up from the side of the vehicle. If the flood was really still rising, it would be flowing over into the interior any minute.

"Let's go!" Ellis dove into the water and swam in earnest, slicing hands and paddling feet. Lincoln, who was never much of a public pool kid, opted to continue wading with the husband until he had no other choice but to swim. The water stung the crusty bullet graze across his shoulder.

They arrived just behind the cop, who gripped the undercarriage and peered down through the open door. Lincoln did the same.

A woman with short chestnut hair and a bloody gash across her forehead lay against the passenger door—now the floor of the vehicle—in a puddle of water several inches deep. She looked small curled up down there, wearing sandals with white capris pants and a pink spaghetti strap top. Her head came up when their shadows appeared. She began to cry and cough.

"Thank God, thank God, please help me, is Randy out there?"

"Yes baby, I'm here!" Randy shouted, directly into Lincoln's ear.

"How are you trapped, ma'am?" Ellis asked.

"My arm!" Her right appendage was tucked awkwardly behind her, and looked to be caught between the seat back and the door, which had partially caved in when the car turned over. Luckily for her the window hadn't shattered, or she'd have drowned already. "I think it's broken!"

"Please, help her!" Randy pleaded.

"We can't like this. We've got to get this car back on its wheels, see if that takes the pressure off her arm so she can get out."

"But the water will come in! She'll drown!"

"The water's already comin in!" Lincoln gestured at the lip of the door, where the flood spilled over to drip down on Randy's wife. "He's right, we gotta get her free!"

Randy thought about this for a moment, his thin, freckled face in anguish. "Okay. Whatever you think."

"Here's how I want this." Ellis swam a little ways back from the vehicle. "You two get on the other side of the car. Brace yourself against the wall and when I say, 'push,' you shove this thing as hard as you can and get it turned back over."

"Gotcha." Lincoln and Randy thrashed their way to the other side.

"Miss, what's your name?"

"Heather," she called miserably, and then coughed again.

"Heather, when you hear me tell them to push, I want you to take a deep breath and hold it, all right? You're gonna feel the car come down and there'll be a lot of water, but I'll be right there with you to get you out."

"Please hurry."

Ellis looked across the car at Lincoln. "Let's get this done. On three. One…two…three…PUSH!"

Lincoln braced his shoulder against the roof of the car and pushed against the brick wall with his legs. Randy helped. The car was light, and the operation took very little effort in the water.

He felt the metal slip away from him as it rolled, and then the vehicle sank quickly under the water amid a flurry of bubbles. Ellis took in a lungful of air and slipped beneath the surface. Maybe he wasn't such a chickenshit after all.

Several seconds went by, during which Randy nearly clawed Lincoln's arm off. Then, with an anticlimactic pop, Heather's head broke the surface, gasping for air.

"Oh, honey!" Randy swam out to her. "Are you okay?"

"No, my arm, my arm is broken, I can't swim!" Her husband grabbed her around her waist and tried to keep her above the surface.

Ellis still hadn't come up.

"Where is he?" Lincoln demanded.

"I don't know, he helped me pull my arm out and then pushed me past him! I thought he was right behind me!"

"I'll...I'll go back for him," Randy panted.

"No, get her outta here! I'll go down!" Before they could argue any further, Lincoln dove.

The thought of opening his eyes in this filth made him want to gag, but he forced himself to. Everything was hazy green, but he caught sight of the car's roof just before he ran into it. He kicked hard, propelling himself down onto the open driver's side.

A foot lashed out of the murk, almost cracking his chin. Lincoln grabbed it by the ankle and held it away from him as he swam into the car.

He could see the fear on Ellis' face in the gloom. The cop was caught on something by the back of his shirt, and struggling too much in his panic for Lincoln to see what. He shouted something that came out like whale song.

Lincoln could already feel his lungs burning. He didn't waste any time, just grabbed the front of Ellis' black uniform shirt and pulled, popping buttons down the front. Ellis jerked his arms out of the sleeves and shot out of the car for the surface in his undershirt.

They breached together, sputtering, and neither said anything as they swam after Randy and Heather. And it truly was swimming this time; the water had risen too much for even the tip of Lincoln's toes to touch.

Exhaustion had crept into every muscle by the time they reached dry land, considerably further up from where they started in. All four of them flopped onto the concrete and lay on their backs to rest.

"Thank you, thank you, thank you," Randy repeated over and over again.

"No problem," Lincoln answered on their behalf. Heather was coughing and crying all at the same time, and Randy rolled over to see to her. Lincoln watched them for a moment, the reunion igniting some small, warm fire inside him that he would never admit to, because it was totally non-gangsta.

Then he thought of Mr. Kim for the first time all day, the look on the shopkeeper's face as Lincoln's bullets struck him, and that fire sputtered out.

He looked at Ellis. Forced himself to smile. "I think I just saved your life again, copper."

"Yeah, yeah. I bet you're real proud of yourself."

"Now, unless there's someone else that needs a hero, can we please get goin to your car?"

Ellis shook his head. "That's not an option anymore."

"What? That's bullshit! You're a lyin mother—!"

"Goddamn it Lincoln, take a look at me. I just lost everything that identifies me as a cop."

Lincoln stared at him, understanding all at once. This was the same street they'd entered the water from, but it had risen so much the utility belt and weapon he'd left behind were gone. Without his uniform, he just looked like a black man in a thin cotton shirt and wet dress pants.

"We can't risk going back for my car, not with both of us unarmed. And I don't even know for sure if it would still be above water by the time we get there."

"So what then?"

"We don't have any choice. I guess we'll go to the Dome."

WHITNEY +14:03

Carter and Hernie consumed the last of the water just after nine o'clock. Both their bellies growled so loudly that thirst was a secondary priority anyway. The cityscape became slightly less deci-mated further inland, going from the rich suburbs that bordered the coast, into blue collar tract housing and the first commercial properties around the downtown area. The damage was still severe, with wreckage across every surface, but here every second or third house stood to some degree. No other people yet though; they'd been the only two dumb enough to be this close to the sea. The ini-tial rush of water from the coast had finally trickled to a stop also, and for a while the journey was dry.

"I'm hungry, Mr. Carter."

Carter sighed and kneaded at one of his shoulder muscles. This was one of two phrases his new albatross had repeated over the last several hours, the other being variants of, 'Where do you think Hatch is?'

"Hernie, what did I say I was gonna do if you told me that again?"

"Uh…turn the car around and take us home?"

"That's right. And since you still don't see the humor in it, I guess I'll just shut up." They reached another intersection between tightly-packed houses and started across. The sidewalk on the far side was too cluttered to use, so they drifted into the street and made their way along the curb. Somewhere on one of the streets ahead, the comforting purr of several car engines passed by.

"Okay. But Mr. Carter…I sure am hungry."

The constant use of 'mister' reminded him of Rosa. He hoped the woman was okay. If only he'd listened to her, he'd be in Fort Worth now, with a full stomach and probably even a working tele-vision, not stumbling through the post-Whitney apocalypse. "I know Hernie, and I promise, when we find something to eat, you get first dibs. Tell me this though; aren't you usually hungry? Liv-ing on the streets and all?"

"Nah uh, me and Hatch eat all the timey-time!"

"Oh really? Since you're the expert then, where does the dis-cerning hobo get his chow? Feel free to lead me there."

Hernie stopped and dropped behind. Carter glanced over his shoulder at him as he kept walking. The younger man's face wrin-kled in concentration as he looked around. "I don't see any garbage cans anywhere."

Carter gagged beneath the rebreather. "My own fault for asking. I mean, you're homeless, where did I expect you to get chow, Red Lobster?" He stepped over the trunk of an uprooted tree and jumped when something smashed into the ground beside him.

He looked down. At his feet lay the plump carcass of a jet-feathered crow. It had hit the ground head first, snapping its beak. Trace amounts of blood dribbled from its tiny skull.

Before he could even get worked up about this hotbed of germs, there was another *ker-splat* to his left, one more in front of him, and then the air was full of fat crows or ravens or grackles or whatever they were called, plummeting out of the clear blue sky to splatter on the ground. He shrieked and dove under the twisted overhang of a nearby bus stop, and Hernie ran in beside him.

The rain of birds lasted only fifteen or twenty seconds, but in that time a flock of at least a hundred disgusting corpses had fallen. Carter forced himself to stand still and breathe. Sudden nausea turned the world to a sickening angle.

Hernie didn't seem as bothered by the disease factories. He stepped into the rough circle of dead birds and squatted to look at one runny corpse. "Wow! Look at all of 'em!"

"I don't want to." Carter kept his eyes closed until he felt at peace. Some perverse part of his OCD commanded him to count all of the corpses, but that was one he denied.

"You think the government men killed them with their lasery-lasers?"

"No, I don't." He started walking again, once more keeping his eyes up on the horizon and glancing quickly at his feet to navigate a path that wouldn't crunch any delicate bones. "It probably had something to do with the hurricane." He was almost sure it didn't, but he didn't want to play the Hardy Boys and the Mystery of the Lyme-Disease-Covered Biological Missiles.

"Poor birdies. You don't think it hurt them, do you Mr. Carter?"

"Oh, no. I'm sure it was as peaceful as a bottle of Kentucky's finest and a handful of Sominex, Hern-ster."

This seemed to tickle his companion's funny bone. He laughed and skipped a few paces to catch up. They left the last of the corpses behind. "You sure talk funny, Mr. Carter!"

"Thanks. I always wanted to be a stand-up comedian."

"No, I mean you use big words. And you talk to yourself. I talk to Hatch sometimes, but he listens, so it's not the same. Mostly I don't understand what you're saying."

Carter didn't know whether to take this as compliment or insult. "I've only had myself to talk to for a long time. I guess I kinda got used to it."

"You can talk to *me* all you want!"

His eagerness made Carter crack a smile. "Thanks. I'll keep that in mind."

Hernie broke into another of his deep, rumbling coughs. He'd been issuing these for a while too, and while they didn't seem to be slowing him down, they sounded meaty and full, like a terminal cancer patient getting ready to spit out a lung.

"You sure you feel okay?"

"Yes. My throat hurts, but not too bad. I was much sicker than this one time."

That may be, but Carter's hand stole up to the rebreather across his face anyway, almost unconsciously. He checked the straps, made sure the device was tight enough around his head that the rubber rim of the cup pushed almost painfully into the skin around his nose and mouth.

The Lucid spoke up, in Doc Pellner's voice. *The sooner you accept that you ultimately have no control over the world, the sooner you'll be able to stop wearing a jock strap across your face.*

But he didn't want to accept that. It felt too much like surrendering, going down with the ship.

No Carter. Surrendering *is giving in to your neuroses.* Surrendering *is allowing yourself to live in fear.*

"Oh God, now I'm psycho-analyzing myself," he muttered.

"What Mr. Carter?"

"Nothing. Just some ghosts that don't know when to keep their mouths closed."

A section of wooden fence lay in the street in front of Carter, propped at an angle against a chunk of shingled roof. They both scrambled up and over it. One thing he'd discovered: being around another person made the last of his agoraphobia disappear entirely.

He hadn't felt dizzy once as they made their way north. The reprieve was heavenly, but he didn't expect it to last.

The neighborhood street and surrounding yards were a junkyard of debris and vehicles, some of the piles of rubble deposited so high and dense they would have to find a path through or go around. They were forced away from the curb even further as the size of the wreckage in the gutter grew, until it was almost like walking next to a barricade of garbage. But Carter didn't notice this. The land ahead had opened up, giving them their first clear view of downtown.

"Hernie, check it out!" He took a few steps further, past a wide gap in the line of rubble beside them that opened onto a driveway. He stopped on the far side, next to a torn-up Mitsubishi nearly buried in loose boards and aluminum siding up to his shoulder. "We're not as lost as I thought! We can reach downtown in another couple of hours! And the Dome is just on the other side!"

"Then we can eat and look for Hatch some more?"

"You got it, buddy!" Carter turned around and held up his hand, so jubilant he was willing to engage in his first high-five since elementary school.

Hernie grinned ear-to-ear, started forward to meet him, and then crumpled over as a gunshot came from Carter's left.

WHITNEY +14:15

"Man...I don't think...I can swim no mo'," CT wheezed.

Mac's own muscles had started aching long before, so he knew the shrimp must be in pain. He halted his steady, right-armed strokes and treaded water. The brackish fluid around them was a cloudy greenish-brown. Impossible to see anything beneath the surface, and that made him feel a little green himself. It also had a vague smell to it that he couldn't identify. Or maybe it was *absence* of smell; it lacked the salty tang of seawater that his nostrils had become accustomed to from a life in this city. Mac turned to C-Tone and patted the wooden surface bobbing on top of the water beside him. "Come grab on this and rest for a few minutes."

"Just be careful you don't dump me," Charlie said quickly. The cop lay spreadeagle on the only buoyant transport they'd been able to find: an old door from the house they'd spent the night in, torn off its rusted hinges with little effort. His weight made it precarious in the water. He stretched out on his stomach gripping both sides while Mac towed him with one hand and swam with the other. As he turned and held on to the side of the makeshift boat to rest his limbs and lungs, Mac gave the old cop another inspection.

His face was deathly pale, hair and brow damp not with flood-water but sweat, and even after a half bottle of aspirin his jaw had been constantly clinched in pain since they'd left the house an hour ago and started swimming west toward the heart of the city, stopping to rest on every rooftop and telephone pole they came across. Mac didn't have a fancy medical degree or an office where he got to look at women's private parts all day, but he was fairly sure Charlie would be unconscious before too long.

Then maybe you oughta let it happen. He ain't exactly plannin to give you a medal if you save his life.

Too true. Mac was pissed off at the way Charlie was reliant on them, but still insisted on turning them in for their supposed 'crimes.' He'd forced them into labor so fast, they might as well be on a cotton farm, circa 1850. Old coot was so comfortable ordering around black folk, Mac almost believed his geriatric ass was there for the real thing. That gun on his hip might give Charlie some power over them on dry land, but Mac knew he could flip the flimsy island over and he and CT could be halfway to the horizon before the cop could do anything about it. Shit, with that bum leg, he'd probably sink like a stone.

Nevertheless, he liked the guy. It was rare to find a respectable cop.

CT caught up with them and flailed onto the door, nearly toppling it over in the process. Mac and Charlie both let out a squawk.

"Sorry." The boy sounded sulky even during out-of-breath gasps. At least all this exercise was probably helping him work through whatever withdrawal jitters he had. "You got any idea where we at?"

"Don't know," Mac answered. "Everything looks the same."

They'd tried to swim along the streets, but as less and less of the houses protruded from the water, they had little to navigate by except for the occasional treetop. Looking around now was a little like being dropped in the middle of the ocean, with water stretching to the horizon on all sides. Mac might've worried they were swimming in circles if not for the view of the Chantilly's to their right, which gave them a northern bearing as sure as a compass.

And there were bodies. *Lots* of bodies. Drowned corpses lying facedown, not even bobbing in the stagnant, currentless water. Most of them black, the poor citizens of the city who just couldn't make it out. Mac stopped counting them somewhere in the teens.

"Jesus H son-of-God Christ." Charlie lifted his weary head to look around. "If you see a guy in an ark with a buncha animals, you might wanna flag him down."

"It's gotta be…what, like twenty feet deep?"

"I'd say about that. We're just in the worst of it though. This part of the city is low elevation. We go far enough west…we'll come out of it eventually."

"What if we don't?" CT's fear made the question sound halfway respectful. "What if…the whole city looks like this, and we swimmin toward nuthin?"

"Then it wouldn't be any different if we stayed and drowned at that house. At least this way we have a chance. Now let's get going. I don't want to be out here if another storm rolls in."

"No!" CT pushed away from the floating door, causing it to rock. "That's easy fo' *you* to say, we the ones drownin out here while yo' white ass lays there!"

"CT, we gotta keep movin," Mac said.

"But what about the crew? If all this is flooded, you know base is too! They could be…"

Mac didn't need the sentence finished; he had long ago made the connection between the drowned bodies and the fact that all his brothers-in-arms might be floating somewhere, but he just couldn't acknowledge it. "They're soldiers the same way we are, and they can take care of themselves. We couldn't even find base in this, so the best thing for us is—"

He was cut off by a distant whine, like the buzzing of a mosquito. As it grew louder, they all realized what it was at the same time: an outboard motor. Not far away, maybe just on the other side of a row of treetops poking out of the water to the north.

"Hey!" CT shouted suddenly. "HELP!"

Mac exchanged a look with Charlie. They needed to be careful about who they accepted help from, but the dire level of the situation overruled caution at this point.

"Over here!" Mac joined in, and Charlie followed suit. After a few yells, Mac broke into a coughing fit that nearly drowned him until he grabbed on to Charlie's surfboard.

They saw the boat as it shot into view, hardly more than a speck in the distance. Mac thought he could see a lone occupant, but it was just too far away to be sure. In any case, the boat sped across the water without giving the slightest indication it had heard them.

"Goddamn it!" CT's voice cracked. "We gonna *die* out here!"

"Maybe he knows somethin we don't," Charlie said. "Follow that boat."

WHITNEY +14:21

Carter watched as Hernie was flung like a spindly ragdoll, arms flapping as he staggered several steps sideways and then collapsed to the pavement on his stomach at the foot of the driveway. He stood frozen, hand still hung in the air for that unrequited high-five, until a second gunshot blasted in his direction. The back window of the vehicle beside him, mostly buried in a pile of wreckage, blew inward with a high-pitched tinkle.

He dropped, more out of instinct than rational thought, curling into a ball next to the back tire of the Mitsubishi that just saved his life. Someone was actually shooting at him, that much he understood, even though the very concept was alien.

He tried to move. Couldn't. His body did its best turtle impression, locking him in a fetal position.

A third shot sounded, raining debris and wood chips from the top of the barrier down on him. The noise came from somewhere on the other side of the car, but he couldn't get more specific with his head between his knees.

"*Mister...Carter...*"

His whimpered name got him to uncurl. Carter looked toward Hernie, staying so low he scraped the rebreather cylinder across the pavement in the process.

Hernie was alive. They were at eye level now, only about two yards separating them. Hernie reached one hand out toward him, grimacing with pain. His eyes were wide and confused as he pleaded, "*Please, Mr. Carter...help...*"

"Just stay there," he begged. "Be still!"

Carter pushed up on his elbows, eyes fixed on the other man. The back of Hernie's trenchcoat was even more shredded than usual, a large patch of blood seeping through the material. He was still in the gap in the debris barricade, but at least he was out of the line of fire, shielded by the house scrap littering the street.

Until their attacker changed his/her/their vantage point. Which could be happening right this second.

"Hello?" Carter shouted cautiously.

In response, the rear of the vehicle spanged with scattershot. Carter kissed pavement again.

"*Damn it, why are you shooting at us?*"

"This is MY property!" a male voice shouted. Again, the only location Carter could determine was somewhere in the debris field, on the lawns between the edge of the curb where he and Hernie lay and the houses they backed up to. The wreckage was so thick, he gained nothing by looking under the vehicle. "You can't come on my property!"

"What? What property?"

Another boom. "*My* house! *My* lawn! *My* property! You have no rights here!"

"Well, unless you own the street too, I don't think we're ON your property!"

"I know what you're after! You're trying to take my food!"

"Are you nuts, we were just walking by!"

Their attacker fired again...and this time Carter felt the heat from the shot. Pellets ricocheted across the pavement between he and Hernie, in the undercarriage of the vehicle, off the rear bumper.

"Look, we'll leave! Just stop shooting at us and we'll go!"

"You'll never take my SUPPLIES!" the voice screeched.

"Great, we ran into Port Allen's answer to William Wallace," Carter muttered.

But the intent was clear: this lunatic really meant to kill them. *Would* kill them, if they just sat and did nothing.

"Stay here," he whispered to Hernie, so quiet he was practically mouthing the words. Hernie shook his head insistently, and, though Carter felt bad for him, there was no time to console. To get the point across, he pointed a stern finger at him and then jabbed it at the pavement. Hernie's puppy dog eyes were as wide as full moons.

Carter turned and slithered in the opposite direction. He could hear the shooter babbling now, something about how they were the first but others would be coming, everyone would want his food after they saw there was none to be had in all of Port Allen. The guy made Hernie' paranoid government babble look completely rational by comparison. But that was good, let him talk all he wanted, it just let Carter know where he was.

He worked his way to the front of the car. The debris cleared here, enough for him to push up on hands and knees. He squatted on his haunches, and peered around the corner.

Too much storm litter in the way for him to get a sense of the situation. It looked like Dorothy Gale's house had smashed into the lawn in front of him at terminal velocity, spraying chunks of sheetrock, siding, and roof in all directions. A maze lay between him and where he thought the shooter's voice drifted from, one with no guaranteed solution.

So just go. Leave the hobo. The nutball with the gun will never even know you left.

The drowned body in the gutter floated through his mind, followed by all the petty worries he'd made his sole concern over the last eight years. He'd locked himself away from the world, escaped all those insignificant moral decisions that regular people faced on a daily basis, and now he was being forced to make up for lost time.

If he stopped to think up an actual plan, his OCD would start throwing switches in his head until he wound down. So instead, he pushed to his feet and just started running.

Carter felt the urge to yell something during his charge—'Excelsior' came to mind—but denied himself this bit of psychological bravery in favor of surprise. He dodged around pieces of house, hurdled over rubble, the mindlessness of the act kind of liberating. Making a conscious decision to save Hernie's life was one thing, but this wasn't him, Carter Vance didn't do things like this even when he used to be normal and sane, Carter Vance read comic books and watched cartoons and thought *Andromeda Strain* was the scariest movie ever made...

The gun gave its rough song once more, the sound much closer, and then Carter careened around the edge of a long piece of house siding and onto the driveway they'd been attacked in front of. The guy who apparently thought Campbell's Soup and Fig Newtons were more important than human life stood just a few yards away, a double-barreled shotgun clutched in both hands. He was old, full of wrinkles and white hair, in chinos and a green and white Hawaiian shirt. Could be somebody's grandfather, if not for the crazed look in his eyes. He was at the perfect angle to fire upon anybody wondering through the gap in the hurricane wreckage at the end of his driveway, and Carter wondered if he'd actually set all this up as a trap. The idea was only reinforced by the presence of a folding chair and cooler behind the whacko.

The old guy's head whipped around when Carter came out in front of him, eyes widening in surprise. He started to swing the shotgun around.

Carter charged again, and this time he did yell, a bellow meant to sound like a tiger's roar but came out like one of those weird laughs Pee Wee Herman used to give. He waved his hands, wondered briefly what he was going to do with them, and then came to the sudden understanding that he wasn't going to make it in time to do *anything*, that the old paranoid fart would have the gun turned on him and the trigger pulled before he could cross half the distance between them.

A wave of vertigo hit him as hard as a punch in the face.

The world was sucked down a drain. For a second, up was down, left was right, the sky opened up to swallow him, and he was reminded of precisely why he'd remained indoors for most of his adult life.

Carter collapsed on the edge of the grass.

He heard the shotgun go off again just after he fell out of its path. His lungs were locked even with the rebreather on, the same way they did when he tried to go for the package outside his gate. He writhed on the ground, trying to get the attack under control.

A brittle snap came above him, the sound of the shotgun breach opening to accept more shells.

He rolled on to his back. Opened his eyes.

He saw the world through a funhouse mirror. The shooter stood over him, stretched and disproportionate, moving in slow motion. He frowned at Carter suffocating on his lawn while he fumbled two more shells out of his shirt pocket. Beyond him was the sky, that impossibly open expanse, smeared with a delicate layer of vapor.

The panic attack wasn't real, not as real as the attack that would come out of the end of that gun. All in his head. Hadn't he proved that already today?

His lungs loosened, allowing in a trickle of air beneath the mask, not a complete victory but enough to snap the world back into focus.

Carter reached for the barrel of the shotgun, grabbing high up to avoid the heated metal. He pulled and rolled onto his knees at the same time. The old guy was yanked forward by the sudden motion, the shells spilled through his fingers, and the shotgun snapped closed. Carter tried to pull it away from him. The other man grabbed the stock with both hands and jerked, engaging in a tug-of-war for the weapon. He growled, "That's mine, that's my property, you have no right to touch it!"

"I'm getting real sick of hearing about what belongs to you, so I'm just gonna tell you the same thing my mother used to tell me." Instead of pulling, Carter drove the butt of the gun into the man's chest with all his might. He took it hard, expelling his air with a whoof, and then plopped to the ground on his ass. Carter stood over him with the shotgun across his chest. "If you can't play nice with your toys, they'll be taken away."

"Give that back," the old man choked, trying to catch his breath. "Give that back to me!"

"So you can keep shooting at us? Survey says: no frakkin way, pal." Carter bent, retrieved the shells he dropped, and loaded the weapon, managing to look competent despite the fact he'd never handled a gun in his life. "Now get out of here, or I'm going to use *you* for target practice!"

The old man obviously wanted to keep harping about his property, but the loaded weapon now in Carter's possession changed his mind. He got to his feet, then cut across his lawn and onto the street, throwing fearful half glances over his shoulder every few steps.

Carter climbed over the little ridge of garbage where he'd left Hernie. He would be dead now, he knew it, and all of this would be for nothing.

But Hernie looked up at him weakly. "That was a bad man, huh Mister Carter?"

"Yeah, it sure was. How do you feel, Hernie?"

"My back burrrrns."

Carter looked around once more. He could see no one else on the street, and the old man appeared to be gone. "All right. Let's get you inside and have a look at it."

He helped Hernie to his feet, and together they hobbled into the little house the crazy coot had been defending.

WHITNEY +14:46

Chris could get only the vaguest sense of direction as they walked. He knew most of the streets around their apartment from riding his bike up and down them, trekking with his friends to various stores, taking the bus to school, but Whitney had changed the topography of Port Allen overnight. Without landmarks and familiar buildings, the streets were smothered in storm wreckage and water. He and Tangela picked their way across it, navigating only by keeping the sun to their right until they could clear enough of the city to see the Chantillys to the north.

"Chris, I'm tiiiired." Tangela plodded through the water, which had risen to the level of their knees. It made each step even harder, the walk into a hike, draining them of what energy they had. The girl had tied Mr. Softy around her neck by two corners, so it hung down her back like a superhero cape.

"I know. I am too."

"Can't we sit down for a while?"

He sighed his annoyance away. "Not yet."

"But I'm hungry and thirsty too."

"We just gotta keep going." He wiped sweat from his brow. They'd left home over an hour ago according to his watch, and had yet to see anyone else or any shelter sturdy enough for him to trust, not even any payphones to check. Not that he would know who to call if there were. Like Tangela, he was hungry also, his mouth tasted like charcoal from thirst, and Mr. Z's tiny shoes were giving him blisters, but he couldn't do anything about any of it.

And you don't even want to think about being out here in the dark.

No, he didn't, and he didn't appreciate his imagination conjuring the image every chance it got. The idea of the two of them alone in the abandoned city at night was too eerie to contemplate. He saw several drowned corpses as they wandered (went out of his way to make sure Tangela didn't) and it was too easy to picture them all standing up in the dark, shuffling after them through the watery streets.

"But where are we going?"

"I told you already, we're gonna walk until we come to the freeway, and then follow it until we cross the bridge over the canyon. I'm sure there'll be people there, and they'll help us find my dad."

Tangela took a splashing step and tripped over something beneath the surface of the water. Chris leapt forward just in time to catch her. She coughed in his arms, dry rattles that shook her entire body, then looked up at him with moist eyes. "My throat hurts too, Chris."

"We'll find you some medicine too, just hang on a little…"

The thought was forgotten as Chris glanced over her shoulder to the side of the street. A lamp post stood just a few yards away, rising up from the dark water in front of a pile of bricks that still had the vague shape of a house.

Leaning against this pole was the ravaged body of a young white woman.

She lay sprawled across a pile of detritus around the base of the lamp post, just high enough to keep her above the level of the water, so she almost appeared to float on the surface. Below the waist she wore only sneakers and blue shorts, exposing tanned and toned legs, one stretched out straight in front of her and the other curled awkwardly beneath. A light yellow top once covered the rest of her, but the front was utterly shredded, revealing a gaping hole into the depths of her stomach.

Even in the quick glance Chris took before averting his eyes, he saw the ragged edges of the wound and shattered remains of her ribcage.

Little remained inside the cavity itself; all the fleshy gears and motors that kept her body machinery working had been ripped out. What was left more closely resembled a chunky tomato stew than viscera.

She'd been eaten, torn into with ravenous frenzy by some scavenger. Yeah, that idea was bad, close to vomit territory, but as his gaze traveled up her torso he found a sight that dropped his blood temperature another ten degrees.

The woman had a narrow face, framed by lank, chin-length blond hair. Undoubtedly pretty (for a white girl anyway; he wasn't too much of a judge himself) but now her features were forever frozen in a mask of terror, eyes bulging, brow drawn, mouth hung open in a silent scream. The late morning sunlight kept even a hint of shadow off her face, making every angle stand out in stark detail.

This was another survivor just like the two of them, and that expression told him this atrocity was visited upon her while she was still very much alive. Judging from the blood flowing from her hollowed out core to mix with the surrounding water, it had happened very recently.

"What's wrong, Chris?" Tangela hung on him, struggling in his arms to turn around and see what had hypnotized him.

"Nothing, don't turn around!" He grabbed her by the shoulders and forced her to meet his eyes. "Tangela, listen to me, do NOT look!"

A warble floated through the air, seeming to come from nowhere and everywhere.

"What is that?" Tangela whispered, her eyes round balls of terror. "Chris, what is that?"

Chris didn't answer. He continued to hold the girl as he glanced around. Both sides of the street were crowded with half collapsed houses and piles of rubble; altogether too many places for whoever—*what*ever—did this to hide. Everything felt too closed in, suffocating, an animal's den.

The high-pitched noise sounded again, echoing off a thousand surfaces. The sound was no more sinister than the cry of a songbird crossed with a yodeler's call, but it plucked every nerve in his body. There was an angry undercurrent to it, as though whatever made the noise was mad its lunch had been interrupted.

He could feel eyes crawling over him, but couldn't tell from where.

"Climb on my back!" he told her.

"Huh?"

He spun around and squatted low. "Climb on my back and hang on!" Thankfully, Tangela slung her arms around his neck without arguing and held on as he rose and lifted her off her feet. He wore her now the same way she wore Mr. Softy. Chris took off, splashing through the water. He went around debris, careful to keep out of reach of anything that might be waiting on the other side. He panted from exertion within minutes but adrenaline spurred him on, that and the splashing footsteps he could swear were just at his heels…

He carried his step-sister nearly three blocks from the partially-consumed corpse, until he was on the verge of collapse. He cut to the left, hurtling onto the sidewalk and across a short patch of what felt like lawn beneath his sneakers, then into the shadowy, open maw of a garage attached to a shredded and partially collapsed house. Once hidden, Chris came to a stop at last, every muscle in his body screaming, and lowered Tangela to the watery concrete floor of the garage.

"What was that, what was that?" she asked, clutching at him.

"Shhhh, be quiet!" A stitch in his side made each intake agony. Now that they'd left the grisly scene behind them, he felt silly for overreacting. Maybe the look on the woman's face hadn't been fright. Maybe some stray dogs had just found someone who drowned and decided to make a meal.

When his lungs no longer felt like hot coals inside his chest, Chris crept past Tangela to the edge of the garage and peeked around the corner at the littered stretch of road. That sensation of being watched was gone. He waited, listening for another of those weird bird songs, and studied the street.

But, of course, when the attack happened, it came from behind.

WHITNEY +15:03

The noise grew so gradually, it never even registered with Maryland. They made a left turn at the next street from where she and Tom heard the monotone announcement over the stereo, and headed east, deeper into Port Allen. Finally Tom stopped and asked, "Do either of you hear that?"

As soon as it was called to her attention, it was impossible for Maryland not to hear it. She even recognized it: the clamor of many people shouting and jabbering until it becomes one big wall of sound, like the continual background roar at a sporting event. This one echoed from somewhere ahead, several streets away.

"C'mon," Gerald said, breaking into an easy run, leaping and dodging around the junk in his path like an Olympic medalist. The amount of debris—not to mention the size of the pieces—strewn across the land had increased drastically after their direction change, putting to rest her hopes that Whitney had been all bluster and no bite. Maryland started after him, but when Tom tried to match their pace he broke into a string of half-wheezes, half-barking rasps. She slowed down to wait for him.

"You feel okay, Tom?"

"I'm fine." He waved her on.

"Are you sick, or...?"

He gave a thin smile. "Yes, I have a disease called *living-fossilitus*. It strikes men over the age of 60 and shows up most prominently when they forget that fact."

Maryland shook her head. "I'm serious. I'm...worried about you." The sentiment surprised her. She wasn't used to taking to people quickly, but then again, the only acquaintances she'd made throughout most of her adult life were Bryce's band of faux friends.

Tom took her hand as they speed-walked after Gerald. "And I appreciate your concern. It's not often I have women half my age fawning over me. But it's nothing, really. I may've caught a cold from our little camp-out last night, that's all."

She cast a doubtful look on him, but said nothing.

They caught up with Gerald at the end of the next corner. He leaned against a waist-high chain link fence next to a small residence entirely tilted at an amazing 45 degree angle, a regular middle America Tower of Pisa. In the sky, the dark clouds hovering to the south all morning had made noticeable advances; rain would be upon them again in short order.

On the other side of the fence was a sheer concrete drop down to the next cross street, at least six or seven yards below. The surface was covered in a foot of floodwater that spread across the land to the east as far as Maryland could see, turning the area into a giant mirror. The sparks of sunlight kicking off the surface were almost bright enough to blind.

But none of them dwelled on any of this for even a second. Their eyes were drawn to the opposite side of the wide thorough-fare, to the source of the noise.

A Bowden Super Marketplace sat directly across from them, a long building with a rectangular front made almost entirely of glass. From their high vantage point, they could see the outer roof was stripped away, revealing a complicated surface of pipes and steel girders beneath. The corner on the left end appeared to be sagging from lack of structural support, the wall beneath folding in on itself.

Most of the plate glass along the front was broken out, but the interior was obscured by a crowd of hundreds of people scurrying in and out of the building and across the flooded front parking lot. Folks streamed out with carts and arms overflowing with goods, pushing through the mob, dropping items in the water only to have them snatched by other hands.

"Goddamn looters," Gerald muttered.

"They're probably just as hungry as we are."

"Maybe, but that's not just food they're taking down there."

Maryland gave the crowd more than just a cursory glance. Gerald was right; she saw people clutching clothing, electronics, and housewares from the superstore. A few fled with their spoils, satisfied with an armload and splashing off in all directions, but most people carried their loot away from the building or dumped them in vehicles and then waded back into the growing fray.

Violence was everywhere. Looter stole from looter, pushed one another, tussled in the water for every dropped scrap. She saw one black man punch another in the face and yank a flat screen monitor out of his hands. The victim didn't fight back, didn't get angry, didn't even appear to notice; he just looked around dazedly and then plowed back into the store, shoving another woman out of the way.

The collective of jostling bodies reminded Maryland of an angry wasp hive, buzzing and full of venom. She looked away in disgust and saw Tom do the same.

"We better get down there while there's still something left."

Gerald hopped over the top of the chain link to the narrow embankment on the other side.

"What?" Maryland grabbed at him. "Are you crazy?"

Tom shook his head emphatically. "We don't want any part of that."

"Let me paint you two optimists a picture," Gerald said through clenched teeth. "We get to this Dome place to wait for these buses, right? Only they never come. And the food and water that's sent isn't enough to go around, or, worse yet, there isn't any at all. We don't know why, and no one will tell us anything. We all just sit there, wasting away, waiting for help that never comes because some bureaucrat somewhere fucked up the rescue operation, until we start dropping dead." He looked over his shoulder at the riot. "That down there might be the last meal we get for a while. And I don't intend to miss out on it."

"But it's stealing."

"No, it's survival. You were set to defend them a second ago when you thought they were just stealing food. Well, if you don't wanna feel guilty, then keep your hands off the silk panties and DVDs and take what you need to live."

Maryland opened her mouth but found no argument. She looked to Tom for help.

"He does have a point," the little Englishman said with an uncomfortable shrug.

Maryland faltered, looking away from both of them, back toward the store. She considered herself a bleeding heart, understanding of the father that takes bread for his starving family, but she'd never been in a position where she was forced to do so. Despite the fact that she really wasn't Mrs. Decatur anymore, she didn't *feel* impoverished, even with the steady gnashing in her stomach.

"I don't care. I'm not going to...to..."

She broke off. She'd been staring at the mob as she spoke, perhaps to remind herself of just what she didn't want to become, when a man in a familiar blue uniform forced his way through the crowd and into the store.

"Police," she said in wonder. "A cop, down there, I just saw him!"

"What? Where?"

"He just went into the store!"

"Goddamn it, we gotta get down there before he breaks the whole thing up!" Gerald plopped down at the edge of the concrete embankment, dangled his legs, and then pushed off, plummeting out of sight. They heard him hit bottom a second later with a splash and a grunt.

Tom, at least, was thinking the same way she was. "He might be able to tell us just what's going on around here, and when relief is coming."

"We have to go over to that store. I don't trust Gerald enough to find out."

"I don't trust *him* enough not to make the situation worse than it already is. In any case, I can't make that jump. I'll have to look for another way down."

"Oh." She smacked her forehead for not realizing this. "Do you want me to stay with you?"

"I do, but I really think haste is of the utmost importance at the moment. Just don't leave the vicinity until I've joined you."

"Okay, I won't."

She started to clamber over the fence herself—with much less grace than that damn Adonis they were traveling with—when Tom grabbed her arm. "Please, Miss Williams. Please don't...leave me."

Maryland laid a hand on his shoulder. "Tom...I promise, I won't go anywhere without you."

This seemed to satisfy him. "All right. Thank you. Do be careful."

She got over the fence, and then jumped without looking back.

WHITNEY +15:17

"H-hi kids."

The voice—high and reedy and out-of-breath—was little more than a whisper, but because it was spoken right into Chris' left ear while he leaned around the edge of the garage door, it was more startling than an air horn. He jumped, scalp tingling, and felt Tangela do the same next to him.

A squat, overweight white man stood behind them, wringing pudgy hands together hard enough to turn the flesh red. Maybe half-a-foot taller than Chris himself, dressed in stained and ripped brown suit pants and matching jacket, with a white dress shirt beneath. He was almost entirely bald, his face puffy and round, cheeks so rosy and convex he appeared to be perpetually holding air in them. Small eyes darted back and forth between the two of them, above a piggy, twitching nose. As Chris and Tangela turned to face him, his fleshy lips pulled up in a nervous, quivering smile.

"Oh, oh, I'm sorry, I didn't mean to frighten you," he said, in that same squealing, hyperventilating tone. "I was stopping to r-rest, and I'm just, I'm so happy to see someone else who-who-who survived the hurricane." Still grinning, still squeezing the palms of his hands as though trying to strip the flesh off. His eyes couldn't stay still, roaming all over them.

Chris reached over to take his stepsister's hand. His first impulse was to babble, to tell this man about the body just a few blocks behind them and the burbly cries they'd heard, but sudden caution sealed his mouth. "Um, yeah. Us too."

"Are you both all right? You c-came running in like that and almost-almost scared me into a heart attack!"

"We're okay."

He gave a sympathetic frown. "This place can b-be pretty spooky, huh? The storm was just dreadful last night, just d-dreadful! And the bodies I've seen this morning…!"

"Hey man, go easy with that." Chris nodded his head to indicate Tangela.

The fat man turned his attention to her—or as much of it as he could with his eyes ricocheting off everything—and cooed, "Oh hi honey, what a lovely little g-girl you are! What's your n-name, sweetie?"

"Tangela," the girl answered, before Chris could stop her. "I'm Tangela Kittrick."

"How lovely!" He paused in his wringing long enough to clap his hands together once to emphasize this. He bent over, reached out, and stroked her short hair, which she accepted with a shy giggle and an uncomfortable glance at her stepbrother. Chris saw that the fat man's hands were shaking. "What an un-un-unusual name, dear! My name is J-Jacob Quinlan. What about you son, who are you?"

"Bartholomew." He didn't know why he said it; it just popped out before he could stop it. He saw Tangela open her mouth to correct him and squeezed down on her hand.

"Bart, just like the-like the *Simpsons!* Well, Tangela and Bart, where are your p-parents? Surely you're not out here all alone!"

Tangela started to shake and sniffle again. Chris was sure this guy meant well, but damn him for getting her all worked up again. "My mommy died last night!"

Quinlan's nervous smile faltered. "Oh dear. Dear, dear. I'm s-so sorry to hear that. I know it probably doesn't seem like it n-now, but it will be okay eventually." He knelt and held open his arms and Tangela—now in full sobbing mode—submitted to him this time. She hugged the man, and he enfolded her in his massive append-ages.

"We're trying to get out of the city," Chris said. "To get to my father."

"No, no, t-that's much too dangerous." Quinlan released Tangela and stood up to begin wringing his hands and wheezing again. "You need to stay with me, until I can-I can get you some-place safe. Are you h-hungry? You must be after the ordeal you've been through. I have s-some food inside. Not much, just some crackers and soda, but y-you're welcome to it."

"Yeah Chris, let's go!" Tangela rubbed the last of her tears away. "I'm so hungry!"

Chris hesitated. He was so relieved to see an adult, and his own stomach fired up at the mention of food, but there was something about Quinlan that just put him on edge. That, and the fact that he didn't want to stay so close to that hollowed-out corpse up the street, and whatever had made those noises. Adult or not, he didn't think this waddling tubbo would be much protection from *that*. "All right," he agreed reluctantly.

"Goody!" Quinlan held out a hand that Tangela accepted.

He led them further into the dank ruins of the house attached to the garage. The roof was caved in far enough that it felt more like a sagging tent in here, and Chris wasn't entirely sure it was safe. Pale light filtered through cracks in the boards. The wind had stripped the interior to bare walls and wiring.

But Quinlan had created a little nest for himself. He was using a cardboard box for a table, where the promised crackers were laid out with a flashlight beam across them. They both hunkered down, grabbed handfuls and scarfed them greedily.

"Oh, the soda!" Quinlan edged out of the ring of illumination provided by the flashlight. "I l-left it in the refrigerator in the-in the kitchen. The power's out, but I f-figured it would keep cool. Just take me a second."

When he was sure the man was out of earshot, Chris whispered, "Finish eating Tanj, and then we need to go."

"Why?"

"Because I don't trust this guy."

"But I'm tired! He'll take care of us! I don't wanna leave!"

He glared at her. "For once, would you just do what I ask?"

"No Chris, I'm not going!"

By that point, Quinlan returned with a plastic two-liter bottle of Coke. He put it on the table. "S-so h-how are you-are you two doing? Those c-c-crackers g-good?" He seemed especially nervous again, his speech even choppier.

"They're real good!" Tangela declared.

"That's great. Y-you poor t-thing, you're clothes are all-all dirty. H-hey…I t-think there are s-some clean ones in the other r-room that might f-f-fit you. Why don't you come w-with me and we'll s-see?"

"Okay." She stood up.

"No." Chris jumped also. "I'll take her."

"D-don't be r-ridiculous, Bart. Y-you s-stay and eat and we'll-we'll—" He paused to gulp air, his panting finally reaching the point where he was too winded to speak, and Chris realized that what he had taken for nervousness was actually *excitement*. "We'll be right back."

"I don't think that's such a good idea." Chris grabbed Tangela's hand.

"B-but we have all sorts of g-games we can p-play. All three of us. D-doesn't that sound n-nice, Tangela?"

"We're not playing any games with you," Chris snapped.

Quinlan stared at him. "Your br-brother isn't very nice, is he?"

Silence ripened in the ruined house. Tangela picked up the torn end of Mr. Softy's hem dangling off her back and plucked at it nervously. Quinlan went back to wringing his hands as he contemplated them, now as sinister as a spider that's just caught its next juicy meal.

"We need to go." Chris turned toward the open maw of the garage and the flooded street beyond, preferring to take his chances with whatever was out there. The horrible thought occurred to him that maybe this man was responsible for the dead girl. He pulled his stepsister with him. "C'mon Tangela."

"Don't go." Quinlan was fast for his weight, coming around to block their path. Tangela shrank against Chris. "I just w-want to make sure you're s-safe, and to p-play some games."

Quinlan advanced on them, forcing them further into the dark recesses of the room. One hand stole down and rubbed the front of his bulbous crotch in slow circles.

"We can't," Chris said. "We have to leave."

"Please let us go." Tangela clutched Mr. Softy to her chest with her free hand.

"Don't be scared," Quinlan said, leaving the bulge in his pants to paw at them. His palms were slick with sweat. Everywhere they touched, Chris' skin felt dirty. "Don't be s-scared, I won't hurt you, I would *never* hurt you, we can have so much f-fun if you just do exactly what I say. Look, I have c-candy, too!" He reached into his pants pocket and withdrew a handful of assorted hard candies in colorful wrappers.

And all at once, Jacob Quinlan wasn't so scary to Chris. Something about this fat man offering them candy—*candy* of all things, the sex predator's clichéd weapon, retired years ago in favor of such hi-tech arsenal as Facebook and Rohypnol—struck him as pathetically funny. He laughed, giggles that trickled out of the sides of his closed mouth before he could stop them.

Quinlan's fat face fell, smile vanished. He scowled. "What's so funny?"

"I was just thinking," Chris said, and now he was snorting, Tangela looking at him like he was crazy but smiling a little herself, "maybe you have a van with tinted windows we could climb into?"

"Stop laughing." No more panting, no more stuttering, now that all the fun was out of it for him. "Stop laughing at me, you little bastard!"

"Let's go, Tangela. Mr. Quinlan has a date with Rosy Palm and her five sisters." He walked around the fat man, leading Tangela behind him.

Quinlan's hand shot out. He clamped onto Tangela's other wrist and pulled her in the opposite direction.

"Hey, let go of her!"

"*You* can leave, Bart! Tangela is staying with me, aren't you?"

"No, leave me alone!"

Quinlan pulled hard, yanking the girl out of Chris' grasp. He walked fast, lugging her with him further into the house, like a troll beneath a dank bridge. Tangela screamed.

Building material was scattered everywhere. Chris snatched up a length of two-by-four as long as his leg. That anger animal was back, making him shake with rage.

"Let go of her, you fat pervert!" He brought the wood down across the arm holding his stepsister.

The length of wood snapped…but it wasn't the only thing. The sound of Quinlan's arm breaking was loud in the stillness of the garage.

"Oh, *shiiiit!*" he howled. He released Tangela and then sank to his knees, holding his crooked appendage to his chest. Chris gawked at the damage he'd done. "Goddamn kids, I wouldn't hurt you, I love children!"

"Yeah, a little *too* much, I think!" He felt giddy.

"Jesus, you broke my arm, you broke my fuckin arm!"

"You come near us again, and I'll aim higher." He dropped the remains of the wood and grabbed Tangela's hand again. He was careful to keep a confident pace as they left the garage, but once he was sure they were out of sight, they hustled again, splashing down the driveway and further up the street.

"*I'll find yooooou!*" Quinlan screeched behind them. "*You'll be* SORRY!"

They went another two blocks before Tangela looked back over her shoulder and blurted, "Chris, wait! Mr. Softy's gone! He fell off back there!"

The loss was bitter, but Chris shook his head. "We're not going back."

She sniffled. "I'm sorry. I tried to keep him."

"Don't worry about it. It's not your fault."

"Thanks, Chris. Thanks for saving me."

"What are brothers for?" he replied, but that was a question he wanted the answer to himself.

WHITNEY +15:23

"Charlie, you ever see *Jaws*?"

By the time he asked this question, Mac was dragging both the cop and CT on the door behind him while he paddled on, using limbs that felt more numb and leaden with each stroke.

"I was…always…more of an *E.T.* guy," Charlie gasped, somehow sounding more out-of-breath than Mac. "But I know enough. What about it?"

"That shark, man. That shark came right up from under 'em and started takin bites. But at least they was in the *ocean*. They could see that muhfuckah comin. But this shit…" He splashed a hand angrily at the dark water. At some point since they saw the boat pass by he'd gone from uneasy to downright claustrophobic about swimming in this murk. He recalled creepy stories about entire towns being flooded out when a nearby river was dammed, houses and streets and even cars left to rot far beneath the surface. That's what they were suspended above now.

And the downtown buildings in the distance didn't seem to be getting any closer.

"You fuckin stupid, fool!" CT laughed. "Ain't no sharks out here!"

"CT, you say one more word, and I'm gonna hold you underwater till you drown or grow gills."

"Mac, I'm tellin you…watch who you talk to like that."

Mac stopped swimming and spun in the water to look at the kid clutching the far end of the wooden door, next to Charlie's injured leg. He was exhausted and irritable and hungry, his throat slowly roasting, but he wasn't about to back down. CT met his gaze without blinking, not even jittering anymore, anger lighting up his eyes like a fire in the windows of a house. "Oh yeah, nigga? And just why is that?"

"Because one day…it's gonna come back to bite yo' ass. Promise you *that*."

"Now, children, if you don't stop, I'll have to separate you."

Charlie, still on his belly, shifted on the door and grimaced. "One in the Pacific and one in the Atlantic."

They ignored him, still glaring at each other openly with the mutual hatred they'd concealed for so long. The jack-in-the-box had popped now, and there was no putting it back. It was going to be war until one or the other of them was gone, and in their lifestyle, there was usually only one brand of 'gone.' "Well, until that day comes, shut up, or I'm gonna make you into a pool toy. Float around on yo' lazy ass for a bit." Mac broke the staring contest and resumed swimming. "Besides, I wasn't thinkin 'bout sharks. I was thinkin 'bout alligators. Or water moccasins. Anything could be creepin up on us in this mess."

Charlie grunted. "Stick to worrying about the stuff you can see, kid."

"Shit, I'm more worried about the stuff that can see *me*."

This got a weak chuckle from Charlie. Mac opened his mouth to keep talking—talking kept the panic at bay—and snapped it closed when CT shrieked, "*SHARK! Oh shit, you was right, shark!*"

Mac paddled in a circle, intending to beat the younger boy bloody, but saw immediately that CT wasn't joking. The kid splashed violently and then grabbed hold of Charlie and tried to shimmy his body on top of the door and the officer both.

"*Get off me, you punk! You're killin my goddamned leg!*"

The whole door started to tip, would've gone over and dumped them both if Mac hadn't grabbed the other side and put his weight on it. "CT, stop, what's wrong with you?"

"Over there, man! There's a shark!" He pointed over his shoulder, across the water.

Mac scanned the smooth surface to the south. Some distance away—he couldn't tell how far, with nothing to compare it to for size—was a triangle jutting up from the water, curved on one side, like the characteristic shape of a shark fin. It was the only thing they'd seen for a while, the rising water having swallowed up the last of the trees.

"I don't think that's a shark."

"How you know? You a marine psychiatrist now or some shit?"

"For one thing, it's blue. Last I checked, sharks didn't come in

Crayola, moron. Now get off him 'fore you tip this whole thing over."

CT slid back off the makeshift raft. The motion caused Charlie to whimper in pain, his breath coming in pants. Mac squinted at the discovery. Dark clouds were sweeping in, slowly robbing them of daylight, and he couldn't get a sense of the thing.

"C'mon. We gonna check it out. Maybe it's somethin I can rest on for a while."

It took about five minutes of swimming to get them close enough to see what the object sticking out of the water was. Even so, his brain wanted to deny it.

The triangular object CT had spotted was the prow of a small, fiberglass rowboat protruding vertically from the water, standing straight up so rigidly it barely swayed in the gentle waves moving through the flood water. It was painted that bright blue that made it so visible in the first place, and had one oar still attached to the side. Mac let go of the door-raft and swam over. He gave it a push. It drifted the tiniest bit and then returned to its original position.

"It's tied up," Charlie said, and Mac felt like an idiot for not seeing it himself. "Somebody had that thing in their backyard, tied to a trailer or somethin on a helluva long cord, and it floated until it reached the end. Must be enough air caught in it to keep it buoyed, that's the only reason it hasn't sunk already. If we can turn it loose…we've got ourselves a real ride."

Mac's exhausted body gave an anticipatory sigh of relief. "How we do that?"

"One of us has gotta swim down and try to get it free. I'd volunteer, but…" He pointed at the tourniquet on his leg.

"Afraid you was gonna say that." The thought of diving down into the brackish depths made Mac's intestines knot. "Don't suppose I could convince you play submarine, can I CT?"

CT stuck out his jaw and looked away, toward the horizon behind them, where those rain clouds crept closer from the direction of the Gulf.

"I'll see what I can do," Mac said.

"Just…try to see if you can figure out what's holdin it." Charlie held his head up enough to look at Mac, but was so weak he flopped back down after a few seconds.

Mac gave the cop one last perusal, took a few deep breaths, and dove.

He kept his eyes closed, used his hands to guide him down the side of the half-submerged boat until he reached the stern. His lungs, already tired from an hours-long workout, ached by the time he found the rope holding the boat. It felt like it wound through two O rings screwed into the lip of the stern. He had to pull himself deeper, below the boat and down the taut length of the cord, to reach the point where it knotted. He wrapped one forearm around the rope to give leverage and keep from floating back to the surface.

His hands pried at the tangle, which felt as big as his fist, a slippery conglomeration of threads. Mac fluttered his eyelids, terrified to open them but doing it anyway so he could get an idea of what he was dealing with.

He could see his hands, less than a foot in front of his face, but the rest was a brown blur. The cord stretched away below him, disappearing into the drowned world beneath. He could imagine the other end being held by bloated and rotting fingers, hands that were even now climbing up it toward him. He tried to just focus on working the knot, which looked more manageable now that he could see it.

His lungs ached, throat throbbed. He coughed underwater, spilling a stream of precious air bubbles from his mouth.

Mac kept pulling, trying to get his thick fingers into the knot. Finally, a loop of rope squirted out from the main mass. He tugged. The entire knot disintegrated, as only the best tied can, and the cord shot by so fast it gave him a friction burn around his arm where it was looped around. The boat blasted away from him, pulled to the surface by the air in it. He turned to follow, coughing all the way.

His head broke the surface. He sputtered and sucked in air.

"Look out, kid!" he heard Charlie shout over his coughing. Before he could wipe his eyes to clear them, something heavy clocked him across the bridge of the nose, hard enough to break it.

The pain burst through his skull like a camera flash. Mac cried out while still hacking. He flailed, trying to put distance between himself and the source of the pain. An avalanche of blood cascaded down his lips and chin. He felt dizzy as he kicked away and wiped at his face.

CT treaded water in front of him, the gun from Charlie's belt held high above the water in one hand and pointed at an awkward angle down at Mac. He realized he'd just been pistol-whipped.

"*What was you sayin?*" the boy screeched, jabbing the gun at him in a shaking hand. "*You was gonna* drown *me, was that it? Use me fo' a pool toy?*"

"I'm sorry," Charlie shouted from the raft. "The little shit jumped me as soon as you went under, grabbed my gun before I could stop him!"

"You keep yo' fuckin mouth shut, or I'm comin fo' you after I finish with this beeyitch!"

"You're already in enough trouble you punk, just gimme back that gun!"

"Stay outta this for a sec, Charlie," Mac told him. "CT don't wanna hurt anybody. Right C-Tone?"

"Oh no, I wanna hurt *somebody*." CT showed pearly teeth. "I been wantin to hurt you fo' a *long* time. You and Links think you can just shove me around, *hit* me? There's a change comin in the crew, been comin for a long time, and that change is *me!*"

"What makes you think they'd follow you, Tyrone?" Mac used the boy's real name for the first time since he'd met him. "Half of 'em think you Links' bitch, and the other half think you a psychopath."

"They'll see! After I keep 'em alive and get 'em out the city!"

It was a pipe dream, a perfect example of how immature he was, but his belief in it, coupled with that anxiety from his withdrawal, made him dangerous. "Okay, Tyrone. Maybe they will. But there ain't no need to hurt us to get it."

CT sneered while he treaded water with his legs and one arm, the gun still held up high. "They think *I'm* Links' bitch? Shit, look at yo'self sometime, Mac. Protectin this pig fo' Links, and he ain't even here. He and that other oinker prob'ly dead. Now get the fuck away from my boat!"

"CT—"

"I said *get the fuck away!* Or I *will* shoot you!"

Mac paddled away from the boat. CT kept the gun on him the whole way and then, when he deemed the distance far enough, tossed it over the side of the fiberglass rowboat, slung a leg up after it, and pulled himself inside. Once he was sitting on the bench, he detached the oar and slid it into the water on first one side and then the other, propelling the boat west, in the direction they'd been heading.

Mac wanted to swim after it, wanted to drag the little fuck out and find out whether he could crush his trachea before he drowned, but knew he was too tired. The boat glided across the water, moving smoothly away from them.

"You better hope I don't find you!"

"Best keep yo' mind on swimmin, fool," CT said over his shoulder, "and save the threats fo' God, when you see Him!"

"Charlie, what're we supposed to do?" he asked, heading back toward the raft. His arms weighed a ton, his big feet felt like they were dragging him under. "I don't know how much further…"

Mac paused in the water, holding onto the wooden door as lightly as possible to keep it from tipping.

Charlie was unconscious.

WHITNEY +15:29

Coincidentally, the old man *did* have Campbell's Soup and Fig Newtons amid the considerable stockpile of non-perishables throughout his kitchen. Whether he actually bought them for the hurricane was another matter. A layer of dust and dead bugs covered the tops of some of the cans close to the back of the pantry. Still, maybe the old guy wasn't so crazy. Surely there would be people somewhere in Port Allen desperate enough to kill for these kinds of stores. He was willing to in order to keep them, after all.

Carter gave the supplies only the quickest check on his first sweep of the house, to ensure he and Hernie were alone. He didn't want to be ambushed by any other survivalists holing up in here, for the little time he planned to be inside. The structure withstood Whitney with only a few roof leaks to show for it. The elderly owner had boarded up every window, turning the place into a fortress. When he'd checked every room and closet with the shotgun (and knocked on doorframes enough to leave his knuckles sore), Carter ransacked the bathroom for medical supplies and returned to where he'd left Hernie.

His homeless friend was stretched out on his stomach on the lime green sofa in the living room, crying softly. The entire room was decorated with a nautical theme, boats and the ocean recurring in everything from paintings to clocks to decorations hung on the walls. There was a weird ceramic bust on the television of two intertwined dolphins who appeared to be mating as they leap from the ocean.

"It's like a Florida retiree became the Omega Man," Carter mumbled.

"I...I know him," Hernie said between sobs. "He's that blue guy in the video game, huh?"

"That's just *Mega* Man, Hernie, but close enough." Carter knelt beside the couch and set the heavy shotgun aside, glad to be rid of it.

Hernie coughed, his entire body spasming from the force of it, and then moaned in pain. "Am I...am I going to die?"

"Someday probably, but let's have a look at this wound before we start engraving the tombstone."

He pulled on a pair of latex gloves from the bathroom, and together they delicately pulled off the remains of Hernie's trenchcoat, and the filthy sweater beneath. Carter pushed mental catalogs of germs out of his head and leaned over the flesh to have a look.

Hernie's entire back was a roadmap of old scar tissue, but the upper portion was dotted with tiny puncture wounds, the scatter becoming less concentrated as it went further down toward his waist. A few of them still oozed blood, but even the worst was clotting. Carter caught the glint of metal in a couple where shrapnel was embedded.

"This doesn't look too bad, Hern-ster. I think you were too far away from the shot for it to do serious damage."

"Are you sure? Can you see if the government put any trackers in me?"

"I'm pretty sure that guy didn't work for the government either. Then again, maybe he was Dick Cheney. Now stay still while I clean this. It might hurt a little."

He used the supplies to first clean the blood away from the wounds and then—with a pair of tweezers and more willpower than he knew he possessed—extract all the bits of scattershot he could see.

Hernie kept up a continual stream of whimpers, but they seemed to be theatrical, since he did little moving throughout the operation.

Band-aids came last. Once he'd done all the doctoring he could, Carter took the opportunity to study the twisted tangle of old scars running in raised lines across the younger man's back and sides.

"Hernie...what happened to you?"

The other man still had his face buried in the couch cushions, but he turned enough to ask from the side of his mouth, "What do you mean, Mr. Carter?"

"These scars. What are they from?"

Hernie was silent long enough for Carter to see he'd touched a nerve. His hand stole up to tap next to his eyeball. "Punishment," he said finally.

"Punishment for what?"

Tap, tap, tap. Harder, faster his fingers moved. "I was bad."

"What do you mean, who said you were bad?"

"My momma."

"Really, you have a mom? Wait, that came out wrong, of course you have a mom, everyone's got a mom. What I meant to say was, where is she?"

"I don't know." Carter saw his lip quiver. "The government came and took her away."

The government, the government, always his obsession with the government. It was so hard to sort out what was fantasy and what was truth with his paranoia in the way. His hand was beginning to really whap the side of his head, and Carter grabbed it to make him stop before he gave himself a concussion. "How long ago was this, Hernie?"

"I...I don't know. A long time. I...I remember school...and the playground..."

Carter leaned sideways, so he could look Hernie in the face. His eyes peered out from beneath greasy locks of his hair. "Did you see them take her away?"

He sniffled. "They came and they tried to take me too and she fought them and fought them and then they grabbed her and started pulling her away and she told me to run and so I did and..." His chest hitched again, and he squeezed his eyes shut against the memory.

Carter grimaced, reached out a latex-covered hand, and laid it cautiously on his bare shoulder. It felt awkward; he hadn't comforted anyone in a long time. "But Hernie, what makes you think they were government?"

He sniffled and coughed a bit, almost causing Carter to jerk his hand away. "Because she said they would come. She said they didn't like her punishing me, and the government takes kids away from their parents for that."

An avalanche of understanding dumped over Carter. The poor guy had to be talking about Child Protective Services; his mother had referred to them generally as 'the government' and, in so doing, engendered a lifelong fear of such agencies. The extent of their influence had been trumped up by his imagination and inability to determine reality, and now he blamed anything that went wrong on them, like whatever happened at the seawall.

However, judging by the scars on his back, being taken from her might have been the best thing in the world for him.

"So…you just ran away and never came back? And you've been on your own ever since?"

"Yes. I couldn't let the government get me. Not ever. Mom said that was the worst thing that could ever happen to poor people like us."

The story was too fantastic to be believed; more like something a charity organization would use to drum up funds. A mentally challenged child surviving alone on the streets for probably the better part of a decade, simply slipping through a crack in society. Carter wanted to say more, wanted to explain the truth to him, but somehow he didn't think it would do much good. A lifetime of screwed up thinking couldn't be undone in one afternoon; no one should know that better than him.

Then again…maybe it just depends on the afternoon.

"You're all finished. Why don't you sit up and see how that feels?"

Hernie did as told, always agreeable as long as he trusted you, even if you were beating the hell out of him. "It hurts, but not so bad."

"I don't have much experience, but I'm pretty sure you can't ask for anything more from a gunshot wound."

And that's when Hernie attacked, leaping off the couch and practically into his lap, throwing his bare arms around Carter's neck. Something so innocent in the gesture, but he was too horrified to do anything other than cringe.

"You saved me. You're my friendy-friend…right, Mr. Carter?"

"Yes. Yes, Hernie. I'm your friendy-friend."

"Okay!"

"Um, now why don't you let go of me, okay? We can be friends who don't hug. Or touch one another. Ever."

Hernie climbed back onto the couch and reached for his sweater. "Hey, wait. Before you do that, let's see what our shoot-first-ask-questions-later-minded host has in the way of new threads."

They spent the next ten minutes raiding the old man's closet for clothes that might fit Hernie. What came out the other end looked like a Mexican day laborer on vacation: a crème-colored, polyester Guayabera shirt and white slacks so creased the pleats appeared to be at perfect right angles. He put his boots on over this to complete the look.

"Definitely stylin," Carter told him, and Hernie agreed by way of dopey grin.

The old man also had both a ground line phone and fully-charged cell on his dresser. The ground line produced only an open hum with no dial tone, and the cell claimed to be getting no reception. He left them where they were.

They took to the kitchen next, and Carter fixed Hernie a quick lunch of cold soup, warm Dr. Pepper, and cookies, the shotgun close at hand the entire time. His mouth watered at the sight of the food, but he couldn't bring himself to remove the rebreather again. He became more nervous with each passing second they remained in the house. A medal case in a small study beside the bedroom had several awards of the Navy persuasion, which explained not only the homeowner's zealous overaggressiveness, but his fascination with the sea as well.

And a man with that sort of training would find a way to take down a noob like Carter, even with shotgun advantage.

"You just about ready?"

"Are we going to find Hatch now?"

"I was thinking more along the lines of the Civic Center, but who knows, he might be between us and it. It's just important that we get there before nightfall."

Hernie looked disappointed but agreed.

They left the house by the front door and found the sky overrun with angry clouds once more, the air heavy with the promise of rain. By the time Carter realized he'd left the shotgun next to the kitchen table where they had lunch, they were already four blocks away.

WHITNEY +15:37

Gerald was halfway across the flooded lanes of traffic by the time Maryland landed with a splash in the water covering the road. Her ankles weren't strong enough to take the impact, and she went down on her knees and bandaged hands. The water was just cold enough to be a shock, but she wouldn't get hypothermia anytime soon.

She scrambled up and sloshed after him, looking both ways before crossing the wide boulevard, even though the only three ve-hicles she could see on the road were abandoned at its sides. Old habits died hard, even when the rules of civilization were officially out the window.

The parking lot of the supercenter was just ahead. She spotted Gerald as he pushed his way into the crowd like a crazed rugby player, throwing himself between two black men and body check-ing a sallow white woman who got in his way just before he reached the threshold of the nearest broken plate glass window. He disap-peared into the store's interior without a backward glance.

She reached the edge of the mob, thinking of her near-trampling last night. The wide window frames were jammed with people try-ing to enter and exit simultaneously, a knot of thrashing, flailing, punching, kicking, and even biting bodies. Bryce Syndrome at its ugliest. Their noise, audible from several blocks away, was now a constant ringing in her ears.

Maryland worked her way to the end, wanting to slip in at the furthest edge of the building. A gap appeared, and she tried to slide through. Two men carrying boxes of tract lighting shoved past her, driving her back outside, and the hole she'd been working into was filled. She tried again, this time laying her hands on the backs in front of her and gently pushing, and received an elbow in the stomach.

"Goddamn it, MOVE!" She grabbed hold of one man's shoulders and hopped, digging knees into his back and clawing her way over his head. She fell into the throng of people on the other side, jostling heads and hands that tried to get her off and bounced her along as a side effect. Maryland crowd-surfed into the store and was thrown to the tile floor in front of an aisle that once held toilet paper, but now looked as picked clean as a turkey carcass after Thanksgiving dinner. She landed on her left hip and elbow, lighting both up with equal amounts of pain, but the store was elevated enough that at least there was no flooding to soak her again.

The interior was dim with the electricity out; the gathering clouds outside let just enough light through the front windows to allow her to see the chaos as she turned onto one of the main aisles. People were everywhere, throwing items into shopping carts when possible but mostly just filling their arms without even looking at what they took. The shelves at the front of the store were bare—even the cigarette bins, she noted with dismay—and the main mass of looters was now toward the back. She wandered in that direction, looking for Gerald and keeping an eye out for the police officer.

She passed a circle of six or seven people fighting over a 12 pack of water bottles. As she watched, the plastic wrapping split, spilling bottles in all directions. These were scooped up and gone almost faster than she could blink.

A few loose fingers of fear tickled her insides. For the first time, she wondered if Gerald could be right. To have survived the hell of the previous night and then starve to death in the next few days would be a shitty waste of irony.

She found him on an aisle close to the back, working his way into a crowd clogging the canned-good aisle. Maryland laid a hand on his shoulder to get his attention. He spun, one fist raised, and then lowered it when he saw her.

"*Any luck?*" she shouted over the din.

"*The only thing I've been able to snag were these!*" He reached in the pocket of his gym shorts and handed her five energy bars in bright red wrappers. "*Don't let anyone see them, for Chrissake! These people are animals! Put them in your pocket!*"

Maryland stuffed them in the back of her jeans. "*We can't live on just these! Can't you get anything more…substantial?*"

Gerald grinned, gloating over her. "*Is the idealist finally starting to get the picture? Feel free to wander around and see what* you *can get!*" He turned and waded back into the crush of bodies fighting over what appeared to be creamed corn.

She turned around, retracing her steps to see what else the store had to offer, but was just in time to see that blue uniform go shooting by the opening of the aisle. Maryland broke into a run, turned the corner, and headed deeper into the store after it.

If she thought the previous skirmishes she'd witnessed were vicious, the one in the deli was a show stopper. The crowd here reminded her of the mindless hordes in a zombie movie, all packed together and vying for meat. The front coolers with the packaged cold cuts were empty, and now they were fighting over whole sides of beef and pork from the walk-in freezer behind the butcher counter, carrying the raw slabs over their heads like Aztec sacrifices. She came around a caged pyramid display of white, cylindrical propane tanks ('Just in Time for Summer!' the sign above them read, but nobody had told them Whitney was canceling summer this year), and slid to a stop on the slick tile, looking for the cop.

He was just a few yards away, a tall, lanky officer in a rumpled uniform. He pulled at people towards the back of the crowd, prying them away from the herd, attempting to break up the riot.

Relief warmed her. She came forward to clutch at him, grabbing one arm to get him to turn around. "Officer, officer, please, I need to talk to you—!"

She never saw the blow coming, which was probably why it hurt so much. Her face blazed, agony spiking so fast it was accompanied by a blinding mental light. Maryland flailed backward, falling against the metal cage around the propane tanks. The wire was flimsy, and shifted enough to knock the whole display over. She sat in the floor, clutching her aching face, as the bass gongs of the tanks collapsing rang out like a discordant pipe organ.

"*Get off me, lady!*" the cop screamed down at her, rubbing the knuckles of the fist he'd just socked her with, and then launched into a coughing fit.

She'd never been hit in her life; not even Bryce was that kind of asshole. She looked at him through the haze of tears in both eyes, seeing him from the front for the first time. His uniform shirt was ripped, badge hanging sadly from one pocket. His face was red and his eyes bugged out with the force of the rolling barks issuing from his open mouth.

"But…but you're a police officer."

He snorted crazed laughter. "Not today! I fucking *quit!*" He turned back to the crowd, punched the nearest looter in the back of the head, and she finally understood: he wasn't stopping the riot, he was trying to get to the front of it.

"GET OUT OF THE WAY, I'M A COP!" He pulled the pistol from its holster on his hip and fired two rounds into the ceiling.

This broke the spell of berserk looting. The mob broke up amid shouts, people shoving and stepping on—and tripping over—one another in their haste to get out of the area, but always keeping hold of that all-important merchandise. She scuttled out of the way before she really did reenact last night's run from the landslide.

From the far side of the loosening crowd, someone yelled, "*Fuck you, pig!*" A hail of fast gunfire erupted.

The chaos increased exponentially. Maryland flattened herself to the floor and watched as the rogue cop returned fire at whoever was shooting. Wave after wave of fleeing looters crumpled, caught in the crossfire, bodies falling to the floor. Was it really possible for things to degenerate this far, this fast?

"*That food is MINE!*" the cop shrieked, emptying the magazine of his pistol across the store and reaching for another.

Maryland turned her head, trying to find a way out, the confusion and noise making her brain hurt. She spotted Gerald at the opening of the cross aisle, pushing his way through the crowd moving in the opposite direction. His eyes swept the back of the store, taking in the situation, and then happened to lock on hers.

"*Help!*"

He looked at her, looked at the cop opening fire just a few feet away…then turned and bolted.

"You miserable bastard!"

The crowd thinned, leaving the cop and his adversary alone on the wide stretch of bloody, body-littered tile to blast away at one another. Now that it was safe, Maryland crawled, scrabbling through the minefield of white canisters toward safety.

"Shiiiiit!" she heard the cop scream. She glanced back and saw him fall over backward, dead or injured, arms held out like he was ready to make a snow angel. The hand with the gun struck the floor and let off another shot in her direction.

One of the propane tanks in the cage to her left jumped. A jet of blue flame poured out of a new hole in the side, along with an ear-splitting squeal, rising in pitch and intensity. The force of the released gas was like a jet engine, causing the tank to spin on the floor amid the other canisters.

The shriek grew even louder, impossibly higher.

Maryland scrambled away on all fours and then gained her feet, bullets and punched faces no longer that important, and sprinted for the front of the store.

She was barely two yards up the middle aisle when the tanks started exploding.

The blasts came separate at first, but then they blended into one general roar. Heat bloomed across her back, followed by the concussion a split second later. She was lifted off her feet, slammed into another person, and smashed against a shelf, sliding back into the floor.

Maryland opened her eyes in time to see flaming shelves falling on her.

WHITNEY +15:52

Chris and Tangela fled north, emerging from the destroyed neighborhood with the mangled corpse and sexual deviant onto a wide, flooded thoroughfare of small shops, gas stations, and strip malls, all in fair condition. Chris didn't recognize any of it, but just the sight of construction that wasn't in shambles comforted him, an oasis in the middle of deadly jungle. The first drops of a light drizzle coated their skin.

Tangela stopped first, amid a flurry of dry whoops that left her breathless. "What's that?" she wheezed, pointing to the east.

A thin column of black smoke rose into the sky, mixing with the heavier clouds rolling in from the same direction. The source appeared to be only a few blocks away. Now that he was paying attention, Chris thought he could hear the crackle of flames, as well as shouts from that direction.

"There's people!" Tangela exclaimed. "Let's go down there, Chris!"

"Yeah, okay." He contemplated the last person they'd run into. Quinlan had made him a little skittish about strangers, probably for the rest of his life. But there would be fire fighters there too, someone who could help them without the stipulation of nudity.

The noise and smoke led them another two blocks along the wide street. They came to an intersection whose four-way streetlight lay shattered in the inches of water on the road. The buildings on the left side opened up, and they had a clear view of the disturbance.

A Bowden Super Marketplace sat on the corner of the next block, and suddenly Chris knew where they were. He and his father had shopped here many times, before Nichelle took over such duties.

Hungry flames consumed the entire back of the store. People streamed out the front, running in all directions with their arms full, taking to the streets without looking back.

Chris' stomach growled at the thought of the food in that place. "Tangela, I want you to stay here, okay?"

"What? No, Chris, don't leave me!"

"It's just for a minute! I want to see if I can get us some food before that place burns down! You'll be able to see me from here. Just don't go anywhere, and don't talk to *anyone*, okay?"

She was crying, which started her coughing again. "Okay."

He wiped rain from her face, gave her a stiff hug, and took off.

Chris stuck to the side of the road opposite the store, running along the bottom of a high concrete embankment. He was almost across from the store when he noticed a figure in front of him, hobbling in the same direction.

Even from the back, he could tell the man was white and bordering-on-elderly. He would splash a few paces, slow down to catch his breath and let loose a string of dry gasps and snorts, then attempt jogging again. Chris caught up with him quickly, so he angled across the street, toward the store, meaning to avoid him.

"Wait! I say, wait, boy!" the man called out. Chris thought the noise from the fire must be affecting his hearing, because he sounded *British*. "Please, I need your help!"

Chris slowed but didn't stop, turned around so he walked backward through the water. "What is it?"

The old man stopped on the other side of the street and bent over double, coughing and clutching his stomach. He was small-statured, but his dress slacks looked two sizes too big for him. After he caught his breath, he pushed his glasses up on his nose and said, still doubled over, "I fear my friends may be in this market! Please, would you give me some assistance? I've been running for eight blocks to get here!"

Holy crap, he *was* British. Chris hesitated. Memories of Quinlan scratched at his brain.

He looked around. A shopping cart sat abandoned in the middle of the next lane, filled with looted bottles of glass cleaner that someone had abandoned. He splashed over, threw the blue containers out onto the waterlogged street, and pushed the cart back to the old man. "Climb in!"

Baggy Pants hesitated. "Well, I..."

"What did you expect, a limo? It's either this, or a piggyback ride, and I've been groped enough for one day!"

The old man drew his brow together in amused confusion. "In that case...many thanks, young sir. I appreciate the valiant effort."

An involuntary smile cracked Chris' face. "Yeah, yeah, would you get in already?"

Baggy Pants tried to get a leg into the metal basket, failed, and ended up tipping over the side head first. As soon as his feet were off the ground, Chris reversed directions, pushing the basket across the wide traffic lanes. It took some muscle to get it moving with the added weight and resistance of the water, but once momentum was on his side, the tires threw up plumes to either side. His passenger twisted in the cart until he was sitting up, short legs hooked over the end.

They reached the parking lot of the store, which was now shrouded in a thin pall of smoke. Chris coughed a little himself, until he pulled the neck of his t-shirt up over his mouth and nose. Looters scurried in all directions, like cockroaches after the kitchen light comes on.

"Over there!" Baggy Pants pointed into the crowd with one hand while covering his own mouth with the other. "Head toward that man!"

Chris changed directions, plowing forward between parked cars. His passenger shouted and waved his hands. "Gerald! Gerald, over here!"

A thirty-something white guy in athletic clothes turned his head. He glanced around—guiltily, Chris thought—and moved another few paces with the flow of the crowd, as if undecided if he should just keep going. He finally broke off and came toward them.

"Where is she?" his passenger demanded.

"I-I don't know," Gerald told him, and even Chris could tell he was lying. "I didn't see her inside, she must've—"

"Don't you *dare* say she left." Baggy Pants scowled. "She promised me she wouldn't, and I trust her word far more than yours."

Gerald rolled his eyes, and Chris realized he had an immediate disliking for him, but in a much different way than Quinlan. This guy was just an asshole. "Fine. I saw her inside. But there was nothing I could do, the whole place is catching fire after those explosions!"

The British guy struggled up out of the cart before Gerald could finish.

"C'mon, what the hell are you doing, old man?"

Baggy Pants gained a semi-solid footing, grabbed the younger guy before he could react, and shoved him backward. The force was barely enough to drive Gerald back a step, but there was a parking space bumper behind him, mostly submerged in water, and it tripped him up enough to cause him to splash back on his ass.

"*That's* for calling me 'old man' again. You'll get worse than that if any harm has come to Miss Williams." He turned and started into the store.

Chris exchanged a look with the shocked man still sitting in the water, then followed Baggy Pants.

"Where do you think you're going?" he asked Chris.

"To help you find your friend. I was headed in here anyway to grab something to eat."

He expected an argument, but received only a grim head nod.

The interior of the store was nearly empty of people now, the last desperate looters clearing out the dog food shelves at the front. The smoke in here was concentrated and much thicker than the cloud over the parking lot, and Chris' eyes burned and watered after a few seconds.

Baggy Pants coughed again, eyes bulging behind his glasses with the force. "Miss…Williams!" he tried to shout, as they went deeper into the store.

"HEY MISS WILLIAMS!" Chris bellowed. Somewhere ahead, the crackle of flames was like crinkling tin foil. An angry red haze burned through the smokescreen, towering over the tall supermarket aisles toward the back of the store.

"I'm here!"

The shout was distant, almost lost in the roar. Both heard it at nearly the same time and rushed forward.

Halfway down the wide middle aisle, they found the woman. She lay on the supermarket tile, trapped by one large section of charred shelf lying across her thighs, pinning her to the floor. By this point, sparks and bits of burning paper wafted through the air around then, which now felt too hot to breathe.

"*Tom, get me out of here!*" she screamed at the man with Chris.

"*Count of…three,*" Chris choked out, bracing his shoulders against the shelving unit. Tom did the same. "*One, two, THREE!*"

They lifted and pushed, the woman under the whole mess trying to help, but the shelf wouldn't budge. It was just too heavy. Chris' jaw worked in circles until he had the solution. He grabbed a nearby shopping cart, flipped it on its side, and drug it over next to the edge of the obstruction. Tom and Maryland watched him helplessly as the fire inched closer. Another shelving unit had collapsed down the aisle, and Chris lifted two of the flat, metal racks and carried them back, laying them side-by-side over the top of the cart and wedging them under the obstruction to form a lever. Tom got the idea now, and the two of them put all their weight on the raised end of the shelves. The mess lifted just enough for her to squirm free. Tom helped her up and kept an arm around her as they left the supermarket.

Part of the Bowden's collapsed as they exited. The three of them made it a safe distance into the parking lot and then fell into the water, hacking to get the smoke out of their lungs.

Chris thought he'd recovered enough to attempt speech when he sensed another presence to his left, and looked up to find that Gerald guy leaning over them.

"Are you all okay?" He sounded as out-of-breath as they were. "I went back into the store to look for you, but—"

The woman Chris just helped rescue was a blur as she rose and jabbed a finger in his face. "Don't give me that, you bastard, you left me in there to die!"

"Those guys had guns! What the fuck was I supposed to do?"

"You're just a selfish prick and a coward! You let an old man and a little boy do a man's work, I hope that makes you feel real good!"

Gerald stood uncomfortably, looking anywhere but at the screeching woman in his face.

"Miss Williams," Tom said gently, "You might want to…clean yourself a bit. You seem to have been…ah…quite frightened by your ordeal."

Chris saw what he meant. The seat of her pants was stained a dark brown. She put a hand back there, right in the middle of the mess, and brought her gooey fingers in front of her face. Then she popped them into her mouth.

All three of the males gathered around her winced in disgust.

"What? It's chocolate. I had energy bars in my pocket."

"Thank God." Tom stood and Chris did the same. "For a second there, I was starting to believe everything my mother told me about you Americans. Are you all right though?"

"Well, I got punched in the face by a rogue cop—that's something I thought I'd never hear outside of a Bruce Willis movie—but I didn't burn to death, thanks to you."

Tom put a hand on Chris's shoulder and gave it a squeeze. "You'll have to thank my new friend here, whose name, I'm ashamed to admit, I never even inquired."

"Chris Sloan, ma'am." He held out a hand.

She surprised him by brushing it away and embracing him instead. "Thank you. You're a much bigger man than some other people I could name. I'm Maryland Williams."

"Um, it was no problem, Miss Williams."

She released him and stepped back. "Just call me Maryland. Only Thomas Winston Cruise over here calls me Miss Williams."

Tom offered a hand which Chris did shake. "I can't thank you enough for what you did, young Mr. Sloan. I shall put your name in for some manner of honorarium once the city government is functional again. Might I ask how you came to be at our disposal?"

"I just saw the smoke and happened to come by with my...oh geez, Tangela!"

Chris looked down the street to where he'd left the girl. He couldn't see her. He was on the verge of running that direction when a small voice asked from behind one of the cars parked in the flooded lot, "Can I come out now, Chris?"

He sighed. "Yeah, come on out." Tangela emerged from hiding and wrapped her arms around his waist. "This is my stepsister, Tangela Kittrick."

"Nah-uh!" She jumped past him into the middle of the group and, as usual, the center of attention. "My name is Tangela *Sloan* now!"

Maryland laughed and patted the girl's head with a bandaged hand. "Last name problems, huh? That's all right, I can relate."

"Nice to meet you as well, young lady," Tom said. "But allow me to clarify my earlier question: how is it that you came to be here, all alone? Where are your parents?"

Tangela's energy drained away. She looked to Chris, who said, "My father's out of town. And, well, her mother—my stepmother—was killed last night in the hurricane."

"Oh Lord, how dreadful." Tom bowed his head.

Maryland knelt and took Tangela in her arms. Chris heard the girl sobbing again. "Oh honey, I'm so sorry. Is there anything we can do?"

"No, I don't think so. We're just trying to get to the bridge and leave the city. I figured it would be the quickest way to find my dad." Chris caught the look that passed between Maryland and Tom. "What? What is it?"

"I hate to the bearer of more bad news for you, Mr. Sloan, but you won't be escaping Port Allen that way."

"The bridge was destroyed last night," Maryland interpreted, stroking Tangela's braided hair.

"How do you know?"

"We were there when it happened. We came from there."

Chris sensed tears of his own coming and pressed the balls of his palms into his eye sockets. Despair descended, cold with an iron-solid core. His father; what if his father had been on the bridge? He'd felt so in control with this plan as a bearing, almost resourceful enough to live up to all that APTITUDE and POTENTIAL. Goddamn Whitney, and goddamn Port Allen. He just wanted to sit on the curb and be the one to cry and stamp his feet like a kid, instead of having to figure out what to do next.

"I think you should come with us," Tom told him.

Chris took his hands from his eyes. "Where are you going?"

"To the…what was it called, Miss Williams?"

"We're going to the Dome. The Civic Center downtown. There was a broadcast on the radio telling all survivors to head that way. Tom is right though, you have to come with us. We'll help you find your father."

"Really?" Tangela pulled her face up to look Maryland in the eye.

"Of course, sweetie. It's not safe for the two of you to be wandering around by yourselves. There should be food and water and someplace you can sleep until we get this all sorted out."

"Oh so now we're taking responsibility for two kids?" This was Gerald's first contribution to the conversation since Maryland attacked him.

"*You're* not taking anything. In fact, if you know what's good for you, you'll stay ten yards behind the rest of us at any given time, because if I see your face anywhere near me again, I'm going to pull out your tiny brain through your eye socket."

Gerald grumbled something about liking to see her try.

"What do you say, Mr. Sloan?" Tom asked. "Will you and your sister come with us?"

"Please Chris, can we?"

Chris took one last look around the smoky parking lot. They

were the last ones here, the looters all having fled, and the flames of the store guttered in the rain. He couldn't help but notice the lack of firefighters, or even any sirens in the distance. That fact scared him even more than realizing they were trapped within the city.

Plus, he was still starving.

The first rumbles of thunder came from the clouds sweeping in overhead.

"I don't really think we have a choice."

"Okay, good." Maryland put a hand on Tangela's shoulder. "No more stops. We can be at the Dome in a couple of hours if we hoof it."

They fell into a line, Tangela holding Maryland's hand in front, Tom and Chris side by side next, and Gerald bringing up the rear with a scowl.

"So Tom Cruise, huh?" Chris asked. "Is he big in England or something?"

WHITNEY +16:18

Randy and Heather Rampy—as their last name turned out to be—attached themselves to Ellis and refused to let him out of their sight.

At first their gratitude for Heather's rescue was nice, but it became annoying when they wouldn't let him step into an alley for thirty seconds to take a piss. It made him think of the crowd that surrounded him earlier, pleading for him to solve all their problems just because he wore a badge. Yes, he was a cop, he was used to being seen as an authority figure, but that level of dependence was more than he was comfortable with.

He no longer had that problem after the four of them made their way back out of the swamped warehouses where they left the Rampys' vehicle and onto the main streets with the rest of the survivors drifting toward the Dome. Without that all-important uniform shirt and badge, he was just another heathen on his way to Purgatory, and that was exactly the way he wanted it.

Randy talked incessantly as they walked, at first about themselves (Ellis now had enough information about the young couple to write a term paper, if not a book; him a financial adviser, her a salon technician, both lifelong residents of Port Allen) and then finally turning the conversation to him as light rain swirled down again.

"So how long have you been a police officer?"

"Let's…let's talk about that another time." He glanced around to see if the question was overheard. They trudged along in a loose knot of people down the middle of the street, the towers of downtown visible to the south on their right, but most of these people were more concerned with putting one foot in front of the other than with conversation. Ellis' stomach had been grumbling for the past hour, so he could relate to the general malaise. Every few minutes a car would putter past, the drivers forced to slow so the walkers could part in front of them, like sheep on a New Zealand road.

"What about you?" Randy asked Lincoln, who had been quiet on the trek. "How long have you been an officer?"

"Ha! Me, a *cop?*" Lincoln plucked at the front of his wet shirt. "Randy, tell me dude, do you really think *I* could be po-po?"

"But the two of you…I just thought…" Randy coughed into his hand, but Ellis couldn't tell if it was prompted by embarrassment or physiological need. A lot of the folks around them were coughing, to varying degrees, but none as severely as Heather. Had to be a lot of germs in a situation like this, and the cold rain couldn't be helping. "Then…what do you do?"

Ellis saw Lincoln wince. "I'm…self-employed."

"Oh, really? That's great, good for you! Tell me, is someone handling your investment portfolio?"

Ellis wasn't sure where the laughter started. First he and Lincoln were releasing hesitant snickers, the kind that come through the nose, then they were chuckling, their amusement building off one another, and within seconds they roared with laughter. Randy gave them a confused look, but didn't seem to take offense. Several people in the crowd glanced over and either frowned or scooted away from the lunatics.

"What's the name of the firm handling your investments? Dewey, Cheatum and Howe?"

"Naw, more like Smith and Wesson!"

"Oh, you're brothers," Randy said, and their howling cut off with the suddenness of a stopped tape. He added quickly, "Not, you know, brothers like…'*black guys*'…but brothers as in, from the same mother. I don't know why I didn't see it before."

Ellis looked at the X-Dawg, who stared back at him, and that was all it took to break them up all over again. This time, when he could stop laughing long enough to speak, he said, "No, Randy, we're not brothers. We're just walking to the Dome together, just like you."

"Randy, my arm hurts so *bad*." Heather stopped to cough so hard she had to double over. The interrogator excused himself from the current line of questioning and dropped back to see about her.

She looked pale. They had used part of one of her pant legs and a strip from Randy's shirt to fashion a make-shift sling for her broken arm. The gash on her forehead had stopped bleeding, but Ellis knew the cracked limb must be killing her. They listened to the sound of Randy soothing her with hushed words for the next few minutes.

"What happens when we get there?" Lincoln asked him suddenly. "When we get to the Dome?"

"I'm hoping we get her some medical attention, and some food and water for all of us."

"That's not what I'm talkin about. I mean me and you, and your brothers in blue." He frowned. "That wasn't supposed to rhyme."

"I already told you, I'm gonna make a report to whoever I can, and get someone out looking for Sturney and his crew, my partner, and your friends."

"Yeah, I know, and that sounds all good on paper, but the mechanics're a little more complicated than the blueprint, if you catch me."

Ellis sighed and shrugged. "No, Lincoln, I don't catch you."

"Look, I ain't naïve enough to think they're just gonna take your word and start lookin to arrest those four assholes without a shitload of questions 'bout what happened last night. I wanna know what you're gonna tell 'em 'bout me and my boys."

"Nothing. You three were in the wrong place at the wrong time."

"Don't feed me fairy tales," Lincoln snapped. "At the very least, we were lootin, and you know it. Even if I trusted you enough to think you'll stick to whatever story we come up with, what happens if your partner is found, or even Mac or CT, and they tell a different one? Or what if they *already* reported in?"

"You're right. So we tell the truth. We have nothing to hide. We were perfectly within our right to let you guys go. None of us did anything wrong."

Lincoln rubbed a hand across the back of his neck. "Now hold up a sec, I didn't say that either. Yeah, *we* know we're innocent, but you gotta admit, even the truth is pretty sticky for me."

"Hold that thought." On the sidewalk to the left, next to the crumbled wall of a Shell station, was an intact payphone. Ellis angled through the thin crowd over to it, Lincoln, Randy, and Heather following.

He'd checked every one they came across, and all had the same odd open-line hiss as the one in the upstairs warehouse office. No harm in trying though. He picked the receiver up from the cradle and placed it against his ear.

No dial tone. Like the entire city's telephone network had been knocked off the service grid. He hadn't seen anyone with a cell phone to ask if they were faring any better.

Lincoln saw the disappointment on his face as he replaced the handset. "That's another thing. What if we get to the Dome and there ain't no one for you to report to? How sure are you those guys already packed up and left, and ain't out cruisin the streets for us right now?"

Ellis balled his fists and then swiped at the moisture collecting on his face. "Lincoln, *I don't know!* I'm not a fortuneteller, I have no idea what's going to happen! What do you want from me?"

"Honesty." The boy stared into Ellis' face with more intensity than most grown men. Jesus, this kid did *not* act like other gangbangers. "The way I figure, I'm in this neck deep. I shot one of 'em last night, and if we go the official route, I have to explain that. Maybe pay for it. But that's only if your piglet friends don't catch us first. So if I'm gonna die or go to jail, I'd kinda like to know why."

Ellis broke contact with those fierce, too-old eyes. Randy and Heather stood just a few yards away, watching them warily. The thing was, he couldn't disagree. If anyone deserved real answers—more than Charlie and Billy, that is—it was the kid who'd been forced to risk his life to save theirs. "C'mon. Let's keep walking while we do this or we'll never get there."

They rejoined the stream of pedestrian traffic. Cars passed steadily in the street now, and people walked in the gutters to allow them room. Ellis maneuvered them into a relatively empty patch of walking space. He looked back and saw the couple had retreated a polite distance out of earshot, but still within visual range.

"Everybody just kind of figured Sturney and his guys were on the take," he began. The last person he'd said these words to was an internal affairs investigator from Houston who disappeared with the information, never to be seen or heard from again. "It's not too hard to figure out when a beat cop starts buying up real estate like donuts. I don't know if he was being investigated already or what, so don't even ask. All I know is, one night I'm on patrol by myself. My partner, Charlie, he worked an earlier shift cause we had two guys call out. I'm driving around Bedford Park over on Chatham—"

"I know that park. That's Bloodwhip territory."

"That's right. They're pretty much the only heroin distributor in the city, and that park is where they do most of their business."

"So what happened?"

"I see two of them jumping the fence in the middle of the night with a duffel bag almost bigger than they were. Gotta be either drugs or money to buy drugs, and either way it means a major deal. So I call for back up and go in on foot on my own so I don't lose them."

"You can just skip to the end. The deal was with Sturney, right? And you saw it and turned him in. I've seen *Training Day* enough times to know how it works."

"Good for you, but what I saw…it was closer to *Scarface*." Ellis swallowed. His throat felt a little raw. He'd changed his mind, he didn't want to relive this. "Those two Bloodwhips *were* there to meet Sturney. I don't know if the deal went bad, or if he set the whole thing up with the intent to doublecross them. But I watched from the bushes a few yards away, waiting on my back up, while those two boys showed off what was in that duffel: enough dope to make Pablo Escobar jealous. Then Sturney and Drano killed them without provocation while McNamara and Meyers watched and laughed."

Lincoln waved a hand. "Okay, I know it's bad because they're cops and everything, but you been makin 'em sound like the boogieman. People get shot in cold blood a lot where I come from. Bam, bam…execution style.”

“Can I maybe finish telling you this, or do you want to take it from here?” After Lincoln shrugged, Ellis said, “I never said they shot them. I said they *killed* them. Sturney held them at gunpoint and made them turn around. Then Drano pulled a knife and slit one of their throats with a grin that made me feel sick. A kid younger than you, and he opened his neck up like a can of beans.”

“Jesus. Were they tryin to keep quiet by not usin the guns?”

“I thought that too, at first. But they liked it. They did everything but play in the blood.”

“So what happened?”

“The other banger wasn’t stupid, he saw what was coming. He tried to break away, and Sturney clubbed him in the head with the pistol until he went down. Then he took the knife from Drano and…ah God, he carved that kid up. He took his time. I think by the end, McNamara and Myers were a little queasy, but Drano watched the whole operation. Now…have you ever seen any ‘executions’ like that?”

Lincoln shook his head. “I take it back, man. In my hood, it’s get in and get out. That’s like serial killer shit.”

“Yeah, that’s exactly what it was like.” Ellis tried to clear the accompanying imagery from his thoughts, and continued the story. “They cleaned up, packed up the money and the bodies too. I didn’t know what to do. I jumped out, got my gun on Sturney, told him to freeze. He laughed in my face. I think he probably might’ve shot me, if we hadn’t heard the sirens just then. They all ran for it.”

“Then why’re those motherfuckers still wearin badges?”

“Because I didn’t say anything. Not at first. I was scared. Told everyone I lost the two kids. Then, two days after it happened, I find an envelope waiting in my locker at the station. With ten-thousand dollars inside.”

“Hush money.”

“Damn right. Only it had the opposite effect on me. It made me feel so guilty I could barely look at myself in the mirror. So I went to IA and told them the whole thing. Problem was, Sturney had three days by that point to erase the evidence trail. They never found the drugs, although I doubt he's had time to get them out of the city. Anyway, it came down to my word against his. Said I had a grudge against him. Maybe some money changed hands, who knows? I'm so paranoid these days I see him in every shadow."

"I'd say last night proves you ain't paranoid."

"For what good it does me. While they come up with enough evidence, he gets to keep his job. And if they build a case against him, guess who's gonna be the star witness?"

"So he takes last night as an opportunity to get rid of you, and the rest of us are all collateral?"

Ellis gave him a hard smile. "You're a little more than that now, at least from Sturney's point of view. Welcome to the witness pool."

A hand fell on Ellis' shoulder. He jumped, causing Lincoln to do the same.

"Sorry," Randy said sheepishly. "I just wanted you to know we're here." He pointed ahead.

Over the tops of the last few buildings, they could see the rounded dome of the Port Allen Civic Center through the increasing downpour.

WHITNEY +16:29

By the time Mac spotted the first houses ahead, he was ready to let the water take him.

He clung to the door-raft now more than he pulled it, drifting in the flood, alternating between half-hearted kicks and one-armed paddling. His muscles, when they weren't numb, felt like fire beneath his skin as they cramped. The pain in his broken nose—which he could no longer breathe through—infected his entire face, drowning out his raw throat. Fear had given way to despair long before the bruised skies opened and dumped more rain.

And Charlie was still unconscious, moaning in his sleep every few minutes. Several times, Mac considered just rolling him off the door and using it to save himself, then felt guilty for it.

His exhausted brain reduced the first downtown building on the horizon to no more than a geometric concept. Just a square, something else to focus on, half-imagined amid the sheets of rain.

Only as he got closer did he understand what he was seeing. By this point, he could make out the curve of the Civic Center dome. Partially flooded houses appeared on both sides of him, rising out of the water like waking leviathans, and then he was swimming on an actual street again.

"We made it, Charlie," he gasped. "We...we fuckin did that shit."

His foot hit something hard and he yelped; thoughts of alligators had never entirely left the back of his mind. He kicked out again, questing with his toe.

Solid ground.

He would've cried, if there was any moisture left in his dehydrated body. He put both feet down, but his overtaxed legs refused to support him. He thrashed ahead, and after a few more yards his knee could reach bottom. He crawled onto the land like the first fish to ever breathe air, pulling the door a good distance up the concrete beach. It produced a terrible squall against the pavement.

Mac collapsed on his back across the yellow stripe dividing traffic lanes. He closed his eyes, let the rain fall on him, and coughed until he saw stars. He never wanted to move again, he wanted to lay right here and fall asleep and never go for a swim again as long as he lived.

Charlie.

No man, fuck Charlie, he'd gotten the pig this far, and he wasn't claiming responsibility for him any more.

Fine then: Links.

If anything could get him moving, it was that name. CT was out there somewhere. And a platoon of crooked cops. He had to get to Lincoln first. Mac rolled onto his aching side, muscles screaming, and looked around.

He had no idea where he was. Some middle class residential street just northeast of downtown, where the land rolled uphill and gained elevation fast. Outside of X-Dawg jurisdiction, for sure. The Dome took up most of the skyline to the north.

"Charlie, wake up." Mac flopped back the other way to face his companion. The cop was so pale, his breathing no more than flutters. His leg wound still oozed beneath the tourniquet, the blood washed away by the rain in diluted trails. Mac hadn't made much of an attempt to wake him before, but now patted his cheek with increasingly harder slaps. "Charlie, c'mon man, you gotta wake up, I can't carry yo' ass no more!"

Charlie muttered something, but his eyes stayed clamped.

Mac got to his feet. His legs shook, but remembered how to work. His whole system was out of whack, muscles tighter than drum skins, threatening to cramp up. He might be able to walk, but running was out of the question. He gritted his teeth in frustration.

He didn't know where to start looking for his friend, but Charlie needed help right now.

"All right, old man. Let's get you some place dry."

He bent, got one large arm under Charlie's knees and the other under his neck and lifted. The weight set off a round of shrieks throughout Mac's back and legs that forced a little moan between his lips. He was glad the cop was unconscious, or they'd both be hollering.

Mac carried him up the sidewalk, to an undamaged house several lots away from the water's edge. All the windows were shattered, and the front door hung open. He walked inside the dark, dank interior, stepping over debris and bumping into furniture until he found a couch in the middle of the room. He lowered Charlie onto the cushions just before his arms gave out.

In the kitchen he found a plastic cup and filled it with water from the sink. He held this to Charlie's lips, tilting his head up to meet the rim, and sighed in relief when he took a few swallows. His eye fluttered open, wobbled a bit, and then focused on Mac.

"W-where are we?"

"Somebody's house. I hate to do this, man, but I gotta leave you here and try to find some help. But I'll back. Just…hang on, man."

His eyes were closed again before Mac could even finish talking.

He left Charlie on the couch and went back out into the rain, closing the door behind him as best he could. He checked the house number, committing it to memory, and when he reached the corner, he did the same with the street sign.

If anything happened to him, Charlie would die, forgotten in this house.

Now, where was he going to get help?

The Dome stood largest and closest on the horizon. He started in that direction at a limping trot.

SICK, SICK, SICK

The Port Allen Civic Center was a circle of steel and concrete, the outer façade gray with towering brown support pillars set at regular intervals reaching all the way up the curved dome of its roof, and one wide, turnstile-gated entrance for each cardinal direction. It was mostly used for conventions and indoor sporting events, with the interior capable of seating 30,000 people, not counting the space used as the arena floor.

And it looked like every square inch would be needed.

Ellis and the others approached from the northwest on Whiteman Avenue. They could see storm damage on the roof from blocks away, but it seemed superficial. The thin layer of aesthetic texturing across the dome had worn off, leaving dull metal shell and thick skylight glass to gleam in the drizzle.

The straggling line of pedestrians mingled with cars turning in from side streets now, honking horns and revving engines at the traffic backup, all one big procession leading into the vast parking lot, where they got their first real look at the Dome and the surrounding area.

"Christ Almighty," Randy whispered. "Would you look at that?"

Ellis thought at first he meant the crowds—the two gates they could see for the north and west were clogged with people waiting to get inside—but then he looked past them to the far side of the parking lot.

An ocean of floodwater led right up to the eastern edge of the building, a lapping shoreline that cut across the lot on a diagonal where the land went downhill. It made the flooding they'd seen pale in comparison. Drowned vehicles were parked in several of the far rows and a few rooftops poked out like ships on the horizon before the water claimed all as far as they could see. Everyone pulling into the lot now was forced to park on the western side, and the spaces were filling up fast.

"What happened?" Lincoln sounded awed.

"I told you, that's the lowest elevation in the city." Ellis held a hand over his eyes to shield them from the rain, but it gave him no sight advantage. "Might be flooded all the way to the shore."

"My…my home was out there. My crew…"

Ellis grimaced. "They could be all right."

"I…I shoulda been there…"

"You couldn't have done anything. You think you could've held back this flood all by yourself?"

Lincoln whirled on him. "Don't talk to me like I'm a five-year-old. Everybody I know could be dead right now."

"I'm just saying, you can't blame yourself."

"Let me ask you somethin, *Officer*." His eyes blazed. "Is your house out there, in all that? Naw, course not, you wouldn't be caught dead on this side of town 'less you were doin the job. You think it's any coincidence that *this* gets flooded, where all the poor, black folks live?"

"Oh, c'mon Lincoln, you can't believe—"

"Don't tell me what I can't believe. Everything else mighta just got taken from me, but not that."

He led the way onward with shoulders hunched, through the tangled mess of the parking lot, but their progress came to a halt when they reached the line for the north entrance to the Dome. They waited miserably while the rain got heavier, inching their way closer to admittance. Heather huddled against Randy, her cough getting worse, and Lincoln stood a few feet away, gazing out at the lake smothering the east side of the city.

After another half hour, they were finally able to enter the turnstile into a hallway that ringed the outer edge of the building all the way around. Just to have the rain off their heads was a blessing, but the inside was dim and sweltering from lack of electricity and smelled of packed bodies. Some backup emergency power source lit a large red EXIT sign above the door, and every fifth fluorescent bulb gleamed weakly. A gaunt woman stood just inside the turnstile, yelling directions to the refugees as they entered.

"Head straight and onto the civic center floor if you want a cot and something to eat! Go right and follow the outer hallway if you need medical attention!"

Ellis noticed the majority chose to go right, where another line stretched out of sight around the inner curve of the building. The cloud of coughing in the hallway brought to mind 17th century British plague wards.

"Officer Wright, I've got to get Heather some help," Randy said. "Would you come with us?"

"Just a sec." He broke from the others and approached the woman directing the masses. "Excuse me, ma'am, can you tell me who's in charge here?"

"I have no idea."

He sighed and tried once more. "Then who do you report to?"

"'Report to?'"

"Who told you to stand here and tell people this?"

She gave him a brief, annoyed glance. "No one did. Sir, I'm just trying to help get people organized. If you want to complain about something, I don't know what to tell you."

Ellis looked over his shoulder once, at the crowd, and leaned closer to her. "Hey, it's okay, I'm a cop."

She looked at him again, a bit longer this time, but with no more sympathy. "Then shouldn't *you* be telling *me* who's in charge?" At his pained expression, she softened and said, "Look, talk to Doctor Kordi around the corner. Maybe he can help you." She went back to directing human traffic, and Ellis walked away.

Heather was coughing again, utterly bloodless in the face. She shivered against her husband. "I d-don't feel so good, honey."

Randy looked at him, eyes pleading. "Officer Wright, please, can't you do something? It's gonna take all day if we wait in this line. I think she's really sick!"

"What can I do? All these people are waiting for the same thing."

"Why are you such a pussy?" Lincoln demanded suddenly. "You need answers, right? So let's take these two and go get 'em!"

Ellis scanned the heads of the crowd in front of him. Lincoln was right; he needed to speak to whoever this doctor was, find out who else had come into the city with him and what they were using to communicate, report the incident with Sturney, and get some new orders. That took precedence over the ailing survivors in this line. He would probably find himself posted at another door somewhere, and, even as exhausted as he was, he would do it and be thankful to have a purpose.

"All right, follow me and stick close."

He led the other three out beside the line and started down the hallway past the waiting. They received boo's and angry curses—and a few thrown objects—but kept their heads down and followed the curving hallway around to the head of the line.

An open door stood on the right, next to a plastic sign that said 'KITCHEN.' The man at the front of the line, burly shoulders and a hefty stomach paunch, threw out an arm to block the way, coughing into the breast of his Dallas Cowboys jersey the entire time and glaring from red-rimmed eyes.

"I'm a cop, let me through."

"Bullshit, you're a cop."

A voice thick with Middle Eastern accent drifted out through the open door. "If he says he is a police officer, let him through!"

Beefy relented, moving his arm. Ellis and the others entered.

The room beyond was little more than a concrete square with a built-in slab table, some sort of prep room connected to the kitchen for the use of the concession stands scattered around the Dome and the catering staffs at the fancier events. A girl close to ten or eleven sat on the table, a woman beside her clutching her hand. Bent over the girl and peering into her mouth with a tongue depresser was a man in chinos and a white dress shirt with the sleeves rolled up to his elbows, skin the smooth color of well-creamed coffee. Ellis couldn't determine his nationality.

The doctor glanced up at them, scrutinizing Ellis' stained undershirt and uniform pants. "You tell me now, are you a police officer, or not? Because I have no time for lies, my friend."

"Yes, I'm a cop."

"Thank heaven above. Stay there one moment, please." He turned around, squatted, and reached into a giant pill jar on the floor amid a number of other medical instruments. He pulled out a white tablet and handed it to the woman. "Give her half now, and the other in about six hours, with plenty of water. Try to find a cot and let her rest. I'll make some rounds out there as soon as I can to check on her."

"Thank you. So much." The woman choked back tears as the girl hopped down and leaned against her. They walked past the four of them and out of the room.

The man came forward and held a hand out to Ellis. He was probably forty or so, with curly, jet-black hair and a tidy circle of facial hair around his mouth and chin. "Eraj Kordi, M.D. General practitioner." His accent clipped each syllable.

"Officer Ellis Wright, sixth precinct. I've got a woman here I need you to see about."

"Let me guess: severe cough, flu-like symptoms?"

"That and a broken arm."

"Get her on the table."

Randy brought Heather forward and helped her onto the concrete slab. Kordi started a quick examination, swabbing at the gash on her forehead, and Ellis asked, "I need to know if you've seen another police officer come through here. He would've had a gunshot wound on his leg, might have been with two black kids, one really big?"

"No, no gunshot wounds at all, thankfully." Kordi took Heather's temperature and gave several other tests, then examined her arm. "Looks like you've already done about as well a job as I could on this. Some pain medication should take the edge off. Other than that, I'm going to give you some high strength cough suppressant laced with antibiotics and tell you the same thing I've told everyone else: get some rest and hang on. You're an advanced case, so it's especially vital you heed this."

"Can I get some of that pain medication, doc?" Lincoln asked. And then, at the look from Ellis, "For my shoulder, asshole."

"What's wrong with these people?" Ellis jerked a thumb over his shoulder at the hacking chorus drifting in through the open door. "*Is* it flu? Pneumonia?"

Kordi gave a grunt of laughter. "I wish it were that simple! This is more like a virulent strain of bronchitis far from anything I have ever seen. My best estimates say seventy to eighty percent of the people here are suffering from it. And there's just not much I can do with what I have at my disposal."

"Where's the rest of your team?"

Kordi paused in the act of digging through the medical supplies lining the wall and looked up at him with a dark eyebrow raised. "Team?"

"The other volunteers or medical staff that came into the city with you. Surely they didn't just send one person!"

Understanding crept into the doctor's face. "My friend...I am *from* Port Allen. My medical practice is three blocks from here. I arrived this morning, seeking asylum the same as everyone else, and found only the accommodations the people organized for themselves. I saw the need for medical aid and filled it. All of these supplies are from my own office."

Ellis could only blink at the man.

"So what you tryin to say," Lincoln began, coming to stand behind Heather so he could see the doctor, "is nobody's here, right? No government or fuckin Red Cross. Right?"

"As rain."

"Man, I knew it! Katrina all over again!"

"Wait a minute, wait a minute." Ellis leaned on the table with one hand. He felt dizzy all of a sudden. "Why is everyone here then? Who the hell told all these people to come to the Dome in the first place?"

"You mean you don't know?"

Ellis shook his head. "We heard by word of mouth."

"There is some kind of automated announcement playing on every available airwave. Find someone with a portable radio out there and listen for yourself. It promises food, water, and transportation out of the city, but no one here knows a thing about any of it. The only foodstuffs we have came from the Civic Center reserves, and that which people were kind enough to bring in."

"I...I don't understand, that makes no sense! It's going on twenty-four hours since Whitney made landfall, and there's not a single rescue worker in this city? How could they not be here?"

Kordi shrugged, an exasperated and somehow hopeless gesture that told Ellis how close to collapse he was. "I only have what information I have gotten from the people coming through here. I have heard from many sources that the Rugg Canyon bridge is out. There are cars abandoned on the freeway for miles."

"*What?*" This from Randy, looking interested in something besides Heather for the first time. "How?"

"Again, I do not know. It was supposedly destroyed just before the hurricane hit."

"That explosion last night." Lincoln's brow drew together as he looked across the table at Ellis.

"Yes, that is what the witnesses have said. We still have no power, no phones—"

"That's landline though, right? What about cell phones?"

"As far as I know, no one can get a signal. For all intents and purposes, Port Allen is cut off from the outside world."

"No, no that's not right," Ellis argued. Dread as thick as syrup rose, threatening to mire him. "There's still the northern pass, through the Chantilly's."

"Yeah, and you gonna take a nice little swim to get to it?" Lincoln asked. "In case you forgot, this place is beach front property now."

"Don't get me wrong." Kordi looked from Lincoln to Ellis. "I'm sure help is coming even if they have to clear a path through the mountains or come in by boat from the Gulf side, but until it does, we are on our own, and the situation is becoming more dire each passing hour. We need someone to organize those people still well enough to go out and bring back all the supplies they can find, from hospitals and grocery stores."

Kordi stopped and stared at him expectantly, but it wasn't until the three other sets of eyes in the room slid over to him that he understood what the doctor meant.

"What, *me?*"

"Of course, you're a police officer! I have my hands full here, and you are the first government official in any capacity I have seen! If these people don't get some leadership soon, sickness and starvation will be the least of our worries!"

That dread was over his head now, impossible to swim in, and when he opened his mouth, he felt it seep into his lungs and try to steal his breath. "No, no, I can't...I'm just a cop..."

"I think what the doc means is that we'll take whatever we can get," Lincoln said.

Ellis had to get away, had to escape the weight of those eyes. They expected him to fix all this, just like the mob that tried to tear him apart earlier, but he wasn't a savior, he wasn't a leader, *Charlie* was a leader, Ellis was just the kind of cop that needed his orders, which was why the Captain said he'd never make sergeant…

"Officer Wright?" Heather spoke up from the table, her lip quivering from sickness or emotion. "You saved me. I won't ever forget that."

"That's right," Randy added. "We can never repay you."

"This isn't the same." His hands shook, and he clenched them into fists to keep it from showing. "I'm sorry, I can't do this."

Ellis turned, walking quickly from the room and back into the hallway filled with coughing and the stink of sweat. He got no more than a handful of paces before a hand grabbed his arm and pulled him to a stop.

"What the fuck is wrong with you?" Lincoln forced him to turn around and face him. "You're a *cop*. These people need you, or they're gonna start tearin each other apart."

He shook the boy's hand off. "Do you see a badge pinned to my shirt anymore?"

"That don't change a goddamned thing."

"You're real high and mighty for someone who was looting convenience stores this time yesterday. You wanna do a good deed, be a superhero? Then *you* take charge." He stalked away, continuing toward the exit to this hellhole.

"What about my boys? What about your partner?"

"They're dead, Lincoln."

Ellis pushed through the crowd and out the revolving turnstile into the rainy afternoon beyond. He was so consumed by anger and guilt that he bashed into the broad chest of someone standing just outside the door.

"Scuse me," he murmured, without looking up.

"That's okay," a familiar voice said. Ellis raised his eyes, saw the badge pinned to the black shirt, and froze.

"After all," Sturney continued. "I 'as here lookin fer you, anyway."

WHITNEY +17:11

Lincoln watched Ellis go and then stomped back to the room where he'd left Randy and Heather with the doc. He wanted to be mad, but from what he knew of the man, this was no surprise. If Ellis had been one of his crew, Lincoln would've pummeled him until either his fear was dead or he was.

But he ain't one of your crew. You prob'ly don't have a crew no more.

Randy had an arm around Heather and was helping her out of the room by the time he got there. "We're going to find her a bed."

"A'ight. I'll check in with you guys later." They left the room, and he turned to the Middle Eastern doctor. "Sorry 'bout that. He's just scared, I guess."

"That seems to be going around also. Come here and I'll take a look at that shoulder."

Lincoln took a seat on the table. Kordi sat on a stool to swab the scabbed-over wound with alcohol and then prodded the flesh. "How did this happen?"

"Gunshot."

"Then you're lucky. This appears to be more burned and torn than punctured. Who shot you?"

"That's a long story that you really don't want an answer to."

"I can live with that. Normally I would be forced to report this to the police, but they just walked out the door."

Lincoln grinned and then sucked air through his teeth as Kordi finished up the exam with something that stung and slapped a large bandage over the wound. "Tell me Doc, how bad is that thing Heather and all those people got? Could they…you know…*die?*"

Kordi's dark eyebrows pulled together. He opened his lips to answer and let them hang. When he finally seemed on the verge of speaking, he was interrupted by two men that pushed their way into the makeshift examination room, past the bruiser in the football jersey.

"You will have to wait your turn gentlemen, just like everyone else."

Both men were Caucasian, but white even for that. The one in front, blue jean jacket and greasy hair in his face, coughed for nearly ten seconds into his forearm and then rasped, "You got medicine in here?"

"Yes, and it's being administered on a first-come, first-serve basis."

His eyes flicked from Kordi, to the pile of medical supplies on the floor and back again. Junkie eyes; Lincoln had watched his mother and now his cousin succumb to addiction, so he ought to know.

"Not anymore, it ain't." He reached into his denim jacket and pulled out a Glock. He trained it with one wavering hand on Kordi. "Give it to us, right now."

"What are you—?"

"*I said give it to us!* Zeke, get over there and grab the stuff while I cover this Arab piece a shit!"

Zeke had a blond mullet and a Drist t-shirt. He slunk around the outside of the room, on the far side of the examination table, and knelt amid the medical supplies, grabbing pill bottles and shoving them in his pockets and tucking the large jar of tablets under one arm.

Kordi stood up slowly. Denim Jacket followed him with the twitching pistol. "First of all, I am *Persian*, you redneck. Second, there is nothing here that you can use to get high, these are *life-saving medical supplies!*"

"Do I look like a fuckin crackhead to you?" Denim Jacket coughed again, and wiped at his eyes, probably believing drug addicts came in one color only. "You wanna save someone's life, how 'bout ours, huh? How 'bout my daughter? We're bad sick and we're tired of waitin for some help!"

"Fine, if that's the case, then let me give you what you need and leave the rest here for others!"

Zeke finished with his raid and, instead of going back around the table again, he pushed between Kordi and Lincoln. The doc was forced to stand against the wall, and once again the gun tracked him, completely ignoring Lincoln. Zeke took up a place behind his partner and gave a nervous glance into the packed hallway.

"No way. Can't afford for you to run out if we need more. Sorry, but me and mine are gonna make it through this. Let's go, Zeke."

Lincoln lunged.

Denim Jacket realized his mistake at the last second and tried to bring the pistol back to bear on Lincoln. It was far too late. Lincoln grabbed him by the wrist and smashed the hand against the wall twice. The gun fell. Kordi scrambled for it while Lincoln punched the would-be robber in the stomach, sending him to his knees.

"The other one, don't let him get away!" Kordi shouted while turning the pistol on the recovering thug.

Lincoln spun. Zeke was gone with the medicine, abandoning his friend.

He charged into the hallway. The guy was only a few yards away, running down the corridor past the line of sick people. A few of them realized what was going on and made feeble attempts to stop him, but he hurtled on.

Lincoln's moist sneakers slapped the concrete. Zeke might be sickly, but the fucker was still fast enough to keep him from gaining any ground. He sprinted all out, sucking in air and concentrating only on the back of the fleeing thief.

A turnstile exit was ahead. The gate was clogged with people shoving to get inside. Zeke jerked to a standstill, scattering bottles and plastic-wrapped syringes as he looked for a way out. After a few unsuccessful attempts to push through, he kept running, this time with Lincoln hot on his heels. He cradled the big bottle of pills like a football under his arm.

Metal doorways appeared at regular intervals along the inner wall of the corridor. Zeke hit one of these, pushing it open, and charged through. Lincoln plunged into soupy shadows after him.

It took only a few seconds for his eyes to adjust to weak halogen bulbs above him, running off the emergency generator. He was on a railed catwalk, over which was a steep drop into pitch black. He could hear Zeke stumbling somewhere ahead of him, the catwalk rattling with each step.

Lincoln chose his footing carefully. The catwalk ended in a staircase, and he took them as fast as possible. Another walkway turned back beneath the first, and he caught sight of Zeke's shadowed form at the other end, just a few yards away, descending even further.

He launched himself over the corner of the railing. His wounded shoulder hit Zeke in the side, toppling the other man down the last few steps in a heap and sending a jolt down Lincoln's spine. He braced himself for the impact of whatever cruel surface lay at the bottom, but was surprised when the two of them splashed down into a cushion of liquid.

Lincoln got to his feet. The water down here—or whatever it was—came up to his waist. He just hoped it wasn't sewage.

Zeke thrashed to his left. Lincoln grabbed him by the shirt and punched him in the face. "This is for makin me get wet, AGAIN!" Another right-cross, and he felt the body go slack in his hands.

From above came the sound of the metal door opening again and then Kordi's voice. "Young man? Lincoln? Are you down there?"

"I'm here!" he called out, his voice echoing. Now that Zeke was out of the picture, the dark pressed in on him. "You got a flashlight up there?"

"Hold on! Someone, hand me a flashlight!" A few seconds passed, and then a beam of light blazed on above him, revealing the doctor and several others in silhouette on the highest catwalk, leaning over the railing. "You all right?"

He hefted Zeke by his shirt to keep his unconscious body out of the water. "Better than him! What is this place?"

Kordi swept the beam downward, giving Lincoln a general impression of the room. The catwalks led down from the level of the Dome floor to the flooded chamber he stood in. The water was murky. The medical supplies Zeke had taken and other bits of garbage floated in it. And ahead of him, on the opposite side from the catwalks...

"Holy shit," Lincoln whispered.

The chamber opened onto a low, arched tunnel that led away into pitch black. Pipes and thick ductwork lay along the top, and water covered the bottom half as far as he could see in the slanted beam of the flashlight, leaving only a misty air pocket along the top. It looked hellishly claustrophobic.

Kordi and several others came down the metal trellis behind him and splashed into the water. "It is some kind of maintenance tunnel beneath the center." When he reached Lincoln's side, he shone the flashlight down the rounded tube. It illuminated several branch-offs further along, but even the strong beam wasn't enough to reach whatever end the tunnel met. "It must run into the sewer somewhere along the way. Either that, or all that flooding is seeping through the water table and beneath the structure itself. God, if it rises anymore in here, we could lose the entire Dome."

"One thing at a time, Doc." Two of the people that came down with Kordi took Zeke and carried him out. Several others went about gathering up the medical supplies before they floated away. "What'd you do with the other one?"

"Our large, next-in-line friend was more than happy to keep him subdued. I offered him the gun, but he seemed content to sit on him."

Lincoln snorted. He took a few steps past Kordi toward the staircase out of this watery pit, but the doctor put a hand on his shoulder. "You did good here, young man."

"No problem."

"You asked me a second ago if I thought these sick people could die. There's no way of telling that just yet. But I think the real danger at this point is people starting to *believe* they could die from it. Do you understand what I mean?"

"You're talking about the Dumb Twins here, right?"

"That's right." Kordi bit the inside of his cheek. "What I said to your friend is still true, you know. This is exactly the sort of anarchy I feared. These people are desperate for some authority, for law, for something to remind them they still live in a civilization. And it doesn't have to be an officer that gives them that."

A smirk tugged Lincoln's mouth to one side. "You sayin I'm the man for that job?"

"I don't see too many other people stepping up to do what you just did."

Lincoln shook his head. Would this man still be asking him to do something like this if he knew Lincoln had been leading an organized looting less than twenty-four hours before? That he'd shot and killed one person; maybe two, if the pig from last night hadn't made it? "What about you, Doc? They already know you."

"I have my hands full. I have someone that's about to start giving out medication for me so I can make rounds on the floor. I can't do all that and keep the peace at the same time."

Lincoln started up the stairs. "Sorry Doc. I got other people that need me, and I don't think I'm gonna be stickin around too much longer. Nobody's gonna listen to a nigga gangbanger anyway."

When he pushed back through the door and stepped into the sunlit corridor, he met applause from a huge crowd blocking both sides of the hall as far as he could see. He smiled awkwardly and held up a hand. It was more attention than he'd ever gotten for anything in his life. He found it a little embarrassing.

He heard Mac in his ear, telling him he could leave this life, if he wanted.

"In a situation like this, people can be whoever they want," Kordi whispered over his shoulder as the applause died down. "And no one is going to need you more than the people right here in this building."

Lincoln Briggs: Sheriff. The idea was so stupid he smiled. Then Mr. Kim flashed through his head, those bullets tearing open the Korean's narrow chest, and the smile faded.

"I just don't know, man..."

"I think there's even some two-way radios we can use in the business office."

Lincoln laughed. "Well, if it's like that Doc...okay. I'll be the law round these parts."

WHITNEY +17:20

The rain went full throttle on Hernie and Mr. Carter soon after leaving the old man's home, and they were drenched to the bone in minutes. Their previously cheerful walk became a forced march, but Hernie was just glad the wind wasn't as severe as the previous night.

He kept his head down and followed close behind his new friend, trying to ignore the constant ache in his throat and the fire in his upper back where he'd been shot. As much as he trusted Mr. Carter, he wasn't entirely convinced the old man hadn't been working with the agents from the seawall, and that one or more of the feverish holes across his back didn't have a tracking device in it. He checked over his shoulder constantly, looking for dark figures to come sweeping out of the rain.

And he looked for Hatch, of course. The dog's absence made his other pains all the worse.

They left the suburbs behind and passed through downtown. The empty streets were frightening. Hernie could usually find food and shelter here, or, at the very least, sit and watch people go by and pretend he wasn't alone in the world. Now the sidewalks were vacant, save for the few folks they glimpsed on adjacent blocks, all headed in the same direction. The rain formed a raging torrent in the gutters which overflowed onto the sidewalk. They were forced to slosh through ankle deep water once more.

As afternoon eroded and darkened somewhere above the layer of relentless clouds, they turned right past a bank building and caught a sliver of the Dome on the horizon.

"That's it!" Mr. Carter shouted. "We can be there before dark!" The rain made it hard to hear him, but with the mask-thingy over his mouth, it was nearly impossible. Hernie wished he would take it off sometimes, but he didn't want his new friend—his only friend—to get sick.

Not sick like him, anyway. Hernie tried to answer, but coughed instead, coughed so hard he saw two of everything. He bent over with the force of it, wet hair falling in his face, rain streaking down his forehead into his eyes. Mr. Carter pounded him on the back till it was under control.

"Hernie, how do you feel?"

"Not...too good."

"Just a little further, okay? When we get there, we can get you dry, and someplace warm to sleep. Just hold on!"

"Okay." Hernie wanted to believe this, but even he could hear the desperate hope every time Mr. Carter made these claims.

The buildings along both sides of the road became seamless commercial blocks, stores crammed together with little space in between. Their storefronts faced the opposite direction however, and they saw only rear exits which opened onto this narrow street to give access to dumpsters. The land sloped steeply downhill as the Dome got closer, and Hernie had to fight to keep his footing as rainwater sluiced past them in fast waves. He walked with his head down and arms around his aching body and almost ran into his companion before he realized Mr. Carter had come to a stop.

The street turned into an open four-story parking garage for the downtown area ahead. It blocked the entire passage, the right side edged up against a retaining wall that formed the base of a building high above them, the left lost behind a three-story shopping concourse that the garage wall lay flush with, giving access to each level. A billboard for an action movie called *Killing Blow* looked down on them. The land sloped even sharper, a short ramp down to the first floor of the garage, built in a concrete pit partially below ground level.

Hernie peeked around Mr. Carter's side and down the ramp. The entire lower floor of the structure had flooded. Just a few yards ahead of them, the rain flowed into a dark lake that left only a few feet of clearance between the top of the water and the bottom of the second level of the parking structure.

It looked like a cave. A wet, concrete cave.

Mr. Carter knelt and looked into that gap under the second floor. "I...I think it's open on the other side, too. We can cross it!"

"No!" Hernie clutched his arm as he stood up. "No, no, please Mr. Carter, I can't go in there! I can't swim!"

"You're not gonna have to swim, Hernie! It can't be that deep! If I thought it was over our heads, then I couldn't go in with this!" He thumped the clear plastic mask over the lower half of his face.

"But I can't, I'm *scared* of water! Can't we just find another way?" Even as he said this, he looked around. There hadn't been a turnoff to this street for a while. It seemed the whole reason for its existence was to lead shoppers into the garage.

"It's gonna take us a lot longer to backtrack! The Dome is *right there*, right on the other side!" He pointed, and Hernie realized he could see the Civic Center through the open back of the second and third floors of the garage. "The whole thing couldn't be wider than ten car rows! C'mon, we'll just wade through and be done with it! We can't get any wetter than we already are!"

Hernie shook his head. He wanted to pull free, to run away from Mr. Carter and all that inky water under there and look for his dog, but that soothing voice in his head was telling him that was a bad idea.

"Hernie...twenty-four hours ago, I was terrified of a puddle in my living room floor. If *I* can do this, trust me, you can too."

"Will you…hold my hand?"

After a second's hesitation, Mr. Carter reached down and grabbed Hernie's wrist. "All the way across!"

They walked forward, down the ramp toward the admittance for the garage. The black maw opened to swallow them. Mr. Carter splashed first one foot and then the other into the water. It rose almost immediately past his ankles, shins, knees and up to his crotch. He held his hands out of it, looking like a tightrope walker, and tugged on Hernie until he reluctantly followed.

The water was freezing, bringing shivers and making the back of Hernie's throat feel even worse, but he shuffled on, keeping the sole of each boot in constant contact with the ground. He could still feel the smooth tarmac beneath him, but he was scared something down there would trip him.

They were almost directly between the two concrete pillars marking the opening of the structure when Mr. Carter yelped and jumped back against Hernie, nearly causing an accident right in his pants.

"*What is it?*"

Mr. Carter blew air into his mask in a quick exhalation. "The damn gate bar."

He lifted one leg up, swung it over, and then did the same with the other. Hernie came forward until he felt the padded obstruction against his thighs, then stepped over also.

The murky afternoon light and drum of the rain dropped away once they were beneath the garage overhang. The shade held a muggy gloom. The sound of dripping water echoed from all directions. Hernie's heart knocked against his ribcage as they continued forward, still on a decline. The water level crept upward, past his waist and chest, stinging against the wounds on his back. Now Mr. Carter had his arms held straight up above his head. He had explained his fear of germs and, though Hernie thought it was silly at the time (not nearly as rational as being afraid of government agents) he also kept his free hand above the water.

Finally, the surface tickled his armpits.

Reminding him that he couldn't swim.

"Mr. *Carter!*" Each syllable stuttery with cold.

"Just a little farther!" Mr. Carter, who was several inches short-er than him even walking on his toes, had his head held back to keep the mask above water. He gave up on keeping his hands dry and brought them—and Hernie's—down for splashing balance. "I think it's bottoming out!"

The ground leveled as they reached the floor of the garage. The water topped off close to Hernie's shoulders and the shelf of Mr. Carter's jaw.

Now they just had to walk through to the other side.

"Aw God!" Mr. Carter moaned. "C'mon, Hernie, *let's go!*"

They continued. After Hernie's eyes adjusted, he was able to pick out the roofs of several SUV's parked around them, the lug-gage racks poking up like twisted fingers. Mr. Carter grunted as he banged into a smaller, submerged automobile, and they skirted around it into the next row.

"We're almost there. Can't be too much farther." Mr. Carter seemed to be talking to himself again. Now that Hernie saw he didn't have to swim, this wasn't so terrible. The darkness was bad, so dense it was more like fog, but if it got too scary, he only had to close his eyes and let Mr. Carter lead him.

They continued in this fashion, step after agonizing step, weav-ing their way through vehicles left when Whitney blew through. Or maybe these people had parked them here hoping the garage would protect them. At one point, Hernie dared to slit his eyes open and was delighted to see the blackness in front of them had brightened. They must be close to the end.

Behind them, there was a huge splash.

A tidal wave washed over them a split second later. Mr. Carter made a gasping noise and hopped a little to keep his mask above water.

"What was that?" Hernie whispered. He looked in the direction he thought the noise and wave came from, but the dark hadn't gone away, only circled around to their backs to lie in wait.

"Sounded like a cannonball in the deep end of the pool."

A noise echoed across the underground parking structure. Hernie didn't possess the vocabulary to describe it, but if he wanted to imi-tate such a noise, he would produce a warbling note while flopping his tongue against the roof of his mouth. It made him feel uncomfortable, even afraid, although he had no idea why that should be.

"Woah." Mr. Carter's voice was a gruff whisper under the mask. "You hear that, Hernie ol' buddy? Cause, in this case, it's okay to tell me I'm going insane."

"Uh huh."

"'Uh huh' as in you heard it, or 'uh huh' as in I'm crazy?"

"I heard it!"

"Okay, *specifics*, my man: they're not just for nerds anymore!"

The noise came again, accompanied by the sound of wet splashes. Something was coming right at them.

"Come on!"

Hernie's hand was jerked as Mr. Carter bolted, and he almost lost his grip. They moved through the garage in liquidy slow motion, bumping into other vehicles. Water splashed across his face every time he tried to get a breath. When that noise came again, he looked back, and, for just a second, thought he saw something silhouetted on top of one of those SUV's, a figure crouched low and watching...

"Oh shit!"

Hernie fell against Mr. Carter, his head sliding below water level before he could jerk upright. They'd reached the back of the parking garage, had actually emerged from the overhang of the second floor into the pound of rain.

Instead of another gate, a concrete wall sat in front of them, leaving a narrow walkway three or four feet wide around the perimeter of the garage. Hernie looked up. He could see sky between the wall and the overhang, but the barrier reached as high as the second story, far too much for them to climb over.

They were trapped.

The splashing got louder, along with another, higher-pitched squeal growing beneath it. Hernie backed up against the wall and stared into the garage.

Something moved in there. Mr. Carter squeezed Hernie's hand hard enough to hurt, but that was okay, because he was applying at least as much pressure right back.

Hernie saw them even before they entered the light. Because of their eyes.

Hundreds of tiny, red eyes.

A plague of rats came boiling out, furry bodies jostling over and under one another as they swam, their voices blending into one unharmonious shriek. The creatures swarmed toward them. Hernie let go of Mr. Carter's hand to fend them off.

Tiny claws and gnawing teeth dug into his fingers, his palms, and then up his arms. He shook them off, but for every one flung back into the water, three more paddled forward to take its place. They surrounded him, everywhere he turned, until the entire surface of the water teemed with angry rodents. He heard Mr. Carter shouting, but now they'd reached Hernie's face, got tangled in his long hair, fought to be king of the mountain on top of his head.

Terror overrode every thought. He opened his mouth to scream and felt squirming limbs fill it.

Hernie fought to get a breath as the weight of the rats pushed him beneath the water.

WHITNEY +17:28

"Thought this might be a good place ta start fishin fer ya," Sturney said, when Ellis still hadn't found his tongue after fifteen seconds of stunned silence. He showed off his big, pearly teeth, flecks of peppermint visible in the crevices. "Guess I was right, cause I dropped my line and, lo and behold, pulled me out a blackfish less'n twenty minutes later."

The burly officer stood facing him under the awning beyond the turnstile, just out of the rain. To Ellis' left, more refugees made progress past them through the door he'd just exited.

"Let me…" He cleared his throat, and tried again. "Let me go, Sturney."

He tried to step around the man and found his path blocked.

"You're not goin nowhere. Yer under arrest for the murder of Harold McNamara."

"W-what? McNamara's dead?"

"Shot durin yer escape. Don't pretend like ya don't know."

"*I* didn't shoot him!"

"Mebbe not. Mebbe it was one of those new friends ya made

last night. Who were they, by the way?"

"Just some punk teenage looters! And you know damn well you weren't trying to arrest us!"

Sturney chewed, cracking another piece of candy, and gave a polite nod and smile to the line of passing hurricane survivors. "Keep yer goddamn voice down so this can stay between us, all right? Be a shame if somebody else had ta get hurt cause yer a chickenshit, backstabbin scab."

Ellis lifted a shaking hand to rub at his jaw.

"Now...those gangbangers inside, Wright? What about Charlie, where's he?"

The news that Charlie was all right—or at least that he'd escaped them last night also—was a fast shot of relief, but Ellis didn't let it show. "It doesn't matter. I already reported in," he lied. "I told them everything, Sturney. About what you did to Billy. They're on their way here now."

He expected fear to cross the man's thick jowls, got amusement instead. Sturney lifted his nostrils and sucked in a great rush of air. "Whew, boy, *that* bullshit is thick! Every phone in the city is down, Wright. Radios don't even work 'cept on local channels. Figure I got more'n enough time to square away our business fer good." He reached out, clamped down on Ellis' shoulder. "C'mon. Let's take a walk."

Ellis shoved his hand away. "No."

Sturney rested a casual palm on the pistol butt at his hip. "Then I'll just have ta make ya. And I gotta tell ya...I don't mind that at all."

"What are you gonna do, shoot me in front of all these people? I'm a cop!"

"Are ya?" Sturney gaped at him up and down like a Playboy centerfold. "Cause ya sure don't look like one right now. Just look like another poor nigger. Ya think if I did put a bullet through yer head right now, any of these sad sacks would bat an eyelash?"

Ellis glanced over at the people passing them. The few whose weary eyes even lifted from the ground to take them in looked at Sturney like he was the returning Messiah. That badge represented security to them, a dam against chaos. It meant someone was looking out for them when God had turned His eyes away.

Even if it was worn by a murderer.

He thought of what he'd said to Lincoln and felt ashamed. By refusing the job, he'd left Port Allen in the hands of men like this.

"*S-someone* will find out, Sturney. What you did to Billy Dunham. And you'll pay."

"I've heard about all outta you I'm gonna."

He grabbed Ellis' left forearm and stepped around behind him, attempting to pull the appendage into a painful hold. Ellis brought his elbow up, subverting the move and clipping Sturney under the chin. He turned to run, and received a brutal blow to the kidney.

He heard the click of handcuffs. Metal pressure on his wrist.

"You have the right to remain silent," Sturney said loudly, more for the benefit of his audience than his prisoner.

"Officer, officer!" A little old lady fall upon Sturney, clutching at his arms and chest. "Please officer, you have to help me, my husband is missing!"

"I'm a little busy here, ma'am!"

The hysterical old lady shoved between them, one hand on the collar of Sturney's shirt, the other clutching a handful of his cheek to get his attention. "Help me, help me, I don't know what to do!"

"Get the fuck outta my face, ya old bat!"

Ellis jerked, his arms ripping free from Sturney's grip during his distraction. The handcuffs dangled from only one hand. He charged into the rain.

Sturney was after him as soon as he could shove the old woman out of the way. Footfalls pounded across the wet pavement behind him, but the other cop didn't bother to yell halt.

Ellis wasn't too much more fit than his pursuer, but he had weight on his side. Adrenaline coursed through him, and when he glanced back, he saw there was no way for Sturney to catch him unless he opened fire in front of all the people milling outside the Dome.

Then he hit a patch of oil-slicked water on the parking lot tarmac and his foot slid out from under him.

Ellis fell hard on his stomach, bracing himself with his hands to avoid smashing his face. That was immediately undone, however, when Sturney landed on him a few seconds later, bringing a knee down on his spine and shoving his head to the concrete. Ellis shouted in pain.

"You make me...run again...and what's comin...is gonna be a lot more painful than it has to be," Sturney panted. He yanked Ellis' arms behind him once more and snapped the cuffs into place on his other wrist. "Git up, damn it."

Ellis was manhandled to his feet. His back was agony, his side still throbbing. Sturney pulled his radio. "I got Wright in custody. Both of ya, meet me back at the cars." He gave Ellis a shove to get him moving and kept a hand around the cuff chain.

They crossed the crowded parking lot, moving around the curve of the civic center toward the outlying spaces. Two patrol cars sat side-by-side, alone in the middle of rain-swept concrete.

Two other figures were crossing the lot on a path to meet them, wearing orange police slickers, the same type Ellis and Charlie had abandoned the night before. Even shrouded at a distance, he recognized the forms of Drano Jenkins and JD Myers. From the direction they came, it appeared they'd been staking out all the ways into the building.

Sturney and Ellis reached the cars first. Sturney opened the back door of the closest one and shoved him inside, banging his head on the door frame and giving him a kick to the ass for good measure. Ellis squirmed onto his sore back and looked up at him in silence while Jenkins and Myers came to stand beside their leader.

Drano was just as pristine as Sturney, but the younger cop looked like reheated death beneath the hood of his slicker. Dark circles sat under his watery eyes, and he coughed into his hand every few seconds. Just like Heather. Ellis realized he would probably never see her or her garrulous husband again.

"Let's do him now." Drano's greedy eyes bored into him.

"Hold yer goddamn horses and let's not get hasty. That's how we got in this mess in tha first place. We got one of 'em here, but there's still four loose ends floatin around out there. Loose ends it'll be a lot easier to tie off now than when they're in a courtroom."

Ellis lashed out with his foot, coming pitifully short of hitting any of his captors. "Leave them alone, they had nothing to do with this!"

Sturney knelt in the open car door, coming to eye level with Ellis. Rain coursed down his face, into his eyes, but he never blinked.

"They're witnesses, same as you. Ya made them into witnesses with yer tattletalin. Now, tell me who they were."

"I don't know!"

Sturney rose and leaned over him in the backseat, their faces coming close enough for Ellis to smell that sickly sweet scent of peppermint wafting from the other man's gullet. His shadow blocked out the weak afternoon sunlight. One hand reached beneath Ellis.

"Hey, what are you doing? Stop it!"

Sturney found his cuffed wrists, and his palm encircled the pinky of Ellis' left hand. The officer wrenched. There was a brittle snap, and the world turned into a blurry red film through which every detail of the day seemed too sharp. Ellis wailed.

"Now," Sturney said, once he'd quieted, "I'm willin to believe ya might not know where Charlie and those other two boys are. You sure left 'em fast enough. But last I saw, you and that one darkie were makin fer the hills together. I already figgered they must be X-Dawgs. Who is he? What's his name?"

Ellis bit down on his quivering lip, tears rolling across both sides of his face, and closed his eyes.

"Ya got nine more, Wright, then we start on the toes."

"Lincoln. His name's Lincoln Briggs."

"What happened to him? He inside the Dome?"

"No. He...he ran off during the storm last night. Left me."

The grin on Sturney's face this time was of the variety usually reserved for lottery winners. "See...*that* I'm willin to believe too. Ya save his life, and he abandons ya. Yes sir, another negro with no allegiance or honor—even for his own kind—don't surprise me one little bit. All the same...I think we'll go have a look-see."

He stood and slammed the car door, sealing Ellis in the rear of the cruiser.

"No, wait!" Ellis thrashed upright, banging his shoulder against the door. They ignored him. He put his ear to the glass and strained to hear their conversation.

"We're gonna make a quick run through the Dome, look fer the others, and then get him outta here."

Myers turned his head and hacked onto his shoulder. "I don't know Sturn, I really don't feel so hot. I'm dizzy as hell. I need a doctor."

"That's gonna have to wait a little longer, JD. But I'll tell ya what, I don't like leavin him here by hisself. Why don't you stick around to watch 'im." Sturney turned to Drano. "You take the west side, I'll take the north. Be careful ya don't get mobbed. These folks're hungry fer some authority." The two of them walked away from the car, splitting in opposite directions.

Myers opened the driver's door of the cruiser, crawled inside, and closed it. He slumped across both seats, head on the passenger side, legs curled up in front of the steering wheel.

"Myers, listen to me, you can't let them do this!"

"Shut up Wright, just…shut up."

"They can't contain this anymore! They'll never find Charlie or those kids, so there's no point in killing me! If you help them do it, you're gonna be in this just as deep as they are!"

Myers covered his ears with his hands like a child, gave another deep, phlegmy rattle, and closed his eyes.

WHITNEY +17:46

It was Chris who spotted the ladder when the streets flooded.

Maryland thought he and his sister made a wonderful addition to their growing natural disaster family. Tangela jabbered on at her constantly about anything that crossed her mind—steering clear of any topics related to her mother, she noticed—while Chris debated the merits of *Return of the Native* and other books from his advanced English class with Tom. Both were precocious and outgoing children, the kind Maryland always envisioned having herself one day, although how she ever figured to do so with Bryce as daddy material (hell, with Bryce as *genetic* material) she didn't know. Now that she thought about it, she realized this part of the fantasy was always a blank, even during their early years together.

The rain from the new band of storms grew fierce, nowhere near as bad as its big sister Whitney, but frightening in its own right. The roads north of downtown became a maze as more and more of their paths were blocked. Every low-lying area filled up, water creeping down each street and connecting at the intersections like blood in sluggish arteries. At first, they walked with several other groups from the riot, but as the weather worsened, they dropped off one-by-one, seeking shelter in the surrounding buildings, until the five of them were all alone again.

"I'm not stopping!" This from Gerald of course, shouting over the downpour as he shivered in his soaked shorts and t-shirt. "We're almost there, right? Who knows how long we'll be stuck here if we don't get on one of those transports!"

They stood under the torn metal awning of a multi-story strip mall to have this debate, where an upraised concrete entrance kept them elevated. The street in front of them held nearly two feet of rushing water, and appeared to get even deeper toward the next intersection. After the tidal wave that almost carried her into the gorge last night, Maryland had to remind herself that this kind of flash-flooding could be just as dangerous, especially for the kids. The Dome lay somewhere to the southeast, she was almost sure of it, but unless they took a detour due south to search for a higher ground approach, they would have to push through this mess.

"Tom can't stay out in this forever!" She put a hand on the Englishman's shoulder, whose eyes were so sunken they almost floated in their sockets. "And Tangela's cough is getting worse!"

"Then go find someplace to tuck them in and feed them chicken noodle soup! When are you going to get it? We're not chained together here! But if you stop, this is where I leave you!"

"He's right, I don't want to be a bother," Tom said.

"He's never been right about anything in his miserable life!" She pulled wet hair out of her face and tucked it behind both ears before turning back to Gerald. "If memory serves, wiseass, you had a chance to ditch us after leaving me for dead, and *you're* the one who followed us like a little lost puppy dog!"

"Don't flatter yourself, we're all headed in the same direction here!" He smirked. Why did the pretty ones always know how to smirk so effectively? "Unless you think I'm gonna wait while you play nursemaid to Tommy and the kindergarteners! Then we're going our separate ways in a hurry!"

She stood rigid and snarled in his face, "God, I *loathe* you!"

"Right back at you, rich bitch!"

"*Rich bitch?* What the hell makes you think I'm a rich bitch?"

"I could smell money on you the second we met!"

"Funny, I didn't think you'd be able to smell anything with all that water up your nose!"

"Jesus, you women never let anything go, do you? 'I made the bed, I cooked dinner…*I saved your life and then you abandoned me in the middle of a firefight!*'"

"Leave her alone!" Tangela pushed between them, hands on hips, glaring up at Gerald.

"This isn't helping anything," Tom groaned.

"Hey," Chris interrupted, and, when they continued to bicker, "Hey, check it out!" They all looked at where he pointed: a fire escape ladder bolted to the brick wall of a building beside them.

"That's great, kid." Gerald waved him away. "You use the nice ladder and let the adults talk."

"No, we can *all* use it." The boy's tone—patient and condescending at the same time—almost made Maryland laugh. "All these buildings through here are connected, or have narrow alleys between them. So we travel on the rooftops as far as we can, since the streets are too deep. At the very least, we might be able to see how much farther it is to the Dome."

Tom smiled and nodded. "Some good thinking, son. I'm willing to give it a try."

"Me too." Maryland blinked wet eyelashes rapidly at Gerald. "Not bad for a kindergartener. But please feel free, as the band once said, to go your own way."

It took them a while just to get up the slippery ladder, Maryland and the kids first, followed by Gerald and then Tom. She was afraid her friend wouldn't be able to make it. He wheezed and whooped by the time he reached the top, and she and Chris had to drag him onto the wet gravel rooftop.

"There it is!" she yelled in delight, once they had a chance to take in the scenery from their new vantage point. The curve of the Port Allen Civic Center was visible just a few blocks away. The sense of accomplishment at actually leading them in the right direction was more exhilarating than anything she'd experienced in the last decade. Tom gave her a pat on the back and she put an arm around his narrow shoulders.

"Will our daddy be there?" Tangela asked.

Maryland shot an uncomfortable look at her brother. "Well, sweetie, I don't—"

"No, Tanj," Chris cut in. "He's probably still outside the city. But they'll take us to him."

It was easier going now that they weren't wading, even with the rain slapping at them. They crept along the rooftops as far east as possible, then hopped across a foot wide gap between the edge of one roof and the overhang of the next, passing Tangela along. A two-foot high brick wall surrounded this one at its edges. A billboard for that new flick *Killing Blow* sat next to the building, meant to catch the eye of those passing by the mall but, from their perspective, it appeared that hammy star Derek Mahoney was peeking over the edge of the roof at them. They reached a corner that brought them parallel to the third floor of a huge parking structure.

"This is it." A mutter of thunder emphasized Gerald's words. "We get over to that garage, find a way down on the other side, and that Dome place is just up the street."

"Then show me some wings, Wonder Boy, cause the edge of that thing is a good ten feet away."

He pointed further along the rooftop. "Don't need wings when I can walk."

She leaned over the edge of the mall, peering through the rain into the narrow space between the garage and the building. The second floor of the parking garage was connected to the mall by way of a covered metal footbridge. A curved glass ceiling stretched over the top and sides, making the walkway into a see-through pipe.

"What, you want to break into the mall and walk across the bridge?"

"Not across it. On *top* of it."

She stared at him until she understood what he meant, and then whipped her head around to the bridge again. The top of the glass tube reached up to just a few feet below the top of the roof's wall. Rain ran off its sloped sides in sheets.

"Are you suicidal, we can't walk across that!"

"Why not?"

"Look at it, it's barely two feet wide, and slippery as hell!"

"I haven't seen any way to get into the mall from up here! So it's either that, or look for another ladder to get down, and go back through the streets."

She slumped against the short brick wall and sighed. The rain had slowed to a depressing trickle, or she would never even have considered it. When she looked back up, it was at the rest of her group. "You guys think you can do it?"

"No problem," Chris answered.

Tom shivered, then coughed. "We d-don't really have a choice. Let's not dawdle debating the issue. Sooner begun, sooner done."

"That-a-boy, Tommy. I'll tell you what." Gerald swept Tangela up and slung her onto his back, allowing her to cling to his neck with a nervous giggle. "If it makes you feel any better, I'll even carry the girl scout here across."

"Damn it, be careful with her!" Maryland shouted.

Gerald held the girl in place with one hand, clutching the point where her wrists crossed under his chin. He climbed over the ledge, sliding carefully down until the toes of his sneakers touched the glass surface, and crossed slowly and deliberately, sliding each foot forward a little at a time. When they reached the far side, he lowered Tangela down from the glass roof to the concrete floor of the garage and then jumped down himself.

"Piece of cake!" he shouted. The girl gave a huge wave.

Chris slung a leg over. "I'll go next."

"No," she snapped. "You're going with me. I want to be able to hold on to you. Tom, do you want to go before us?"

"Last, please." He stared at the glass walkway warily.

Chris lowered himself down from the edge of the building, and she followed. The distance to the ground telescoped once she was off the stable surface of the roof. She looked away. Derek Mahoney's lopsided smile from the billboard mocked her, and that was no better. She decided to concentrate on what was right in front of her. The glass squeaked and squelched beneath her shoes.

She almost couldn't let go of the rooftop. Chris took hold of her elbow, tugged at her gently. She finally released the wall and sank her fingers into his narrow shoulders.

The boy led the way, him with his lower center of gravity, and after they'd gone what felt like a football length, she chanced a look back. Tom scooted off onto the walkway just a couple of feet behind them and shuffled in their wake, arms held out for balance, like an elderly surfer.

After that, she kept her eyes on the end of the walkway, which inched ever closer.

"Almost there," Chris muttered. "We got this. We got this."

A gust of wind hit them hard. Up here, with nothing to hold on to, her imagination turned it into a bulldozer. Maryland's left foot rocketed down the slick side of the curved glass. Her lungs locked as she lost her balance and felt gravity take over.

As tightly as she clung to him, it might have been the end for both of them, if Chris hadn't reacted with unnatural speed. As soon as she jerked, the boy surged forward, pulling her with him. He dove for the end of the walkway. Instead of her dragging them both off the side, his weight served as a counter, throwing them full out across the glass onto their stomachs. The air whooshed out of her. For a moment, Maryland's legs kicked free in midair—*please God, please don't let me die next to a billboard for a summer popcorn flick*—and then she rolled back onto the slick surface and fought for a breath.

Tangela screamed, Tom yelled, but all she could do was hold still until her lungs worked again. Chris dragged her toward the garage side, chanting something that sounded like, "Not again, no, God, not again!"

She crawled this time. Chris jumped from the walkway glass onto the parking structure. She tumbled after him and lay curled up on the cold concrete while they helped Tom down.

They gathered around, demanding to know if she was okay. She told them she was to get them to leave her alone, but Jesus, she was tired of this, tired of Maryland's Adventures in the Real World, and she couldn't for the life of her remember why she'd left that big, beautiful mansion in the first place. Had that really been *her* that told Bryce their things didn't matter? She couldn't do it anymore, if this was what life was like when you didn't have money—being wet and miserable and insulted and punched in the face and shot at and almost burned to death and falling from rooftops—then she would crawl back to Château Decatur and beg to be forgiven for having the audacity to expect her husband to be faithful to her.

That's when she decided. She would get the rest of them to the Dome, make sure Tom and the kids were cared for, and then...she would go back. She would have to beg, and spend the next year making up for the loss of the Bentley with endless blowjobs. That awoken Amazon in her brain screamed in rage at the idea, but even that tough bitch sounded damn tired.

It was this surrender that got her back on her feet, not their spurring. She followed them through the garage in a beaten trance, Tangela holding her hand and Tom fawning over her. When they heard the screams from below, she broke into a run with the others, but the only thought in her head was of soft beds and stocked pantries and closets full of dry clothes.

WHITNEY +17:57

The mask kept the disgusting vermin out of Carter's mouth, but the suckers climbed up his head in their panicked need to find high ground. They writhed on his crown like a living toupee. Raked furrows in his scalp. Bit his ears. Filled every wound with germs there weren't even names for.

And, in a supreme twist that had to be his imagination, they all sounded like they were *coughing*.

Bubonic, oh god, it's bubonic plague and black death and probably hepatitis C all rolled into one.

Carter kept his eyes closed and flailed, lost to terror and disgust, bucking off the ones without a firm grip and ripping away the ones that did with his bare hands to toss back like a catch-and-release fisherman. Except these fish just kept coming right back. His toes could barely touch bottom, and the few parts sticking out of the water were layered with jittering fleshbags. Their tinny shrieks filled his brain.

Nowhere to go, no place to escape, but to completely submerge.

He couldn't take the mask under. This fact stayed imprinted even in his full-out panic. The rain hadn't seemed to hurt it, but dipping it in water? Probably ill-advised. It wasn't some two-cent snorkel, after all. And if he lost the rebreather, he had a feeling the tide of phobias he'd managed to keep at bay would come spilling out and leave him a quivering ball.

Either that, or these Nimh-rods are gonna whittle you down till there's nothing left, Cart.

He sucked in a hurried breath, preparing to plunge beneath the surface.

"Hey!"

Carter froze.

"Hey, give us your hand!"

He shoved an arm across his brow to clear his vision, dislodging several rats fighting for a perch on the nose of the mask, and looked up.

A row of people leaned over the edge of the second floor like spectators at a dogfight, staring down with hands outstretched.

"Hernie!" He'd lost track of the guy. He spun in circles as more rats closed in.

Something clawed at his waist.

Carter yelped as Hernie surfaced beside him, shoving rodents away on miniature wave crests.

"Please, please, Mr. Carter, don't let them get me, don't let them get me, dontletthemg—!"

"Hernie, *stop!* Look up!"

The homeless man continued freaking out, so Carter grabbed his arm and lifted it out of the water for him. When he felt contact with the people above, Hernie finally stopped yowling and clutched at the offered hands.

Hernie was yanked up and out. Carter watched him disappear over the lip of the next floor before he went back to playing Whack-a-Mole with the enclosing rodents.

"Here, here! C'mon buddy!"

The man holding out his hands was probably about his age, but far more muscular. Carter grabbed at him, felt himself lifted. Rats fell away from him in clumps, hanging to his clothes and a few with claws sunk into his flesh, determined not to give up their ride to safety. He kicked, causing his body to rock in their grasp.

His stomach slammed into the concrete ledge when he swung back, pushing air out of his lungs. Carter lifted a leg up, found leverage, and tumbled forward, rolling onto his rescuers.

He came to rest on his forearms, with a body under him. He looked up and found himself face-to-face with a woman.

She was thin, with wet auburn hair hanging in her face. Hazel eyes. Nice cheekbones, besides the slight puffiness to her right eye. He couldn't get a look at the rest of the package at the moment, but her breasts felt more than adequate pressed against him. Not supermodel material, but considering she was the first woman besides Rosa and his mother he'd seen in person in a decade, and the first one he'd been within kissing distance of since his last girlfriend in college…

An eyebrow raised, surprised at first, and then, as seconds dragged, her lips pursed. Carter opened his mouth, never wanting a perfect opening line so bad in his life.

He was beaten to the punch as a hefty rat squeezed out from between their bodies and scampered over her face.

Then they were both yelling and rolling across the floor of the garage, her beating at her own head like a mental patient. He sat up and smacked the creature off her. It tumbled across the concrete and then skittered around a pillar and out of sight.

She glared at him. He grinned sheepishly and shrugged. "Sometimes Willard just doesn't listen."

Her angry expression didn't change.

"You know…*Willard…rat…*"

"Yeah. I got it, thanks. Just didn't feel like joking after having my face nearly clawed off. And for the record, Willard was the name of the *guy*, not the rat."

Carter felt the king of all dopey grins tug at his cheeks. No woman had ever bested him at pop culture trivia.

He scrambled to his feet so he could help her. Her hand seemed to linger in his, but it could've been wishful thinking. Time seemed to have slowed down all of a sudden. "Um…I'm…heh…Carter Vance."

A sculpted eyebrow raised as she appraised him. "Are you sure?"

"Fairly."

"Maryland Williams. That's Gerald, Tom, Chris, and Tangela."

Carter peeled his gaze from her and gave the motley assemblage a quick wave. "Thanks for the assist. We really appreciate it, don't we Hernie?"

His sidekick still lay on the garage floor, shivering. "Please Mr. Carter, please don't make me go through there again."

He knelt and pulled Hernie to a sitting position. "Not in this lifetime, pal."

"Are they…" Hernie leaned forward and whispered, "…*government?*"

Carter looked around at their rescuers: Maryland, the athletic guy, an older man twice his age and half his weight, and the two black kids that stood peeking from behind him, eyeballing them suspiciously. "I think they're safe."

"What were you doing down there anyway?" the jock—Gerald, if he'd attached the names correctly—asked.

"Just trying to get through to the Dome."

The black boy took a step out from behind the older man he was using as a shield. "Were you…swimming under the water?"

"Huh?"

"That thing. On your face."

"Oh!" He touched the plastic surface of the mask and felt his cheeks redden. Carter glanced at Maryland, saw she was interested in this answer as well. They all were, he could feel their eyes, and, for the first time since he started having dizzy spells in public, he was embarrassed. "No, this is…you see…I have…uh…asthma."

"Mr. Carter's scared of germies." Hernie wrang out his new threads. "Like *really-really-real-real* scared."

"Thank you, Hernie. Yes, there's that too."

Gerald grunted. "Yeah, well, you're just lucky those big suckers didn't tear you apart."

Carter used the bottom of his wet t-shirt to dab at blood that flowed from nicks and scratches all over his hands. For a few minutes there, he'd actually forgotten that ever present fear, but now every inch of him burned with the bacteria that was even now building entire civilizations on his epidermis, like a billion needles poking at him. He forced himself to play it cool, but was helpless to stop his hands from rubbing compulsively at the wounds. "It wasn't for lack of trying. My kingdom for some Bactine."

The older guy, Tom, stood at the edge of the garage, coughing like a lifelong smoker. When he spoke, Carter did a double take at the British accent. This was just getting too weird. "Something certainly got to them, to cause them to swarm you like that."

Carter went to stand beside him, forcing his arms to his side and counting his steps to make sure they were even instead, a sort of mental disorder tradeoff. The rat pack had hit the parking garage wall, and were trying to claw their way up. Their squeals still sounded a little like chirping coughs to him. He noticed several of them floating dead in the water, and thought of the crows that had kamikaze'd him and Hernie back on the street.

"There was something down there!" Hernie cried. "We heard it, didn't we Mr. Carter?"

"We heard…I don't know what. Then those rats just came out of nowhere behind us." Another mental snapshot pinged in his head, one thrown at him entirely by the Lucid: the dark shadow in the hurricane-swept street the night before.

"They're on the run," Tom told them. "Rats are very instinctive, you know. They flee from danger well in advance. These were probably taking shelter from the storm in the rafters."

"And something caused them to abandon ship." Carter was getting this tingle in his stomach, the kind he usually got before the vertigo attacked, but he didn't think this had the same cause.

That noise, warbling through the garage.

"What did it sound like?" Chris asked suddenly. The kid's dark eyes were penetrating.

"Like this!" Hernie eagerly produced a sound like a Shiite woman's ululation.

"Is he all right?" Gerald asked. The question was pointed enough that Carter caught his drift.

"He's…a little challenged. Upstairs. But he's right. It sounded like Flipper on crack."

The boy was breathing hard.

"Chris, honey, what is it?" Maryland put a hand on his arm and he jumped.

"I…we…heard it before." He glanced at the little girl—his sister?—and said, "Cover your ears, Tanj."

She scowled but did as told.

"We found this person that had been…eaten."

"*Eaten?*" Carter echoed.

"What do you mean?" Maryland asked.

"A woman, just lying in the street, back where it was flooded. She was…cut open."

Either the story or his severe cough caused Tom to gag. "Good Lord."

Gerald laughed, a derisive, mean-spirited sound. Carter decided he didn't like the guy. He'd known too many like him throughout high school and college, the ones that always made his life a torment. "So we're gonna tell spook stories now? Should I light a campfire?"

Maryland rolled her eyes. "Christ, do you need a license to be that obnoxious?"

Carter suppressed a snicker of his own.

"How come we haven't heard about this before, huh?"

"Man, that was the least of what we saw before we ran into you guys." Chris gave a full-body shiver that Carter could identify with. "I just sort of forgot about it until he said that."

Maryland grabbed Tangela's hand and led her across the floor of the vacant garage. "Look, it was nice meeting you both, but we have to get going. We're on our way to the Dome also."

"I suppose we're taking the retard and the germophobe with us?" Gerald called after her. "What's next, a quadriplegic with a death wish?"

Carter's face burned beneath the rebreather.

"Feel free to ignore him. The rest of us do." Maryland flashed a tired smile over her shoulder, and those squeamish needles under Carter's flesh melted away.

The new group all trudged on, toward the painted arrows showing the way to the exit.

Hernie grabbed his hand. "I like them, Mr. Carter. Are we going with them?"

He took a long look at Maryland William's departing backside. "Sounds like a plan to me."

WHITNEY +18:08

It took Mac an hour of shuffling south along Port Allen's new eastern coastline—and stopping every time his muscles cramped—before the rainy streets opened onto the corner of the lot surrounding the Civic Center. His eyes widened. He had hoped for *someone*, at the very least a phone, but he was shocked to find a crowded parking lot and lines stretching from every entrance except the one where water led right up to the doorway. He limped through the tangle of cars to the end of the closest line.

"What's this for?" he asked aloud, to no one in particular.

"Waiting to get in," a man huddling under a torn umbrella answered. "Supposed to bus us out from here. And they have food inside."

"What 'bout a doc? There doctors inside?"

The guy looked him up and down, took in his hunched posture and swollen nose, and shrugged.

Mac continued up the outside of the line. "Yo, is there a doctor?" The loud words clawed at his raw throat, brought tears to his eyes. "Anyone a doc? My friend needs help!" No one answered. Most barely even glanced at him.

He charged forward, making his way to the front. They would listen when he shoved them aside. No way was he waiting to get in there, this was a medical emergency and...

A cop stood beside the door, scanning the faces of those that went through. Mac was just a few people back from the turnstile when he caught sight of the figure. At first he was excited, and then sudden caution made him drop back and duck behind a tight knit group just before the head swiveled toward him.

The face beneath the slicker was young and sallow, with dark circles under the eyes. Mac couldn't be a hundred percent sure—seeing as how he was cuffed and drowning at the time—but he thought this was one of the two who'd boxed them in around the patrol car last night. As he watched, the figure underwent a coughing fit even worse than Mac's, all while studying the faces of everyone that went through the turnstile with more than passing interest.

"Thought you said they'd be gone, Charlie," he whispered. The woman he was attempting to hide his massive frame behind shot him a look.

The line lurched, and with it went his cover. The cop would've seen him, if the radio at his collar hadn't crackled to life. He bent his head away to speak into it, then turned and started away, into the parking lot.

Mac watched him go, letting his gaze drift back to the door and whatever help lay inside. The clock in his head seemed to be flying, counting down the time Charlie had left. But if this really was one of the cops from last night, if they'd hung around just to keep looking...he could be the best shot at finding Lincoln.

Mac cut through the line, forced his aching legs to carry him across the lot. He set his path at a steeper angle, to bring him around the cop's far side but stay in his blind spot at the same time. Wherever he was headed, his direction carried him away from the curved outer shell of the building, and into the sea of cars. Mac kept low and followed.

The cop in the slicker made his way toward two patrol cars isolated at the far edge of the lot. With no cover, Mac was forced to wait and watch over the rusted hood of an ancient Cadillac. From the opposite direction came two other officers, one of them pushing a black man in handcuffs. Mac strained, but at this distance and with the clouds dampening the afternoon sunlight, it was impossible to tell who it was.

They threw the prisoner in the back of one of the cars. There was some talking, then some screaming. Then two of the cops started back toward the Dome and the third, the one that Mac had followed, got into the front seat and disappeared below the level of the window.

So where was the fourth?

Mac waited until the other two were lost in the crowds and then took off across the open stretch between him and the patrol cars. A muscle in his calf locked up hard after only a few yards, squeezing like a bear trap. He came to a halt and bit the inside of his cheek to keep from crying out. He limped on, bending over as he got closer to the patrol car, moving in a rough semicircle to come around behind the vehicle. Only when he was crouched next to the trunk did he take a minute to catch his breath and let the cramp ease.

The rain slackened, winding down to a light patter. Mac could hear no voices inside. He slowly rose up until he could see through the rear window.

The figure in the cage wasn't Lincoln; he could tell that from the back of the head alone. But when it turned, looking out the windows toward the civic center, he thought he knew who it was. The cop in the front must've been lying down across the seats, because Mac couldn't see him at all. He circled around to the rear door on the left, closest to the prisoner, and peered in.

The guy in the back seat jumped when Mac's face appeared in the window. His mouth opened but then clamped shut again, eyes flicking toward the front of the vehicle. Mac's suspicion about the prisoner's identity was correct: it was the other cop from last night, Charlie's partner, Elroy or Ellis or something, now stripped of his uniform. Mutual recognition bloomed in the other man's face.

Get me out! He mouthed the words large and slow on the other side of the glass.

Mac glanced around, toward the building. He moved to the front window. The pig in the front seat appeared to be in pretty bad shape. He lay on his right side, stretched out across the bench seat in his rain slicker, but every few seconds his body shivered in swift jerks. He looked as unconscious as Charlie had when Mac left him. Mac slid back to the rear door again, grasped the handle, and lifted it when the rain was at its hardest.

It came open with surprisingly little noise. Ellis squirmed, swinging his legs out, and slithered onto the wet pavement with his hands shackled behind him. Mac pushed the door closed enough to seal but not latch it. They knelt together beside the tire.

"Where's Links?"

"He's inside the Dome! They're going to look for him now!"

"Aw, shit!"

"They don't know for sure that he's in there, I...I refused to tell them!"

Mac saw the guilt written across the other man's face. "What did you tell them?"

"Nothing! They broke my finger and...!" His eyes widened. "Wait a minute, is *Charlie* in there?"

Now it was Mac's turn to squirm. He wiped rain out of his eyes, mostly to hide them. "No, he's...someplace safe."

"All right then, go get the handcuff keys!"

"From where?"

"Myers, he should have some!"

"What, the other fuckin cop? Nigga, you got us in enough trouble to last a lifetime, and you want me to go pickpocket that side of bacon?"

"I can't help like this! If you hurry, we can...we can...I don't know, do something!"

"*Something?* That's yo' plan? Ain't you General Patton?" Mac turned his head from side to side, cracking the joint there. This had gotten all messed up. He couldn't keep track of who he was supposed to save anymore or how he was supposed to go about doing it.

Lincoln first. Always been that way, always would be. That simplified things.

"Where the keys at?"

"He should have a set of universals in a pouch on his belt!"

Mac turned and pulled open the front door the same as he'd done the rear.

This time the dome light popped on. And these hinges squeaked. *Loud.* The sound probably wasn't enough to be heard over the rain, but to him it was a fire whistle.

But neither of these made a difference. The prone figure coughed, hoarse and dry, but still didn't stir.

Mac leaned into the vehicle over him, past the computer console jutting from the center of the dash. He lifted one flap of the cop's rain slicker enough to expose the utility belt around his waist. Three leather pouches lay against the man's left hip, right behind his holstered pistol. Working as carefully as his thick fingers allowed, Mac unsnapped the cover of one, found it empty, tried another and got a tube of that super pepper spray they'd used on Charlie. On a whim, he pocketed this and went in for his last try.

The third pouch held handcuffs and, Velcro-ed to the inside, a set of two keys. He pulled them off and turned back to Ellis with the ring dangling from thumb and forefinger.

Ellis' eyes grew huge and flicked over Mac's shoulder.

"*Whathefu?*" Myers heaved himself up. He stared at them through the open car door with wobbly eyes. Blood dribbled from one corner of his slack mouth.

He and Mac sprang into motion at the same time, the cop going for his gun and Mac leaping back on top of him. Under normal circumstances, the man wouldn't have been a match for him in a strength contest, but both of them were on their last leg. They struggled for a second in the confined space of the car, prying at each other's fingers as the gun slipped out of its sheath, snarling like animals, and then Myers froze. A look spread across his features so wall-eyed and glassy it caused Mac to stop fighting.

The cop opened his mouth and coughed a scarlet mist into Mac's face.

He dropped his hold on the weapon and recoiled in disgust, spilling out of the vehicle onto Ellis. Myers let go of the pistol too—if fell out of sight into the floorboard—and then clutched at his throat as he dry-heaved reams of blood across the interior. He fell back across the seat and spasmed violently, shoes drumming against the leather seat.

"*What's wrong with him?*" Mac wiped at the blood on his face. The rain washed it away, but not fast enough. He couldn't take his eyes off the seizing figure.

"I don't know! The keys, where are the keys!"

He'd dropped them when he went for the gun. He fished them out of a water puddle beside the tire and set about unlocking Ellis's cuffs while Myers continued to flail and hack.

The radio in the dashboard crackled to life. Mac recognized the Southern-fried voice from the bullhorn. "Myers, we're goin in, give us a shout back."

Ellis had the cuffs off. They stood up, and the roof of the vehicle mercifully hid the jerking body from view. All except his feet, which were beginning to slow.

Mac went into his own coughing fit, long enough to leave him wheezing when it passed. "I didn't do that to him, man, you saw it!"

"I know, it's not your fault!"

"Myers, you there?" the radio asked. "Wake up, boy! Don't make us come all the way back there!"

"We've gotta get out of here." Ellis pointed toward the end of the parking lot behind them, and the first streets leading away to the west of the Dome. "We can hide out there."

"No fuckin way, I'm not leavin Links to these guys!"

"Listen, they want me more than any of you! We can lead them away, and they'll have to follow! They won't even go in the Dome if they think we're not in it!"

Mac hesitated. "What about...him?" He pointed into the open car door. He didn't like these piggies but...goddamn, *no one* deserved this.

The radio came to life one last time. "Goddamn it! Drano, meet me back at the cars!"

"They'll get him some help! Now come on!" Ellis took a few steps and turned back, waiting.

Mac glanced once more into the vehicle, where Myers lay completely still. He couldn't tell if the man was even still alive. He had just been sick one minute and then...

Another raw chuff worked its way up his throat. Mac swallowed heavily to force it back down and then loped along after Ellis toward the outlying buildings around the Dome.

WHITNEY +18:21

The lines to get into the Dome stretched for a quarter of a mile. Maryland and the others emerged from a side street and drifted across the parking lot to the queue leading into the south gate. Others did the same, parking cars in the closest available spots or scurrying from buildings and alleys all around, many of them with coughs that sounded very similar to Tom, Tangela, and the Hispanic half of the parking garage duo. The rain was unrelenting, but at least the temperature had warmed up enough to where they weren't shivering.

Gerald stood as far back from them as possible. The kids had taken a liking to Hernie, and they busied themselves trying to teach him a hand game that looked like a distant cousin of Paper, Rock, Scissors. Tangela giggled every time he messed up, then both of them would hack until they were breathless. As bad as they sounded, Tom was definitely a higher priority. His face would make a good Halloween mask at the moment, pasty and sunken, with circles that looked like bruises beneath his eyes and cheekbones. His throat was so raw he could barely talk, and his frequent coughs had begun to sound like more like windy whistles. After making him take shelter with some other folks nice enough to give him space in their nearby vehicle, she turned to the last member of their group.

Carter Vance. She really didn't know what to make of him. He was on the skinny side, awkward, dressed like somebody from her high school A/V club, and that futuristic mask over his mouth and nose was kind of on the creepy side. And on top of all that…he kept sneaking glances at her every few minutes, looking up to moon at her beneath the wet hair hanging in his face. It wasn't even so much the looking at her—she knew she was passably pretty, and guys had been checking her out ever since her tits started to point up—as it was the fact that his eyes always returned to the ground at his feet so *intently*, as though he could actually grip onto it just by staring.

The line started forward at a slow but steady pace. As they shuffled, she decided to take a chance and moved up next to him.

"Your friend seems to be a real hit." They both looked back at Hernie and the kids, now engaged in animated conversation about cartoons. "I'm glad someone else is here to take their mind off things. They've been through a lot."

He answered without looking at her, hands shoved in his jean pockets and rain dripping off the edge of his plastic-covered chin. "Yeah, as long as he doesn't kick them, we'll be okay."

"Huh?"

"I…you see…heh…you had to be there, I guess."

"Riiiight." Total freak. Great. She was hoping to leave the kids with this guy and Tom when she split to go home, but that idea was evaporating. "You two known each other long?"

"Hernie?" His voice was nasally and muted from the pressure of the mask on his nose. The clear plastic fogged with each breath before the moisture filtered out through the gadget attached to the side. The thing was sophisticated for a germ mask. "Just since this morning. Course, that feels like an eternity ago. He's homeless. I picked him up down south by the coast just before I started this way."

"Who's this 'Hatch' he keeps talking about?"

"His dog. Or so he says. Claims he lost him this morning while he was fighting James Bond at the seawall."

"Okay…you lost me again."

He shrugged one shoulder and gave her another one of those quick glances, up to her face and then back down at the pavement. "Long story short, he's paranoid delusional. Very Mel-Gibson/ *Conspiracy-Theory*-ish. He's harmless though. So long as you don't jump out at him looking like one of those scientists from *E.T.*"

"You name drop a lot of movies, Carter, you know that?"

"I tend to make pop culture references when I'm nervous."

She cracked a smile at that.

"But something did happen to the seawall this morning," he continued. "I left my house, heard some kind of explosion, and that's when the city really started flooding."

"Really? An explosion?"

"Yeah, why? You know something?"

"No, not really." She pulled her wet hair back, tucking it into the collar of her shirt. Something felt wrong to her, in the same way it had felt wrong last night while she sat in traffic. The face of the fleeing Guardsmen recurred, her imagination adding more detail now than she could've possibly seen in the few seconds of pouring rain. Some part of her subconscious—maybe that Amazonian goddess working so hard to keep her out of trouble—was convinced it was important. "It's just…there was an explosion on the Rugg Canyon bridge last night too, just before the storm hit. I was there, but I have no idea what caused it. The bridge completely collapsed."

"Woah. The bridge is out?"

"It was…awful. Full of cars when it happened. I just can't stand to think…" She closed her eyes and let the rain sluice across her skin, not wanting to relive the experience in front of him. "So you live close to the seawall? Where at?"

"Teague Street."

"That's really close to me! I live in Manchester Heights!"

This time his look lingered a bit longer before plummeting. "You're a Manchester Heights chick? What are you doing out here then? Your helicopter out of fuel or something?"

Her tongue wagged for a few seconds before arriving at a mumbled answer that sounded like, "It's complicated."

"Yeah, with a boyfriend like that, I guess most things are."

"I swear to God, a person needs a roadmap and compass to talk to you. What boyfriend?"

He pointed at Gerald, milling in the parking lot on the edge of the line, that eternally sour look on his chiseled face. "Sorry, is he your husband?"

"Ha! *Him?* I just woke up with him this morning!" Another swift look complete with arched eyebrows. "No, no, Jesus, not like that, I mean I just met him this morning, he was there when I woke up and, you know, maybe he's my type or whatever, but I didn't...*you know*, and why do you keep doing that with your eyes, anyway?"

"Doing what?"

"You keep doing this thing where you flick them up for just a second and then look back down real fast."

"Am I still doing that? Damn. I thought I'd stopped."

The lined worked on another few steps before she prompted, "You can explain anytime."

"Well, I'm, uh, agoraphobic."

"Wait, I thought you were *germ*ophobic. That's why you're wearing this lovely selection from the Michael Jackson fashion catalogue."

He inspected one of the rat scratches on the back of his hand, covered it with his other palm, then seemed to think better of it. "I'm kinda both, actually."

"Agoraphobia. That's, what, fear of crowds?"

"That's one type—and trust me, all these people are really not helping—but mine is more open places. Outside. I don't like the sky. Hence, the keeping-my-eyes-on-the-ground thing. I get panic attacks, vertigo, loss of breath...it's not pretty."

"That's...interesting." *And complete bullshit, my scrawny, nerdy, little friend.* She'd had a roommate named Tallulah during her first—and only—year of college that claimed to have as many dysfunctions and disorders as this chump, including claustrophobia, xenophobia, and something called ataxophobia: fear of untidiness, which made her the extreme wrong choice of roommate for 18-year-old Maryland Williams. The pale girl had failed out of school for excessive absences (Maryland did too, but that was from excessive *partying*), and spent most of the day in bed with the shades drawn, sniffling. It had all seemed so fake, so forced, especially the one time she'd nearly gone into convulsion when Maryland left out a pair of day-old panties.

But she hadn't spared Tallulah's feelings and she wouldn't baby this Carter fellow either. She watched him from the corner of her eye, wanting to gauge his reaction when she said, "I can't say I believe it though. I think a lot of that stuff is all in a person's head."

He never missed a beat. "Of course it's in a person's head. It's a mental disease, where else would it be?"

"You know what I mean."

"Yeah, I know what you mean." He held a palm out in front of him, letting water collect in the middle, then turned it over to let it dribble off the side. "This is the first time I've been out of my house in eight years. How's that for 'all in my head?'"

"*What?* Are you serious?"

He didn't answer, just put his hand back in his pocket and plodded along with his head craned down.

"So why now?"

"Whitney didn't really give me a choice. My house looked like a bowl of spaghetti when I left."

"You got a lot of problems, Carter. You ever consider becoming a blues musician?"

He looked up, and this time his eyes stayed rooted on her. She saw they were baby blue and surprisingly clear. "You should hear me play harmonica."

The line just ahead of them was moving through the turnstile. Tom, Hernie, and the kids crowded back in with them as they entered, cutting off the conversation.

"At least we'll be dry for a change," Chris remarked.

"I *hate* the rain," Tangela declared.

"Yeah," Maryland agreed. "I don't think I could stand being out here for another minute."

So of course, as they passed beneath the awning just outside the doorway, the downpour came to an abrupt halt. All of them groaned.

Before they entered, Carter broke away from the group, walked to the edge of the wall, and knocked four times.

"Just...don't ask."

WHITNEY +18:27

Sturney and Drano wove their way through the parking lot back to the patrol car to find the door open and Myers lying stretched across the front seat. His eyes were almost popped from their sockets, teeth gnashed in an eternal grimace, every muscle in his body seized up, as though rigor mortis was already setting in. Fresh blood coated the vehicle in gushes and sprays, like an arterial fire hose had been turned loose on the interior. They couldn't even tell what the younger officer had died from, and Sturney didn't feel like crawling in the car for a closer look.

"Christ." Sturney popped another peppermint. It was a little known fact that he had Irritable Bowel Syndrome, and he swore the candy settled his stomach. "Someone came back here and let Ellis out. Had to be one'a tha others. Prob'ly watching us the whole time. But what the fuck did they do ta Myers?"

Drano frowned, but only because that was what was expected of a human being when faced with this much carnage. The gleam in his eye when he looked at the blood was all animal. "They might've sprung him, but they didn't do this. Not one of them has the balls for wetworks like this."

"Well, whatever. We can ask when we get 'em back. They couldn'ta got too far."

Drano turned his hawkish eyes to Sturney. "Sure you don't wanna just leave town? Call Merced and get him to set us up down south somewhere with all that H? We'll never be able to explain this even if we do find Ellis and Van Ness, not five officers going missing."

"Look around you Drano." Sturney reached carefully into the blood soaked car, grasped the keys still dangling from the ignition and pulled them free. His fingers squelched in blood coating the metal. One of them might have to drive this vehicle later, especially if they pressed on with a cover-up. His stomach gurgled at the idea. "I don't know what the fuck's goin on in Port Allen, but there ain't no leavin, not yet. The bridge is out, the pass is flooded, communication's down, and we ain't seen so much as a Red Cross helicopter."

"Still the western trail, don't forget."

"Yeah, and we'd need something heavy duty just to get up it. With our luck, we'd get halfway and run into the rescue crews comin up the other side. No, we can worry 'bout makin a run for it later. Right now, we got some time to kill, so let's use it findin *them*."

Drano sighed, obviously displeased with this answer. He was bloodthirsty but not stupid, a fact that both pleased and worried Sturney. "Okay. What's the plan then? Back to the Dome?"

"Naw, that chickenshit ran with whoever helped him. But they'll pop back up eventually. Right now, I kinda just wanna git away from here." He looked back at the Dome. "Cause I got a baaaad feelin 'bout those people crammed inside there."

WHITNEY +18:36

Inside the Dome, weary helpers shouted directions. The press of bodies was even worse in the cramped and dim quarters, and his old pal vertigo made the edge of Carter's vision go fuzzy. His windpipe clamped. Judging from the way his companions wrinkled their noses, he was just thankful he had the mask to filter out the smell of unwashed bodies.

"Medical help is on the other side of the building, follow the hallway. Food and beds are inside the main floor of the civic center for as long as they last."

Maryland started down the hall. "Tom, we have to get you in to see someone."

The older man shook his head. He looked like death, if death died, came back undead, and then got run over a few times. He was swaying on his feet even now. "I'm just not up to being poked and prodded, Miss Williams. Please…just get me somewhere I can lie down. Some sleep would do wonders, I'm sure."

She eyed him a moment and then shrugged helplessly. "Fine. Whatever. Men are too complicated for me anymore."

"I'm fairly one-dimensional," Carter offered.

She rolled her eyes. "I want to take Tangela to see a doctor."

"I'm okay too!" The girl could barely get the statement out around a series of brittle coughs. "I don't wanna see a doctor, I want my daddy!"

"Young lady, you're coming with me right now, and that's final. I may not be able to make these big boys listen to me, but you're a different story."

"Hernie, what about you?" Carter asked. "You want to see a doctor for your cough? Or your back?"

The homeless man shook his head till his long hair whipped. "No, I feel better, I promise."

Carter had his doubts, but turned back to Maryland. "If you want to take her, I'll go with everybody into the Dome to eat and find Tom a bed."

"Thank you." She took Tangela's hand and led her up the corridor, in the direction an alarming number of people were headed.

"Bye Tanj," Chris called to his sister. Hernie stood behind him, giving a forlorn wave. "I'll see if there's someone who can help us find Dad."

Carter was about to speak, when Gerald pushed past him. He'd been out of the conversation thus far, but only because he'd been engaged in animated debate with a group that came in after them. Now he marched up to one of the door attendants. "Hey, buddy, is it true the north pass through the hills is flooded?"

Tom and Carter exchanged alarmed glances.

The door attendant, a thin guy with bags under his eyes, winced at the loud demand. "Please sir, keep your voice down…"

"Don't tell me to keep my voice down! Is the pass out or not?"

"That's…that's just what I heard, okay? That, and the Rugg Canyon Bridge."

"No shit, I was there for *that* fireworks show! Correct me if I'm wrong, but aren't those the only two ways in or out of this dump? How are they planning to bus us out of here?"

"Sir…I don't know. Please just go inside and—"

"No, you get me somebody in charge, right fucking now!"

Carter brought a hand up in front of the man's face, feeling like he was offering the appendage to a hungry badger. "Hey, c'mon, give the guy a break."

Gerald redirected his fury. Carter was only too aware of the muscles rippling in his biceps, and how hard they could probably propel the fist at the end of them. "Get your hand away from me, germboy, or you're gonna lose it!"

The door attendant turned and shouted, "Lincoln! Need some help!"

On the opposite side of the turnstile, a black youth was talking to another group of worried people. At the attendant's yell, he ushered them through the wide entrance of the Dome floor and then started in their direction. He was at least five years older than Chris, and looked as hard as concrete chiseled from a Compton sidewalk. He crossed his arms as he came to stand in front of them. "What's the problem?"

"Who're you? I want someone in charge of this place!"

"I'm as 'in charge' as you gonna get. Now…what's the problem?"

Gerald gave a bitter squawk of frustration. "The problem is, you guys are keeping me here against my will! I want out of this fucking city, like yesterday, and now you're telling me we're trapped here?"

Lincoln didn't bat an eyelash while Gerald yelled in his face. The more Carter looked at him, the more he really did look like a gang member. Then again, his experience was based on episodes of *The Shield*, so what did he know? The teenager stepped forward, bearing down, forcing Gerald to back up if he didn't want their noses to touch. "Sir, we doin the best we can. Help ain't here yet, so we all havin to manage." He raised a single finger and drilled it into Gerald's chest. "But the last thing we want…the thing that's in *nobody's* best interest…is for a riot or some shit to break out up in here. I'm in charge of makin sure that don't happen, of makin sure everything stays in harmony. Right now, you're fuckin up my harmony. So unless you wanna find your ass gagged in a closet…I suggest you move along. *Sir.*"

Gerald stared at him a second longer, eyes flicking between the younger man's stony face and that finger in his chest. Carter waited for a swing. Finally Gerald threw up his hands and mumbled, "Goddamn it, I told her this is what would happen!" He stalked off.

Carter went up to the young man, who was still watching Gerald. "I'm sorry about that. We don't really know him."

He looked at Carter. Squinted at the rebreather. "We don't need that kinda attitude here, know what I mean?"

Carter felt the press of bodies around him, fought not to let his breath catch. "Yeah, I know what you mean. Listen, we have some kids here without a guardian, but their father should be coming to get them. Is there some sort of list or registry of the people here at the Dome?"

Lincoln looked over Carter's shoulder at Chris. "You lost, little soldier?" Chris nodded. "Naw, we ain't got nothin like that. Just not that organized yet."

"Is it true—" Tom began and was interrupted by a fit of vicious hacks. "Is it true what he said though? Are all the ways into the city blocked?"

Lincoln considered before answering. "It's true."

Carter asked, "And there's no help here yet?"

"No one."

Tom shook his head. "That's impossible. The radio broadcast we heard—"

"Nobody knows where it's comin from or who's sendin it. We got no phones, no cells, and no electricity. And those're just a few of the hundred problems around here, like the maintenance tunnels of the Dome are startin to flood, and we runnin out of food. So if you want somethin to eat, I suggest goin in."

Tom tried to speak again, but this time the coughing fit was so bad he doubled over, and Carter and Hernie both slid a hand under his arms to help him back to his feet.

Lincoln uncrossed his arms. "Hey, you really bad off, man. You been around to get some medicine?"

Tom flapped his arms like he was trying to fly, his weight—what little there was—entirely resting on Carter and Hernie. "I just... want to lie down..."

"C'mon. I'll find you a cot and call for Doc Kordi."

The four of them followed him through the swinging doors onto the Dome floor, coming out through a gap between elevated bleachers. The room ahead was a typical spectator ring, maybe a hundred yards across, with a metal-ribbed ceiling that arched high overhead into a series of strip skylights. The polished wood floor contained rows upon rows of brass cots.

There was a little more elbow space in here than in the packed hallway, but not much. People squeezed in along the walls and staked out places amid the aluminum benches and reclined on the cots. This Lincoln kid was right: there was no way to take census of a mess like this. Most of the light came from cloudy sun beams through the Dome's narrow skylights, but portable generators had been set up around the room with spotlights and industrial fans attached. Even so, the air was thick and muggy, and Carter was again thankful the rebreather was pulling double duty by filtering out the stink of sweat. He shivered from the idea of all the bacteria in this room, piling up in a huge, invisible swarm. Forty-eight hours ago that image would have wilted him like a hothouse flower, and he suspected it still might if he didn't keep his panic under constant check.

In mask we trust, he thought, and on the heels of that, almost automatic: *I'm okay, you're okay, the universe is center.*

"Tell me this," he said aloud. "If there's no outside help here, where'd all the supplies come from?"

"Most of it was here already. The Dome's always been a disaster relief center. The rest was brought in by folks and donated."

A buffet line began to their left, leading up to gas grills where amateur chefs fired up chicken legs, hot dogs, and burgers. Carter wasn't hungry with the meal he and Hernie had just eaten at the old murderous fart's place, but even if he was, visions of ptomaine and salmonella prevented his appetite from revving again.

Lincoln waited with Tom, talking on a battery-operated walkie-talkie, while they went through the line. Chris and even Hernie piled Styrofoam plates high with potato salad from tubs and cookies from cellophane packages of Oreos and Keebler. The boy fixed a plate for his sister, while Carter tried to juggle food for Maryland and Tom, in case he felt up to it.

"Geez Hernie, how can you eat again already?" Carter asked, before realizing the homeless man probably didn't eat as much in a week as he had today.

Hernie shoved a couple of cookies in the breast pocket of his spiffy new Guayabera. "Those are for Hatch later, when we find him."

"Right. *Hatch*. I'll grab something for the Easter Bunny, then."

Chris reached for the last slice of bread in a torn package, only to have it snatched away by a beady-eyed old woman. "You're not going to have any, Mr. Carter?"

"No, I made a New Year's resolution to avoid Listeria infections."

"Wha Li-eria, Misher Car-er?" Hernie asked around a mouthful of crusty potato salad.

"It's… Just eat, guys. Food poisoning's pretty long term thinking, at this point."

His mouth watered a little bit at the sight of the flame-cooked food at the end of the line.

Don't think it will be here later, when you finally do *get hungry.*

He took a few pieces of barbecued chicken.

They grabbed warm bottles of water, and then Lincoln led them to an empty cot. In the bed next door was a blond woman with skin as bloodless as paper, and a man in a chair beside it holding her hand.

"These are some friends of mine," Lincoln told them. "Randy and Heather." Randy gave them a wave, Heather a weak smile. "Oh, hold up, I never got your names."

Introductions were made all around, and Carter found a place to set their food down and then helped Tom into the cot, where he fell asleep almost at once with his glasses on. Carter took them off and slipped them in his own pocket.

The man named Randy gestured to Tom. "Is he…?"

Carter looked between him and Lincoln. "Is he what?"

Lincoln only stuck out his jaw. "I called Doc Kordi on the radio. He's makin rounds in here someplace. Let me see if I can find him." He squeezed past the line of beds and into the crowd on the outskirts of the room.

"Do you know something we don't?" Randy asked, after he was gone.

Carter frowned. "Huh?"

Randy tapped his upper lip just below the nose. "The illness that's going around. Has that mask kept you from getting sick?"

"Oh, I…I don't know…*illness?*"

"You're friends have it too, don't they?"

"We figured it was just the flu."

"Well, the mask is probably a good investment anyway. Who does your portfolio?"

The woman holding his hand coughed, and he turned his attention to her before Carter could tell him Merrill Lynch.

Lincoln returned with a Middle Eastern man carrying a heavy plastic bag. He bent over Tom, pried open his eyelids and mouth, looked inside. While the examination was going on, Maryland arrived with Tangela in tow.

The doctor placed a stethoscope on Tom's upper chest. "He is coughing?"

"Yeah. A lot," Maryland said.

"For how long now?"

"At least since early this morning."

He pulled a syringe from his bag and eased it into Tom's upper arm. The man stirred but didn't open his eyes.

"What's that? They only gave Tangela some pills." To Carter, she added, "I got some for Hernie too."

The doctor withdrew the needle, covering the dot of blood with gauze. "This is a prescription antitussive so strong it's not even on the market yet. It's a Hydrocodone derivative only two molecules away from heroin. I only have a few samples, so I'm administering it to the more advanced stage patients. It's going to knock him out completely for a few hours, but I find it gives them some strength back. Just keep him resting, and try to get some food into him when he wakes up."

"What about Heather?" Randy's voice quavered. "Is there anything else you can give her?"

"I'm afraid if she takes anything else, it's going to be worse than if I gave her nothing at all."

Maryland sent Tangela to go and stand with Chris and Hernie, out of earshot. "What is this, doctor? Do all these people have the same thing?"

"It would appear that way. The supplies I have access to seem to put off the symptoms, but only for a while."

Carter suddenly wanted to claw at his skin, to run from this place, to seal himself in a hole away from other people and the disgusting microbes they carried. For the first time, he truly regretted leaving the shambles of Mitch Connelly's house this morning. "H-how bad is it?"

"Symptoms continue to worsen, but…" Kordi's eyes became dark, haunted pits without bottom. "I have no idea what an end stage to this thing will look like."

From the next bed, Heather began to sob.

WHITNEY +22:04

CT needed a fix. *Bad.*

The cravings had been occasional and merely annoying during the long night of the hurricane and his even longer swim this morning, mostly because his mind was occupied. But now that every second wasn't about survival, and his brain had time to turn on itself, the ache in his veins blossomed into a constant and unbearable agony, a hunger that would devour him if not sated.

He'd rowed the boat ashore this morning on a street he didn't recognize, and left the thing in someone's front yard. He brought the cop's pistol with him, experiencing one last savage moment of glee at the thought of the old coot and Mac stranded in the middle of the flood. Lincoln was probably dead, and soon Mac would be too. He just wished he could be there to see that giant fucker drown.

He was the Big Man now. The Boss. The Man with the Bulletproof *Cojones.*

He truly intended to find the rest of the crew and take his cousin's place, just like he'd told Mac, but first things first. He needed a serious dealer, one that had more of a selection than the tiny bit of weed the X-Dawgs dealt in. A Bloodwhip had been supplying him previously, but he held no hopes of finding the kid now.

CT set off into the ravaged city. It was deserted. He checked every alleyway that was still standing for blocks and didn't even see any winos. A few hours later, his hands were starting to shake when he finally came across a group of people heading to the Dome, and he went with them.

Once they reached the crowds at the convention center, he knew he'd hit the jackpot. Where there were this many downtrodden people, there was a drug dealer; it was just a fact of life. Sure enough, he spotted one leaning against the side of the building between gates. Just a scuzzy Mexican kid in a ripped t-shirt and doo-rag, smoking a cigarette, but CT's trained addict eyes knew how to pick out a bliss merchant like he used to when reading those *Find Waldo* books. He was practically drooling as he approached the guy.

"I'm buyin," he muttered.

"Whatchoo want, *homes?* Dime?"

"Naw, man. I need me a rock."

The Mexican kid nodded. "Got that. Twenty."

CT stared at him blankly. Some part of his brain had known he would need cash for this endeavor, but the cravings had been so severe he'd somehow glossed over the fact he was flat broke. He licked his lips. "Hey, lemme owe you."

"*Owe me?*" The dealer smirked and flicked his cigarette away. "Shit, get the fuck outta here."

"C'mon, man, I'm an X-Dawg! I'm good fo' it, I swear!"

The Mexican kid came off the wall for the first time. "*Cabron*, I don't care if you're Donald fuckin Trump. No credit today. Lotta hungry mouths to feed out here that *do* have cash, so get outta my face."

For a second, CT considered pulling the pistol. He was the Boss now after all, and that was no way to talk to the Boss. He wanted to see that grin fall off the kid's face, to let him know he was dealing with the guy that was about to take over this city. He could rob this fool for his whole stash, then make it last until regular distribution was set up under his leadership.

But there were too many people around, and all it would take is one cop to get him right back in boiling water.

So he turned and strode away. He waited in line to get into the Dome, looking for other dealers. He spent a little time panhandling—a decidedly un-Boss-like activity, which just fueled his anger—but after an hour came up with a whopping 42 cents. The need was getting worse, making him feel cornered, an itch under his skin that jumped every time he scratched at it. He felt like he was going to vomit soon, and part of him was surprised his addiction had gotten so deep without him even realizing it.

CT came around a curve of the outer Dome hallway and almost passed by a small room with a line stretching out of it. He peeked around the curve of the doorway.

"What's in there?" he asked a man nearby.

"Vending machines. They're almost out of food on the Dome floor. This is pretty much all that's left."

CT's burning thoughts went in a new direction. He smiled, then shoved through the line.

"Hey, what are you doing?" someone shouted.

"Free enterprise," he said, heading toward the glass-fronted machines.

WHITNEY +22:14

Imogene's eyes fluttered open. Her chest hurt, throbbing in rhythm with the working of her lungs. She recognized the signs of an attack too well after all this time. Janie had gotten her back into bed and was probably fixing her steaming hot tea right this second.

She tried to sit up, and a firm hand pushed her back down. "Not just yet, ma'am. I don't want you overexerting yourself." The voice was unfamiliar, the accent foreign. She realized that there was a mask over the lower half of her face feeding her oxygen, instead of the nasal tubes.

This wasn't her daughter's home. The ceiling was curved steel girders far above her, the surface she lay on was too uncomfortable and lumpy to be her bed, the noise of many people pressed in around her and...and...

And Janie left you to die.

The fog in her brain lifted at this cruel reminder. She turned her head one way and then the other against the pillow. This room was dim, but she could see rows of beds stretched out away from her. She thought at first she was in a hospital, until she saw they were little more than brass Army cots. But, more immediate, were the younger men on either side of her, squeezed in between her cot and the next. Imogene only recognized one: to her right was the man in the John Deere hat that rescued her from the roof of her flooded home. He sat in a folding chair, bushy eyebrows raised. On her left, bent over her midsection, was a Middle Eastern fellow listening to her chest with a stethoscope.

"You're at the civic center," this dark-skinned man answered her unasked question. "I'm Dr. Kordi. Your friend here undoubtedly saved your life by giving you CPR until you stabilized, and then brought you here."

Imogene turned to the Cajun man in the overalls, held out a hand, and gave him a shaky smile. He took her fingers in both of his and held them.

"Even still, you're incredibly lucky, Ms...?"

"Freeman." The word came out as a shredded croak. "Imogene Freeman."

The doctor pulled the stethoscope away and stood up straight to look at her. "I diagnosed what I could with you unconscious, and there just happened to be an emergency oxygen tank in the first aid supplies here. Tell me, is it Pulmonary Disease?"

"Good ol' COP'D. Never leave home without it."

Her hero chuckled from the bedside, but it quickly turned into a rumbling cough.

Kordi glanced at him. "Tell me, Ms. Freeman, are you experiencing any other symptoms?"

"I...I don't think so."

"Coughs, throat pain, dizziness, anything like that?"

"Just my usual collection of aches and pains, sugar."

Kordi rubbed the space just above his right eye with two fingers, and then stifled a cough of his own. "Interesting."

Imogene let her hand fall away from the other man's grasp and turned a little more in the cot, following the tube from the oxygen mask down to its terminus on the nozzle of a green tank on the floor.

"It's not a C-PAP machine like I'm sure you're used to, but it should suffice, as long as you're not too active."

"Wasn't thinkin about that, doc. Just wonderin how much juice this little gizmo could possibly have in it."

"At least eight hours. But don't worry, I'm sure help will be here before then. The mouth of the northern pass is flooded, but they'll launch boats from it eventually."

Imogene maneuvered her arms under her and pushed, forcing her body upright on the cot. This time, Kordi didn't stop her. A wave of dizziness passed over her, but her lungs continued to function without a hitch. "That's a pleasant thought, but I'm not so sure it's right. There was an explosion in the pass last night. I imagine the whole shebang is clogged up right now."

Kordi shook his head. "No, no, you must be mistaken. The explosion was on the *Rugg Canyon* Bridge."

Now that she was sitting up, she could see more of the room. Cloudy, early evening light came through the skylight windows, which meant she'd slept away most of the day. Portable lamps cast severe wattage illumination in swatches across the ceiling. "Hate to argue, but I saw it, with my own two eyes. The pass is kaput."

"S'true," Cajun added.

"Dear God." Kordi's voice was a contemplative whisper. "But how could—?"

There was a burst of static from the floor beside her cot. The doctor reached down to pick up a walkie-talkie, turned away, and spoke through it. When he was finished, he gathered up his supplies. "I'm sure someone will be here soon, even if they have to fly in. I'll be back to check on you soon."

Imogene watched him go, and then favored her new friend with another grin through the oxygen mask. "Thank you. For everything."

"Like I said, ain' no big deal."

"But it is. I don't even know your name."

"Jer' Lay-mur." This came out in such a muddle, she had him spell it: Jerry Lemiere.

"Well, Mr. Lemiere, it's a pleasure to meet you."

"Likewise." He bent to the floor and picked up a Styrofoam plate loaded with all the makings of a perfect barbecue: basted chicken, and a mound of potato salad and coleslaw. "Feel like eatin? Li'l cold, but I wanted to make sure you had sum'n."

She felt her eyes well up at the tenderness. So many tears lately, for so many different reasons. "Thanks, but I'm not up to it just now."

He set the plate back under his chair, opened his mouth to say something else, and was interrupted by the woman on the cot to Imogene's right, who began a brutal wheezing spell ending with a ragged moan. So many people in here were sick; the sounds echoed from all around. Her husband served in the Korean War, and the description he'd given her of battlefield triage tents seemed a close match to this.

Lemiere caught her dismayed look. "You wan' get up? Ge' some air?"

"I wish I could, but I can't walk, remember? The bed is probably the best place for me."

Lemiere displayed every crooked tooth in his head as he stood up and reached behind his chair. "T'at ox'gen tank ain' the on'y t'ing in the first aid." He brought out a collapsible wheelchair and held it in front of her.

"My, my, Mr. Lemiere, when you give a lady the knight-in-shin-in-armor treatment, you really go the distance, don't you?"

He tried to hide it, but she saw his grin become sheepish as he unfolded the wheelchair.

After the contraption was ready, he lifted her up and placed her on the padded seat, and then slipped the oxygen tank into a kangaroo pouch on the back. Not as comfortable as her own, and a little rickety, but this was a beggar/chooser situation if ever there was one. She gave the wheels a few turns to test the mobility, intending to roll herself, but Lemiere quickly got into pushing position behind her.

She had no idea who he was, or why he was helping her, and she was too scared to ask. If he suddenly saw her as dependent on him, it might scare him off, make him decide she was too much trouble. After all, if her own offspring could abandon her, then it certainly wasn't a stretch to believe a man she'd known a total of twenty minutes might do the same.

And she really didn't want to be alone anymore. Her ordeal the night before had reinforced her belief that she wanted to have a say in when it was her time to go.

Lemiere pushed her through the endless rows of people hacking and writhing on their makeshift beds. She tried not to look. They passed the buffet line, where slumped hurricane survivors waited for food that was rapidly dwindling. She realized she was more thirsty than hungry, but even if they got in line now, the last of the water bottles would surely be gone before they got through.

"Did the doctor really say the Rugg Canyon Bridge was out too?"

"Yes'm."

"So what's happenin? Is someone gonna bring more food, or do they want to cart us outta here?"

"Don' know. Heard folks say a lot of t'ings while you 'as out, but nobody know fo sho."

Lemiere wheeled her through one of the Dome floor exits and into the hallway beyond as she thought about this.

They wandered down the passage. The only light out here came from glowing red exit signs and every fifth fluorescent, plus daylight through wraparound windows and the wide turnstile exits, but the latter two were fading fast as twilight came on. It was more than enough for her to see the people sitting against the wall with their food or talking in groups. A preacher gave a hushed sermon to a congregation of ten. Another man angrily railed against the government to more than double that. As they passed two men, a fistfight broke out that no one tried to break up.

"It's a powder-keg," she whispered.

"What's t'at?"

"Cram enough people into one place, don't give 'em any hope, and sooner or later…you get an explosion."

As their walk progressed, she heard the clamor of children somewhere ahead. The curve of the hallway gradually revealed a crowd of six or seven, plus a few adults. She heard pleas from the kids and a few angry words from the adults, but it wasn't until they were nearly on the edge of the small group that she saw the situation.

They stood clustered around a black boy with cornrows, probably only a few years older than her granddaughter Alice. His bare arms were filled with miniature snack packages and several soda cans. He grinned around at the children as they begged. "I said twenty bucks, or you li'l niggas can piss off!"

"They're kids, you scumbag," one of the women in the crowd shouted. "They just want something to eat!"

"Shut up, muhfuckah! It's a hundred fo' *yo'* fat ass!"

"You believe this?" A man in a Stetson turned to Imogene and Lemiere and hooked a thumb over his shoulder. "Little punk broke into the vending machines and stole everything. Now he's trying to extort people."

Imogene's cheeks heated up. She grabbed the rims of the wheelchair and pushed, propelling her out of Lemiere's grip and into the midst of the children. They grew quiet as she rolled through, and the black boy stopped his teasing long enough to look her in the face.

"Whatchoo want, Grandma?"

"I'm no grandmother of yours. I woulda drowned any of my offspring that acted like you."

The children all went, "*Oooooo*," in unison, and the boy's eyes opened wide enough to show the whites.

"You're gonna give me one of those sodas, because I'm thirsty," she continued. "And you're going to give everything else to these children."

"Says who?"

She opened her mouth to tell him exactly who, but someone else did it for her.

"Says me," a voice on the other side of the crowd commanded. "Give the woman a soda, CT."

WHITNEY +22:58

Lincoln had been run ragged over the last three hours, putting out fires—some figurative, but a few literal—before they could burn the place down around them.

Everywhere he looked, exhausted faces glared. While the line of those waiting to get inside had finally played out, there were still more trickling in every few minutes with their own stories and rumors to add to the mill, like dirty clothes in a washing machine. These people were out of food, out of patience, and out of hope, hanging on with tattered fingernails to a ledge that was slowly eroding.

There was theft and some vandalism. An attempted rape. Fights broke out everywhere. The more charismatic tried to form mobs, although what they thought this would do for them he didn't know. Lucky for him, most of them knew him by now, and problems dissolved upon his arrival. He threw himself into the work, mostly to keep his mind off Mac, CT, and the rest of his soldiers.

Kordi was right. No one cared if he was a gangbanger yesterday, they were just content to have someone to believe in today. In a way, it was more responsibility, but this seemed *real* and important, in a way that being an X-Dawg never had.

The doctor had contacted him over the radio about some kid price-gouging refugees with the vending machine staples. He recognized the back of his cousin's cornrowed head immediately, and felt weak with relief. Finally, he would find out where the others were.

"Give the woman a soda, CT."

His cousin turned. Lincoln wasn't sure exactly what to call the emotion that swept over his face, but it was close to surprise. "*Links?*"

Lincoln kept his face hard. "Give that food to these people. That's an order."

CT stared at him like he'd just crawled out of the closest toilet. He seemed to be shaking all over, his face drawn and pale, and Lincoln bet it wasn't so much from Kordi's mystery disease as it was a clean and undiluted bloodstream. "But Links—!"

"We can talk after you give it up."

He thought the boy was still going to put up a fight, but he finally opened his arms and let the goods spill to the floor with a scowl, even the canned drinks. The children swarmed over him like a broken piñata, grabbing what they could. The crowd dispersed. The old lady in the wheelchair was handed a Sprite by one of the kids with all the reverence usually reserved for superheroes and gods, and she rolled forward to give Lincoln a pat on the arm as she passed. She had an oxygen mask on too, like that guy Carter, except not so much like something out of *Star Trek*. "Nice to know someone's still lookin out for the less fortunate, sugar."

Lincoln smiled at her as she rolled away, and then faced C-Tone across the hallway. He suddenly didn't want this confrontation to happen.

"I thought you was dead, Links!"

"And yet you don't seem too happy to see me."

CT rolled his eyes around, scratching at his arm, his shoulder, his chest. "Yeah, well, whatevah."

"When did you get here? Where's Mac and that cop Charlie?"

"I don't know!" he answered, and then eagerly, "Links, man, you got some cash?"

"Wait, what do you mean, 'you don't know?' What happened?"

"Just a few bucks! I'm...*I'm hurtin real bad!*"

"I can see that." Lincoln looked around, then took his cousin by the arm and led him to a dark spot further up the hallway. "Jesus, CT, look at you! You so strung out, you can't even sit still!"

"I know, man, I know, it's wrong, I gotta get off the stuff, but please, I need it, just a little to get my head straight!"

Lincoln took one more furtive glance around. He wasn't going to get any answers with the kid in this state of mind. He reached in his pocket and pulled out a disposable syringe with a miniscule amount of morphine that Kordi had given to him for emergencies.

CT didn't even ask what was in it. He snatched it from Lincoln's hand, jammed it into the crook of his arm, and depressed the plunger. His eyes rolled back. The look of relief on his face was like someone taking a piss they'd been holding a long time. But when he spoke, he voice was calm. "What's the deal, cuz? How come you playin Robin Hood?"

"I'm in charge of security in the Dome."

"Security?" CT's cheeks puffed out. "What dumbass gave you that job?"

"It doesn't matter. You've had your fix, now tell me where Mac is!"

"Mac, Mac, Mac. That's the only thing out yo' mouth, cuz. You wouldn't be so eager to find that muhfuckah…if you knew what I did." He smiled and closed his eyes, riding the high.

Lincoln shook him out of it. "What are you talkin about? Answer me!"

CT opened his heavy-lidded eyes wide, but just a ghost of a grin stayed on his lips. "I left him behind after he told that pig every-thing with Kim was *yo'* fault."

The words didn't seem to fit together. Lincoln could only stam-mer, "W-what?"

"Get it through yo' head! *That pig found Kim's body!* He want-ed to arrest us! Mac saved his own ass by tellin him the whole thing was you! He did everything but raise his right hand and swear to tell the whole-truth-and-nuthin-but! All I could do was run!"

"Mac…squealed? On *me?* No, that's impossible."

"I know you don't wanna hear that cause he's yo' boy and all, but it's true, I was there, and—"

Lincoln shoved him against the wall with a forearm on his neck. He knew he shouldn't, he was supposed to be an example for these people now, but his blood had reached boiling point in record time. Part of it was that smirk on his cousin's face, as he told Lincoln that the one person he trusted in all the world had sold him out at the drop of a hat. CT's head bounced off the painted cinderblock wall. "Understand this, he is *NOT* my boy, he's my goddamn *lieutenant*, and what you're talkin about is *treason!* So you better be fuckin sure about it!"

CT's upper lip stiffened, smoothing out that secret smile. "Every word."

"Shit. *Shit.*" Lincoln released him and leaned against the wall on one elbow. This was too damn much, a betrayal that couldn't be more severe if it came from his own hand. That whole speech of Mac's at the convenience store about Lincoln being too good for the crew...what a load. "Where was the last place you saw him?"

CT shrugged. "It was, you know, down south, few blocks from here."

"When?"

"Couple hours ago. I been tryin to find the rest of the crew, but I ain't seen nobody. You think...?"

"I don't know CT, you're the first X-Dawg I've seen. The whole east side of town is flooded. I got my hands full just tryin to keep these people from killin each other."

"Yeah, but *why?* You a 'banger, not a cop. Whatchoo doin here, Links?"

That question seemed more important now than ever. Had part of him believed that being a glorified bouncer would make up for what happened at Kim's? That the cops would just count all this as community service hours? If that other cop, Charlie, really knew what happened, then they would come here and arrest him and none of this would make a difference.

A vivid image slammed into his thoughts: him in a courtroom with Mac on the witness stand, pointing him out as the killer.

And deep down, he knew he deserved nothing less.

From down the hall, someone screamed his name, cracking the layer of dread solidifying over him. He looked away from CT to find Carter running toward him, panting into his plastic mouthpiece.

"Lincoln, you've got to call Dr. Kordi!"

"Jesus, man, what's wrong?"

"It's your friend, Heather. I think she might be dying."

WHITNEY +23:07

The line to get into the Dome restrooms was almost as bad as the one to get into the Dome itself. Maryland waited the better part of an hour for the ladies' room, but when she finally got in, she decided to hold it a little longer. Every stall overflowed with a mixture of sewage and toilet paper. The stench around them was nauseating. Someone had cracked open the frosted windows to try and let in some fresh air, granting a view of the flooded parking lot and the dwindling rain.

She tried to bum a cigarette off a woman with a fresh pack, and was flatly denied. Before leaving, she turned to one of the mirrors above the row of sinks to take a look at herself.

A haggard stranger stared back. The swelling around her eye had gone down, leaving a faint ring, but the bags under them were like two dark blood clots and her hair was a tangled nest. Her hands were still bandaged and she was covered in a menagerie of fresh bruises. She couldn't ever remember looking this bad, during or before Bryce.

God, she wanted to go home.

She trudged back out to where the others had set up camp. Tangela lay sprawled in the narrow aisle between Tom's bed and the next row, and Maryland stretched out beside the girl. They'd tried to find Tangela a cot as the medicine took effect, but there were none close and she refused to leave the rest of the group. At least her clothes had finally dried out. Chris and Hernie were on in the floor a few beds down, leaning against one another as they dozed. Everyone fell asleep in the Dome as exhaustion overpowered their nerves, the level of noise in the room declining to a subtle drone. Gerald wandered by every half-hour or so, asking if they had any updates and muttering that he told them this would happen.

Carter reclined across from her. He'd waited until everyone else was passed out before picking up the plate of food he'd gotten earlier. She watched as he raised a barbecue chicken leg to the plastic mask, started to lift the plastic, gave up, and then approached from a different angle. She grinned and shook her head.

He let go of the weird little cylinder on its front and the mask—what had he called it? A rebreather?—pushed deep into his face. "What?"

"C'mon Carter, cut the crap and tell me what's up with that thing."

"I already told you." He set the plate on the waxed hardwood floor and sat up. "Not my fault if you don't believe me."

"Surely you weren't always like this. You didn't slide out of your mother wearing a tiny oxygen mask, did you?"

"No. It...started just after I graduated from college. I was always a little OCD, but I started getting these fears. Stuff most people would call irrational."

"Of germs and open spaces?"

"That all came later. It started with...weird things. Things that just came out of nowhere."

"Give me an example here."

He pulled his knees up, rested his chin on them. He looked so much like a teenager when he did that, but she'd heard him tell Chris he was thirty-one. Essentially the same demographic as her and Gerald, but he might as well have been from a different planet. "Okay. I can't wear dark over light."

She frowned. "What does that mean, like layers?"

"No, I mean my shirt can't be darker than the pants I'm wearing. I don't like it. Freaks me out."

She stared at him for three long seconds before slapping a hand over her mouth to halt the laughter bubbling up.

Carter grimaced. "Yeah. That's how most people react."

"I just can't believe there's no medication they can give you or some kind of therapy or something."

"I've tried everything. When it first started happening, I was going to group therapy—"

"There's enough of you to make a *group*?"

"They called it a club, but yeah, I guess so."

"What, the Fear Club for Men? Not just the president but also a client?"

He smirked. "Funny. I'll just shut up now."

"No, I'm sorry, I'm not laughing at you, I'm really not. Please, go on."

He watched her for a few long seconds. "Anyway, when I stopped leaving the house, I started seeing a psychiatrist by tele-conference. He thinks it's all psychosomatic too, but..." He let the sentence hang with a shrug.

"You're out right now, aren't you?"

Before he could answer, Tangela shifted against her, coughed and then resettled.

"She's...um, she's a cute kid," Carter said.

Maryland watched the steady rhythm of the girl's breathing. She felt peaceful with her, stroking her hair, almost hypnotized. There was such innocence in those young features, and Maryland wanted to grab her and warn her about the older men with money, about the dangers of letting yourself get too comfortable with life. If there couldn't be a happy ending for Maryland, at least there could be one for her. "Yeah, she is. She's been through a lot."

"Did I hear her say something to Hernie about her mother dying?"

"Last night. In the storm. She's so strong. I wish I had that much strength. I would've left Bryce a long time ago." The last sentence was out before she realized it, her subconscious speaking while she was too relaxed and sleepy.

"Bryce?"

Oddly enough, she realized she hadn't wanted Carter to know about him. "My husband."

"So you *are* married?"

"You make it sound like herpes." His lip curled beneath the clear plastic at her choice of words. "Sorry. But it kind of was like having herpes. Not that I've ever had herpes. It was just...embarrassing and annoying and you never knew when problems would flare up."

"So...you're not with him anymore?"

She looked up at him, *really* took him in, like he was the new Gucci purse that she was evaluating for purchase. She usually didn't have to put that much thought into men; first glance had always told her everything she needed to know about their prospects in her future. *Yeah, and look where that got you.* "Carter, look, you're nice and we're hanging out cause we're in this situation, but it's not gonna happen, all right? You're not my type."

His eyeballs ballooned in his head, and his breath plumed so fast it fogged up the inside of the rebreather. "Hey, no, you got it wrong, I'm just making conversation! What, you can pry into my life story and I can't do the same?"

She sighed. "Fair enough. In that case, I'm going through a divorce. Kind of. It's complicated. The truth is, I'm thinking about going home."

"Like after this is all over?"

"No, like right now. I just…can't do this. I can't be here anymore. I wasn't made to live like this. If I'd stayed put and ridden it out, I would be lying in bed in that storm-proof fortress Bryce built, eating chocolate-covered strawberries and watching TV on the generator."

"You've really got to hook me up with your architect."

She gave a thin-lipped smile. She suddenly wanted just a cigarette, nothing more than that, and the fact that life couldn't see fit to just make one appear in her hand after all it put her through seemed monumentally shitty. "I left behind my house and my clothes and my cars and my…my *everything* and I thought I could make do but I can't. I just can't. Not if this is what life is like without them."

He raised an eyebrow. "I'm the last person qualified to argue this point since, obviously, I'd rather be home playing World of Warcraft right now, but you want to go back even if life *with* all those things is like herpes?"

Something about that cut her. Not just because he was right, but because she suddenly understood that hers and Carter's basic problems were the same: they both were too afraid to leave the lives they'd built. She rushed to defend herself. "Bryce isn't that bad. I just need to learn to stay out of his way and let him do what he wants."

"Gee, marriage sounds great. Where can I sign up?"

She snorted and said nothing.

"So…why don't you go then?"

Maryland moved her hand from Tangela's hair over to her forehead to feel for a temperature, even though the doctor told her not to expect one. "I keep trying to force myself to get up and leave, to walk out of here and right back into my old life. But every time I think about it, it's like my legs won't obey me."

"Like that *Buffy* episode where they're stuck in the house after Dawn makes the wish…!" He trailed at the look on her face.

"Carter, can you be serious for like five minutes?"

"This *is* me being serious."

"Okay, fine, just forget it."

There was commotion from the bed next to Tom's. The wife of the stock broker guy, Heather, launched into an endless coughing spell. They hadn't heard a word from her in hours—she'd been unconscious as long as Tom—but Randy had kept up a steady stream of chatter until they all started falling asleep. Now his head came up off his arm and he repeated her name, louder and more shrill each time. Heads popped up from all over the Dome floor like prairie dogs.

Tangela opened bleary eyes in Maryland's lap and blurted, "Mommy? What's going on?"

"Nothing, sweetie," she answered for the absentee woman. Chris pulled his head off Hernie's shoulder and wiped at the drool he left. Everyone started waking in the cots around them, sitting up in alarm, all except Tom. She helped Tangela stand and then looked over the foot of the cot.

Randy sat hunched over his wife, who was coughing so hard her eyes looked like eggs about to slide out of a chicken. Her back arched, pushing her breasts up from the bed, and her good hand was a claw against the thin blanket, hooked into the fabric hard enough to show every muscle in her delicate fingers. The broken appendage flopped in its makeshift sling.

"Heather!" Randy screamed into her face. "Oh God, baby, stop, STOP!"

She gave no sign she even heard him. Her entire body was committed to the harsh barks coming out of her mouth. The rigidity left her spine, and she went into a flopping seizure.

"Jesus." Carter unconsciously reached to touch his precious rebreather.

Randy had her by the shoulders now, either trying to hold her down or shake her out of it, but her motions were too violent to tell. Heather's coughing stopped momentarily as she drew in a deep breath through a mouth stretched to impossible width.

And then she spewed a geyser of blood into her husband's face.

Tangela jumped and buried herself in Maryland's side. "What's wrong with that lady, what's wrong with her?"

"Don't look!" Maryland grabbed the girl, leading her away from the bed. All around them, people backed away, but none could take their eyes off the writhing woman. "Hernie!" The dopey-eyed Hispanic man looked up. "Listen to me, Hernie! Take Tangela and Chris! Get them away from this and don't let them see!"

"Yes ma'am," he whispered in awe. He took each of their hands in his and pushed through the aisle.

"Don't let them out of your sight!" she shouted. Chris looked back over his shoulder once before they waded into the gathering crowd.

"What's wrong with her?" Randy looked up at them, wiping blood from his eyes. Heather went back to flopping like a water-deprived fish. "God, *what do I do?*"

She grabbed Carter by the shoulders. "You have to go and find that doctor!"

His eyes slowly focused on her. "Kordi? Right. Uh, where is he?"

"Lincoln will know!" Randy screeched. "Please, hurry and find Lincoln!"

After he left, Maryland slipped between Tom and Heather's bed, next to the husband. "Move out of the way for me, Randy."

"No, no, I want to be close to her!"

She looked him in the eye to make sure she had his attention. "I know you do, but you're getting hysterical, and that's not going to help her."

Tears escaped him, melting into the slick coating of blood across his cheeks, but he abandoned the chair to give her access.

Maryland leaned over Heather. The woman was still spasmodic, cracking down hard enough with each wet cough to jerk the little cot across the floor. Her eyes rolled back in her head, and, Christ, blood was seeping from her nostrils and ears too. Red tears appeared at the corners of her eyelids.

"Somebody hold her down! We have to make sure she doesn't swallow her tongue!" Hands appeared on Heather's shoulders, pushing her body into the thin mattress. She looked up to find Gerald staring grimly back at her from the other side.

Randy slipped off one of his wife's shoes. "Will this work?"

It would, but as Maryland pushed the tip of the sandal into Heather's mouth, she realized that swallowing her tongue was impossible with the series of brittle rasps coming out of her. The shoe was ejected amid a gush of blood that splashed across Maryland's hands and wrists.

From inside the woman's heaving chest, there was a loud *snap!*

"*Do something! She's DYING!*"

Maryland only stared at the wet tide that had stained her bandages a brilliant crimson. Randy's voice sounded far away.

The crowd formed a periphery around them several yards back, but they parted now to admit the doctor, followed by Carter, Lincoln, and another much scrawnier black kid that was probably closer to Chris' age.

"Keep holding her!" Kordi ordered. Maryland snapped out of her daze and grabbed Heather, applying her full weight along with Gerald. The doctor rummaged through his plastic bag of supplies, filled a syringe with something, and jabbed it into her upper arm. Her motions slowed drastically, and he bent over her. "How long?"

"What?"

"*How long has she been seizing?*"

"J-just a few minutes!"

"What's wrong with her?" Randy demanded.

"She's hemorrhaging. Every major vessel in her throat and head must be rupturing simultaneously. I've never seen anything like this."

A maroon stain seeped across the bedsheets under Heather's head like a halo, but her movements continued to wind down.

"She'll be okay though." Randy's eyes pleaded with the doctor. "You gave her something to help…right?"

Kordi's eyes came up and locked onto Maryland. She became acutely aware that she had a dead woman's blood on her. He turned to the young investment banker. "I…I'm sorry."

Randy howled in anguish, but for some reason, it echoed.

Then she realized it wasn't just him screaming, but someone else up in the bleachers. Before any of them could turn, the noise was repeated from the opposite direction, a few rows away, and then another from elsewhere.

There were more people going into convulsions.

"It's Ebola!" someone shouted.

The room erupted into hysteria so suddenly a starter pistol might've signaled it. The level of noise increased to ear-splitting as people cried out. The crowd surged, breaking and reforming from people shoving toward the exits. She thought of the grocery store riot, of the stampede on the freeway.

The world seemed determined to trample her before this was all over.

"Wake Tom up!" she shouted at Carter and Gerald. She didn't wait for an answer before running in the direction she'd sent Hernie with the kids.

She saw his face amid the throng. Maryland pushed through the mob to him. "Let's go, we have to get...!" Chris stood close on one side of Hernie, staring around at the terrorized crowd with wide eyes. On his other side...was no one.

Tangela was gone.

WHITNEY +23:13

"I don't know how long this cover story can hold," the liaison told Kyler over the comm board, which played through speakers in the command trailer. "The attention on this city is worse than we expected, even with the devastation Galveston sustained. People are camped out on this side of the bridge and along the freeway for miles, the media is demanding to know what's being done and why the airspace is closed, and nobody is listening to stories about 'debris disturbance' anymore."

Kyler rummaged through cabinets in the makeshift BOO Aurora had established in the rolling hills along the western edge of Port Allen. Someone had stocked them with cranberry juice. He hated cranberry juice. He had an ex-wife that got urinary tract infections just about every other week and drank the stuff by the gallon. Toward the end of that marriage of inconvenience, he thought about stabbing her all the time, just to see if the blood that came out was watered down cranberry juice.

"Uh, sir?" the liaison prompted, and Kyler realized he'd been frozen, staring into the cabinet and daydreaming for the better part of a minute.

Fugue, his mind corrected. *Not daydreaming. First step toward a monikered strait jacket and a steady dosage of Thorazine.*

"Just change the story," he recovered.

"Uh...change...change it to what...?"

"Insurgents. There's a buzzword for you. The American public *loves* insurgents. A group got their hands on some weapons, military hardware, whatever, and they're shooting at anything in sight, including pesky news choppers."

"But sir, wouldn't that ultimately raise a lot more questions than—?"

A ping from another monitor. *The* monitor. "Tell them they're rioters. Or drug addicts. Identities unknown. I don't know, you guys write this stuff, that's why we pay you! You just worry about keeping the airspace clear until tonight and then none of this will matter." He turned off the link and moved to the next console, displaying an incoming message from his faceless superiors.

He put in his six access codes and entered the conversation.

Status report on current population density requested.

He rechecked the satellite data and typed, *Estimates place 78 to 83 percent of remaining population within the civic center.*

The response took less than five seconds to return. *This is lower than original projections.*

Incident with the incentive this morning. Seawall blown improperly; flooding occurred in unreliable manner. Two men lost. He knew they wouldn't give a shit about the loss of personnel, but they also wouldn't want it left out of his report.

Cause?

Unknown. Investigation in process. He held his breath as he awaited the reply.

Green light on Initiative A.

Kyler smiled. Exactly what he'd been waiting for.

But another line of text appeared. *Secondary objective: capture and detain subjects fitting the following descriptions during sweep-up.*

"Goddamn it, just let me do my fucking job." Kyler scrolled through their grocery list, which read like Noah's ark manifest: two late-stage subjects, two asymptomatic subjects, two women, two men, two children of either sex, two African Americans, etc. He groaned. That left him with the problem of finding someplace to keep all the civvies they abducted, and trucking in some scientist-types to start taking data.

Well, if they fell into his lap, great; if not, Aurora could do without. He would just rattle the ant farm and see what shook out.

Kyler picked up the phone. Dialed a number. Tried in vain not to notice the way his hand wobbled.

"Get those birds in the air, Mattinson. The Dome is yours."

SLEEP NOW IN THE FIRE

The motion was so fast, Tangela was still confused about what happened and whose arm was wrapped around her waist, lugging her awkwardly. One second she was beside Hernie, straining to see through a forest of legs. The next, an appendage snaked around her midsection and snatched her up. She had time to see that her absence hadn't even registered with her brother or her new friend before they were lost in the crowd.

She squirmed, trying to understand. The hip pressed against her was fat—*really* fat, like more-than-Santa-Clause-fat. She bounced as the person wove their way through the crowd. A piggish snorting drifted down from somewhere above her, but she couldn't turn enough to see the person's head.

Then she was plopped down on her feet, and two eyes set in mounds of chubby, quivering flesh moved in front of her. "Y-you just keep s-still, Tangela!"

She recognized the voice first and then the piggy face. It was *him*. The fat man that tried to hurt her this morning in the old house. He scowled down at her, the arm that Chris broke held in a makeshift sling against his round chest. She recoiled in horror and tried to run.

He reached out with his good hand and clamped onto her arm, as he'd done last time. "H-hey, wait, we're gonna have f-fun! See, I brought this back to y-you!" With his bandaged arm, he held up Mr. Softy.

She continued to fight, finally bashing against the injured appendage. He let go of the blanket with a barked curse and dragged her toward one of the exits from this big room.

"Help!" she screamed. The people around her were going the other way, hurrying to watch that bleeding lady, and the few that paid her attention were lost in the crowd. She tried to yell again, to reach out and grab at the people flying by her, but the fat man let go of her long enough to administer a dizzying blow across the back of her head. Tears welled. She coughed and coughed, coughed so hard she couldn't catch her breath. Before she could get it under control, he tugged her along again.

She looked back and caught a glimpse of Mr. Softy lying on the gymnasium floor far behind them.

WHITNEY +23:22

"Where is she?" Chris shouted. "Hernie, *where is she?*"

Hernie looked around himself at the floor, as if he expected the girl to materialize. His eyes were large as he shook his head and said, "I don't know!"

"Jesus!" Maryland spun in a slow circle and called his sister's name. Her voice was lost in the uproar that followed Heather's death as people made for the exits. The place was turning into a riot. Long-brewing fights broke out everywhere. Sick people were helped to their feet by family and friends only to be bowled over as panicked runners plowed into them. People took whatever they could get their hands on, and a full-scale war was being waged over the remains of the food and bottled water.

The Dome's capacity was 20,000 people, but Chris would guess there was far more than that in here right now, fighting to get out.

As the floor around them cleared, Chris spotted a familiar bundle on the floor yards away, would've glanced right over it if not for the checkered pattern. He ran over, picked it up, then held the fabric in his hands as its meaning dawned on him. "Oh, God, he's got her! That son of a bitch found us!"

"Who? Chris, what are you talking about?"

"This big fat pervert named Quinlan! We met him earlier to-day, and I think he's dangerous! He must've taken her this way!" He pointed across the floor in the direction the blanket suggested, toward the north end of the building. "C'mon, we have to find her before he gets too far away!" He started to run, but Maryland grabbed him around the shoulders and held on.

"We'll find her, I promise, but we have to leave before we get trampled!" There was a crash of breaking glass nearby as one of the portable lamps was knocked over. The room was getting darker in increments. "And we have to get *every*one out of here! Tom's still unconscious!"

Dr. Kordi shook his head. "I don't think it's a good idea to move the sick!"

"They're tearin this place apart, Doc!" Lincoln said. "We can come back later once all this calms down!"

Kordi put a hand to his forehead and squeezed. "Yes, all right! The south exit is the closest!"

"I'm NOT leaving here without Tangela!" Chris fought against Maryland. He couldn't lose Tangela too. The thought of her in Quinlan's hands made him ill.

"I would never leave her, Chris!" Maryland said in his ear. "I'll go and look for her myself, but you have to leave, it's not safe!"

"I'll go with you!" Carter's declaration sounded mechanical, more automatic than planned.

"Me too!" Frustrated tears rolled down Hernie's cheeks as he spoke. "I don't want nothing bad to happen to Tangela, Mr. Carter, she's my friendy-friend too!"

"Okay, fine!" Maryland turned to the rest of them: Kordi, Gerald, Lincoln, the other black boy, and Randy, still sobbing over the corpse of his wife. "Can the rest of you get please get Tom out of here?"

"Man, fuck this!" Gerald stretched his hands to the ceiling. "Why am I even still here with you losers? I'm grabbing what food I can and finding a way out of this goddamned city!" He turned and made for the food table.

"I'll get your friend outside," Kordi assured her, "but then I have to come back and help what wounded I can! I have a respon-sibility! Here, take my radio with you!"

He handed his walkie-talkie to Carter and then he and Lincoln each grabbed one of Tom's arms and lifted the unconscious man from the bed, resting their necks in the crooks of his armpits. Tom's head lolled, jaw hanging slack.

"Randy, you have to go with them!" Maryland said.

"Oh God!" the man wailed. "I can't leave her, I can't!"

From somewhere in the building came a quick series of pops. All of them recognized gunfire.

"NOW RANDY!" Maryland let go of Chris, grabbed the man's arm and pulled him to his feet. He held on to Heather's hand as they dragged him away, kicking and fighting. "Someone take him!"

Chris grabbed his hand after he finally calmed, leading him away from the cot and after the others. At least this was someone he *could* help. "Please…you have to find her!" he begged one final time.

"We will! You take care of them!"

"We'll wait for you at the south edge of the parking lot!" Lincoln yelled.

The six of them plunged into the stampeding mob, and Maryland, Carter, and Hernie, turned away to look for the missing girl.

WHITNEY +23:26

Jacob Quinlan had spotted Tangela and her meddling brother upon first arriving at the Dome. His arm throbbed, but his frustration was worse: why did they never understand that he didn't want to hurt them? He would never hurt a child, he *loved* children, especially little girls.

He just wanted to make them part of him forever, couldn't they see that?

And now that Port Allen had fallen, now that there weren't any rules, he didn't have to be ashamed of that fact anymore. He didn't have to drive miles outside of town to hide his love, like he did with all the others. To meticulously plan out each encounter and get rid of the…*waste*…that was left over, so he wasn't persecuted by those who didn't understand.

Little Tangela. It looked like she and Bart had made some new friends since leaving him. It hadn't taken long to find somewhere private inside the Dome, and then he watched from the edge of the room, waiting for the perfect opportunity to separate her from her hateful brother. There were kids all over the place, others he probably could've snatched much easier, but it was her that drew his eyes again and again.

Now he led the girl by the wrist, off the Civic Center floor and into the dark hallway outside. If anyone out here thought anything of a rotund white man dragging a sickly black girl behind him, they didn't show it. Understandable. They had their own problems, after all. Most of the tightly packed mobs were trying to go into the Dome's main floor, seeking beds and food and to find out what the uproar was. They were met with a wave of panicked people trying to go the other direction. Quinlan managed to get out with his new friend just before the way became clogged with bodies.

The two of them reached a metal door marked 'Maintenance.'

Quinlan pulled this open. There was deeper darkness inside, but he'd snagged a flashlight in his travels today and used it to scout the place. He pulled the girl inside and let the door swing shut, sealing off the sound and meager light from outside.

"Y-you've been a b-bad girl, Tangela," he panted. He couldn't help it. He always stuttered and got short of breath before he shared his love. Mother always said it was good to be so eager, on those nights when she brought him into her bedroom.

He pushed her roughly along the metal catwalk leading from the door. She fell down the first short staircase, crying out as she hit bottom and then beginning to cough. He pulled the flashlight out of his torn pants and flicked it on so he didn't do the same. She blinked up at him in the light, tears in her eyes, and tried to crawl away.

"You and y-your brother hurt me. I just, just, just wanted to be your friend. To l-love you."

"Leave me alone!" she pleaded. As though she had reason to be scared of him. He would make her understand though. She reached the next staircase and fell into the water that flooded the bottom of this room before even realizing it was there. She came up sputtering.

"Y-you're mine now, Tangela. We can be together down here…"

He hauled her up by the back of her blouse with his good hand and held her against him as he stepped down into the cold flood water. Something in his arm boiled with pain, but he barely noticed in his excitement.

"I know you want this." Breath so fast, he was almost snorting. Ecstasy washed over him. "They a-always want this. You'll see…"

The water came up to his waist, her chest. He tucked the flashlight into his sling so it shone down into her face. She squinted and flailed weakly, but the fight was going out of her, just like it always did. He pawed at her, tearing her shirt around the collar as his hand slipped beneath. Soon she would see, soon she would love him too —

A hooting cry echoed through the maintenance tunnels.

WHITNEY +23:30

"We find Lincoln and the others, then you're gonna take me right back right to where you left Charlie, you understand?" Ellis pressed at a stitch in his side, careful not to jostle his broken finger.

Mac ran next to him, his huge strides barely enough to make him break a sweat. He was having trouble breathing through his crushed nose, however. It had puffed up so much the skin was splitting along the top, causing his voice to come out distorted and his frequent coughs to sound like honks. "For the thirtieth time, that's the plan. I swear. You make it sound like I'm holdin him for ransom or somethin."

The two of them had hidden in a storm-gutted store a few blocks from the Dome, watching the rain trail off and waiting for dark to give them some cover before venturing out. It was torture, especially after the gangbanger told him about leaving his comatose partner in an abandoned house somewhere north of the civic center.

"You really think your cop friends cleared out by now?"

"They must have. I mean, they can't just keep hanging around. Sooner or later, *someone* is gonna come looking for us."

"Funny. That's what Charlie was tellin me the whole time we was swimmin through the hood. And look who was here to welcome me."

Ellis said nothing. The shops along both sides of the street ended in another block, and across the intersection was the parking lot around the Dome. They could be there in minutes.

Mac stopped running.

"What are you doing, c'mon!"

"You hear that?"

Ellis didn't have to ask what he meant. From over the rooftops to the west came a mechanical *WHUMP-WHUMP-WHUMP* noise, growing steadily louder. The clouds had cleared again, and they both looked up, into the darkening sky, where the last thumbnail of daylight was bleeding out.

An oblong shape roared overhead. Pitch black and moving so fast it was almost impossible to see against the backdrop of the night, but flying low enough to bathe them in the whir of its rotors and the backwash of air from its passage. The helicopter disappeared from view over the other side of the buildings, heading in the direction of the Dome, the sound of its engines fading.

"Let's go!" Ellis took off again, his various aches and pains forgotten.

"What the hell was that?" Mac yelled as he caught up.

"*That*, my friend, is the cavalry!"

WHITNEY +23:33

The old man weighed next to nothing, but he was out *cold*. Lincoln and Kordi kept him balanced between them as they fought through the mobs trying to push their way off the Dome floor.

"Stay close!" Lincoln turned his head in Tom's armpit as much as he could to check on the others. CT clung to the back of his shirt to keep from being separated. The kid, Chris, was to his left, still leading Randy by the wrist, who walked with shuffling steps and head down.

More gunfire somewhere outside, muffled by the walls. A renewed cry of fear swept through the crowd like the wave at a ballgame.

The doorway into the outer hall ahead was choked with people. Lincoln saw refugees tripping, falling to the floor, and being covered by waves of unrelenting runners. Bodies were actually piling up at the front of the line where it bottlenecked, a human barrier of thrashing limbs like some bizarre orgy.

"We're not gonna be able to get out this way!"

"There!" Kordi pointed with the arm still holding his plastic bag of medical supplies. "Those air ducts! They must lead through to the hall!"

Lincoln saw where he meant. They broke away from the main group and headed along the bleachers until they reached a bare portion of wall. Along the way they passed a man convulsing on the floor, blood spraying from every orifice. Kordi turned his head to follow him as they went by.

"You can't do anything for them, Doc!"

"I know! That's what scares me!"

They reached the air duct, a three-foot square metal screen just a little over chest level. When Lincoln pulled himself up to look in, he could see through to the outer corridor, just a few feet away. A straight shot.

They put Tom on the floor, and with Lincoln, Kordi, and CT hauling at the long slats together, they were able to bend the metal enough to get it pried away from two of the four screw mounts. They boosted the doc up first, and he kicked at the covering on the opposite side until it broke away. Chris went next, then CT and Lincoln manhandled Tom's unconscious form into the air shaft and pushed him through until his feet disappeared out the other side. He moaned once during this operation, eyelids fluttering, and then went back to snoring. CT crawled through, and then Lincoln turned to Randy.

The man was staring across the Dome floor, which was more or less clear except for the scattered disease victims and the people still rioting at the exits. Nearly all the portable lamps were out, casting a miserable pallor over the room. A fire had started in the corner from one of the overturned barbecue grills.

Randy pointed in the direction of his deceased wife.

"Please," he whispered, so low Lincoln almost couldn't hear him. "We can't just leave her here."

"We'll come back." Lincoln knew that wasn't true, not for him, at least. He had decided to turn himself in after they got out of this. His sheriff days were over. "I'm sorry, man."

Randy climbed into the air duct. Other people were starting to get the idea now and heading in their direction. Lincoln pulled himself up and squeezed through before he could be mobbed.

The other side was just as bad. The hallway was packed. Here people got caught at the turnstiles. They pushed into the crowd as far as they could, but were stopped yards short of the exit by more shoving.

"Man, fuck this!" CT pulled out a pistol from his pocket and fired two rounds over the top of the crowd at the closest window.

It collapsed, dropping a glittering rain of thick glass. The people around them screamed and scattered, then immediately swooped back in toward the new exit.

"*Are you crazy?*" Lincoln snatched the gun away, nearly dropping Tom. He tucked it in his waistband. "Whose gun is that?"

"I took it off that pig befo' I left him and Mac! Worked, didn't it?"

Lincoln supposed you couldn't argue with results. The turnstile was emptying as folks made for the broken window or attempted to smash open others. Automatic gunfire sounded behind them. The six of them pushed through, out into the night air and the parking lot.

"Let's just get away from the building and give this a chance to calm d—!"

A light blazed in their faces from above.

WHITNEY +23:39

Tangela cried and coughed and shook under Quinlan's disgusting touch. She wanted more than anything for this to end, for her momma to come and save her, and when she realized this would never happen again, she just sobbed harder.

A noise came floating out of the dark cave that began just in front of them. To Tangela, it sounded like cartoon Indians when they hit their palms against their mouths, only way higher. It made her feel as uncomfortable as Quinlan, but in a different way. She remembered it from earlier, when Chris carried her on his back, just before they met this horrible man.

"What was that?" Too dark to see Quinlan's face, but she could hear the fear in his voice. That was worse somehow; as much as she hated this man, he was still an adult, and adults weren't supposed to get scared of noises in the dark.

It came again, *wah-wah-wah-wah-wah*, closer this time, echoing all around. There was a deep *KER-SPLASH*, the sound of something heavy dropped in a swimming pool. A wave surged out of the opening of the tunnel and broke over them.

"W-who's there?" the fat man shrieked. "I d-didn't do nothin, I swear!" He let go of Tangela as he fumbled for the flashlight he'd tucked in his sling. Her weak legs gave out, dropping her into the cold water. She floated beside him, caught between her fear of him and whatever else was in here.

She shivered in the dark while he blubbered. He swept the flashlight around the opening of the flooded corridor, which stretched far beyond its range, the walls fading into gray obscurity just yards away. Everything else was layered shadows. She could see the glassy plane of the water, the dark blob that was the fat man, and—

As she watched, the water behind her captor parted to make way for a hulking silhouette.

It grew and grew, so sleek the water couldn't even cling to it. It rose up silently until it towered over the fat man, a shape so awkward she couldn't make sense of it. An acrid smell hit her nostrils, sharp enough to singe nose hair. Two beady yellow eyes gleamed at her over Quinlan's head.

Just seconds ago, she thought there could never be anything worse in the world than him. Now, here it was, every boogieman that ever hid under the bed or in the closet. She felt her bladder let go, momentarily warming the water around her.

The yellow-eyed thing fell on Quinlan, dragging him beneath the water so fast the first scream had barely left his lips. The flashlight bobbed to the surface, throwing sparks of light in all directions.

Tangela scrambled to her feet and splashed toward the staircase. Behind her, the fat man broke the surface, screeching like a cat. She glanced over her shoulder as she climbed out of the water, tripping on stairs. She could see him wrestling in the light of the spinning flashlight, trying to break free as the monster tore at him. It made that sound again; this time there was savage triumph in it.

She was crying again, sobbing and coughing. She reached the landing and started up the second set of stairs toward the door. Quinlan fell silent. She looked below.

The monster was coming. Scrambling up the stairs after her. Snorting in high-pitched bursts.

She screamed for the first time. The door they'd come through was ahead; she could see slightly brighter light flowing under it.

A crash at her heels as the monster landed at the top of the stairs. That awful hooting noise resounded. Tangela reached the door, pulled it open, and careened through. After being in there, even the dim evening light in the corridor blinded her. People ran by her, and she joined the crowds. She was still crying, but she knew she was safe now; monsters—at least, *this* kind of monster—never, ever showed themselves to this many people.

There was new commotion behind her. Shouts turned to screams. Followed by the monster's bubbly cry, rising above all else.

Apparently, this one didn't know the rules.

She could see the top of its scaly head above the other people in the hallway, all of whom were now scattering as they saw what walked among them. The monster dove into the crowd, like an excited kid in a ball pit. The hallway filled with fear so fast it smothered her.

Tangela kept running as a crazed stampede picked up renewed energy around her.

WHITNEY +23:41

The crowds trying to get out on the north side of the Dome flowed fast, with no blockages. Carter hurtled through the door ahead of Maryland and Hernie—denying the insatiable urge to rap his knuckles on the outside—but was almost knocked down by a wave of people that crashed into him from the right. It was either go with the flow or get run over by it, so he kept pace.

He saw the other two swept up as well. Maryland managed to grab his arm to keep from being separated, but Hernie was shoved to the side and flattened against the wall.

"*Mr. Carter!*" he yelled, as the tide of bodies pushed them apart.

"*Just stay there, Hernie!*" Motherfrakker, there wasn't any room to maneuver out here, or to stop, or to think. All of these people were touching him, grinding their disgusting bodies against his. The noise of shouts and pounding feet in the darkened corridor was deafening. This, he decided, must be what hell is like.

"*What's going on?*" Maryland stumbled and almost went down, but her grip on Carter's shoulder kept her upright. "*Is this because of what happened to Heather and those people?*"

"*If it is, then why aren't they trying to get out?*" He got his feet planted and stood his ground long enough to look back over the chaos. It was an endless hysteria parade coming toward them. A few people actually made it through the turnstiles beneath the glowing red exit sign, but most just seemed to be bolting in whatever direction was open, resulting in a human traffic jam of screaming, colliding bodies. If he squinted in the dim light, he could almost make out a ripple moving through the center of the mob toward them.

As he watched, an object sailed above the crowd. It was small and round, about the size of a human head...

Scratch that; it *was* a head. He saw the torn skin around the neck as it passed under one of the emergency lights, a bit of spinal column protruding and blood droplets following behind like the tail of a sperm. He followed it as it struck the wall to his right and then fell into the crowd, inciting fresh cries and a change in fleeing direction.

"No way did I just see that," he murmured.

"*There she is!*" Maryland let go of him and plunged crossways through a gap in the crowd before he could stop her.

"*Maryland, wait!*" Carter tried to go after her, but was shoved violently back the other direction and further down the hall. He fought against the crowd. Just too many bodies packed into the narrow passage; it was like fording a deep, fast river. Claustrophobia closed in, followed by waves of revulsion at all these people touching him. His lungs seized. He looked back again, standing on his toes, and caught a glimpse of something huge squirming through the mass of people just yards away. The crowd parted and shifted, people throwing themselves against the walls to get away from it. The screams were piercing.

Someone hit him hard, upsetting his precarious balance. He fell flat on his back. Feet kicked him in the side as those behind him went down. A thrashing tide of bodies sprawled over him, and then his fear didn't have to steal his breath because their sheer weight was doing it. He couldn't see anything except the sweatsuit-clad ass in his face, pushing the rebreather mask painfully into his skin. His arms were pinned, his lungs screaming to inflate beneath the crush and God, they were going to *squish out his insides like a tube of toothpaste...!*

Hands slid beneath him, gripping him by the arms. He squirmed, and, with the extra help, he was able to slip out of the dogpile. The rebreather skewed sideways, and he held his breath until he could get it refitted. Filtered air filled his chest, but the black spots still swam through his vision as he sat up and turned to the owner of the hands.

He expected Hernie or Maryland.

Instead Gerald stood over him, a plastic bag of water bottles slung over one shoulder.

"*You?*" Carter choked.

"*That's twice I saved your ass! So tell those other guys, I'm not a total—*"

The sentence was cut off as a monstrous form rose up behind him and tore his throat out.

WHITNEY +23:46

Mac's coughs felt like punches to the chest by the time he reached the end of the block behind Ellis. From here, they had a downsloping view of the north side of the Dome and the surrounding parking lot, now a maze of haphazardly-parked cars.

Helicopters hovered in a rough semicircle around the Dome, at least eight of them. They were just a little ways off the ground, at about the level of the roof. People streamed out of the civic center on all sides in an endless procession, but stopped when they saw the choppers. They reached hands up to the sleek, black machines like ancient people worshipping a flying god. The helicopters switched on searchlights and swept them over the assemblage.

"They here…to start flyin…people out?" Mac wheezed.

"I…I don't think so. In fact, they look more like—"

Flaming projectiles broke away from two of the choppers and streaked toward the convex roof of the Dome.

WHITNEY +23:48

Lincoln shifted Tom on his shoulder and held a hand up to block the light from his eyes. When it swept away, he saw the source hovering just outside the exit from the Dome.

"*Links!*" CT shouted over the noise of the vehicle's engine and the crowd gathering below it. "*That's the fuckin pigs! We gotta go!*"

"That ain't the cops!"

"Whoever they are, they're making things worse!" Kordi yelled from Tom's other side. The people under the helicopter climbed on top of one another to reach it, forming a human pyramid that crushed those at the bottom. The black chopper remained just tantalizingly out of reach, as though trying to draw as many as possible. Its tinted canopy was dark enough to reveal nothing of the pilots.

Randy waved to get Lincoln's attention. *"Maybe we should just wait here!"*

"I don't wanna get in the middle of that with him!" He raised Tom's limp hand and waggled it. *"Let's just get to the other end of the parking lot and wait for the others!"*

They skirted the mob and made their way further out. They had just reached the first row of cars when all five of them were knocked flat by a concussive wave of sound and heat.

WHITNEY +23:49

Lemiere pushed Imogene's new wheelchair fast down the hallway in the middle of a great mass of people. She held onto the oxygen mask with one hand, the seat handle with the other, and tried not to hyperventilate. They'd been at the makeshift dispensary when the riot broke out, trying to get medicine for Lemiere's cough. Now they were running with a thousand other people toward the south exit, and they didn't even know why.

They careened around the last curve of the hallway just as gunshots sounded. Glass shattered ahead. She could see people fighting to get through the turnstiles and breaking the windows to make new exits.

A man with a semi-automatic rifle lurched out of the crowd at them. *"Gimme that!"* he barked, blood running from his nose. He reached for the oxygen bottle tucked into the pocket on her wheelchair back.

"Ge' back!" Lemiere stepped between him and Imogene. The man swung the barrel of his gun up, but there wasn't enough room between them. Lemiere grabbed the stock and held it down. The man pulled the trigger, rattling off a chain of shots into the floor by

Imogene's foot. She screamed. The crowd around them broke like startled birds.

The recoil threw the man off balance. He staggered away from Lemiere, gun arm swinging wild, finger still on the trigger. Bullets sprayed the people passing by. Blood flew as they fell.

"*You crazy sumbitch!*" Lemiere leapt at him with an angry, Cajun cry, hitting him midsection with his shoulder and driving him to the ground. They struggled for a moment before Lemiere wrenched the weapon away and smashed the butt across the maniac's cheek, knocking him unconscious. He stood up, checked some chamber on the shaft of the rifle with quick precision—obviously a man who knew more about firearms than she did—and held it to his chest.

By now the crowds were clambering through the broken windows to get out, leaving a trail of trampled bodies behind. Lemiere positioned himself behind her once more, secured the gun through a crossbar on the back of her wheelchair so it jutted from both sides, and charged into the fray. They were able to maneuver their way to an opening after a few minutes.

People at the window pointed into the sky. A bright searchlight caught her attention from above, and she saw helicopters outside the building.

"*Thank God!*" she yelled over her shoulder. "*We're saved!*"

The crowd was still shoving from behind, desperate people grasping and heaving. Lemiere wrapped his hands around the wheel spokes and lifted her, chair and all, and dropped her roughly on the concrete walkway on the other side. She bounced on the thinly padded seat. Her weak lungs hiccupped. People poured out of the window on both sides of her and streamed into the parking lot, waving at the helicopter. Lemiere had just hopped over himself when a deep rumble went through the ground.

She turned her head up to him. "What was that?"

It came again, closer this time, a shockwave big enough to cause Lemiere to fall against her.

Then a blast of heat hit her from behind, and she was flying through the air.

WHITNEY +23:52

Maryland shoved her way through the throng to where she'd glimpsed Tangela. This was worse than the freeway last night or the grocery store this morning; something had these people utterly terrified, and, in the dusky, confined space of the corridor, it was like too many starving rats poured into the same tiny cage.

Tangela cowered in a small niche in the outer wall, coughing and watching the crowd with wide eyes. She began to cry when she saw Maryland.

"It's okay, sweetie, I'm here!" She snatched the girl up.

Tangela was repeating something over and over, but the noise in the hallway was so loud Maryland couldn't hear it until she pressed the girl's mouth against her ear.

"Monster," she whispered. "Monster."

Something large brushed past Maryland, close enough for her to catch a whiff of putrid fish. She spun in time to see a shadow sweep by with the fleeing crowd, something that moved with serpentine grace. Low and hunched, its length was several yards from the end of its snout, down through its sinewy body, to the tip of its broad, flat tail. As it passed beneath one of the few fluorescents still powered by the emergency generator, she got an impression of leathery skin and delicate, wafer-thin spines growing like porcupine quills from its back. It lashed out with muscled arms, claws raking flesh to draw blood. The raw power of it tossed people through the air. There was something almost gleeful in the havoc it wreaked.

She blinked stupidly after it, sure she was hallucinating. Something about it was like a dinosaur appearing at one of the charity dinner parties she'd been to with Bryce.

The hallway cleared in the wake of the (*monster*, tough Maryland whispered, using Tangela's word)...of whatever it had been, and commotion on the far side of the corridor drew her attention. People sprawled into one tangled knot like a Twister game from hell. She saw Carter helped from the bottom of a pile of downed refugees by Gerald, of all people.

But she wasn't the only one that noticed. The creature circled through the mob and made a beeline for the easy targets.

As she watched, that black shape reared up behind the athletic guy that she had—against her will—been mentally undressing all morning. One of the overhead lights shone directly down on it, but its mottled skin and multiple protrusions made a mess of the illumination. Its misshapen head turned, snapped forward, and jaws like an alligator's clamped down around Gerald's neck. The creature jerked once, and flesh came off in one meaty rip. He jerked spastically for a few seconds before collapsing at the monster's feet.

Tangela screamed in her ear. Then she realized the girl was turned backward over her shoulder, and that the piercing shriek was her own.

Carter sat dazed on the ground, but at the sound of her voice, he looked up from the body. So did the monster. Its face was painted in shadow, but its yellow eyes glared with malevolence.

It came barreling at her, weaving from side-to-side.

She stood frozen.

Before it could reach her, a sonic boom raced through the building, the force of it enough to push her against the wall. Memories of the bridge explosion rushed her. Everything shook. She clapped hands over her ears as the tile beneath her feet rocked. The creature stopped, turned its narrow head up, and then bolted with incredible speed, back down the hallway in the direction it had come, shoving people out of its path.

Another tremendous blast vibrated the air. The walls cracked, chunks of plaster from the ceiling fell on the heads of the crowd. This time Maryland did go down, making sure not to land on the girl. The explosion was accompanied by a wave of heat. Flames belched from the exit of the Dome floor they'd just come through, incinerating those around it.

Carter appeared above them, helping them to their feet. The hallway filled with smoke and the roar of fire. The crowd fought to get through the turnstiles and broken windows, treading over anyone that fell. The three of them made their way toward the nearest.

"*Wait, Mr. Carter, wait for me!*" Hernie caught up to them just as they clambered over the windowsill and into the parking lot.

A helicopter hovered above a multitude of people just yards away from them, a searchlight over the whole group as they ran toward it. It was black and long, with short wings attached to both sides. Maryland stopped with Tangela still draped over her shoulder and Carter's arm around her.

"*Are they here to help us?*" she shouted to him over the roar of noise.

"*Those don't look like any Red Cross choppers I ever saw!*"

The helicopter tilted forward, so its nose faced down at the crowd, and two cylinders mounted under the wings spit fire. There was a prolonged purr, the kind of sound she imagined a robotic cat might make, and the people reaching for the hovering machine were chewed apart by invisible teeth, going down in a bloody, gouged line.

"*Jesus, they're firing on them!*"

Carter gave her a shove in the direction of the parking lot. "*Run!*"

WHITNEY +23:57

The resulting fireball when the missiles hit the top of the Dome blossomed into the cloudy night sky like a flaming rosebud. The sound of it expanded across the city, a thunderous rumble that went on and on. Ellis and Mac watched as the curved roof collapsed, caving in at the middle. The image made Ellis think of a wilting soufflé. A heat wave washed over them even at this distance.

One of the helicopters circled around and loosed another missile directly into the western section of the circular outer wall. A boil made of fire grew on the concrete before it disintegrated, raining fire and destruction on the people still trying to get out.

"*FUCK!*" Mac screamed. "*Why are they doin that?*"

"I have no idea," Ellis whispered.

People already outside the building seemed to be getting the idea that the gunships were no saviors. They backed away from the growing fires and the helicopters, but far too slowly. The choppers turned, tracking them, and opened fired from side-mounted machine guns. Chained gunfire rolled across the parking lot, combining with the undergrumble of the explosion.

"They're *killin* 'em!" Mac jaw fell open. "Oh God, Lincoln!"

He took off across the street. Ellis hesitated for only a second before going after him.

More missiles screeched into the night.

WHITNEY +23:58

"I scrounged us up s'more beans from that school bus of Oklahoma disaster volunteers, man," Burt Weaver said as he walked back to the campfire with his arms loaded.

Daryl Sloan sat huddled on one side of the meager flames, next to a paper plate of untouched food. He hadn't been hungry enough to eat since yesterday, so the extras made no difference to him, but the rest of their roadside community sent up a cheer and clapped the hippie on the back as he walked through.

People had banded together all day as they sat next to the freeway and waited for something, *anything*, to happen, forming small collectives if only for the company. When the rains started up earlier in the day, they broke and made for the cars, but once it cleared everyone emerged again, sharing food and updates. Daryl and Burt fell in with fifteen or so other stranded motorists and played cards to pass the time. A woman named Yolanda had canned food in her minivan, which they cooked over an open flame started by a gruff Port Allen oilman named Bernard.

Burt plopped down next to Daryl. He had yet to figure out the man's age. They guy looked pretty ripe, weather-beaten and crow-footed, but talked like a teenager. Well, a teenager circa 1969, anyway. "C'mon Daryl, you gotta eat somethin, dude. Your family is fine, I promise."

"I know. I know they are." Daryl didn't, not at all, but it seemed the thing to say.

"Wanna play some more rummy, get your mind off it?"

"No thanks."

"That guy Cecil has some righteous board games in his trunk. I think I saw Connect Four, man!"

Daryl shot him a smile. "No, really, I just kinda want to…sit."

"Suit yourself, friend."

"They got no right! No fuckin right!" This from Avery, a muscled-up guy in a cowboy hat on the far side of the fire. His girlfriend Crystal, dressed in cutoff shorts and a neckerchief top that covered half her breasts, reclined against him. "They can't keep us from goin into the city! It's illegal!"

"Oh, will you give it a rest?" an older man moaned. "You've been saying that every fifteen minutes all day!"

"That's because it's true!" Burt chimed in. "This is all part of the government's plan to distract you from the real problems: global warming, pesticides, and the fact that laser eye surgery is makin the hole in the ozone layer worse!"

Everyone groaned at that.

"Maybe," someone shouted, "but you two idiots talkin about it all the time ain't makin this traffic move!"

Daryl sighed. They were still in the same place. Ever so often, a car would pass them going the opposite direction, but they assumed these were people who'd had enough of waiting and turned around to spend their time elsewhere. At first they tried to flag down these vehicles to see what they might know, but none of them stopped.

Avery muttered something and pulled his cowboy hat lower over his face. Crystal reached up to rub his neck.

"I think I'm gonna go back to my car and get some sleep," Daryl told Burt. He wasn't really tired, just sick of other people. "Will you wake me if something happens?"

"You got it, man."

Daryl stood, stretching muscles sore from sitting on the ground, and heard a commotion behind them. He turned in time to see a skinny white youth come pelting out of the night along the side of the freeway beside the stalled cars, shouting, "It's out! It's out, the bridge is out!"

Avery climbed to his feet. "Got another town crier."

The rest of their group stirred, getting to their feet. Rumors had run rampant all day, some filtering from group to group, others heralded by self-proclaimed messengers who ambled through the waiting people on both sides of the highway screaming. The bridge being out was just about neck-and-neck with one about Whitney starting the Rapture in Port Allen.

Yolanda waved the kid over with offers of bottled water. He angled toward them, panting and out of breath, and was surrounded by the rest of the group.

"Now son, what are you hollerin about?" Bernard asked.

"Yeah, we already heard the one about the bridge, dumbass," Avery added.

"It's out, I saw it," he said between gulps of water. He had to be under the age of twenty, a few years older than Chris. The thought of that sent another pang through Daryl's system.

"No way! Rugg Canyon is another *fifty* miles up the road! You expect us to believe you ran all the way here?"

"I've been going around since noon to tell people."

"Then why hasn't it been on the news?" someone asked. "I've been listening to the radio all day!"

"There's an army blockade or something to keep people from getting too close, and they grounded all these helicopters from the news and the Red Cross that offered help. I even saw this one get forced away by Army choppers. The only reason I know is because I circled around to the north with some friends early this morning and then snuck into the perimeter they set up." He wiped water or sweat off his upper lip and looked around at them. "Trust me, the bridge is gone. Completely. Everybody on it fell into the canyon. I saw the bodies."

The people from the fire sat in a moment of stunned silence, broken when Yolanda moaned, "Oh, *Dios!* My husband called me from the bridge! I haven't talked to him since!"

"Now we know for sure what all this is about." Bernard said solemnly, sweeping a hand past the waiting vehicles clogging the road. "And we're probably not moving anytime soon."

"But what are they doing?" Daryl demanded. "What are they doing about getting us into the city? About getting out the people that are still in there?"

The young doomsayer shrugged, and Daryl had the urge to grab the kid and shake answers out of him. And if they were the wrong answers, he'd keep shaking until they were right.

"No Fly Zone," Burt said, as if tasting the words. "Sounds like someone's got somethin to hide."

"You're bein paranoid," Crystal told him.

Avery put an arm around her bare waist. "Yeah, what could possibly be that bad in there?"

"I heard..." the kid said softly, eyes glittering in the firelight, and all heads swiveled back to him to soak up each word, "that the whole city...is *radioactive.*"

"That's a loada crap," someone declared, and just like that the group dispersed, people heading back to food and the fire, and the kid went on to enjoy his fifteen minutes of fame.

Daryl stood talking with Burt a moment longer and was just about to head on to his car when a hand grabbed his shoulder. He turned around to face Avery.

"Hey guys." His cowboy hat was in hands. He played with the brim nervously as he glanced around. Avery was a big guy even without the hat; Daryl had to look up to meet his eyes. "Daryl, you said you got family inside the city, right?"

"That's right."

"Well...Crystal and me...we were thinkin about goin in. Just gonna see if you wanted to come along. You too, Burt."

Daryl put a hand on his temple and held the other up. "Look, I know you don't believe that about the bridge, and you could be right, but even so, there's obviously no way in up there."

Avery waved the words away. "Naw, I'm not talkin about the bridge, I'm talkin about the old western pass. The turnoff for it is just a few miles back."

"That old trail?" Burt shook his head. "No dice, man, they have another roadblock set up there, I remember passin it last night in the storm. Besides, you'd need somethin heavy-duty to get through, especially if there's storm damage."

"See that Hummer?" Avery pointed at a black and yellow monstrosity far back on the road, but still visible above the roofs of all the other vehicles. "That's mine. It's fully gassed and more than enough to get us over the mountains. If we cut overland early tomorrow morning and meet up with the western trail in the foothills, we'll go around the roadblock and they won't even know it."

Daryl frowned. "Okay, even if all that's true, why are you offering to take *us*?"

The cowboy shrugged, cut his eyes away, and smiled sheepishly. "Just be nice to have some backup, that's all. An extra hand in case, you know, somethin comes up in there."

"You mean someone else to share the blame in case you get caught."

"That too."

Daryl shook his head and sighed. The need to get into Port Allen, to take some kind of action, was driving him insane. This was the exact plan he'd considered earlier this morning, but now that the military was involved, it was a whole different ballgame.

"I'm in if you are," Burt said. "*Viva la revolución.* Down with the man, man."

Daryl opened his mouth to give an answer, but was stopped by a distant grumble that swept across the plains from the east. Everyone around the fire and by the side of the freeway looked up, toward the Chantillys.

The low ridges of the mountains had disappeared as night fell, slipping into a pocket of cloud-borne shadows, but now it was visible again, backlit by a soft glow. Another muted crack drifted over it to them. The whole scene reminded Daryl of war movies where the fighting was happening far in the distance.

"Okay," he said. "But I want to leave as early as possible."

WHITNEY +23:59

Lincoln landed hard on his stomach, with Tom's unconscious body slumped on top of him. God, this guy could sleep through anything. "*Everybody okay?*" He received a chorus of affirmatives and then pushed the Englishman off so he could look back at the Dome.

Or the fiery conflagration that had once been the Dome.

By the light of a blazing fire at its center, he could see there was hardly anything left of the building. The curved top that had given the civic center its nickname was gone, and the outer walls were either collapsing or on fire. Tongues of flame lapped at the night sky. He saw people crushed by an avalanche of falling debris, others on fire as they made it out. Even as he watched, another helicopter hovering over the flood on the east side of the building fired a missile into the growing pile of rubble, throwing up a cloud of wreckage and bodies on a burning carpet.

It was so hellish, he couldn't even take it all in, much less figure out why it was happening.

He glanced at the exit they'd just come through. That last explosion had knocked them down, but those closer to the building had been launched through the air by the shockwave. People were regaining their feet beneath the eyes of the merciless helicopter.

Lincoln spotted the little black lady in the wheelchair, the tough old broad that had stood up to CT, now lying on the ground and struggling to crawl across the pavement on her belly. Something in the pit of his stomach wrenched at the sight.

"*Take him!*" he shouted at CT, putting a finger on Tom's chest. "*All of you, get away from the building! Wait for me out in the parking lot!*" He stood up.

"*Where are you going?*" Kordi yelled.

"*I have to help someone!*" He dove back into the melee surrounding the building.

Smoke was heavy here. All around him were shouts and screams, burn victims, people flopping like epileptics as they coughed and bled out, utter chaos. He focused only on the prone figure, who writhed on the ground.

He reached the old lady and turned her over. Her eyes were clenched shut, her mouth twisted in a snarl of pain. Her hands clawed at her own throat.

"*What is it?*" He thought at first it was the disease, but she wasn't coughing up blood, or even coughing at all. "*What's wrong?*"

She mouthed one word between gasps. "*Air.*"

He remembered the mask she'd been wearing, the clear plastic cup and hose. He looked around helplessly. "*I-I don't know where it is!*"

Someone grabbed him by the shoulder and shoved him back. He looked up to see the skinny white guy in the John Deere cap that had been pushing her wheelchair. He squatted beside them, her collapsed chair in tow. He pulled a small, green tank out of the back pocket, slipped the band over her head, and adjusted the cup on her nose and mouth.

She still looked to be in pain, but at least she wasn't choking anymore. She gave them a shaky thumbs up.

"*Let's get her out of here!*" Lincoln shouted. The other guy started to unfold the wheelchair, but Lincoln just tucked the little oxygen tank under his arm and then picked the woman up. She couldn't weigh more than 70 or 80 pounds, less even than Tom. He draped her over his shoulder like a caveman. The other man picked up her chair and what looked to be an automatic rifle.

The rest of the dazed crowd made its way out into the parking lot, away from the building. As the three of them turned to do the same, the helicopter over them opened fire.

Three people to Lincoln's left evaporated in a mist of blood. He yelped and jumped away, holding the woman on his back.

"*Go, go!*" The crowd scattered in all directions amid wails. The sound of the machine guns rose above it all, smooth and even, a mechanized whine. All around them, people fell as limbs were severed, bodies burst open by the force of the weapons. He saw motion above and looked up to see another helicopter circling in from their right to aid in the slaughter. Bullets tore up the pavement in a zig-zag in front of Lincoln, and he veered in a different direction with the old woman flopping against his back.

The first cars in the lot were just ahead, the only cover around. He made for them with his head down, not daring to look back. The air was alive with screams and that constant droning gunfire. And then they were in the midst of the cars and Lincoln ducked beside the trunk of a Taurus, making sure the lady's head was down low enough to be hidden. John Deere Cap came to a panting halt beside him. They rose up enough to read the situation.

Most of the helicopters had flown away from the Dome and roamed the parking lot, spraying bullets at anything that moved. Every few seconds, gunfire would find the gas tank of one of the vehicles and an explosion lit up the night. They saw one of these flip end-over-flaming-end, landing on a group of cowering refugees. The helicopter that caused this fired on the survivors before moving on.

"They're exterminatin us like cockroaches," Lincoln whispered. The woman clinging to him shivered. John Deere Cap watched him with hooded eyes. "C'mon. We gotta get away from here."

Lincoln got on all fours, repositioned his passenger so that she balanced on him like a horse, and began to crawl down the rows of cars, all the while telling himself that the slight tickle in his throat was his imagination.

WHITNEY +24:00

The light wind coming off the ocean blew the smoke from the growing fires northward. Carter and the others rushed through a black haze in which cars and bodies drifted like debris from a shipwreck. Explosions thudded, distant fireworks, echoing too much to determine a direction. Screams blended into one long, warbling note. They held hands to stay together; him in the lead, then Maryland with Tangela slung over her shoulder, Hernie following. All three of them coughed as they tried to get clear air into their lungs, and he was once again grateful (or was that *guilty?*) that he had the rebreather.

At least the smoke served to mask them from the helicopters. They heard the blades spinning overhead several times as the machines whirred past, saw ghostly sparks as they opened fire. Then Carter's eyes started to burn from the smoke and he couldn't see anything at all through his tears.

"*Carter!*" Maryland tugged on his hand. "*Where are we going?*"

He didn't know. God, he didn't know anything. Some piece of him, the Lucid maybe, far back in his head where the panic couldn't reach, had been trying to come up with a reason for all this—the helicopters, the explosions, that *thing* in the hallway—and was drawing a great big, fat blank. Even with the mask on and the smoke obscuring any view of the sky, he felt a mother of a panic attack coming on.

A parked truck swam out of the fog and he stopped running, leaned against the hood, and closed his eyes to focus on one breath at a time.

"*What are you doing?*" Maryland charged past him without slowing, still holding his hand. The force of her momentum pulled him off his perch and into the concrete on his knees. The world gave a sickening spin.

"Can't." He squeezed her fingers with his own, still cognizant enough to marvel at what delicate little digits they were. "Having… an attack."

"*Don't you fucking do this now, you chickenshit!*" She lashed out with her foot, catching him in the side just under the arm she was holding up. "*Get up! Get up or we will LEAVE YOU HERE!*"

"*Get up, Mr. Carter!*" Hernie wrapped an arm around his waist and heaved.

Get up, you unbelievable prick! the Lucid bellowed.

With lungs still in protest, he got up.

Time sputtered, black spots growing in his memory like burn marks on a movie reel. Every time his eyes opened, a new scene presented itself: running with them again, legs on autopilot...the smoke thinning...two black men—one of them huge—looming out of the murk...falling into this behemoth's arms...and then, as he was carried away, a final view of the Dome and its surrounding lot ablaze, a giant bonfire with angry bees buzzing around it, before he winked out for good.

HUNTED

SHOOT TO THRILL

WHITNEY +24:28

The ringing in Carter's head gradually separated into distinct voices. Angry voices. He sat up and wished he hadn't.

The melon atop his shoulders weighed at least fifty pounds. Even in the dark behind his eyelids, the world lurched sickeningly, like a good, all-night bender. Except this wasn't from alcohol. Oh no; that throb on the inside of his skull was brain damage brought on by oxygen deprivation.

Better watch those stubborn lungs, the Lucid warned. *You don't have many brain cells to spare.*

As long as I kill the one you *use...*

Carter felt for the rebreather, found it still in place and functioning. Finally he took in the scene change, moving only his eyes instead of his head to keep the pain at bay.

He was indoors now. A small, square room with a tipped metal shelving unit wedged between the narrow walls over him, and a litter of cleaning supplies across the floor. A janitor's closet. It was dark and dank, probably would've smelled like wet plaster and mildew if not for the mask. He repeated the Okay Mantra until he no longer wanted to clean the place with a blowtorch.

The voices drifted through an open doorway to his left. He could hear enough to tell they were two distinct pitches, but the words all blended together. Neither was familiar.

He grabbed the edge of the doorframe and used it to claw his way to his feet, kicking a wet roll of toilet paper out of his way. For one second, the pain in his head peaked so hard he was sure he would vomit. Then it passed, worming into the back of his brain to sulk. He gave four soft knocks on the wall and then stepped over a pile of more substantial wreckage just outside the door.

Beyond was a short, littered hallway, and he followed it toward the voices. He came out behind a clerk's counter. In front of it was the interior of a gas station: a few aisles of short shelves, most of them overturned, the entire front wall of glass panels shattered and collapsed, the ceiling in shreds. Through the hole in the building he could see gasoline pumps in the distance. It was fully dark now.

The arguers were on his right. Two black men, one a bit shorter than him, the other massively larger. He recalled them from the last hazy moments before he conked out. Maryland stood against the wall beside them, arms wrapped over her chest.

"Carter, thank God." Relief flooded her face. She came behind the counter and threw her arms around him, but he was too groggy to enjoy it. "You wouldn't wake up, I didn't know what to do! Are you all right?"

"Hulk smash." His tongue was thick, mouth full of cotton. "Where are we?"

"A gas station, just a few blocks from the Dome."

"How long was I…?"

She shook her head. "I don't know. Couldn't be more than a half-hour or so."

An open plastic bottle of Dr. Pepper sat on the counter. She handed it to him and, after a guilty few seconds of inner warfare, he lifted the corner of the mask to drink. The cola was warm, but heavenly. "Where's Hernie? Tangela?"

"In the manager's office, right next to the supply room you were in. They're still sick, so we kept you separated, just…just in case."

Carter let his bleary eyes drift to the other two men. They stared back, checking out the rebreather.

Maryland gestured to them. "Carter, this is Mac and Ellis. Ellis is a police officer. They helped us get away."

"'Helped' might be an understatement," the big one rumbled, "considerin I carried yo' ass."

"I remember. Sorry about that. But thank you." Carter came to the counter and forced himself to hold a hand over the top. Why the hell not, he was covered with grime anyway. The rebreather was the important thing now, the lynchpin of his sanity. Mac came over and shook with one massive meathook. Even in the dark, he could see the guy was no more than a kid with the proportions of Donkey Kong. His face was a mess though, the nose swollen up so big it looked like an imbedded sausage. Carter repeated the offer to the other man.

"Thanks, but no. Broken finger."

"Looks like you guys have had it even rougher than us."

Mac grunted. "Those are long stories we don't got time for. I got a friend somewhere down in that mess at the Dome, and I'm goin back to look for 'im!"

Ellis rolled his head back to stare at the ceiling. "For the last time, *we don't know what's going on down there*. We should just stay away. What I want you to do is take me to Charlie."

"I gave you the address!"

"But I don't know where that is! *You* need to show me! I'm… I'm…" The guy gritted his teeth and stamped his foot while he searched for words. "I'm *ordering* you to take me there!"

Mac gave a hard-edged grin, and then shook his head. "That's not workin today, Officer. We're all equals when the sky's fallin. If you don't care about my people, why should I give a shit 'bout yours?"

"Because if my people die, you're responsible for killing a cop!"

"Fuck him and fuck you too, pig! I never shoulda listened to you!"

"Okay, just stop." Carter held up a shaking hand. "We've been through enough without the Laurel and Hardy routine."

"They've been fighting like this since we got here," Maryland told him.

"You guys obviously have some issues to work out, but before we get out the padded bats, can you please just tell us what happened back there?"

They both digested this with a few seconds of ashamed silence. "No clue, man." Mac coughed against one fist, the sound dry and raspy.

"What about you?" He pointed at Ellis. "You're a cop, don't you know what that was all about?"

"Why does everyone assume that just because you're a cop, you gain clairvoyance in any given situation?" Ellis shrugged. "I haven't been in touch with any of my superiors since before Whitney. I know about as much as you do."

"Which is what, exactly?" Maryland's voice quavered in a way that Carter didn't care for. "Let's just make sure we're all on the same page here before we decide what to do."

Ellis took a few steps in their direction. "Someone with helicopters and a lot of firepower came in and…just blew up the civic center. We saw it happen from a distance, got the whole show. They fired missiles at it with all those people still inside, then they…shot at the ones who made it out."

Maryland nodded. "Okay, good, we can all agree on that. Now the obvious question is: who did it?"

"I think *why* might be a bit more pressing," Carter added.

Mac was stomping up and down one of the few open aisles. He swiped something from one of the soggy shelves, tore open a wrapper, and gnawed into a hunk of chocolate. "It's the same answer to both questions. Terrorists."

Maryland groaned. "That's ridiculous."

"I don't know," Carter mumbled. "Didn't seem to be much motivation. Who picks on a bunch of hurricane victims besides terrorists?"

"There is no way a foreign military force with that much hardware could be operating within American borders," Ellis said.

"Maybe they came in from the ocean side right after the storm."

Maryland walked to the counter and placed her hands on its scarred top, bandaged palms down. "We all saw the helicopters, so no matter who they were, we can all agree they're a danger. We just can't do anything about them until help arrives. In the meantime, we might have bigger problems. If you guys were out here, then there were some things going on *inside* the Dome you have no idea about."

"Like what?"

Her face was a haunted oval in the pale moonlight coming in the front of the store. "People were getting sick."

"No shit, lady!" Mac shouted from the other side of the room. "I'm sick, that little girl and your friend in the other room are sick, *everybody's* sick!"

"Would you keep your voice down!" Ellis hissed.

Maryland continued. "No, I mean they were…dying. This woman next to us, she was coughing one minute, and the next she just…just started bleeding out. Hemorrhaging. She went into convulsions and died."

Carter saw the other two exchange a knowing look. "What?"

Ellis grimaced. "We saw that happen to someone this afternoon. Another officer."

"Yeah, well, in the Dome it started happening to a lot of people. All at once. It caused a rush for the exits, which is why so many people were outside when the place went up."

They were quiet until Mac started to cough again, trying desperately to keep them in but succeeding only in wheezing through clamped lips. One by one, they turned to look at him. "What? You sayin I got this disease? That what happened to them is gonna happen to me?"

No one answered.

"Fuuuuuck that!" He stalked toward the station's shattered front. "I'm goin back to the Dome to see if those helicopters are still there. And once I find my boy, I'm gettin to a hospital!"

"Wait, just wait!" Maryland pleaded. "We have friends we need to find too, but Ellis is right, it's not gonna do any good if we run back there without thinking this through!"

"You just told me I'm dyin!"

"I never said that! I don't know what the sickness was! There was a doctor at the civic center that had medicine to slow it down! He was with the people we're looking for last time we saw him!"

Mac glared at her across the station for a long minute before surrendering. "Fine, I'm listenin."

"Thank you."

Ellis came to the counter. "You're talking about Kordi, right? The doctor?"

"Yes, that's him!"

"I met him. He told me about this disease, but no one had died from it yet. I didn't put two and two together when we saw Myers bleed out." He turned to Carter. "Is that why you're wearing the mask? Do you know something about it?"

"Nope, I'm just..." He was aware of Maryland's eyes on him. "Germophobic."

"That's convenient," Mac muttered from his position by the hole in the wall. "You think it's contagious? You think you can catch it from me?"

Just him saying it gave Carter the sudden urge to claw at his skin where they'd touched. He imagined he could feel every microbe this guy was breathing into the air, coating every inch of exposed flesh, suckling at the scratch marks the rats had given him. But it really didn't matter. He'd been traveling with Hernie all day, then Tangela and Tom, so anything he was going to catch was probably already in his system. That was the Lucid's opinion anyway, but Carter still felt like taking a bath in hydrochloric acid.

To keep his mind from turning on itself, he said, "Discussing that is as pointless as trying to figure out where the helicopters came from. But there's still one other thing that happened inside the Dome that I'd like to bring up." He looked down at Maryland beside him. "And you know what I mean."

She covered her eyes with her fingers, like a kid trying to shut out the sight of the shape in the closet. "I know, but that…what we saw…it couldn't be real. I'd rather think we hallucinated it."

"Hallucinated what?"

Maryland didn't answer, so it was Carter's turn to give story time. "During the mass exodus, there was…something in the crowd. It was too dark to really see it, but it looked like some kind of…*monster.*"

He was met with stone silence until Mac demanded, "What the fuck're you talkin about?"

"I don't know where it came from or where it went. It was fast and big. Kind of leathery, like an alligator or something. It just…ripped through the crowd. Like a lawnmower through grass blades."

"It tore out our friend's throat." Maryland shrugged. "Well, our acquaintance anyway. I don't know if I'd call that asshole a friend."

"This thing was vicious, an animal or something. Not only that, but…I think I've seen it before."

Maryland looked horrified. "*When?*"

"Last night, during the storm. It was just a shadow in the street, but it had that same bulk, that same awkward shape."

Mac slammed a fist down on a nearby shelf. "Man, we don't need to be tellin no ghost stories!"

"You're right, I'd rather think you hallucinated it," Ellis said.

"Even if that's true, what does that have to do with the helicopters or the sickness?"

Carter shook his head. "Maybe nothing. But, as supremely *Lost*-ish as it sounds, it *did* happen. And maybe you want to think about that before you go charging back down there like the world's most pathetic cavalry."

"I don't care if it's the devil," Mac whispered. "I gotta find Lincoln. I gotta know."

The use of the name wiped all expression off Carter's face. "Lincoln? Muscular black kid?"

In unison, Mac and Ellis asked, "You know him?"

Maryland jumped away from the counter, waving her hands in excitement. "He's with the people we're trying to find too! Wait a minute, Carter, *the radio!*"

He'd completely forgotten he had it. He pulled the rectangular hunk of black plastic Kordi had given him out of his pocket, expecting it to be broken. It looked intact. The one thing he was sure they were all thinking was that Lincoln and the others were most likely dead. But he refused to be the one to say it and spoil the illusion. So he fiddled with the radio while the others gathered around him at the counter.

"Lincoln has the other one?"

"Last we saw." Carter turned a knob and static burst from the single speaker before evening out into a dull hum. He pushed a button on the side and said, "Hello? Hello?" Nothing. "Lincoln, Kordi, you guys there?"

"You're not doin it right!" Mac snatched the walkie-talkie away and repeated the same procedure. "Why ain't it workin?"

Maryland said, "Maybe he doesn't have his on, or maybe he's out of range."

"It says right here, five mile radius!"

"Then I don't know! Turn it off so we don't waste the batteries!" She reached to take it from him.

He stepped back and held it over his head. "No way! This stays on till we hear from him!"

Maryland opened her mouth to argue—if there was one thing Carter had gleaned about this woman, it was that she didn't back down—when a short scream from outside cut her off. They held their breath and stared at one another.

"What was that?" Ellis whispered.

"It was outside."

All four of them duck-walked to the hole at the front of the station, peeking around the torn exterior to see outside.

A young woman limped down the middle of the street that bordered the station, trying to run while looking behind her every few steps. She jumped at every shadow.

Maryland looked at them. "We have to get her in here."

Mac shook his head. "Screw that, we don't know her!"

"I didn't ask your permission." She leaned out and called softly, "Hey! Hey, over here!"

The woman uttered another shriek at the sound of Maryland's voice. She looked around until she spotted their waving hands, then hobbled over and collapsed in their midst.

"Oh God, oh God, I've been r-running for so long!" She was early twenties, dark hair back in a ponytail. She wore torn up jeans and a blouse stained with blood.

"What's your name?" Maryland asked.

"S-Sharon." She started to cry, big blubbery sobs that brought coughs with them. "My parents…I think they're dead. We got out of the civic center…we were hiding from the helicopters…but they landed. These people got out and started walking through the parking lot…" She sat up like she was on a spring and clutched at them. "Jesus, they're shooting *everyone!*"

WHITNEY +24:43

There was no clearance under the van. Barely any room to breathe. Lincoln's face pressed into the muffler, some other part of the undercarriage jabbed his stomach. He thought it was a Previa, but didn't have time to look before jamming himself beneath.

The old lady was next to him on his left, sucking air heavily through her oxygen mask with her eyes closed. On the other side of her was the scarecrow-ish guy in the John Deere hat, with her wheelchair beside him. If he tilted his head back against the wet pavement, Lincoln could see CT and the younger black kid lying on their stomachs under the car parked behind this one, with the British dude's still sleeping form crammed in beside them and halfway sticking out into the space between vehicles. Their eyes were huge, round O's. Randy and Kordi, the widest of their group, had been forced to squeeze beneath the SUV next to them.

And immediately to his right, deep in the narrow shadows of a Honda hatchback, was another man that had taken shelter when they did. Lincoln couldn't see any of this guy's details, but he alternated between hysterical panting and quiet sobs.

Lincoln had caught up with the others soon after saving the old woman. They'd tried to make it out of the vicinity of the Dome, but the helicopters roamed the parking lot like angry hornets, forcing them to ground in the sea of vehicles. They lay quietly, not speaking as the firing continued, then the choppers pulled back toward the ruined civic center. The sound of their blades faded. The night quieted, save for the crackle of fire.

They almost tried to leave then, until more screams and gunfire reached them. Every few minutes there would be a renewed rattle of automatic weaponry, softer and shorter than the machine guns on the helicopters.

And it was getting closer.

"Lincoln!" Kordi finally whispered. "We can't just lie here all night!"

"Yeah, so? Whachoo want me to do?"

"Go up and see what's going on!"

He wanted to snap at the man. He'd helped out in the Dome, been the sheriff, but he never volunteered to be leader of this group. The doc was right though, they needed to know what was up. And if no one else was willing to do it…

"Just stay here and keep quiet." He wriggled out from under the vehicle on the driver's side door. Being able to inflate his lungs fully was a relief. He crawled on hands and knees to the front tire and rose up slowly until he could peek over the hood.

Too many cars in the way to see anything other than the remaining walls of the Dome rising above them, like the crumbling remains of the Coliseum in Rome, and the huge bonfire still burning at its center. It threw blades of shifting light across the entire parking lot. A column of oily smoke drifted up from the remains and blended into the cloudy night sky. He stood up further, an inch at a time, and nearly shrieked when someone bumped into him. He looked over and saw John Deere next to him, the automatic rifle clutched to his chest. The man gave him an encouraging nod. Together they straightened up and looked out over the parking lot.

The helicopters sat next to the Dome. Distant figures milled around them, backlit by flames. More were spreading out, patrolling the rows of cars, but they were too far away to see clearly in the dark. John Deere tapped him on the shoulder and pointed left.

There were more on this side, close enough that Lincoln ducked again out of instinct. In the residual light from the Dome, they looked like black shrouded ghosts, their faces covered over with a slick sheet of plastic or glass that reflected the fire, and cylinders jutting from their chins. They were armed with submachine guns. They walked between the cars, crisscrossing back and forth across each other's paths. He recognized the system, because he'd trained his own soldiers to use it when looking for rival gang members in their territory.

They were searching. Combing the parking lot like sentries, heads up and alert, occasionally stopping to bend over and look under a car.

Lincoln was on the verge of turning away when there was a shout. One of the figures closest to them, only six or seven rows away, came up from a crouch dragging a man out from beneath a vehicle. "Let me go!" he yelped, as he was pulled to his feet. He struggled, trying to break away, until the figure raised its weapon and fired. The man jerked along with the short burst and then fell over.

A few cars away from this activity, there was more movement. Someone else making a break for it, a woman carrying a child over her shoulder. One of the other figures rushed to cut her off. She turned back the other direction, but was surrounded as more of them closed in. They could hear her sobbing, pleading for them to leave her alone between snorting coughs. Lincoln waited for them to kill her, but they closed in instead, one of them yanking the child away and another grabbing her by the hair and hauling her away in the direction of the Dome.

John Deere removed his hat and held it forlornly to his breast. Lincoln was surprised to find a blaze of anger warm his cheeks.

"What's happening?" the person hiding under the car next to them asked loudly.

"Shhh!" Lincoln told him.

"Please come back, don't leave me alone!"

"Dude, *shut up!*" He studied John Deere. The guy didn't seem scared in the least. "They gonna find us eventually."

Deere spoke in a thick accent. "We need ge' movin, try to—"

The sound of rotors swept over the parking lot. More helicopters from the east, flying over the flooded part of the city. Lincoln and John Deere fell to their knees to watch.

These were different than the others. They weren't sleek gunships, but wider, squatter conveyances. John Deere confirmed this when he whispered, "Troop carriers."

Seven of them came in low over the Dome. Like the others, they were all black, no markings. They split in different directions, a few of them heading further into the city. One moved on a diagonal course past them, to the southern edge of the parking lot, hovered above the concrete, and offloaded at least twenty more of the black figures.

"Ah *shit,*" Lincoln groaned. "We're ain't gonna make it past them!"

The helicopter lifted off, its former occupants spreading out to tighten the net drawing closed around them. One of the new arrivals had a megaphone. It raised the horn to the plate over its face and shouted in a squalling, amplified voice, "*Attention, anyone still taking shelter within the sound of my voice! Come out immediately, and you will not be harmed!*"

"Shyeah, I believe that." It reminded Lincoln of Sturney the previous night, spewing his lies during the standoff to get the younger cop to come out. For the first time in a while, he wondered where Ellis was. If he'd just listened to the cop, been selfish instead of a hero, he wouldn't be here right now.

The stranger poked his grimy head out. "Did you hear that? He said we could come out!"

Lincoln grimaced. "Don't listen to that, he's lyin!"

"I-I have to go! I can't stay under here, they can help me find my kids!" He squirmed out from under the vehicle.

Lincoln fell on him, pinning him to the pavement. "Man, don't be stupid! They not gonna help you!"

"Get off me!" the man screeched, thrashing under him. "Help, *help!*"

"Be quiet, you gonna tell 'em where we at!"

"Let 'im go!" John Deere barked, grabbing hold of Lincoln's arm and pulling him away. "He wanna ge' hisself killed, t'at's his choice."

The man scrambled up and took off, weaving between cars toward the figures. The two of them raised up just enough to watch. More people were coming from all around. The figure that made the announcement lined them up with their hands on the back of their heads, seemed to perform a quick inventory from a clipboard, and started pointing. Roughly half the crowd was led toward the Dome. The rest—including their guy from the next car—were shot with their hands still behind their heads.

"Fuckin bastards," Lincoln growled. His hands fisted at his sides.

"Nuthin we cou' do. Better he go t'an take alla us with 'im."

"What's goin on, Links?" CT's voice drifted up.

Lincoln sank down and lay full out on his stomach on the wet pavement so he could look at the entire group at once. John Deere did the same.

"The helicopters landed and whoever's inside is killin everybody." From their grim faces, none of them looked surprised. "Pullin people out and gunnin 'em down, or draggin 'em away. They gonna find us if we don't do somethin."

"So let's shoot 'em first!" CT said. "You got that pistol from me, and he got that machine gun!"

"There's too many. As soon as they know we here, a whole *army's* comin after us."

"He's right," John Deere confirmed.

"Then we have to go," Kordi said. "Right now. Crawl if we have to."

"I don't think we can sneak through. 'Specially not when we got Tom unconscious and this woman in a wheelchair."

CT uttered laughter with a hysterical edge. "Fuck that! Yo, I'm sorry grandma, but I ain't dyin for *yo'* crippled ass! Let's leave 'em here and get goin!"

"I-I don't want to sound cruel, but he may be right," Randy whispered into the concrete.

Lincoln looked over at the woman he'd saved. She was ancient, probably the oldest black person he'd ever seen. Life expectancy in the hood, even when you weren't in a gang, wasn't exactly overwhelming. She removed the oxygen mask from her face long enough to gasp, "Leave me."

John Deere shook his head. "I ain' doin it. You folks wanna go, then go."

Lincoln sighed and rested his forehead on the ground. He'd done more in the last twenty-four hours that he regretted than in the nineteen years that came before it. He thought the old woman's kind eyes might haunt him for the rest of his life if he left her, even if that was only for another few minutes.

On the other hand, he was out of ideas.

"What about a diversion?" Chris asked. They all looked at the kid. "Maybe we could start a car or something."

CT punched the younger boy's arm. "Now you thinkin, son!"

Kordi waved a hand. "I would offer my vehicle, but it's parked on the other side of the lot. Lincoln, can you hotwire a car?"

"Oh, what, because I'm black and in a gang, I must know how to hotwire a car?"

"That's what I'm implying, yes."

"Well, I don't. CT does."

"Soon as t'at engine starts, t'ey gonna be comin, fo sho." John Deere rested his chin on his forearm. "Whoever do it, gonna be a sittin duck."

"What if we all tried to just drive out?" Randy asked. "Get in a car and just floor it?"

Lincoln shook his head. "Can't all go, we'd never find a car big enough. But if someone drove one as a diversion...took the guns, maybe...the rest might make it."

"Yeah, but who's stupid enough to do that?" CT asked.

"I'll do it," John Deere said immediately. "Long's you promise to take Imogene."

There was a long, relieved silence that no one wanted to break. Finally, Lincoln said, "Wait." He was going to hate the next words from his mouth. "I'll go with you."

"You don't have to do t'at."

"If you're gonna stand any chance, you need someone to drive and someone to shoot back at those guys."

More gunfire, startlingly close.

"No time to argue." Lincoln sat up. "I get to drive."

"Le's do it then." John Deere smiled and clapped him on the back. "Take t'at SUV, case we need to go offroad or jump some curbs."

The vehicle was a Bronco, the same one Randy and Kordi were currently under. They slid out, and Lincoln handed the pistol to the doctor. "We'll lead them away, toward the far side of the Dome. Just stay low and try to get outta the parking lot. Head for the buildings."

"My clinic is on Hollister and Shoreway. We'll try to make it there and wait for you."

"What about my sister?" Chris' brow wrinkled. "And Hernie and Maryland and Carter? Do you…think they're still alive?"

"I almost forgot." Lincoln pulled out his radio and handed it to the kid. "Try to reach them on this once you get away from here."

He crawled toward the driver's side of the SUV with CT. John Deere hung back to gently slide Imogene from under the vehicle, and Lincoln watched as she touched his face and whispered to him. Then she looked at Lincoln with grateful tears in her eyes.

The doors of the vehicle were locked. CT picked up a chunk of Dome wreckage from the ground and reared back. "Gonna have to break a window."

"Hol' up." John Deere produced a pocketknife, went to work on the lock, and had the door open in seconds. He looked back at them. "I know a few tricks too."

"Damn, we need this fool as an X-Dawg."

Deere slithered inside with the rifle and ducked low in the passenger seat. Lincoln got behind the wheel. CT worked beneath the dash and finally ripped out two mangled wires. "All you have to do is touch these together. Sure you wanna do this, Links?"

"Go with the others," he said. "Wait for me. Don't make any trouble. That's an order."

"Man, whatevah." CT crouched with the rest of the group.

Lincoln closed the door without latching it. He and John Deere poked their heads over the dash. The narrow aisle they would be turning onto was clear, but they could see an entire squad of the black sentries on the next one, well within firing distance. Lincoln cleared his aching throat.

"Name's Lemiere, by da way," John Deere told him.

"Lincoln Briggs. It's been a pleasure dyin with you tonight, Lemiere."

The man laughed, a brittle—but friendly—sound. Lincoln looked out his window, at the expectant faces of the others. Randy already had Imogene's wheelchair unfolded, and they'd put Tom in it, his head lolling. All of them raised a solemn hand.

Lincoln reached down, touched the two wires together, and heard the engine rumble to life beneath the hood of the Bronco.

WHITNEY +25:08

They left Sharon with Hernie and Tangela in the gas station after she calmed down. The young woman was convinced her parents were dead, and none of them found the energy to tell her otherwise. Maryland made her lie down on a mat made of dog food bags across the room from Tangela, where she passed out.

She checked on the little girl next. It was dim in the back office, but the others wouldn't let her light so much as a matchstick. As if they had one. Tangela was still sick, but she was more alert. She watched Maryland with red-rimmed eyes as she went about her impromptu and, for the most part, utterly useless examination. The symptoms were the same, and she didn't know what to do about them.

"Is Chris here yet?"

"Not yet, sweetie. We're going to look for him now. I want you to stay here with Hernie and this other nice lady, okay?"

The girl stuck out her jaw and wrapped herself in a tight embrace. "I want to go home. I want my mommy. Please, Maryland..."

She couldn't give this girl either of those things, and it broke her heart. "I know. I know you do. Tangela...what happened to you? At the Dome. Where did you go, sweetie?"

The flesh across her dark chin puckered. Her eyes glazed with some memory, and then she shivered and turned over against the wall, coughing hoarsely.

Maryland decided not to press. She turned toward the door where Hernie hovered, shuffling his feet against the ground. He looked up uncomfortably as she came over.

"I'm sorry, Mary-land," he said, emphasizing the 'Y' in her name. "I didn't mean—" He stopped to cough for several long seconds. His words were a rough whisper when he started again. "I didn't mean to let nothin happen to her, no way, she's my friendy-friend. You're all my friendy-friends."

She put a hand on his stubbly cheek and forced him to meet her eyes. A part of her recoiled—after all, he was just as sick as Mac—but that kind of thinking was too much like Mr. Hypochondriac in the other room. "It's not your fault, Hernie. Will you stay here and look after her? We won't be gone very long. You just have to be very quiet. Can you do that?"

"Yes, I can do it, we'll be so quiet, not even a mouse will hear us!"

"And if anyone else comes…you run, okay? Wake up Tangela and just run."

His face clouded. "Those bad government men?"

She started to shake her head, but, after a pause, said, "Yes, Hernie. Them or anyone."

Maryland slipped out to where the others waited. Ellis asked, "Will they be all right on their own?"

She shrugged. She was hesitant to leave the girl at all, but they had no choice. They had to do *something*, and they sure couldn't drag along a sick little girl, a mentally challenged man, and a hysterical young woman where they were going.

God, she was so tired. She'd never wanted a smoke and a shower so bad in her life. On the way out, she grabbed a pack of Virginia Slims from the shelves behind the counter. Now all she needed was a working lighter to make at least half that dream come true.

Maryland forced her feet to keep moving, following the three men as they crept along dark storefronts. The street elevation through here was high enough to be dry. There was no further conversation after they left the gas station, only the sound of Mac stifling his coughs and trying the walkie-talkie every few minutes. He walked at the front of the group, and everyone had—either consciously or not—given him plenty of space. Even Ellis, who was clearing his throat every few minutes.

"They can't still be there," Carter whispered to no one in particular. "All the explosions and the gunfire. Someone on the outside of Port Allen must've heard that. Someone *must* be coming. I mean, are we the last people on earth here, or what? Did Whitney suck us into an alternate dimension? There was a *Sliders* episode where—"

"I loved that show!" Ellis exclaimed. "Just wasn't the same after Rhys-Davies left though."

"He didn't leave, he got fired. The network—"

"Guys, can we *please* hold the nerd convention for another time?" Maryland pleaded.

The street dead-ended where it met Gulf Terrace, which circled the Dome parking lot. The mouth was choked with storm rubble. On the left corner was a GNC missing all its plate glass windows, but on the right had been a two story law office that partially collapsed in the storm, dropping large debris across the road. The front of the building was sheered off neatly, revealing a cross section of desks and cubicles. They got down on hands and knees, crawling through wreckage until they were under the dark streetlight. Across the intersection and down a steep but short decline was a perfect panoramic view of the Dome and its parking lot.

The helicopters were still there, on the ground now, clustered around the crater that had once been the Port Allen Civic Center. Most of the smoke had blown away. They could see tiny figures moving through the sea of cars, and flashes of light when they fired their weapons. Just as Sharon had said.

How many people had died there when the Dome collapsed? Thousands at least, judging just from the cars in the parking lot, undoubtedly more than had died on the bridge last night. And now the survivors were being ferreted out and gunned down.

When she'd seen enough, Maryland rolled over and lay on her back behind a three-foot high section of brick wall. "If this was a terrorist attack, shouldn't they be running by now? They don't even look like they're in a hurry!"

Ellis nodded. "I don't get it. It's like they know no one is going to stop them."

"Maybe no one can get into the city with the roads out," Carter said.

"No, that can't be it." Maryland thought back to what Tom had said, when they first woke up beneath the overpass. "There should've already been helicopters here. *Our* helicopters, I mean. Red Cross and FEMA, people like that. All of this is so messed up. Hell, maybe we *are* the last people left on earth."

Mac swiveled his head from side to side, the cracks from his joints making her wince. "Whatever's goin on, we gotta do somethin. They're killin those people."

Ellis threw out a hand. "You wanna go down there and ask them to stop, be my guest."

Maryland leaned toward the two of them. "We need to get help." Carter's hand pawed at her shoulder from behind, and she shrugged it off. "Find a way to call someone, get them to—" The hand was back, tugging at her hair. "Ow, Carter! Jesus, *what?*"

She turned back, found his eyes huge in the late evening light. He clamped a hand over her mouth and pointed.

Dark alleys fed onto the street from between every building. To their right, on the other side of the debris field, a silhouette emerged from the closest of these crevices, a shadow against shadows. It slid out onto the sidewalk with measured steps. Her mind kept trying to imprint a picture of that monster from the Dome onto it, all spines and rough angles, but as it entered a patch of moonlight, she saw that it was definitely human.

Not that she could feel much better about that fact. The figure looked like an escapee from one of the action movies Bryce was always watching: black from head-to-toe, some kind of skintight latex material, with a flack vest, belt, and mirrored faceplate with tubes sticking off it where the mouth would be. And an extremely big gun. It stopped against the front of the GNC on the corner, just eight or nine yards from them, and turned its shielded face to scan up and down the street.

Maryland locked up. Afraid to even breathe. She turned her head back to Ellis and Mac and saw they were both watching the new arrival. Ellis raised a finger to his lips.

The figure was still in the same position, a silent sentinel. Mac squirmed away, toward the hulking ruins of the buildings on the opposite side of the street. Ellis rolled onto his belly and followed.

Maryland stayed stock still.

Carter leaned against her. Pushed the cup over his mouth against her ear and murmured, "*Go.*"

She shook her head, more of a twitch than anything. She was frozen by terror. She imagined she could feel its eyes on her, behind the glass or plastic or whatever covered its face. It might look human but it wasn't, it was a creature with heightened senses and ESP, it knew they were here somewhere and was hunting them right now, zeroing in like a heat-seeking missile…

The black figure pulled one arm away from its weapon and scratched its ass.

Maryland had to clamp a hand over her mouth to keep from laughing out loud. It was just a guy, some dude that probably left the toilet seat up and skidmarks in his underwear, and suddenly he wasn't so scary anymore. He didn't know they were there, couldn't see them amid all the building rubble. She eased over on to her stomach and crawled.

It was a tedious trek. She had to follow a path that kept her hidden from the figure's view, and go slow enough that she didn't disturb the smaller bits of wreckage. Her bandaged palms were fine, but several times she felt something sharp slice into her knees and stomach through her shredded clothes.

Eventually they reached the shadows of the gutted law office. Ellis and Mac crouched on the other side of an overturned desk.

"Just wait and he'll go," Ellis whispered, his wide eyes floating in his dark face. The others gave silent agreement.

And then the radio in Mac's pocket, turned to full volume, began speaking.

WHITNEY +25:11

The engine of the Bronco gave a few robust chugs and then cut out.

On the next aisle, heads whipped in their direction.

"Try again!" Lemiere shouted.

Lincoln touched the two wires CT had given him together. The engine gave a whine but didn't start.

He peeked over the dash. A swarm of mercenaries was descending on them, rushing between cars with brutal determination.

"We didn't happen to come up with a Plan B, did we?" Lincoln rubbed the wires together once more while pressing on the gas.

This time the Bronco opened up with an angry purr. Lemiere scrambled for the button to roll down his window. "DRIVE!"

Lincoln threw the vehicle into gear. They lurched out onto the narrow aisle. His first instinct was to turn left, away from the faceless wraiths honing in on them, but that would only bring the soldiers sweeping down on Kordi and the others. Instead he spun the wheel right and floored it into their midst.

The black figures moved out into the middle of the aisle ahead of them, blocking the way, bringing up their weapons.

"Hit 'em!"

"Just like bowlin," Lincoln muttered, and slouched down in the seat.

Several of the men leapt out of the way at the last minute, but Lincoln was doing at least forty-five when he struck two of them, one getting his leg torn nearly off as he jumped to the side, and the other falling under the grill to bounce their vehicle a foot in the air.

"STRIKE!" Lincoln shouted. Lemiere whooped.

Too early for victory cheers. Sharp rattles sounded all around them. Bullets thunked into the side of the Bronco with a series of hollow pings. The window behind Lincoln blew out, chunks of glass striking the back of his head.

Lemiere turned his cap around backward and leaned out his side with the automatic rifle. He returned a short burst of fire. "T'at'll give 'em somethin to t'ink about!"

They reached the end of the aisle. Another line of cars cut them off ahead, with narrow access to either side. Lincoln slowed down and turned right once again, heading back toward the section of parking lot directly west of the Dome. He could see whole platoons chasing after them in the mirrors, and hoped it had given Kordi the opportunity he needed to get the others out.

More soldiers closed in on both sides. These guys were everywhere, popping up between cars. They came to the edges of the aisle without stepping out this time and fired at the vehicle as it passed. Lemiere took pot shots back at them, managing to hit two or three.

"This car's startin to look like Swiss cheese!"

"T'en get us outta here!"

"I'm tryin! This parkin lot's a maze!"

No one had parked within the painted boundaries, especially up close to the Dome, where it was all a general mishmash of vehicles. If they turned down a dead-end, it was over. All Lincoln could do was just stay in motion, taking whatever turns would get them closer to the edge of the lot.

In the distance to their right, something sleek and dark lifted off from the ground and swung in their direction.

"Oh hell!" Lemiere screeched.

The aisles around them were clear of soldiers now as they backed off, making way for the helicopter. Lincoln took a turn fast enough to bring the SUV up on two wheels, and suddenly the endless rows of cars thinned out, giving them room to maneuver between. They had a clear path uphill to the end of the lot.

The chopper swept in behind them, low enough to show up in the rearview. The sound of its blades was rhythmic thunder. The pavement ahead cracked and exploded as the heavy guns opened fire. Lincoln hit the brake and swerved, bringing them away from the path of the bullets. Lemiere was thrown against him, then leaned back out to shoot at their attacker. The high-pitched ricochets off the aircraft's metal hull were scarily close.

A curb loomed, marking the end of the huge civic center parking lot. Gulf Terrace ran along the other side, a street Lincoln actually knew. If they could get out onto a main thoroughfare and into the city, maybe they could ditch the Bronco and lose the helicopter on foot. He increased their speed, putting a short burst of distance between them and the chopper as it readjusted its course to come after them.

The SUV hit the curb at sixty miles an hour. All four tires left the ground...but only three came back down.

One of the rear wheels shredded on impact. Rubber slapped the undercarriage. Metal screeched.

Lincoln's control over the vehicle disappeared. The Bronco tried to slew to the right. He wrestled the wheel to keep it on course. They rocketed onto the next street, buildings flashing by to the left and right.

The helicopter swept in from above on the passenger side, spewing death. Lincoln did everything he could to swerve around the next corner, but he could feel the SUV getting away from him.

"I can't hold it!"

The world tilted as the Bronco tipped over.

WHITNEY +25:22

Dr. Kordi and the white gentleman named Randy lifted Imogene and put her in the lap of the sleeping fellow slouched in her wheelchair. She didn't know these people, couldn't think of a reason why they should help her, but this fact didn't seem to matter to them any more than it had to Lemiere. Imogene clung to the oxygen tank as tightly as she'd noticed the boy holding on to his checkered security blanket. This was the hardest workout her lungs had gotten in more than a decade. The pain was excruciating, clawing up from her chest into every muscle and nerve ending. Unconsciousness—or worse—was just around the corner.

She could hear the car's engine growling as Lincoln tried to start it, and then the vehicle pulled forward and left the rest of them behind. Imogene said a silent prayer for he and Lemiere. She *did* feel useless now, a tired old woman that was dragging these people down, and yet those two were risking their lives for her.

Maybe Janie was the smart one after all...

"Let's go!" Kordi whispered. "Keep low and move fast!"

She wanted to tell them to leave her, she was only dead weight, but she refused to let Lemiere and Lincoln's sacrifice be in vain.

The black boys went first, followed by Randy, and then Kordi pushing the two of them in the cramped wheelchair. She felt the bony body under her shift, and the man uttered a low groan.

"Not now," Kordi pleaded. "I really don't have the time to explain, so just stay out a little longer."

Her vision blurred as they navigated through an endless lot of cars. She closed her eyes and wished it all away. Gunfire ratcheted across the parking lot, but they kept moving. When Kordi got winded, Randy took over the pushing.

A hand snaked out from under a car as they passed by, grabbing at their ankles. Kordi jumped and turned the pistol on it, but it was only a man and his son, wearing similar expressions of terror. They put their hands up and begged not to be left behind. The doctor helped them up and they went on.

Imogene saw other people crawling from under vehicles to join their escape. When they reached the edge of the parking lot, a few of them scattered, but most continued with their group. Kordi gave directions, pointing them through turn after turn until they reached the edge of the heavy floodwaters on the east side of the city, and followed along it toward his clinic.

Finally, when all of them wheezed and coughed, Kordi called a halt. The group wedged themselves into a tiny dooryard to rest.

The younger black boy—Chris, she thought his name was—sat down on the curb next to her wheelchair and rubbed at his feet. He reminded her of Alice, her oldest grandchild, sweaty and exhausted after one of her soccer games. She was glad to see he wasn't associated with the other one, the one that had tried to extort people at the Dome for sodas.

He noticed her. She gave a frail smile through the oxygen mask. In one hand he held the blanket, and in the other the device Lincoln had given him.

She lowered the plastic from her face. "That's a very nice blanket, sugar. You had it a long time?"

"Yeah, but it's my sister's now. I mean…as long as she's…okay."

Imogene pointed at the radio. "She on the other end of that thing?"

He nodded.

"Why don't you give it a try then? I think we're safe for the moment."

He smiled a little and turned knobs on the device. Children always knew how to work such newfangled things. He brought the black box to his mouth and spoke into it.

"Hello? Is anybody there? Maryland? Mr. Carter? Anybody?"

It was Chris' voice coming through the speaker clipped to Mac's waist. The problem was, it was amplified to godlike proportions from their volume meddling, echoing through the ruined office.

"They're alive!" Maryland cried.

Ellis grabbed for the device. "Turn it off!"

"I'm tryin!" Mac found the power button and the boy's pleas cut out.

But the damage was done. Thudding footsteps came from outside.

"Uh…I think it's time to go," Carter told them.

They scrambled to their feet in the debris. The sound of the figure's approach came from the gaping hole in the building's exterior. They turned toward the wall behind them and an open door to the interior of the office block.

Maryland and Ellis hurtled through first. Mac tried to go through at the same time as Carter, then elbowed him aside. Carter stopped, raised a hand to knock on the door jamb, the compulsion too automatic to be denied, then looked over his shoulder. The armed figure gave a cautionary peek around the corner, spotted him through the mirrored faceplate, and then jumped completely into view, spraying bullets in a high arc.

Carter scurried into the hall. Plaster exploded from the place where his head and chest had been; he felt chips sting the back of his neck. This weapon made the one the old man had fired at him and Hernie sound like a cap pistol.

In the hall, Mac's huge silhouette was the only thing visible. Carter chased after it. "He's coming, he's coming, go faster!"

Mac's response was a litany of coughs.

Carter dared a look back once more, and hit a wall before he could turn forward again. The hallway dead-ended. The impact sent his brain caroming off his skull like a racquetball. Mac's hand snaked out of a doorway to his left and pulled him through, tearing his shirt sleeve in the process. He slammed the door shut.

They were in a dark, windblown office complete with a desk and overturned file cabinets. At first Carter thought his rattled head was playing tricks, because everything he could make out in here looked skewed, but then he realized the building's structural damage had caused the walls to buckle and lean.

No other doors and only one window. Ellis was already at it, breaking the glass with a desk lap in his good hand, and then kicking at the sheet wood nailed across the outside. Mac got behind the desk—

the kind of heavy oak model that lawyers just loved—and shoved it against the door, then began piling everything he could find on top of it. Carter and Maryland helped, lifting up the file cabinets and chairs.

They heard the doorknob turn on the other side of their barrier. Without warning, their pursuer opened fire.

"*DOWN!*" Mac screamed. They all hit the floor, Maryland coming down right in front of Carter. The fire outside was so steady, it became one long, vibrating drone. Bullets chewed through the wood and plaster of both door and wall, pinged off the metal filing cabinets, and even finished the job Ellis had started on the window, turning the last of the obstruction into wooden confetti. The firing stopped, and Carter was left with ringing in both ears.

"*I'm a cop!*" Ellis shouted from beneath the window without raising his head. "*Stop shooting, I'm a COP!*"

Maryland peeked between her fingers. "I don't think it matters to them!"

The gun started up for a few more seconds, raining splinters down on them. Carter hissed, "In a few seconds, he's gonna be able to crash through that wall!"

Mac scooted toward Ellis. "He's just pinnin us down till more of 'em have a chance to get here!"

Carter and Maryland joined their huddle. "What is that thing, an automatic *bazooka?*"

Ellis sat up and wiped dust out of his eyes. "On the count of three, we go through the window. Ladies first, of course. When you hit the ground, keep running and don't stop."

"Screw the counting!" Maryland stood up, grabbed the sill, and hopped over the ledge as neatly as Bo Duke ever did into the General Lee. The three men stared at one another before clambering out after her.

Carter went next, with Mac so close behind he was almost crushed beneath the huge teenager when they landed. It was a six foot drop to a wet concrete landing, enough to give him a dizzying flush of vertigo. He sprawled to his knees, feeling something in his leg give.

The alley here was a split level. It led to the right back toward the street they'd come from, but along the building's brick wall to the left, a narrow staircase went from the landing down to a flooded lower passage connected to a road that ran through the next block over. Maryland had already regained her feet, flown down the steps, and was sprinting for the mouth of the lower alley.

Before Carter could follow, a powerful searchlight hit him from above, illuminating the patch of concrete around him hard enough to sting the eyes. Bullets thunked around his feet and off the metal railing around the landing, throwing up sparks. Judging by the angle, they seemed to come from the next rooftop over. Carter flattened against the wall of the building, under a thin concrete overhang where the light couldn't touch him.

"Sorry man, good luck!" Mac charged forward, hurdled the railing, and dropped down the side of the staircase, into the safety of the alley. A line of shots trailed him, but he moved too fast for the shooter to get a bead during his exposure. Carter caught a glimpse of him splashing down the water-choked corridor to the left after Maryland.

Ellis jumped from the window and landed next to him. Carter pulled him up and out of the way just before those deadly shots could take off his kneecaps.

"God, these guys are everywhere!"

"We can't stay here, they're battering down the door!"

Carter looked around frantically. Everything was happening so goddamn fast, but he'd never felt so sharp and focused in his life. The stairs would expose them for too long and he doubted Mac's trick would work again, even if they didn't break their legs when they landed. There was only one other direction to go.

"C'mon!" he shouted over another burst of automatic fire from above. The concrete overhang ran along the building to their right, in the opposite direction Mac and Maryland had gone. It would give them cover, but the further they went, the more likely they would give the shooter an angle on them. But if they could get some distance from that glaring searchlight, they might have a chance to surprise him when they made a run for it.

Ellis got the idea. The two of them crept along the wall like escaped cons in an old prison movie. When they'd crossed half the length of the building, one of the gunmen shouted from the window behind them in an electronically amplified voice.

Carter stepped away from the wall and bounded for the mouth of the alley. The light swung wildly as it tried to track them. An endless chain of gunfire followed. Ellis cried out as they reached the edge of the building and turned the corner. Carter stopped to look at him.

"I'm okay!" Ellis wheezed. He looked fine, no visible blood anywhere, but there was a blank, hollow look in his eyes. "Just keep running!"

But he couldn't. Both of them were exhausted, and Carter's lungs were on fire. God, why hadn't he bought a treadmill during his years indoors? Whoever these commandos were, they were fast, coordinated, and ruthless, and the only thing they wanted from them was death. He couldn't think of anywhere to go, any plan besides more running, and that would only work for so long. They needed a miracle.

And then one came screaming around the corner of the intersection ahead of them, in the form of a blue and white SUV with one rear tire dragging the pavement. The turn was too sharp for its limited traction. He could see the driver's face behind the wheel as the vehicle crashed over on its side, skidding toward the wall of the building across the street.

"Was that—?"

"Lincoln," Ellis confirmed, and then they were running again.

WHITNEY +25:38

Mac splashed out onto the flooded street from the narrow alley. This was still a commercial district, with tightly packed storefronts. He didn't recognize any of it. The smooth sheen of water reflected the backlit clouds, creating the disorienting optical illusion that he was standing in the sky. Maryland had turned right; he could see her ahead on the sidewalk in the dark. For a half second, he considered going the opposite way, but then stumbled after her.

Every breath dragged across his raw throat, bringing renewed hacking. He clamped a hand over his mouth, trying to hold them inside. His palm came away smeared with blood that looked black in the night.

"No," he whimpered. "Fuck, no." It might be holdover from his broken nose, but ever since they'd told him about that disease, all he'd been able to think about, even while being chased by this death squad, was that cop bleeding out in the squad car, coughing God-knew-what germs in his face.

Even impaired and gasping for air, his longer legs caught up to Maryland in a hurry. She ran with militaristic precision, arms and legs pumping, regulating her breathing with quick, rhythmic pulls. Probably a jogger.

"Where we...goin?" he gasped.

"Hernie," she said from the side of her mouth. "We have to get back to Hernie." She glanced at him and then over her shoulder. "Carter...?"

He blanched. "I don't...know...if they made it..."

"Jesus, I think I'm gonna be sick." She halted at the next intersection and stood in the shadowed entry of a shop. The glass doors were shattered, and she stepped through the frame.

Mac ducked in beside her. It was an ice cream shop, with a glass sneeze guard running the length of the counter. The smell of spoiled milk drifted out from further inside. He popped his head out to have a look at the ground they'd just covered. The street was getting even darker as clouds overhead thickened, but he didn't think they'd been followed. Yet. "I couldn't wait, I saw an opportunity and I took it. I don't know if those fuckers got 'em or not." The distant purr of those heavy machine guns drifted through the store, followed by what sounded like a car engine and something heavier.

Maryland leaned over with her hands on her knees, staring into the water around their feet. Her shoulders shook. He thought for a moment she was crying, but when she straightened back up again her face was neutral. "We can't help them now. We have to get back to Hernie and Tangela. Goddamn it, *where are we?* Why does everything in this city look the same?"

Mac slumped against the inside of the doorframe and tried to get air into his lungs. "I can't run anymore. I'm dyin, I know it. I gotta get to that doctor *fast.*"

"Try the radio again."

He pulled the walkie-talkie out and turned it back on, being sure to keep the volume low this time. "Hello? Anybody there?"

The answer he got was immediate, and sounded like a kid's voice. "Who's this?"

"Let me see that." Maryland reached out and Mac reluctantly put the radio in her shaking hand. "Chris, it's Maryland, are you okay?"

"Maryland! I knew you were alive, I just knew it! We're all right! Tom is awake again! Did you find Tangela?"

"Yes sweetie, Tangela's fine."

"What about Hernie and Mr. Carter?"

Maryland squeezed her eyes shut. For the first time, Mac wondered if she and the skinny dude in the weird oxygen mask were hitting it. They looked like they were from two completely different worlds, but he'd seen stress do some crazy shit to people. "They're fine, we're all fine. Where are you?"

"Tell him to get Lincoln!" Mac said. She held up a finger to silence him.

"We're almost to Doctor Kordi's office! Will you come here?"

"I'll try. Put the doctor on for me, okay?"

"Okay!"

There was a pause and then another voice thick with accent crackled from the radio's speaker. "Thank God you made it!"

"That's a little too early to say. We're lost somewhere in the city close to downtown, and we're being chased by some people dressed in black with very big guns. They're all over the place."

"Yes, we've seen them. We barely escaped them at the civic center."

"Chris said you're going to your office. Where is that? Is it safe?"

"For the moment. My clinic is just a few blocks south of the Dome, off Shoreway. The flood has swamped most of the buildings in the area, so I don't know how long we'll be able to stay. I could try to send assistance if you knew where you were…"

"I appreciate it Doc, but I don't think there's anything you could do. Please just stay there and keep everyone safe. We'll try to make it to you."

Mac waved a hand in her face.

"Oh, could you put Lincoln on? I have someone here that wants to talk to him."

The silence on the other end chilled Mac, made his guts feel blended to a watery purée. "Lincoln and another gentleman created a diversion so we could escape. I haven't seen him since."

Maryland was quiet, studying Mac. "Doc, we're gonna turn our radio off unless we need something. Please keep yours on."

"Will do."

She turned off the walkie-talkie. Mac said nothing. The awful idea that he was the last X-Dawg had suddenly occurred to him.

"Mac, listen to me." In the gloom, he could see only one of her eyes, and he focused on that. "I understand he's your friend, but whether he's alive or dead right now, you can't change that. But there's a little girl that needs our help. And Hernie and Sharon, too. Keep it together, and let's get back to them."

He shivered. "Damn sister, you sure know how to pep talk a guy."

"Do you remember where the gas station is?"

"It's on one of the higher streets. I think it's a few more blocks up and maybe one or two over."

Maryland went back to the door, but didn't step out. "Well, we're not going that way."

He looked over her head. Three more of the commandos eased around the corner of the building across the street and stood, scouring the area.

"Let's see if this place has another way out."

They retreated deeper into the shadows of the shop.

WHITNEY +25:44

The Bronco entered a new intersection as it went up on two wheels and then tipped over completely. There was a bone-jarring thud as it came down on the passenger side, followed by the squeal of metal as it scraped against the street. Lincoln was tossed out of his seat, sprawling across Lemiere.

"Hold on!" he heard the Cajun shout over the sparks flying in his window.

Lincoln twisted around. The windshield fractured upon impact, but through the spider web of milky cracks, he could see a brick wall rushing at them. He squeezed his eyes shut and braced himself between the now vertical dash and ceiling.

The crash wasn't as bad as he anticipated, but the sudden stop propelled him forward, banging his grazed shoulder against the glass. The engine sputtered and died. Bricks dumped across the hood of the Bronco, and then everything fell silent.

His vision swam when he opened his eyes. The crumpled nose of the SUV had knocked a hole through the wall they rammed. Smoke or dust drifted in through the vehicle's a/c vents. He couldn't help but cough, which set his sore throat on fire, and then he was hacking because of that instead. Time to face facts: he was sick too, sick with whatever had killed Heather, who he'd first met in an overturned vehicle much like this one. Lemiere was beneath him somewhere in a tangle of limbs, groaning softly. He rolled off the man, using the steering wheel to stand.

A mechanical roar came from outside as the helicopter swept overhead.

"We gotta go, dude!" Lincoln raised a hand, reaching for the driver's side door handle above his head, but it was pulled out of his grasp. The door swung up, letting in watery, thin moonlight. He fell back, raising an arm to shield himself from the bullets that would come pouring in.

Instead, it was a floppy-haired white guy with a stupid-looking plastic mask over his mouth that looked down at him.

"Carter?"

His acquaintance from the Dome reached inside and offered him a hand. "Unless you wanna keep playing tag with that helicopter, I suggest you come on. Otherwise, you're about to be it."

Lincoln took the hand and pulled, bracing one foot on the steering wheel and the other on the headrest so he could climb up and out. Various parts of his body squalled, but he ignored them. He jumped down from the Bronco, and was shocked all over again when he found himself face-to-face with Ellis.

"*You*, with *him*? Goddamn, this day just keeps gettin weirder."

Ellis gave him a forced smile. He looked sick, too. "Your friend…Mac…he was just here…"

There was no time to ask what that meant, or if it was the preamble to those three mythic words: YOU'RE UNDER ARREST. The very surreal thought occurred to him that all this—the commandoes, the helicopters, the guns and missiles—were all just an elaborate scheme to put him in a cell for the murder of Mr. Kim. Part of him knew that was paranoia talking, but nothing else about this situation seemed logical.

Carter pulled Lemiere out of the SUV. The Cajun came up still clutching the assault rifle just as the chopper ripped over the rooftop of the building they'd crashed through. It hovered overhead, tilting downward to face them.

They all leapt away from the Bronco a half second before the helicopter opened fire. Bullets ripped the vehicle's side open like tin foil. Lemiere gave them a shove toward the cover of the nearest alley, but Carter shook his head. "Nah-uh, trust me, you don't want to go that way! Across the street!"

They charged in the other direction. The piercing rounds found the Bronco's gas tank when they were a few steps from the sidewalk. It went up with a roar, throwing heat and light across their backs. Lincoln focused only on the alley ahead, and kept running.

One of the blacksuits emerged from the storefront to their right. He saw them, turned to bring up his weapon, but, thank God, Lemiere was faster. He sprayed a short burst from the assault rifle and the commando fell backward, blood bursting from his chest. It was just good to know they were human beings under those masks and rubbery jumpsuits.

"How many bullets you got left?" Lincoln asked.

"Few," Lemiere answered, without looking at him.

They were in another narrow alley. Lincoln was sick of them by now. Ahead was a darkness they could hopefully lose themselves in. But at the first door on their right, hanging open on one hinge, Lemiere pointed. "In here!"

Carter hopped from foot to foot. "No, don't stop, there's more of these guys! They'll keep coming!"

"I know, and t'is is da last t'ing t'ey expect!"

"If it means no more runnin, I'm in," Lincoln agreed. Ellis said nothing. His eyes were sunk deep into his skull, and his skin was ashy gray in the pale light.

They followed Lemiere into the building. It was too dark to see what sort of place it was, but Lemiere led them through small offices and narrow hallways as decisively as if he came here everyday, holding his weapon Rambo-style, checking around each corner before sliding smoothly around. *Who the hell* is *this guy?* Lincoln wondered, as Lemiere pushed open a door in front of them and checked every corner of the room beyond. Finally they came to a door with a window in it, and Lemiere stared through for several long seconds before easing it open.

On the other side was an open loading dock. Two large trucks were backed up against the drop-off into the concrete bay, their rear loading doors lined up perfectly with the lip. Both had green cabs and rectangular white cargo areas emblazoned with *Monarch Trucking* down the side.

Beyond that was the street they'd just come from. Lemiere had led them in a circle.

Lincoln could see the twisted, burning remains of the Bronco to the extreme left. The attack chopper had settled in the middle of the street, landing neatly between the light posts. Its whirring rotors were just coming to a stop. A canopy on the dark vehicle slid back, and two pilots climbed down, wearing the same biohazard ninja suits as the others.

More commandos gathered around them; three now, but even as they watched, two more approached carrying the body of the one Lemiere shot and laid it on the street. They gestured to each other and pointed in the direction the four of them had gone.

"They still lookin for us."

"Yeah, but t'ey gonna be doin it faaaar away from here, fo sho." Lemiere closed the door again and released a long, loud cough that rattled as it came up from his chest. "T'ink about it: if you t'em, would you expect us to be right across da street?"

Carter demanded, "But what are we gonna *do?* We can't just sit here, we have friends out there!" He said to Lincoln, "*Your* friend, Mac, he's out there!"

Lincoln felt the emotion fall off his face. "He ain't no friend of mine."

"Well, he seemed pretty concerned about you! We just got separated from them a few minutes before we saw you!"

Lemiere pulled out a clip on the assault rifle and glanced inside with a grimace. "Wha' you wan' me to do? I can't work no magic, say POOF and make t'em gone." He slapped the clip back into the weapon and looked at Lincoln. "You know t'ese two?"

"Yeah, I met the germophobe here at the Dome, but this other guy is a cop..." He hooked a thumb over his shoulder and turned to look, before realizing Ellis wasn't there.

The cop lay facedown at the far end of the hall, with what looked a large bloodstain spreading across the back of his filthy undershirt.

WHITNEY +25:56

Hernie stood watch over Tangela and the new girl as they slept. He was unaware of the passage of time, or how long the others had been gone. His poor brain had so much shoved into it over the last twenty-four hours. He'd never met so many people all at once, or had anyone who could stand to be in is company for so long. The only way he could focus with all this excitement was to repeat Mary-land's final instructions to him, over and over, mostly in his head with an occasional mutter slipping out.

Look after Tangela. Stay quiet. Run if anyone else comes. He couldn't fail these people again, not the way he had Hatch. The thought of the dog sent another splinter of worry into his jumbled thoughts, but he forced even that aside. Stifling the constant string of coughs that wanted to come up his aching throat, he stood just inside the door of the tiny gas station office, hugged his chest, and tried not to go to sleep.

He was swaying on his feet, eyes fluttering, when a rumble brought him around. Thunder? No, this had been too close.

Hernie looked across the room. Tangela's eyes were closed, but she coughed hoarsely every few minutes. Sharon tossed and turned, weeping in her sleep.

Another noise from outside made him jump. *Pop, pop, pop, pop*, very fast and faint.

He crept out of the office and into the hall, inching toward the front of the gas station. In the main room, every shadow leered. He hated nighttime enough before the storm, but now it was down-right scary. He'd seen that monster back at the Dome, had stood against the wall while it tore a man in half right in front of him, and he was certain it was unleashed by the government to track him down.

More of those pops, even closer. Hernie reached the glass front of the station and peeked out.

His eyes wandered the street, searching for any sign of Mr. Carter's return. Even though everyone else had been nice to him, Mr. Carter made him feel most comfortable. Movement on the next corner caught his attention, and his heart surged before he realized it wasn't who he wanted it to be.

Three figures. All black, with masks over their faces.

Just like the two at the seawall.

Hernie's skin went cold. His brain twisted into knots. He couldn't think what to do. Get the others and...run. Run where? Suddenly Mary-land's instructions seemed a little vague. He could feel himself getting flustered, fingers dancing against his skull as he tried to do the one thing that was always hardest for him: think.

Stay calm and watch, that gentle voice told him. It sounded more like Mr. Carter than his mother now.

He stepped away from the glass, further into the station. Outside, one of the agents pointed first down the street, and then right at him. Hernie jumped before he realized the gloved finger was circling the gas station in the air. The trio broke up, heading in different directions. One of them trotted across the street, heading right for him.

Hernie crossed the station's main room in three leaps and then scurried into the hallway. He entered the office at the back just as broken glass crunched under booted feet behind him.

He stood in the middle of the room, wringing his hands, trying to decide what to do. Tangela and Sharon slept on. Even if he woke them, there was no way out of this room aside from the door, and that only led back to where he could now hear stealthy steps approaching.

If he couldn't run like he'd been instructed, he would just have to fight.

Against the wall opposite the door sat an overturned bucket and mop. He hefted the mop. It was wooden, but he didn't think it would be enough. He scurried to Tangela's side and covered her all the way up with the towels Mary-land had found, pulling the makeshift blankets over her head, and did the same for Sharon, turning them into a bundle of rags. He stepped back to examine the camouflage. Neither looked like a bed to him, and he'd slept in some pretty weird places. He squeezed into the dark crevice behind the door with the pitiful mop and prayed so hard that he wouldn't have to use it.

The agent was coming. His footsteps whispered in the hallway. They were tracking him somehow, he just knew it, otherwise how else would they know to come here? It wouldn't matter how much hiding he did, they would find him. They always did. Hernie wiped sweat out of his eyes and then held his breath.

The figure stopped just outside the threshold. Hernie could see him through the gap between the door and jamb; that smooth, featureless plane where the face should be was the worst of all his nightmares. He could hear the man's breath hissing through the cylinders that jutted from the bottom. Blood pounded in Hernie's ears so loud he was sure it must be audible. The moment held until he thought he would pass out.

Then, as quietly as he'd come, the agent turned around and started back down the hall. Hernie let out half the breath and then stopped when he felt another whoop coming on.

Across the room, Sharon moaned in her sleep again.

The sound of it hung in the air for half a second before the agent burst into the room, squashing Hernie with the door but moving too fast to notice. Hernie peeked around the edge. The agent stood scanning the room, undoubtedly with heat or x-ray vision.

Sharon sat up suddenly, throwing the blankets off. Her eyes landed on the shadow standing several yards away, and she shrieked. This woke Tangela up, and she did the same.

"Well, what have we got here?" The agent's voice buzzed with the ear-splitting whine Hernie remembered. "Looks like a couple of keepers to me. Hey, Sergeant Barnes, get down here to this gas station and—"

"Leave them alone!" Hernie jumped from behind the door, swinging the mop in an arc. The part of the handle just above the head struck the agent across the skull, snapping the wood in half.

The agent stumbled a step forward with an electric grunt, but didn't go down. He turned and brought up his gun.

Hernie took the remains of the mop handle and used it as a spear. The splintered end hit the agent in the left shoulder, piercing the black suit and penetrating the flesh beneath. He screamed, the droning sound enough to vibrate Hernie's vision. He kept driving the weapon forward, pushing the man back until he was pinned against the far wall between Tangela and the still screaming Sharon.

The agent pulled the trigger of his gun, firing wildly, the flash from each bullet like a camera going off in the dim room. Hernie pulled his mop handle back and jabbed again. This time the agent dropped his gun and reached for the wooden shaft jutting from his shoulder.

The seawall, Hern-ster. Remember what scared them at the seawall?

He did. Hernie reached for the dark glass plating strapped over the man's face.

"*Nooo!*" the agent howled, and gave Hernie a shove. He fell back, kicking the gun on the floor halfway across the room. With the pressure gone, the agent yanked the mop handle out of his shoulder and tossed it away. "You fucking asshole!" He brought up covered fists, now slick with his own blood. "Let's go, you little fuck."

"You give me back my MOTHER!" Hernie wailed, and leapt on him.

They rolled across the floor, a ball of flying fists and feet. Hernie got in a few good punches to the agent's ribs beneath his rubbery suit, but then the man pinned him against the floor by the throat and delivered a series of brutal blows to his head. The room spun by the time he was released. He lay limp on the floor as the man's weight disappeared. From somewhere at the end of a long, echoing tunnel, he could hear Tangela calling his name.

The agent retrieved his weapon and pointed it at Hernie. "Sorry pal, but there ain't no retards on the list."

A huge shape hurtled in through the doorway and slammed into the agent. Hernie recognized Mac only when Mary-land came through right behind him. The big, black teenager yanked the gun from the agent's hands and then hit him in the stomach with the butt, sending him to his knees.

Mary-land edged past the fight to pick up Tangela. "Hurry, there's more coming! We have to go right now!" Sharon jumped up from the dog food bags and headed toward the door.

"Did I do right?" Hernie asked.

She smiled down at him and offered her free hand to help him up. "You did perfect."

Together they went after Sharon. Mac left the unconscious agent on the office floor and followed them with the gun. They exited the front of the gas station through the hole in the exterior into the deepening night beyond.

WHITNEY +26:12

Lemiere propped the assault rifle against the wall and dropped to his knees beside Ellis. He placed two fingers against the cop's throat. "What da hell happen' to 'im?"

"I-I-I don't know!" Carter sputtered. "He yelled out when we were being chased by those guys, but he said he was fine!"

"He been shot." Lemiere pulled his greasy John Deere hat off and tossed it away, unleashing wispy strands of brown hair as fine as spiderweb, then grabbed Ellis' shirt at the neck and tore it down the middle. Low down on his dark back, close to the junction of hip and spine, was a hole the size of a quarter. Liquid bubbled out, looking black in the dim light. It certainly put the graze on Lincoln's shoulder in perspective. Lemiere looked up at Carter and said, "Find a bathroom. See if t'ey's a first aid kit, some towels, anyt'ing. Go, now!"

Carter's eyes were fixed on the blood pouring from Ellis, but he finally turned and started checking doors along the hall.

Lemiere pulled out a pack of cigarettes and a lighter from his breast pocket. He held the latter up to Lincoln. "G'down here close."

He came forward and crouched beside Ellis, flicking the lighter on and holding its weak light over the wound. Something hot and sick uncoiled in Lincoln's stomach, but he didn't look away. He'd spilled too much blood himself today to let something like this put him off.

"I found these!" Carter came back with a bottle of rubbing alcohol and a stack of folded t-shirts emblazoned with the trucking company's logo. "But I can keep looking!"

"Have to do." Lemiere unscrewed the cap and poured the clear liquid directly onto the wound, washing away the blood to reveal a ragged tear in the flesh. He slid the cellophane wrapper off his cigarette carton, flattened it, and pressed it over the hole, then picked up one of the shirts and cut off a small, circular piece with his knife. He repeated the process, working fast.

Carter turned away. "Ugh, I'm gonna sit this one out. I've already treated my gunshot wound for the day."

Lemiere took a bundle of the fabric pieces and laid them over his plastic seal, putting all his weight down on his arms. Lincoln watched this process with interest.

"What 'bout the bullet? Shouldn't we try to get it out or somethin?"

"T'at's movie stuff. Nev' go pokin 'round in a gunshot wound less you know what you doin. 'Sides, t'is is a ricochet, oth'wise, he'd already be dead, with t'ose chest-bursters t'ey usin. Right now, it's da shock we gotta worry about."

"How you know all that?"

"Jus' t'ings I picked up here and t'ere."

"You in the Army?"

Lemiere smiled. "Somet'in like t'at. Hand me t'em chairs."

Lincoln released the lighter and grabbed the two wooden desk chairs to his right. Lemiere made him keep pressure on Ellis' back while he broke the backs off with his foot, snapped away the legs, then proceeded to tie the padded sections tightly together with strips of t-shirt, creating a makeshift stretcher. Lincoln watched in amazement. For the first time since joining and then taking over the X-Dawgs, their whole military schtick felt kind of lame. He and Mac and CT and the others had only been playing soldiers, but Lemiere was the real thing.

"We gonna have to move 'im. Bleedin's slowin, but we gotta get to your doctor friend's clinic."

"That's easier said than done, MacGyver." Carter peeked out the window in the loading dock door. "There's even more of those trigger happy Cylons arriving out there. Looks like they're combing the area, and you got us trapped in here. So how do you expect us to stroll out?"

"Not stroll." Lemiere pointed at the pegboard mounted next to the door, from which keys hung. "Drive."

"Uh, remember that helicopter outside?" Lincoln asked. "It's just gonna take off and come after us again, and then we're right back where we started."

"Yep, been t'inkin about t'at too." Lemiere favored them with a snaggly grin and held up the bottle of rubbing alcohol. "Don' suppose t'ere's any cleanin supplies where t'is came from?"

Five minutes later they crept through the door to the loading dock, carrying Ellis facedown on the stretcher. He was already coming back around. They rolled up the cargo door on the closest truck and laid him inside. Carter sat with him.

Lemiere squatted in the doorway. "Jus' sit tight. If t'is don' work and t'ey catch us, maybe t'ey won' even know you back here."

"So wait in the dark to be found and shot. Got it."

Lemiere gave him a thumbs up.

"What about the others?"

"T'ey could be anywhere by now. Gotta save who we can."

Lemiere started to slide the door down, but Lincoln whispered "Hey!" through the narrowing gap. "Was Mac really lookin for me?"

Carter smirked through his facemask. "I knew the guy for about an hour, and for most of that, the only thing he talked about was finding you."

Lincoln swallowed and helped Lemiere latch the door.

The truck was stick diesel, so Lemiere took the driver's side this time. Lincoln crept down the side of the truck and climbed up next to him carrying another shirt they'd turned into a sling to carry their new supplies. They both cranked down their windows. Almost directly ahead sat the black helicopter that had chased them, with several guards around it. The others had been deployed, he assumed to the surrounding blocks.

"As much fun as driving through crowds of machine-gun-carrying maniacs is, I really want it to be the last time we try this, okay?"

Lemiere grunted and cleared his throat. "You only gonna have one shot. You miss...we dead."

"No pressure, huh?"

Lemiere started the ignition and threw the truck into gear. Once again, commandos zeroed in on them. They chugged out of the loading bay, Lemiere trying to coax speed as quickly as possible from the heavy engine.

Bullets spanged off the truck grill and punched holes in the windshield before tearing through the roof of the cab. Lincoln crouched below the dash, but Lemiere propped the assault rifle out the window and returned fire with the last of his ammunition. He directed the vehicle to pass as close to the right of the helicopter as possible. "NOW!"

Lincoln reached into the shirt satchel and pulled out the Molotov cocktails Lemiere had created from caustic cleaning supplies. He lit the shirt fuses with the lighter and tossed one out his window, arcing it over the hood of the truck. The commandos had already scattered from Lemiere's cover fire, but now they turned heel as a patch of the street burst into flame. He threw another one and caught one of the black figures on fire. It ran in burning circles.

They pulled up even with the helicopter, Lemiere gunning the engine and shifting gears so fast the clutch groaned. Lincoln lit two fuses at once. Here was the critical juncture, what Lemiere claimed would make or break them. With the shooting stopped, Lincoln was able to lean far enough out his window to almost sit on the edge of the door, and look over the cab of the truck. A motionless helicopter rotor swept just a few feet over the top of his head.

The canopy of the helicopter was still open. It was nearly level with his eyes. Lincoln hurled first one and then the second cocktail without a pause as they passed by. The first exploded against the side, spattering fiery oil against the metal without much effect.

The second dropped down into the delicate—and very flammable—interior of the cockpit.

Flames burst up like an erupting volcano. Lemiere cackled between coughs. Lincoln smiled and gave the recovering commandos the finger as he ducked back into the cab.

"We gonna be able to get to the clinic in no time with this thing!" He patted the dash of their new ride.

"Don' ge' too com'table. We use t'is to put some distance between us and t'em, lead 'em in da wrong direction. Then…we back on foot 'fore they ge' another bird in da air."

WHITNEY +26:28

The smoldering wreckage that had once been the Port Allen Civic Center was already cooling when the turbid skies opened up for a brief but fierce downpour the night after Whitney. The remaining fires sizzled and went out. The floodwaters rose, working to swallow the building. And, in the parking lot, Aurora agents finished their sweep for survivors.

A contingent was designated for clean-up duty while the others reported back to their team rendezvous for another project. There was a lot more city to search, and not much time to do it in. Field Agent Zachary Garmon was one of the lucky winners picked to stay behind and haul bodies.

As ten o'clock neared, he was still loading executed corpses from the edges of the parking lot onto a flatbed transport. It was hard work (physically and mentally), but he shuddered to even think what it would be like to dig all those crispy critters out of the Dome itself. He and the other agents kept their fingers crossed that the official sanction would be to leave the charred remains as-is, so the media boys could draft a convincing cover story about a gas leak.

Garmon dragged the body of a teenage girl up the ramp onto the transport and laid her down with the others he'd collected. She flopped limply. She'd been pretty—cute little face, platinum blond hair, long legs revealed by holes in her pajama bottoms—but all that was ripped away by the bullets that had shredded her torso. Christ, give her another few years and she wouldn't look too far from his last girlfriend in D.C., the one he was still begging to take him back.

He tried to block out the sight of her open, staring eyes. He was certain she wasn't one that he, personally, had shot, but there were plenty of other lifeless faces here that owed their deaths to him. The latex of his bodysuit was half an inch thick, but even so he imagined he could feel the dead girl's blood on his gloved hands. He held them up to the driving rain to wash them off and headed back down the ramp.

Another agent named Treemont met him at the bottom. Rather than use the comlink in their headset, the man turned on his buzzing exterior speaker—meant to keep their voices from showing up on recordable devices—and asked, "Hey, did you hear about Barnes' team?"

"No, what's up?"

"Remember that SUV that shagged ass outta here? I heard from someone that knows a guy on Barnes' team that a fucking *armed* civilian resistance took out the helicopter they used to go after it." Treemont sounded positively giddy, but his face was hidden behind the reflective faceplate. "Can you *believe* that? Who would've thought we'd see some actual action on this assignment!"

Garmon shrugged noncommittally, because, frankly, he didn't know if he did believe it. He was envisioning ragamuffin hurricane survivors with homemade RPG's made out of oatmeal cans and cherry bombs, striking from the shadows like Robin Hood's merry men. He just wanted some sleep, a cigarette, and out of this suit, although not necessarily in that order.

But if it *was* true…he didn't know what to think. After a day like this, it was hard not to feel a small thrill. He knew plenty of agents, himself included, that regretted accepting the offer to transition from the armed forces into the agency known only as Aurora.

Or more specifically, the branch that was under the command of James Kyler.

"Garmon," a new voice said into his headset over the radio. He recognized his own team commander. "Get those bodies over to collection and then report to the west side rendezvous."

"Yes sir."

He and Treemont lifted the transport ramp, gave each other a curt wave, and Garmon climbed into the driver's seat. He drove the vehicle through the rows of cars, weaving to a spot close to where the south side of the civic center met the climbing water.

Here was a pile of bodies rising to the sky, like a mountain of garbage at a town dump, twice as high as the bed of his transport. Air carriers were supposed to fly in and cart them all off for good sometime during the night. A few last sheets of rain dropped as Garmon parked next to two other transports that had been working other sides of the lot and got out to help the collection agents offload his cargo.

Rather than drag corpses to the top of the heap, he pulled them around to the far side, where the floodwater lapped at the concrete just a few feet away. On his second trip—with the pretty blond girl, who seemed to be accusing him with her glossy, angry eyes—he tossed his burden down and noticed something curious as he turned away.

The corpses beneath and around her were missing flesh. On arms and legs, torsos and heads. In some places, stark white bone gleamed in the moonlight. He didn't think bullets had caused this kind of damage, even those M7 Series Rippers they'd been outfitted with. If anything, this looked *gnawed*, like a gazelle carcass after a lion gets finished with it.

There was a quick flash to his left. It startled him so bad, he tripped over a gnarled arm and fell backward into corpses.

Something huge splashed away from him, diving into the flood covering the east side of the city. He had time to catch a blurred glimpse of something long and scaly before it submerged.

Garmon scrambled out of the body pile and looked over the water. Nothing. An alligator maybe, venturing out for an easy meal? Lucky the thing hadn't taken his leg off. He didn't know they could jump like that, but it was the only thing that made sense. He'd have to warn someone in Operations.

His team commander interrupted his thoughts again. "Okay ladies, all lethal weaponry is a no go until further notice. Switch over to nets and tranqs. The top brass want us to finish their scavenger hunt."

Garmon headed for his transport and took one last look over his shoulder. Nothing out there.

But as he walked away from the pile of bodies he'd helped create, he thought he heard a weird hooting cry drifting over the face of the water.

COME TOGETHER

Carter and the others arrived at the clinic just before eleven according to Lemiere's watch, all of them panting from carrying a fully-conscious Ellis through the rain. They'd driven the truck south and west through the city for several more blocks, away from their standoff, then circled down and around on foot, approaching their destination from the opposite side of the Dome by slipping from shadow to shadow. Lemiere scouted ahead and then signaled them with two fingers twirling in the air.

All of the blocks surrounding Eraj Kordi's place of business were covered by a foot and a half of water. They trudged through, lifting Ellis high to keep him out of it. The night was muggy after the last spate of rain, and Carter was sweating from places he didn't know sweated. But the dark sky and renewed cloud cover kept his vertigo at bay, tricking his mind into believing the sky had been erased.

Lincoln pointed out a long, rectangular building with a stone-wall exterior and a gray corrugated metal roof. The narrow windows that faced the street were boarded over, and a Family Healthcare sign in front was bent and leaning. The building was up out of the water though, built on a high concrete slab, the front door at the top of a short staircase.

A roly-poly man in a flannel shirt jumped out with a shotgun when they tried to enter and demanded identification. Before they could convince him, Kordi emerged from the gloom within the building carrying dry towels. "Let them through, Mr. Turner!" They quickly entered the building, Carter pausing to wrap his knuckles on the glass. 'Turner' regarded them with hollow, sunken eyes before going back to guard duty.

"My friends, it is wonderful to see you!" Kordi exclaimed while they dried their wet clothes and hair. The doctor had some eye luggage also, and his words were riddled with hoarse, chesty coughs. He'd changed into a white lab coat, which Carter found a little funny under the circumstances. It was the routine things that kept you going sometimes; he could relate. "Lincoln, Mr. Lemiere…I can't thank you enough for what you did. Everyone here owes their lives to you."

"It's cool," Lincoln said to his shoes.

Kordi turned to Carter next. "And I'm happy you found your way here as well. The others thought you'd been killed when you separated."

"The others? You mean Hernie and Maryland?" He tried to keep excitement out of the words. "Are they here?"

"They radioed me a little while ago for directions. They're several blocks away, all of them."

His relief was immense. Cripes, one day out of the cage and he was developing attachments to people he'd just met? He could imagine Pellner calling that overcompensation or a new security blanket, but right now, he was just glad to hear they were alive.

"We got a hurt man here, Doc," Lemiere drawled in his Cajun accent. "Gunshot wound."

"*Ricochet*," Ellis corrected sulkily from the stretcher. "I'm fine, I just got a little dizzy. They said if I didn't lay on this, they'd strap me to it."

Kordi looked him over with a flared nostril. "Ah yes, the police officer. Ellis, correct? Bring him in and I'll take a look."

Kordi took one side of the stretcher and he and Lemiere started down a hallway to the left. Before they disappeared into what Carter presumed was an examination room, Ellis turned his head on the gurney. "Lincoln, I'm sorry. For leaving you at the Dome. Outside, when Sturney had me…I gave him your name. He knows who you are now. I'm so sorry."

The young man looked past Ellis, to some undefined point in the distance, and then shrugged. "We all got stuff to regret, man. No beef here. Can't say it really matters, since we got bigger bacon to fry than those pigs."

Carter and Lincoln ventured to the right, into the waiting room of the clinic that occupied this entire side of the building. The air was warm and stale without the a/c, just short of stifling. Padded chairs and benches sat in facing rows, with lit candles lining the small tables where the magazines usually rested. There was a small reception area to the left, a vending machine that someone had pried the door open on, and all around the room were framed inspirational posters with pictures of cyclists and mountains on them. Other than that, it wasn't much different from the way things had looked at the Dome towards the end, just on a much smaller scale. There were ten or so people in here that he didn't know, huddled together around the wan candlelight. They coughed and hacked, some of them spread across the padded seats and covered in blankets. Carter caught frowns and suspicious eyebrows as they took in his rebreather.

There were familiar faces mixed in. Tom squinted at him from one of the seats, then finally stood and hobbled over to shake his hand. There was more color in the man's cheeks than the last time Carter had seen him, but his coughs sounded both dryer and deeper, chopping their way out of his lungs. "Sorry, I wasn't sure if that was you, dear boy. I seem to have misplaced my—"

Carter held up the spectacles he'd had in his pocket since leaving the Dome. One of the lenses had cracked sometime during his adventures, but they were intact otherwise.

"You are truly a prince among men." The British man slipped them over his squat nose.

"Just promise to never make a sequel to *Eyes Wide Shut* and we'll call it even."

Chris was right behind him, carrying the walkie-talkie and chattering about the imminent arrival of his stepsister. Randy gave a sullen greeting without getting up. The other young black kid that had been at the Dome sketched a salute at Lincoln with two fingers, and an old woman in a wheelchair with an oxygen mask rolled over and grabbed the teenager's hand. "God bless you, boy."

But the real reunion came fifteen minutes later when the other group entered the building. They were trapped in the vestibule for ten minutes while excited greetings were exchanged. Chris and

Tangela embraced, as did Tom and Maryland. Hernie threw his arms around Carter in another of his patented bear-hugs, and he was too tired and relieved to see the man to care. He noticed Mac try to do the same to Lincoln, but he turned his back and walked away without a word. The look on the big lug's face—confusion melting into sadness—was heartbreaking.

Finally, Carter found himself facing Maryland.

"Hey, Fear Club." Her hair was lank, wet strings, her clothes were soiled to the point of no return, and she was smudged with dirt across her makeup-less cheeks. She looked gorgeous. "Thanks for leaving me for dead."

"*What?* I didn't—! *You* left *me!*"

"Carter, I'm kidding."

"Oh."

"Don't get the wrong idea or anything, but...I was worried about you."

"Yeah? Me too." He rubbed the back of his neck and grinned. "So is this the part where I kiss you?"

"Didn't I just say not to get the wrong idea?" She breezed past him. "Besides...you'd have to take the mask off for that, and I do *not* want to be responsible for your next therapy bill."

He followed her back into the waiting room in time to catch the beginning of a growing commotion. Everyone that had the energy had formed a shouting semicircle against the far side of the room. From what he could see, Mac had the younger gangbanger, CT, up against the wall. Carter saw one of his huge fists rear back and punch the kid in the stomach. He doubled over in the bigger guy's arms.

"You little shit!" Mac slammed CT upright and held him against the wall with a hand on his chest. He backhanded the kid across the face with a noise like the crack of a homerun hit. "Thought you could get away with it? Thought I wouldn't *catch you?*"

Carter and Maryland joined the group trying to break it up, but most of the people were scared to get between the behemoth and his target. The smaller boy leaked blood from nose and lips, his face puffing, body sagging in Mac's grip...but there was a savage grin on his lips. Carter would have a hard time trusting anyone showing that much teeth. Lincoln was suddenly there, muscling his way through the crowd.

"Mac, stop! Let him go right now!"

Mac paused with hand cocked to deliver another slap and glared at Lincoln. "This motherfucker tried to kill me, Links! He broke my nose and left me and that other cop to drown!"

"That's not the way I heard it! He also had some things to say about you!"

Mac hesitated. "What're you talkin 'bout?"

At the other end of Mac's arm, CT chuckled through his split lips. "I told him, Mac...'bout how you turned him in. How you told that other cop everything."

"Does anybody else feel like they're coming in on the middle of a soap opera?" Carter asked aloud.

Mac's jaw slowly came unhinged. His thick brow lifted in alarm as he looked from CT to Lincoln. "It-it wasn't like that! You don't understand!"

"So it's true?"

"No, no, it's...I...whose word are you gonna take, Links, mine or his?"

"So far you haven't given me any word *to* take." Lincoln grimaced. "But it don't matter. Right now, I don't trust either one of you." He grabbed Mac's hand and pried the fingers loose from the other boy. "But we ain't doin this. We got enough problems right now without killin each other."

CT's legs wobbled as he was released. He leaned on the wall and grinned. "Yeah, niggah, you heard the boss."

Lincoln jumped at him. "And if I find out you lied to me...I'm gonna let him finish what he started."

The younger kid's eyes flashed; rage boiled across their glassy surface. He said, with stony conviction, "Ain't neither one of you touchin me again. *Ever.*"

Lincoln let go. "Just stay the fuck away from each other. And me."

Mac turned and pushed out of the ring of people without a word. CT's grin grew wider as the knot of onlookers dispersed, but Carter was one of the few people to see it.

"If I could have everyone's attention!" Kordi called, coming down the exam room hallway holding a candle. Lemiere was with him. "Now that everyone's here, I think it would be beneficial if we all sat down and talked. About what's going on and what we should do next."

There was mumbled assent. People grabbed waiting room chairs and scooted them into a cluttered group facing the reception desk.

"Carter," Maryland whispered to him before they joined the mass. "I was thinking, these people have been through a lot. We should probably just focus on what's important and try not to confuse them, so...let's keep stories about the killer monster to ourselves, okay?"

That awkward, hulking shape flickered through his mind—watching him in the street with yellow eyes, rampaging through the crowd in the Dome—and he grimaced. "I couldn't agree more," he said, and pulled up a chair between her and Lincoln.

WHITNEY +27:47

"Wright's in there." Sturney plopped down in a chair in the dark bakery across the street from the clinic. "He's in one a the rooms in tha back. Saw 'im through the winda."

Across the table, Drano hacked until he doubled over. On the table was a box of stale donuts he'd found in the shattered display case. He took one of the pastries with a shaking hand and took a humongous bite. "Those black boys, too. All three of them, with about twenty others."

Sturney slapped his knee in excitement and grabbed his own donut. "See, I told ya! I knew I heard tha name Lincoln on the radio!" They'd picked up the broadcasts by accident over the police band while searching for chatter that might tell them what in holy hell was going on. There was nothing on the airwaves except dead static, like a giant lid had been clamped down on the entire city to keep signals from coming in. The lone voices they'd picked up gave them directions to the healthcare facility across the street from where they now sat.

"I didn't see Van Ness, though."

"Cause he's prob'ly dead. If he wadn't in tha Dome when it blew, those boys in the black pajamas got 'im."

Neither of them knew what to make of the commandos. They'd thought at first it must be the long overdue arrival of the military, and Sturney started to force himself around to the idea of living the rest of his life in Mexico, selling blow to tourists for enough scratch to visit the whorehouse. But they watched the helicopters come in from afar, and the subsequent attack on the civic center, and knew something else was up. An entirely new ballgame, whose rules they didn't know. Once the choppers and troops started to expand through the city, performing block-by-block searches, they abandoned their patrol car and continued on foot.

"Looked like they're having a meeting in there." Drano jerked a thumb toward the clinic. "And they have a guard posted at the door. We could flash the badges, show a little muscle, see if we can walk out of there with all four of them."

"*What?*" Sturney pursed his quivering lips in disgust, dropping donut crumbs across his lap. "Jesus, Drano, use yer head! That's all we need, a room fulla witnesses connectin us ta them!"

"You were willing to take them at the Dome."

"Yeah, but this ain't the same as a buncha strangers, these folks *know* 'em, and they'll remember us later on!"

"Unless we walk away, and let those gunmen finish them all off."

"Can't take that chance. These boys could pack up any time. 'Sides, this ain't a normal situation. Who's to say that us havin badges is gonna mean jack shit ta them?"

"Then goddamn it, Sturney, what do you want to do?"

Sturney leaned an elbow on the table and cupped his meaty chin while he thought. It was high time to end this business, no more mistakes. Both he and Drano were sick, probably with whatever crud Myers had before Wright killed him. Those commandos were gunning down anyone they came across. The sooner the two of them finished Wright off, the sooner they could concentrate on finding a way out of Port Allen and start working on an alibi.

"Didn't I see a sportin goods store when we was on our way here? Reckon they have some ski masks?"

Drano coughed again. His rasp made his inflectionless voice even more dead than usual. "Sturn, if we're going that far, why not just shoot them through the window? Or burn the whole goddamn place down?"

"And risk bringin them goobers in black down on us before we can get out? No, we go in anonymous, use some force to get everybody meek, bring 'em outside and gut 'em. And kill anybody else that gets in our way."

The mention of guts grabbed Drano's full attention. "Okay. I can handle that."

Sturney stood up from the table, unbuttoned the front of his shirt, and removed his uniform, stripping down to his undershirt. Drano did the same, and they crept out of the bakery, leaving the donuts on the table.

WHITNEY +28:05

Kordi resembled a teacher at the front of a classroom to Lincoln. Which was a weird comparison for his mind to jump to, considering he hadn't seen the inside of a school in four years. The doctor held a candle under his face, the pale light deepening the sickly shadows beneath his eyes, and waited patiently for everyone to settle. The only ones not participating in the meeting were the little girl, Tangela, who was passed out on a bench with Hernie by her side, another unconscious woman bundled in blankets and stretched across several seats on the far side of the room, and Ellis, who hadn't come out from wherever they took him.

From things the cop had said on the way here, Lincoln was mostly convinced he didn't know anything about Kim. Whatever Mac had tattled, it was limited to the older officer, Charlie, who he'd seen no sign of. Lincoln didn't know what to do—make a run for it or stick it out—and he was getting a headache from the indecision.

"Perhaps we should start with introductions. Most of you know, I'm Eraj Kordi, MD, and this is my clinic. If you could, I'd like to know who you are and...well, how you feel."

They worked their way through the assemblage in rows, giving names and brief stories of how they came to be here, all in the hushed tones of Jews huddling in an attic. Everyone reported symptoms of varying degrees, the best off seeming to be Maryland, Carter, CT, Imogene, Chris, some of the new folks, and Lincoln himself, although he did admit his throat has been ticklish for a while. Two rows up, Mac told the doctor he'd coughed up blood, and Kordi promised to get him some medication as soon as they were finished.

Lincoln also tried to catch the names of everyone he didn't know. Sharon, the jittery girl Maryland had brought in with her group, and Turner, the heavyset door guard with the shotgun. He'd been separated from his wife at the Dome riot and had no idea where she was. The Frakes were a family of four that escaped the civic center parking lot with Kordi: Sara and Walter, and their twin teenage sons Doug and Dan. These two looked about Lincoln's age, but he could never really gauge white people. Barry wore slacks and a tie and talked in a mumbled, shell-shocked voice; Fernando, a thin Hispanic man, coughed too much to give them anything more than his name; Nancy looked like someone's grandmother and kept saying how confused she was; and Justin was a badly burned black man caught in the fire at the Dome and now covered in white bandages around his face and hands. No one knew the name of the unconscious woman. She'd joined Kordi's group somewhere on the streets between here and the civic center, and passed out when they reached the clinic. Kordi gave her a shot of the strongest medication he had left, and told them solemnly that she was in the last stages of the sickness.

Twenty-five people, by Lincoln's count, including Ellis. Two of them children, one mentally-challenged, one in a wheelchair, and at least one too sick to go anywhere.

"As you also know," Kordi continued when the last person finished, "we have two problems facing us. The first is, of course, this illness that seems to be affecting almost everyone without exception."

"It's fatal, isn't it?" Sara asked in a trembling voice. She was petite, limbs as thin as twigs, in jeans and a pink sleeveless shirt. Both her boys cleared their throats discreetly every few minutes. "It killed all those people at the civic center…"

"I'm afraid I just don't have an answer for that," Kordi said quickly. "We can discuss it all you want, but the simple fact is that I don't know what it is, or how to cure it. Oddly enough, it seems to be nothing more than increasing symptoms without any underlying cause. The coughing worsens until it triggers severe hemorrhaging. The initial medication I've given most of you abates the symptoms, eases the throat, until eventually the sickness overpowers it. I have a few doses of a second-tier treatment I've reserved for the more severe cases that, again, only seems to *delay* and not *combat*." He held up a firm finger. "But…all of this is not to say it will necessarily be the same for everyone. We have no way of knowing whether the terminus will be as extreme for each person."

"But if it—," Sara began, before her husband—a curly-headed, professor-type with round-frame glasses—cut her off.

"Doctor, if it is the same, how long are we talking about?" Walter asked. "How long until…?"

Kordi squirmed at the front of the room. "Obviously this affects people at different rates."

"Give us an estimate!"

"I don't want to speculate."

"Speculate!" Maryland told him.

"Tell us something, *anything!*" someone added.

"Well…keeping in mind I'm a general practitioner and not a CDC official…hours. Every person who is coughing in this room could very well be dead by noon tomorrow."

The room exploded. Everyone talked, over-talked, and then resorted to shouting. Sharon bawled. Chris grabbed Tom's hand. Sara clutched her sons to her while her husband demanded—from who, Lincoln didn't know—that something be done.

Lincoln jumped to his feet. "*Hey!* Shut up and keep quiet!" Enough of them still knew him from his work at the Dome so that they obeyed. "What the hell's wrong with ya'll? Ya'll saw what happened at the Dome. The doc's not tellin you anything you didn't already know, so let's calm down and talk about this."

They sat in uncomfortable quiet for a minute. It was broken when Fernando stood up and pointed to the back of the group. He stopped coughing long enough to ask, "I wanna know about *that* guy! What's that mask he's got? Do we need to be wearin those?"

Lincoln looked over at Carter as he met the faces turning to him. Candlelight flickered off the plastic mask in question. "Look, I'm just germophobic. I'm not wearing it because of *this* sickness, but just sicknesses in general. See?"

"That doesn't matter," Kordi said. "Yes, if this disease is airborne, that mask might be keeping him from inhaling the same germs as the rest of you, the same way that Miss Freeman's oxygen would. But—."

"Oh, you don't know shit," Walter muttered.

"—*but* if you've already had exposure, like most of us, then we need to focus on the next step, and that is receiving some real medical attention as quickly as possible."

Nancy asked, "Can't we call an ambulance?"

"How you gonna do that, lady?" CT jeered. "The phones're still out!"

"Even if they weren't," Tom spoke up from Maryland's other side in a voice hoarse from coughing, "I think it's safe to say there aren't any hospitals currently functioning within the city limits."

Walter had his arm around the shoulders of his closest son. "If we can't bring help to us, then we have to go to the help! We've gotta get out of the city!" Everyone nodded heads and buzzed in low tones.

Kordi held his hands up to get them calm. "Yes, that would be the ideal option, but that brings us to our second problem. As we all know, we seem to be under attack by well-equipped forces, to say the least. No one knows who they are or why they're doing this, but they killed many innocent people this evening with the most systematic methods imaginable."

"And they're not leaving," Maryland said. "On the way here, we saw more of them. They're searching for other survivors, going through each block."

"We have to go," Walter demanded. "We have to go right now!"

"Hold on, hold on," Kordi argued. "Maryland may be right, but if we run out there without coming up with some sort of plan now, while we have the chance, they *will* catch us. So let's talk about our assets. We're not completely defenseless. I have a pistol, Mr. Turner has a shotgun, and this gentleman," he pointed at Mac, "has brought back one of the machine guns these people were using."

"They'll go away though, right?" This from Sharon, squeaking from the end of their row. "Or someone will come for us, the army or somebody, they have to!"

"That's right!" Turner was the only one not sitting. He stood against the wall between them and the front door of the clinic, his big hands white as they clutched the pump-action shotgun. "These people are going to pay for what they've done, goddamn it!" He finished this up with a hearty round of wheezing that had people on his side of the room leaning away.

Kordi coughed into his fist. "Yes, I certainly believe that's the case as well. The best idea is to hold out as long as we can, and surely the government or the military will...will..."

Lincoln saw a single hand go up at the front of the crowd, slowly but with rigid assurance. After Kordi acknowledged him, Lemiere stood up and turned to look over the people with a scowl. Finally his grim lips opened, and he said, "I don' wanna bust anyone's daydreams about the gub'mint sweepin in on a fleet of unicorns to save us...but have you considered da idea t'em men out t'ere might *be* da military? As in, *our* military, da *U.S.* military?"

This was met with utter stone silence for a period of perhaps three seconds, before another eruption happened, this one inter-mixed with coughing and gasping. Lemiere waited for it to stop on its own.

"I was in da service for fifteen years. I don' know who t'em boys are or what branch t'ey reportin to, but t'ey gub'mint trained. *T'at* much I know."

"That's ridiculous!" Walter argued. Several others echoed this sentiment, including Maryland and Barry. "They're terrorists or something! Our own government would never do the things we've seen those men do tonight!"

"How's it feel to be so naïve?" Lincoln asked him, and Walter scowled through the sea of heads at him. He didn't know if he be-lieved it either, but he didn't like seeing Lemiere treated like he was nuts. "Ever hear of a little thing called Vietnam?"

Walter's mouth caught momentarily, then clamped shut. He said, much more solemnly, "I meant to *us*. Why would they do this to Americans?"

"Didn't say I knew t'at," Lemiere continued, still standing. "But lemme ask you folks a question: why were you at da Dome?"

"Some other people told us to go there," Walter answered. "Some neighbors from down the street."

"Why, I heard it on my little portable TV!" Nancy said. "It was a message from that Emergency Broadcast System, I think, the one that makes that loud beeping noise!"

"Car stereo." Maryland shot a glance at Tom. "It was the only thing we could get."

Lemiere was nodding. "T'at's the only thing bein broadcast, in any medium, since da storm hit. Even without power, we oughta be gettin outside radio and television now on batt'ry-operated devices. And cell phones, if some of t'ose towers outside da city're still standin. We haven't even seen anyone else come in because da bridge was destroyed last night in a convenient explosion."

"And the northern pass too!" Imogene pulled her oxygen mask away from her mouth to shout. "I saw the explosion myself!"

"T'at's right. So instead, we all herded toward da Dome, packed in good and tight, and what did we find when we got t'ere? Nothin. None of t'at promised help and food. Just t'ose helicopters blowin the hell outta us once most of da survivors were in t'ere. So ask yourselves, who has da power ta do all t'at? Ta put a clamp on t'is city so nothing comes in 'cept the messages t'ey want? Ta keep us trapped here while enough hardware ta outfit a small nation come flyin t'rough like da angel of death hisself?"

"Oh my God," Maryland whispered.

"C'mon!" Carter groaned. "This is absolute paranoia! Now you're beginning to sound just like..."

He trailed off. Brow furrowed. Twisted in his seat. Most of the others followed his gaze to the shadows on the far side of the room.

Where Hernie sat cross-legged on the floor.

WHITNEY +28:19

Hernie tried to keep up with the debate, but he got too confused, his mind wandered, and eventually he just contented himself with watching over Tangela again. His eyes were heavy, his throat burned, and before long he was dozing on the floor against the chair next to her.

A tap on his shoulder brought him around. When his eyes fluttered open, he found Mr. Carter and everyone else leaning over him in the dim room. He jumped.

"It's okay, Hern-ster." Mr. Carter brushed something off the carpet and then sat down on the floor so they were eye level. "This is very important, my man. I need you to do something for me."

The voice his friend used was more serious than normal, but even if it wasn't, Hernie's answer would've been the same, and just as immediate. "Yes, Mr. Carter, I can do whatever you want!"

Mr. Carter smiled. "That's good, Hernie. What I want you to do is tell these people what you told me when we first met. About what happened to you this morning."

"This morning?" He bit his lip and frowned.

"At the seawall."

"Oh! About the government agents and the lasers and—?"

"No." Mr. Carter stopped him gently with a pat on the knee. "I need you tell us…the truth. *Exactly* what happened to you. Just the facts and nothing else. If possible, try not to use the word 'government' at all. Do you understand?"

He shifted uncomfortably. All these people were staring at him, all these strangers and Mary-land and Doctor Kordi and Chris and Mr. Tom Cruise (but not the one from the movies), and their eager eyes made him feel nervous.

"C'mon, Hernie." Chris slid into the floor next to him. "You can do it."

Hernie closed his eyes. Tried to focus on this morning. His hands stole up and his index and middle fingers began tapping a slow beat against either side of his head, like Native American war drums. Everything was there, he could see it fine in his brain, but his tongue couldn't form the words to make it all come out. He thought of his mother, about holding her hand in a way that was more dream than memory, and then that gentle voice was speaking the words into his ear for him to repeat.

"We were in the oil re-fine-ries," he said. "Me and Hatch. And I wanted to get the muddy-mud off me, so I climbed up on the sea-wall…and then they came."

"Who came?"

"Gov…*people*. Dressed in black. With masks over their faces."

He saw Mr. Carter glance around at the others. Mary-land asked from over his shoulder, "Like the men that we saw, Hernie? Like the one you fought at the gas station?"

"Yes, just like that."

"You're sure?"

"Very sure."

"Oh c'mon, you're leading him!" a man near the back called out.

"Mr. Frakes, please be quiet a moment," Doctor Kordi told him.

"What did these people at the seawall do?" Mr. Carter again. "Describe it."

"They had these…things. Little black circles. Like a CD, only a lot thicker."

"Like a hockey puck?" Lincoln offered.

"Huh?"

"Don't confuse him!" Mr. Tom Cruise swatted him on the shoulder. "Go on, Hernie."

"They…stuck it to the seawall. Then they waved a magic wand over it…and it lit up. Green and red, like Christmas."

"T'at's a detonator, used to sync up explosions." This came from the man with the hard-to-understand accent standing in the middle of the group. "Sounds like high-grade plastique, maybe C4."

He was near the end, the words were there, and Hernie stopped tapping his temples and let them spill out in a rush before he could be interrupted again. "Then they saw Hatch and they were gonna hurt him, shoot him, so I jumped on top of them and it made an explosion and then there was a lot of water and…I lost Hatch."

From the expressions on the faces staring down at him, he couldn't understand if he'd explained it right or not. Some of them looked angry, some scared, some confused.

"That's really good," Mr. Carter told him, and he relaxed. "Is there anything else you can remember? Anything at all? Did they say anything?"

This was even harder. He could remember them talking, their buzzing voices, but the words were such minor details and there were so many of them that he had to think hard to find the ones that felt important. "They said…the blast had to be just right…so water didn't wash the city away. So it could drive them toward the civic center. Is that where we were, Mr. Carter?"

His friend looked pale when he answered. "Yes, buddy. We were there. You did a good job, Hernie. Thank you."

Mr. Carter got to his feet, and the crowd started to back up. With the pressure of their eyes gone, it was a little easier to think, and Hernie's memory gave him a sudden poke.

"Oh, wait, there's another thing!" They turned back to him. "I broke one of their masks, and he started screaming a whole bunchy-bunch! He said he was…what was the word?…condom… uh…nated?"

"You mean 'contaminated.'" Chris said quietly.

WHITNEY +28:33

Ellis listened to the conference through the open door of the exam room where Kordi and Lemiere had left him. After getting him rolled onto his stomach, the doctor had examined the gunshot wound while Lemiere told him his ricochet theory.

"This is a little outside my area of expertise," Kordi had said, "but I think you're right. This can't be too bad. The bleeding's stopped for the most part, and I think I can see the bullet just in the subcutaneous layer. With the projectile's speed already slowed, that could have served to cushion the impact and stop the bullet before it reached the organs."

"'Subcutaneous layer?' You're saying I was saved by back fat?"

"Someday modern medicine will recognize the benefits of love handles," Kordi muttered wistfully, and Lemiere chuckled. "Now get ready. We don't have time for anesthetic and this might sting a little."

Kordi also turned out to be a master of understatement. It felt like a red-hot skewer shoved into Ellis, only slowly. Lemiere just about sat on top of him while he clamped his jaws against a scream. The doc played Operation in his back with a pair of forceps and a candle until he found the bullet, pulled it out, and cleaned up the new gush of blood.

Lemiere examined the warped metal. "Sum bitch, dis is serious ammo. Just 'bout blast a hole t'rough steel. Musta bounced quite a bit 'fore hittin you."

"I'm not going to stitch this, because the bleeding should stop again on its own," Kordi said. "But I certainly recommend you stay off your feet to ensure it doesn't tear open. I also have a spare shirt on the back of the door you can wear. Now, if you'll excuse me, I have a waiting room full of near-hysterical people."

After they were gone, Ellis ignored the ebbing throb in his spine and the growing one in his throat as he listened, trying to envision the faces of the new people from their voices. As soon as Lemiere gave his theory about the commandos—or maybe 'soldiers' was a better term—Ellis was in instant agreement. It was the only thing that made sense.

The debate became hushed for a while, but now they were back, words drifting down the hall to him. Against doctor's orders, he sat up carefully and slid off the table. The pain was bad, but not crippling. He pulled on the shirt Kordi had left for him, a solid blue, short sleeve pullover that actually matched his uniform pants. He looked through the cabinets along the wall until he found a brace for his broken finger and wrapped the digit as solidly as possible, then poked his head out to watch.

"T'ey was here da whole time." Lemiere was speaking to the entire assemblage. "Least since t'is mornin. T'ey ain't responsible for da hurricane, but t'ey are for everyt'ing t'at's happened since. T'ey blew da seawall ta force us all toward da Dome, where we'd be easy pickins. And keep in mind, t'ey was speakin *English*. Not too many terrorists gonna be doin t'at, 'less you t'ink da British are invadin." He glanced at Tom with a grin.

"That doesn't prove anything!" Someone else—it sounded like that Walter guy—stood up. "That guy's retarded, for Christ's sake!"

"Sounds ta me like t'ey knew 'bout t'is illness, too," Lemiere pushed on without acknowledging him. "Maybe t'at's even why t'ey here."

"What are you saying? That we're under quarantine?"

Lemiere took his time answering. Candle glow created flickering pools under his eyes. "Maybe."

"I refuse to believe that!"

"It doesn't matter!" Kordi pounded the reception desk, and the room got quiet. *Between him and Lemiere*, Ellis thought, *they got this show pretty much covered.* He remembered what the doctor had asked of him back at the Dome, to be a leader, and felt his cheeks flush as much at the idea as the memory of running away. They didn't need him, not when they had these two.

Lincoln had told him about Heather Rampy on the hike to the clinic. That was what happened when you followed Ellis Wright. God, *no one* needed him.

Well…almost no one.

Kordi was still talking when he tuned back in. "So whether you want to believe it or not, the problems are still the same! We need help, either a way to get to it or a way to bring it to us. Does anyone know of any vehicles close by we could use, anything that might get us at least part way up the mountains?"

Everyone mumbled their answers. The consensus seemed to be, if someone's car had survived Whitney, then it was currently residing in the lot at the Dome. Lost to them, in other words.

"I do own a small boat at the marina though." Barry smoothed his hair back with shaking hands while he spoke. "I have no idea what shape it's in after the hurricane, but maybe it's still seaworthy."

"Yes, yes!" Sharon held her hands over her face and rocked back and forth while she squealed.

"That's it!" Walter spun to look at them all. "We get in this boat and sail away from the city! Come back in further down the shoreline, away from these people!"

"No." Lemiere stopped to cough. "The chance is slim t'at it— or anyt'ing else down t'ere—is still even in one piece. 'Sides, how many people will t'is t'ing hold?"

"Eight or nine. A dozen, maybe, if they're light."

"See? T'at's leaves half the group behind."

"Hey, I'm sorry, but I have to say, screw the group!" Walter clutched at one of his boys' shoulders. "I got a family here, buddy, we should be allowed to get on it! Along with women and children, of course."

"You get on t'at t'ing, you gonna be a sittin duck on the water, case t'ey got anyone patrollin out t'ere. And it's gonna take you a good bit of sailin to reach somewhere you guaranteed ta find help. Da doctor said we have *hours*, people, not days!"

Ellis hobbled out into the hallway, cleared his sore throat. "I have an idea."

They turned to stare. "Who's this guy?" Fernando demanded.

Kordi came to stand next to him. "This is Officer Wright, of the Port Allen police department."

Just as with the people in the street earlier in the day, they drank him in like the resurrected Messiah. All it took was the title, not even a badge. "My precinct is on the southern edge of town, off Parson Street, if it's still standing. Probably a few hours from here by foot. There's radios, communication equipment and a generator to power them. I'm sure we can find something to send a distress call."

Barry shook his head. "But I thought they had the whole city on lockdown. Nothing in or out."

Lemiere told him, "Not necessarily. Cell towers're simple ta take down, and it's a lot easier to jam signals comin *into* a certain area, 'specially when you know what channel t'ey usin. If we had an outgoin line powerful enough and t'ey didn't know about it to override…we coul' reach someone on the outside."

"That's a good idea," someone muttered.

A man with bandages across half his face spoke in a timid, slurred voice. "But…if that's really the military or the government or whatever that blew up the Dome and is keeping us in the city, then let's say we make it to your precinct. What then? Who do we call? More cops? How do we know they wouldn't just tell these guys where to find us? For that matter, how do we know you're not part of this?"

"Do I look like I'm part of this?" Ellis limped forward, the ache in his back ratcheting with each step. "Look, I don't know who to call, but this is the only option I can offer you. I think we can all agree there's no way the outside world knows what's going on, that American citizens are being gunned down like dogs. This is a hush-hush operation, that's why they're not letting anyone in or letting us get word out. We just need to find someone that cares, with the power to do something. It's the only shot we have. At the very least, there's other weapons there to defend ourselves. Maybe make a stand."

He waited for someone to argue, but people only looked at one another imploringly before turning back to him. Lincoln gave him a thumbs-up from the back of the room.

"This is excellent." Kordi checked his watch. "It is just past midnight now. If we start soon and you lead us there, we will have the advantage of night, and we can get some distance from the area these soldiers are searching."

Ellis was already shaking his head. There was that word again, 'lead'. As in, 'take responsibility.' Fortunately, he had an excuse. "No. I'll give you directions, draw you a map if you want, but I can't go. Because that punk right there is going to show me where he dumped my partner this afternoon." He leveled a finger at Mac, who slouched in his chair.

"Of course," he heard Kordi say. "Why am I surprised?"

"I really think *you* should take us there, Ellis." Maryland raised her eyebrows and cocked her head to the side.

"Dr. Kordi and Mr. Lemiere will be able to get you there just fine."

"Yes, but you're the only one that knows for sure how to get there, where the communication equipment is, and how to operate it," Tom pointed out. "Of all us, you're the one essential in this plan."

Walter stood up. "You need to go with us! You have a civic responsibility! We...we pay your salary!"

"We could sue the police department!" Barry yelled.

"Would you listen to yourselves?" Ellis grabbed his forehead. "You're talking about lawsuits when it's life or death out there! In case you hadn't noticed, someone called time out on the rules of civilization in this city yesterday afternoon! Now, my partner is lying somewhere near-dead, and I'm not going to leave him!"

The uproar continued, people talking to each other, shouting and pleading with him. He stood there dumbfounded, trying to figure out how to explain to them that he was the last person they wanted in charge, until Lemiere broke away to come toward him. "Le' me talk ta you a minute. You too." He beckoned to the huge gangbanger.

They stepped away from the group, into the hallway, while Kordi tried to keep order and conduct the debate about the soldiers. Lemiere asked, "Wha's t'is all about now?"

"He was with my partner the last time I saw him. He told me he left him unconscious in one of the houses along the edge of the floodwater, somewhere north of the Dome."

Lemiere looked at Mac. "Wha' was wrong with 'im?"

"I don't know, he got shot in the fuckin leg. He went into a coma or somethin yesterday. I stashed him in this abandoned house and went to the Dome to get help and then I kinda got a little distracted." He glared at Ellis. "Savin you from your pig friends."

"How do we know he ain' already dead then?"

"We don't." Ellis swallowed thick, guilty spit. "He's my partner, all right? And everything that happened to him is my fault. I have to go after him to make sure."

"And t'ere's no way I can talk you outta it?"

"None."

Lemiere thought for a minute, scratching the thick stubble along his jaw line. "Okay t'en. If t'at's da way it is, you lead t'ese folks to your precinct, and let me go find your partner."

"*You?* Why would you go?"

"Because t'ese people need you, need what you stand for. T'ey'll follow you ta safety."

"But they're following you and Kordi!"

"No, t'ey *listenin* to us, and t'ere's a big difference. T'ey trust you, and right now t'at's what t'ey need, someone ta bring t'em together."

Ellis shook his head rapidly. "I can't ask you to do that. You're just as sick as anybody else here, you need to go with them in case they find help."

"I got more life in me t'an you, at t'is point. 'Sides, I stand more chance of gettin ta your partner and back out. I have a little motorboa' docked just north of here. I can use it ta pick 'im up and get away from t'ose troops. You ain' in no shape ta go sneakin around. Lemme do t'is."

Ellis grimaced. The Cajun was right. Again. He was the best chance Charlie had.

But still, the job he was leaving Ellis seemed much more terrifying.

Lemiere took silence as consent. "Can you tell me how to ge' to 'im?" he asked Mac.

"I memorized the address, but I got no idea where it is! I kinda figured I'd be comin back myself, so I'd know it when I saw it."

"Then you just volunteered to go with me."

Mac didn't hesitate. "Okay, man. I'm down with that. I wanna save him just as much as you do, and I ain't got shit else to go on for."

The three of them went back into the waiting room and Lemiere announced that Ellis would be leading the group south. The relief on their strained faces made Ellis queasy.

"Okay," Kordi said. "I want to administer some medication before—"

He was cut off by the sound of brutally sharp coughing from across the room. On the benches, the nameless woman flopped. Her head crashed up and down as blood spewed from her mouth. Tangela, several seats over, woke up and screamed. Hernie picked her up and carried her away.

Kordi flew across the room, with Ellis and Lemiere behind him. The rest of the group kept their distance, watching in horror. They tried to hold her down while the doctor worked, but it was evident after a few seconds there was nothing he could do except ease her pain while she bled out. After it was over, the slick leather beneath her dripped with crimson and pooled into a dark stain on the carpet. They looked at each other in the candlelight, faces spotted with this woman's blood.

Something in Ellis broke at the sight of her pain-twisted features. They were all going to look like this before long, if not shot by those mercenaries.

He stood up and looked out over the survivors huddled across the room.

"Five minutes," he said. "Gather up anything you think you'll need, and then we're getting the hell out of here."

WHITNEY +28:57

People scurried around, collecting what few belongings they had. Most of them clustered around Kordi, pleading for medicine, supplies, clothes, food, anything he might have in the clinic. He snapped his fingers at Chris as he walked by. "I will make up a list and then I want you and those twins to go in the storeroom and gather everything on it!"

"Sure thing, Dr. Kordi." As the man scribbled on a pad at the reception desk, Chris continued over to where Tangela sat propped against the wall with Hernie.

"Hey sis, I forgot to give you this earlier." He held out Mr. Softy, which had been under one of the waiting room chairs since he arrived at the clinic. "I rescued him."

"Thanks." The utter lack of feeling was so unlike her. She wrapped the thin security blanket around her shoulders and shivered. "I want Mommy."

"How do you feel?"

"Sick."

He believed it. Her usually dark face was at least four shades lighter, her eyes sunken jewels in bruised-looking sockets. She coughed every few seconds, pitiful, strangled sounds that caused her to wince each time.

Really, there wasn't much difference between her and the woman that just died. Chris' skull squeezed till he thought he could feel the bone cracking like ice in a drink. Tangela was going to die if they didn't get help; that was obvious even without Kordi telling them. But this helplessness was more than he could take. He needed to fix this, but he couldn't think of a single thing to do, not even with all his damn APTITUDE and POTENTIAL, which his teachers said would come in soooo handy in the real world. If this wasn't the real world, he didn't know what qualified.

For the thousandth time, he wished his father was here. He probably couldn't do much more than any of these other adults, but it would make him feel better all the same.

"Just stay here and keep still. I'll see if I can get you some more medicine, okay?" He said to Hernie, "Please keep an eye on her. If anything happens…make sure you get Dr. Kordi first, and then find me."

After he got an agreement, he went to accept the list of items and a couple of flashlights. Dr. Kordi pointed out a door at the far end of the hall, past the exam rooms, and explained how to find things in the storeroom.

Doug and Dan were with Sharon when he found them. She was crying about her parents, and they flanked either side of her, rubbing her shoulders, trying to assure her they were still alive. Chris had talked to them some on the way to the clinic. They were two months short of their eighteenth birthday, and he'd noticed them using any excuse to talk to the college girl. If teenage hormones could make you think about girls just a few minutes after someone told you that you were going to die, he hoped he skipped the end of puberty entirely.

"Dr. Kordi asked if you guys would help me find some stuff in the storeroom."

"No problem," Doug, the shyer of the two, said.

Dan turned to Sharon, leaning on the counter so his bicep flexed. "Hey Sharon, you wanna come with us?"

She dried tears on her sweater sleeve and smiled up at him. "Okay."

Chris rolled his eyes as he turned away, but Dan caught the look. "What is it, pipsqueak?"

"White people are weird."

He led the way to the door the doctor indicated. On the other side was a narrow staircase leading down to a long basement storeroom running the length of the building. It was flooded by a foot of water. They clicked on the two flashlights they were given and swung them around. Rows of free-standing, backless shelves stretched away, filled with medication samples and supplies. File cabinets stood at regular intervals along the periphery. There were windows high up, near the ceiling in here, but at outside ground level. All of them had been boarded over for the storm, but they leaked water around their seals in continual streams down the cinderblock walls. The sound was like a hundred faucets going at once.

They took off their shoes (Chris' feet thanked him after being scrunched into Mr. Z's footwear all day), rolled up their pant legs, and waded into the chilly water. The cold concrete numbed his toes. Chris tore the list in half, and he and Doug took one piece while Sharon and Dan grabbed the other. Dr. Kordi had arranged the list sequentially, and they had no trouble finding the supplies.

He and Doug worked their way toward the back, finding most of their items on the outside aisle against the left wall. Their arms filled up fast. Doug was juggling a load of mediation samples when he dropped their flashlight into the water. The light stayed on for a second before flickering out, and they were plunged into muggy black.

"Goddamn it."

"Smooth," his brother told him from somewhere on the other side of the metal rows.

"Shut up, Dan. Here Chris, give me your stuff. I'll take it all back up and see if they have another one." Chris piled all he could in Doug's arms. A few seconds later he could hear the sounds of the twin splashing away from him and then running up the stairs.

Chris waited. Without the flashlight to rely on, his eyes adjusted. Through the gap between shelves, he could see the other light bobbing around Sharon and Dan. He thought the boy had his arm around her. He shook his head and smiled, turning away to give them privacy in case they…

Crunch.

Chris yelped and jumped away.

"You okay?" Sharon asked, her voice instantly screechy with fear.

"Yeah, I think so. I just stepped on something sharp." He lifted his foot and gingerly probed the sole. He thought he was cut, but it was too wet to be sure. Chris swept his toes along the ground. Beneath the water beside the wall was a field of glass shards. He squinted into the shadows to look for where they might've come from, first at the supplies closest to him and then gradually swinging around to the window above.

There was no board covering this one. He could barely see the outline of a few pieces of jagged glass caught in the frame. Flooding from outside poured over the edge in a miniature waterfall.

Before he could consider this, one of the shadows to his left stirred.

It stepped from between filing cabinets, blocking his exit. Chris backed away. The shadow reached for him, and he thought of the gutted woman in the street.

"Sharon, Dan, there's something in here!"

He splashed down the aisle, the sounds of pursuit mirroring those of his flight. Chris reached the end of the aisle—catching sight of the cinderblock just before smacking into it—and turned right, squeezing between the end of the shelf and the wall. His pursuer was too big to fit. He felt fingers pawing at the back of his shirt, heard a grunt of frustration. "Catch 'im!" a voice commanded.

Chris kept moving, slipping through the narrow end of each shelf, working his way along the back of the storeroom. "What's going on?" Dan called, and then Sharon screamed.

He moved into their aisle. Ahead of him, by the wildly swinging light of Dan's flashlight, he could see a burly figure wrestling with Sharon. "It's *them!*" the girl cried. "Don't let them get me!"

Chris knew who she meant, but he didn't think it was right. From what he could see, this person was wearing a stained white shirt and dark slacks, and the black mask over his face wasn't so much *hazmat* as it was *ski slope*. Sharon struggled, and the two of them slammed against a shelf, spilling goods into the floor.

Chris leapt onto the figure's arm, prying at the fingers around Sharon's wrist. He sank his teeth into a fleshy forearm. The figure gasped, let go of Sharon, and shoved him. He fell into the water at Dan's feet, the cold a shock to his system. Somewhere behind him, Sharon sobbed as she ran for the stairs.

"What the hell?" Dan demanded. He looked big, probably a football player for Allen High, where Chris would be next year. Dan waded into the figure, swinging the flashlight like a weapon. The first few blows were deflected, and then the figure reached behind him. When the hand came forward again, Chris saw the frigid glint of a knife.

"Look out!" he yelled. Dan swung the light at the figure's face, and, at the same time, it thrust upward with the blade, catching the boy in the gut. Dan whimpered, a high, reedy noise, and let go of the flashlight. The last thing Chris saw before the lights went out was the look of confusion on the twin's face.

He scrambled up and away, heart racing. There was a giant splash as Dan toppled over, and then the sounds of his killer coming after Chris. He forced himself to be quiet and inched his way toward the direction of the exit.

Chris felt the edge of the wall where it turned inward at the staircase when an arm slid around his waist. Something deathly cold and wickedly sharp pressed against his throat. He gasped.

"All right, ya l'il fucker, you wanna go upstairs? Then let's go upstairs."

WHITNEY +29:15

As soon as the rest of the group gave him some breathing room, Kordi led Maryland and the little old black grandma named Imogene to an exam room. Everyone else milled around the windows, peering through small cracks around the boards to watch outside. The nameless dead woman had been laid in the records room behind the reception desk. The twins' mother, Sara, was appointed travel agent, and went from person-to-person, accounting for mobility. There were two other wheelchairs besides Imogene's at the clinic, and the decision had been made to give one to the badly-burned Justin and the other to Lemiere in case he needed it for the other police officer. They tried to give it to Tom, who swayed on his feet every time he stood, but he flatly refused.

One of the Frakes' kids—Doug she thought—blew past them from another dark doorway ahead with his arms full of supplies. "Do you have another flashlight, Dr. Kordi? It's kind of flooded down there."

The doctor sighed, but it had a good-natured ring. "I think my secretary bought some of the big waterproof kind. Check in her desk." The teenager hurried away, and Kordi led them to the doorway of the last room on the left. He stopped and exclaimed, "What are you doing?"

Maryland looked over his shoulder.

Lincoln's cousin—the kid that had gotten into a fight with Mac—was rifling through one of the overhead cabinets. At the sound of Kordi's voice he jerked away, spilling individually wrapped syringes onto the countertop. He coughed. "Nuthin man, I wasn't doin nuthin!"

Kordi stood aside to let him pass. "There is not anything you can get high with in here. Get out, right now. Do not let me catch you taking anything else."

CT sauntered out, shoving his face into Kordi's as he passed. The doctor pulled back, and the black boy laughed. Maryland saw the way his eyes jittered.

When he was far enough down the hall, Kordi told them, "We are going to have a problem with that one. His habit is bad enough to cause withdrawal pains. People in that position get desperate."

"Greeeeat."

"If he gets any worse, we have the choice of either giving him something to dull his senses, or watch his symptoms play out."

Imogene gripped the armrests of her wheelchair till her bones showed through her leather skin. "Let the li'l bastard suffer."

"Trust me, I would like nothing more, but we will eventually be carrying him. At least when he is high, he will be functional. Now please, come in."

Maryland pushed the elderly woman to the padded exam table. Kordi lit a few candles and then rummaged under the sink until he came up with an even smaller oxygen tank in a pouch with a strap. He cleared his throat into his fist. "That one is probably ready to give out. This one should give you another five hours. Plus it will be easier to travel with." They set the bigger canister she'd been using aside, and fitted the new one over one shoulder. She gave the doctor a nod as she breathed through the new mask.

Maryland grabbed the handles of the chair to direct her back out, and winced when she closed her hands too tight around the plastic. Kordi noticed. "Come on then. Let us have a look at those hands."

Imogene wheeled out of the way, into the corner. Maryland placed her bandaged hands palm-up on the exam table and let the doctor unwrap them. The flesh beneath was still a thrashed mess. He gave them a gentle cleaning with alcohol that stung far less than she expected. "What did you do?"

"Slid down a concrete embankment."

"Do not do that anymore." She gave him a smile that he returned. "They will be scarred permanently, but you shouldn't have any lasting problems. They've closed up as well, so the risk of infection is minimal. Leave the bandages off and let them get some air."

She looked into the man's gaunt, drawn face. "Thank you."

"Not a problem."

"No, I mean, *thank you*. For everything you've done. A lot of us wouldn't be alive right now if it weren't for you."

"That's right," Imogene agreed.

She thought Kordi blushed, but his skin was too dark and the room too dim to tell. He cleared his throat again. "It is just...my job."

Maryland started to tell him how wrong he was, when she was cut off by a scream.

"They're here! Oh God, *they're here!*"

She'd come to know that alarmist voice all too well. Sharon had jumped at every shadow on the way to the clinic, like a kid watching her first horror movie. Now she flew past the open door of the exam room, screaming that the soldiers were here. Maryland pushed up from the table and headed toward the hallway. "I swear to God, I'm gonna put a muzzle on her."

She stepped out. Chicken Little ran toward the waiting room on her right. Before Maryland could go after her, there was the sound of clomping footsteps on her left, from the storeroom.

Two dirty, disheveled men in ski masks emerged right next to her, spreading out once they were in the wider corridor, one of them with a beer gut hanging out from under his shirt that would put Bryce's to shame. This fat one had a hairy arm across Chris' chest, and a knife at his throat. The boy's face was terrified.

She couldn't react. Couldn't think what to do. That decisive inner Amazon was out to lunch.

The thinner one rushed her, eyes gleaming through the holes in his knit mask. She saw the pistol in his hand a split second before he grabbed a handful of her hair and pulled painfully, twisting her head until she was forced to look away from them. She felt the gun barrel dig into the base of her neck and went cold as he pushed her forward. "Move, bitch!"

Kordi stepped out. "What is going on?"

"Get your ass down there! Right now!" The doctor was shoved hard enough to make him stumble, and then herded toward the waiting room beside her.

Ahead of them, Turner spun around, circling from the glass front door of the clinic. He started to raise his shotgun, but the fat one barked, "Nah ah ah. You drop that scattergun, maestro, or I'm 'onna turn junior here into a sprinkler system. Got me?"

Turner clutched the shotgun, weighing options. The man with the pistol let go of his death grip on Maryland's hair and charged him. He smashed his weapon across Turner's face. Turner fell to the ground, clutching his cheek, the weapon tumbling from his hands. The gunman swept it aside with his foot. It rolled into the sea of chairs they'd used for their meeting.

The fat one let go of Chris long enough to give Maryland and Kordi one last push into the waiting room. Everyone froze in a rough semicircle, watching events unfold with dulled eyes. Sharon had reached the reception desk and cowered behind it, clutching Doug. Tangela shouted her brother's name and tried to stand, but Hernie held her back. Other than that, no one protested. As Maryland walked a few paces forward, she scanned the room, trying to place the important faces. Lemiere was in a far corner with Mac, but neither of them was holding the machine gun as she'd hoped; Ellis stood amid the larger crowd at the windows, looking dumbfounded. She even sought out Carter, but not because she believed he'd be any help. He watched her from a chair next to Tom, that baby-smooth face of his wrinkled with confusion. Maryland spun to face their attackers, standing side-by-side with Kordi.

"Ever'body face down on the ground, right now!" the fat one hollered. No one moved.

Turner was on his hands and knees, trying to crawl away from the duo. The thin one gave him a kick in the side. He grunted and collapsed, wheezing on the thin carpet. "You heard him! Lay the fuck down or I start shooting!" He swept the crowd with his gun, and people screamed and fell to the floor.

All except Kordi, who remained standing with his hands held up. He glared at the two men. Maryland found herself still on her feet beside him. Tension had locked every muscle and joint in her body.

The doctor spread his fingers in the air. "What is this about? Robbery?"

"They stabbed Dan!" Chris shouted. "He's hurt, they—!" His words were cut off as his captor clapped him on the side of the head.

Sara jerked up from the floor. "My son! Where's my son?"

"If you hurt my boy…!" Walter yelled from somewhere in the room of facedown survivors.

"If that is true, let us give him first aid!" Kordi told them.

The thin one opened his mouth to answer and began hacking instead. His eyes bugged out through the mask and he clutched at his throat with his free hand. The fat one said, "Nobody's goin anywhere! Just shut up, all of you!"

Kordi watched them. "You are sick. Let the boy go, put down those weapons, and I will treat you. I am a doctor."

"We're here on other bidness." He grabbed Chris by the roots of his short hair and jerked the boy's head all the way back, exposing his neck so far the Adam's apple stood out like a knot on a tree. "Ellis Wright, if you don't stand up and get over here right now, you're gonna see the inside of this kid's throat."

In the seconds of silence that spun out after this request, Maryland realized an interesting fact.

Imogene was not with them.

WHITNEY +29:28

Ellis went to the floor along with everyone else, but it took longer with his back wound. As he sank to his knees, he found Lincoln just a few yards away. The young man lifted an eyebrow and nodded at the gunmen.

Ellis lay stretched out between Walter Frakes and Nancy, cheek pressed against the carpet, and listened to the short exchange between the doctor and the masked man he figured to be George Sturney.

And then came his own name.

"I know ye're here, Wright," that redneck voice coaxed, just as it had drawn Billy Dunham from the cover of the patrol car during the storm. Sturney squinted around the dark room full of prone bodies. "Be a man and come on out. Don't make this little negro take what you got comin."

A ripple of motion as heads swiveled to him. He raised himself up by his forearms. "I'm right here." Sturney and Drano honed in on him. Ellis stood up even slower than he'd gone down. "Let the boy go. There's no need to involve any of these people."

"Ellis, do you know these men?" Kordi asked. "Are they with those soldiers?"

"No. They're just a couple of crooked cops."

"Hey!" Drano shouted.

"You best shut those big lips of yers right now." Sturney punctuated this by pressing the blade harder into Chris's neck. A single bead of liquid rolled down his skin. He gasped. "Otherwise, ye're gonna get aaaall these nice people in the same trouble ya got those three 'bangers into. Lincoln Briggs, idn't that what you told me, Wright? Where are ya, boys? Didn't think we'd forgot about you, did ya?"

To Ellis' left, Lincoln rose, shooting him another look. Across the room, Mac stood up.

"Where's the other one? Scrawny kid."

CT was pressed into the base of the wall, trying to hide behind Randy. Lincoln nudged him with his foot. "Stand up, cuz."

The youngest X-Dawg slammed a fist against the wall and hopped to his feet. "Man, *fuck* you," he muttered. Then louder, "I ain't got nuttin to do with this! I ain't gonna say shee-it!"

"No, you sure ain't," Sturney agreed. "Cause you're gonna step outside with me, one at a time, nice and easy, while my friend here keeps a watch on everyone else. You first Wright, let's go."

Kordi shook his head. "No one is going anywhere until you tell us what this is about."

"Goddamn it, if that sand nigger opens his mouth again, PUT A BULLET IN IT!"

"No, don't!" Ellis held both hands straight out in front of him, as though they would be able to stop the projectile if Drano fired. He couldn't let anybody else get hurt over this. These people were already his responsibility, had been from the moment he entered their midst as a hunted man. And since death was still a less scary prospect than leading them into whatever future lay ahead, finishing this Sturney's way was just killing two birds with one stone. "I'll go with you."

"Good man. Get yer hands up and come over here."

Ellis did as he was told. When he'd crossed in front of Kordi and Maryland, Sturney let Chris go. The boy lurched forward and then sat down heavily in a chair, coughing and holding his bleeding throat.

Sturney pointed at the front door of the clinic with his knife. "Outside. Go. I'll be back fer the resta ya."

Ellis went behind Drano and pushed through the door of the clinic. Sturney was so close he could feel the man's breath on his neck. Just before he stepped over the threshold, he caught activity from the corner of his eye.

At the far end of the hall, a wheeled shadow rolled cautiously into the corridor.

He didn't pause, didn't let himself look, he just stepped out into the wet night beyond with his fellow officer right behind him.

WHITNEY +29:32

Imogene huddled in the exam room, listening to the newcomers that had stormed the building. She pushed herself to the door, waiting for the wheels of the unfamiliar chair to squeak. They remained silent. She leaned around the corner, the new oxygen tank slung over her shoulder. The two masked men were at the end of the hallway with their backs to her, shouting at the crowd in the waiting room. One of them had Chris with a knife at his throat. Her heart broke at the sight.

There was never any doubt of what she had to do. Only the question of how.

She rolled around the room, looking for anything her frail arms could use as a weapon. She found a drawer of syringes, stripped off their wrappers, and grabbed as many as her skinny fingers could fit around. By the time she went through the door, one of the gunmen was forcing that nice police officer outside the clinic. The other remained behind, holding the rest at bay with a gun.

Fear squirmed through her heart like a worm in moist dirt. She ignored it. If this world was truly done with her, then being shot while trying to save lives was a hell of a lot better than being left by your own family to drown. At least this would be on her terms.

The doctor and Maryland were the only two she could see, just beyond the masked man. She caught the doctor's gaze as she left the exam room, saw it widen and then sweep quickly away from her. She inched down the hall, tire treads whispering against the carpet. Her breathing roughened inside the oxygen mask, but she forced her lungs to function. COP'D wasn't going to spoil this for her. Kordi was talking, something to keep her target's attention on him, but she didn't listen. Her vision narrowed almost entirely to the gunman's vulnerable back.

She coasted to a stop behind him. Squeezed her fistful of syringes as she lifted them above her head. Said a silent prayer and a goodbye to her grandchildren.

And brought the wickedly sharp needles plunging into the base of the gunman's spine.

WHITNEY +29:34

Outside, the water had risen past Ellis' calves. This whole area would be swamped soon. He walked down the front steps of the clinic and stepped into it. It soaked through his shoes, chilled his skin. The night was still and the cloud cover had broken for the moment, giving them a clear expanse of starlit sky.

All things considered, it was a beautiful canopy to die under.

Sturney stepped down behind him, hefting the knife. He reached up and pulled the ski mask off. Underneath was a gargoyle's face of disease. His eyes were glassy, skin pale, but that snake's smile was still on his fat lips, even as he coughed.

This is all Ellis had thought about since that night in the park. Dying at the hands of this man, carved up like what he'd done to those drug dealers. But even as he'd feared it, he never—not deep down—thought it would actually happen.

"There's just one thing I don't understand. How'd you find us?"

"You jackass. You dipshits're broadcastin yer location to anybody with a short wave. Yer lucky those fellas in black ain't already burned this place to tha ground."

"Ah," was all Ellis murmured.

Sturney held the knife out at arm's length between them, the tip pointed at Ellis' chest. "All right, let's do this."

Ellis looked from his expectant face to the knife and suddenly felt like laughing. "What, you expect me to throw myself on that thing? You're gonna have to work for it, fatboy."

Sturney shrugged. "More fun for me."

Round Two between them was just as short as the first, but this time Ellis was actually fighting, instead of just trying to escape. Sturney slashed out with the blade, nearly catching him across the chest. He splashed backward. The wound in his back admonished him with sizzling lightning bolts. Sturney advanced, swinging like a fencer. Ellis waited until an arc passed by him and Sturney was on the backswing before jumping forward to grab his arm. He tried to use a subdue technique to disarm the other man. Not only did this start his broken finger shrieking, but Sturney countered easily, seconds away from breaking free.

So instead, Ellis reared back and punched the man in his thick jowls. Sturney stumbled back a half step, piggy mouth agape.

And from that look alone, Ellis realized how badly he still wanted to live. If only to see it again.

Before Sturney could collect himself, Ellis swiped out again, this time going for his throat. His open hand landed across the man's Adam apple like a karate chop. The savagery felt liberating. Sturney coughed explosively, still backing away and holding his meaty neck.

From inside the clinic, there was a gunshot, followed almost immediately by another.

"Sounds like your boy couldn't even handle a little crowd control." Even though Ellis itched to get back in the building and find out what was going on, he waited to see what the other cop would do.

Sturney wiped at tears in his eyes, looked from him, to the building and back again, jittering with indecision. The knife vibrated in the air. "Fuck it all!" he snarled. "This ain't over by a long shot!"

He turned and made for the clinic.

Ellis went after him.

WHITNEY +29:37

Maryland's mind was like glue as she tried to work out some action—any action—to take. She still felt paralyzed, just like at the bridge. Then she saw Imogene roll into the hallway behind the remaining gunman. Kordi must've seen it to, because he took a deliberate step forward with his hands still raised. The pistol—which had been aimlessly roaming the room and lingering on the gang members—swung back in his direction. "Stay the fuck back!"

"Why are you doing this? What do you want these men for?" Kordi's hands lowered, coming from shoulder level toward his waist. Imogene was halfway down the hall. What did the old woman think she was going to do?

"It's none of your business!" the masked man shouted.

Three-quarters.

"These people are my patients, so it very much is my business." Still Kordi's hands glided downward, as slow and steady as a glacier, and Maryland thought his arms must be tired until she noticed they were actually moving past his sides and toward his back.

And then she saw the lump beneath his white lab coat, just about at waist height.

Imogene stopped behind the gunman. Her bony arm raised, and something glittered in her clenched fist.

Suddenly Maryland understood what was about to happen with crystal clarity; no, more than understanding, this stark knowledge bordered on *clairvoyance*. She wanted to stop it, wanted to beg them not to resort to this, but her tickling throat was clamped up as tight as the rest of her.

Then the frail lady in the wheelchair stabbed the gunman in the back, and the chain of events Maryland foresaw set off with lightning speed.

The gunman bellowed. He spun around to his attacker with a collection of what looked like syringes sticking out the back of his filthy undershirt. Imogene charged forward to ram him. While reaching for the needles with one hand, he used the other to grab the arm of her wheelchair and dump her into the floor.

At the same time, Kordi's dexterous, physician hands completed the circuit they'd started, sweeping aside his lab coat and pulling out the pistol tucked into the waistband beneath, like an Iranian Wyatt Earp. He brought the weapon in front of him and squeezed off a single shot. She'd watched Bryce shoot enough to know Kordi was an amateur; his eyes clamped shut in anticipation before he ever pulled the trigger.

The glass door of the clinic turned into a spiderweb of cracks a foot to the left of his target.

The gunman leapt for cover while returning fire from the hip.

Something wet splattered across Maryland's face, breaking that statue-like hold on her nervous system. She jerked.

Kordi keeled halfway around to face her, and she saw the upper left half of his face was gone, sheared away, nothing but a mess of exposed bone and runny fluids and half an empty eye socket. His right eye found her, his mouth opening to form an expression of sadness. He collapsed at her feet, spilling chunks of something slimy across her shoes.

Sharon screamed, the first of a series of caterwauls from the rest of the group.

The gunman still fired as he dove into the nearest exam room, random shots that exploded all around Maryland. The clinic door opened and the fat one burst through, sans mask. He took in the situation in a heartbeat and roared, "*Goddamn it, just kill 'em all!*"

Everyone got up, shouted, ran for cover, the room boiling into utter chaos. She saw Hernie grab Tangela and run with her. Someone else appeared at her side: Lemiere retrieving the pistol from Kordi's limp hand. The gunman shot wildly, into the mass of people, and Lemiere tried to find a hole to fire back.

Someone else tugged on Maryland's elbow. Carter, trying to pull her to safety.

Ellis charged in the front door of the clinic and ran into the fat man. They toppled over the wheelchair and Imogene's unmoving form, wrestling on the ground.

And before she even knew what she intended to do, Maryland pulled free of Carter, fell to her knees, and crawled through the firefight, toward the chairs just to the right of the hallway. The rest of the group was gone, in the records room on the far side of the reception desk she thought. Lemiere had taken cover behind a padded bench to exchange shots with the gunman. The hollow booms made her ears rings. The air was already acrid with gunsmoke. She saw Ellis get punched in the face, and then the fat one was on top of him, straddling his chest, pushing his knife down while Ellis held his wrist.

She was in the chairs now, the legs like a metal forest. Turner's shotgun lay ahead. She grabbed the stock and pulled it toward her, then reversed directions fast.

Maryland rolled, keeping her head low, moving toward where Ellis was losing his arm wrestling match. She came up in a crouch, just as the fat one pulled his hand back to escape Ellis' grasp. He raised the weapon over his head to drive it down again.

She took hasty aim and jerked the trigger.

The weapon slammed against her shoulder, threatening to topple her. She saw the fat man's hand disintegrate from the wrist up, the knife disappearing. Blood spurted once from the wound in a low arc like a drinking fountain.

He wailed and clutched the limb to his chest, jumping up. Lemiere and the other gunman had taken a break from firing, and the fat one charged into the room where his friend had disappeared, screeching like a rocket. After a few seconds, they heard glass and boards break. Lemiere went to the doorway, peeked inside, swept the room with his gun, and called out, "T'ey gone! Out da window!"

Maryland slumped, the tension that had made her so rigid the last few minutes now fleeing to leave her practically boneless. She let the shotgun fall and buried her face in her hands.

WHITNEY +29:44

People crept out from the records room to gawk at the devastation. The walls of the clinic were peppered with bullet holes, several windows broken, but that was the least of anyone's worries.

Dan was dead. Walter carried his son up from the storeroom with a look on his face that would've melted rock. Cords stood out on his neck like iron bands, either from the strain of carrying the huge body or the crushing grief and fury that warred across his features. He, Sara, and Doug gathered in one of the exam rooms and closed the door. Every few minutes a banshee's wail would split the air, high and tormented.

Turner's jaw had a knot on it the size of a baseball from his beating, and the joint was so sore he could hardly talk. There were some stepped-on fingers and lots of bruises.

Barry had taken one of the stray bullets in the gut during the charge for cover. He writhed on the floor, screeching in pain until Randy found what he thought were vials of morphine. At first Lemiere worked feverishly to stop the bleeding, to no avail. They shot him up with painkillers until he could rest easy, and Nancy and Tom held his hands while he passed on.

Imogene, however, was fine. She'd suffered what they thought was a sprained wrist in her fall. The tough old bird shrugged it off without even accepting an aspirin, but she wept when she saw Eraj Kordi.

The doctor still lay where he'd fallen, now covered in red-stained blankets. Maryland knelt by his side and led a silent vigil of those who wanted to pay their respects. Ellis knelt beside her and bowed his head.

Lincoln broke the silence first. "It woulda been all four of us if not for him and Imogene."

"It's my fault." Ellis hung his head. "Oh God, this is all my fault."

"No, it's *their* fault." Maryland spat each word through clenched teeth. "Who were those men?"

"Like I said, just a couple of crooked cops."

"Isn't that just a fucking trend with you donut jockeys? I saw another of Port Allen's finest looting a grocery store yesterday morning, and shooting anyone that got in his way."

"I don't know anything about that, but these two weren't looters. The fat one was George Sturney, and the other one was Mike 'Drano' Jenkins. They're after me because…" He paused and glanced at Lincoln. No reason to keep it secret anymore. "Because I saw them kill someone a few months ago and steal a ton of drugs, and the storm was the perfect cover to get rid of me. They want the X-Dawgs because they witnessed their first attempt."

"What about the rest of us? Do we all have a big target sign on our backs now?"

"They can't kill us all. They'd be really stupid to keep trying."

Lincoln cleared his throat. "That's what you said last time, man."

Ellis squeezed the bridge of his nose and remained silent.

"Danger, Will Robinson," Carter muttered. "I mean, is anybody *not* trying to kill us at this point?"

Maryland released Kordi's hand so she could close her own into fists. The wounds along her palms reopened from the pressure, dribbling blood through her fingers. She said to Ellis, "I shot that son of a bitch. Blew his hand right the fuck off."

"Don't feel guilty about that, you saved my life."

"*Guilty?*" She barked laughter. "I don't feel guilty. I wish I'd aimed lower and gotten his piggy head."

Ellis sensed someone at his side. He looked up to find Lemiere leaning over him.

"We all nee' to get movin. Soon as possible."

"You think they'll come back?"

"Not so much worried about t'em as anybody else who might've heard da OK Corral here."

"Oh. Right." Ellis tried to stand, almost toppled, and accepted the assistance that Lemiere offered. He was running on fumes, exhausted, hungry, and hurting. They all were. "You'll get my partner then?"

"If he's alive. Me and the boy're leavin now. T'at pistol's empty, so we'll take da machine gun, your group takes da shotgun. I split up the flashlights, and I t'ought you might want da last of t'ese."

He held out a black medical satchel with the initials EK embossed on it. Ellis took it and lifted the flap, then gave an appreciative whistle at what was nestled inside. "They might come in handy."

"Just stick to da shadows and move fast. Hopefully with you goin south, you'll stay one step ahead of da searches. We'll meet you at your precinct soon as we can, but try to reach us if t'ey's a change in da iten'rary."

"That reminds me, don't say too much over the radio. Sturney said that was how he found us. If he listened, you never know who else might be."

"Point taken." Lemiere coughed for a full fifteen seconds, then smoothed down the wild hairs growing across his balding pate. "Be careful, policeman. Don't be 'fraid to lead t'ese people, and anyone else you find. Lord knows, t'ey gonna need it."

"I..." He meant to say 'I will,' but he was tired of lies, tired of platitudes, tired of anything but naked truth. "I'll try."

The rest of the group drew together in the waiting room near the door, clutching bags full of supplies, everyone seeming to understand it was time to go. Ellis thought many of them would be hesitant to leave this sanctuary when the time actually came, but Sturney and Drano had burst whatever bubble of perceived safety they once had. Now, they were just eager to leave it behind.

"I promise you, the men who did this will pay. And we'll come back for the bodies, as soon as this is over." Ellis said this to them all, but looked specifically at the Frakes. Kordi, Barry, and the nameless girl really had no one here to speak up for them.

No. That wasn't true. As he looked around at all the weary faces, he realized they were all connected by this situation, as much as any battlefield brotherhood.

"Let's go. Turner, when we get outside, you keep the shotgun and stay up front with me. The rest of you stick close, and if anything happens, be ready to run for the closest cover."

"Wait, wait!" Sara interrupted. Her eyes were still moist, but clear and resolute once more. "I made a roll earlier! That way we won't forget anyone if we call it before we leave and arrive someplace!" And, after a long few seconds of silence, "What? I'm a kindergarten teacher."

"Go ahead," Ellis told her.

She took a folded scrap from her jeans pocket. After the deceased were removed, there were twenty-one names on it. As they were called, every last one had a corresponding, "Here!" called out.

Except one.

"Who's *C-Tone?*" Fernando read over Sara's shoulder.

Everyone looked at their neighbors and then glanced around the clinic for the thin black boy with the perpetually angry eyes.

Ellis held up a hand. "Okay, when was the last time anyone even saw him?"

"When those guy told him to stand up!"

"No, I remember seeing him in the records room with us during the shooting!"

"And he was here when we came out," Lincoln added.

Ellis shrugged. "Then wherever he is, he left of his own free will. We can't afford to wait for him."

"Good fuckin riddance," Mac muttered.

They filed through the front door in two rows, blowing out candles as they went. Ellis and Maryland were last, and both cast a reluctant glance back at the covered form in the floor.

The wind picked up again outside, another stormline blowing ashore in the wake of Whitney, but for now the sky was clear, and a waxing moon shone still and bright. A fog bank hung heavy across the face of the floodwaters where once a full-quarter of Port Allen had lived, a grounded cloud creeping toward them on billowy feet, and it looked like it would arrive a lot sooner than the rain.

On the flooded sidewalk in front of the clinic, eighteen members of the group headed south, while the remaining two turned north.

WHITNEY +30:07

Drano Jenkins stumbled into the swamped alleyway blocks away from the clinic with Sturney's good arm slung over his neck and the man's moans echoing in his ears. Sturney gave another tormented bleat as he was dropped onto a chunk of brick and masonry torn from the wall of a building further down. Only then did Drano tend to the business of removing the syringes still protruding from his back like porcupine spines.

Sturney whimpered and doubled over, his lips peeled away from locked teeth. The pain was so vivid and intense he wanted to knock himself unconscious to escape it. Luckily, the blood loss was probably about to take care of that for him. He'd taken off his white undershirt and wrapped it around the stump of his right arm to staunch the bleeding, but it had already soaked through the cotton and left a trail of dribbling maroon until they reached the flooded area. He had his left hand clamped around the wound like a bracelet, attempting to squeeze the shredded ends of the appendage shut. "Gonna…gonna….kill that bitch," he panted.

"No, you're not." Drano snagged the last needle and yanked it free. He stood up straight and tore off his ski mask. "We're getting out of town and heading south, like we should've done yesterday. This is officially over."

"The fuck…it is. They'll pay. They'll ALL pay. Ellis Wright… and that fuckin cunt who shot me…are gonna die…"

Drano leapt across the narrow space and grabbed Sturney's shoulders without warning, then slammed him back against the wall. He cried out and tried to hold his hurt arm away. Drano leaned in, let loose a cough that could rattle windows, and then screamed more words than Sturney had every heard him string together at one time. *"You fucking hillbilly, this is DONE! We just got our asses handed to us! They used me as a pincushion and they crippled you for life! We'll never be able to explain all this, so going after them is just about revenge, pure and simple! You got ten million dollars worth of dope just waiting to help you live out the rest of your life on the beach, so what'll it take to get you to cut your fucking losses and WALK AWAY?"*

"Get. Yer. Hands. Off. Me."

"*Psssst!* Hey!"

The voice came from the end of the alley, where tendrils of wispy fog had grown. Drano let go of Sturney to whip out his service pistol and pointed it into the night.

A shape came toward them, obscured by mist. By the time they could recognize the form, it was only a few yards away.

One of the black gangbangers. The younger, rawboned and mean. Sturney's kind of guy, if his skin color was a little lighter.

"I been chasin you muhfuckahs fo'evah!"

"*You?*" Drano pulled the hammer on his pistol with his thumb. "Oh, you're dead!"

The kid jerked his hands up in the air. "Don't shoot! Just hear me out, I came to make a deal!"

Drano glanced at Sturney, who stared at the boy and twirled the first two fingers of his remaining hand in the air. He was woozy now, the alley listing from side to side like a boat, but no way was he going to show it in front of this bastard. "What're ya talkin about? What deal?"

"First, you tell me…you guys *really* got some drugs? That black oinker said you did, and I just heard that dude say somethin 'bout dope. Man…I-I need some, bad. Whatever you got."

Sturney panted his way through a smile. He should've been able to tell the look of an addict before. "Maybe we do, maybe we don't. You don't start talkin, then you ain't never gonna find out."

"Okay, okay! I know where they goin! I'll tell you! You hurry, you'll prob'ly beat 'em there!"

"And let me guess. In exchange fer this information, we give you something to get high on, plus you get to live, correct?"

"Yeah, well…all that and one more thing."

Sturney arched an eyebrow, his curiosity overshadowing his pain for the moment.

"Look, if you wanna kill those other two pigs—and they goin to get the old fart right now—that's fine with me. But if you plan on takin out my cuz and Mac, well, then…" A grin split his face, feral and wild, the kind of grin that used to be at home on Drano's face. "I wanna help."

"Bullshit." Drano shook his head. "Let's kill him and go."

Sturney contemplated the boy for a long minute, cleared his throat, and spit out a thick wad of gelatinous blood. "Gimme that goddamn gun."

Drano Jenkins snarled one last time at the gangbanger, lowered his weapon, and put it in Sturney's good hand. Sturney promptly placed the barrel against the side of the officer who was not only his partner for thirteen years, but also best man at his wedding and godfather of his kids. He pulled the trigger. The blast ripped out most of Drano's guts and threw him against the opposite wall. He slid to the ground, muttering curses at Sturney the entire way. Sturney put another shot in the man's head to shut him up.

He struggled to his feet, jaw clenched, mangled arm leaking blood down his side. He was in bad shape, no doubt, but he thought hate might keep him going just a little bit longer. Sturney gave the boy a look that could freeze gasoline.

"I usually don't work with niggers," he rasped. "But in yer case, I'm gonna make an exception."

THE NEW POLLUTION

Lemiere carried the machine gun and the walkie-talkie, and Mac stayed close behind, lugging the collapsed wheelchair from the clinic and a flashlight that he wasn't allowed to turn on. The Cajun was careful to stress this fact, and that Mac should try to hold in his coughing as much as possible. The latter wasn't so easy. The doc had given him some medication before the shootout that made him feel better (or less dead on his feet, anyway), but that burning itch in his throat was just getting worse.

Neither of them talked about it, but the idea that they could drop dead any second was an invisible, ticking clock over their heads.

They made it only a few blocks when they heard the pounding footsteps behind them.

The streets were filling up with floodwater and fog rolling off the ocean, the world going from midnight black to murky white as it trapped and reflected the available light. Visibility was no more than twenty yards, and even that was closing. Sounds echoed, making it impossible to tell which direction the running thuds came from. The two of them had been walking beneath the brick-pillared overhang of a long strip mall, and Lemiere pulled him around the nearest corner and pressed into the shadows.

Someone belted up the mall sidewalk and skidded around the corner they crouched behind. Lemiere swung the gun up, yelling for the other person to freeze.

"It's just me!" Lincoln hoisted his empty hands. "Damn Lemiere, you a li'l high strung, ain't ya?"

Lemiere pulled the weapon away and grabbed at his own nar-row chest. "Jesus, you was 'bout a hair away from havin dinner with Babe Ruth! What da hell you doin here?"

Lincoln's gaze flicked to Mac over Lemiere's shoulder. "I told Ellis I was comin with you."

"Why didn't you say t'at back at da clinic?"

"Because I figured you'd say no."

Lemiere grinned his snaggle-toothed grin and shrugged. "You wanna put your head on da choppin block, don't mean nothin to me." He put a hand on Lincoln's shoulder. "But just in case we need a getaway driver, I'm glad to have you."

They kept to the shoreline that now cut through the middle of the city, sometimes with water lapping at their feet, sometimes forced to go around whole blocks to avoid shops that were either destroyed or slowly being flooded out. The fog here was thickest, encasing them in a bubble of eerily glowing white from which can-tered lamp posts, storm debris, buildings—and occasionally bloated corpses—would loom without warning. None of them said a word, did their best to keep quiet, and Mac noticed Lincoln was careful to keep the Cajun between them. Every few minutes they would hear a noise—clangings, distant pops, splashes—and Lemiere would hold up one fist to signal a halt.

Eventually he led them into the deep archway of a Mexican food restaurant called El Perro Gordo. "Stay put while I take a look 'round. I'm pretty sure I left my boat on da next block, but da Dome ain't too far on da other side." He disappeared into the fog, leaving them to stare at one another.

When the silence grew too much for him to bare, Mac asked, "So why'd you come? Why didn't you go for help with everybody else?"

He was hoping for a roundabout apology for the fight at the clinic, but instead his best friend answered coldly, "So I can find out for myself what you told Charlie. 'Bout me and Mr. Kim."

"Man, I told you, it ain't like that, Links!"

"Then explain it."

Mac turned around and put his fist through the soggy, exposed drywall of the restaurant out of frustration. "I ain't gonna explain shit to you! We been like brothers since we was kids! That fool cousin of yours ain't nothin but a connivin drug addict! He knows he's lyin, that's why he ran off! Why ain't my word good enough?"

Lincoln didn't answer. He stood rigid across the entryway, watching Mac the way somebody might look at a math problem.

"What's it matter anyway?" Mac was acutely aware that this fight had become about more than just the two of them. "Look around! This shit don't matter anymore! We about to die and you holdin a grudge against me for somethin I didn't even do!"

He rushed forward, planted his palms on Lincoln's chest, and shoved. The other boy hit the brick wall hard and rebounded back on his feet, then jabbed a finger up into Mac's face. "You better take your hands off me son, and remember who the fuck I am!"

"You ain't *nobody!* Not anymore! You the leader of a gang that don't fuckin exist! If we even survive all this, then you just gonna be another homeless black kid, no better off than that Hernie fool! So why do you give a shit 'bout goin to jail?"

Lincoln lowered his hand. The look on his face was beaten and weary. "I don't care 'bout jail. And I don't care 'bout dyin; I never thought I'd live this long anyway. All I care 'bout is knowin who my friends are, who's got my back. I guess now I know. So let's just get through this, and then we never have to look at one another again."

Before Mac could even think of a response, Lemiere popped his head around the corner. "Let's go, but real quiet now. T'ey sweepin da blocks ahead."

Without a word, they followed the Cajun. The distant sounds of automatic gunfire warbled out of the fog and grew gradually closer. Lemiere kept them in the shadows, moving between structures.

A scream floated to them from somewhere close, cut off by a bullet. They watched from behind an overturned dumpster as a contingent of six soldiers marched out of the mist, appearing a piece at a time. Their masks were cold, expressionless sheets, turned pearl-colored by the mist. One of them carried an electronic device in his hands, and he kept bowing to study its small screen every few seconds.

"What're they lookin for?"

"No idea." Lemiere checked the volume on the radio clipped to his belt, making sure it was low enough not to repeat what happened to Mac earlier.

The one carrying the gadget gestured, but if they spoke, Mac couldn't hear them. They broke into two groups of three and headed in opposite directions on the street, fading away into the white wall.

Lemiere's hands twisted on the handles of the machine gun. "When I say go, keep movin right behind me."

"Maybe we should stay here a little longer."

"My boat is just 'round da corner. If t'ey find it, who knows what t'ey do? And if we can't see t'em in t'is mess, t'ey can't see us. Even infrared gonna have trouble with t'is kind of fog."

He lit out from the dumpster, and they kept up with the pace he set. They rounded the edge of a building and found a small motorboat ten yards out from the water's edge, moored to a signpost by a loose loop of rope. It was much bigger than the one Mac had released from the depths of the flood, a sleek silver machine striped with red flame. By the time they waded out to it, the stagnant water—which had developed a pungent, piss-like smell since the last time he took a swim in it—came up to their chests. Lemiere held the gun and radio above his head and put them in the boat when they reached it. It took both Mac and Lincoln to lift the wheelchair up and slide it inside.

Lemiere's pale face floated in the wisps of fog. "When I tied it off, t'is was da shoreline. Water's still risin."

They clambered into the boat as quietly as possible, sopping wet now, and Lemiere untied them. He rummaged behind the back bench and came up with two oars that he handed to Lincoln and Mac.

Lincoln accepted the instrument. "What's this?"

"What's it look like?"

"Just start the engine!"

"Well, why don't I draw t'ose soldiers a map of where we at? 'Sides, I only have a li'l gas left, and it's for an emergency."

Mac dipped an oar into the water on his side, propelling them silently forward. "Yeah, but how come *we* gotta do the labor? As in, the two black guys?"

"Cause da captain of da ship don't row, boys."

They paddled into the night.

WHITNEY +32:09

The caravan headed south until the encroaching water forced them to turn west, deeper into the city. The street flooding lessened, and the cover of fog shredded to tatters like overused tissue paper the further they got from the water. With the next band of storms moving in, it wouldn't have lasted long anyway. The buildings of downtown stretched against the night sky to their right, giant silhouettes in the dark, powerless city.

They were picking up other people as they scurried down the sidewalk, like a magnet sucking up metal filings. At first this fact was almost overlooked, but when Sara attempted to run through her roll again, she discovered five extra heads that weren't on her list. The next time it was eleven. They crept out from forgotten corners of the city, burrowing out of the wreckage of homes and buildings, slinking out of alleys and the backseats of stalled cars. Some of them knew about the sickness, the destruction of the Dome, and the soldiers prowling Port Allen's streets, but even those with no first-hand knowledge realized things were amiss. A few inquired where they were going, but most seemed content to be with other people.

And one of them—an overtly gay man named Stewart—started spreading a story about his mother being taken by some kind of sea monster close to the floodwater's edge after their escape from the Dome. Maryland worked quickly to hush him up.

At some point, after her legs felt like rubber and the ache in her throat forced her to give out tiny coughs that hit with the suddenness of sneezes, she made her way to the front of the straggling caravan just behind Ellis and Turner.

"There's thirty-four of us now. A lot of people are wanting to know when we'll get there."

Ellis turned around to gawk. She didn't envy his role. If leading these people to safety required walking through fire, they expected Ellis to slap on the suntan lotion and get moving. "Wow. Tell them it won't be too much longer. We made faster time than I thought."

"Okay. That's not all, though. At least three of them have guns of their own."

"Shit. Not that we don't need more weapons, but I don't like the idea of not knowing the people who have them. I don't suppose any of them would be willing to turn them over for redistribution?"

"Way ahead of you." She handed over a Beretta and extra magazines she'd confiscated from a man in a camouflage jacket, eager to be rid of it. The memory of Kordi's brains spilling over her shoes and Sturney's hand disintegrating after she pulled the trigger of the shotgun were permanent mental scars. "The other two said—and I'm not paraphrasing—that you'd have to pry them from their cold, dead fingers." Ellis took the weapon, checked the clip, and then shoved it in his pocket.

She dropped back, checking on people along the way. Tangela was draped across Imogene's lap, with Chris flanking one side of the chair and Hernie pushing. With her sprained wrist, the old woman could no longer get herself around. The girl was coughing, her skin clammy, on the threadbare edge of unconsciousness. Chris held her small hand as Maryland checked the knife wound on his neck.

Tom limped along behind them, and she matched his pace as she fell back abreast of him.

"How are you doing?"

The pupils he turned to her were green islands floating on a bloodshot sea. His mouth was slack. When he tried to speak, all that came out was a series of barks as dry as a rattlesnake's tail. Droplets of blood no bigger than pinheads dotted his lips.

"Here, drink this." She dug a bottle of warm water out from the pocket on the back of Imogene's wheelchair, part of the rations from the clinic's stores. She had to unscrew the lid for him, and he shook so badly getting the rim to his bloody mouth she thought she might have to hold it for him too.

When he finished, and the coughing stopped, he whispered, "I don't think…it's going to be too much longer for me, Miss Williams." His voice was like sandpaper rubbing a rough stone.

She felt hot tears, and wiped them away with the heels of her hands. "Please Tom, don't say that. We'll be there soon, we'll call for help…"

He placed a liver-spotted hand on her forearm. When he spoke, his words were still quiet, but she thought now they were that way to keep anyone from overhearing. "Even if that does happen, I doubt I'll be around to see it." He let go of her and reached into the back pocket of his baggy pants, then drew out a folded, wrinkled sheet of paper. "I took the opportunity while we were at the clinic to write out something for my sister in London, part will, part farewell. Will you hold onto it, just in case…?"

"Of...of course."

"Thank you, Miss Williams. For what it's worth, I want you to know you've been a wonderful companion to have on this little adventure. I sincerely hope you make it through and find some peace in this world, away from your husband."

His words arrowed through all her tightly woven defenses and almost knocked her heart right out of her chest. Maryland stopped walking and hugged him, quick and fierce, wrapping her arms around his bony neck. He grunted with the force of it, and returned the gesture.

So much death. She didn't know how she could take any more. These people were the closest thing she'd had to friends in years, and she was watching them get ripped out of this life one at a time. Eventually it would be her turn. Looking over the straggling line of Port Allen survivors, she knew they were all probably seeing their last night on earth.

Well...maybe not *all*.

She caught sight of him as she let go of Tom, him and his smug little mask and hair that stuck out everywhere and I'm-nerdy-but-it's-cute attitude. And as she watched him breathing—not the same contaminated air as the rest of them, but his precious filtered oxygen—she suddenly felt as mad at him as she had been at Bryce, and wishing for a few priceless baubles to chuck at Carter Vance.

After giving Tom one more encouraging pat on the back, she let him continue walking, and dropped back even further in the lineup, past Sharon and Doug holding hands, Justin being wheeled by Walter, and back to where Carter walked alone.

"How does it feel?" she demanded without preamble.

"Um, is 'good' the right answer?"

"How does it feel to know you're going to be alive when all these people are dead?"

"What?"

She reached out and flicked the metal tube attached to the outside of his rebreather. He jerked his head away as if her hand was a piranha. "*This* thing. Bet you feel real justified you spent the last decade scared of your own shadow, now that your phobias are gonna save your life."

"Hey, don't blame me because I plan ahead."

"But you *didn't* plan ahead! It's just stupid luck! Talk about being right about the wrong thing! It's like skipping your flight because you don't like the meal and then watching the whole plane go down in flames! It doesn't make you clairvoyant, it just makes you a picky eater!" She realized she was shouting at him.

"C'mon, would you stop it? What's wrong with you?" He stopped on the sidewalk next to a boarded up bookstore and squirmed. The buildings were starting to spread out again away from downtown. She crossed her arms and faced him while other members of the caravan passed by. Sara gave her a questioning look. "We don't know that this thing will keep me from getting sick. Kordi didn't know for sure that it was airborne, he was just guessing. For all we know, it was something we all ate at the Dome."

"Oh really? Well, how do you feel?"

"Honestly? I feel…fine. And I can't even begin to tell you how weird it is for me to be the one saying that."

She started to cry now, still furious with him but knowing it was stupid. What did she want him to do, take the damn thing off? Throwing his life away wouldn't help her or Tom or Tangela or anyone else.

Carter crossed his arms and fidgeted, glancing down at the ground again. "Look, no one is going to die, okay?"

"Not going to…? People are *already* dead! *Dr. Kordi's* dead! What kind of delusional world do you live in? Is *anything* real to you?"

For the first time since she'd known him, genuine anger flashed across Carter Vance's face. "Okay, you wanna know how real this is to me? For the last three miles of our forced march, I've been thinking about something Lemiere and Ellis said back at the clinic: that we're under quarantine, and that the rest of the world doesn't know about it."

"Yeah, so?"

"So if that's really why the soldiers are here, because of this disease, then it's bad enough for them to not only keep us isolated, but shoot us on sight. That's not quarantine, that's eradication." He held up a rigid finger. "But what if that's the only option, because whatever this thing is, it's too dangerous to be allowed outside the limits of this city, into the general populace? What if we've got the doomsday virus to end all doomsday viruses right here? What if those soldiers...what if *they're* the good guys, not us? What if we reach out and touch someone from Ellis' precinct, and the world just shrugs and says, 'Better you than us'? At that point, this mask isn't gonna make any difference." He started away from her, mixing back into the caravan, but just before he disappeared, he turned and shouted back, "So don't tell me I've got my head in the clouds, because I'm probably one of the few people not fooling myself!"

Maryland watched him go. For the first time, she wondered if Bryce was sick back at the Château, and was surprised at the pang of fear it caused. He was still her husband, after all, the man who had given her the world but never himself. Part of her still desperately wanted to go home, though whether it was for the money or for some long dried-up kernel of love, she didn't know. Maybe she would still go back after this was over, but for now, survival was about taking the next step, and the next and the next.

The end of the caravan was almost upon her, and she spotted another familiar face. She matched Randy Rampy's step, needing human companionship.

"Hey, buddy, you okay?"

The man whose wife's blood was still under her fingernails looked up from his perusal of the concrete. "Her body. I was going back for her body...and they blew it up."

"Oh Randy, I can't tell you how sorry I am. Is there anything I can do?"

He mumbled three syllables that might have been the beginning of an answer, but then something long and cylindrical was jutting from the side of his neck, almost materializing out of thin air, something jet black with a circumference as big as a penny.

His sad eyes rolled back, the lids fluttered closed, and Randy the financial adviser collapsed into an unconscious bag of bones on the sidewalk.

WHITNEY +32:25

"I can't see shit in this fog!" Lincoln exclaimed, shoving his oar into the water. They'd been rowing for an eternity. He'd tried to maintain the same steady, broad strokes as Mac, but his biceps—as nice as they were—just weren't a match for those tree trunks his former best friend was packing. The result was that their boat pulled continually to the right, and Lemiere made Mac stop rowing every few minutes so Lincoln could correct their course. He didn't even understand how the Cajun could tell where they were when every direction held only the same shade of gray.

"T'at's good. We need da cover."

"But Lemiere," Mac argued, "how am I supposed to find the place where I left Charlie if I can't see land?"

Lemiere bobbed his head back and forth a few times. "Okay, bear to da left. Just be quiet and take it slow."

Once again, this called for Mac to ease up on his side while Lincoln put his back into a left hand turn. He stole a sidelong glance at the other teenager while he rowed. It hurt, fighting with Mac like that, especially when he might be telling the truth. Lincoln would see what Charlie had to say, and make his decision then.

And what if Charlie's already dead?

"Woah, woah, boy, stop!" Lemiere broke into his thoughts.

He looked ahead. A brick chimney stuck out of the water like a huge finger directly in front of them. Lincoln reversed his rowing while Mac pulled harder. They swung by the obstruction close enough for it to squeal again the boat's hull.

Lemiere armed sweat from his forehead. "Guess we gettin close."

The fog thinned almost immediately after that, the colors of the night bleeding in like a black marker held to paper. They raised their oars up and let the boat coast silently through the water.

They emerged from the mist all at once, sailing suddenly into a clear night. The floodwaters ended several hundred yards away, the land rising steeply up from the murky depths before leveling off into a concrete beach. Even in the dark at this distance, he recognized the crowded parking lot he'd escaped from hours before. Off to their left, the smoldering remains of the civic center were backlit by a series of searchlights gathered around the far side.

Lincoln looked around. The fog stood in a smooth, solid wall around them, stretching out in either direction, forming a wide, unnatural semicircle around the section of coast containing the Dome.

"It's da heat," Lemiere said, as though reading his mind. "Dome's still too hot. It's burnin up da water vapor before da fog can reach it."

Mac leaned forward and squinted. "What are they doin over there?"

Far down the shoreline, on the southern edge of the Dome they'd passed in the fog, they could see figures scurrying between a large helicopter and a huge pile of garbage that reached above their heads. They picked flopping bundles from the pile, carried them to an open cargo compartment in the vehicle, and tossed them inside.

Lincoln saw them throw one that had appendages attached to it. "Are those what I think they are?"

"T'ey gettin rid of da bodies," Lemiere confirmed. "Least da ones t'ey had anyt'ing to do with. T'is is one surgical operation, boys. Now, hurry up and get us back in da fog before t'ey see us."

They resumed rowing, spun around and disappeared back through the wall of white mist. Just as it closed around them, Lincoln heard a splash somewhere on his side of the boat. He peered into the distance, but could see nothing. When it didn't repeat, he threw himself back into the rowing.

This time they maneuvered the boat closer to shore. Sunken houses emerged from the fog like the wreckage of ships, separated by streets running right down into the water below them. Mac studied each intersection, sweeping the flashlight beam around to try and find something he recognized.

"Thought you said it was only a few blocks from the Dome," Lincoln grunted.

"It was, but everything looks the same, okay? I was exhausted from swimming for like three hours!"

"No, you just fucked up and brought us out here to die!"

"Knock it off, you two!" Lemiere scolded.

"Wait, right *there!*" Mac stood up so fast his oar almost slid into the water. He pointed. "The water's come up a lot, but this was the street we came out on! I left him in a house right at the end of this block!"

They steered the boat in until the bottom scraped against the concrete. Lemiere tied them off to a fire hydrant that would soon be underwater, and they headed up the sidewalk with the wheelchair, surrounded by fog and storm-damaged suburbs.

The house that Mac led them to probably belonged to a happy family currently somewhere far outside of Port Allen. If they were lucky. All its windows were busted, and the front door was closed but unlocked. They burst into a dark living room that smelled of mildew.

"Charlie, I told you I'd be ba—!" Mac left the sentence unfinished, his jaw hanging open.

The room was empty.

WHITNEY +32:41

Like so many of the awful things that happened since Whitney evicted Carter from his reclusive, germ-free existence, the attack on the street was heralded by a scream.

After snapping at Maryland (and what right did she have to attack him anyway, her with her perfect…well, *everything*…just because he'd taken some precautions against Armageddon), he forged up the middle of the trudging survivors. He saw new faces on this cattle drive everywhere he turned, more people to stare at his mask; with envy now instead of suspicion. Most of them looked more like hacking, wheezing pillowcases that had been filled with manure and then stomped by cleated shoes. They were sick and exhausted, but more than anything, they were scared.

That, at least, he could sympathize with. Fear had been his *raison d'être* for the past decade. He could show them recipes for it that would blow their minds.

He tried to lose himself in the crowd, gaze firmly rooted on the ground and stepping at least three times in every square of sidewalk to soothe his nerves.

Somewhere near the back, a feminine screech pierced the air. The caravan came to a straggling stop.

The north-south street they'd turned onto some fifteen minutes before was a narrow two-lane, with short blocks of boarded up businesses facing one another. Storm damage was negligible; peeled shingles here, a sagging wall there, but nothing compared to what he'd seen further south. They walked along a short strip of side-walk next to slanted parking spaces in front of the stores. All of the alleys on their side of the street were blocked off with high board fences.

Carter turned, as everyone around him was doing. At the same time, there was a whisper of motion past his head, a quiet *shhhhk* next to his ear, and suddenly the person in front of him—some newcomer to the parade with a Houston Astros ball cap pulled low over his brow—had a small, black cylinder thunk into his back. The guy made a weak attempt to clutch at it before his knees pud-dinged and he fell down in a twitching heap.

The woman next to him asked, "Jim? *Jim?*" She knelt, pulled out the black cylinder, and held it up to Carter between her fingers. "He's asleep!" Carter raised his hands in confusion, then looked in the direction the scream had come from, trying to pick out Mary-land.

But a transformation was underway. The idea they were in dan-ger crept into the crowd's bleary heads as slowly as the herd com-prehending a wolf in their midst.

"*Look out!*" a voice yelled.

That was the only thing required to steal the small measure of civility these terrified people had mustered.

They jumped for cover, going for the shops next to them, but every door and window was nailed over with a layer of wood. Some tried to scramble over the high fences. When none of that worked, they just tried to run, in different directions. Carter could hear Ellis screaming for people to come to him near the front of the line, and the blast of Turner's shotgun, but otherwise the street was eerily quiet during the siege.

He spun in a confused circle as people pushed past him on the dark sidewalk in all directions. His chest tightened, the big sky above him spun, and he fought to stay calm. If he gave in to the mass hysteria, then tranquilizers wouldn't be needed to put him on the ground.

Something else flew through the night, big enough to catch his eye and just slow enough to follow. It seemed to unfold in midair, making a complicated shape, and then shot a good three yards in front of him to make rough contact with the wall of a storefront. He stared at it, stupefied.

Fernando was pinned to the wall by a rope net anchored into the brick by metal prongs. The Hispanic man struggled beneath, one arm pinned awkwardly between him and the wall, the other flopping at his side. The net was taut enough to make his pudgy face ooze between the woven strands.

"Get me out, get me out!" he pleaded.

Carter ran over and tugged on the straps holding him. They were made of tough nylon, and the metal spikes at the end of each strand bit deep into the brick. He looked up and across the street, in the direction the net had come from. On the one-story roof of the opposite building a figure stood outlined in a shaft of thin moonlight. Two others waited along the edge, both with long-barreled rifles pointed down at the line of survivors. One of them fired— only a distant *twang!* and a minute jerk of the barrel tip—and Fernando's cries ceased after a dart appeared in his shoulder.

And suddenly, Carter understood. The narrow street with no outlets. The high ground taken by the enemy. This was an ambush by their friendly neighborhood disaster militia, no different than what he'd organized countless times on Halo to take out all those annoying brats on Xbox Live.

Only now these soldiers weren't shooting to kill. They wanted them alive.

"They're on the roof!"

People were still scurrying, running into one another in their search for safety, but the street was just too open with nowhere to go. A few of the smarter one snatched up wood and the other garbage littering the street to use as shields. One of the other survivors that joined them since leaving the clinic pulled a revolver from inside his jacket and returned fire at the figures Carter pointed out. The soldiers dove for their own cover.

But there were more to replace them, popping up all along the roofline and from store windows to take hasty shots before diving back down. This abandoned street had just become a Western on downers.

Carter headed toward the last place he'd seen Maryland, pushing past frightened people huddled in doorways and whatever shallow depressions in the building façades they could find. She was coming his way, dragging a prone body by the arms.

"It's Randy! They shot him!"

"They're just tranquilizers!"

"I know that, but we have to get him out of here!"

"We can't do anything for him! Come on!" He grabbed her arm and tried to pull her away, but she wouldn't budge. "They're going to get us all if we don't do something!"

A fire blazed in her eyes. "Tangela, where's Tangela?"

He took off without another word, and this time she came with him. They went toward the front of the line. Carter shouted for people to follow. He spotted Walter and his remaining son trying to herd people in that direction also. *Git along, li'l doggies*, he thought crazily, his head drunk with an impending vertigo attack.

Sleeping bodies littered the sidewalk. He couldn't even tell who they all were. He spotted Nancy facedown, and several others netted and unconscious like flies in a giant spider's web. He hurtled them all, not slowing. The air was full of zinging darts now, shooting past to quiver in the plywood across the shop windows or bounce off brick. Ahead, he could see a mass of their people ducked behind a low concrete wall in front of a local copy shop, and he and Maryland dove in with them.

Most of the others cowered here, tucking in body parts to keep anything vulnerable from exposure, but there wouldn't be room for everyone still trickling this way. Ellis and Turner took turns popping up to shoot at the soldiers on the opposite rooftops. When he saw Carter and Maryland, Ellis shouted, "You gotta get these people off the street! We'll hold them off so you can get a head start!"

"Get them *where*?"

"I have no idea!"

Hernie waved from the far side of the barrier to get his attention. "Mr. Carter, Mr. Carter!"

"Not now, Hernie!"

"We can go through the wood fortress! Me and Hatch used to sleep in there!"

"Huh?"

"He means the lumberyard!" Ellis gestured at the board fence between the copy shop and the next building, where hinges in the wood revealed an entrance. "It runs behind all these stores! If we can bring the fence down, everyone can just run through!"

Carter nodded, and Ellis tapped Turner on the shoulder. The big man rolled as close to the fence as possible with his shotgun and fired three shots in quick succession. The first two blew holes in the wood as big around as a basketball, but the third split the whole blockade down the middle, revealing a passage that would leave them exposed for at least a few seconds.

Ellis rose up enough to squeeze off a round from his pistol. "There's a big Presbyterian church a few blocks further up on the next street over! Wait for us there!"

Carter took a deep breath that shuddered in the rebreather. He could feel his brain misfiring like an ill-tuned engine, all those paranoid voices insisting that his lungs were going to lock, that he was going to pass out again.

Then he rammed a mental fist into them, pummeled them down into a bottomless well in his mind, and jumped to his feet.

"COME ON!" he bellowed.

The space between the two buildings was narrow but short, a cinderblock corridor that banished the last of his vertigo. He led a conga line through it at breakneck speed. Faces swirled in and out of his vision, but there was just no time to take another role call to see who they were missing. The sound of coughing in the tight space was an echoing roar.

They emerged on the other side, and Carter understood what Ellis had intended. The copy shop backed up against a sprawling lumberyard whose main building faced the next street over.

But their exit strategy had been ruined by a mean shrew named Whitney.

The yard was now a muddy pit. Lumber of all sizes had been strewn like Legos by an angry child. Where once there had been neat rows of planks and passable aisles, now entire stacks of cut wood had tumbled into sodden, broken heaps. A rusted chain link fence marked the end of the yard to their right, festooned with windblown garbage and leaning under the weight of overturned wood.

"Oh my God," Maryland moaned.

"Doesn't matter. We gotta go through it."

They started in, moving as fast as possible. The yard was flooded; mud sucked at their feet and made pushing the wheelchairs near impossible. Justin chose to walk, Maryland picked Tangela up, two strong men he didn't know carried Imogene, and they collapsed both chairs and dragged them along. Carter led the way, trying to keep the chain link to his right as a guide but often forced to go deeper into the yard to avoid impassable spills of lumber.

It was as they came around a leaning stack of four-by-four's that he heard the snuffling on the other side of the fence.

He stopped. The chain link was obscured by a thick layer of spilled plywood and trash, but gaps in the debris along the bottom revealed a low, alien shadow. Something splashed over there, and then came the sound of muffled snorting.

"H-hello?"

His question was immediately met by an explosion of frustrated scrabbling at the base of the fence.

Too primitive to be human.

A shiver of pure, adolescent terror gripped him. All he could think of was the thing from the Dome, tearing people apart with manic glee. He turned to Maryland, sure his eyes must be hanging from their sockets, and saw the same thought reflected in her trembling face.

"*Go,*" she told him.

He moved on, pace renewed. They were trapped in a long stretch between wood stacks with no cross aisles. Whatever was on the other side of the fence followed; he could hear its quick, somehow excited footsteps. The end of the lumber yard was visible ahead, another fence and then the street beyond, but if this thing found a way through before they could reach it...

The upper half of a huge pile of sheet lumber had slid off ahead of them, creating a triangle-shaped corridor that had partially crushed the fence. A figure charged out from the deeper shadows under the spill, almost running into him. Carter saw the breathing mask, black suit, and large weapon held across its chest. The soldier jerked, obviously surprised to see them, and started to swing the gun around.

A scratching noise came as the creature on the opposite side of the fence came up the ramp of downed wood. It paused at the top, snarling, and then leapt straight at the face of the soldier.

It took Carter several seconds to realize that their monster was a large, dark-colored dog.

"*Hatch!*" Hernie shouted in delight.

The dog hit the soldier full in the chest with its front legs outstretched, the weight enough to knock him over with an outraged electronic squall. The weapon spun away. The back of the soldier's head caromed off a chunk of wood, and he fell unmoving into the mud.

Hatch turned around to stare at them innocently, tail wagging. Hernie ran to him, squatted, and threw his arms around the animal's neck.

"I don't believe it," Carter said in amazement. "He *is* real."

"Of course he's real! He came back here to find me!"

"Well, uh…good dog, I guess."

Walter pushed by and scooped up the long, black gun. "C'mon, there's probably more of them!" Everyone broke, not caring who the leader was but just grateful for someone to give them orders. A few paused to give the dog a pat on the head. Tangela reached out a weak hand from her place in Maryland's arms to brush along his mud-encrusted back, and then the animal fell in beside Hernie. Carter started to go on as well, then paused.

Maryland grabbed at him. "Carter, let's get to this church before they find us!"

"Hold on a sec. Give me one of those wheelchairs!" He looked down at the unconscious soldier in the soggy earth. "I think it's time we get some answers."

WHITNEY +33:04

Ellis flung his arm over their barrier and fired one more shot without looking, just to keep the soldiers at bay. A tranquilizer dart clinked against the concrete an inch from his hand as he withdrew it.

To his right, Turner performed the same maneuver with his shotgun, then produced more shells from the pocket of his shirt. He seemed to have an endless supply of them. "Can't hit nothin at this range." The words were garbled through his swollen lips. A hush fell once they stopped firing; the weapons their enemies used barely made a sound.

"I don't care if we hit them, I just want to keep them back long enough to give the others a chance."

"They're gonna flank us sooner or later, if they haven't already."

Ellis nodded. "All right, let's make a run for it."

"What about them?"

Turner pointed at the trail of bodies leading up to their cover. Ellis counted at least ten people spread out on the pavement, a few actually snoring audibly. Every one of them his responsibility.

But sometimes leadership had those executive decisions, too.

"We can't do anything for them. It's not like we can carry them out of here ourselves, and even if we could, the second we set foot out there, we'll just be joining them. As it is, we'll be lucky to make it past the fence without getting tranqed."

"Okay, let's do it. I'll follow you."

Ellis checked the medical satchel Lemiere gave him to make sure the strap was secure over his neck and shoulder. The objects inside clinked and sloshed. "Fire another warning shot when we stand up and then *keep moving!*"

They stood in unison with a war cry ferocious enough to frighten a grizzly bear. They fired at the few figures still on the rooftops across the streets, forcing them back, then charged through the gate amid a flurry of darts. Turner snatched a piece of the fence and used it as cover until they reached the lumberyard.

"Dear Christ," Turner muttered, when he saw the state of the place.

"Don't stop, we can't risk leading them back to the others!"

They hurried into the closest unobstructed aisle to find two soldiers creeping toward them from several rows down, these with pistol-sized tranquilizer guns. Ellis and Turner made a hasty zigzag and took shelter behind a heap of spilled wood before the pair opened fire. Ellis kept moving, back screaming, taking turns into the twisted maze of lumber to lose their pursuers. Every second they remained in the lumberyard was more opportunity for the soldiers to tighten the perimeter around them.

Another popped up from the top of a precariously balanced stack of wood and fired a net down at them from a four-pronged weapon that looked like a sci-fi ray gun. Ellis half-jumped, half-fell out of its way, but his trailing right hand and both legs became ensnared. The force of the projectile spun him in a partial circle and threw him against a broken pile of plywood, where the edges of the net attached themselves. His lower body was left suspended, while his upper half collapsed into the mud. The satchel slid off his neck.

Turner pointed his shotgun up and fired, blasting the soldier off his perch in a misty burst of blood, then knelt to help Ellis get loose. "They've got us cut off, there's no way we'll make it through here!"

"Then we'll just have to give them something else to worry about." Ellis yanked his hand free of the nylon straps with Turner's help. "You got a light?"

After he finally wriggled out of the net and came up slathered with mud, he pulled the remaining makeshift Molotovs out of the satchel. There were five of them in all. They lit the fuse on two and tossed them on the two biggest woodpiles around. The lumber was damp, but the flash of fire when the chemicals ignited dried it enough to catch.

More soldiers came from their right. They both discharged weapons to keep them back. Ellis clambered over a river of plywood onto the next aisle, tossed another chemical grenade at a trio trying to get in front of them, and started a fresh fire. They continued weaving across the yard, the fire behind them spreading through the loose wood, and used their last two cocktails to cut off their attackers' advances.

By the time they reached the selling office, the entire yard looked a lot like hell. The wood blazed, flames and smoke crawling into the night sky, more lumber tumbling over to block pathways and destroy the aisles between. The soldiers had enough trouble getting away without catching fire in their rubber suits, which apparently weren't flame-retardant. But from the look of the clouds that were almost here, it wouldn't last long.

Ellis and Turner climbed the fence at the front of the property, took one last look back to make sure they weren't followed, and slunk away.

WHITNEY +33:27

As Lincoln, Mac, and Lemiere stared at the empty couch where Mac had left Charlie unconscious yesterday afternoon, there was a creak in the hallway behind them, one that led deeper into the house. Their nerves were ratcheted so tight, they all leapt for the ceiling, and this time Lemiere squeezed off a short burst of automatic gunfire that rattled the few remaining windowpanes.

Charlie didn't even flinch, barely reacted to the tattered line of holes in the plaster that stopped just inches from his chest. He stood in the dark, hunched over like a ghoul, staring at them with feverish eyes. The badge on his wrinkled uniform shirt hung pathetically limp.

Lincoln pushed the gun away. "God Lemiere, you almost killed the guy we're here to get! Maybe you wanna let someone else have a turn with that thing?"

Lemiere engaged the safety. "Sorry."

"Charlie?" Mac asked. "You okay? I thought you was in a coma!"

"Pee," Charlie answered in a husky voice. "Had to p-pee, Johnny." He limped forward, favoring his injured leg heavily until he could grab a recliner. He was drenched in sweat, shaking badly, his rough face aglow with fever. He coughed, wiped at his mouth with a trembling hand, and said, "Where's your mother?"

"Huh? My mother?"

"He delirious," Lemiere said. "Get him in t'at wheelchair 'fore he falls over."

"Oh, right!" Mac rushed forward, unfolding the wheelchair. "Um, here—*Dad?*—sit down in this."

Charlie complied, collapsing backward into the seat. "I...ain't your dad, punk."

Mac leaned over his shoulder to look the cop in the face. His eyes were a little more focused deep in their sickly wells. "Charlie?"

"So you actually came back. F-figured I was gonna rot in here."

Mac spun the chair around to face them. "Yeah, we came. Ellis sent us."

"Ellis? He's alive?"

"He's at your precinct. We're gonna take you to him right now.

There's a lot of shit goin on, but we'll explain later. You sure you're okay? Last time I saw you, you was pretty close to dead, man."

The cop's head was a stone on his limp neck. "I'm…driftin in and out, but I could tell I was slippin away. Kept tryin to picture my kids…you know, give me a reason to stay alive. I think I was ready to take that trip to the big beach party in the sky and…" He trailed momentarily, eyes swimming. "And then that owl interrupted my beauty sleep."

"*Owl?*" Lemiere asked. "What owl?"

"Don't know, some damn owl hootin right outside. Been hearin it all night, I think. Hard to keep track. Annoyed me so much I couldn't even die in peace. Surprised you guys didn't hear it, sounded like it was right there before you burst in." He gestured at the broken window next to the front door.

Mac frowned. He glanced at Lemiere, who shook his head minutely and tapped his temple twice. "Uh…am I Johnny again, Charlie?"

"Kid, I got a goddamned bullet in my leg that's goin gangrenous, I feel like someone took a blowtorch to my throat, and I can barely see three feet in front of me. But I know an owl when I hear one!"

They were silent for a moment, listening without even realizing it, and, though the night beyond the threshold remained as oppressively quiet as ever, a finger of icy dread caressed the back of Mac's neck. The city seemed empty even with the army of faceless mercenaries prowling its streets, a kingdom of the dead in which they were the last holdouts, and that quiet suddenly felt expectant. Waiting.

Hungry.

"Maybe we should just get outta here," Lincoln said.

"I second t'at."

"Let me give him these first." Mac held out two pills that Doc Kordi had given him before everything went to shit at the clinic. Charlie regarded them warily. "One's an antibiotic. The other's somethin to keep you awake and alert until we can get back."

"Don't know if I wanna be 'awake and alert.' Rather just sleep till it's all over." But Charlie scooped them out of his palm and dry swallowed both. Mac pushed the wheelchair through the door. Outside, the fog was still a white curtain, but the sound of many booted footsteps echoed through it.

"Move," Lemiere growled. They ran back down the sidewalk in the direction of the boat. Every time a crack in the pavement jostled the wheelchair, its occupant whimpered.

"You fellas wanna t-tell me what the rush is?"

"*Shhh*, be quiet!"

"Later, man!"

By the time they reached the shore, where the sloped street took a header right into the water, droplets of light rain pattered against their faces. Lemiere's boat floated next to the almost covered fire hydrant. He waded out in water up to his waist, untied it, tossed the gun inside, and dragged it closer to shore.

"Jesus, no, not more water." Charlie moaned as the three of them lifted him up, wheelchair and all, and positioned him in the bow of the boat. His head lolled, eyelids half-closed. "Johnny...tell your mother you're not supposed to need a chainsaw to cut Christmas ham..."

Lincoln and Mac clambered into the boat. Lemiere pushed them out into deeper waters and then slid over the side himself.

He squatted in the bow, shaking off water like a dog, and dug the hand-held radio out from under one of the bench seats. "Ellis, you t'ere?" No answer but static. "If you can hear me, we got your partner, and we gonna circle da coast and come up to you from da south." Still nothing. "T'ey prob'ly outta range by now." The Cajun replaced the radio, straightened up, and ordered, "Okay, grab t'ose paddles and let's—"

The water behind him erupted. A nightmare shape rose up next to the boat, wrapped a scaly appendage around Lemiere's waist, and drug him into the depths of the water before he could even scream.

WHITNEY +33:39

Ellis expected to see the spire of the Third Grace Presbyterian Church as he rounded the next block up from the burning lumber-yard, even with the rain pounding. He and Charlie patrolled this neighborhood at least once a week, and the church tower was visible from any point in the surrounding area.

When they arrived at the huge, elegant structure—panting and hacking so bad it stung his eyes and made his chest cramp—he understood why. Whitney had stopped to give her thoughts on religion before moving on.

The church was constructed from two stately, snow-white wings, set at an acute angle toward the street, with columned promenades built onto the ends and stained glass windows of simple design adorning both sections. The sanctuary stretched from the middle toward the parking lot in the back, turning the building into a capital 'Y'. At the juncture of the three parts rose a glittering glass pyramid, from which a black iron spire reached toward heaven.

Now it jutted upside down from the arched roof of the left wing at a drunken angle where the storm had blown it, puncturing the ceiling like a pin in a balloon, its severed end a crooked lightning rod. The glass pyramid was gone, either blown away or collapsed. Most of the stained glass was gone despite the boards nailed across them, and the walls were stripped of that gleaming white paint the church administration reapplied every spring.

The damage would get worse the further they went toward the coast. For the first time, Ellis wondered what they would do if his precinct really was no longer there.

He and Turner entered through one of the broken windows and made their way toward the lobby, where a field of glass crunched underfoot. Rain flowed in through the hole in the roof, creating a circular waterfall that splashed and pooled on the carpet. The door to the sanctuary was open. They eased inside.

This room was huge, half a football field in length and width, with a vaulted ceiling that yawned overhead. The stained glass here was broken too, leaving multi-colored teeth to chew at the edges. Pews marched away in two rows, facing the raised pulpit and altar at the front. The first four rows were occupied by people, some sprawled out, some actually praying. Sara stood at the front of the group, talking softly. Maryland and Carter spotted them and came running down the aisle.

"We have to go back!" Maryland coughed into a curled fist. "We have to go back right now!"

Turner shook his bruised head. "They're everywhere back there! We barely got away!"

"Then I'll go myself!"

Carter squeezed the back of his neck. "I've been trying to talk some sense into her."

Ellis grabbed her shoulders, forcing her to look at him. "Maryland, what's this about?"

Her face scrunched in anguish. "Sara took roll. Chris isn't here. He must've been one of the ones they…" She flung her hands back and forth at the wrist. "In the confusion, I didn't realize it! Maybe he's still back there, maybe he's…!"

"There's nothing we can do," Ellis said. "It's awful, I know, but that place was crawling with those soldiers, and we burned the lumberyard down behind us. They have him by now." He released her, but stayed ready to grab her if she tried to run. "But there's no reason to think he's dead. They tranquilized those people for a reason."

"And somehow, that's even more terrifying," Carter mumbled.

"Maybe, but it still doesn't change the fact that we can't help him if we get ourselves caught too."

Faced with blunt truth, Maryland finally nodded. The desperation on her face smoothed out a little. Turner excused himself to go and sit down with the rest of the group.

"How many other people did we lose?" Ellis asked.

Carter frowned. "From the original clinic group? Three: Fernando, Nancy, and Randy. Plus most of the medical supplies we brought from the clinic. Overall though…we *gained* people."

"Gained?" Ellis looked past him, reevaluating the pews full of heads. Upon second inspection, there were a lot of people down there. "How many—?"

"Thirty-eight now. Thirty-nine, if you include Hernie's damn dog. We picked up more on the way, and there was already a small group in here when we arrived. Sara's filling them in on what we know and where we're going."

"Well, get them all up. We don't have time for another summit meeting. Those soldiers will comb the area until they find us. We have to go before they get organized."

"They won't," Carter said firmly.

"You don't think they're gonna come after us?"

"No, because they won't have to. That was obviously an ambush back there. They were set up and waiting for us. They *knew* we were coming somehow. So before we go rushing into another trap, maybe we oughta stop and think about our next move."

"These people are exhausted," Maryland added. "Most of them haven't slept or eaten in more than twenty-four hours."

"And they're gonna have to suck it up a little longer! Look, my precinct is just blocks from here! We can be there in another twenty minutes if we leave now!"

Carter sighed and pushed wet hair away from his eyes. "There's one other thing you need to see."

They led him down the aisle, through the throng of new faces. Sara gave him a quick introduction to the new members. Those that had been on the street clapped when they saw him. He waved uncomfortably. Carter and Maryland led him up the stairs that wrapped around the pulpit stage to a door on the left. It opened onto a baptismal lit by some of the candles they'd taken from the clinic. Carter gave the door a shove and stood aside to reveal a scene from a Quentin Tarantino movie.

A wheelchair stood in the middle of the floor, with one of their mystery soldiers slumped in it, head on his shoulder. No, more than slumped; Ellis could see straps of cloth tied around the wrists and ankles, securing the sleek, black form to the seat. The chest inflated, faint breath rasping through the weird tubes growing out of the faceplate, which reflected their three silhouettes in the doorway.

As they stared at it, the head abruptly lifted and a male voice—muffled by plastic—shouted, "You can't keep me here like this, you have to let me go *immediately!*"

Ellis yelped and jumped out of the doorway, back onto the stage, and retreated to a far corner behind the altar. Carter and Maryland came with him. Inside the baptismal, the secured figure continued to rant.

"Are you insane? Where did he come from?"

"The lumberyard," Maryland answered. "He was alone. We figure they were sending troops in to take us from behind and he was just the first to respond."

"Okay, but what're you doing with him?"

"Getting some answers." There was a ridiculous hint of pride in Carter's voice as he declared, "We're gonna interrogate him! I get to be Bad Cop!"

"Interrogate—? Get this straight, *I'm* the cop, not you! I can't condone this, it's illegal! I'm going to set him free!"

He started to walk away, but Maryland's hand fell on his forearm. Her nails hooked into his bare flesh. Her eyes were bloodshot, but it could've been from sickness, exhaustion, or the sheer willpower blazing in her. "The rules of civilization are on hold right now, you said so yourself back at the clinic. This is war, and that man in there is our prisoner. If you want to survive this, we need to see what he can tell us."

"They're going to be looking for him!"

"They're already looking for all of us. Having him here can't make it any worse."

"Unless he calls them somehow!"

Carter held up a black, rectangular box a few inches in length and width, with a few unlabeled switches and torn wire attached to the ends. "I found this right under his faceplate, where it attaches to the rubber. I'm pretty sure it's a radio transmitter of some kind. He's not calling anybody."

Ellis looked from one to the other and shrugged. "All right, fine. By all means, go in there and talk to him. But you're still crazy if you think he'll tell you anything."

"Oh, he'll talk." Maryland marched past them into the small baptismal. "When I get finished with him, he'll be spilling his guts. Either metaphorically or physically."

Carter and Ellis exchanged a look comprised of raised eyebrows and hurried after her.

WHITNEY +33:45

"LEMIERE!"

Lincoln leapt for the side of the boat where the man disappeared and leaned over the edge. He could see nothing but the greenish-black surface of the water sloshing against the fiberglass hull. Rain splashed against the back of his scalp as the skies opened.

"What was that?" Mac screamed. "*What the fuck was that?*"

"I don't know!" He wanted to thrust an arm into the murky liquid to feel for Lemiere, but was too scared of what he might encounter. That shape, it wasn't human, there wasn't even anything recognizable in it…

"Are we almost to Palm Springs?" Charlie asked dreamily from his wheelchair.

Bubbles erupted a few yards out from the boat. Lemiere's balding head broke the surface, gasping and spluttering. Blood leaked from a new slash across his forehead. "Help, Jesus, *HELP!*" The terror in the Cajun's usually reserved voice made Lincoln's testicles draw up. He swam for the boat as the rain fell faster.

Lincoln held out a hand, intending to help him over the side when he got close enough, and saw another disturbance in the water just past Lemiere, something sinewy that parted the waves behind him. "Hurry up!"

Lemiere reached the boat and grabbed his forearm with both hands. Lincoln pulled. He had the man halfway over the side when another hand rose up from the dark depths next to them.

He saw it clearly, even in the early morning darkness. Seven inch long fingers with tissue-thin webbing between them, chipped and filthy claws curving off the end, all attached to a hand whose elongated shape made him think of monkeys and vampires from old black and white movies. The flesh was plated with dark green scales the color of swamp muck.

"Oh my God." He wanted to go for the gun, but he couldn't let go of Lemiere. The alien hand scrabbled at the Cajun's vulnerable back for purchase, those nails flaying open the flesh in bloody trenches.

Lemiere wailed. He let go of Lincoln with one hand and twisted to flail at the thing. It battened onto his arm at the wrist and wrenched. The force of the maneuver rocked the boat violently and almost yanked him—and Lincoln—back into the water. The whole boat bobbed sideways, away from shore and into deeper water.

"*Get me out!*" Lemiere howled, and Lincoln braced his feet in the bottom of the boat so he could haul at him just as Mac came to help in the tug-of-war. Together they succeeded in dragging Lemiere another foot out of the water.

But the owner of that horrible hand wasn't giving up. Lincoln could see it twisting and jerking. There was a horrific crack.

Lemiere's screams reached impossible decibels. A seam appeared in the flesh above his elbow, a red slit as neat and even as a shirt sleeve. The rippled muscle beneath was revealed a split second before the bone popped like a champagne cork and the entire appendage tore away.

They tumbled back into the boat with Lemiere on top of them. Lincoln felt a warm gush as the Cajun's blood washed over his torso. The man rolled away, screaming and holding his stump.

"Take care of him!" Lincoln shouted to Mac. He scrambled to his feet, his sopping shirt stained pink below the waist. Rain rolled down him. He wiped it out of his eyes, then grabbed the machine gun and spun in a circle.

The water was undisturbed in all directions. The fog was still thick around them, but the steady rainfall was beginning to dilute it. Between the skittering sound of the rain against the water and Lemiere's hoarse screams, it was hard to hear anything else, but he caught the steady *thup-thup-thup-thup* sound approaching from the direction of the shore.

"Links, we got company!" Mac yelled from the bottom of the boat as he tried to hold their injured friend down.

A helicopter swept by overhead, one of the black gunships that had fired on the people at the Dome. Whether it was coming specifically for them or just happened to be passing by, Lincoln didn't know, but they'd made enough noise the last few minutes for half the city to hear them. The fog, their only cover, blew away like dandelion fluff from its whirring blades. He thought for a minute it might not have seen them in the dark, but then it banked and started to circle.

Mac slapped his leg. "Get us outta here!"

"Engine!" Lemiere choked out between gulping breaths. "Start...engine!"

Lincoln lunged for the outboard motor attached to the back of the boat. He knew little about them, but recognized the pull-cord when he saw the dangling knob. He grabbed it and then stopped cold.

Two yellow eyes glared at him from below the surface of the water right next to the engine.

Something exploded upward, lunging for him with spiny, malformed arms. No time to get the gun up. He yelped and stumbled backward over Mac and Lemiere's legs. Claws swiped within inches of his nose. The pull-cord from the motor reached its length and tore out of his hand, but it was enough to start the engine. Suddenly they were in motion with no one at the helm.

The creature was gone.

Lincoln scrambled up. Wind rushed over him, flapping his clothes. They were picking up speed fast, probably thirty miles per hour and climbing, the boat shuddering over uneven patches of water. The helicopter rushed after them. They couldn't outrun it like they did in the SUV, not in this thing. He shot off a burst from the machine gun at it, and the force of the recoil nearly tossed him in the water. This was a *serious* weapon. He planted his feet and fired again. The helicopter veered away this time, not damaged but reevaluating its tactic. It bought them only a few extra seconds, but at least that was something.

The steering handle on the engine flopped with no one manning it, sending them on a haphazard course. Lincoln plopped down on the bench beside it. When he looked back, he thought he saw something in their wake, a sleek form breaching the surface before diving back under. He swallowed sour spit that had been collecting in his mouth for the past ten minutes.

Charlie was passed out in the wheelchair at the opposite end of the boat. The doc's medication must not have made it into his system. In the floor, Mac straddled Lemiere, trying to tie off the torn end of his arm with a shirt. Blood pumped from the wound in rhythmic squirts, enough to fill the bottom of the boat. The Cajun hacked and flopped.

No time. The helicopter's mechanical growl was back, and this time the big guns spoke, the bullets marked by a trail of tiny water spouts. Lincoln gave the steering handle a massive shove, turning them toward shore and out of the chopper's sights. Houses and streets flashed by to their right; he thought they'd already passed the Dome, the speedboat carrying them across a distance in minutes it had taken them two hours to row. The helicopter corrected its course to cut back across them on a diagonal.

What was he supposed to do now? Zig-zagging would only keep them safe so long, and what happened when they finished the gas off? They were still a little way from the shoreline, but maybe he should slow down and try to find a place to dock. He looked around desperately, searching for inspiration.

Which was why he didn't see the long, wooden box floating atop the water in front of them until it was far too late.

The boat was at top speed when it struck the heavy obstruction on the left side, directly under where Charlie slumped. There was a whiny, chalkboard squeal. The bottom of the boat buckled and their momentum was robbed. The back end flipped up like a catapult. Lincoln felt himself go airborne just before slamming into cold floodwater.

WHITNEY +33:53

Maryland entered the room with their prisoner and went to stand in front of him. She glowered and put her hands on her hips, but that felt silly, like she was doing a Wonder Woman impression, so she clasped them behind her. She really didn't know how to stand. This was, after all, her first interrogation.

C'mon, you've seen Bryce do it a hundred times in the courtroom, and, as we all know by now, whatever he can do, you can do better.

Carter and Ellis lingered just inside the baptismal doorway. The figure in the chair was silent, but she could feel him watching her from behind the reflective plastic shield. Candlelight from the shelf behind her danced across its surface. She put her hands in her pocket, knowing it was a self-conscious gesture, and felt a familiar cellophane-wrapped shape that made her heart leap for joy.

Maryland pulled out the crumpled pack of Virginia Slims she'd taken from the gas station earlier. She'd completely forgotten about them. She opened them casually, found the only one in the pack that wasn't crushed or shredded and lit it from one of the candles.

Aaaaah; that was the stuff. The rush of nicotine irritated her sore throat and left her dizzy but completely confident.

"Who are you?" she asked.

"That's classified," he answered, before the words were even out of her mouth. "You people...you need to let me go right now or...or you're gonna be in *big* trouble!"

Maryland laughed harshly, even though it stung her throat even further. "What, like twenty years in prison? That sounds a lot better than the death sentence you bastards are doling out right now!"

The figure was silent again, which meant he might have some actual brains. Then again, anything could be going on behind that mask. She'd watched *CSI* and *Law and Order* enough to know that body language was a big part of this process (did the eyes go up or to the side during a lie? She couldn't remember...) and he had the advantage in that department. She clamped the cigarette between her lips and walked toward him, hands outstretched toward his face.

"What are you doing?"

"Pulling back the curtain on the great and powerful Oz."

His demeanor change was sudden and drastic enough to startle her. He thrashed in the wheelchair. The fabric bonds at his wrists and ankles creaked but held. He pulled his head away from her. "Don't! Don't touch me! Please, leave it alone!"

She glanced back at Carter and Ellis, but their faces were unreadable. "Why not? Afraid you're going to catch this persistent little cold the rest of us can't seem to get rid of?"

Again, he was quiet.

She lowered her arms, blew smoke at him. It curled up against the faceplate before dissipating in the muggy air. "Look, you will answer my questions and tell me what I wanna know, or I'm gonna take off that ziplock bag you're wearing a piece at a time. That simple enough for you?"

"You can't do this," he murmured, almost too quiet for her to hear, the wonder in his voice suggesting she'd just levitated.

"It's being done, so deal with it. Now, who are you people?"

"I...You have to understand, I can't tell you that. If I do, *I* die. Or my family does." He sounded sincere. And scared.

"Okay then, are you with the government? The *United States* government, or maybe the military?"

"I can't say."

"Well you better give me something, or the mask is coming off, buddy. Worry about me or worry about them."

He hesitated, shifted in the wheelchair. "Garmon, all right? My name is Zachary Garmon. Is that enough, can we compromise here?"

She sighed and tapped ash on the floor. "It's something, I guess. So *you're* American then?"

"As apple pie."

Carter came forward and jumped between them before she could say anything else. "How'd you find us, Garmon?"

"What?"

"Back there, on the street just now. That was an ambush, am I right? You guys knew we were coming, and you found the perfect place to strike. How?"

"I don't know what you're talking about."

Carter flew into a frenzy, waving his fists in the air and then kicking the side of the wheelchair repeatedly like a caveman. "Don't give me that, you're just hoping they'll be able to find us again and then you get a big, fat rescue! That's it, *I'm* taking this thing off!" He reached for the mask.

Garmon squealed. "No, no, fine, I'll tell you!"

Carter watched him a moment, then turned his back and stomped toward the corner of the room. On the way, he mouthed *bad cop* at Maryland. She rolled her eyes.

Garmon panted in fear, his breath snorting through the filters on his mask. "Does one of your group have a radio on you? Probably one of those cheap two-way deals?"

Ellis pulled the device from his pocket and held it up by the antenna. "Right here. But we were careful not to broadcast our location."

"With one of those, it doesn't matter. If it's on, it's pushing a constant radio pulse. We just triangulated it, that's all. They were tracking another one, last I heard." He paused. "You people are the ones that blew up the helicopter, aren't you?"

This time they ignored him. Ellis looked at the walkie-talkie in his hand disgustedly. "This thing has cost us nothing but trouble. Thank God I turned it off when Turner and I were on our way here." He brought it to his mouth, spun a dial, and said, "Lemiere, if you can hear me, turn your radio off. Get rid of it. They're tracking us by them." He clicked the device back off and tossed it to

Carter. "We need to send someone out to bury that, just in case he's lying."

The interrogation was waning—as was her cigarette—so Maryland took charge again. They couldn't let the fire cool under this guy's soles for a second. "We've already figured out why you're here, so I won't drag that answer out of you. We'll get to that in a second. But first I want to know, the people you were tranquilizing: what happens to them? Why weren't they shot?"

"I don't know."

"Garmon, I'm done threatening you."

"*I don't know!* I don't get an explanation for everything, I'm just a fucking grunt! I get orders, I follow them! The bosses said to bring in some sick cases, so that's what we did!"

Her cigarette was down to the filter. She dropped it to the tile floor, ground it with her heel, and came forward again, slow and deliberate. She put her sore hands over his wrists on the armrests. The rubber was cool and slick beneath her touch, kind of like how she imagined a seal's flesh would feel. Maryland put her weight on them and leaned over until her forehead was almost against the plastic plate even with him pulling away. His breath exhaled through the tubes on the bottom, warming her neck. This close, the dark tinting failed, and she could see the eyes of the man inside watching her with brow drawn.

"We're not stupid, soldier. We know why you and your friends are here. We know you're wearing this suit because of whatever's making us sick. Whatever's...killing us. I have friends dying out there. So I'm not gonna tolerate any wiggle room with this next question: what is it?"

"That's classified, ma'am," he whispered.

"Is there a cure?"

He laughed, but it came out a squeaky huff. "You don't need a cure. You need a fucking *antidote*."

WHITNEY +34:01

The sound of coughing in the church was driving Hernie crazy. Sometimes he thought it almost had a melody to it: high-pitched squeaks, lower throat-clearings, long hacks, short, rapid-fire coughs that were more like sneezes. They all blended together and echoed off the high ceiling.

He thought even Hatch was sick. The dog sat next to him, at the end of the pew, and every few seconds he would open his mouth and give a strangled wheeze. Hernie was just glad to have him back. He gave the animal another rub behind the ears and looked around the big church.

He hadn't been in one for a long time. They intimidated him. Even this dark one, with its broken windows and soggy carpet. That nice lady Sara was at the front, answering questions. Lots of people were praying with their heads bowed, but he didn't know how to do that. Mr. Carter and Mary-land were in the other room with Officer Ellis and the government agent they'd kidnapped. It made Hernie very nervous knowing that one of the people who'd chased him his whole life was within shouting distance. Imogene was back in her wheelchair, drawing deep, shuddering breaths from her oxygen tank every few minutes. There were a lot of people now that he didn't know. They draped themselves over the pews and tried to sleep.

Tangela was beside him on the thinly padded seat, clutching her blanket. Tom was on her other side, curled up and shivering. The three of them were sickest, and Hernie noticed that everyone except Imogene seemed to avoid them, the way Mr. Carter had at the beginning.

Hernie's throat burned so bad he couldn't swallow anymore. Every few coughs brought blood.

Tangela stirred. She sat up and hugged her blanket tighter to her chest. "Is Chris here yet?"

"Uh uh."

Imogene raised her head. "But he will, child. I just know it. God watches over the young, I've always believed that."

Hernie sat up excitedly in his seat as idea came to him. It wasn't often that happened. "If Hatch came back, so can he!"

Tangela put her head against his shoulder. He felt her begin to shake with sobs. "He's dead, Hernie."

They contemplated this silently. Hernie understood exactly what death was, knew people all around them were dying from whatever was making him cough, but for him it seemed unrelatable, like watching a TV show about people that lived far, far way. Somehow the idea that it would eventually reach himself or those closest to him—the people he considered his friends—was an entirely new concept.

"I'm gonna die too," Tangela whispered miserably.

"No." Tom reached a shaking hand out to her.

"No," Imogene repeated.

"*No,*" Hernie echoed, with more defiance than he'd ever uttered anything in his life. He could feel tears running down his own cheeks. "No, that won't happen, I'll never let it happen." Because he couldn't be alone again. That thought scared him more than his own death.

"It's okay," she told them. Her voice sounded old to him. "I want to die. At least then I can…be with my mommy."

"Please don't leave me." It was barely loud enough to hear himself. He put an arm around her and rocked her back to sleep.

WHITNEY +34:07

"An antidote is for poison," Carter said.

"Yeah, no shit," Garmon agreed, as Maryland finally stood up straight again. With her out of his face, their P.O.W.'s rubber-covered head turned to take all three of them in. He sighed. "You seem like smart people, so I'm gonna tell you this only because I hope it'll make you see how pointless fighting is. And how your best shot at surviving is to turn yourselves in, the sooner the better.

"None of you is sick. It isn't any disease causing this. It's called P3. They codenamed it Project Mercury, because of how fast it works, but the lab guys that invented it say it's a 'Cumulative Bio-Pollutive Compound.'" These words were said with the air of rote memorization, but Carter thought he could detect sarcastic disdain in the last few. "Yes, it's a poison, and once it's in an organism's bloodstream, its kill rate is 100 percent effective on a long enough timeline. By now, it's spread to every corner of this city."

"Wait a minute, are you saying this was let loose *intentionally?*" Maryland sounded repulsed. "That we're…guinea pigs or something?"

"Would that really surprise you?" Carter mumbled.

"No, it's not intentional that it's here, it's just an accident caused by Whitney," Garmon said.

"Then how the hell did it get here in the first place?"

"It's *made* here, right in your own backyard. And don't ask me why Port Allen, because I don't know. That part of it didn't concern people at my level, but as operatives in the field, we were fully briefed on P3."

"Then you brief us," Carter told him.

Garmon flexed his hands a few times beneath their straps, probably trying to figure out exactly how much he really wanted to blab. Carter thought they would have to prompt him again, but then he started speaking. "It's an 'engineered pollution.' A compound that bonds with—and hides in—the same kind of elements usually associated with environmental deterioration. Except it's much deadlier to carbon-based life forms."

"The birds," Carter murmured.

"What?"

"We were dive-bombed by a flock of dead birds yesterday morning. And ran into a horde of rats. Looked like they were coughing and bleeding out the same as us."

"That would be P3. Smaller, weaker, unhealthy specimens always succumb first. They haven't found a single creature that can withstand the effects. Except cockroaches, of course. Because it's not technically a sickness, there's no cure, and because it blends with pollution that's already existing, it's nearly impossible to detect."

Maryland frowned. "But why would someone create something like that? What's the point?"

But Carter thought he knew the *why's* already; just because he'd sat out the last few rounds of Earth dodgeball, didn't mean he hadn't watched the news. "It's for third-world countries, isn't it? Nice, easy, seemingly natural population control."

Garmon didn't bother to confirm. "It's mostly inert and useless in a functioning, self-cleaning ecosystem, but where there's stagnation and corruption—be it from too many people shitting in the streets or, let's say, a city that's just been devastated by a hurricane—it goes bug-nuts. Imagine a bubble of it over the entire city."

"That's sick," Maryland said. No feeling in it, just a simple statement. "You made something to kill people more efficiently and then when it got loose, you came in to clean up the mess. I thought we'd seen just about the lowest humanity could go, but this is a chart topper."

"I didn't have anything to do with it lady, so talk to them."

"I would, if you'd tell me who 'them' is."

"Enough." Ellis spoke from the doorway. "Okay, we know what it is now. So *is* there an antidote?"

Garmon raised his shoulders; it was awkward in the wheelchair with his wrists tied. "They told us just to be damn careful we didn't get contaminated, so I honestly don't know. And neither will you, unless you turn yourselves in. I could've called my people and had them here in minutes if the boy genius over there hadn't pulled out my suit's transmitter."

"Oh yeah!" Carter gave exaggerated nods. "I'm sure they'd slap a band-aid on us and send us home with a kiss after everything we've seen!"

"I can't guarantee what they'd do. But it's your best shot at getting some help."

"So after the lion bites your hand off, you stick the other one in its mouth and ask for a ride to the hospital? I don't think so, pal!"

Maryland said quietly, "Let's say we decide to do it."

"Oh c'mon, you can't seriously be considering that!"

"Shut up, Carter," she told him flatly, without turning from Garmon. "If we decide to turn ourselves in, we have people here with us that...might not make it that long, until we can get treatment. A little girl. Isn't there *anything* we can do?"

"Absolutely. Get the surplus P3 out of her system."

"What?"

Garmon spoke fast. "P3 has to be ingested or inhaled, depending on the pollutants it's attached itself to. The trapped water around here will be lousy with it for a long time, but give the air in this city a few days to replenish, and it'll be gone. Of course, by that point, you would've all died anyway. And my people mean to you have you swept out long before even that. But anyway, that's not the point. Like I said before, P3 is also *cumulative*. Meaning the more exposure you have, the faster you go downhill. Once you're contaminated, you'll always have a baseline, but you can slow and even reverse the symptoms that it causes."

"*How?*" Maryland demanded. "Quit talking like a goddamned scientist and *tell me what to do!*"

Garmon calmly lifted a finger from the armrest he was tied to and pointed at Carter. "Correct me if I'm wrong, but that's a Care-Plus B7 series rebreather, right? That's an advanced little piece of machinery. About a half-step down from what I have in this suit right now."

Carter felt like he was at the end of a long, long corridor as Maryland and Ellis slowly turned to face him.

"You're saying that thing could help people get better?" Ellis asked.

"That, or pretty much any source of clean oxygen. As long as they're not eating or drinking anything contaminated, it'll bring them back to baseline. Once you take them off if though, the process will start all over again, and the length of time till…expiration…will depend entirely on how much P3 is in their environment."

"Sure, that's great for them, but what about me?" Carter asked.

"You'll pick up a baseline. But you'll be just starting out, in the initial stages. While you're getting worse, a lot of other people can be getting better."

"I don't *want* a baseline!"

But you already have one, the Lucid whispered. *Just think Cart, how many times did you take the mask off, just for a sip of water or a bite of food? How much of this P3 do you have in your system right* now?

His vision blurred from the idea. It might not be germs as he had always feared them, but it was close enough to kickstart the fiercest panic attack of his life.

Garmon gave another of those disjointed shrugs. "You asked for a way to prolong the lives of those people until you can get some help. I gave it to you."

"Carter," Maryland said evenly. "Let me have your mask."

She might as well have asked him to pluck out an eye and hand it over. "What? No!"

She advanced on him, palm held out. "C'mon Carter."

"How do you know he's telling the truth?"

"If there's even a chance, we have to try."

He backed away, out the door of the baptismal, and Ellis joined her, the two of them like men with straitjackets maneuvering to surround an escaped mental patient. "She's right, people need that."

Carter clapped a hand over the plastic, half-afraid they really meant to take it from him by force. "I don't give a smurfing smurf what they need, this mask is *mine!*"

They were out of the baptismal now, on stage between the altar and pulpit at the top of the short staircase leading down to the pews. Carter glanced around and saw their own little congregation watching. He kept backing up and the other two kept following.

"Goddamn it!" Maryland banged a fist down on the dais. "Give it to us, Carter, I'm not playing with you!"

"No! All you need is fresh oxygen! Use…use Imogene's tank!"

"She's a sick old woman with a medical need, you bastard! You've had your phobias like a five-year-old, that's fine, we indulged you since it didn't affect anyone else, but—!"

"You didn't indulge me, you just made fun of me and now you want me to share? Screw you Maryland, I don't owe anything to you or anybody else!"

"*We're* actually dying! *You're* not!"

"I will if I take off this mask!"

"No, it'll just put you in the same boat as the rest of us! Once you start getting worse, we'll give it back to you and you'll get better! Are you really going to look these people in the eye and tell them you're too selfish to save them?"

Carter turned, intending to do just that, to scream it at them if he had to, but there were an awful lot of eyes bearing down on him and he didn't know where to start. Younger eyes than his, like Doug's and Sharon's. Innocent eyes, like Hernie's and Tangela's.

Beautiful eyes, like Maryland's.

So he ran. His feet were moving before he was even conscious his brain had commanded them to, and they carried him down the aisle through the middle of the pews and out of the sanctuary without even a pause to knock. In the flooded vestibule he realized someone was chasing him, but he didn't stop until he'd pushed through the double doors at the front and into the muggy night beyond. The little moonlight left to this night filtered through the evaporating clouds.

"Carter, wait!" Maryland had to stop and stifle a coughing fit.

He stopped at the edge of the muddy church lawn and turned to look at her. It was just the two of them out here; no one else had followed. "I'm not doing it! I've made more advances over the last twenty-four hours than I have in the last five years, but I'm not ready to give this thing up yet, I-I can't!"

"Yes, you can! Grow up and stop trying to take the easy way out of everything!"

"Easy…?" He gave a forced hiccup of laughter. "You're one to talk, rich girl! What about your plan to slink home to hubby? To put up with the shit just because the money's good? If that's not the easy way out, I don't know what is!"

She looked stung by this, but he tried not to let it steal his anger. "It's not the same! Your fears are *imaginary*, Carter!"

"Not anymore they're not!"

"You know what I mean."

He threw his arms open wide. "Why are they imaginary? Because they're in my head? Because they have no basis? By that definition, just about *every* fear is imaginary, Maryland! We don't know why have them, we just do! Haven't you ever been scared of something—*really* scared—and not known why?"

"Of course I have, everyone has, but we don't give up and lock ourselves in our house like you did, we confront them every day! We fight them and we *don't stop!*"

He swallowed. Swiped at his eyes. "You don't understand what it's like. You never will."

"Carter…we need it. Tangela needs it. *I* need it."

She knew what to say to hit him hardest, and he hated her for that. "I'm sorry." He started away from her again.

"Where are you going?"

"To get rid of this radio."

"But you can't! Those soldiers are still out there!"

"That's good, maybe you can truss yourself up and stick an apple in your mouth to save them the trouble." He dropped the sarcasm and said, "I'll just…find Ellis' precinct and meet you there. Unless you decide to go with Garmon, that is."

Carter didn't look back as he started up the street away from the church, mostly because he was afraid of something else: that the look on her face would make him surrender the one thing keeping him sane.

CEMETERY GATES

Lincoln went deep, driven into the water like a torpedo. Chilly, oily liquid encompassed him. He flailed, unable to determine which way was up, his lungs pleading for air and his raw throat giving up what little he'd managed to gulp. He was on the verge of giving up when he found the surface.

He spit out the rank taste of floodwater and coughed until every vein in his eyeballs floated across his vision. When he could finally breathe again, he took stock.

The rain had slackened and the last vestiges of the fogbank clung to the surface of the water. The overturned boat bobbed about thirty feet behind him, its silver belly showing. He could see a crumbled dent in the hull where they'd struck…whatever that thing had been. The engine casing, now submerged, made a sickly chugging noise around a froth of bubbles. The helicopter was too dark for him to pick out against the backdrop of the night, but he could hear its grumble somewhere further out on the opposite side.

No sign of anyone else. He'd lost the gun, too.

Lincoln paddled in a circle and caught a flash of cloth in the murk, just a few yards away. He swam to it. A body floated face-down. He grabbed the torso and flipped it over.

Lemiere's sightless eyes stared up at the grimy heavens without blinking. The torn end of his missing arm floated against Lincoln's chest, no longer pulsing blood. Lincoln patted his cheek, felt for breath and pulse, but the man was just gone.

He was surprised by sudden grief. "I'm sorry, man. You deserve better." He let go, and the Cajun's body floated away.

"Lincoln!"

He searched the night for the distant voice. Eventually he spotted Mac waving, the black curve of the shoreline rising from the mist behind him.

Lincoln kicked hard in that direction as the sound of the helicopter closed in. Mac treaded water, the unconscious Charlie held in the crook of one arm. "We lost the wheelchair! And I can't find Lemiere!"

"He's dead! Swim for shore! We gotta get outta here before they see us!"

They paddled, putting distance between themselves and the wrecked boat. Lincoln looked over his shoulder to see the helicopter hovering above it. The pilot opened fire, the chain guns punching holes in the aluminum big enough to put a fist through. Lemiere's motorboat sank fast, the bow rising up before it slipped beneath the surface for good. Then the chopper turned in a slow arc, the cockpit sweeping the area around it.

"Stop! Stop moving!"

He and Mac froze, Charlie suspended between them. The helicopter continued swinging, hovering in each cardinal direction before moving on. They had to know the boat crash hadn't killed them, but they had no exterior light to search with. Lincoln was just thankful morning hadn't come yet. After a few minutes, the chopper flew north, in the direction of the Dome, and they continued paddling toward shore.

Both of them were coughing by the time Lincoln's sneakers squelched into a semi-solid surface. Felt like grass or mud down there. Might've been a lawn, but he could see no houses. In fact, there was nothing on the horizon except some thin, narrow shape climbing a few yards straight out of the water a little ways ahead, but it was too obscured by the last of the fog to tell what it was.

So where in Port Allen were they coming ashore?

They kept walking, and the water fell to chest level. "Ow!" Mac exclaimed. Lincoln whirled, already envisioning the owner of that demonic hand and those yellow eyes. "I hit my knee on somethin! Feels like a slab of concrete stickin out the ground!" He edged around, hoisting Charlie's body up to keep his head out of the water, then stopped again. "There's another one over here!"

"Just keep goin and be careful! We gotta get—" Something bumped into him from behind. He spun to find a long, rectangular box floating just in front of him. It was made of slick, polished wood, the top curved upward.

"What is that?"

"I don't know." He gave it a shove. It was heavy, but it bobbed in the water. "Looks like the thing we crashed into."

Mac came over to join him. They felt along the sides until they found a seam. There was a rusted metal latch that almost came apart in their hands when they pulled at it. A lid swung up on squalling hinges.

Inside, a skeletal face leered at them.

"Jesus fuckin Christ!" Mac leapt away. Charlie moaned in his arms.

Lincoln took in the rotting corpse, dressed in the remains of a vintage suit from the 70's, nestled into the silk-lined interior of the box. "It's a coffin," he said, beginning to understand. The coffins, the slabs sticking out of the ground... He squinted at that shape ahead, and, now that he knew what to look for, he could make out the solemn lowercase 't' formed by two bars of stoic concrete. "We're in Parkland Cemetery. The flood loosened up the ground, and all the coffins are floatin to the surface."

"Yeah, cause *that* ain't creepy as hell!"

"My precinct," Charlie wheezed, coming to life in Mac's arms. "It's not far from here."

"Parkland's *huge*, Links! How we gonna find our way outta here?"

"Don't know." He'd only been inside the city's graveyard twice, the first-time for a barely-remembered funeral of some relative when he was in elementary school, the other on a bravery test when he first joined the X-Dawgs. It was nothing but several miles of fancy tombstones and mausoleums on a slight downhill grade, surrounded by a wrought-iron fence. "But we ain't gonna do it standin here."

They set off again, carrying Charlie. They made it only a few steps when a new sound reached their ears: the whine of another motor.

A new speedboat cruised toward them from further down the shore, and, unlike their friends in the chopper, this one had a great big searchlight mounted on the front.

WHITNEY +34:19

Maryland watched Carter disappear on the next block and then stomped back into the church. She'd just delivered a whole series of low blows, but she felt worse about using his obvious feelings for her.

Feelings? He hasn't known you long enough to have feelings. *He just wants to jump your bones like any other guy. You did what you had to do.*

The people in the church mobbed her instantly—the group bigger and more intimidating than the one at the clinic—and they demanded to know the meaning of the argument they'd witnessed. She realized only now it might not've been a good idea to let them hear this, but she'd been so furious. She gave Ellis, at the back of the crowd, a questioning look. He shrugged as if to leave the decision up to her.

"All right, listen carefully. The man we captured, his name is Garmon. He told us what's making us sick. It's some kind of chemical that's in the air and water. Once it's in our systems, it's there permanently. He told us our best chance of getting any help is…to surrender ourselves to the other soldiers."

A voice called out, "The same guys that have been shooting at us all night? No thanks!"

"Where did Carter go?" Walter demanded.

"He…left."

"Is what you said about his mask true? Can that thing make us better?"

"Garmon says that clean air might help some of our symptoms. Give us more time. Not a permanent solution, just something to keep us from dying. But anything from him is, of course, highly suspect. So all of us have a decision to make."

The crowd parted. Imogene rolled through, struggling to push herself with her one good hand. She met Maryland's eyes intently as she slipped the elastic band over her head and held up the plastic cup of her oxygen mask. "Will this help the girl?"

"Imogene—"

"Will it help the girl or not?"

"It might," Maryland admitted. "But we can't take that from you. Unlike Carter, you actually need it."

"You're not takin it, sweetheart, I'm *givin* it to you. As long as I stay still and calm, I might not have an attack."

Maryland shook her head.

"*Lord Almighty, if this is my time, let it be my decision!*" the old woman shrieked, stunning them all.

Before she could answer, someone coughed once, the sound echoing off the high rafters of the church. It was followed by a whole piercing string that didn't stop. Her heart thumped, filling her stomach and chest with ice water. She knew the sound of death rattles by now.

"Mary-land!" Hernie shouted. His dog howled beside him, and someone rushed to shut the mangy thing up.

She elbowed through the crowd with Ellis limping beside her, arriving at the aisle where Hernie and Tangela sat.

Tom convulsed on the floor, clawing at his throat and spraying blood in all directions.

They pulled him out into the aisle as the crowd regrouped. "Get back, give me room!" She swung a leg over him like a bicycle and straddled his hips to hold him down. He bucked beneath her with a strength his small form didn't look capable of, his eyes wild and rimmed with blood. "No, Tom, not now, *stay with me!*"

"*Here, here!*" Imogene held out the oxygen tank and mask.

Maryland snatched it away and pressed the cup over Tom's mouth and nose. The clear plastic turned tomato red on the inside almost instantly. "Breathe!" she commanded. "*BREATHE!*"

His narrow chest hitched between her thighs, and she thought for a second his eyes cleared. He gazed up at her, raised one hand to clutch weakly at her arm, then his whole body went slack. His upraised arm wilted to the floor with a wet smack. A last exhalation forced a dribble of blood from the seal around his mouth. It oozed down his cheek like a maroon teardrop.

She stared down at it and realized she was completely numb. And exhausted. Her throat burned even worse and she wanted to cry tears that just weren't there.

But she no longer wanted to go home. Home—and the entire

life she'd lived with Bryce before this hell—seemed as imaginary as Oz at that moment.

She stood up without speaking. She left them all watching after her as she went to the front of the sanctuary, up the stairs, and back into the baptismal, where Garmon waited. It was obvious he'd been trying to get loose. She continued her silent march as she crossed the room and grabbed hold of the rubber garment stretched over his head while he struggled.

Maryland hauled at it until the rubber tore, starting at the back of his neck. She felt savage, her teeth as tight as steel pegs in her jaw. Tubes and wires built into the fabric of the suit shredded. She was vaguely aware she was coughing—big whoops that felt wet on her lips—and that Ellis was trying to pull her off of him, but the cop was no match for the fury seeping into her to fill up those numb spaces. She kept tearing until the whole mask ripped away, taking a generous hunk of the man's hair with it.

"*Nooo!*" Garmon slammed his body side-to-side in the wheel-chair hard enough to lift the tires off the ground. They had their first real look at him. He was younger than her, probably mid-twen-ties, with a blond buzzcut and ears that stuck out too far. Not the face of evil she'd expected. Just another grunt.

"Maryland, what did you do?" Ellis asked in awe.

"You fucking crazy bitch, you just ruined that rebreather and *you contaminated me!*"

"Good," she spat, shaking Ellis off. "One of my friends just died from your 'contamination,' and you're no better than he was."

"I'm sorry for that, but it's not my fault! I was just trying to help!"

She dropped the mask and clamped down on those protruding ears. He gasped. She snapped his head up to face her. "Now you're gonna help yourself. You're gonna tell us goddamn *everything* or we will leave you here tied to this wheelchair so your precious P3 can eat away at you. You can see which gets you first, that or the dehydration."

Something in her spiel must've gotten through to him. "O-okay."

"Who are you assholes?"

"We're called Aurora. It's part of the US government, but out-side normal reporting channels."

"Who's in charge?"

"I have no idea. It doesn't work like that. The guy that's leading this operation though, his name's Kyler."

"Where is he?"

"They have a base camp set up somewhere in those hills, just inside the city limits. I'm not sure where."

"Okay. You passed the easy questions, so let's try the hard stuff: now that you have your very own spiffy 'baseline,' do you still want us to march ourselves up to the nearest Aurora soldiers?"

He thought about this long and hard, his upper lip trembling. "I...I don't know."

"I didn't think so, you asshole."

"I don't know what the standing protocol is!"

"Which means you don't know if they'll just shoot us on sight."

He thought about this, the gears of training in his head grinding in the opposite direction as the gears of common sense. "But it's the only thing we can do, the only chance we have at getting help!"

She yanked his ears harder; he whimpered. "Some of our group were tranquilized and left behind when you attacked us on the street. I'm gonna ask you again, what happened to those people? Where are they?"

Garmon took a deep, shuddering breath, probably thinking about all that P3 he was inhaling. "I don't know. But wherever they are...I'm sure it's not very much fun."

WHITNEY +34:23

"Another cookie?" the man in the white lab coat asked.

Chris shook his head, his vision blurring. His chin felt wet, and when he wiped at it, his hand came away slick with drool. He wanted to close his eyes and go back to sleep. He coughed, and the sharp burn in his throat woke him up a bit.

He was in a square room, the walls bare and sterile, but he couldn't figure out how he got here. Across a plain, white desk sat a person who had given him orange juice and the most delicious chocolate chip cookies his ravenous stomach could ask for. In addition to the lab coat, the man also wore a clear mask over the lower half of his face. The item was very familiar for some reason. Hadn't he just met someone that wore one of those?

Chris knew all the way to his bones that something was wrong with this scenario, but he was too sleepy to care.

"Okay then, I have just a few questions for you, then we'll get you into bed. How does that sound?"

"Great."

The man in the lab coat and breathing mask gave him a friendly grin, looked down at a sheet of paper on the desk, and held a pen at the ready. "What is your name?"

"Christopher Mark Sloan."

Scribble, scribble, went the pen. "Your age?"

"Fourteen."

"Do you smoke, or take any drugs or alcohol?"

"No."

"Prescription medication?"

"Nope."

"Have you had the chicken pox?"

"Yes, sir."

"And does your family have a history of any hereditary disorders? Diabetes, heart disease, cancer? Anything in your personal medical history, like asthma or Hyper-Activity Disorder?"

Chris felt a goofy grin steal onto his face. "We learned about brown hairy tongue in Health." The man waited, smiling pleasantly but with a touch of impatience. "No," Chris amended. "I broke my arm when I was nine, though."

"Excellent. Tell me Christopher." The man in the white lab coat leaned forward over the desk, like a vulture over a fresh carcass. "How do you feel?"

"Tired."

"Apart from that."

"Oh. Pretty sick. My throat hurts bad, and I can't stop coughing." He demonstrated this with a hack that felt like he'd swallowed needles.

"Good, good." The man made checkmarks on the paper.

Chris sensed someone beside him. Another lab-coated man rolled up his sleeve and plunged a needle into his arm. He gave an automatic gasp before realizing he was too numb to actually feel it. "What's that?"

"He's just getting some blood from you." The syringe filled up with red liquid and then the second man vanished. "Can you tell me how long these symptoms have been occurring?"

"I dunno. What day is it?"

"It's Wednesday."

"Um, since early this morning? Wait...are you a doctor?"

"I'm a kind of doctor, yes."

"Are you gonna give me medicine?"

"Well...we'll see." He made one last note. "Finished here. You can take him."

Hands slipped under his arms and lift him out of the chair. His weak neck couldn't support his head; it lolled back. Shrouded forms leered down at him from both sides, men wearing camouflage and gas masks that covered their entire faces. He squirmed as they carried him out of the room, through a set of metal doors that led outside.

It was still nighttime. Crickets chirped. The air tasted thin and there was a chill that brought out goosebumps on his skin. He was dragged across a short stretch of sparse grass, through a barrier of some kind, and then dropped unceremoniously. Chris sprawled to his knees in the dirt. He heard someone come running, and a voice yelled, "You bastards! He's just a kid!" There was a snorting chuckle as the figures retreated, closing the gate they'd brought him through.

Someone turned him over and patted his cheeks. A white face swam out of the haze of his vision, one he recognized. "Randy?"

"Chris, thank God!"

Pieces came to him, like lights coming on in a dark house. "What's...what's wrong with me?"

"It's the drugs, they haven't worn off yet. Can you sit up?"

He gave it a shot, leaning against the investment banker, and took a look around. There was just enough moonlight to see that they were in a rectangular enclosure formed by razor wire stretched taut between wooden posts, like a cattle corral. He could see other people milling up and down the length of the pen, some sitting against the posts, all of them coughing. Looking through the fence, he could see similar cages standing in parallel lines next to this one, containing even more people. They appeared to be in a field, with fancy travel trailers closing in three sides of them—he assumed this was where his interview had been conducted—but on the fourth side, rising above them like the shadow of a giant, was—

"Are those the Chantillys?" He gazed up at the rolling ridge-backs just a few hundred yards away.

"Yeah, we're somewhere up in the hills." The melancholy cloud around Randy Rampy had lifted a bit. "Probably along the western trail; it's the only place cleared out like this."

"What happened? How did we get here?"

"I don't know for sure. One second I was talking to Maryland on the street, the next I woke up strapped to a gurney being offload-ed from a helicopter. From what I've found out, they shot us all with tranquilizer darts and then brought us here." He cleared his throat and then massaged the flesh with one shaking hand. "Every-body here is sick, just like at the Dome."

The word 'sick' backed a dump truck of memories up to Chris' tired brain. "Oh man, where's Tangela?"

"I haven't seen anyone else from the clinic. Maybe they got away…"

Chris stood, his legs shaky but holding him upright. He screamed, "*Tangela!*"

"I don't think that's such a good idea." Randy cast a glance at the trailers. "They have guards patrolling…"

Chris went to the edge of the enclosure and reached through the razor wire. He waved until he got the attention of a sickly-looking woman with glasses in the next pen. "Is there a black girl over there? Named Tangela?" The woman shook her head. "What about the next one? Can you find out?"

It took a full five minutes to get the word back. There were no little black girls at all, let alone one named 'Tamara.' He slumped back to the ground and sat with his head on his knees.

Randy joined him. "I'm sorry. But don't assume the worst just because she's not here. They could still bring her in."

"I hope they don't. She's better off out there."

"You don't know that. Maybe these people are going to help us. The only thing we can do is cooperate, give them what they want, and hope for the best."

"Screw that." His head cleared with each passing second, the engine he always imagined in his brain cycling back up to its regular running speed. Here was a problem his APTITUDE and POTENTIAL could actually solve. "As soon as it gets light enough, I'm finding a way to bust all of us outta here."

WHITNEY +34:25

The boat cruised through the flooded graveyard, the spotlight on its bow sweeping the misty surface of the water. It illuminated buoyant coffins and dappled along the tall tombstone that rose from the depths. They'd been heading toward higher ground, but the water was still up to Lincoln's shoulders when Mac grabbed his arm and pulled him and Charlie into the dark crevice behind a granite cherub. The fat little stone angel seemed to dance atop the water's surface.

Scarcely a heartbeat later, the searchlight cut through the area, casting moving shadows that reached out like twisted hands. Mac squatted until only his broken nose and bald head stuck out of the water. He took Charlie down with him. The cop sputtered awake again as the water hit his face, and Mac slapped a hand over his mouth before he could cough.

The boat puttered by just on the other side of their hiding spot. Lincoln peeked beneath the arm of the cherub to watch, then turned to Mac and Charlie.

"It's them, the soldiers," he whispered. "There's five of 'em."

"What s-soldiers?" The medicine finally seemed to be bringing Charlie around. "Someone wanna tell me what's goin on?"

"Later, old man," Mac said. And then to Lincoln, "Let's just wait till they go away!"

"I don't know if they will. They sent that boat out here cause they know we ain't dead." Lincoln stood up to see where the craft was headed, and the world spun. He threw out a hand to the statue's leg to catch himself before he fell over.

"Links, you okay?"

"Naw, man. Felt like shit ever since we got dumped in the floodwater." The back of his throat was hot enough to fry bacon—a direct contrast to the chilly water—and he kept getting lightheaded.

He couldn't figure out which he wanted less: to be gunned down by the soldiers, or go out in bloody convulsions like those people at the Dome. *If you're* really *lucky, maybe you'll get both.* "It's gonna be morning soon, and then they got us dead to rights. We gotta keep movin, swim under the water if we have to."

"How we supposed to do that with Charlie?"

"Leave me." The cop's heavy breaths sprayed water. "You guys got me this f-far, but I'm weighin ya down."

Lincoln rolled his eyes. "Nobody's gettin left. We didn't come all this way just to abandon you now."

A quavering screech rolled across the cemetery like some alien bird call. All three of them grew still. Lincoln understood why Charlie had said it sounded like an owl. His flesh crawled as he thought about that shape swimming in the wake of Lemiere's speedboat, as nimble in the water as a dolphin. What the hell had it been? Something else the soldiers had sent after them?

The cry attracted more than just their attention. The boat's motor revved. The searchlight swung around as the soldiers swerved back in their direction, picking up speed.

"*C'mon!*"

Lincoln waded from cover, staying hunched in the brackish water, moving toward what instinct told him was dry land. Mac followed close with Charlie in both arms. Lincoln's feet encountered smaller gravestones every few steps, tripping him up, forcing him to go slower or bruise up his shins.

Suddenly his shadow was thrown long in front of him.

The gunfire started before he could shout a warning, the deafening sound of those huge guns lessened by the open cemetery. Lincoln threw himself behind a cross grave marker. Bullets thunked into the other side of the the concrete shield. The boat's momentum carried it past, and he caught sight of a couple of the passengers jumping over the side as it turned to track him. He took off in the other direction.

He didn't know where Mac and Charlie went, and he was too afraid to call out and betray any of their positions. He dodged from cover to cover, trying not to splash.

Ahead was a large area packed with jutting tombstones, statuaries, and floating coffins; far too dense for the boat to follow. On the far side, he could see one of several crypts that dotted Parkland's landscape, a squat, circular brick building with a steepled roof. The lower half was under water.

He pushed through the sea of coffins, held tightly together in their corral. They rubbed against one another when he brushed past, creating a domino effect of chittering squeaks. The water was at chest level now, and the field of caskets made an excellent hiding spot.

Lincoln found a dark corner in the shadows between a floating mahogany coffin and a rusted metal butterfly with the words "FOR CAMILLE" engraved on one wing. He took a breath and submerged, then let loose the cough building in his throat, hacked until he almost choked. A wave of nausea came with it, making his head swirl. He rose back up as silently as a submarine periscope.

The boat chugged along somewhere in front of him, circling the tight perimeter of graveyard decoration. Their searchlight was a beacon, playing across the tops of the tombstones. It swept over one statue of a little girl reaching toward heaven, and then backlit an ugly gargoyle perched atop the narrow ridge of a tall tombstone. Why anyone would want such a hideous thing looking down on them for eternity was beyond him.

And then it moved, turning a spiny head.

Lincoln's heart sped to an uncomfortable rhythm.

Those yellow eyes he'd seen before picked him out. An elongated muzzle beneath them opened, and the creature's head rocked back and forth, like a mamma bird about to regurgitate a meal. That yodeling squawk came from its throat, and instead of Charlie's owl, this time it reminded Lincoln this time of the noise a seal makes. The cry broke into a series of harsh rasps near the end, rough noises that sounded like growling coughs.

He didn't know if it was comforting or not that monsters also got sick.

The soldiers saw it too. One of them shouted, "There!" amid a squall of buzzy static. Their machine guns fired. The creature on the tombstone became a blur, jumping onto the nearest coffin and then careening down the line of floating crates directly at Lincoln. Its claws gouged holes in the polished wood as it charged. It reached for his face.

If he'd hesitated even a second, the thing would've taken his head off. He dove beneath the surface as it swept past.

Lincoln opened his eyes in a world of pitch-black murk. He pushed off from the tombstone he'd been leaning against, sliced through the water with his hands and kicked hard, swimming beneath the jostling layer of coffins. He couldn't give the thing a chance to get in the water with him.

The grave markers of long dead Port Allen residents surged from the black, in his face before he could see them. His lungs ached. He tried to come up. Hit his head on a casket. He wedged his fingers between them, trying to shove them apart to make room, but they wouldn't budge. He thrashed in the water, swimming further, looking for a spot to surface, and when he looked back, he saw the glowing eyes of that thing coasting toward him at top speed...

He collided with a pair of legs headfirst and surfaced, gasping and coughing. He found himself face to face with one of the soldiers, who seemed just as surprised to suddenly have a black kid's head in his crotch. The glistening figure flailed, trying to get its gun up. Lincoln pushed him out of the way.

There was an eruption beside them. The creature shot out of the water. It latched on to the soldier before he could open fire. The man screamed, the buzzing through his mask enough to make the bones in Lincoln's skull vibrate. He saw the beast's claws sink into the soldier's face and throat, tearing through rubber and flesh alike, and then it buried its snout in the gushing wounds and tore away a football-sized hunk of gore.

Lincoln waded toward the crypt as fast as he could.

WHITNEY +34:27

Mac never stopped running when the boat opened fire. He couldn't see what happened to Lincoln. Charlie was a rag doll in his arms, his weight made lighter by the water's buoyancy. The cop looked up at him as Mac pushed toward the small building he could see against the midnight blue horizon.

"Déjà vu," he said, with a dreamy smile.

Mac didn't know if the man was hallucinating again, but he whispered, "This is the last time I drag yo' ass through the water, Charlie."

He glanced back. One of the soldiers was off the boat and coming after them, but Mac's long strides helped them pull away. The opening to a brick mausoleum was just ahead, short enough that Mac had to duck his head. Grass was replaced with concrete beneath his sneakers. It was even darker inside this flooded, circular room, but he could see the small metal squares lining the walls for ashen remains.

And something else. Far in the shadows against the wall were six hairy domes floating on the water like turtle shells. As he watched, one of them rose up to reveal a sunken-eyed, male face.

"Get outta here!" the guy hissed. "This is *our* hiding place!"

"Well I got one of those soldiers right on my ass, so you gonna have to share!"

Mac delved further into the crypt, where the rest of this man's party hunkered, two females and four males, all of them smothering coughs. He took Charlie over to an outcropping that served as a shelf for flowers and candles and said, "Can you hang here for a minute?"

The cop grabbed hold, leaning heavily to keep from slipping under the water. From outside came the crack of more gunfire.

"Just stay down!" Mac took up a spot next to the chamber's only exit. As he flattened against the wall, something in his jeans pocket pressed against his leg. His hand stole down to feel the unfamiliar bulge.

The soldier passed by Mac as he eased into the crypt. The flashlight on the end of his weapon picked out Charlie and the other group almost immediately. He raised the rifle butt to his shoulder.

Mac leapt on his back before he could mow them down. This soldier was a better hand-to-hand fighter than the one in the gas station. He tucked and twisted, trying to sling the weight off. Mac tore at the rubber over his head until he'd made a hole.

Then he brought up the object he'd found in his pocket; the pepper spray he'd taken off the dead pig when he freed Ellis. He jammed it into the mask and depressed the trigger.

The result was instantaneous. The soldier bellowed and dropped his gun. The flashlight on the end of it was still visible as it sank to the floor of the crypt, giving the whole room a greenish hue. The soldier beat at the tinted shield over his face. His screams of pain, amplified by whatever speakers were in the mask, echoed in the mausoleum to head-splitting proportions.

"What did you do?" The guy that had told them to get out slapped hands over his ears.

"Oh my God, shut him up!" one of the women pleaded.

But Mac only watched as the soldier tore at his head until Lincoln splashed through the door of the mausoleum. Several of the other people gave a startled cry.

"It's coming! The thing that killed Lemiere, it's here, it's—"

Something brushed Mac's leg beneath the water. He saw a shape glide through the muted, underwater glow coming from the dropped weapon. The screaming soldier—who had ripped the faceplate from his mask so he could splash water into his swollen eyes—was yanked under. A stream of bubbles rose to the surface.

The silence in the crypt was all-consuming. An eye-watering tang filled the air: the scent of dead things at low tide. Mac strained his eyes against the black water around them, searching for motion, every nerve twitching with dread.

And then the monster, something that looked like four-hundred pounds of scales and spines, rose up in front of the door, cutting off their only exit. Lincoln jumped away. Now everyone was screaming, crowding toward the back wall, and the creature closed in with—Mac could swear it—a grin on its dripping muzzle.

"You can have a taste of this too, shithead!"

Mac loosed a stream of red foam from the nozzle on the pepper spray canister, holding the button until it ran out. The mess splattered across what passed for the thing's visage. It gave a screech and shook its head, then, as the burn really set in, it brought up the twisted spikes on the ends of its fingers and clawed at its own face, digging bloody furrows in the leathery flesh. Mac saw its yellow eyes pop like egg yolks.

"Run!" he yelled. "Go, get out!"

They made a rush toward the door, giving the monster a wide berth. It thrashed, slashing out in angry, blind circles, and caught one of the other survivors across the stomach, disemboweling him in one swift stroke. Mac and Lincoln held Charlie between them and waded past while the creature ripped apart the poor bastard.

Outside wasn't much better. The boat and its remaining three occupants sailed around the corner as the crowd of refugees fled the mausoleum. They unslung guns and opened fire. The five people left from the other group were caught in the open and went down in a blaze. Mac, Lincoln and Charlie turned away, seeking cover around the side of the tiny brick building.

A warbling roar split the night. The monster exploded out of the crypt, a blur in the water. It made a beeline for the boat.

The soldiers watched as it reached them in seconds and jumped into the boat, then began to slash and bite anything it could get its hands on. One of the soldiers tried to dive in the water and was dragged back in by his head, just before the thing twisted it off like a bottlecap.

Lincoln moved on. "C'mon, let's go before it finishes."

They slogged through the water, carrying Charlie with an arm slung over both their shoulders. The screams continued behind them for several more minutes before cutting off. The flood level dropped further, and, as they spotted the black fence that marked the boundary of Parkland just ahead, they stepped out onto soggy graveyard soil.

Mac and Lincoln pushed until a storm-damaged section of wrought iron fell over. Both of them coughed throughout this operation, pausing once so Lincoln could vomit up blood. Neither commented as they dragged Charlie out of the cemetery.

"You think we lost it?" Mac gasped.

The answer came behind them: a reed-thin hoot with a sizzling angry undercurrent.

~ ~ ~

WHITNEY +34:28

It took Carter less than twenty minutes to get rid of the radio over a backyard fence and then find Ellis' precinct, but it felt like eternity with the Lucid riding him every step of the way.

You can't do this you coward, you have to go back!

I can't give them the rebreather, he thought back stubbornly.

But you have to see it now, Maryland's right, it was always a sham! An excuse! You conquered the agoraphobia in less than a day when you had to, and that house was obviously never germ-proof!

It's not about the phobias anymore. They were just warm-up. Practice for the big game. Now it's real. And I'm swinging for the fences.

Sports metaphors? Are you even hearing how ridiculous you sound?

And he couldn't make it stop. For the first time, he could see this being *actual* schizophrenia, a disorder that had crept in the back door while he was busy with all the others.

So he sang instead. Every song he could think of, as loud as he could, while he strolled down the decimated streets just a few miles from the shoreline. Shifting gears from Elton John to Tool to Moby, as long as it drowned out the Lucid. He would've been an easy target for any of Garmon's buddies, tripping over wreckage while he screeched whatever came into his head, but he didn't care. Getting gunned down or tranquilized might be the lesser of two evils.

He was still singing when he spotted the only building that could be a police precinct. A three-story middle structure, with two shorter, smaller levels sprouting from the sides. The roof and most of the walls were torn off the top floor, and every window was broken, but it appeared stable. He took the paved path from the street, hollering some Creedence Clearwater now. The sky lightened by degrees, drifting toward morning blue.

The front doors were locked but the glass was missing, leaving just two latched together frames. Some deeper part of his brain than even the Lucid tried to give a warning that there was something wrong with this picture, but the singing drowned out all advice from his medulla oblongata up. He knocked on one of the doors, then stepped through into a large, cheerful lobby.

His singing drifted into humming and then tapered altogether while he took a look around. An elevated front desk sat ahead with a Port Allen Police Department seal on the wall behind it. The tile floor was scuffed and covered with a layer of mud and trash, blown in through the missing front windows. There were doors that led out of this room on both sides, and two behind the desk, but he couldn't even begin to guess where they might lead.

He was here. Now what?

Well…he would wait until the others arrived, of course.

What if they don't come, Cart? If they've all turned themselves in to get the help you wouldn't give them?

Carter spun, trying to think. Maybe he should go back to the church. The walls wavered. His breath stuttered. Vertigo, even though he was indoors. He needed something to take his mind off it. A plaque on the wall beside the front doors listed the officer's code of conduct, a collection of virtues to make him feel even more guilty, but he read them all, honor and integrity and—

And how was he reading it from across the room?

For the first time, he realized *why* this lobby was so cheerful. The overhead fluorescents were on. Besides the lamps at the Dome, his eyes hadn't used man-made illumination since before the power went off back at his place. But if the lights were on here, it meant they were getting electricity, maybe through a generator. Was it automatic or did it mean—

Something slammed across the back of his neck. He fell to the dirty tile on hands and knees, and then a booted foot smashed into his solar plexus. He gagged into the mask and collapsed on his side, curling into the fetal position.

"'Zat one of 'em?" a male voice asked above him, somehow coughing while it spoke.

"Yeah, he yo' girl's boyfrien or some shit."

Carter recognized that one.

"What's that thing on his face?"

"Shee-it, I don't know, he weird. 'Fraid of germs or somethin."

The pain ebbed, and Carter tried to open his eyes. Someone grabbed him, lifted him up by the front of his t-shirt, and shook him. "Where are they?" A pale, flabby face hovered over him, and he caught sight of CT standing just behind the shoulder it was attached to. The young gang member wore a cop's gun belt with a holstered pistol.

"Hey, look at me." The fat man shook him again. "Where are they? Where's Wright and that bitch who shot me?"

"I don't know," Carter answered honestly, holding his bruised stomach.

"Boy, what little patience I have is *loooong* gone. Ya better tell me while ya still got all yer important parts."

"I don't know," he insisted. "They…they said they were coming here." This got him dropped to smack his head against the floor.

"Want me ta take care of 'im?" CT asked, coughing himself.

Carter could see the other man now that he stepped back. He was thick and squat, and appeared to have only one hand. The other arm ended in a nub wrapped in bloody towels, held in place by thick, office rubber bands around the wrist; the Skywalker home amputee kit. He shook his head and gave another massive rumble that sounded like a jet engine in his chest. "We may need 'im, if he's really her boyfriend. Throw 'im in one of tha cells and then get these lights turned back off. We don't do a goddamned thing 'til we have tha others."

WHITNEY +34:36

Turner busted into the baptismal as Maryland finished with Garmon.

"Two guys just stole Imogene's tank!"

"*What?*"

The sanctuary was in uproar all over again. Ellis noticed Tom's body had been confined to the side of the room and covered with a blanket. People gathered around Imogene as she lay back in her wheelchair, staring at the ceiling and taking slow, measured breaths. "What happened?"

Sara stood close by, wringing her hands and rocking on the balls of her feet. "We were trying to clean her tank, to get the blood out, and these two men—two of the ones that were already here at the church—they just grabbed it and took off! It was so fast, we didn't know what to do!"

"I woulda shot 'em, but I didn't want to risk bringin the soldiers," Turner added.

"You did the right thing. We don't need any more violence." Ellis raised his voice to address the entire group. "Listen, the goal hasn't changed, people. We just need to get to my precinct. We can still try calling for help, and we have emergency equipment there, including oxygen tanks and breathing masks. More than enough for us to share."

Justin spoke from a nearby pew. "What about turning ourselves in? Are we giving that any more discussion?"

"There's nothing to discuss. If you feel your chances would be better going to the soldiers, nobody will stop you. Is anybody prepared to do that?"

No one said a word.

"Okay then. Let's get moving."

"Ellis." Maryland said his name from the edge of the crowd, leaning heavily against Imogene's wheelchair. "Maybe it would be better if we didn't *all* try to go. This is too big a group to hide. If we take everyone and they find us again, it could be worse than last time."

He considered this. "Would everyone be okay sitting tight here until myself and maybe a few others can come back with equipment and weapons?" No argument; they were too tired to put up a fight. Most people started to drift back toward the pews to collapse.

Ellis went to kneel beside Imogene. "Do you want us to take you with us, so we can get you to one of those tanks?"

She shook her small head emphatically. Those labored breaths worked her narrow chest like a bellows. When she spoke, the words rode each crest of breath like a surfer on a Hawaiian wave. "Better not to move…or get too excited. Let me stay here…and concentrate on breathin.'"

"I'm coming with you," Maryland said. "And we're bringing Tangela and Hernie. They need fresh oxygen fast."

"What about you? You haven't been looking so hot, Maryland."

She wiped sweaty hair back out of her face. "I'll be fine. Worry about the others first."

"I'm going also," Walter said over Ellis' shoulder.

"You don't have to. We'll go, see if Lincoln and the others are there, try to make the call, and bring the equipment b—"

"I'm *going*." Walter put one arm around his wife's waist, and the other over his son's shoulders. "I've already lost one member of my family tonight, I won't lose any more. I want one of those tanks, Officer Wright. You *owe* me one."

Ellis winced at the implication. He bit the inside of his lip and nodded. "Okay. Bring that gun you took off Garmon then."

He stood. Turner was the last one left to address. He put a hand on the man's shoulder. "You're in charge here. Don't let the prisoner out of your sight for a minute. And if Aurora shows up…just do what you think is best."

It took the five of them just a few minutes to say their goodbyes, bundle up Tangela, and slip out of the church.

WHITNEY +34:41

After leaving Parkland, Lincoln and the others headed a couple of blocks west, in the direction of Charlie's precinct. These neighborhoods were destroyed, Whitney hardly leaving enough behind to tell what had once been here. Now that Charlie was conscious and coherent, Mac and Lincoln used the opportunity to fill him in on the soldiers, the disease, and what had occurred at the civic center and Kordi's clinic.

The sky went from black to dark blue to rich violet without a single cloud, and a cool breeze blew in from the south; all the precursors to a gorgeous day, but, one way or another, Lincoln didn't think they'd see much of it. They were all coughing up blood now, at a fairly steady pace, and the old cop said he could no longer feel his bad leg. They checked the wound when they dared to slow down and found the veins around it a livid green and purple, the whole leg as bloated as photos Lincoln had once seen of a rattlesnake victim.

Their scaly friend from the graveyard had yet to put in another appearance, but they heard it. Sometimes it was that awful, bubbly cry echoing over the wreckage, but more often it was the same sound the three of them made: sharp, pathetic coughing.

As they rounded the corner onto a residential street full of overturned trees and half-standing houses, Charlie strung between Lincoln and Mac, they found themselves facing an entire battalion. A few blocks down sat two helicopters and at least twenty-five soldiers from the biohazard army. They ducked back before they were seen.

After lowering Charlie gently to the sidewalk, Lincoln crept back to the corner of the closest crumbled wall for another look. The main group broke into smaller units, spreading out in a tight line over several blocks and then moving in their direction like hunters flushing out game. They stopped to sweep houses and hiding places in the wreckage, working in coordinated teams.

Mac kicked over a pile of bricks. "They got us cut off! Goddamn, is this *ever* gonna end? What are they even doin here?"

"They probably wanna know what happened to the five guys they sent to find us." Lincoln held his head as he spoke, eyes squeezed shut. "You know, the ones that ended up in that monster's stomach?"

"That thing..." Bloody saliva leaked from the corner of Charlie's mouth and got caught in his mustache. "It looked like...some kinda fish. With arms and legs. I never heard of anything like that. Outside the tabloids, I mean."

Lincoln squatted and leaned back against the gnarled base of an uprooted tree. His throat felt like throbbing hell. "Did you see the way it blinded itself?"

"Can't blame it for that; I know what that spray feels like."

"Yeah, but you didn't claw your own eyes when it happened to you."

"Extreme reaction to pain just shows it's an animal. Same way a raccoon in a trap will gnaw off its own leg. And if it's an animal, we can outsmart it."

"*Outsmart it?* Shit, it seems to be following us okay without any eyes."

"Sound or smell, kid. No trick to that. The soldiers were firing from the boat, and it passed us by and went for them."

"But what do you think it is, though? Where'd it come from?"

"Wait a minute! Holy shit!" Mac waved his hands to get their attention. "Carter and Maryland, they said there was some kind of...of *creature* inside the Dome, just before it blew. I thought they were crazy, but...you think that thing could be what they were talkin about?"

"Well I hope to Christ there ain't more than one of 'em." Charlie reached down, took hold of the tarnished badge that clung to his uniform shirt by one torn slip of fabric, and ripped it loose. He held the hunk of metal in front of his face and stared at it. "I don't know if I said it before—my mind's a little muddled right now, if you hadn't noticed—but…thank you. Botha you. Cause of you, I get a chance at seein my kids again. Hell, even the ex would be a sight for sore eyes."

"Don't worry about it." Lincoln waved away the sentiment.

But Charlie wasn't finished. He slipped the badge into his pants pocket, wincing as his leg shifted. "You're good young men. I see that now. Maybe not so much the other one that stole my gun, but you guys are all right. I still don't understand what happened with that Kim business—"

Lincoln squirmed and looked away.

"—but I don't think you killed him on purpose. And I'll testify to that."

Lincoln stared intently at the ground in front of him, cheeks burning as fiercely as his throat.

Mac watched him, broken nose like a cucumber in the middle of his face. "I didn't mean it," he said, picking up the thread of their earlier argument. "You *are* somebody. You gonna *be* somebody, even if I gotta hold you in a headlock 'til you are."

Lincoln climbed slowly to his feet, using the uprooted tree as support. He held out a hand and gave Mac a weary grin. "Gotta stick together, right?"

Mac took the hand but used it to jerk him closer and sling an arm around his neck. "So we good?"

"We always good, bitch."

"All right, all right," Charlie interrupted. "I didn't mean to start a homo love-in. If Ellis and these others people are lookin for help, we better catch up to 'em."

Mac released Lincoln. "I don't see how we gonna do that. These soldiers got the whole street blocked."

"So…we go under." Charlie raised an arm toward the street running beside them, where an open manhole interrupted the otherwise smooth pavement.

"What, the sewer? No fuckin way!"

"It ain't the sewer, kid. Sewer pipes run deeper'n that. It's the flood control system and the maintenance tunnels they use to get down to the sewers."

"If it's the flood control system, then what if it's flooded?"

"Then you better be able to hold your breath for awhile."

Mac shook his head.

"Look, we got eight or nine blocks to my precinct. That's it. We can go right under their feet. There's even a drain that lets in through the prisoner hosedown we might be able to get open. It's either that, or start tryin to work our way around those soldiers by goin blocks out of the way. And *all* of us might be dead by then."

"He's right. It's the only chance we got."

Mac stared at the dark circle in the street. "All right, fine. But if I end up walkin through shit, I ain't gonna be happy."

The screech of the creature from a block back got them all up and headed for the manhole.

WHITNEY +34:56

Hernie refused to leave without his dog, and Ellis grudgingly allowed the animal to come along. He feared it would do something to get them caught, and Walter remained vocal about the same, but Hatch was surprisingly obedient, trotting alongside his master and never straying ahead. The six of them—Ellis, Walter, Maryland, Hatch, and Hernie carrying Tangela—circled around through a neighborhood to the south and approached the precinct from the rear. The route cost them an extra ten minutes, but Ellis wanted to give the areas to the north a wide berth in case the Aurora agents had spread that far.

They were close enough to the shore now to catch the clean smell of the ocean on the breeze. According to their prisoner, that same wind would eventually cleanse the city of this deadly chemical, but not fast enough for them. The coming dawn revealed that the precinct was still standing, although the third story looked like it had been the victim of a flat wrecking ball that sheared off the entire level.

Walter was in the best shape of any of them, followed by Ellis, whose back hurt far more than his throat. Tangela drifted in an out of consciousness, breathing shallow, gripping her blanket tight around her. Hernie coughed continually, barely on his feet. Even the dog kept lowering his head to give a few rattling chuffs. And as for Maryland...

She was going downhill practically in front of their eyes. All Ellis could think about was Doc Kordi's assertion that the illness affected different people at different rates, and how Garmon had said that smaller, weaker specimens succumbed first. Did Maryland's smoking put her in that category? As they crept through the shadows along the edge of the eastern wing toward the garage, she went into a fit and doubled over, her whole body cramping, and Ellis thought it was the end for her.

He grabbed her by the arms and eased her back against him. The others stopped to watch.

"It's okay. It's okay, I'm all right."

"We need to get you on some clean oxygen. Right now."

She shook her head. Blood leaked from her nose. She wiped it away. "Tangela first."

"They'll be plenty for all of us. We have a whole armory full of riot gear and 02 tanks."

"Carter. We have to find Carter."

"We'll look for him. Can you get up?" She grimaced and wobbled back to her feet.

Walter held his weapon in one hand and beckoned. "C'mon let's keep going! My wife and son are dying back there at the church!"

"Hold on a sec. I want to do this quick, so here's how it'll work: we go in through the garage, and I'll look for a running vehicle big enough to hold all of us and the supplies."

"Anything with an engine is going to draw these Aurora guys right to us!"

"I thought about that, but I don't see any other way to get everything back. While I'm doing that, the rest of you go to the armory on the first floor and start bringing the tanks and all the guns you can find out to me. Once we're loaded and ready to roll, I'll check the broadcasting equipment on the second floor to see if I can contact someone outside the city."

"What about Lincoln and Lemiere and the others?" Maryland asked. "Your partner. They were supposed to meet us here, too."

Ellis sighed. Even before getting rid of the radio, they hadn't heard one word from the Cajun and the two gangbangers. Odds were, they were probably dead, along with Charlie. Just something else to hang on his conscience if they made it out of this. "If they're here, they're here, but we can't afford to wait for them or Carter or anybody. Especially after I start broadcasting our location."

They rounded the corner and faced the wide garage doors of the repair bay. The iron shutters were down and locked; Ellis was never privy to a key and even if he was, he'd lost his key ring around the time he and Lincoln took shelter in the warehouse during Whitney. A smaller door stood at the building's edge, metal with a reinforced window. He used his pistol butt to batter at it until he could reach through and thumb the lock.

The repair bay was gloomy; the only illumination came through thin windows near the ceiling. Most of the vehicles had been driven out of the city to spare them hurricane damage, but the shapes of a few patrol cars and a S.W.A.T.-style van were still here. Three inches of water stood in the floor. Jerry, the city's mechanic, was going to throw a shit-fit when he saw this place. Ellis led the way across to a platform for the industrial backup generators in the far wall.

"When the power grid is running off these, all the electronic keycard locks in the building automatically stay open, except for the armory. The only way you can get in is with the keypad." Ellis worked the lever to prime the generator. He was glad he'd paid attention through the training class to know how to operate these monstrous suckers. They primed faster than what he'd been told, almost as if they were ready to go. He flipped the failsafe switches, then pressed the ignition on the generator. It fired up with an electric *whoosh* and then hummed along quietly. He pointed to the door that led into the stationhouse. "Go through there into the main building, and the lobby's at the end of the hall. Head through the double doors behind the front desk to the squad room, and just follow the signs to the armory. The code is 74893. I'll have a car ready by the time you get back."

"Be careful," Maryland told him, coughing once.

"Get those tanks on before you start carrying the rest out. That's an order."

They hurried through the door, Hatch bounding just ahead. The lights were still off in the garage, and Ellis intended to leave them that way.

The only vehicle big enough to carry five people, a dog, and enough weapons and 02 tanks to outfit a scuba-diving army was the S.W.A.T. van. He jogged through the water, rolling tool carts out of the way. He would have to look for the ignition keys in the racks against the far wall, but at least he could get it ready for loading. Ellis grabbed the handles of the rear door and flung them wide.

A form inside leapt out at him.

He jumped back, heart racing. Only after he'd taken a breath did he realize it was a person that had flopped halfway out of the van. He squinted, straining to see in the dim light.

The face of Billy Dunham stared up at him. The rookie still had that look of surprise in his raised eyebrows and wide mouth. There were more shapes in the vehicle's floor beyond, and Ellis leaned over him to have a look.

Someone had turned the van into a hearse. The bodies of Harold McNamara, JD Myers, and Drano Jenkins were piled inside like kindling, arms and legs intertwined at awkward angles, faces streaked with dried blood, just one big pile of dead officers. Next to them, within easy reach of the door, was a long duffel bag that he had seen once before, in the arms of two teenage drug dealers. Ellis tugged on the zipper, and stared at the tightly-packed white bricks inside.

Full clarity dawned on him, and he saw the flaw in his master plan: the same place he'd been drawn to for refuge would also be where his fellow brothers-in-blue would go to ground. Just the fact that Drano was here meant George Sturney must still be alive after Maryland shot him.

And Ellis had led the others right into the man's hands. Or hand, as the case may be.

He spun, preparing to go after Maryland and the rest of the group, when a voice drifted down from somewhere on the dark catwalk running around the top of the repair bay.

"*Oh Officer Wriiiiight,*" Sturney sang. "Not so fast. We got a *LOT* ta talk about."

WHITNEY +35:00

This operation had gone solidly FUBAR.

Kyler wouldn't say the situation in Port Allen was out of his control—he would never admit something like that—but he was willing to concede that mistakes had been made, timetables misjudged, and a few specific events had been labeled with his least favorite thing of all: a question mark.

The same mark that had been branded on his face for the last twenty years.

He had reports spread out on the desk in his command trailer, but he was having trouble focusing on them. One second he would be reading, and then he would come back to himself with a start several minutes later, sitting back in his chair and staring off into space. He couldn't even remember where his mind wandered on these little detours.

Jesus Chris, what was *wrong* with him?

He was off on one such mental excursion when the sound of an insistent buzz brought him back. His eyes focused and then swept the room, finally landing on the red phone on his communication console.

The device was just a plastic handset, no buttons whatsoever, meant only for inbound calls. One of these phones had been in every Aurora command post he'd ever been in charge of, but he'd never heard one ring. He walked stiffly over to it. His hand shook as he reached out. He despised the low feeling of fear that grew in the back of his skull.

"We're going on 35 hours since the hurricane hit, and you're still keeping the general public out of an American city. This was supposed to be finished in less than 24." The voice was smooth and calm, not a shred of emotion or inflection. Could've been a robot, for all he knew. Just the fact that Kyler was hearing it—receiving personal contact from whoever squatted above him on the all-powerful chain of command—meant his personal world had wobbled severely out of orbit.

"I am aware, sir."

"Are you planning on living in that damn town, Kyler?" Even the sarcasm had no life to it.

"I intend to have this finished up shortly."

"'Shortly' is no answer." At these words, red flashed behind Kyler's eyes, a red so intense it could've been from a fresh nuclear blast. He clapped his free hand to the side of his head, as if he could snatch away the pain, but it faded on its own. "You told us this would be finished up when you had those people crammed into the civic center, so you could blow them all up. What happened?"

"By the time the choppers arrived, people were evacuating the building. We don't know what caused the scare. And there have been other complications—"

"We know all about your complications. One lost helicopter, three men confirmed dead, another six missing in two different engagements."

They *knew*. Of course they did. Secrets went up in Aurora, never down. "We believe—" he had to check the dossier on his desk for a name, committing the picture of the goofy-looking FNG that came with it to memory, "Agent Garmon might've been taken prisoner. As for the other five..." Kyler actually didn't know *what* to say about the team that disappeared in the swamped cemetery. They were five of his most seasoned men. He'd heard the radio playback of their screams just before contact was lost. In his line of work, he'd seen and done a lot horrible things, but those shrieks had spooked even him.

"Taken prisoner? Aren't we talking about a bunch of hurricane refugees, Kyler? Does this sound like the tidings of a black operation to you?"

"No sir." *It sounds like an androgynous bureaucrat yammering in my ear.* He was horrified to hear one of those grunted giggles come spilling out of his mouth before he could stop it. He rushed on. "There seems to be a small but organized resistance in the city. We're still trying to pinpoint the exact location. But the test subjects are all here, as ordered."

He spread the blinds across the trailer's window with one hand as he said this, confirming that, yes, the temporary holding pens were still full of Port Allen citizens. The way things were going, he half-expected them to be gone, spirited away by fucking pixie dust. He could see his men patrolling the perimeter of the base camp, and, in the background, the rounded peaks of the glorified boulders the locals called a mountain range. They had set up shop in the higher elevation where P3 concentration would be nil, a miniature valley that looked down on the city to the east.

"We want this finished, Kyler." There was a dangerous edge to this voice. "We want those test subjects delivered to the lab in New York. We want the rest of Port Allen emptied, by any means necessary. We want the neutralizer deployed, and all traces of P3 scoured from the earth. We want you and that patchwork army you call a special unit out of that city. We want all of this to happen by 1200 hours, or your involvement with Aurora will be terminated. Is that clear?"

"Clear, sir." The phone went silent.

Kyler slid his chair to the communication console and checked the clock. Five and a half hours. Then…disavowment. He brought up an open line to the corporal overseeing field directives.

"Send Mattinson to my trailer immediately," he said. "This ends now."

WHITNEY +35:12

Maryland's lungs felt ready to collapse. Each breath was agony, enough to make her never want a cigarette again. A horrible sore throat combined with an even worse flu.

And, of course, the knowledge that it was neither of those, but something well on its way to killing her.

She could imagine the P3 coursing through her bloodstream, shredding her insides or however the hell it worked, and suddenly she knew what it was like to be Carter Vance.

As they entered a mud-slathered lobby—Walter carrying their only other weapon, Hernie still clutching Tangela's limp body, the dog panting and gagging, the stench of death hanging around them in an almost palpable cloud, all that was required was some cartoon vultures to make the image complete—she went into another coughing seizure. This time a red mist coated the air after each violent cough. She stumbled and fell, banging her knees on the tile.

Hernie stopped, retching also. "Mary-land!" His voice came from the far end of a tunnel.

Her legs wouldn't work. "Keep…keep going, Hernie! I'm all right!"

Don't you quit when the finish line is right in front of you! Get your ass up and keep walking!

A hand lowered in front of her face. She looked up at Walter and accepted it, gasping at the wrenching pain in her muscles.

They followed Ellis' directions, through a set of doors behind the front desk. It was dark except for weak emergency lights, but they didn't stop to try any switches. Carter was nowhere to be found, and she didn't care. She hoped him and his mask rotted together.

The squad room consisted of rows of low cubicles, partitioned with cloth-covered temp walls and topped with glass windows. They hurried down the middle aisle, toward a fierce metal door on the back wall that said "Armory." A keypad on the wall glowed red, the only proof Ellis had gotten the power restored. Walter input the code, the red light turned green, and the door swung open on pneumatic hinges to reveal racks of neatly stacked weaponry and equipment.

"Stay put. I'll find the oxygen tanks," he said.

There was no warning before the shots sounded behind them. Her tired mind recognized the gunfire, but she still stood agape as the glass in several of the cubicle walls exploded, and a hole the size of a half-dollar opened up in the plaster next to the armory door.

"Get down!" Walter dove for the floor.

She flopped down gracelessly behind the nearest cubicle partition, pulling Hernie and Tangela with her. Hatch gave a few weak barks, then stopped to whimper.

"Get the fuck away from there!" someone shouted across the room.

"Is that them?" Maryland whispered. "Aurora?"

Walter shook his head, holding the large machine gun against his chest. His bookworm look didn't mesh well with the weapon. "I don't think so." He rose up on his knees just enough to peek over the edge of the cubicle. She did the same. She could see nothing but rows of dark desks.

Walter yelled, "Who are you? What do you want?"

"Come out wit' yo' hands up!"

"We don't want any trouble! We have an officer here with us!"

"Stand the fuck up and get out here, bee-yitch!"

The pronunciation of that last word rang bells in Maryland's head. "Where's it coming from?"

"Somewhere on the other side, close to the door we came in. We don't have time for this!"

Maryland turned to Hernie. "Take Tangela and Hatch and go into this room. I'm gonna close the door. Do *not* open it until I tell you, okay?"

He crawled through the open doorway of the armory with the dog at his heels. She took a moment to check Tangela's breathing, then passed the girl to him and pushed the heavy door shut. The keypad turned red again.

Walter told her, "You can go in there too. There's not much you can do without a gun."

"I'm not getting stuck in there and not know what's happening. Let's just try to make it to the door, and get Ellis."

He nodded. "I'll go down this row, you go down the next."

Maryland scuttled forward on all fours. The partitions stood on little brass legs, leaving a gap at floor level. She could see Walter's hands as he crawled on the other aisle of desks.

She didn't know what exactly happened next. Blackness crowded out her vision. Her head came down against the rough carpet while her body was still moving, giving her a friction burn across the forehead. She stayed in this hunched position as time spun out, trying to find the will to get moving. The sound of gunfire brought her back.

Maryland straightened up enough to see. Walter had made it several desks farther, and was firing a burst at someone in the next row. The muzzle flashes lit up the room. She caught the shadow of their attacker as it ducked behind a computer monitor that exploded when Walter's bullets hit it. The figure popped right back up and squeezed off a single round in return.

Walter cried out, clutching at his shoulder. She saw his teeth come together and he made a buzzing *nnnnnn* sound as he dropped out of sight.

Running footsteps as their adversary circled around to her.

She crawled, looking under the cubicles until she spotted Walter. He lay on his side, the gun beside him. She slid into the tight space under the closest desk and reached through, trying to grab the weapon.

A hand closed around her ankle.

"No!" She thrashed and clawed at the cheap carpeting as she was dragged out. The gunman flipped her over, dropped a knee on her stomach, and then she felt the stingingly hot barrel of a gun against her chin. She stopped struggling and looked up at the face above her.

"CT?" she asked in relief. "You're Lincoln's cousin, right? Remember us, we were at the clinic with y—?"

"I know who the fuck you are!" he snarled. He was only two years or so older than Chris, but it had been two years of rough living. He looked like an animal now, eyes jittery and blood crusted at the corners of his mouth. There was a manic energy about him, and she remembered how he'd been trying to steal drugs from Kordi.

My God, he's higher than a kite. Like stratosphere, gone.

"Get movin, back to the door!"

His weight lifted. She was too disoriented to do anything but comply, but when she tried to stand, he shoved her back over with his foot and made her crawl back toward the armory. He walked behind her and crooned, "Mmm, that's a sweet little piece. I *defin'ly* want a turn befo' Sturney gets holda you."

The name rocked her. Ellis, and his damn rogue cops. The man from the clinic whose hand had disappeared like a magician's rabbit when she pulled the trigger on the shotgun. She didn't understand the how's or why's, only enough to realize things had just gotten so much worse for them. "Oh Jesus," she moaned.

"That's right, him and me're runnin the show up in here! *I'm* the boss now, just like I told 'em I would be! And he's out there takin care of yo pig friend right now!"

When they reached the door, he made her sit beside it while he brought Walter. The man was conscious but in pain, his glasses cracked. He held the wound in his chest and looked over at her with glossy eyes.

CT banged on the door to the armory. "Open up! I got both yo' friends!"

"Don't do it, Hernie!"

The black kid turned and grabbed her by the cheeks, squishing her face into parody. "What's the code to get in there?"

"Go to hell, you little weasel!"

Without hesitation, he put his gun to Walter's other shoulder and pulled the trigger. Blood exploded against the wall behind him in a Rorschach pattern. Walter screamed. So did Maryland.

"You gonna tell me now, bee-yitch?"

"*Why are you doing this? What did we ever do to you?*"

He didn't answer. There hardly seemed enough of a human being left inside him to formulate a rational response. He turned back and kicked at the heavy door in a frenzy, screeching, "*You hear that, muhfuckah? I'm gonna keep shootin off pieces if you don't open...this...DOOR!*"

There was a long moment of silence, in which Maryland prayed Hernie was smart enough to stay barricaded inside. She imagined him in there, hitting his head as he tried to decide what to do. Then the light at the keypad turned green, and the door swung open. Hernie looked out timidly.

"D-don't hurt my friends."

CT shot Walter once more without even looking, in the middle of the chest this time. He jerked once and then slumped, leaving a red smear on the wall.

"I give the orders around here, retard!"

"You son of a bitch, *he has a family!*" Maryland tried to hit him, but he pushed her back down.

"Bring that girl and get out here."

"Leave her alone!"

Hernie came out and stood holding Tangela, wrapped in her security blanket. Hatch followed, growling with hackles raised.

"Yo man, keep that dog the fuck away from me!"

"Listen, we know what the disease is now," Maryland pleaded. "Just let us get one of the oxygen tanks out of the armory. Tangela is going to die if you don't! We all will, even you!"

"You ain't gettin nothin 'til Sturney says! Now get up! Let's go, alla you, *move!*"

They left Walter's body, and the boy walked them at gunpoint back out of the squad room. In the lobby, they went to the right, through a hall opposite the garage. She looked back at the door. Had Ellis heard the gunshots? Was he even still alive?

After going through another corridor, they entered a long, harshly-lit room with two rows of jail cells facing one another, the paint on the bars fresh and white. Another set of swinging doors stood at the far end, marked "Showers." As CT forced them in, someone in a cell on the right jumped to the door and stuck an arm through.

"Maryland!"

"Carter?"

"He's working with the guys from the clinic, the ones that killed Dr. Kordi!"

"I know!"

CT planted a hand in Hernie's back and shoved him and Tangela inside the tiny cell across from Carter's. Hatch bared his teeth. The boy delivered a brutal kick to the dog's hindquarters. He yelped and jumped inside with his master. CT slammed the door shut on its sliding track. For the first time, Maryland noticed the ring of keys dangling from the bottom of the gunbelts around his waist.

He turned to her, grabbed her by the throat, and drove her back until she hit the metal bars next to Carter's cell. The pressure on her throat was just too much. She tried to cough and choked; her eyes rolled back as she fought against unconsciousness. She could hear Carter shouting for him to leave her alone.

"Where's my cuz?" CT growled, letting up just enough for air to seep into her lungs. "Where's Links? I want him and Mac, they supposed to be *mine*, Sturney said so!"

"They-they both went after Ellis' partner. We haven't seen them since."

"Yeah…That's what yo' boyfriend over there said." He leaned close enough for their lips to brush, reeking of body odor and another, muskier smell that she could only associate with stark raving insanity. "*You* belong to Sturney…but he said I could have some fun while he finishes his other bidness. He *really* wants you ta hurt."

She rasped, filament-thick strands of gooey blood running from her mouth and nostrils. She might not have worked a day in her life since she married Bryce, but she was on P3's clock now, and it was almost quitting time. "Maybe that's because I forced him to jerk off with his left hand for the rest of his life. Which I sincerely hope is short."

The black boy snickered. "You don't look like you gonna make it too much longer, either. Maybe we better get the party started now."

"If you touch her, I swear to God, I'll kill you!" Carter waved a fist through the bars of the cell beside them.

CT ignored him and pressed the gun hard into her ribcage. She barely felt it. "Whacha ya think, baby? Wanna give him a show?"

She closed her eyes. "Not here. Not in front of the girl. Please."

"A'ight. You want a private room for me to tap that ass? Let's go."

Maryland Decatur would've pleaded; the Mary Williams that existed before her would've cried in terror. But the new and improved Maryland just led the way to her rape while the voices of her friends echoed off the cold jail walls.

WHITNEY +35:16

The tubular sewer passages reminded Lincoln of the maintenance tunnels beneath the Dome, except much smaller and tighter. After crawling down the metal ladder and then lowering Charlie through the manhole, they found only a foot or so of liquid in the bottom, but it looked like flooding rather than sewage. Even the smell wasn't bad. He wasn't about to live here any time soon, but they could do a lot worse for an escape route even though they had to keep their heads ducked as they ran.

Strangled cries bounced through the sewer tunnels in hot pursuit, a sound like the gobbling of a turkey. No light down here except dawn breaking through the overflow grates they passed. Lincoln didn't even know where they were going, he just kept splashing down the corridor with Charlie's arm slung around his neck, past branch-offs and tunnel intersections, trying not to cough.

"Wait, stop!" Charlie told them, after they hurried by another offshoot.

"I don't think stoppin's such a good idea." The warbling of the monster seemed to come from right behind them, but when Lincoln looked back all he could see was the tunnel ending in black gloom a few yards back. The echoes in here were too confusing.

"It is if you don't wanna get lost down here. Take me over to the wall."

They carried the cop over. Watery morning light shone through a curbside drain above them, revealing gunmetal gray walls covered in rust and dark green mold. An aluminum plate was screwed into the wall. Charlie let go of Mac and reached out with a shaking hand to brush at the grime caked on it.

Lincoln had to squint to make out the writing engraved on it. An arrow pointed at the tunnel intersection next to them with the word "Sunset," and two others pointed both directions in their corridor, with "Tilton 1500" marking one, and the other with "Tilton 1600".

"What is it?" Mac whispered.

"Directions. This is how the sewage maintenance workers find their way around down here."

"How do you know that?"

"I helped look for a kid that went missing down here a few years back. This means we're under Tilton, right at the sixteen-hundred block. Sunset Terrace is that way, meanin we need to make a turn. We're almost to my precinct."

A series of quick splashes echoed in the tunnel from all directions.

"Go!" Mac yelled.

Lincoln turned into the branch-off, pushing and panting, dragging Charlie, who tried to use his one good leg to hobble as much as possible. Mac ran backward to watch their rear.

"Is it coming?" Lincoln asked.

"I don't know, I can't see shit!"

Ahead was another four-way intersection of tunnel branches. Lincoln dragged Charlie straight through.

He caught sight of a hulking shadow against the side wall of the passage to their right. It uncurled, releasing spindly limbs, and came slithering at them.

"Look out!" He jumped ahead, trying to pull Charlie with him, but the weight was too uneven. Both of them crashed into the hard floor, sending a wave of rank water over their faces.

The monster squealed as it entered the tunnel, separating them from Mac. That rotten fish smell was nauseating in the enclosed space. Lincoln turned over in time to see the slimy thing standing over him, its body perfectly still but its head turning from side-to-side with quick precision. At first he was puzzled by the birdlike actions, but then a dribble of black ichor ran out of its empty eye sockets to splatter on his knee, and he understood.

It was listening. Swiveling its head like a radar dish.

Lincoln could see Mac under the thing's arm, creeping backward one slow step at a time. The creature quested out with one of its deformed hands, putting it against the slick, curved wall and feeling downward like a blind man with a cane. Lincoln eased his foot out of the way before it could touch his sneaker.

Charlie choked on a cough next to him.

The creature went berserk, throwing its arms in wide arcs as it had in the mausoleum. Lincoln scooted away. He grabbed Charlie's arm and tried to pull him further up the tunnel, but the monster's claws found the meat of his thigh and latched on. The cop screamed as it tugged him toward the depths of the black tunnel it had come from.

Mac jumped on it from behind, bringing his hands down in a combined fist right on the back of its lumpy head. The creature gave a squawk of either surprise or pain and lurched forward, then dropped its catch to spin around. It hissed and scuttled down the tunnel toward Mac, slashing out blindly. He was forced to back up.

"Go on!" He narrowly avoided a flash of claws across his face. "Get to the precinct, I'll lead this thing away and catch up to you!"

Lincoln wanted to call out, but couldn't risk bringing the thing back after them. Mac disappeared into the darkness, with the monster chasing after him.

Lincoln went to Charlie, who was sobbing as he grabbed at his new injury. It was the same leg as his bullet wound. The back of the muscle was shredded; he would undoubtedly lose the appendage. As Lincoln knelt beside him, the cop coughed out a stream of blood into the water.

"C'mon Charlie, you gotta get up!"

"I can't, I can't go on, just l-leave me here—!"

"Goddamn it Charlie, I ain't playin with you, get the fuck up! I gotta go back for Mac as soon as I get you someplace safe!" Lincoln slid an arm under him and lifted. After a few minutes of grunting and struggling, Charlie was once again upright. He hopped down the tunnel, hanging from Lincoln's neck.

They continued for another few minutes, stopping to check the direction plaques mounted on the wall at every intersection. The water got deeper and more filth-ridden, and the flow picked up speed. Lincoln started to get scared they might be swept away. Finally the tunnel flattened drastically and flowed out into a series of sprawling parallel concourses separated by heavy mesh. Thick concrete columns ran from the sewer floor up to a low, concrete ceiling. They would have to drop to hands and knees to go on, and crawl through the rank sludge.

"This has gotta be the substructure for the precinct!"

"I can't go in there, Charlie!"

"We have to!"

They got down and slid into the narrow space. Charlie was able to pull himself along behind Lincoln. There was barely enough room to keep their heads above water, breathing the foul air that hung against the ceiling. If the level in here rose at all, they would drown. The confined quarters made Lincoln's brain burn with panic.

He saw light ahead, probably just a dribble but startlingly bright in the sunless world beneath the city. It came through a square drain above them, about two feet wide. They worked their way under it and looked up into a tiled room.

"That's the prisoner hosedown!" Charlie exclaimed.

Lincoln hooked his fingers through the grate. It was solid and bolted from the other side. "It won't budge!" The desperation he heard in his own voice just heightened his claustrophobia.

"It's to keep people from gettin out, not in! If we smash at it from this side, without that concrete lip giving it support, we should be able to force the damn thing open!"

Lincoln didn't waste time talking; he had to get some fresh air before he blacked out. He turned over on his back in the filthy water, braced his head against the nearest concrete post to keep from drowing, and kicked at the grate corners with the heels of his sneakers.

He'd already gotten two loose when a distant, anguished scream rolled through the dank sewer system.

"Mac," he whispered, then went back to work.

WHITNEY +35:19

"C'mon bitch, *come and get me!*" Mac taunted, reliving the playground days of Marco Polo with a creature that looked like it crawled out of the ugly end of the primordial ooze. "I'm the one that caused you to pop your eyeballs, muhfuckah!"

Its blind head swiveled toward every sound, drool and bloody pus running out of various holes in its face. It seemed to be adjusting to its blindness. Mac ran backward for a while, leaping out of the way every time it fired an arm out, but then it snarled and darted forward in frustration, and he bolted flat out with his back hunched in the low tunnel.

He had a plan. No way was he letting this thing take him out in a fucking sewer, not when there was a perfectly good army topside willing to blow him away, and a disease eating holes in his lungs and throat. Fishboy back there would have to wait his turn.

He would go a block or two down, lead this thing away, maybe lose it altogether. He would go in a big circle, and hopefully Lincoln and Charlie would have the way cleared for him.

Mac took the first left turn he came to. He couldn't seem to gain any ground, and he was so exhausted. The beast stayed on his ass, crawling on all fours through the muck lining the bottom of the sewer. Its gibbering echoed all around, like madhouse nonsense. He could see no more than a few feet in front of him, so Mac concentrated on making sure each running step splashed down solid and his cough reflex didn't overpower him.

There would be another turn ahead. It would take him back to the original tunnel, and then he would go after Lincoln. He had told his best friend that he could get out of the gang life, make something of himself, but hell, Mac was only *nineteen* himself, and he still had shit to do.

He just had to outrun this thing. Overcome. Some people had monkeys on their back; he had a fucking alligator.

Mac poured on the speed, running toward his new life, and stumbled when the tunnel widened out into a small, square room where he could stand upright again.

This was a dead end. An overflow grate along the right hand

side of the ceiling gave him enough light to see, but it was far too narrow for his wide torso to fit through.

The back wall was a few yards ahead. He stopped in front of it, put his palms on it as though to verify its reality. He was panting hard, each breath wet and coppery with blood.

A scuttling noise came from behind him, followed by a soft coo like a pigeon.

He turned.

The monster emerged from the mouth of the tunnel, its empty eye sockets boring into him. It went slowly, taking its time now, seeming to sense the dead end that had trapped its quarry. Mac wondered if those warbles were a kind of sonar. If so, then the loss of its eyes wasn't so much a setback as a nuisance.

For the first time since they'd encountered this creature, he had time to study it. It was an amalgam of parts, the animal kingdom's version of Frankenstein. Scale-plated skin a mottled green and brown and purple. Shimmery somehow, like oil in a rain puddle. A head and broad tail with the vague shape of a gator, spiny quills jutting from its back and sides that reminded him of the venomous spikes on a lionfish. Something about its underbelly and the way it carried itself was like a snake, but its darting movements were entirely birdlike. Its breathing sounded as broken and painful as his own.

As he watched, it planted the webbed appendages of its feet in the chamber doorway and spread its thick, ropy arms out.

Charlie was wrong. The thing *was* intelligent.

It came forward a step at a time. Its gnarled fingers left barely a foot of clearance to either side. Mac would have to duck under or brush by the thing to get out of here, and then it would be on him. He was afraid to even breathe.

There was really only one thing he could do.

Mac stepped forward, cocked one of his huge fists, and let fly. The blow glanced off the side of its toothy muzzle and rocked its blind head back. It slashed out at him. He sidestepped.

"You cocksuckah, let's do this!" Mac brought a foot up and kicked it in the rough skin of its belly. He jabbed at it again, aiming for its throat, and caught it instead in the temple as it whipped around. It roared and stepped back. They circled, moving around the outer edge of the room, and if he could just keep this up until he reached the exit…

He tried to punch it once more, but it was ready. When the blow landed under its long chin, one of its arms whipped up, grabbing him around the wrist. Its other appendage wrapped around his neck and pulled him close. His face was shoved against its broad chest, the scales rough on his skin.

Sudden, sharp pain ripped into him as it bent his arm the wrong direction. Its strength was phenomenal. His elbow shattered, shards of bone shredding the skin. Mac bellowed, screaming until his lungs hemorrhaged and blood flowed from his open mouth. He didn't want to die, but he figured as long as Lincoln had gotten away, it was worth it.

He leaned his head back. The vision in his left eye was almost gone, but he could still see up into the creature's slimy face.

"I bet…I taste…like shit."

Mac thought the creature grinned just before it wrapped those enormous jaws around his neck, and pulled most of his spinal column out.

WHITNEY +35:24

Ellis ducked beside the bumper of the S.W.A.T. van. Pulled the Beretta from his waistband. He had no idea how many bullets he even had left in the weapon. He strained his eyes in the dim garage, scanning the catwalk that ringed the upper part of the room near the windows. Sunny morning light streamed through them, filtered through dirt-streaked panes of glass.

"Sturney! We know what's going on! We know who the soldiers are and what this disease is! I can help you!"

A loud *SP-TANG* off the metal bumper next to his shoulder. The crack of the shot didn't even register. Ellis threw himself into the several inches of water on the floor and crawled into the wide space beneath the vehicle.

"Oh, you can help me, Wright? You can give me back the life ya stole from me? Cause a you, I'm never gonna see my kids again! Cause a you, I gotta run from this city with my tail between my legs!"

Pure, undistilled anger walloped Ellis. From under the van, he yelled, "I didn't steal a goddamned thing from you, you fat piece of shit! *You're* the crooked cop! Did you think you'd be able to go around robbing and murdering drug dealers forever without any consequences?"

More shots, splashing into the water on the right side of the van. At least now he knew which side of the room the man was on. Ellis slunk to the edge and peeked out at the rafters, waiting for him to speak again.

"I *RUN* THIS GODDAMN TOWN!" The fury in his voice was uncontrolled. "And I ain't gonna let you change that just cause you think you know the badge better!"

Ellis saw the rotund shadow up there, leaning over the railing to shout at him. He took careful aim and fired.

He couldn't see where the shot went. Sturney swung around one of the narrow catwalk support beams and took shelter behind a stack of boxes with a curse about Ellis' mother.

"I have other people here, Sturney, all of them with guns! When they get back, you'll be fighting all of us! Just throw your weapon out and come down! You're the only one that wants this to end in bloodshed!"

"You mean that li'l cunt that took my hand?" Sturney gave what was either a cough or a laugh. "Don't worry about yer friends! My new partner's takin good care of 'em! Got all the time in the world, you and me! So let's get this barbecue started!"

A small object the size of a baseball sailed over the railing of the catwalk. It bounced off the side of the van and clunked down into the water beside Ellis' face.

His jaw dropped.

They weren't the only ones dipping into the armory. Apparently, Sturney had already visited.

Ellis scooted the other direction, trying to claw his way from under the S.W.A.T. van as the riot grenade Sturney threw went off behind him.

WHITNEY +35:29

Carter raised a foot and kicked at the barred door of his cell over and over again. Yeah, it was juvenile, and resulted in little more than a bruised foot, but it was either that or go back to read-ing the graffiti off the cinderblock walls.

Maryland and Lincoln's cousin—who had apparently gone full Scarface from whatever drugs he was on—left five minutes and an eternity ago. The thought of something happening to her was un-bearable, and Carter had come to the decision that it would be his fault. Terror and guilt gnawed at him.

Congratulations, your first real *fear. Welcome back to the land of the Lucid.*

"Mr. Carter!" Hernie, in the cell across from him. He knelt by the bunk in his cell, leaning over Tangela. His hoarse, cough-wracked voice rang in the corridor. Everything in here was made of something hard, either brick or tile or steel, even that putrid toilet in the corner, right next to where the occupant of this cell was expected to sleep, and Carter couldn't help wondering why they always said prisoners wanted to come back. He'd been fighting to stay indoors for years, but less than an hour in this place made him yearn for wide open spaces. "Mr. Carter, what do we do?"

"It's okay, Hern-ster!" He reared back for another kick at the door, which barely quivered. "I'm gonna get us out of this!"

Carter stopped kicking and pulled at the bars instead, trying to pry them apart like Superman, and prayed for one of those adrena-line bursts that allowed mothers to lift cars off their children. He was only granted forearms that felt like warm tapioca. "Isn't there anyone else here that can let us out?"

"He killed Mr. Walter!"

"Aw, God. Where's the rest of the group?"

"They stayed at the big church! Only Officer Ellis came with us!"

"What about him, then? Where was the last place you saw him?"

Hernie didn't answer, and when Carter looked up from his fu-tile escape attempts, he found the younger man doing his *Rain Man* bit, rocking back and forth on the edge of the bunk and tapdancing on his temples.

"C'mon Hernie, stop doing that and answer me!"

"In the garage!"

A distant boom sounded through the corridor, rattling the doors to their cages. He might've been inclined to believe it was more thunder, if the ceiling hadn't rained down a fine mist of loosened plaster. The lights dimmed.

"Ah, what *now?*"

"Mr. Carter, Tangela has more blood coming out of her mouth!" Hatch howled along with his master.

"I know, Hernie, *what am I supposed to do?*" In utter frustration—and again, the need to take *some* kind of action—Carter stepped back to resume his pitiful kicks at the door.

This time, however, the clang of impact came first.

Carter stopped, foot raised behind him for the swing, and heard the noise again. It came from outside his cell, somewhere to the right. He smushed his face between the bars to get as wide a line of sight as possible. Another clank followed by a metallic squeal came from behind the closed doors leading to the inmate showers.

"Who's in there? Please, we need help!"

One of the double doors swung open cautiously, and the filth-streaked face of Lincoln Briggs peeked around the edge.

WHITNEY +35:32

CT stayed close behind Maryland, using one hand to press the gun into her back and the other to grope at her, squeezing her breasts and ass like he expected to find gold in them. She was too tired, numb, and sore to care. And anyway, it was a more adept showing than Bryce's idea of foreplay.

She was nearly dead on her feet, but as much as she hoped for it, unconsciousness stayed away. If this was really happening, she wanted to sleep through it.

They made their way back toward the lobby, but instead of going all the way to the muddy reception area, he pulled her through a side door into a stairwell. He forced her up, but after a few steps, even he seemed exhausted. They made it to the landing where the stairs turned back on themselves before he pushed her against the wall face first and then flattened his body against hers.

"Far 'nuff." He was a good foot and a half shorter than her, and the erection bulging in his baggy jeans hit her just above the knee.

So this was it: she was going to be raped by a midget crackhead on a stairwell like any typical New Yorker. She always figured if this happened to her, it would be more of the classier date rape variety, so at least she'd get a meal and drinks beforehand. Maryland giggled.

He stiffened against her and snarled, "We'll see how much you be laughin in a minute. Get those pants down, bitch."

There was a rumble from elsewhere in the building. The ground beneath their feet shook; the lights flickered. CT stepped away from her to look back down the stairwell. "What the—?"

She threw out an arm and shoved him. Her muscles were weak, the effort nearly enough to wind her, but he was unprepared. CT flailed at the edge of the stairs and then went over backward.

The fall was short and violent. His legs folded, bringing him down hard on his butt. He rolled down the last few risers on his side, giving short yelps and grunts. He hit bottom stretched out flat, still clutching the gun, but scrambled up again. Whatever drugs he was on had supercharged his system.

"*You fuckin dead, you ho!*" Against the orders of his new master, he fired the pistol up at her.

But Maryland was already gone, limping up the last half of the stairs toward the second floor.

WHITNEY +35:34

Lincoln pushed through the swinging doors, still supporting Charlie with one arm, leaving the bare shower room where they'd crawled from the flood control system. They hobbled down the tile corridor between the jail cells until they reached Carter.

"Lincoln, c'mon, c'mon, you have to get us out of here, *right now!*" Carter hit the bars of his cage to emphasize each word.

"What's goin on?" Lincoln wanted to laugh at the sight of him and Hernie, of all people, in lockup, but he was too afraid it would start him coughing. "Why you guys in there? With a dog?"

"Your psychotic cousin locked us up and took Maryland!"

"*CT?* He's here?"

"Yeah, and the kid's on enough drugs to make Hunter Thompson look like Mother Theresa! He's working with those crooked cops that came to the clinic!"

"Slow down, that don't make no sense!"

"*We don't have TIME to slow down!*" Carter bellowed. "There's only one of them now, the fat one! He promised your cousin he'd get him out of the city or something! They're going to kill Ellis too, if they haven't already! Just let us out so we can find them!"

Lincoln put a hand against the metal. "Charlie, how do we open these?"

"If the electronic locks are out, you gotta have a key. All of 'em were taken when they cleared out the precinct before Whitney except for one spare ring, but damned if I know where it would be."

"CT has it, I saw it on his belt!" Carter gripped the bars so hard his knuckles stood out in white lumps. "Where's Lemiere? Maybe he can jimmy the lock or something!"

"Lemiere's dead. We been chased halfway across the city by the soldiers and some kinda fish monster! We left Mac in the sewers with it just a few minutes ago! I gotta go back for him!"

Carter reached through the cell door and grabbed Lincoln's hand. "Please. He said…he was going to rape her. We know what the disease is and who the soldiers are. We have an actual shot at saving ourselves. Please don't let this happen to her."

His face beneath the rebreather mask was broken and desperate, and Lincoln suddenly understood something that had slipped by him before: the hypochondriac was in love with Miss Richie Rich, to a degree he probably didn't even realize himself.

As much as he wanted to go after Mac (except that scream told him—deep in his heart, where even the most awful truths can't be denied—that there was nothing *left* to go after), Lincoln couldn't say no. CT was his problem, a rabid dog that should've been put down long ago.

"A'ight. I'll take care of it."

He helped Charlie into the cell next door and lowered him onto the bunk. His leg was still dripping blood. "You gonna be okay?"

"Sure, kid. But don't you go after Sturney. That guy is way outta your league."

Lincoln tried to leave, but the man caught him by the shirttail. "I'm sorry about your friend."

He said nothing, because anything would just be a confirmation he couldn't deal with yet. He left the cell door open and headed toward the other end of the holding block. Just before he went through, Carter yelled, "I don't know where they went, but he's not playing around!"

"Neither am I."

WHITNEY +35:35

The grenade went off as Ellis used the door handle of the next vehicle over to pull himself up.

Riot bombs were made for concussion, light and sound, a souped-up flashbang, but Chief Tyler had ordered them discontinued because the explosions did too much damage at close proximity.

The shockwave pitched him forward into the patrol car. He shattered the driver's window with his chest and took a bruising blow from the door frame in the neck. The rear end of the S.W.A.T. van behind him jumped a foot in the air, the back corner swinging around and denting the side of the patrol car; another foot closer and it would've been his torso. The sudden noise was so loud it shorted out his hearing. He spat blood.

Ellis stumbled out of the open end of the V formed by the two vehicles now. The grenade had also damaged the generators, probably from flinging high velocity debris. Even from across the garage, he could see the outer casings were punctured and several of the industrial cables shredded. Both threw sparks of electricity and billowed caustic electrical smoke.

Sturney jogged around the catwalk, trying to get to a new position. Ellis could hear his footsteps on the metal walkway. "That li'l riot buster didn't kill ya, did it? Wouldn't want the fun to end yet!"

Ellis swung his gun around the upper part of the room, trying to get a fix on the man's location. He worried that gunfire might bring Aurora down on them, but if the explosion hadn't already done it, this couldn't make it much worse. Too late, he spotted the barrel of a shotgun leaning out from the railing above him just before it went off.

He was peppered with a thousand tiny balls that raised painful welts and ricocheted off the side of the S.W.A.T. van hard enough to leave divots in the black metal. Rubber buckshot; Sturney had opted for all the non-lethal methods to stretch out the pain.

His body slowly turning into one big bruise, Ellis stumbled back against the van. The pistol—his only weapon—slipped through his fingers and plopped into the water at his feet.

WHITNEY +35:37

The door from the second floor landing of the stairwell led onto a dark, sweltering hallway with nothing but closed doors on either side. Maryland pelted down the corridor, unable to catch a full breath and sounding like a hiccupping pig. The sounds of CT's pursuit echoed up the stairs after her.

A larger staircase waited at the far end of the hall, ascending to the ruined third floor of the precinct. Wispy daylight streamed through, but she didn't think she'd be able to make it before her pursuer was in firing distance. She rattled knobs as she went, but all the doors were locked.

She finally found one ajar and slipped inside just as the stairwell door slammed open. She eased it shut and searched for a lock, but there wasn't one. Maryland wiped sweat out of her face, stuck a fist to her mouth to muffle her coughing, and hurriedly took in the small room she had chosen for her last stand.

Its construction was easily recognizable. A small desk and chair on the far side, and a bench immediately in front of her, facing a dark-frosted window that took up half the wall. On the other side of the glass was a larger area with its own entry from the hallway, containing nothing but a metal table and four chairs.

An interrogation room. The glass probably looked like a mirror from the other side.

BANG, BANG! "*Where you at, bitch?*"

Maryland jumped. The voice and gunshots came from right outside the door, undoubtedly intended to flush her out. She crouched behind the desk and opened drawers in search of a weapon.

Quick footsteps passed her hiding spot, toward the far end of the hall, then came back this way. She picked up the desk lamp and turned it over, preparing to use its heavy base as a bludgeon. She moved back to the door, put her back against the glass, and waited with her weapon held over her head.

A door opened elsewhere. She could hear him moving close by, trying to stay quiet.

A shadow flitted over her shoulder.

Maryland spun. Somehow kept from screaming. He stood inches away, face pressed against the one-way glass, trying to peer through. She reached for the door knob to run while he was distracted.

A convulsion hit her like a jolt of electricity.

Maryland tottered back. Something clenched in his midsection, a fist that grabbed her guts and squeezed. She bent and wretched, letting loose a steady stream of thick blood from her mouth with as much pressure as a garden hose. Her vision grayed at the edges. A horrible fire raged through her as every muscle in her body cramped.

"No. Not like this."

She thought of Heather, a woman her own age that she'd barely known, whose blood had spilled across her hands. Of poor Tom, dying on the floor of a church thousands of miles from his home while he was supposed to be on vacation.

She would rather let the crazy crackhead shoot her than die from Garmon's P3.

Maryland crawled toward the door as the cramps sank their claws into her.

WHITNEY +35:41

"Mr. Carter, my throat hurts so bad, and Tangela's still bleeding! What do I do?"

Carter put his head against the bars. "Hernie, I can't do anything from here! Just hold on and Lincoln will be back with the keys in a minute!"

He heard the cop in the next cell grunt, "Let me take a look at her."

"I don't know, you're on your last leg yourself—no pun intended. Maybe you should just stay still."

"I've been shot and dragged across the city, chased by soldiers in biohazard outfits and some damn thing that looked like the Creature from the Black Lagoon's uglier cousin, and I just got finished crawlin through most of Port Allen's crap. If I ain't dead yet, I think I can make it over there."

Carter gave a weary grin and watched as the officer limped to the door of Hernie's cell. He grabbed the bars for support, his face screwing up every time his bad leg jostled. "Here, bring her over to me."

As he reached through the bars, Carter asked, "So you're Ellis' partner?"

"Yeah, Charlie Van Ness."

"I'm Carter. That's Hernie and Tangela." There was a low *woof* from the floor. "And Hatch."

Hernie held the girl up, wrapped in that blanket, while Charlie checked her over. "What's with the mask?"

Carter sighed laughter. "It's a drool cup. I spit a lot when I talk. Is she okay?"

"She's barely conscious, but she's alive. She got this same sickness Lincoln was tellin me about?"

"Everybody does, including you. And if you don't get your very own drool cup pretty soon, you're gonna be just as bad off."

Charlie leaned against the front of the cell, forehead bathed in sweat. The guy shook so bad, he practically vibrated. "You saw this monster?"

"At the Dome, during the rush for the doors."

"It actually came out *into* the center? Around all those people?"

"It didn't strike me as the bashful type. Why?"

"I assumed we were safe after we got outta the sewers, but if it was willin to show itself in there…"

A warbling screech bounced through the holding cell corridor from the direction of the showers. Something in there scratched and scrabbled at the tiles.

"Oh God, you brought it here. Right to us." Carter shrank into the shadows.

Charlie hobbled back to his own cell. "Not a word! It can't find you if it can't hear you!"

He just made it back inside when the door to the showers swung open again, but this time a nightmare crept through.

WHITNEY +35:42

Lincoln followed the signs that pointed to the lobby, and almost passed the stairwell door until the sound of gunfire drew him back.

He took the stairs two at a time and eased into the second floor corridor. Everything was quiet up here, all the doors closed, and he worked his way toward the opposite side, where the hallway opened onto an elevator lobby and a high-ceilinged reception area for the office of someone important. A fancy staircase ascended to the third floor, and Lincoln could see bright morning sunlight filtering down.

A door creaked open behind him.

CT stalked into the corridor, muttering under his breath. There was a pistol clutched in one bone-thin hand. He saw Lincoln standing at the far end, and his snarling face melted into a smile.

"Hey cuz." The boy hopped from foot to foot, like a marathon runner warming up. Every part of him seemed constantly in motion. He would crash out hard from this trip, if he ever came down at all. "Didn't think you was comin."

Lincoln shrugged casually, but the sight of the gun turned his insides cold. For the moment, the weapon was still pointed at the ground. Lincoln made a conscious effort to keep his eyes locked on his cousin's, but it was hard when they jittered so much. "Yeah, here I am. Glad you made it, too. I was worried when you disappeared."

"Bull-*fuckin*-shit." CT shook his head and swung his arm out like he was trying to punch an invisible person. "You prob'ly didn't even give me a second thought. Too busy butt-fuckin Mac, like always. He here?"

"He's dead." The simplicity in the answer stung him.

The boy's wicked smile grew even wider. He sputtered and used the back of his free hand to swipe at something wet across his lips, blood or drool. "Good. I hope it was *real* painful."

"Where's Maryland?"

"Don't know. Bitch got away from me."

Lincoln raised his palms. "CT…what are you doin? You workin with that cop that tried to kill us?"

CT performed an odd, shuffling victory dance. "That's right! Muhfuckah ain't so bad, neither! He got enough drugs to last me fo'*evah*, and he gonna set me up down south! I'm gonna be a dealer, big time!" He jabbed the pistol at Lincoln. "See, I don't need you! You ain't nuttin but a punk!"

His cousin advanced, and Lincoln backed toward the staircase. "You don't actually believe that, do you? He gonna kill you as soon as he done with us."

CT's face drew together, teeth bared. He brought the gun up again and held it on Lincoln this time. The barrel wavered. "*Shut the fuck up, Links! You don't know jack shit! I'm the Boss, I'm the Big Man! Fuckin bulletproof! No one's gonna treat me like a little errand boy evah again!*"

"It ain't like that." Part of Lincoln still hoped to talk some sense into him, but another, deeper part had known this was coming. His heel was against the first stair leading up to that bright third floor, and CT was seven or eight yards away, closing the distance. "I always treated you with respect, even when the rest of the crew was laughin at you! Now put down the gun! That's an *order*, Tyrone!"

"That's the last time you gonna say that, fool!"

Lincoln turned and climbed the stairs almost on hands and knees. A bullet hole appeared in the riser to the left of his head, but he didn't stop. The sound of CT's gun followed him all the way, but every wild shot missed. The sunlight grew brighter until Lincoln burst out onto the plane of the third floor and blinked around in confusion.

No ceiling up here, and only a few broken walls; Whitney had ripped them all way, leaving a splintered, sagging platform with a few overturned desks and chairs and a layer of debris covering everything from edge to edge. The sky was a beautiful shade of aquamarine, barely a cloud to impede his view of the city. Light wind whistled across the barren surface of the missing third floor, stirring scattered paper.

As his murderous cousin closed in, Lincoln hurried out onto it, searching for some place to hide.

WHITNEY +35:43

Ellis knelt to search for the gun just as a pair of shoes splashed up next to him.

He came up swinging. A fist grazed along Sturney's jaw, but Ellis' head still reeled too much to put any force into it. Sturney's one hand whipped around in a solid sucker-punch directly into his stomach. He doubled over.

"Boy oh boy, Wright, why'dja even become a cop? Ya got about as much guts as a Thanksgiving turkey." Sturney grabbed the back of his neck and brought his knee up into the center of Ellis' face.

The agony was excruciating. He felt his lips split; several teeth snapped. He fell into the water in a crumpled ball. His back wound started up, his finger throbbed, every part of him hummed in tune with the torturous symphony his face conducted.

Sturney stood over him, ghoulish, blood dripping from his mouth. He coughed in a consistent string, his cheeks puffing rhythmically as he tried to hold them back. He lifted the blunt end of his right arm, covered in garbage bags and duct tape.

"I don't even need this ta take ya apart. I'm still more man than you'll ever be."

"Yeah…" Ellis caught his breath through the bloody hole that used to be his mouth. "A thousand donuts a day'll do that to you."

He pistoned out with his foot, catching Sturney in the knee-cap. The man roared. Ellis flopped onto his stomach and crawled through the swamp under the S.W.A.T. van, toward the open expanse of garage on the other side. The room was filling up with black smoke from the damaged generators, making him want to cough even more. He needed some distance, some time to think and regroup…

Sturney dropped and came after him under the vehicle, dragging himself along with one hand and the elbow of his amputated limb. He looked feral, his visage twisted with the desire to destroy, to kill. Ellis remembered that look from the night he'd killed the two kids in Bedford Park. He grabbed hold of Ellis' leg and sank his teeth into the calf right through his uniform pants. Ellis screamed and shook him loose, but the hand stayed firm around his ankle.

Further under the van, he spotted the duffel bag; it must've fallen out when the vehicle was jarred by the grenade. Ellis stretched forward and drew out one of the white bricks of packaged heroine. He twisted around with it still in his hand.

"You want this? This is what it was all about, why you killed Billy and Dr. Kordi and those two kids? Then TAKE IT!" He smashed the packet into Sturney's upturned face. The shrink wrapping tore, and a cloud of white powder billowed out. Ellis grabbed more, one after another, and threw them over his shoulder, spraying millions of dollars in narcotics across the wet floor.

"*Nooooo!*" Sturney released Ellis to grab at the stuff, as though he could catch every white flake.

Ellis started crawling again, but made it only as far as the other side of the van before Sturney's entire bulk fell on his back, crushing him, and a forearm shoved his face down into the oily water.

WHITNEY +35:44

If he went to the far right side of his cell, Hernie could see the creature slinking up the aisle. Its smell preceded it, a tang so volatile it made his eyes water. Bulky on two legs, slightly hunched, skin a mottled green that glistened with perpetual moisture as the dim lights played over it. He remembered it from the Dome. As it got closer, feeling along the front of each cage with gnarled, webby hands, he had to fight to keep from whimpering.

Across from his cell, Mr. Carter pressed into the shadows. Officer Charlie held a finger to his mouth. At first Hernie didn't understand, but the more he watched the monster, the more he thought of some half-remembered cartoon mole from his youth, a mostly blind character forced to use its hands as eyes.

Tangela lay curled on the bunk, breaths quick and shallow. He stood in front of her, and reached down to give Hatch a pat on the head. The dog's lips curled away from his teeth, but he gave not a single growl.

The creature had almost reached them. Hernie could see two empty, blood-rimmed holes where eyes should be. Its head bobbed back and forth in a figure-eight motion. Scaly arms stretched toward both rows of cell doors, and its claws made a *tik-tik-tik* sound as they trailed across the metal bars. Otherwise, the room was silent, and Hernie caught his breath and held it tight.

He squeezed his eyes shut when it passed in front of him. The cloud of fishy stench burned in his nostrils. He heard the monster give a snort before launching into a fit of machine-gun fast squeaks.

Hatch cowered against Hernie's leg and released a puddle of urine across the concrete floor.

The creature continued past. Hernie opened his eyes in time to see a broad, bumpy tail drag past his cell.

Behind him, Tangela moaned in her unconscious slumber.

The monster flew back and thrust its hideous face against the bars, snarling and snapping. It jammed an arm through to grasp blindly at him. In the shallow cell, Hernie felt the edges of its blood-stained claws brush along his chest and threw himself back on the bunk next to Tangela before it could snatch him.

The room erupted. Hatch began to bark, Mr. Carter yelled from across the way, and someone was screaming, but Hernie realized that was just himself. The monster gave off high-pitched screeches and strained against the bars, slashing at the air.

Hernie pushed Tangela as far back as possible, and shielded her with his body. "Go away! You can't have her!"

Even stretching out as far as it could, the creature was still about two feet short of reaching him. It drew back its arm and beat at the cell bars. Hernie watched as they bent and twisted out of shape.

WHITNEY +35:45

Charlie could see only the beast's broad back as it battered the holding cell with the mentally challenged guy and the little girl. Muscles rippled beneath its flesh; the thing was a *powerhouse*. Already the floor-to-ceiling steel bars had developed crooked angles. In a matter of seconds, the creature would be able to just force its way in.

"HEY!" Charlie heard the guy in the cage next to him scream. "HEY, OVER HERE YOU SCI-FI CHANNEL REJECT, COME AND GET *ME!*" It paid no attention.

Charlie's cell door was still open. Because of the narrow width of the aisle, the creature was forced to jam its massive girth sideways. Its tail swished around in the opening of his cell. Before thoughts of his fatherless kids could enter his head, he limped over and slammed the door as hard as he could, squashing the tip of the appendage.

The creature snarled. Turned on him. They faced one another from mere feet away, and God, it was even uglier in the light. The cell door had rebounded off the monster's flesh, and Charlie tried to push it all the way shut to lock himself in.

It thrust a hand into the gap, caught the door, shoved it back the other way. Charlie backed away as far as he could, mesmerized by the brutish freak that stood at least a foot taller than him. He tore his eyes away long enough to look around for refuge, but the cell just wasn't big enough to hide in.

As it entered the small space, Charlie hoped the few seconds he had bought the others would be enough for a miracle.

WHITNEY +35:46

It grabbed Officer Charlie by the shoulders and lifted him off the ground.

Hernie wanted to close his eyes again, but they were glued open. The monster squeezed. Bones broke audibly as Officer Charlie's rib cage collapsed. He shrieked.

"Hernie!" Mr. Carter shouted from his cell. "Hernie, can you get out?"

He probably could. The thing had bashed apart the bars of his cell like they were no more than plastic straws. He could slip right through the wide gap and run while it had its back turned.

But not with Tangela. He would have to either push her out first or try to drag her behind him as he went through, and even he understood that either option would take up more time than they had.

He would have to leave her.

In the diagonal cell, the monster had turned Officer Charlie into a mushy, pulpy shape. His head had swollen from the pressure on his torso, blood pouring from every orifice. He hung limp from its grasp. It grabbed his head and smashed it against the wall, like an exclamation point to the whole attack.

"Hernie, RUN!"

He wasn't going to run…but there was someone else that could.

"Go Hatch!" Hernie pointed at the gap in the bars. "Jump through!"

The Lab never hesitated. He reared back and leapt out of the cell, almost skidding into the monster when he landed. Hatch jumped away as it swiped at him. He ran, barking his head off and crashing through the swinging door out of the holding cell area.

The monster screeched in fury and started after him, moving fast and low to the ground. The sounds of their chase faded down the hallway.

"I'm really beginning to like that dog!" Mr. Carter stuck an arm out of his cell and gestured. "Hernie, take Tangela and get out, right now!"

"Mr. Carter, I can't! She's so sick!"

"Then leave both of us and *go!*"

"No! I won't do it!"

He sat down beside the little girl and cradled her head as she coughed up blood.

WHITNEY +35:47

Tyrone Clancy—once C-Tone or CT to those close to him—no longer felt pain of any kind, not even that constant soreness in his throat. The shit Sturney had given him was Grade A product, the kind you needed connections to get your hands on. But beyond that, he was the Boss now, and he figured feeling this good was just a perk of being in charge. He was *flying*. And even though he'd forgotten what he was doing and even who he was a couple of times in the last few minutes, there was still one thought burning through that beautiful haze loud and clear:

Lincoln Briggs had to die. His cousin had stood in the way of his evolution—his *destiny*—for long enough.

CT charged up the staircase, emerging into the open trash dump of the third floor. The destruction hardly even registered; his vision, like his mind, was narrowed to a pinhole attention span.

"LINKS!" He fired the pistol in the air. "Get out here and take this!"

Steps to his left. He was blowing holes in a pile of wall plaster and cardboard boxes before he realized he'd imagined it.

Lincoln came at him from behind, wielding a bent pipe. He smashed it down on the hand holding the pistol. The weapon was knocked from CT's grasp. Lincoln swung again and hit him across the back. The blow brought him to his knees, but only from its force; he still couldn't feel any pain.

"You lied about Mac, didn't you?" Lincoln cocked the pipe over his shoulder. "It don't gotta be like this! Gimme those keys!"

CT unclipped the ring from his gunbelt and threw them at Lincoln's face, coming in right behind them. As his cousin swatted them away, CT tackled him full body. They rolled through debris, stopping a few feet from the stark edge of the building with CT on top.

"You and Mac, with all yo' bullshit!" His voice cracked, tears working through his blood crusted nasal passages. He pounded his fists down into Lincoln's face, neck, and chest. "Did you think you was always gonna keep me down, Links? That ain't happenin! *I'm the Boss, ME!*"

His onslaught came to a halt when Lincoln caught both of his wrists.

"You wanna be the Boss, crackhead? *Be the Boss in hell!*"

Lincoln bucked, and CT felt himself shifting forward over his cousin's head, sprawling to the ground, only there was no ground to catch him. The long drop to the parking lot yawned in front of him as he slid off the edge of the roof.

For a second, he thought he actually *was* flying, as magical as Peter Pan and Rocky the Squirrel, because surely that was another benefit the Boss was granted for situations like this. But the pavement rushed at him until his amped brain insisted it could see every chip and speckle.

This won't hurt, he thought, *won't even feel it, gonna walk this shit off in no time.*

But it *did* hurt when he struck bottom, and it shocked him to find he wasn't immortal. Most of his ribs shattered, his spine snapped in three places, and his skull cracked open like an egg. He lay jerking on the ground, and watched as a gray, runny mess oozed out onto the concrete in front of him.

WHITNEY +35:48

Lincoln didn't waste time looking over the edge of the building at his dead cousin, the last member—besides himself—of a street gang once called the X-Dawgs. He retrieved the keys to the holding cells and ran back downstairs.

In the hallway he'd passed through earlier, he found Maryland facedown in a pool of her own blood. She blinked up at him with lost eyes, a thread of scarlet drool oozing from each tear duct.

He scooped her up and headed for the stairwell.

WHITNEY +35:49

Hatch understood his master's wishes perfectly, to lead the creature away, but now the pungent scent of the thing chasing him was the only spur needed to keep him moving through the precinct hallways.

He could hear the behemoth at his heels, rushing along the corridor. The delicate blend of pheromones inside its potent smell was an open book to Hatch's canine nose. They bespoke injuries, not just the same weary sickness Hatch and the humans suffered from, but a crippling impairment which slowed it just enough for him to stand a chance.

And he discovered one other fact, hidden deep in the olfactory cocktail. Something the beast wished to keep secret, as most of God's wilder creatures instinctively do when in the same condition. The knowledge was useless to Hatch, but interesting nonetheless.

The corridor ended in a closed door. Hatch stood on his hind legs and pawed at the handle until it clicked open, glancing back as he did. The creature was a black shadow rushing at him.

Hatch pushed through into the muddy lobby. He followed the scent of his own back trail, the only direction he was sure contained an exit. He'd already worked out that his chances for escape would eventually dwindle to zero, the first time he encountered a dead end or a door he couldn't open. If he could make it outside, however, where he had unlimited range of motion, he thought he could lose the handicapped beast.

So he charged across the lobby with the monster in hot pursuit, heading toward the only place with which he was familiar.

The garage.

WHITNEY +35:50

The door into the holding cells opened. Carter figured it was the monster, done using Hernie's mutt as a toothpick and back to finish the meal. Instead, Lincoln stumbled in the room, carrying Maryland's limp body.

A snake with fangs of fear bit him in the neck.

"What happened?" he demanded.

"I don't know man, I think it's the sickness!"

"Did you get the keys?"

"Yeah, the hard way."

"Then get us outta here!"

Lincoln came forward, stopping at the puddle of blood seeping from the dead cop's stall. "Fucking Christ! *Charlie?* You okay?"

"He's dead, Lincoln! The monster followed you out of the sewers! Hernie's dog led it away, but it could be back any minute! Get me out of here, *now!*"

"Shit. *Shit!*" Lincoln tore his eyes away from the mangled corpse and then laid Maryland gently on the tile floor. Carter knelt on the other side of the bars to examine her. Her eyes were closed and puffy, the lower half of her face smeared with blood, but Carter thought she was still more beautiful than any Hollywood starlet on their best day.

"Your cousin, did he—?"

"Don't think he got the chance. She's one badass chick."

Lincoln tried keys from the ring in his hand until one of them popped the lock. Carter slid the door open. The gangbanger turned and released Hernie while staring at the bashed-in metal bars.

On the floor, Maryland gave a vicious, tearing cough and convulsed.

"NO!" Carter jumped on her. The seizures brought her head up far enough to bang back against the hard floor. He held her down. "We need a breathing tank!"

"I know where they are," Hernie exclaimed, "but I don't remember how to get in the room!"

Carter looked at Lincoln. "Go find Ellis! HURRY!"

Lincoln coughed into his forearm as he watched Maryland flop, then took off.

Carter looked down at the woman bucking beneath him. "C'mon Maryland, not now, not when we're this close! Snap out of it!" If she heard him, she gave no indication. She was choking now, her eyes rolling back as crimson tears streaked down her face.

Hernie stood over him, bawling. Carter ground his teeth beneath the rebreather, tears of his own welling. Lincoln had only been gone ten seconds and he was already cursing the gangbanger.

Cart, no oxygen tank is gonna save her even if it's delivered by Speedy Gonzalez. You saw those people bleed out. You know how fast it happens once they get to this point.

He did. Maryland Williams was going to leave this earth in a matter of seconds.

With numb, shaking hands, Carter pulled the rebreather mask over his head, and took his first breath of genuine Port Allen air.

WHITNEY +35:51

When Ellis got finished trying to breathe liquid, he reached up and found the end of Sturney's mutilated arm. He dug his fingers through the plastic wrapping and bandages, into the raw meat beneath. Even underwater, he heard the man scream.

The pressure came off his neck. Sturney rolled away. Ellis surfaced for a sputtering, blood-tainted gulp of air and squirmed away from the other cop.

Ahead of him was the small, raised platform for the generators, just a few inches out of the water. The bitter fumes pouring out of the machines hung in the air like a black cloud. Electrical sparks jumped from the damaged cables.

He tried to get to his feet. Couldn't. His body had just taken too much punishment. Either blood loss or shock or P3 was getting ready to put him down for good.

Sturney was having no such problems. Even being just as sick, even after losing a fucking *hand*, that maniac went right on ticking. He stood in front of the door that led into the precinct and fumbled for his service pistol, having to reach across his gut with his left hand to the holster on his right side.

Ellis crawled forward even though there was nowhere to go. He pulled himself onto the generator platform, determined to at least die dry, and slipped into the small space beneath the trailing cables.

"I hate you," Sturney rasped. He spat out a wad of blood and teeth. "I fuckin *hate* you. Just die." He raised the gun.

The door behind him burst open. Hatch came through, slamming between the officer's slightly spread legs and knocking him off balance. The Lab splashed through the water and hopped into Ellis' lap, where he sat shivering.

A hideous, alien shape appeared in the doorway behind Sturney. It reared up as the cop regained his footing and turned to face it. He stared as it stepped into the water. A look of utter terror transformed his face as he brought the gun to bear on this new threat and opened fire.

The creature took three shots to the chest and then reached out, crossing its huge arms at the joint that must be its elbows. One hand grabbed the officer's right shoulder, the other his left hip.

It yanked.

George Sturney tore in half at the waist as easily as a sheet of paper, unleashing a torrent of viscera. His legs toppled over to reveal the bowl of his wide hips, and his upper half flew across the garage toward the damaged S.W.A.T. van. His arms were still moving when he hit the metal side of the vehicle and fell into a pile on the floor.

Ellis clapped a hand over his mouth and screamed.

Sturney's killer—some hellish thing that looked like putrid fish parts stitched together—turned toward him and bounded forward.

Ellis pushed Hatch out of the way, tore one of the shredded loops of thick electrical cables in half, and stuck the sparking end into the water that covered the floor of the garage.

The flash of blue-tinged light was more blinding than the grenade; the squall of electricity and the screech of the monster was a thousand fingernails on a thousand chalkboards. It jerked and twitched, arcs of energy spearing through it. Something in the generators blew, raining sparks on Ellis as they shut down.

He had time to see the beast stop its electric jitterbug just before a stray bolt jumped from the wire to him, and he was gone.

WHITNEY +35:54

Lincoln wasn't sure what happened in the precinct's garage, but he was glad it was over by the time he got there.

He'd followed the booming sounds of combat, keeping an eye out for the creature. The power in the building failed as he bolted through the door into the garage. The entire dark, sprawling space was filled with smoke from a fire blazing up the wall to his left. The flames flickered through the haze.

Lincoln pulled the edge of his shirt up and covered his mouth, but it was too late. He started coughing, and his white shirt—already stained pink with Lemiere's blood—turned damp maroon. The force of the hacking made spots swim across his vision. He ducked low, where the smoke was thinnest, and could breathe a little easier.

A shape trotted out of the blackness. His heart gave a lurch until a rough tongue drug across his cheek. Hernie's damn dog. He reached out and patted the big Lab's head. It wagged its tail and whined, then backed into the smoke toward the fire. He followed, almost tripping over a pair of severed legs.

His stomach roiled. He recognized the monster's handiwork.

Hatch led him to where Ellis lay curled up in a ball at the base of the burning wall, one hand in a death grip around an industrial electrical cable. Lincoln couldn't tell if he was dead or not, but when he looked around at the water, he pieced together the situation.

A few steps away was a splintered board. He snatched it up, gagging on smoke and blood, and swung it like a golf club, striking Ellis hard in the shoulder. The cop's eyes flew open. He flopped away, looking around wildly until he spotted Lincoln, then clutched at his arm and shouted, "*OW! What did you do that for?*"

"You supposed to hit electrocuted people with wood!"

"*While* they're being electrocuted, dummy! You don't just beat them with a stick after the fact!" His upper lip had been reduced to two bloody flaps, his left eye swollen to grotesque proportions. Ellis pulled the collar of the shirt Doc Kordi had given him up over his bloody mouth and nose. "Good to see you."

"Same here. Can you get up?"

"I don't know. Never been in so much pain."

The fire licked at them and the ceiling was beginning to burn. Lincoln helped him to his feet and away from the strengthening flames.

"Did you find Charlie?"

Too much to explain, and it wouldn't make a difference anyway. "He didn't make it. Neither did Lemiere or Mac."

Ellis winced. "I'm sorry."

"Me too. About your partner, I mean."

"What about Maryland and the others? Have you seen them?"

"Shit man, I forgot! Maryland's havin one of those seizures! Carter sent me to get you so we could grab...an oxygen tank? I don't know how that's gonna help, but that's what he said!"

"Later! C'mon, we gotta get out before the whole building goes up!"

They moved on with Hernie's dog at their side, but on the way to the door, they encountered a huge mass stretched out in the wet floor.

Lincoln felt his balls shrivel at the sight of scaly flesh. The dog growled.

"That thing killed Mac, Charlie, and Lemiere."

"It killed Sturney too," Ellis said between coughs. "I think it's Maryland and Carter's monster."

"You electrocuted the son of a bitch?"

"Yeah. Why, you want to hit it with some wood?"

"No, I wanna make sure the fucker's dead."

Lincoln took a cautious step forward. The monster was on its stomach; he could see its broad shoulders, and its tail stretched out between two squat, bulging legs, but the head was tucked away under an arm. He reached out a hand toward one of the quills jutting from its back.

He was several inches away when the monster gave a full body heave and a fluttery snort before coming to rest again. Lincoln jerked his hand away.

"I don't think it's dead. You got a gun?"

"Somewhere in here. But I don't think it would do any good."

"Then let's get the hell outta here and let the fire take care of it."

WHITNEY +36:00

The cornucopia of scents almost made Carter gag. After having nothing but the metallic taste of filtered air for the last 48 hours—and, really, the last eight years—every other smell fought for dominance in his nose. His own fetid sweat, the tang of Maryland's blood, and the rotten leftovers of their seagoing dinner guest all combined to assail him. Vertigo set in, his phobias trying to stop this revolt against good sense, but he ignored them all and pressed the plastic mask down over her mouth and nose hard enough to dimple the flesh.

"Don't let this be for nothing!" Above them, the fluorescents flickered and went out, the electricity in the building dying and leaving them in the greenish glow from the battery-operated EXIT sign. "You better wake back up right now Maryland, cause I wanna gloat!"

Her chest hitched, her body drawing in breaths only so she could keep coughing them back out. She hacked blood into his mask, and he knew he'd been too late.

"Goddamn it, *noooo*."

The contractions beneath him tapered. She grew still. He slid off into the floor beside her, stretching full length upon the tiles, his hand still pressing the mask to her face. Hernie's sobs grew louder.

"I tried," Carter whispered in her ear, not knowing if he was talking to her or himself. Only it wasn't true, he *hadn't* tried, not when it would've made a difference.

He fought the urge to crush the mask in his hand. Everything he'd said to her outside the church felt so ridiculous. *This* is what he'd been fighting against, taking off this stupid thing? Not just today, but ever since these phobias had crept into his life, turning him into a walking punchline? An act that seemed so simple now that it was done?

I'm not okay, you're not okay, the universe is a cesspool, he thought, letting his head fall in shame.

"S-so Fear Club, does th-this mean…we're engaged?"

The voice was so small, he was scarcely sure he heard it. Carter lifted his head.

Maryland's eyes were open, blinking away red film as she looked at him. She gave a shaky smile beneath the rebreather's plastic.

Carter scrambled up, leaned over her, brushed matted hair out of her face. Hernie joined him on her other side, and the two of them stared at one another for a moment before giggling like schoolgirls.

Carter lifted her head to slip the rebreather strap over. "How do you feel?"

"Like s-someone…used my stomach…for a pu-punching bag." Each breath seemed to be an effort.

"Maybe you better not talk. Or move."

She ignored this, raising one trembling hand to touch the mask over her mouth. "You know…this is the first time I've seen you without this thing. You're…a lot cuter than I thought."

He grinned. "Bet you say that to all the agora-germophobics."

"Just the batshit insane ones. Hey, Hernie. Is Tangela okay?"

"Yes ma'am, she's okay, but real sick!"

She pawed at the rebreather. "You gotta get this off me and put it on her."

Carter shook his head frantically. "No, absolutely not, you're keeping that! You take that off and you might go right back into shock! I'm not—" *losing you again*, he desperately wanted to say, "—letting you do that."

The door to the prison block flew open. Lincoln, Ellis, and Hatch came through, the two humans wearing backpack oxygen tanks connected to gray, rubber breathing masks that covered the entire lower half of the face. They carried three other units. Tendrils of dark smoke crept in with them, tainted green from the light in here. Hernie ran to hug his dog.

"Thank God," Carter sighed. "What about your handless buddy and the Swamp Thing?"

"Swamp Thing?" Maryland asked.

"The former's dead, the latter's unconscious and probably going to wake up with a severe headache any minute. Help Hernie and Tangela get these on." Ellis gave his tanks to Lincoln, then hobbled over and handed the last breathing apparatus to Carter. The cop was beaten to hell and back. He pointed down at Maryland. "She okay?"

"I think she will be. She lost some blood, but it looks like Garmon was telling the truth about the clean air."

"I wish we could let her rest, but we have to go." Now Ellis caught sight of Charlie's body and trailed off. For a long moment he didn't move, just hunched his shoulders and stared at the ground rather than at the twisted mess in the next cell.

"Ellis…I'm sorry. We—"

The cop cut him off by raising the fingertips of one hand at his side. He turned toward them, but the smashed remains of his face were too disjointed to read. When he spoke, his voice had dropped an octave. "The building's on fire. Aurora is bound to see it."

"What about the radio and calling for help?" Maryland tried to sit up, and Carter helped her. "That's the whole reason we came here."

"Everything long range requires power, and the generators are trashed. About the only thing we have time for is getting more of these oxygen tanks out of the armory for the others."

"But *then* what, Ellis?" Maryland frowned and readjusted the rebreather mask. "How long are these tanks gonna buy us?"

"A few hours, at best." A tear slipped from the corner of his good eye. "But maybe that will be enough to come up with a new plan."

"I wouldn't count on it," Carter whispered.

CHÂTEAU DECATUR

JAILBREAK

Mattinson was the definition of a good soldier, loyal and smart as they bred them in this country. He'd once been a highly decorated lieutenant in the Army, but rank and serial number were two things you gave up when you joined Aurora. Kyler never took to him on a personal level. Like all the recruits that came from the Armed Forces, he just seemed…humorless. Not the kind of man you could sit and have a beer with after a hard day of covert ops.

But professionally, the man was as focused as a pit bull.

And Kyler was ready to let him off the leash.

He entered the command trailer without knocking, then stood at attention. Kyler didn't bother to relieve him. Mattinson was more comfortable when he knew what was expected of him. The man wore fatigues and a gas mask; one of the clunky, rubberized monsters they'd been issued in Iraq in case of mustard gas, none of this high-tech, microfilter, $10,000-per stuff they were putting in the bodysuits. Kyler himself didn't have one on, despite the advisement from the techies in the other two trailers. At this elevation, P3 penetration was nil. He only had to look out the window at their collection of lab rats—all of them getting better, instead of dropping like flies—to confirm that. The New York crew would have weeks of fun watching them all die from baseline.

"They found Squad 18," Mattinson stated, without preamble.

Kyler was at the trailer's small closet, pulling out a black sport coat to match the pants he wore. He dropped the hanger in his rush to spin. "Where?"

"The cemetery on the far east side, where they chased that speedboat."

"All dead?"

Something flickered through the soldier's exposed eyes. "Yes, sir."

Kyler had just picked the hanger back up, but now he bent it into a useless shape. "Goddamn these people. They're like the fucking Vietcong. Kill one of them and another pops out of a hole behind you."

"That's just it, sir." Mattinson's voice carried a hint of hesitation, even muffled by the gas mask. "I don't think it was the civilian resistance."

"Care to explain?"

"The bodies...they were torn apart. Some of them looked partially *eaten*. They also found the remains of several others in the same condition, probably civilian. I should have pictures for you within the hour."

Kyler *did* want to see the pictures—he'd found himself staring at a lot of gruesome battlefield photography lately—but the information drew one of those question marks he hated so much.

Those screams. What had scared his men bad enough to make those sounds?

No time to dwell. In three and a half hours, he would be a nonentity. His unit would be redistributed or shut down, and he would be lucky to make it out of the country alive.

He finished dressing and displayed the ensemble for Mattinson. "What do you think? Does this convey contriteness without sacrificing character?"

"Uh...um..." Mattinson stumbled into safer territory. "Are you leaving, sir?"

"Damn right, the second I have confirmation that Port Allen is a ghost town. I'm off to see the handlers in Washington. If I don't make some sweet-smelling roses grow out of this mountain of shit, we'll all find ourselves at the receiving end of a red slip. You know what a red slip is, Mattinson?"

"No, sir."

"It's like a pink slip, except issued in blood. That's the only severance package Aurora will ever give you."

Mattinson's Adam's apple worked beneath the seal of his mask. "The brass aren't happy?"

"Can you blame them? I don't know how a bunch of civilians made us look like green Army dicks—or worse, the FBI—but they did, and we have a little under four hours to get our dignity back."

"What can I do to help, sir?"

"We have to wipe out these civvie guerillas. But to do that, we've got to find them. We lost them at the lumber yard, the same place Agent Garmon was probably taken. By the way, do you know this guy?"

"Only through one of my field directors. He's a newer recruit, they say he follows orders but no real aptitude."

Kyler nodded. "We've swept 85 percent of this city, from the northeast down. The harbor spotters haven't seen them try to leave by the water, which puts these fuckers somewhere along the coast or in the neighborhoods at the base of these very hills. Now, if we—"

The comm console beeped. Kyler leaned to open the local channel.

"Sir, you might want to come outside and have a look at this."

Kyler swept around the console to the door. Mattinson followed. They stepped out onto the dirt of the valley floor. Dead ahead were the pens full of Port Allen citizens, but to his left, past the trailer perpendicular to his own, was a sweeping view of the city spread out below. The Dome was a blackened crater on the far side. The agent that called him stood just beyond the back of the trailer, pointing down the narrow trail that led into that panorama.

Off to the south, somewhere close to where the land gave over to sparkling green Gulf waters, a solitary column of smoke rose from a cluster of buildings. Something about it was beautiful, a scar hanging against the blue morning sky, and he wondered what happen if you slipped a knife into it, what color the blood would be...

"Sir?" Mattinson interrupted the fantasy, and Kyler realized he'd been out of it for...what, 30 seconds? Longer?

"That's them." He rounded, eyes flashing. "No more explosions, nothing high profile. I want you to leave me a skeleton crew and a chopper to start ferrying these guinea pigs to the airstrip. Take every other man in my command, finish the sweeps, and wipe those civilians *out*. Stop at nothing. Hunt them to the ends of the earth if you have to."

Mattinson was moving before the words were out of his mouth, twirling two fingers in the air to rally the others. Kyler started back into the command trailer, then paused to glance over at the holding pens in the middle of the camp, full of unsuspecting norms with no idea the rest of their lives would be spent underground in lightless cells, poked and prodded until they puked their guts out and were incinerated. In the cage closest to him, furthest into the U-shape the trailers formed, a group of these saps huddled close together, several of them looking over their shoulder in a too-nonchalant way.

Not hard to figure out what was going on there.

He would've called a guard to check, but a certain measure of escape plotting was good for prisoners. Kept spirits up, minds occupied.

Still…it was time to get them moved, so he could finally leave this hellhole once and for all.

WHITNEY +36:09

"Wait, stop. *Stop!* Something's going on!"

Randy had said this to the covert assembly of prisoners every fifteen minutes or so, but this time he might be right. Their armed captors streamed from the trailers, past the end of the yard that opened onto the taller hills, and charged to the bank of helicopters parked a few hundred yards from the camp. Even several of the men guarding the pens—now changed out of their traditional camouflage BDU's and back into the sleek, black, latex suits—abandoned their posts and joined in the rush, leaving only a few to continue the patrols.

"Just keep an eye out," Chris ordered the crowd around him. He'd given up telling them how suspicious they looked packed in together, or even explaining how nervous their eyes made him while he performed delicate electronic work. He just prayed for enough time to finish his science project. "Are you sure no one else has a cell phone?"

"I can go back and ask the next cage over again," a tiny, balding man named Polson offered, "but one of the guards could overhear."

"Never mind. This might be enough."

The helicopter engines fired up. The wide personnel vehicles lifted off one at a time and shot into the city, leaving behind only one.

"Boy, *somebody's* got them pissed off," Randy mumbled. He'd seemed much less depressed over their last two hours of captivity, and hadn't mentioned his wife even once. It probably helped that he was feeling better.

They were *all* feeling better actually, the symptoms clearing up, even though most of them had no sleep in the last twenty-four hours. Chris went back to his work, thankful he didn't have to pause to cough every few seconds. His jaw worked in rapid circles as he concentrated.

"Are you sure you can do this, young man?" another woman asked.

Spread out on the ground in front of Chris were objects people had in their pockets when the soldiers tranquilized them. The ones they were able to convince their fellow prisoners to part with, anyway. He viewed it like a puzzle, fitting the pieces together to form a picture that would get them out of here. Some of them were useless—gum, combs, keys, etc—but ninety-percent of the items were exactly what he needed for his invention.

Cell phones that were as useless as paperweights out here.

"Yeah, this'll work." He pulled the batteries out of two more phones and ripped away as many of the tiny wires inside as he could. If they were going to act, it would be best to do so now, before the rest of the troops got back. "Just make sure everybody is ready to run."

WHITNEY +36:13

Daryl Sloan put the binoculars to his eyes again. Rose carefully above the stand of pricker bush and cactus. Took another look at the scene ahead.

"I'm tellin you, man, *that's* a concentration camp," Burt said next to him. "Only thing missin is a big group shower full of carbon mono."

And, Daryl had to admit, it looked that way. The western trail widened at the top of the last rolling crest of the Chantillys, becoming an oval-shaped grass plain boxed in by higher peaks, before turning back into roughshod dirt and rock on the other side and leading straight down into the city. Spread out across this miniature valley was a settlement of some kind, consisting of several long, chrome-plated trailers—like Airstreams, but more high-tech—parked in a U-shape, the open end facing them, and five dogruns in the center constructed of wire and wooden posts. Between thirty and fifty people milled inside each of these perimeters, in loose groups or sitting on the ground.

He could also see soldiers with M16s. Most of them left with the helicopters that had just lifted off, wearing what looked like black scuba-diving suits, but enough stayed behind to maintain the watch.

Daryl lay down on his stomach in the dirt. "I don't get it. Why would the National Guard be holding people captive?"

"Cause that ain't the National Guard, dude! Wake up and smell the greenhouse gases!"

Daryl rolled his eyes. "Okay, the Army, whatever. Why would they stick people in a concentration camp?"

"Don't even get me started answerin that one."

"I meant Port Allen citizens."

"So did I, man. So did I."

Daryl grasped at straws, not ready to slip into the same delusions as his new friend. "Well...how do we know they didn't do something wrong? That they're not in there for a reason?"

"There's little kids in there, man. Can you think of any crime worth throwing a five-year-old in the slammer?"

Grass crunched behind them before he could think of an answer. Both of them flipped and sat halfway up before catching sight of Avery slinking through the bushes. Daryl hadn't realized how spooked he was by all this until he felt the way his heart jackrabbited against his ribs.

"Another patrol just passed by." The cowboy pulled off his wide-brimmed hat and squatted on the heels of his boots. "Didn't see the Hummer though. I'm havin Crystal take it further off the trail as soon as they're outta earshot."

Burt tugged at his greasy mop of gray hair. "Good, cause I think we're past the point of this go-back-the-way-you-came horseshit. They catch us now, we're gonna be tattooed with serial numbers and thrown in the gulag over there faster than you can say 'Abu Ghraib.'"

"Don't be so dramatic," Daryl chided.

Burt held up his hands. "I'm just sayin!"

Avery leaned forward. "Tried callin back to Yolanda and the others to let them know what's goin on, but my cell ain't got no signal at all. Crystal's neither." He pushed his hat back on his head. "You *really* think that chatter we picked up was, like, encrypted code or somethin, Burt?"

"What else could it be?"

"Jesus. What did we get ourselves into, boys?"

Daryl didn't answer. They'd left a few hours before under cover of waning night, taking Avery's mammoth vehicle over open land to avoid the National Guard barricade set up where the western trail met the freeway. Once they reached the hills and started up the steep, rough path, the CB radio in the dash picked up bursts of static-filled gibberish. On a hunch, Avery killed the lights and went even further off road, finding ways to nudge the landcruiser up through boulder-strewn, heavily wooded passages parallel to the main trail.

It turned what would've been a 45-minute trip into a three-hour ordeal, and had Daryl gritting his teeth with impatience. But they were thankful for the precaution when the first armored Jeep rolled through the area. Since then, they'd played hide-and-go-seek with routine patrols that wove through the system of back roads.

Then they'd crested the last rise and caught sight of this camp dead ahead. They parked and scouted ahead on foot to take a look.

"This is some bad karma," Burt whispered to himself.

"What do we do now?"

"Can't you find some way around all this, Avery?"

"Not a chance. I know the Chantillys, I come up here all the time to go muddin. The western trail itself is bad enough; that's why no one ever uses it. We have options comin up or goin down either side, but all the branch-offs narrow through this pass. The mountains are just too steep and the trees are too dense to drive over anywhere else."

Burt blew air across his lips. "And that's exactly why they set up shop here, to make sure no one goes in or out."

"But *why?*" There was a pang in Daryl's voice, an offspring of pleading and desperation. "Why round up a bunch of hurricane victims?"

"I don't think they're gonna hand over the answer to that one, man."

"Well, that's it then." Avery shrugged. "I guess we go back."

"I'm not going back," Daryl declared.

"Daryl, dude, let's just get some human rights violation snapshots on Avery's cell phone and head back to find the media! It's our responsibility to get this into the hands of the people!"

"No, it's *my* responsibility to find my family! If this is the way to do that, then I'll fight across that field with my bare hands!" He took a deep breath. "You guys just leave me here and go back. You're right, it's important that someone knows what's going on."

Avery held up a hand. "Hold up a sec Rambo, we're not leavin you, but what's your plan? Go confront these guys? Cause I agree with Burt on what's gonna happen if we try that."

"I don't want to confront them, I just want to get past and into the city."

"We might be able to sneak around on foot if we leave the Hummer, but then it'll take us another few hours to walk down the other side."

"Too much time. Didn't I see a rifle in the back of your car?"

"Yeeeeah, my huntin gun. A .44."

"Uh uh, no way." Burt clapped hands over his ears. "I ain't gonna be a party to shootin *any*body, not even these fascists."

"I'm not talking about shooting, I'm talking about being ready."

"For what?"

Daryl rose up again and looked through the binoculars, zooming in as close as possible. As he swept across the pens, he caught the briefest glance of a dark face that looked familiar enough to set his heart pounding. He tried to come back and zero in, but whoever it was (*not Chris, couldn't have been, that was just impossible... wasn't it?*) had been lost in a tight crowd in the cage furthest inside the ring of trailers.

"An opportunity," he said. "Let's get the Hummer pulled up here as close as possible."

WHITNEY +36:15

They sent Lincoln to see if he could commandeer a vehicle while Carter and Hernie lugged oxygen tanks from the armory to the curb. They managed to get 17—not including the ones they were wearing—before the fire spread too much to enter the building. Brilliant yellow flames consumed the bottom floor, and undulating smoke snakes curled out of every window.

"That can't be good." Carter wiped soot stains and sweat off his brow. He moved carefully to avoid hitting the rebreather, before remembering it was gone.

Ellis raised his lumpy face from his seat on the grass. He'd stuffed his cheeks with scraps of cloth and his left eye socket was now the size of a golf ball, the flesh stretched so taut it gleamed in the early morning light. As he studied the grayish-black needle hanging in the sky, his head cast a shadow so malformed it could've passed for the Elephant Man. "It might as well be a giant arrow. We have to get away from here."

Lincoln squealed to a stop next to them a few seconds later in a battered mail truck. The blue eagle's head was nothing more than paint flecks after Whitney sanded it away. "Found this at the post office down the street. Keys were still in it."

They slid up the rear door and tossed the tanks inside. Lincoln stayed behind the wheel with his own tank in the floorboard. Ellis curled up in the front seat to give him directions back to the church. Everyone else hopped in the back without closing the door.

Carter and Maryland leaned against the front seats, watching Hernie try to get Hatch to breathe through a mask. The dog would take a few breaths and then shake his head, dislodging the plastic cup from his muzzle. Tangela giggled at his efforts, the ratty blanket still clutched under one arm. The change in the girl over the last fifteen minutes was phenomenal: she was conscious, sitting up, and coughing seldom. Carter hadn't seen her this happy since before the Dome riot.

"How do *you* feel?" he asked Maryland.

"It's incredible." She rubbed a finger across the section of his rebreather that covered the bridge of her nose. "Once that poison is out of your system, the symptoms clear up almost instantly. Don't get me wrong, I still feel like a garbage truck ran me over—"

"Probably from coughing up three gallons of blood."

"—but I think I could be back to a 90 percent after a good night's sleep. Maybe even 92."

"Don't hold your breath. No pun intended."

Maryland squinted. "How is that a pun?"

"I don't know. Leave me alone. I'm so tired I can barely make pop culture references."

She chuckled hoarsely; he loved the sound of it. Somehow, laughter confirmed they were really still alive. The back of her head rolled against the seats and then slid down to rest on his shoulder. "And what about you? Don't you wanna put on one of these tanks?"

Carter made an exaggerated show of breathing deep, filling his lungs to capacity. Even though he could imagine globules of P3 coating his lungs like cigarette tar, he thought nothing had ever smelled sweeter. A tiny voice inside him squealed in protest, but it sounded farther away than ever before. *Eat your heart out, Pellner.* "Not yet. I have a while before I get to your point. I think I'll just enjoy the spring air till then."

Her elbow found his ribs. "There's hope for you yet, young Skywalker."

"I wouldn't go that far." He sighed. He'd been thinking about this for awhile, and it would be best to just get it over with. "Hernie told me about Tom. I don't know what to say. I'm so sorry, it's my fault."

"Don't you take responsibility for this. Aurora doesn't get off that easy."

"But if I'd just given you the rebreather before…"

"Then it might've still been too late."

"You can't know that."

She sat back up. "Who are you looking for forgiveness from, Carter? Me, Tom, or yourself? Because Tom can't give it to you, and you don't need it from me."

He decided to chew on that one for a while.

"So this whole thing, it's just the government tryin to cover up their own mistake?" Lincoln asked in the front seat. Carter and Maryland tuned in to their conversation.

"That about sums it up," Ellis answered. "The only thing I don't understand is how that…that…*monster*…fits into their plans."

"I ain't so sure it does." Lincoln slowed the vehicle and eased into the median to avoid debris in the road. "The soldiers in the graveyard seemed just as surprised by that thing. And it was just as eager to rip them up as us."

"As horrible as ol' Sushi-Breath is—and as much as we'd probably like to pin it on Aurora—maybe it's a completely separate element." Carter knelt between the seats. "No big conspiracy, no hidden agenda, just something else the storm blew in."

"That's some depressingly bad luck," Maryland said.

Ellis shifted in his seat and winced as one of his injuries jabbed at him. "It doesn't matter. We lost it, and hopefully that fire burned it to death. Aurora is our biggest threat now. We have to decide what to do about them."

Lincoln spoke before anyone else could. "If this guy you captured—Garmon—if he says there ain't no cure or whatever, then what's the point of runnin?"

"He didn't say there was no cure, he said he didn't know," Carter clarified.

"But don't you figure there would have to not be? Otherwise, why kill everybody, 'steada just givin us the cure?"

"I don't care if there isn't." Maryland shivered. "Clean air will help us for a while. I'll live in an oxygen tent the rest of my life if I have to, I just don't want to go through that again."

"Yeah, but we still need help even for that. Which is lookin less likely all the time. Our best bet might actually be turnin ourselves in to these Aurora guys."

This was the second time the idea had been proposed, and this time everyone was quiet, including Carter. Ellis said, "We'll give that option to everyone again when we get back to the church."

"Oh shit," Lincoln moaned.

"What?"

"They're here."

He was looking in the side mirror. Carter and Maryland crawled to the open back of the mail truck, past Hernie and Tangela, and peered out into the morning sky behind them. Two black helicopters were sweeping in low from the west like angry dragonflies.

"Uh uh, no way, I'm not doin this again, someone else can drive!"

"Go faster!"

"Swerve around!"

"Calm down." Ellis scooted up to look out his window. "They're not firing."

The two choppers fell into step just above and behind them, but the big guns mounted on either side of the cockpit stayed silent.

"They're following us. Back to the others. Maybe they want to take us alive, like the people they tranq'ed."

"So what do we do? Lead 'em away?"

"The others will die anyway without these oxygen tanks. We wouldn't be saving their lives by staying away. We have to evacuate them before Aurora storms the building."

"Or blows it up," Carter added.

"If we can just get them someplace safe, we can figure something out."

"How?" Maryland cradled her forehead. "We're not all gonna fit in this mail truck, Ellis!"

"I think I got an idea." Lincoln pushed the vehicle as fast as it would go.

WHITNEY +36:19

With so few men at the campsite, the frequency of guards passing their pen dropped to every four or five minutes. Chris counted only seven either in motion or stationed by the trailers, compared to the twenty before sunrise. They—plus however many armed doctors or soldiers were inside the trailers—were all that stood between the prisoners and freedom.

His legs wobbled as he crossed the shorter length of their rectangular enclosure alone. Mr. Z's shoes had given him a nice crop of blisters, but mostly the shakes were just caused by fear.

Mom...Nichelle...if you're watching from up there, and you have any control over what happens down here, *please let this work.*

The gate to their pen opened toward the broad side of the trailer that made up the bottom of the U shape. Nothing more than a wooden frame on hinges, with razor wire stretched across the middle. A chain and large padlock held it closed. These prisons had been constructed fast and easy, a temporary holding solution.

He didn't intend to see what the permanent version looked like.

Chris knelt and gently placed the bundle of cell phone batteries on the ground. The cylinder was as big around as his thigh and tied together with shoelace, a shoddy array of parts and cords that looked like a terrorist bomb from an action movie. Two long wires with bare ends stretched from the middle of the packet, and he wrapped their copper filament guts around links in the chain, then pushed the batteries behind the nearest post, where they would be hidden from anyone approaching on the outside.

He wanted to check his contraption again, but refrained. It would either work or it wouldn't. Booby traps were a little beyond what he'd learned in Mr. Keeler's Advanced Shop, but if they taught stuff like this in those college-level engineering classes his father wanted him to take, maybe they wouldn't be so bad.

When he got back, most of the cage's 28 prisoners were gathered and waiting for him. They huddled around. A smaller group of six stood far down on the opposite end of the cage. "What about them?"

"They want to stay." Randy grimaced. "They agreed not to snitch, but they're making sure they're not affiliated with us in any way. You know, in case there are..." His gaze flicked around the group, and then he leaned forward to whisper, "...*repercussions*."

The word made Chris' nerves frost over. Some of these people still believed this was all routine quarantine, preparation before they were given a cure. Yeah, right, and maybe Santa Claus would hand deliver it along with their Stockholm Syndrome.

But, despite the confidential whisper, everyone else heard Randy, and suddenly there was a lot of shuffling feet and downcast eyes. Chris pushed on before the contingent at the other end of the pen could get any new recruits.

"Okay, once we're all ready, we need some way to get them to open the gate."

"I can fake a heart attack!" someone offered.

"That probably wouldn't make much difference to these assholes," Polson muttered. "'Less they wanna film it for posterity."

A young Mexican girl named Silvia said, "We could start a fight! Or a protest or something!"

Chris shook his head. "We don't want too many of them coming in to break it up. Whatever we do, it needs to draw as few guards and as little attention as possible. I'll take care of the rest. Remember, we have to get out *quietly*. When we're free, the next step is getting the other pens open. Then everybody makes a run for it together. Further into the hills and out of the city."

Everyone nodded. If any of them had a problem taking orders from a fourteen-year-old kid, they didn't show it.

"But...what if they shoot at us?" Silvia asked.

"They won't do that." Randy sounded almost cheerful. "We're limited commodities! They went to a lot of trouble to capture and hold us out here, which means we're more valuable to them alive than dead!"

Chris hoped that was true, but he didn't think so. If it looked like they might actually escape, then their 'value' would drop fast. The shooting *would* start eventually, either bullets or more tranquilizers, and either way it meant death.

But not for all of them. His entire plan relied on chaos, and having enough bodies in motion to confuse the remaining soldiers, so some of them could get away. This was their best hope for escape.

Theirs, not his. He planned to go the opposite direction, back into Port Allen.

"One of them's coming!"

All heads swung around, Chris so fast that the slash across his neck from the dirty cops opened back up and dribbled blood. For the first time since he was brought in early this morning, a guard marched toward the gate of their pen.

"Something's wrong." They knew, they'd watched everything he did, and now they were ready to put a stop to it. He fumbled in his pocket for the cell phone that controlled his invention, but steadied his nerves just before activating it. Timing was crucial. He figured the device had fifteen seconds before it overloaded and blew out.

"C'mon, all of you!" the guard shouted through his gas mask. He stood at the gate, an M16 held across his camouflaged chest. "Line up here, single-file, against the fence! We're going for a ride!"

They all looked at one another and then reluctantly complied, drifting over to form a line against the razor wire.

Chris stood near the front and waited.

WHITNEY +36:20

The name of the agent approaching the pen was Brennan, and he'd been with Aurora for going on a decade. In that time, he'd seen a lot of forced compliance, the most hardnosed individuals brought to agreeable terms by any number of coercive methods. But he thought the folks in the innermost pen were a bit *too* cowed. They lined up on the opposite side of the razor wire without him even having to ask twice, meek as churchgoers.

Kyler had given the order to get them loaded on the helicopter one pen at a time. Brennan was sent to herd this first group out, but something was going on with them; he could practically smell it. Like the anticipation on people's faces while they waited for you to open a present. He debated calling for back up.

Brennan leaned his rifle against the fence so he could unlock the gate. From a pocket, he produced a small ring that held the key to all the cages. He removed the lock and reached for the chain.

The second his skin connected with the metal, instant pain consumed his hand, raced up his arm, and nested in his brain. White-hot distemper, scrambling his thoughts and short-circuiting his nerve endings. He tried to release the source of this agony and couldn't. His hand remained involuntarily clamped to the chain.

A squeal of static in his head, and then the lights went out.

WHITNEY +36:21

3.7 volts.

That was how much potential energy the average cell phone battery had.

Not all that much, but one of the first thing Chris learned in his studies with electricity (taught in an antiquated safety video that probably did more harm than good) was that it didn't matter how many volts went through a person as much as how those volts were *forced* through that person. Lithium batteries already had a notoriously high amperage, and after he'd taken off the safety seals and wired them to overload, the pack he connected was capable of a massive shock to the system. The guard performed a silent, ten second jitter before the batteries overheated and he collapsed, joints stiffened into a gnarled pose.

But the jolt wasn't even close to lethal. Already he stirred on the ground. Before he could sit up, Polson and another man charged the gate and leapt on him. Fists flew, and this time the guard was out for good. Polson snatched up the machine gun.

Chris marveled at how well it worked. So fast and quiet no one else in the camp had noticed. "Now just give me a chance to—" he got out, before his meticulous plan went to hell.

Like runners starting a marathon, his fellow detainees broke for the gate in a helter-skelter mob. They poured around both sides of the enclosure and ran down the narrow aisle between the other pens and the trailers, back toward the open field, presenting a mass of easy targets.

"No, wait!" he shouted after them. No one even paused. He'd been good enough to listen to before, but now that they had their freedom, he was just a kid again.

Randy grabbed his arm. "C'mon Chris, we gotta go!"

"We have to let the others out first!"

From the trailer on their right, the gunfire began.

WHITNEY +36:23

Maryland clutched at Tangela to keep her from falling out the end of the mail truck as Lincoln bounced over the curb and drove onto the muddy church lawn. He slammed the brakes, skidding to a stop in front of the doors. The helicopters shot by overhead and then banked to circle.

"Get everybody out here!" The gangbanger pulled off his oxygen mask and jumped through the driver's door of the mail truck. "Bring the flashlights from the clinic and I'll have us a way out by the time you get back!" He ran across the mud pit, away from the church.

"Grab as many of the tanks as you can!" Maryland command-ed. They pulled them through the rear door of the truck, leaving Tangela and the dog inside. Maryland, Carter, Hernie, and Ellis each grabbed backpacks and masks and hurried into the church.

Turner met them at the door, coughing into the back of his wrist so much he couldn't speak.

"Here, put this on!"

Ellis helped him into one of the tanks. When he could catch his breath enough to talk, he wheezed, "Jesus, who rearranged your face?"

"Never mind about that, Aurora is coming! We have to get everybody out!"

They hurried toward the sanctuary. Maryland asked, "Is Imogene okay?"

"She's hangin on, but we lost two others while you were gone! And we gained about twelve more people who either came in or wandered by! They say those troops have been pushin south all night!"

"Of course, they're trying to drive us into the ocean like a bunch of lemmings!" Carter shouted.

In the sanctuary, they were mobbed with sick people clamoring for oxygen tanks. There were close to fifty people in the group now, more than enough to riot if they couldn't get control. Some of the group was so crazed, Turner had to hold them off with the shotgun just so Ellis could get a few quick words out.

"We couldn't get out a call for help, and the soldiers followed us back! They'll be here any minute, but we're going to make a run for it! Anyone that wants to surrender, now's your chance! I recommend exiting the building after we leave with your hands in the air! The oxygen tanks will be distributed to those coming with us who are most in need first, and rotated out every fifteen minutes! There is NO need to fight!"

This took the tension level down enough for them to dole out equipment, which didn't even cover half the group. Ellis ended up giving his away to an older gentleman and his wife. Maryland held one back for Imogene, but before she could find the woman, Sara came out of the crowd with Doug and Sharon.

Neither of them had to say anything; the truth was written in Maryland's eyes. Details would come later (if there *was* a later), but for now, the confirmation of Walter's death was enough. Sara lowered her head to spill silent tears for her husband, and Maryland took the woman in her arms, wishing there was time for more. Doug hid his face in Sharon's neck.

Imogene was still at the front of the sanctuary, panting like a thirsty dog. Maryland strapped the gear onto her wheelchair and over her mouth. The woman squeezed her forearm and gave a quick thumbs-up before someone else grabbed the chair handles and wheeled her out with the rest of the evacuees.

Which left only one loose end. Carter came with her into the baptismal, where Garmon still sat tied to his chair.

"What's going on, what's all that noise?" he demanded.

Maryland snarled, "Your buddies are here. Provided they don't just blow the place up, they should find you in just a few minutes if you scream loud enough. I hope you rot with them." She turned to go.

"Wait!" Garmon shrieked. "Don't leave me, take me with you!"

She glared at him from the doorway. "Why in hell would we do that?"

"Because you owe me!"

"Oh, you slimy little—!"

"Look, you got me infected! I wasn't lying, I really don't know if there's a cure! And…I don't know what they'll do to me!"

"That's your problem. We can't lug you around, you'll just slow us down."

"Then set me loose so I can keep up!"

"And turn us in the first chance you get!"

His fingers curled over the arms of the wheelchair in desperation. "I have no reason to try anything, I'm in the same situation you are!"

They stared, first at him and then at each other.

"I can help! I know how Aurora operates! You *need* me!"

Carter shook his head. "Do or don't, but we have to go."

She reached for the straps at Garmon's wrists, then stopped. "You tell me one thing first, goddamn it! That fish monster…is that one of yours too? Another Aurora science experiment maybe?"

He gaped at her like a person taking in the freak tent at the carnival. "Lady…I have no idea what the fuck you're talking about."

Maryland was convinced, but even if she wasn't, it would have to do. She untied the straps at his wrists and let him do the ankles. He jumped out of the chair in his rubber bodysuit. "God, thank you!"

"Just don't make me regret it."

Four people stayed behind in the sanctuary. She didn't know any of their names. Maryland looked back and gave them a good luck wave before fleeing the church.

Outside, a few people were shrugging into the last of the tanks from the back of the mail truck. The rest of the group stood at the curb, gathered around Lincoln and staring down at something. Hernie had Tangela slung over his shoulder and Hatch at his side.

Ellis stood halfway across the lawn and beckoned. "*Let's go!*"

Maryland covered her eyes to block the sun and looked up. The two gunships that had tracked them here still hovered in the sky above the church. "*Why aren't they shooting?*"

Ellis pointed over her shoulder.

To the west, a platoon of the attack choppers' fatter cousins swarmed the sky. She could see figures leaning out of the open cargo space.

An entire army descending on them.

When they got close to the others, Maryland saw people climbing down into an open manhole in the street.

"*This* is your big idea?"

"No way." Garmon shook his head. "Do you know what the P3 levels will be like down there?"

Lincoln eyeballed the man. "Who the hell's this guy?"

"He's the agent we told you about. He's coming with us."

"Yeah, well, trust me, it's fine, I was just down in 'em. We have the oxygen tanks, and Charlie showed me how to get around, so we won't get lost."

"But Lincoln," Carter argued, "these tunnels are flooded. I saw it happen when the seawall broke yesterday morning."

Garmon waved a hand. "Actually, that's the one thing we don't have to worry about. The seawall was supposed to come down all at once, so it flooded the overflow systems evenly. But there was some kind of problem with the explosives. The water overloaded the spillways, which is why everything drained to the east side of town. We never figured out what happened."

All of them looked at Hernie, who asked, "What?"

Carter ruffled his hair. "I think you and Underdog just saved our butts again."

The rest of them started down the ladder, after lowering Hatch and Imogene. Maryland was the last one through, and the troop transports were just touching down across the street as she ducked beneath the pavement.

WHITNEY +36:24

A soldier coming down the steps of the trailer to the south spotted the fleeing refugees. His eyes widened above the rim of his gas mask. He shouted, "*Stop!*" which went over about as well as when teachers at Chris' school yelled it in the middle of a good fight. The soldier fumbled for a moment, then whipped his rifle up and fired. The burst cut down a man running past him toward freedom.

That was all it took to push things toward the brink of hell.

Polson, who had just reached the corner of their pen, found the trigger on his commandeered weapon and returned fire. Recoil staggered the little bald man. The shots tore through the shiny aluminum hide of the trailer, but missed their target. They did, however, force the guard to leap back into the safety of the trailer door. Polson bellowed in anger. He looked like a nutso postal worker with the huge gun in his hands.

Randy still tried to drag Chris through the gate of their pen. He wanted to give in to the heat of the moment and just run, let dumb instinct take over, even though, given current circumstances, their chances of making it across the open stretch of field were close to zero. This was an adult telling him what to do, and he was so tired of thinking and responsibility.

Chris glanced back. Grimy, desperate faces watched from the other pens.

"We can't leave them!" He pulled out of Randy's grip and scooped up the key ring from the unconscious guard. Chris sprinted around the side of their empty cage and on to the next one with his cheeks puffing. He was winded after only a few seconds.

Most of their cellmates had already scattered in all directions, but a few hesitated as calmer heads prevailed. Chris moved into the gap between their rectangular cage and the next, arriving at the gate just as the other soldiers stationed around the camp woke up to the prison break underway.

WHITNEY +36:25

Kyler was staring at the lights on the command console when the sound of the first shots reached him, his eyes half-lidded and a thin line of drool edging down the corner of his mouth. Their twinkling had hypnotized him, crossed some wire in his malfunctioning brain. The blasts were so close he jerked out of this fugue and almost fell into the floor, reaching for the sidearm he wasn't wearing. The comm board beeped, and he reeled for a moment before he could reach to open a channel.

"What's going on out there?" His tongue felt fuzzy.

"Sir, there's a prisoner breach! One of the pens—!"

"Wait." Enough information had disseminated across his bleary brain to snap him awake. "Are you…are you *shooting* at them?"

"T-they're armed, sir!"

"*I don't give a shit, you moron, DO NOT FUCKING SHOOT THEM! Each one of those P3 incubators are worth more than a hundred of you!*"

"I…but…what should…?"

The vapid confusion in the agent's voice caused the veins in Kyler's head to feel like they were bursting. "Detain them! Use the goddamn tranqs! FUCK!" He cut the line and ran for the door.

WHITNEY +36:27

Guards chased the prisoners across the field, opening fire at their backs. Polson stood his ground along with some other men, one of whom had taken the sidearm from the soldier they'd electrocuted. Together, they created enough resistance to slow the enemy's advance, but they wouldn't last long in the open. Gunfire stretched across the sunny morning.

Chris knelt at the gate of the next pen and tried key after key while the prisoners gathered on the other side. He spotted the mother of one of his school friends amid the crowd. For some reason, the sight of the woman's tear-streaked face brought the situation home to him in a way nothing else could. Even if he was still alive this time next week, the life he knew was gone. His hands started to shake so bad he couldn't get the keys into the lock anymore.

Fingers folded over his.

He looked up to find Randy standing over him.

"Didn't think you were getting rid of me that easy, did you?"

Together, they had the chain off the door in seconds. Chris knew they needed to change their strategy—that crucial element of surprise was long gone—but events were happening too fast for him to think of a new plan. It was all he and Randy could do to jump out of the way before they were trampled. The citizens went left, away from the fighting. They flocked around the end of their cage and joined the exodus. Chris stood against the post to the right of the gate and watched the action across the field.

Soldiers multiplied from the trailers. They worked to surround Polson's tiny resistance, but the new flood of prisoners divided their attention. Two guards broke off and clomped in their direction. They entered the far end of the dirt lane separating pens, and Chris realized he was caught between them and the crush of bodies exiting the cage behind him.

They raised their guns. He looked away and waited for the bullets.

But there were no shots. When Chris opened his eyes, he found the soldiers frozen with their heads cocked to the side. They glanced at each another, and one of them shrugged helplessly. Across the field, the others halted their assault on Polson's crew with the same confusion.

Something had changed. The energy in the field reversed directions like a thrown switch. Polson's men charged the closest soldier, who seemed to have forgotten all about the automatic weapon in his hands.

"Don't run, we can TAKE 'EM!" he war-cried. Polson jabbed the butt of his rifle into the guard's face as they overran him. From over here, it looked like they were tearing the guy apart.

The soldiers in front of Chris backed away slowly.

It was the very worst thing they could've done.

"Get 'em!" someone from the second pen shouted. The flow of escapees changed directions, and a mob pounded past Chris toward the soldiers, who turned to flee toward the trailers.

He and Randy grinned at one another.

The battle had begun.

WHITNEY +36:28

"What is that?" Crystal leaned over the seat to smack her gum in Daryl's ear. Her breasts just about fell out of the neckerchief she wore as a top and onto his shoulder.

Daryl rolled down the Hummer's passenger window. A distant crackling drifted down the road from the direction of the encampment. "That's gunshots!" Fear gripped him in a clammy hand, and he didn't even know why. He looked to Avery in the driver's seat. "Go, we gotta get in there!"

"I don't think we shou—"

"GO!" Daryl thundered, slamming the vehicle into gear and stretching his leg over to tromp the gas. *I'm coming, baby*, he thought, envisioning Nichelle's face.

The Hummer's wheels spun in the dirt for a second before it shot forward, and everyone in the vehicle screamed.

WHITNEY +36:29

Kyler exited his trailer into chaos.

One of his first assignments upon joining Aurora had been the slaughter of an entire village in Asia, to coerce the local regime dictator into cooperating with a certain foreign policy. His superiors called it 'hard-line negotiating,' and that's how he'd rationalized most of the killing he'd done in his life. The plan had been for a team of six with backpack-fed chain guns to simply mow the place down.

But their targets had organized on the fly, swamped the soldiers, and managed to kill two of them with their bare hands before evac. Kyler learned that day to never underestimate the power of the mob. And if those dirt poor chicken farmers had found the will to survive, then a bunch of fat-cat Americans could spell disaster.

The twenty men Mattinson had left him with were under siege. Most of them were isolated and caught in indefensible positions in the grass field beyond the camp, as ragged civilians closed in and beat the hell out of them. His agents had stopped firing per his order, but they couldn't get back to the weapons trailer to get the tranquilizer guns. Desperation was thick enough to taste. They tried to keep the hordes back with their fists and rifle butts, while the rest of the prisoners that hadn't stayed to fight fled in all directions.

He saw his mistake. A show of force at the beginning might've quelled this, but by taking his men's freedom to pick targets, he'd dealt them a crippling blow.

As incredible as the concept seemed, they were on the verge of losing base camp.

How the hell had this gotten fucked up so bad?

A few yards to his right, the door to the medical trailer flew open, and the staff doctors came stumbling out in their lab coats. They made the same interpretation of the situation, and a few of them actually turned to run. Kyler snagged one of their coattails and pulled the man back to him. He yanked the doc's sidearm out of its holster and used every inch of his willpower not to blow the man's brains out. Instead, he opened his mouth and gave a shrieky burst of laughter.

Kyler released *herr doktor* and charged around the pens. He fired the pistol into the closest crowd of refugees. "Just *kill* them!" he screeched. At this point, he didn't know if losing base camp or the test subjects would make his superiors more agitated.

But killing these yokels...*that* would be immediate gratification.

The agents closest to him got the idea and fought for elbow room to reopen negotiations.

WHITNEY +36:30

Chris and Randy kept their heads low and tried not to get caught in the skirmishes as they made their way to the third pen. This group freed themselves even before they could, battering at the wooden posts and wrapping articles of clothing around the razor wire to pull them down. A fresh wave of reinforcements was added to the cause. By Chris' calculations, the soldiers were outnumbered 8 to 1.

He let out a whoop of joy. Randy laughed and gave him a high five.

Whatever had caused the soldiers to hesitate was over before they could get to the fourth enclosure. Gunfire started up again, forcing the refugees to change tactics. By now, they had stolen enough weapons to make a stand, and as the soldiers regrouped and retreated toward the trailer on the east side of the camp, the prisoners found cover around the west and continued the assault. A stray shot struck something vital, and flames sprang up in the windows next to the citizens.

Randy reached the next gate ahead of Chris. Outstretched hands pawed at the banker from inside the pen. He cupped his palms and shouted, "Throw me the keys!" Chris tossed them down the aisle and doubled over to catch his breath.

Hands grabbed him from behind. He was lifted off his feet and slammed against the closest fence. Razor wire sliced through his t-shirt. Chris screamed as he dangled with his feet kicking.

A soldier held him at arms length, pressing him against the fence with one hand. The expressionless gas mask hovered in front of him.

"Leave him alone!" Randy ran toward them with fists bunched.

The soldier holding Chris whipped up a pistol and pulled the trigger. Randy took the bullet low in the stomach and fell backward.

"*You son of a bitch!*" Chris reached for the man's face. The guard pushed him harder against the fence.

Chris reared back and kicked him in the stomach. The soldier grunted, his grip faltering just enough that Chris's feet could touch the ground again. He squirmed and jerked, getting away but leaving a chunk of his shirt in the man's hand. His first instinct was to run, but already the guard was turning back around.

So instead he dropped to his knees, combined his hands into one fist, and brought them up into the soldier's camouflaged groin. This time he wailed behind his mask. Chris threw his weight against the man's leg, shoving him into the razor wire, then stood up and ran.

Randy's eyes were open and staring at the clear sky. Chris prayed the man was with his wife now and then snatched up the keys beside him.

All across the encampment, the fighting continued, but the revolters were steadily falling to the better trained guards.

Chris opened the fourth gate to add to the anarchy.

WHITNEY +36:31

Once Avery realized he had no choice, he grabbed the steering wheel and drove as Daryl floored the SUV up the road.

"Oh Jesus, man, I never saw Amsterdam," Burt moaned from the backseat.

"Get out that gun!" Daryl ordered him.

They bounced over uneven ruts in the road and crested a last hill.

Crystal screamed.

"Holy shit!" Avery wrenched the wheel. Daryl surrendered the pedals just in time to keep the sudden direction change from flipping them.

Scores of people were running toward them in a big, loose crowd as they fled the concentration camp. They dove to either side of the speeding vehicle, and Avery laid down on the horn as he attempted to steer through.

The knot of people thinned, revealing the camp ahead. Four of the fenced enclosures were empty, and the fifth lay right in front of them. A pitched firefight was underway all across the field, concentrated up by the trailers, two of which were now burning. Avery hit the brakes, throwing them forward in the cabin.

They plowed through the fence, stopping in a snarl of razor wire. The people in the pen clambered over the hood of the Hummer in their haste to get out.

"Hey, goddamn it, watch the paint job!" Avery shouted, as bodies swarmed over his windshield.

Daryl reached over the seat and grabbed the hunting rifle, then cracked open the door.

"*Are you crazy?*" Burt screeched. "*Don't go out there, man!*"

"He's right Daryl, let's just get into the city!"

"I have to know what this is about! What if it has something to do with my family?" He jumped out of the monstrous SUV, dodging the people still escaping from the pen. He went around the back of the vehicle, where Burt and Avery joined him. They stared around at the fighting in confusion.

Bodies lay everywhere, most of them civilian. A contingent of soldiers and men who looked like lab technicians were bivouacked by the trailer to their right, laying down suppressive fire to ranks of people that charged them. A haze of heavy, metallic gunsmoke drifted across the meadow. Pockets of hand-to-hand fighting raged all around, cries of pain and grunts of effort mingling with the flat cracks of gunfire. Daryl had seen documentaries about the Civil War that looked much like this.

"What is this?" Avery yelled over the noise of combat.

"Revolution, man!" Burt wrapped his arms around his own chest. "And not the kind Lennon was singin about!"

Daryl spun in a confused semicircle with Avery's rifle, unsure if he wanted to get involved.

And then a sound reached him that he'd been afraid he would never hear again.

A familiar voice called out, "*Dad!*"

WHITNEY +36:33

Chris had made his way alone across the battlefield to the last pen when a yellow Hummer raced up, crashing through the razor wire and then skidding to a stop. He jumped behind the nearest fence post and peeked around the wood.

The last of the prisoners were getting out through the hole the Hummer had created. Everyone had an equal shot at freedom now, so he could leave with a clean conscience. As soon as he saw the opportunity, he would make a run for it.

The doors on the Hummer opened. Someone got out, but Chris couldn't see through the scads of people and the thin pall of smoke that hung over the entire camp. And when the figure *did* come far enough for him to get a look, he still didn't believe what his eyes told him.

"Dad?" he whispered in amazement. And then louder, "*Dad!*"

The figure turned toward him. It was Daryl Sloan all right, the same man that once spanked him for bringing home a friend's cap gun, now holding a rifle and standing with a man in a cowboy hat and another with scraggly, gray hair. He squinted toward the sound of Chris' voice and then broke into a shocked grin.

No more than thirty yards separated them, most of it occupied by warring factions. Prisoners dropped everywhere, or abandoned the fight to flee. Chris and his father started across to each other, oblivious of any danger.

WHITNEY +36:34

The civilians were running out of ammunition for their stolen weapons.

It was riot warfare now, the last of Kyler's men shooting to kill from cover or fighting for their lives in the field. The trailers were a wash, the fires too intense to put out, but the tides were turning back in their favor an inch at a time. Some of the smarter civilians had decided discretion was the better part of valor. Kyler wished their backsides a fond farewell. As soon as he regained control, all of them would be rounded up again.

In the meantime, Kyler ran unmolested through the mobs. He was in civvies, so these people never suspected the danger. He selectively targeted the most brazen of the refugees and shot them point blank. After his pistol ran out, he jumped into the fray and just started swinging. He might worry later about reprisals but, for the moment, he was enjoying life more than he had in months. The crazed violence and tang of blood in the air made him feel good. A string of constant, high-pitched giggles bubbled in his chest.

And then the goddamned Hummer showed up.

Kyler was trying to stop a feral mob from quartering one of his agents when the vehicle came flying across the field. He thought it was more of his men, the ones patrolling the side of the mountain, finally coming back to see what the commotion was. But the vehicle was stark yellow, and it crashed into the last pen about twenty yards from him.

He had a woman in a sleeper hold, but he let her go to gape. Now there were *outsiders* strolling in here? For Christ's sake, was this a guarded base camp, or a fucking McDonald's drive thru?

Whoever these people were, they had to die. By coming in here with a functioning vehicle, they'd made themselves priority targets.

He watched as a black, middle-aged man got out, holding a rifle. Someone else caught the newcomer's attention, a young boy in the midst of the fighting to Kyler's far left, and the two of them started toward one another with arms outstretched.

Kyler got clear of the jostling bodies, grabbed his agent's assault rifle from the ground, and opened fire.

WHITNEY +36:35

"Look out!" Avery yelled.

Daryl heard rapid shots, and then the cowboy shoved him to the ground. Avery landed heavily in the grass beside him, a ragged line of wounds across his chest.

"Aw, shit." Daryl looked up. Across the field, Chris had stopped running and looked around in confusion. Daryl motioned for his son to drop. The bullets had come from somewhere to his left, but all he could see in that direction was a crowd of people fighting with several soldiers.

The Hummer skidded up next to him, providing enough cover to stand. Burt was behind the wheel, and Crystal leapt from the passenger side before it had even come to a full stop. She collapsed on top of Avery, weeping.

"*Get in!*" Burt yelled through the open door. Bullets thunked into the driver's side and blew out a window. Daryl slung the rifle over the hood and searched for a target in camouflage. Who the hell was shooting?

He tried to grab Crystal, but she shoved him away and stayed hunched over her boyfriend's body. No time to talk sense into her. He jumped into the SUV beside Burt, who was slouched in the seat. "*That's my kid up there!*"

"*I kinda figured!*" Burt gunned the vehicle, staying low until they had some speed. They shot across the last stretch of ground to where Chris lay in the dirt. Daryl kicked the door open and his son jumped into his arms. He felt tears welling, and warm relief that thawed his blood for the first time since leaving the job interview in California.

"Chris, what about Nichelle and Tangela?" he asked urgently. "Are they here too?"

The boy paused for a moment—something in Daryl's subconscious twinged—and then shook his head. "Dad, we have to go back into the city!"

He dragged the boy inside. Someone was still firing at them, and the rear window of the Hummer shattered. Burt tromped the gas, spinning them around. Daryl looked for Crystal, but she'd been swallowed up by the battle. The fighting looked like it was almost over, and bodies lay scattered everywhere. If he had to guess, he would say the soldiers won by a landslide.

"Get us out of here! Head toward the city!"

"Dude, I don't think—!"

"Just *GO!*"

They raced through the crowds, heading toward the far side of the camp.

WHITNEY +36:36

The Hummer would pass right by him on its way out. The surviving agents crept from the trailers to mop up the last of the rabble, so Kyler moved to cut off the vehicle before it could escape. He gritted his teeth. He would put a hundred rounds through the front windshield and see if that slowed the bastards up.

A paunchy, bald guy came out of nowhere on his right, swinging the butt of a rifle like a baseball bat. It caught Kyler completely off guard. The hard edge of the weapon struck him across the temple, knocking the world out of focus.

"*Death to traitors!*" the man screamed with lunatic zeal, before charging off.

Kyler teetered, his own gun dropping. The sounds of battle echoed in his dizzy head. He fell to his knees, sprawled on the grass. The last thing he saw before slipping into unconsciousness was a large tire rolling at his face.

WHITNEY +36:37

Daryl saw the poor guy get clobbered to the right of the Hummer, and then fall into their path.

"*STOP!*" he and Chris yelled together. Burt braked hard, but the vehicle slid another few yards through the grass before coming to a stop.

"Is he okay?" Burt tore at his hair. "I killed him, didn't I? Oh man, I'm gonna be a mushroom in my next life!"

"He's fine! Just go around!"

"Dad, no!" Chris clung to Daryl's arm. "We can't leave him! They're keeping us for some kind of experiment!"

Daryl started to argue. Dozens of people were still in the field, and they couldn't do anything for them.

But at least they were conscious. This guy didn't stand a chance.

Daryl exchanged a glance with Burt. "Let's do it if we're doin it," the hippie said.

They jumped out of either side of the Hummer and went to the injured man lying in front of the grill. Blood dribbled from a wound on his forehead, and he didn't stir when Daryl shook him. "Grab his legs and we'll just take him with us!"

Together, they carried the slack body to the back seat of the Hummer and laid him on the leather. Just as they shut the door, an engine roared to their right, and one of the armored patrol vehicles careened into the field.

Burt sped away, and Daryl pointed out the narrow pass just beyond the trailers that sloped down toward Port Allen. The military car swung in behind them, and a gunner in the back opened fire from the mounted machine gun. Bullets roared around them, sounding like hailstones as they impacted the metal.

All four of the Hummer's wheels left the ground as they jumped the sudden downslope. They flopped around the cabin on touchdown, but Burt kept the SUV moving. A muddy trail wound between scraggy trees and the steep mountain gradient on either side. Daryl kept Chris pushed low as the gunfire closed in.

"Um, Daryl?" Burt pointed through the front windshield. "What about *that*, man?"

Ahead of them was a conical mound of dirt and rock, set up to block the trail.

"Don't stop!" Daryl reached for his seatbelt. He grabbed Chris' shoulders and held the boy to him. "Aim for the side!"

"Please don't let me die behind the wheel of a gas guzzler!" Burt coaxed a little more speed from the engine and twisted the wheel to the right at the last second, aiming for the shallowest part of the obstruction.

They hit hard, but the belt kept Daryl and Chris from slamming into the dash. The Hummer went up on its passenger wheels, riding the sloping dirt mound at close to a ninety degree angle. For one frozen moment, Daryl was sure they would tumble, but gravity and momentum carried them through. They dropped hard on the other side.

Their pursuers tried to copy the maneuver and failed. The military car launched from the side of the dirt mound in a lazy corkscrew spiral. They came down on the roof and skidded into a tree sideways.

Burt cheered as he watched from the rearview. Daryl checked on their unconscious passenger—now in the floor—and then lifted his son up to hug him once more.

"I knew you would come," the boy said. "I *knew* you would."

"Chris…what's going on? How did you get in that place? Where are Nichelle and Tangela?"

His son's face clouded over. "I'm so sorry, Dad…I tried…I tried so hard…but Nichelle…"

Daryl put a hand over his mouth. He didn't need to hear anymore now. Didn't know if he could. The world was a crushing boulder on his chest.

Chris pulled his hand away. "Tangela." He whispered the girl's name. "We have to find her, she's somewhere in the city."

Daryl nodded and tried to swallow the lump of acid in his throat. "What happened here? Tell us everything."

Burt kept driving down the hillside while Chris spoke.

CUCKOO'S NEST

The gay guy—Stewart, if Lincoln had the name right—readjusted the flashlight beam on the rusted wall. "Can you make it out?"

Lincoln could read the small address plaques easily; that wasn't the problem. They just didn't mean anything to him. Neither did any of the views he could catch from the few overflow grates in the sidewalk they passed. The neighborhoods west of Ellis' precinct had a much higher blue-to-blood ratio than he was used to.

They'd kept to a straight line more or less, and without any streets or debris to negotiate, they'd covered a lot of ground in the last forty minutes. But Lincoln didn't recognize any of it.

"Just keep movin." He pointed onward into the dank tunnels. The line of weary Whitney survivors held on to one another's hunched shoulders as they splashed through the half foot of water lining the corridors, their way lit only by the few who held flashlights. Lincoln stood aside in the cramped quarters to let them pass.

A gunshot came from the rear of the line. It sounded like a bass gong against the metal walls. The refugees bleated and quickened their pace, bumping into one another in the dark. Lincoln pulled out a pistol he'd gotten from one of the others, then pushed against the flow. His throat ached again. He could barely suppress a cough. He'd given up his oxygen tank at the last fifteen minute change-up, and the symptoms had come back with a vengeance.

"What's going on? Are they here?" Carter called out from the middle of the line. He had an arm around Justin, helping him along. Hernie was in front of him leading Tangela, and Maryland just behind.

"I don't know! See if you can get to the front! We gotta keep the underground railroad movin!"

"Yeah, but to *where?* Where are we going, Lincoln?"

"Away," he answered.

The group petered out into stragglers as he got close to the back, mostly the decrepit and injured that fell behind in the maintenance tunnels. They'd entrusted the pushing of Imogene's wheelchair to the Aurora dude, who was at the tail end. He'd shucked his rubber suit and wore only a pair of long johns and thick, military-style boots, but he was still sweating from forcing the wheelchair through the rank water.

"Where's Ellis?"

Garmon wheeled the black woman around as Lincoln passed and tried to keep up. "He and that guy with the shotgun stayed back at the last junction!"

Lincoln found them further on, where a tunnel branched to the left at a 90 degree angle. Turner stood against the wall on one side and Ellis on the other, peeking around the corner with their weapons.

"They caught up to us already," Ellis whispered. "They're at the next bend down there, keeping out of sight. We're just trying to hold them off long enough to—" He caught sight of Imogene in the dark and snarled at Garmon, "Get her out of here!"

"Let me help, that's what I'm here for!" Garmon got on his knees and stuck his head into the tunnel branch. Ellis gave a quick sweep of a flashlight beam and received a rattle of bullets in exchange. They ricocheted against the wall in front of the tunnel branch. "Yeah, I see them. That's a small pursuit team. Eight or ten guys, max. They're trying to keep *you* busy the same way you're keeping *them* busy."

Lincoln shoved the pistol in the back of his pants. "Meaning?"

"Meaning there's probably a whole other squad trying to find a tunnel branch to get ahead of us."

"Don't think they can. There's less and less intersections as we go."

"It's because we're still heading west," Ellis said. "Rich side of town. Fewer houses, bigger lots, means less streets."

Garmon ran his hands down the legs of his long johns, leaving black streaks. "If they can't cut us off down here, then they'll find some way to do it from above. Fighting is just a waste of time. Our best chance is to keep moving."

"Yeah, and then we'll have *these* guys on our ass the whole time."

Turner pointed at the wall beside Lincoln. "Well, there is *that*."

Jutting from the corridor wall was a clear, plastic housing fitted into the metal. Lincoln had to squint in the dark to make anything out, but underneath the barrier was a mechanical control of some kind, just two buttons that said 'Open' and 'Close'. "What is it?"

"It lowers that steel shutter," Ellis said. Lincoln had to squint to see the thick metal slab recessed in the curved tunnel ceiling right above his head. A track ringed the entire corridor, a slot only an inch thick that the door would slide into, sealing the tunnel. "Turner thinks it's part of the flood control system, in case Public Works needs to divert the flow of water in here. That's got to be a manual failsafe."

"Don't it need power?"

"Must be on an emergency backup. We already tested it."

Lincoln bobbed his head. "All right, so we close it and cut 'em off."

"That would buy us some time to get ourselves lost," Garmon agreed.

"Only one problem." Ellis closed his good eye; the other remained a distended bulb. "The controls are on *this* side of the door."

Understanding and dread dawned on Lincoln. "Which means somebody's gotta stay behind to destroy them so those assholes can't follow."

Silence fell among them, broken only by the drip of water in the maintenance corridor.

Garmon finally spoke, still kneeling by the tunnel branch. "If that's an option, we don't have a lot of time. You guys better draw straws or play eeney-meeney."

Lincoln jabbed a knee into his chest, knocking him back. "If we trusted you enough, we'd just leave your murderin ass here! Those are *your* homeboys back there!"

The agent thrust his chin forward. "Hey, don't forget, you need me."

"Bullshit, we need you!" He turned away. "Ellis, tell this dude—"

Lincoln realized what a mistake it was to turn his back when he felt a hand skitter down it, then the gun was yanked out of his waistband.

Shit.

He looked back, expecting Garmon to have the barrel in his face.

And was utterly shocked to find Imogene pointing the pistol at him from her wheelchair instead.

WHITNEY +36:57

"Get movin," she rasped through her oxygen mask. "Back into the tunnel. All of you."

"Imogene." Lincoln said her name with dumbfounded awe. "What're you doin, girl?"

"The only thing that makes sense, sugar." She switched the gun between the four huddled men, letting them all feel the business end. The weapon was so heavy, it took both her bony arms to hold it aloft, elbows cocked out to the side and the pistol grip almost against her chest. Her sprained wrist screamed with the effort. "Now go on, boys, and listen to your elder. I'll close the door."

"Put the gun down." Ellis held out a hand as he eased toward her.

"No sir. And you best walk right on by, 'fore I use it."

"That's ridiculous. We know you, Imogene. You're not going to kill anyone."

"You're right, I ain't gonna kill you. That would be stupid, considerin I'm tryin to save you." She dropped the sight on the end of the gun a good foot. "But I am willin to shoot each of you in the knees, if that's what it takes. Way I see it, you stand a much better chance bein crippled and on the other side of that door than if those scoundrels back there catch you."

"There's no need for this, Miss Freeman," Turner said. "One of us will—"

She turned the gun to the wall and pulled the trigger. She'd never fired a gun before. The gunshot blossomed in the dark, the impact throwing her against the vinyl seatback. All the men froze and fell silent.

"I'll be switched if one more of you good people gives your life up for the likes of me. You've done more for me since the hurricane than my own family, and now it's time to pull my weight." She chuckled. "Good thing there's not much of it."

"We're *not* leavin you." Lincoln's clenched teeth were visible in the dim tunnel. "Let's just rush her, she can't get all of us!"

"Go ahead and try then, babies. I may not be Annie Oakley, but I imagine I can shoot at least a couple legs 'fore you do."

They must have seen the determination in her face. The military boy was the first to comply, as she knew he would be, stepping back into the deeper darkness of the tunnel. Turner went next, splashing across the mouth of the offshoot quickly and then sliding by her with Ellis. Lincoln glared at her another second before edging his way to the other side of the metal shutter. Even though the sight of his bottom lip quivering shattered her heart, she remained careful to keep out of his reach.

"A little further now. That's good."

Once they were over the threshold, she held the gun with her wounded hand and used the other to pull off the oxygen mask. Her lungs flared. Not from the chemical that was killing the others— oh no, she hadn't gotten nearly enough of that stuff yet—but just from that ol' reliable friend of hers, COPD, that magician who had trapped her in an invisible cage all these years. She could tell from the pain this attack would be a doozy.

Imogene reached for the tank in the back of her wheelchair. She leaned over as far as her aching back would allow and rolled it and the mask through the water. "Here. Give that to someone who needs it."

"Don't do this," Lincoln pleaded. "You don't have to."

"Yes I do," she wheezed. Breathing was agony.

"*Why?*"

She lowered the gun, but not her resolve. "Because this can still be my choice. Everything else has been taken from me, but, by God, I am gonna *choose* when my life ends."

Their faces were anguished; that big grizzly Turner looked close to tears. She softened and said, "You men have all saved my life. And Lemiere too, God rest his soul. I'm just returnin the favor."

Imogene reached over, unlatched the waterproof lid set into the wall, and pushed the 'Close' button. The shutter trundled down from the ceiling, cutting off her view of them and then settling into the flooded floor. The light from the flashlights went with them, leaving her only with weak sunlight filtered through a clogged over-flow grate.

She held the tip of the weapon a few inches away from the controls. The explosion when she pulled the trigger made her jump, which caused her lungs to clamp down even tighter. The controls sparked and sputtered, no more than a mess of metal, plastic and wires that gave no response when she pressed them.

"*C'mon, you ne'er-do-wells!*" she called. "My lungs couldn't kill me…Whitney couldn't kill me…so what makes you think you can do any better?"

Footsteps splashed up the tunnel offshoot.

She was dizzy, the attack worsening, but she grinned because she'd beaten them. Memories of her grandchildren danced through her head as she spun the wheelchair around and watched the black shapes descending on her.

When their bullets found her, she was still smiling, and already far from this world.

WHITNEY +37:53

The refugees had left the church almost two hours ago. Their pace through the lightless underground was a constant run after Imogene's sacrifice, an effort to put whatever time she bought them with her life to good use.

No time to mourn. Maryland couldn't say this was the cruelest part of their predicament, but it seemed the most unfair.

The tunnel started uphill, and dead-eyed, soul-sucking exhaustion overtook them. The air was thick, moist, hot, and filled with constant coughing and weeping. Maryland would give anything for a single ray of sunlight, but there was nothing to break the monotony, just endless metal on all sides, reflecting the beams of their flashlights into a dull glow. Her back ached from hunching over.

She called a halt, and folks slumped wherever they could find room in the brackish water. Ellis enforced the exchange of oxygen tanks—a high-stakes game of musical chairs—but it didn't matter. The filtered air got them feeling better, but as soon as they came off, they went back downhill fast. She tried to give up Carter's rebreather, but Lincoln wouldn't let her.

Maryland pulled Ellis aside as he stepped over sprawled bodies to get to the front of the line and whispered, "How much longer will these tanks last?"

"An hour and a half. Maybe two."

"Garmon was right: we *need* to get out of these tunnels. Our exposure down here is making everyone sick faster than we can get them well."

"We haven't heard from Aurora in a while, so maybe we've lost them. We'll get out the first chance we get."

"Yeah, and *then* what?"

Ellis sighed, revealing the missing real estate in his rearranged gum line. He had to be in incredible pain, but barely a flicker had crossed his face since leaving the precinct. "Maryland...I'm running just as blind as the rest of you. Let me figure out where we are first." He walked away.

"Good luck with that!" she hissed after him. "There hasn't been a tunnel branch in twenty minutes! We're trapped in here!" She kicked the nearest wall in frustration, then sank down in the tepid, brown water between Hernie and Carter. Hatch gave rough, wheezing pants across from her, and she rubbed the dog behind the ears.

"Are we really trapped?" Tangela asked from Hernie's lap. The two of them were taking turns breathing through one mask. She wore Mr. Softy tied around her neck like a cape.

"No sweetie. We'll find a way out."

"Okay. I have to go pee."

"Might as well just let it flow," Carter murmured.

"That's gross!"

Maryland smacked his shoulder. "Go a little ways up the tunnel, okay? Hernie, would you go with her?"

They left, and she rested against the wall next to Carter. Something in her back popped. Hatch flopped down on her other side and she played with his tail.

"Not to be a downer," Carter said softy, "but I don't see any possible way for us to get out of this."

"All we need is another manhole. Ellis is looking right now."

"I'm not talking about the pipes."

"Oh. Well, if we're gonna die, I just don't want to do it down here in this hellhole." She gave a slow laugh.

"What's so funny?"

"How far my standards have fallen, huh? Twelve hours ago I would've given anything to go back to satin sheets and leather seats. Now I would settle for not sitting downstream from where a little girl is urinating."

"So this is like therapy for both of us."

"Bite your tongue, Fear Club. I'm not nearly as bad off as you."

"I'm serious." He leaned over to look at her. "I'm sorry for what I said earlier, at the church. I made it sound like you were weak, but...you've come a long way too."

She studied him in that weird glow from the flashlights. Really took him in. His smooth face (almost free of stubble even after two days of hard living), his blue eyes, limp hair, that string bean body. He didn't look like someone the Maryland of either last name would go for, and he certainly didn't *think* like one.

But no one had ever given her that much credit in her life, certainly no male. *Definitely* not Bryce. "Thanks, but it doesn't really matter. I'll never get the chance to stand on my own two feet."

"Would you go back now? If life reverted to normal—no more P3, no more Aurora—would you go back to him? To the money?"

She tried to gnaw her lip thoughtfully and got a mouthful of grime. After spitting it out, she asked, "You mean right this second, or if all this never happened?"

"Huh?"

"Do I still have the memory? Cause that makes a big difference in my answer, I think."

"Yes, you have the memory. Quit stalling and answer the question."

She found it surprisingly easy this time. "No. I wouldn't go back."

He nudged her ankle with his foot. "Then at least you can be proud of that."

Splashing came from her other side. Ellis duck-walked up next to them. "You want the good news or the bad?"

"I detest when people ask that," Carter said. "The good."

"Lincoln and I lifted off a manhole cover up ahead. The coast looks clear. No sign of Aurora."

"And the bad?"

"We've run about as far west as we can go. I can see the Chantillys just ahead. I suppose we could find a shallow side and start climbing, but we'd run out of oxygen in those tanks long before we got through the hills. I don't even think all these people are physically capable." He rubbed at the base of his neck. "If only we had somewhere nearby we knew was safe, just to regroup for a bit and figure something out."

"Wait a minute." Maryland sat up. "Where are we?"

He shook his head. "I don't know exactly. I think I can see Manchester Heights to the north."

She snickered, the sound coming out more through her nose than her mouth. It grew though, expanding in her stomach until she had no choice but to open her mouth wide and let it out. The boisterous laughter rang throughout the corridor full of people, and boy, did it seem out of place. Carter, who got the joke, chuckled along with her.

Ellis stared. "What's wrong with you guys?"

Maryland stifled the peals enough to say, "Looks like I'm going home after all."

WHITNEY +38:02

"No sign of them, sir. They slipped through the forward cordon before we could get back down into the sewers."

Mattinson sat in the cockpit of his chopper, holding the radio mic. "Are you sure they didn't get behind us, into the secured part of the city?" If their targets were at large in there, it was game over. It would take them too long to search the swept area, which now comprised more than ninety percent of the city.

Ninety percent of an American city, emptied of every last human being. In less than 24 hours. Those numbers boggled Mattinson's brain, who had initially gone into the military to prevent things like this from happening.

"No sir, not according to the tunnel schematics. They cut themselves off when they closed that shutter. Only way they can go and not run into us is further west. But the P3 concentration down here is off the charts. They're probably all dead somewhere."

"Unless they got back onto the streets.

"We have the surface perimeter too tight for them to backtrack. We'll catch up to them eventually."

"Fine, continue the sweeps. Close up the city, and let me know the minute you find them."

Mattinson put the radio mic back on its cradle in the dash and sat back in his seat. This was bad. Bad because the brass was displeased, but worse because he'd disappointed Kyler.

When he worked up the nerve, Mattinson tried to radio base camp. The call wouldn't go through. No one was answering up there in the hills. They probably had their hands full with the prisoners, but *someone* should be monitoring transmissions.

Fuck it. He would carry out his mission, the way he always did. Mattinson fired up the helicopter and lifted off.

WHITNEY +38:17

The edge of the plateau that held Manchester Heights on its belly lay only three blocks from the manhole they emerge from. The slope was too steep to climb except at the front, where landscaping had created a shallow gradient for the road. Maryland's house stood at the end of a wide lane that, according to her, had once been lined with cherry blossom trees, but now held only a few uprooted stumps. They'd seen no helicopters, heard no engines, not a single peep from Aurora, but took no chances. Ellis moved everyone in small groups. Now he signaled Lincoln with two fingers, which, coincidentally, were also the only parts of his body that didn't scream when he moved them.

The gangbanger sent his squad of twelve hurrying across the last expanse of open ground between a collapsed four-story mansion and the edge of Maryland's property. The rest of the refugees huddled in the shade along the tall brick wall bordering her house.

At first, Ellis couldn't decide if this had been a mistake. He'd never been to this neighborhood, not even for the annual Christmas lights extravaganza, but he knew all the properties looked like something from *Lifestyles of the Rich and Famous*. Or *had*. Being on an upraised plain allowed the wind to blow across this earthen plate, and most of them had sustained hurricane damage as severe as anything on the coast.

But the one on the other side of the wall didn't have so much as a flying buttress out of place. It squatted in the shadow of the rocky hill face rising up behind it, huge and stately and far more extravagant than the others. The entire front was bulging sectioned glass, with Roman columns leading to an off-center, portico-style main entrance and wide front steps that reminded Ellis of New York City office buildings. The rest was white brick with Palladian windows down the sides, a gray gabled rooftop that spiked into multiple peaks, and a single cupola in the middle, like the cherry on a cupcake. The rock gardens that lined the front were even intact, and a wide driveway led up to a five-car, unattached garage. Around the corner from where they stood was a gate big enough to admit a Mack truck, with a ridiculous wrought-iron sign arched over the top that read, 'Château Decatur.' Ellis always thought a 'château' had something to do with grapes.

He found Maryland talking to Sara and brought her, Lincoln, Carter, and—on second thought—Garmon around the corner, just down the sidewalk from the gate. Sweat beaded their foreheads; the sun was really heating up for the first time since Whitney. They were so glad to be out of the flood tunnels, no one cared.

"I don't understand, whose house is this?" Garmon's voice was scratchy.

"Why you so eager to know, company man?" Lincoln snarked. "Gonna get word back to your peeps, so they can sweep in and finish us off?"

"Hey, I have just as much invested as you do! Not only am I AWOL, but thanks to you dragging us through half the sewers, I'm already showing P3 symptoms!"

"Maybe you'll think about that next time you poison an entire city." Lincoln turned to address the others. "Okay, we made it to Richie Rich's hood. What now?"

Maryland sighed. "Now you're gonna see a grown woman grovel."

"Don't," Carter said. "You don't have to, this isn't worth it."

"I'm doing whatever'll get us in that house. This is way more important than any petty bullshit between me and Bryce."

Ellis nodded toward the gate. "Do you really think he won't help?"

"Honestly…the chances are slim."

"But we have hurt people here. Surely—"

"You don't know him like I do, Ellis. He won't give a shit about any of you, probably not even me. We'll have to make him see that it's in his best interest."

"We can do that. He's got to be as sick as we are, if not…" He stopped just short of 'dead,' but he saw her wince anyway. "And he won't have any idea why. We can trade information for asylum."

Maryland touched the base of the rebreather. "I know, and that's our ace."

Ellis tried to rub his back and succeeded only in setting of a firecracker string of pain up and down his side, arm and chest. He'd been pushing through the pain from his Sturney-administered beating, but if he didn't get some relief soon, he would crash out. "Maryland, I don't want to be blunt, but…have you considered the idea that Aurora might already have gotten to him?"

"They haven't," Garmon answered before she could.

"How can you know that?"

"This is one of the last parts of the city scheduled to be swept. We worked east-to-west, starting at the Civic Center. Aurora hasn't been here yet, which means, even if we *did* lose them, they'll still be here any time." Garmon pointed at the people strung along the wall, huddling in the shade and looking around fearfully. "You are looking at what is probably the last civilians left alive in Port Allen, along with anyone smart enough to stay ahead of the search teams."

"None of that matters," Maryland said. "Whether Bryce is alive or dead, we have to get in that house."

"Why? What's so important in there that we had to detour all the way here?"

Maryland broke apart from the group, heading up the sidewalk toward the gate. The men followed. "First off, the place is a fortress. Bryce had it built that way. He's got food, water, working electricity, and enough guns and ammo to outfit an army. And one more thing." She reached the heavy mesh gate set into the wall and looked up the hill at the house. "A radio. A good one, strong enough to call Houston if we wanted."

Garmon snorted. "So what? Any broadcast you make is gonna be picked up by Aurora! Let's say you manage to get in touch with the closest authorities that aren't directly under their control. Do you think they'll make it here before Aurora comes to kill all of us?

Or worse, drag us off to some lab? What cavalry are you gonna call to come save us?"

Ellis gave the answer he'd been mulling over ever since they'd left Kordi's clinic. "The media. We'll tell them all about Aurora's little experiment. There's no reason to kill us if the whole thing's blown wide open."

"Yeah. All right. That sounds like the ending to a great Bruckheimer movie, but that's not how things work in the real world. You say we don't know your husband, lady? Well, trust me, *you* don't know Kyler. If you carry through with this, he'll kill you just for spite."

"Then he'll have to do it with the whole world listening."

"Besides," Garmon pressed, "you think it's so easy to just dial up 'the media' on a ham radio? If you can even find a frequency they haven't jammed, you'll end up contacting every trucker with a CB for a hundred miles!"

"Hey!" Lincoln placed a hand on Garmon's shoulder and shoved. "You got a better idea? Cause all you done so far is tell us how much ours sucks!"

Garmon fumed but said nothing.

Maryland started toward the speaker box set into the brick wall. "Get back so he can't see you. It'll be better if he thinks I'm alone. Bad enough I'm coming back without the Bentley."

WHITNEY +38:21

Now that she was actually here, the strength of how much she did not want to come home surprised Maryland. The most stubborn, childish part of her would rather be back at the police precinct, on her way to get raped by Lincoln's drug addict cousin. That, at least, she could fight against. The inner Amazon—who felt real enough now for her to see, if she tried—raged at the humiliation of asking Bryce for this. The thought of that smug look on his face...

But mostly she was just afraid. Afraid that once she was back in that house...she would never have the strength to leave again.

This was probably how substance abusers felt. She was just a crack addict, too. One with better taste.

On the other side of the gate, the front lawn rolled toward the house. Fifty or sixty yards of grass that still looked as fresh and green as the last time Javier mowed it. The water in the front fountain was off, and the entire top of the concrete sculpture—a thing made of stacked triangles, designed by some new German artist named Sigmund Gross—had crumbled during the storm.

The intercom set off a buzzer in the house. She hit the button and waited to hear her husband's voice.

No answer. She looked into the camera bulb suspended over her and waved, trying to put some cheer into it. She pushed the ringer again, then held it down.

"Well, this was a great use of our last minutes on the planet," she heard Garmon mutter.

Maryland glared at the camera, imagined him laughing in there. She stepped back to look at the top of the eight-foot tall brick wall, and its row of outward curving metal spikes. "Lift me up."

It took some manhandling, but they got her high enough to grab the spikes and swing a leg over the top. She dangled from the other side and dropped to the ground.

Carter hooked his hand through the mesh of the gate.

"I'm just going to talk him into letting us inside," she said. She had the sudden urge to grab one of his fingers, but if Bryce was watching, that would *really* be the end of this expedition.

The walk up to the house was dizzying. Driveway gravel crunched underfoot, and the glass front wall—which looked like a fairy tale when their Christmas tree was displayed—loomed over her. She expected to be met on the front steps, but again, there was no sign anyone was home, not even when she cupped a hand against the glass and peered inside the foyer.

The house had no doorbell. Her keys were long gone, somewhere at the bottom of Rugg Canyon, but she had—unbeknownst to Bryce—put a spare in a fake pebble from the rock garden. She was afraid the storm might have tossed it, but it was mired in muck at the bottom. She turned it in the lock, then glanced back just once at the expectant faces at the gate.

Maryland stood in the door while it swung open. The feeling of cooled central air was heaven. The generator was still running.

Sunlight fell in golden cascades through the glass front wall, illuminating the tile landing in front of the grand staircase and twinkling amid the chandelier crystals.

Beyond that, darkness lurked.

"Bryce?" Her voice echoed in the two-story front foyer. The house always felt like a museum (or maybe a *mausol*eum), the kind where the air was heavy and talking forbidden, but now the silence was menacing. To her left was the fireplace where she'd confronted him two nights ago, the remains of her tantrum still scattered on the floor. The lazy bastard hadn't even swept up the glass shards. Probably waiting for Consuela and Marisol to come back.

The interior was a grid of hallways arranged in a rough rectangle, with an endless array of rooms. Most of them held Bryce's crap. She hadn't even gone in them all. The first light switches jutted from the wall to her left. She flicked them. There was a moment when she thought nothing would happen, but then the ceiling lights above the chandelier faded up.

So where was Bryce?

The automatic switch for the gate was also on the wall. She thumbed the button so Ellis could get the group off the street.

"Bryce?" she asked again, but she thought this time might have been more to calm her nerves. Despite the cool air, she was panting, and the rebreather formed condensation on the inside. She started down the gloomy, arched hallway, turning on lights as she went.

Something was wrong. She'd lived here six years, but the place felt as alien as the surface of a forgotten planet.

In the kitchen, she found a spoiled roast beef sandwich on the counter. The sight of it filled her with dread; like the bridge before the explosion, she couldn't determine why. The thought that Bryce might be dead had been in the back of her head for a long time, but, at her core, she never really believed it could happen. If there were *three* things that would survive nuclear holocaust, it was cockroaches, Twinkies, and her husband.

Nevertheless, she suddenly felt bad about her last name shuffle.

In one of the kitchen junk drawers, she found an old package of her Kools. She lit one, pushed it under the corner of the mask, and smoked nearly the entire stale cigarette in one delicious drag. When her nerves felt steady, she put it out in the sink and edged through the south exit of the kitchen, into a passage that led through the rest of the ground floor.

The closed basement door to Bryce's underground bunker was on the right. Just past it was a splash of red on the wall, like a squirt of ketchup. She stared at it until the stain lost all meaning, until she went colorblind and the maroon turned negative. Fear rushed at her like invaders outside a castle wall, and she spun, wanting out of this place…

She ran into someone and shrieked.

"It's me, it's me!" Carter grabbed her shoulders. "Did you find him?"

"No, I…I don't know. He's probably downstairs. C'mon, let's get everyone inside."

WHITNEY +38:25

When the gate opened, Carter streaked ahead. Ellis told Lincoln to lead the others and hung back to make sure everyone got inside the grounds of the estate. Garmon came up and stood beside him while he tried to count heads.

"I'm telling you, this is a mistake." The young soldier had torn off the sleeves of his soiled long johns. "Our only chance is to stay ahead of Aurora. Digging in is a tactical mistake."

"Look around, Garmon. There's nowhere left to go. We get help or we die, it's that simple." He finished up his count. Forty-eight people. Fifty-two including Maryland, Carter, Garmon, and himself. "Let me ask you this: would it be better if we tried to climb the hills? Every step we get away from Port Allen is another step where the air is cleaner, right?"

"Not necessarily. I mean, as far as the P3 goes, it would initially appear that way. Those that aren't too far gone already would start getting better, losing symptoms. But you would still have a baseline. And the more exhausted you get, the more it would take hold. And from what I understand from my briefing, once the P3 baseline gets its claws into you, no amount of clean air is gonna help."

"But it would keep us ahead of Aurora, which is what you just said you wanted. Maybe it would even give us enough time to get some help."

"Honestly, I don't think so."

"*Then what the hell do you want us to do?*" Ellis growled. He grabbed Garmon by the front of his long johns and shook him. "*You assholes got us into this, and we're just trying to survive, all right? None of us are going to see tomorrow, but we'd like to live every minute we can!*"

Garmon took the abuse without a fight. "It's fine," he said, when Ellis released him. "You're right, this is probably our best bet. So would you mind if I had a gun to help defend?"

"Hell no."

"Why not?"

"Because I don't trust you. You're not with us because you've shown remorse for Aurora's actions, you're with us because it's in your best interest. And if those interests change, I don't want to suddenly end up with a bullet in my back."

Garmon swallowed, but didn't argue. His cheeks reddened, and Ellis hoped it was brought on by shame. "Then can you at least give me one of those oxygen tanks for a while? I'm feeling really sick!"

"You can have a tank when you finally prove why we brought you. There's a lot of other people here that have been breathing this poison longer than you. Just make yourself useful and barricade this gate after I close it, all right?"

"How do I do that?"

"Figure it out! There's a five-car garage up there, drive whatever's inside down here!"

Ellis hobbled for the house, leaving Garmon to sulk.

WHITNEY +38:30

Maryland's kitchen now held what looked like the grown-up cast of Oliver Twist. Filthy, hollow-eyed hurricane survivors (except, now that she thought about it, hurricanes were the least of what they'd survived) filed into the house, too tired to goggle at the opulence like most of their houseguests. "Everyone, make yourselves at home," she told them. "There's plenty of food in the fridge and the freezer, and bathrooms are just down the front hall or upstairs."

It took a few minutes to get them moving, but once someone finally peeked in the fridge, the group turned into a pack of wolverines. The kitchen buzzed with activity, and a chunk of her fifty or so guests left to explore the rest of the house. Tangela perched on the edge of the island, yawning and kneading the flesh just under her chin. Maryland went over and smoothed the girl's hair back. "How's your throat, young lady?"

"It's startin to hurt again."

The oxygen tanks were all in use, and Maryland didn't feel like finagling one. Instead she pulled off Carter's rebreather and slipped it over the girl's face. A wave of dizziness rattled her, but it passed.

"You sleepy?"

"Uh huh. Is my Daddy coming now?"

"I don't know, sweetheart. If you can wait until I get things settled around here, I'll find you to a nice, big bed."

Tangela nodded.

"I can take her," Sharon offered. The young woman sat at the kitchen table with Doug, Sara, Justin, and Hernie. "I could use a nap too, if that's okay."

Tangela shied away. "I don't wanna go without you, Maryland." The plea made her giddy with love for the girl. A tiny part of her—a secret, dark, shameful part—hoped her father was never found.

Then she thought of Chris, and felt instantly guilty.

"You can take Hatch," Hernie offered. The dog chuffed and slunk forward with his head and tail ducked to nuzzle against the girl's leg. Tangela giggled, nodded, and let Sharon pick her up.

"Thanks," Maryland told the teenager. "Use any of the bedrooms upstairs. I'll come find you in a bit."

After they left, she rummaged through one of the kitchen drawers and found a bottle of prescription Percocet from when Bryce had back surgery last September. She was waiting at the door with pills and a glass of water when Ellis and Turner came into the house, with Lincoln at their heel. Both men looked at her with gratitude and took the medication.

"Everyone's inside and Garmon is barricading your gate," Ellis reported.

"I'll see if I can find him some of Bryce's clothes. Those long johns are a little snug and I'm tired of looking at his junk."

"He can wait. Where's your husband?"

She shook her head and shrugged.

"What about this radio?"

"It's downstairs. I'll show you."

This time, Maryland forced herself not to look at the stain down the hall as she opened the basement door. The lights were already on down there. A few wisps of smoke drifted out, along with a distant mechanical squalling. "That's got to be the generator."

They went downstairs single-file: her, then Ellis, Turner, Lincoln, Carter. Even Hernie, Stewart, and several of the others whose names she couldn't remember jumped in line, probably not wanting to be out of sight of their fearless leader. She held the banister in a death grip as she led the way. Dread twisted through her guts.

"Is this a basement or a whole other house you built yours on top of?" Lincoln asked.

"This is where Bryce goes to hide away."

"From who?"

"Me. Everyone. It's also his end-of-the-world bunker. He thinks…"

Her hand slid into warm goo on the banister railing.

She brought it in front of her face. A sticky gel leaked down her palm and dripped from her fingers. She caught the faint odor of seawater and dead fish, like low tide at the pier.

Ellis wiped a finger down the wall next to the stairs, where more of the substance coated the plaster. "What is this stuff?"

She wiped it on her pant leg. "I have no idea."

They continued down, and soon it was on the stairs themselves, squelching beneath her tennis shoes. Stewart made gagging noises. At the bottom, the smoke in the air was a little thicker. Something screeched and thumped from the generator room to their right.

Turner headed inside, waving away smoke to check the machinery. "This thing needs service!" he called. "It's bone dry on oil and nearly outta gas! Lucky it hasn't melted yet!"

"See what you can do," Ellis said. "We need to keep the electricity running. Maryland, get us to the radio."

She knew he was talking to her, but the words might as well

have come from the far side of the moon. The goo was everywhere down here, floor, walls, and ceiling, turning every surface into a blurred smear, like trying to see underwater. But beneath it, just in front of her at the base of the stairs, was a long, amorphous, maroon blotch on the beige carpet.

That sense of foreboding was back, intangible as a cloud, but heavy as stone.

She was *terrified*.

"Maryland?" Carter asked, touching her shoulder. "You all right?"

"Yeah." She shook off the drunk-monkey stare, but the doom stayed cemented in place. "It's this way."

The basement stretched long under almost the entire house, but it wasn't an open space. Thin walls separated each area, creating a meandering path that forced one to look at all of Bryce's toys in order to get anywhere. Maryland took them through a soundproof music lounge, pantries full of non-perishables, a labyrinthine wine cellar that Bryce had installed with low tract lighting and faux cobblestones to give the place a quaint, grotto feel, and the spa and workout area. The clear sludge got so thick it dampened the fluorescent overheads, formed stalactites, dripped onto their heads. In places, the stuff had hardened into a dark, textured shell. Temperatures plunged past the point of air-conditioning, until their breath showed in plumes. The whole experience was like going into a cave.

Each step strangled her a little more. She wished Carter would come up here with her.

Ellis ordered one of the men at the back of the line, "Tell Garmon to get down here as soon as he finishes with the gate. I want to see if he knows anything about this." The messenger took off.

"You think Aurora's responsible for the H.R. Giger motif?" Carter asked.

"If they were developing one chemical here, who knows what else they created? Until we find out, don't touch any more of that stuff."

Maryland reached the last break in the wall. On the other side was Bryce's Last Resort, the room he would fall back to in a worst-case scenario. It was full of more stockpiled supplies, a few weapons locked in an antique oak desk, a computer and the radio they sought, sturdy metal file cabinets full of back-up hard copies of his important case files from the firm, and, most important, his escape hatch. She could remember him showing off this room to her and teaching her to use the radio when the house was first built. Back when love was still a many-splendored thing, and he cared if she lived or died.

She stopped with her foot halfway across the threshold.

The place was trashed.

Most of the lights were broken, creating a dim, brown murk. Crates had been overturned, their contents scattered. Most of it seemed to have been shoved into the far left corner, where a waist-high wall of emergency blankets, canned goods, and thick pads of paper and legal books were constrained by an overturned treadmill from the workout room and several file cabinets. To her right, the five-foot wide metal disk of the escape hatch hung open. It looked like a giant mouse hole, leading into darkness.

And in here, the walls were caked in fecal-colored shell and oozed with slime. That smell—of salt and dense, mulchy fish—spoiled each breath.

Ellis stepped in front of her with his pistol. "What is all this?"

"For the last time, *I don't know*," she snapped.

"I do." Lincoln wrinkled his nose next to her. "I know that smell. And it don't got nuttin to do with Garmon's boys."

"Wait a minute, what's that mean?" Maryland rubbed her upper arms to keep the cold at bay. Her gaze kept drawing back to the open escape tunnel. It made her feel better to think Bryce had gotten out of the house.

"He's talking about our friend, Flipper." When she stared blankly at him, Carter gave a pointed look around at the others. "You know, with the bad skin and the anger management problems?"

Apparently she was just dense, because even Hernie got the gist before her. "No Mr. Carter, I don't wanna see that thing again!" he whimpered. The rest of the group rabbled, asking what they were talking about.

"Let's just do what we came here to do," Ellis said. "Maryland, *where's the radio?*"

His curt words were like a slap. She pointed to the opposite side of the room. "It was set up on that desk. Maybe it got knocked off."

They spread out slowly through the large space, Ellis, Lincoln and a few others wandering through the destruction to search while the more timid hung back in the doorway. Carter gave her hand a squeeze, and she gladly let her clammy fingers remain in his.

She saw Lincoln shine a flashlight beam into the tube of the escape hatch and explained what it was before he could ask.

"Where does it lead?"

"Just away from the house. Out into the woods, toward the base of the hills."

"Then why didn't we come in this way?"

"Because it's supposed to be locked from the inside. Plus, I have no idea where the entrance is."

"I found the radio!" Someone yelled from the wreckage a few yards from the desk. "It looks okay!"

It took two people to hoist the equipment back onto the desk: a microphone and a large casing with a control panel. The whole thing was connected through the wall to an antenna somewhere outside. Maryland ventured into the room to examine it. She could barely remember how to use it, and she certainly didn't know enough to run a diagnostic on it.

"Okay, it turns on here." A red light glowed on the mic when she flicked the power switch. "You just push this button to broadcast...I think...and that dial over there changes the channel."

"Yeah, but isn't that, like, going to tell those government guys where we are?" Stewart asked from nearby. This brought a few other grumbled worries.

"Look folks, I think that's a chance we're gonna have to take," Ellis said. "This is not *one* option, it's the *only* option. They may come for us, but if we don't reach someone on the outside, we die from their poison."

Carter leaned against the desk and gave a small cough. "But that brings us back to Garmon's problem and that immortal Ray Parker, Jr. question: who you gonna call?"

No one had an answer to that, and in the few seconds of silence, Maryland remembered.

"Mayday," she said. "This radio has a setting, Bryce called it a 'mayday'. You record a message...uh...wait...here it is." She punched a button on the control board and said into the micro-phone, "Um, mayday, mayday, this is Maryland Williams. I'm broadcasting from my home at 6520 Rosewood Drive, in the Man-chester Heights neighborhood of Port Allen, Texas. Myself and a group of Hurricane Whitney survivors are under attack from a…a military group, and we need immediate assistance. Anyone that can hear this message, please respond and contact…" She glanced at the others, who all shrugged. "…the authorities, the media, *some-one*." Maryland stopped the recording. "Now, I can set this to play on a rotating basis over every frequency."

"That's practically givin Aurora a map right to us," Lincoln said somberly.

"Then we'll hold them off as long as we can." Ellis nodded at her. "Do it."

She started the mayday broadcasting.

At the same moment, someone yelped on the far side of the room. Stewart had wandered over to the high pile of debris in the corner to sit down, but jumped away now. "*Gross!* There's a dead person over here!"

And all at once, that dark wave hanging over her broke, and Maryland was shocked to understand this is what she'd been fright-ened of all along. Carter tried to hold her back, but she broke free and walked to the corner. Several people followed her.

The debris over here was more ordered than it looked at first glance. The treadmill and cabinets were leaned deliberately she saw now, to support a circular barricade of clutter that divided the cor-ner from the rest of the room. It was a wedge-shaped bowl about six yards across, the bottom covered in that foul muck. Inside this makeshift pit was Bryce's mangled body, no more than picked bones and shredded silk pajamas.

Arranged around his remains were six white, ovoid shapes, each just a little bigger than a football, nestled down into the layer of slime.

"Eggs," Lincoln whispered beside her. "We're in that goddamn thing's *nest*."

From behind them came a garbled hooting, like laughter from an insane asylum.

WHITNEY +38:43

The creature was dying.

The increasing pain in its throat made it realize time was short. Add to that the misery of blindness and the damage to its nervous system from the recent electrocution, and it knew instinctively that even if it reached the ocean, it would never recover.

None of that mattered though. The survival of its brood was all-important. The creature had sated its own post-labor hunger, but the search for meat for the hatchlings was cut short when the hateful land-dwellers burned its eyes. It had been consumed with fury and the need for revenge before pain forced it to retreat to the hasty nest it had prepared. This wasn't the ideal environment for the offspring, but with some saliva and skin excretions, it was almost as moist, cool and dark as their sea floor home would be.

But now, as the creature reentered the place it had left the eggs, its compensating olfactory senses picked up a surprising array of scents.

There were land-dwellers here.

And not just any land-dwellers. Among the intruders, the beast recognized so many: one that helped blind it, one that knocked it unconscious with crackling heat, the others that escaped it in the same dwelling.

The babble of their wretched language drove it mad with the need to protect its offspring. It would have its revenge after all, and a ready supply of meat for the pups, preferably still squirming.

Claws flashing, the creature dove into their midst.

WHITNEY +38:45

Carter saw the hulking shape emerge from the escape hatch. And, even though he had the sudden urge to turn his boxers into a restroom, he realized that it all felt inevitable. This confrontation had been coming since he glimpsed the thing outside his house in the pouring rain. No hurricane to hide him this time, no fleeing crowd to distract it, no jail door to separate them.

"Look out!" he yelled, the words frozen clouds in the air.

The thing bounded toward the sound of his voice.

A tight knot of three people were closest to it, gathered in front of the radio desk. One man was impaled on the end of its claws, another knocked out of the way with enough force to lift him off his feet and send him crashing into the gooey wall beside the radio. It thrashed in a frenzied rage, stomping a third woman until her head reminded Carter of a smashed pumpkin.

"Oh shit, I think we really pissed it off," Lincoln murmured.

Ellis brought his gun up and fired two shots at the creature while it tried to shake a knot of entrails off its hand. Both bullets struck its broad chest, causing it to stumble back, but there was little blood flow. It screeched.

"Run, get out!"

Carter spun, seeking two people. Maryland was still with a couple of others gathered around the nest. Hernie stood a few yards inside the doorway, gawking in horror at the slaughter. There were six or seven others in here that he didn't really know; Stewart and some others they picked up at the church.

The people in the basement broke for the exit. A burning cough rocketed up Carter's throat; his first real P3 symptoms had chosen a bang-up moment to make their debut. He got to the door just behind Stewart and pushed Hernie through, then stopped to make sure Maryland went ahead of him. Ellis and Lincoln brought up the rear, pausing long enough to fire again.

The creature turned its deformed head toward them, gave a twitter, and launched.

The flight back through the twisted maze of the Decatur basement was chaos. Carter could hear people at the front screaming in panic, Maryland shouting directions, Ellis and Lincoln's guns booming. The freezing air burned his lungs, tore at his suddenly sore throat. In the work-out room, an entire wall of mirrors reflected just how close the creature was, slithering after them with winding, serpentine motions, snapping in the direction of any noise. No way could they escape. Lincoln separated from the main group, leading it away. Carter thought he was done for until the gangbanger hurtled over a Nordic track machine just as the thing tore it to pieces. He cut across the space, jumping to the head of the line. The maneuver bought them a few seconds while the monster realized it had been tricked, readjusted its hearing, and took up pursuit.

The next room over contained a sauna that Carter banged his knee on. He dared to look back, and caught a muzzle flash that burst across his vision like a flashbulb.

He stumbled on, momentarily blind himself. He ran into someone's backside and fell, clutching at whatever he could grab. There was an incredible explosion, the sound of glass shattering, and then something cold and heavy hit him in the forehead hard enough to knock him out.

WHITNEY +38:47

Lincoln led the way from the spa into the wine cellar. Ahead of him were shelves constructed of diamond-shaped lattices, with bottles of high-dollar liquor jutting from each hole. This room was poorly lit by faded bulbs only at the junction of each aisle, and he'd lost his flashlight. He had no idea which way to go.

Others smashed into him and each other as quickly as any ten-car pile up. They pushed and squeezed past him, desperate to get away. He heard Maryland trying to tell them which way to go. Lincoln turned around to look for her just as the entire wall to their right exploded inward, throwing plaster and slime in all directions.

The monster entered the room like a wrecking ball. It threw a spiny shoulder into the nearest wine rack. The entire works crashed forward, bringing down the other shelves like dominoes. Glass sprayed. The air was filled with the tart smell of wine. Lincoln saw several people pelted by collapsing debris, another whose throat was ripped out by the same webbed hand that took Lemiere's arm. The rest of the group screamed and broke apart in the tight space.

Lincoln bolted down the wine rows in any path that took him away from the rampage. Several others followed, but he didn't stop to check who. He turned down another aisle and spotted an exit. Through the doorway ahead was another open pantry full of dried goods and then the staircase out of here.

Turner was on the way toward them with shotgun held ready. "What's goin on, I heard gunshots!"

"No time! You gotta get these people outta here!" Lincoln answered. There were four others with him, but no familiar faces. "And swap me guns! I'm goin back to help Ellis!"

And get a little revenge.

Lincoln grabbed the shotgun before the man could protest, tossed his pistol over, and plunged back into the wine cellar.

WHITNEY +38:49

Someone patted Carter's cheek.

Hernie was hunched over him, a finger to his lips, eyes so wide and glassy they almost glowed. The air was still freezing, and the homeless man's panting breath sprayed crystalline drops down on him. Carter raised his bruised head.

He lay on the cobbled floor of the wine cellar, amid pieces of shelf and bottle shards. Another jaunt to the land of unconsciousness. He was used to passing out from hyperventilation, but the clonk-on-the-head version was just as bad. Hernie helped him stand. Carter whispered, "Where is everyone?"

Hernie shook his shaggy head.

The cellar was dead silent now aside from the trickling noise of spilled wine, and he wondered if it was because they were all trying to trick the Creature from the Smelly Lagoon, or if they were already gone. Or dead.

Carter inched forward along the still intact row of shelves, in the direction he thought the exit to Bryce Decatur's basement grotto lay. Hernie followed in his wake, stepping carefully through debris in the dim light. Carter's skin goosepimpled in the cold, a direct contrast to the fire in his throat. All that time pretending to be sick had been no preparation for this. What a waste. He wished he could have his hermetic life back only so he could tear it apart himself.

Hernie clutched at his arm hard enough to leave bruises.

Carter swiveled his head so slowly the tendons creaked.

From the other side of the shelf next to them, a scaly muzzle poked through one of the empty lattices, less than a foot from Carter's face. He could make out the mottled greenish sheen to its pebbly flesh. The nostril holes sucked in air and blew out a rancid whiff of low tide. The breath was wheezy and labored, but the lips peeled back to reveal a row of crooked daggers. A long string of gelatinous saliva uncoiled.

If Carter didn't know any better, he would swear the damn thing was *smiling*.

He yanked Hernie out of the way just as the creature bashed through the shelf, swinging wild. They moved fast and silent down the aisle, which turned left into another row of vintage wines. Ahead was a space in the middle of the room that had been mostly cleared out by the monster's rampage. A battlefield of wood, glass, and alcohol littered the floor. The chardonnays and blancs and grigios all intermingled in a colorful puddle.

Someone who'd been crouched behind stacked wine cases streaked past them. Carter caught a blur of Stewart, but was too slow to stop him. He and Hernie could only stand back as the beast tore a direct path to the noise. It caught up with Stewart as he blundered over debris, swept the small man up in powerful arms, and twisted him in two different directions like taffy. Carter looked away just as a lump of intestines splattered on the floor.

He could see the exit in the wall to their left, right next to where the monster was finishing with Stewart. They would have to brush by it to get out. Maryland, Ellis, and a few others appeared in the aisle on the opposite side, and burning relief made Carter go limp. Ellis waved at them to wait, and began to send the other people scurrying through the door. With a final glance at him, Maryland went next, sliding between the monster and the wall until she could squeeze out, and Ellis went right behind her.

"No Mr. Carter, I don't wanna go by it," Hernie pleaded in his ear.

"It's just like the parking garage." Carter squeezed the man's hand. "Follow me, just like last time. It's you and me, right? Best friends and all that?"

Hernie whapped his temple three times with his free hand and then nodded.

Carter rushed forward, dragging Hernie behind him.

The thing's tail flicked into his path. Carter's feet tangled. He sprawled forward into the narrow passage beyond the wine cellar.

Hernie stopped and tried to pull him up.

"Go Hernie, run!"

A huge shadow fell across them as the creature descended.

Two ragged sneakers appeared inches before Carter's nose. He looked up to find Lincoln standing over them with a shotgun.

"You had this comin a long time." The kid pulled the trigger.

The weapon blasted. Carter got up, and he and Hernie jumped behind Lincoln. The gangbanger cocked the shotgun and fired again. The creature took the blast full in the chest from a yard away. This time when it fell back, Carter saw dimples of thick, black blood dotting its leathery hide. It roared.

"I don't think that's gonna do it," Carter said. His ears rang so bad he could barely hear himself.

The three of them dashed through the last of the basement. The creature's claws scrabbled at the floor as it gave chase. Ellis waited halfway up the stairs. Garmon came in the entry at the top, took one look at what was behind them, and squealed, *"Holy shit, what the hell is that?"*

"GET OUTTA THE WAY!" Lincoln took the stairs two at a time, Ellis hustling to clear the escape route.

Carter looked over his shoulder. The creature was obviously hurting. It was slower, and listed to the side as it loped along. Still fast enough to catch them, but if they could just outlast it…

He mounted the steps, Hernie clutching his shirttail. Carter focused on that rectangle of light at the top.

They were two steps from the basement exit when the hand on his shirt jerked hard enough to almost pull him off balance.

Carter turned back.

The beast was retreating, but it was taking Hernie with it. The creature had him by the leg, dragging him back down like a caveman with his bride. Hernie kicked and struggled as he thumped against each stair, then held his hands out.

"Mr. Carter, help!"

"Goddamn it, *no!*" Carter started after him.

Hands grabbed him around the waist and arms. Held him back. The distance between him and Hernie lengthened each second.

"Let me go!" he demanded.

"He's gone!" Ellis yelled in his ear. "Don't do this, you'll get yourself killed!"

But he couldn't stop. He continued to fight as they hauled him away. The last thing he saw before they carried him from the basement was Hernie dragged into the darkness, toward the monster's nest.

WHITNEY +38:53

"And that was the last place you saw her? With these other people?"

"Yes. Tangela's alive, Dad. I *know* she is."

Daryl Sloan sat on the back bumper of the Hummer and stared at his son. The story was too fantastic to be believed—Port Allen systematically exterminated by paramilitary forces—but it fit everything he'd seen. The boy told them roughly half the tale as they drove down the Chantilly hillside along the rough trail. When he got to the part about the disease, Burt began to retch and gag, and held his grimy shirttail over nose and mouth.

"See, I told you, *I told you!*" he'd shouted, somehow driving, keeping his face covered, and jabbing a finger at Daryl all at the same time.

"Told me what?"

"This is all their fault, man!"

"*Who*, Burt?"

"You know...the *government*...and...and the *corporations!* Global warming, man!"

"You don't even know who you're blaming anymore."

Burt took huge panicked gulps of air through his hand and pleaded, "Can we just save the rest of the story, please? If I'm gonna die, I'd rather not hear the details."

It might've all been hysterics, but Daryl could feel a tingle in his own throat. And Chris had been coughing more the farther they went.

Once inside the city, they turned due north along the foothills and finally parked in a field of boulders so Burt could 'steady his nerves,' an act which resulted in reams of sweet-smelling smoke pouring from the vehicle while Daryl and Chris finished talking outside.

"Chris, I hope...no, I *believe* she is too, but how do we find her? From the way you described it, I think I know which street you were captured on, but even if we could make it back there, these people...the woman, the guy with the rebreather, the police officer...surely, they've moved on since then. And that's only if they weren't killed or captured themselves."

Chris' jaw whipped back and forth like a hand saw working through a two-by-four. Daryl could remember him starting that when he was just about in kindergarten, and the boy was too young to remember his mother doing the same thing when she was angry. The tears welling in his son's eyes meant it wasn't helping him find a solution. "I don't know, but we have to. I gave my word that we would get to you and…she could live with us…"

Daryl got off the bumper and pulled the boy to him, pressing him into his chest as though trying to absorb him. His son; his son was alive. As mad as he was at God right now—and had been for the last several years—he had to be thankful for that much.

"Dad…about Nichelle…"

Daryl's hug tightened, crushing the words out of existence. "Not now. We'll talk about it later."

"I just want you to know, I tried. I tried to save her. I didn't hate her."

"I know that. I always did."

The driver's door of the Hummer opened and Burt sauntered back to join them. He looked more relaxed, but his eyes were little bloodshot marbles. "So what's the story, mornin glory? We got a plan?"

"I think so." Daryl sighed. "I'm gonna find my daughter. You're taking Chris and the Hummer and getting back out of the city any way you can."

"*Dad!*"

He put a hand on the boy's thin chest. "I don't wanna hear it. If I'd known what was going on in Port Allen, I would've sent the two of you in the other direction at the camp."

"But you stand a better chance of finding her if all of us help!"

"My first responsibility is to get you to safety. Once you're out of here, you can get help, tell someone what's going on."

"Don't get me wrong, I'm all for beatin feet outta this madhouse," Burt said, "but how're we supposed to do it, man? The only way out is right back the way we came, and they're bound to've plugged that hole in the dike by now."

"So you take the Hummer right up the side of the mountain as far as you can, and then you walk the rest of the way."

"That's gonna take a long time, Daryl. Too much time to be able to send back help that's gonna make any difference. And that's only if this disease don't kill us first. I'm not sayin it ain't an option, but if we're goin that route, we might as well wait for you."

Daryl opened his mouth to tell them he didn't care, he just wanted at least one member of his family out of harm's way, but before he could speak, he heard a faint, scratchy voice. He frowned and looked at the other two for a moment before realizing it was coming from inside the Hummer.

"The radio!" Burt exclaimed.

They'd kept both the AM/FM and the CB on during the entire drive. Everything across the regular wavelengths was dead air, except the CB which broadcast bursts of that encoded gibberish every few minutes. But this sounded like clear speech. They gathered in the open driver's door to listen.

"…the authorities, the media, *someone*," a female voice drifted down from Avery's CB unit mounted on the vehicle ceiling. There was a burst of static, and then, "Um, mayday, mayday, this is Maryland Williams. I'm broadcasting—"

"*That's her!*" Chris yelled. "They were going to Officer Wright's police precinct to call for help! They must've made it!" He snatched the corded mic from its cradle and mashed the button on its side. "I can't believe it! Maryland! Maryland, it's me, Chris!" The voice continued to talk. "She can't hear me! How do you work this thing?"

"Your guess is as good as mine, little dude."

"Better write down that address," Daryl said, and Burt produced a stained minipad of paper and a pencil stub from his breast pocket.

"I don't understand, why can't we talk to them?" Chris demanded.

"Because it's a recording," a groggy voice said from the backseat. Daryl jumped so hard he banged the back of his head on the Hummer's doorframe. He'd forgotten all about their unconscious passenger. The man sat up, wincing and holding the lump on his forehead.

"Whoa, take it easy there, dude." Burt moved to the rolled-down rear window. "That blow mighta scrambled the ol' upstairs pudding a little."

"A recording?" Chris asked.

"It's a mayday," the stranger clarified. "Probably broadcasting a few times on each channel before moving on. Who are you people? Where am I?"

"I'm Daryl Sloan, and this is my son Chris. That's Burt Weaver. You got knocked out back at that detainment camp."

"Right. The detainment camp. And you good Samaritans stopped to pick me up, eh?"

A sarcastic thread wove through the words. Daryl didn't care for it. "What did you want us to do, leave you there? They would've killed you."

The man's eyes drilled him. There was something hard and flinty in them, like Daryl imagined the eyes of a serial killer or ruthless mob boss would look. Then he grinned, and that trace of unpleasantness was gone. He gave a girlish giggle under his breath; a quick *hee-hee-hee* that chilled Daryl's heart.

Chris looked over the seat. "What's your name?"

The man took a long moment to answer as he probed at the dark purple bruise on his scalp. He had a scar that snarled around the underside of his chin too, but that injury looked years older. "James. James DeWitt. I remember your Hummer now. You came crashing in out of nowhere. Tell me, how'd you get way up there, Mr. Sloan?"

"Call me Daryl. We came up the mountain, through the old western trail."

"Huh. You'd think these guys would've had patrols set up along the way."

"Oh, they did, but we got around them. I don't think these military guys are half as good as they think. Anyway, we made it there just as the escape started. My son orchestrated the whole thing from inside."

Burt added, "Yeah, the little dude is a regular Clint Eastwood. *Alcatraz*, I mean, not *Dirty Harry*."

Daryl put an arm around Chris, who beamed.

"Then I guess I owe my life to you. Thanks." DeWitt smiled good-naturedly, but to Daryl, it seemed forced. His jaw looked clenched hard enough to shatter teeth. "Now, if you could just drop me somewhere, or I could get out here…"

"What? No, are you crazy? You can't stay in the city!"

DeWitt sighed, leaned back, and took a look out the window. "You brought me into the city. Perfect. Not to sound ungrateful, but you know there's a little 'medical issue' going on down here?"

"My son told me. Do you know anything about it?"

"Only that we're all infected now."

"You were *already* infected though, right?" Chris asked. "That's why we were all locked up."

"Right, right." DeWitt flapped a hand at them.

They were quiet a moment, the silence a little unsettling. There were no birds, no crickets, just the distant sound of what Daryl thought might be a helicopter.

Burt finally held up the pad of paper. "Daryl, dude…this address is in Manchester Heights. That's not too far."

"That's where Maryland lives. I guess they went there next." Chris knotted his hands together under his chin. "Please just let us come with you, Dad."

Daryl nodded. "Mr. DeWitt, it might be better if we did separate after all. We're looking for my daughter, and I don't want to drag you into any more danger than we already have. We can leave you somewhere and come back to get you, if you want."

DeWitt still leaned back in the seat, speaking without looking at them. "Where's your daughter?"

"The last place my son saw her is with this large group of Whitney survivors—"

"Large group?" DeWitt sat forward now.

"Yes, the one broadcasting that message. They've been fighting these soldiers since last night."

DeWitt grinned so wide, his face looked in danger of splitting in two. He gave another of those unsettling snickers.

"By all means," he said. "Drive on."

WHITNEY +38:57

Mattinson was attempting to take a piss in one of the bio-containment suits when an agent stomped up next to him with a portable field radio, "Sir, I think you should hear this!"

He jumped, the urine stream cutting off, and listened to the recorded message. "Is this frequency being blocked?"

"No sir. As near as I can tell, everything at base camp is still down, including the jammers. This is going out live to whoever's listening."

"Jesus Christ! What the fuck's going on up there?"

"Should I send a chopper back?"

Mattinson considered. "We have our orders. We can find out what happened after the targets are neutralized." He tapped the radio. "And now we know exactly where they are. Do we have anyone close to this location?"

"There's a foot squad fifteen minutes away. The rest of us can be there in thirty."

"Send them in immediately. Everyone. Shoot to kill, no survivors." Mattinson forgot all about his leak and headed for his chopper. "I want a full report by the time I arrive."

WHITNEY +39:02

Hernie was in *biiiiiig* trouble.

As soon as he felt the hand close around his ankle, he was pretty sure he was a goner. But instead of twisting him out of shape like a Slinky, the monster left him unharmed as it hauled him away from his friends, back into the freezing cold bowels of the basement. He struggled, but it was all he could do just to keep himself from being cut as he was dragged over glass shards and jagged pieces of wood in the wine cellar.

The creature walked on two legs to pull him along while feeling its way forward, but it twitched and stumbled every few paces. It reminded Hernie of the homeless people at the shelter that snuck in booze. It snorted and wheezed, each inward breath as noisy as a car alarm.

It's sick. Sick like us.

The monster dragged him back to the room at the end of the basement, the one that held the radio. It brought him to the junk barrier in the corner. Hernie understood what was on the other side: a nest, just like a mama birdy makes for her eggs.

It released its grip on his leg. Hernie scrabbled at the floor, trying to squirm away, but the creature slammed one massive leg down on his back and pinned him flat.

"W-what do you want?" he asked.

The creature tilted its hideous head and hissed.

Hernie's chest hitched as he tried to draw breath beneath the massive weight. "Mr. Carter's gonna come for me, you bad monster! And then you'll be *sorry!*"

The monster responded by grabbing his ankle again in one hand, his foot in the other, and *twisted*, like someone removing the top from a soda bottle. Bones snapped. Hernie screamed as his foot was turned the wrong direction at the end of his leg.

The monster yanked him off the ground by the mangled limb. He dangled upside down for a second—at one point staring into the slavering maw of the beast—and then was tossed into the nest. He landed on his side hard enough to wallop the air from his lungs. The agony in his leg was all-consuming, the foot flopping bonelessly and the cuff of his borrowed pants turning red.

When he could breathe again, Hernie forced himself to roll over.

A skeleton lay a few feet away, scraps of swollen, purplish flesh still clinging to the bones, but that didn't concern him as much as the eggs.

They were each the size of a volleyball and roughly the same color, but their texture looked like stone. As he watched, two of them shook, the vibrations like a rattlesnake.

The voice of Mr. Carter spoke up.

Hern-ster, I think our aquatic friend intends for you to be baby's first chowdown.

Mr. Carter had a way of explaining things just right, so Hernie could understand.

Blind panic took him. He dug both hands into the mound that formed the edge of the nest and tried to pull himself out. His leg screamed. He couldn't put any weight on it, and the debris was piled too high for him to crawl over. The monster stood over him, making sure he couldn't escape.

He slid back down and lay on his stomach, watched the eggs as they shook. Mr. Carter would come. He had saved Hernie when the old man shot him, and he would do so now. They were best friends.

While Hernie tried to convince himself, he noticed something on the wall that made up one side of the nest. He raised his chin off the floor and squinted at it.

A plastic rectangle with narrow vertical slits running top to bottom, and a button at the bottom. It looked like the thing Mary-land had used at the front gate of this big house, to talk to her husband.

Hernie crawled across the floor past the eggs on his elbows, every inch drenched in agony. At this rate, it would take him a few minutes to get across the space. He kept his eyes focused on the plastic rectangle.

He'd covered most of the distance when a brittle crack issued from one of the eggs.

WHITNEY +39:05

Carter wasn't sure how he ended up in the room of crystal figurines. They sat behind glass on a series of backlit shelves, staring at him from all directions. Dogs, giraffes, and seals. Little girls on tricycles. A bear wearing a fedora. They were kind of cute, until he caught his reflection in the glass covering them.

The ghost of an ashen, slack-jawed thirty-one-year-old stared back at him, a guy that had spent his life playing with dolls and avoiding the sun like a vampire.

A little desk sat in the corner, with a heavy oak chair tucked into it. He grabbed the seat by its back and swung it in an arc.

An entire wall of glass exploded at once. A musical symphony of twinkling crystal rained down around him. But the fury wasn't sated; he felt like it was barely getting started. He heaved the chair up and used it again and again, reveling in the destruction, happy that he was taking something beautiful out of the world.

Sweating and gasping and coughing, he finally let the chair slip from his hands. Shattered figurines lay everywhere. The bear in the fedora—now minus a body—glared at him accusingly from atop a pile of crystal body parts. Amazingly, Carter hadn't been so much as scratched by the flying debris.

"I now see the danger in the phrase 'make yourself at home.'"

Maryland stood outside the room, leaning through the doorframe.

Something in Carter's head snapped, and he looked around as if seeing what he'd done for the first time. "Oh Jesus. Ah God, I'm so sorry. Your figures…"

"Don't sweat it. They were Bryce's."

"They *were?*" He snorted. "Wow, and I thought my collections were bad."

"I'm actually a little jealous. I've had fantasies about doing that for years. How did it feel?"

"Not as good as I'd hoped." He coughed again and shrugged. "I mean, what does it matter, right? A city's worth of people died over the last two days. What's one more homeless retard on the bonfire?"

Maryland entered; her feet made Rice Krispy noises as she crossed the carpet. "He was your friend."

He thought about that. Carter hadn't made any friends—*real* friends, not people he paid for services like Rosa or Doc Pellner— in years. He'd told Hernie they were friends back at the old man's house, and again downstairs, but that was all just talk.

The world looked watery to him suddenly. He blinked until it stopped.

"You couldn't have done anything to help him," Maryland whispered.

"No, of course not!" He gave a heap of glass in front of him a hard, soccer-style kick. Shards flew in all directions, pinged off the walls. "I can't ever help *anything!* This voice in my head had me scared of my own shadow for *eight years!* I'm sick of it! *All of it!*"

She surprised him by coming forward, slipping her arms around him, and putting her chin on his shoulder. He melted, holding her tight and burying his face in her hair. It didn't smell as sweet as he imagined, but he thought he could happily live in it for the rest of his life.

"You saved *me*," she reminded him.

Footsteps pounded outside. Lincoln flew into the room with Garmon and Ellis trailing.

"Hey man, what's all the—? Woah, sorry. We interruptin somethin?"

"Yeah, a WWF grudge match, by the looks of this place," Garmon muttered. "I see the china shop, so where's the bull?"

"Just a little therapy." Maryland gave Carter one last squeeze as she released him.

Ellis nodded. "C'mon you two. I moved everyone out of the

kitchen, made them go over to the far side of the house. We need to clear out before that thing comes up here on another rampage."

"And go where?" Carter asked.

"We…we run for the mountains, I guess."

"What if someone actually responds to our SOS? We came all the way here for the slim hope that radio would do something for us, and now you just wanna abandon it?"

"Yes, since its roommate seems to be a brutal killing machine!"

Carter shook his head. "You said yourself Ellis, this is it, nowhere else to run, last stop on the hellbound express."

"All right then, give me a better idea, or at least one good reason to stay!"

Carter didn't have one. But that was okay, because the voice of God spoke for him.

"H-hello? *Cough-cough!* Are you there?" The amplified words seemed to come from everywhere at once, floating down from the ceiling, and Carter could hear it echoing from the hallway. And man, did the voice of God sure sound a lot like—

"Hernie," he and Maryland said together.

"It's the PA system." She ran out of the destroyed room. They followed. Overhead, Hernie's disembodied pleas for help went on.

The broadcasting speakers were everywhere—from what Maryland had told him of her husband, Carter could imagine how the guy would get off by having his voice boom through the house— but the closest one with a microphone was down one of the two long hallways that ran through the middle of the mansion. Carter jabbed the button.

"Hernie, pal, it's me! You okay?"

"M-Mr. Carter?" Just hearing the little dope call him that again made Carter laugh. "I d-don't want to be here anymore!"

"Where's 'here,' buddy? Did you get away?"

"N-no, my leg, my leg hurts so baaaaad…"

His voice weakened. "Stay with me, Hernster! Where are you?"

"I'm in the nest. Those eggs are making n-noises, Mr. Carter. Will you come get me?"

"Yes! Just sit tight, we're coming!" He let go of the button and faced the others, already despising the look on their faces.

"Carter," Ellis said, "I understand how you feel, just like I did about Charlie, but there's no way you can go down there."

"I'm through running," Carter told them. "And you should be too. Odds are, we're probably all gonna die anyway, but that's all the more reason not to give another inch. That's *our* friend down there, and *our* radio. That *20,000 Leagues* reject is not gonna push us around."

Lincoln lifted Turner's shotgun. "I'd like nothin better than to get some revenge on that bitch, but you just can't kill it. Guns don't do no good. It just shrugged off a blast from this, you saw it, man."

Carter held out a palm. "But that's not true. It bled, and if Arnold Schwarzenegger has taught me one thing besides how to bankrupt an entire state, it's that if something bleeds, it can be killed. And that thing was already hurting, either from the P3 or everything else we've done to it."

He thought for a second, frowned, and then smiled.

"Besides…what if we didn't have to kill it?"

WHITNEY +39:10

Hatch lowered his head to sniff at the crack along the bottom of the basement door, then looked up at Lincoln and whimpered. He'd retrieved the Lab from upstairs because he didn't want to do this alone, and the animal was the only one he trusted not to be a liability. Lincoln bent and tugged the dog away by the scruff of his neck.

"Yeah, I know. This is fuckin stupid. But it's also the best plan we got to save your master. And, as the two fastest people here, you and I just got drafted."

Hatch bowed his brown head, then sat at his heel with a gagging cough.

Ellis approached and held out a fistful of shotgun shells. "That's the last of what Turner had left. He said you better not die, because he wants that gun back."

"Thanks." Lincoln topped off the weapon's breach, replacing the two rounds he'd expended earlier. His hand shook as he pushed the cartridges inside. He shoved the rest in the pocket of his jeans.

"Hey." Ellis waited until he looked up to continue. "You sure you want to do this?"

"No. Not even fuckin close. But who else is gonna do it, gimpy? You?"

"Would if I could."

Lincoln smirked. "Ya know, I mighta not believed that yesterday. But you grew a pair at some point." And then the half-smile faded from his lips, and Lincoln said, slowly and deliberately, "Ellis, I gotta tell you somethin."

"It's okay. I know you did the best you could to help Charlie. If anything, it's my fault for sending Mac and Lemiere instead of going myself."

"Naw man, it ain't about that. I just want you to know—"

Ellis put a hand on his arm. "It can wait till you get back. Okay?"

Lincoln gestured at the closed basement door. "I kinda don't think it can. I need someone to hear this before I go down there."

Ellis studied him with his one good eye and nodded.

"I killed Mr. Kim," he said quietly. The simplicity of the statement astonished him. "Back before the hurricane. It was an accident. He caught us lootin and just…went berserk. That ain't no excuse but…" He didn't know how to finish, didn't even know why he needed to say it so bad. Not for forgiveness. He figured it was because everyone else that knew the truth was dead, and if he went to the grave without passing it on—under false pretenses, so to speak—it would be like saying it never happened.

Ellis continued to stare at him for several long seconds. "Lincoln, everything we did before Whitney…everything we were…I don't think any of that matters anymore."

"You sound like Kordi."

"It's true. This has all been one great big reset button, and if—by some direct-from-God miracle—we survive, the only thing that matters is where we go from here. So tell me, you going back to being a gangbanger?"

"Hell no," Lincoln said. "I've been thinkin 'bout…I don't know…maybe joinin the Army."

"Sounds like a plan. And step one is: make it back out of that basement alive. You hear me?"

"Just make sure I got a clear path."

Ellis nodded, and retreated back down the hallway, through the kitchen entry.

Lincoln's heart jackhammered. He looked down at Hatch, grabbed the doorknob, and pushed open the basement door. Only when he was met with darkness and quiet did he realize he fully expected that thing to be right on the other side, ready to take his head off with those sickle claws.

He started down the basement steps with the shotgun in one hand, barrel pointed at the floor. Hatch matched him step for step, hackles raised. Whatever Turner did to the generator had worked; it hummed along as smoothly as a washing machine behind the door at the bottom of the staircase, leaving the basement as silent as Parkland Cemetery.

They reached the bottom. Lincoln stood in the muck and scanned the darkness that crouched in the recesses. He wished he'd brought a flashlight, but it was too late now.

"Hey yo, Fish-mama!" he shouted. "I'm here! Let's do this thing!"

No answer. He waited a fistful of seconds and then told the Labrador, "Take me to him, boy."

Hatch slunk forward, cautious and low, his breathing husky. Lincoln took up a matching pace on the dog's tail as they started into the pantry full of stocked nonperishables.

The place was bigger than the house he grew up in, with shelves along every wall and boxes of dried food stacked everywhere. The gloom intensified. Most of the lights were busted, and he was fairly certain they'd all worked last time he came through. He hated sneaking around, it was so much more nerve-wracking than running right up to it like he had before. He couldn't make a move until he'd drawn it out. So why couldn't the fucking monster just cooperate?

In front of him, Hatch gave a long, low growl.

Lincoln halted. The Labrador stopped, shoulders hunched into twin peaks. He stared into a far corner of the pantry, where the shadows gathered like a black hole. There was a shape in there coiled against the ground, staying very still. Something large and prickly. He could smell its stench.

His skin went numb, his mouth dry. Lincoln pointed the shotgun into the corner and tried to hold the aim steady.

"I see you," he said. The shape didn't so much as twitch. He inched his way forward, past Hatch. Sweat trickled into his eye. "You killed my best friend."

Still, the creature didn't stir. Maybe it was dead already. He closed the distance to a few yards, the closest he could get and still escape if it rushed him.

"*Damn it, come on! Come and get me!*"

And then it did.

From his *left*.

A stack of cardboard boxes flew in every direction as the creature crashed through them. Lincoln flailed away, trying to get the shotgun turned around. His feet got tangled and he fell into the shape in the corner. The bulky object collapsed under him, and he caught a glimpse of a careful arrangement of foodstuff covered with a tarp, complete with slivers of glass to form a spiny look-alike.

He'd been *duped* by this thing.

He fired the shotgun from the hip with one hand. The blast hit the monster low across one side as it came for him. It screeched and took a half step back, but not enough to give Lincoln room to stand.

Hatch barked and darted in from the other side, nipping at the monster's ankle. It swiped at him. The dog jumped aside, and Lincoln used the opportunity to roll to his feet.

The creature stood between him and the door out. He inched along the wall as it swung blindly, but it was slower than the last time they'd met. Where once there was agility, now there was only exhausted labor, like a prize fighter in his final round. Hatch came in for another bite, and this time the beast spun all the way around in a fury. Again, the claws missed their target, but its broad tail smashed the dog's midsection and sent him flying into the wall. He yelped and left a starburst of blood on the plaster.

Lincoln didn't wait. He took off for the stairs, but paused once to cock the shotgun and fire it in the air. Had to make sure the thing followed him, or they would have to start this dance all over. He didn't have to worry though; the creature charged after him on all fours.

Up the staircase. The sound of it treading wood was like explosions. Lincoln wanted to fire again, just to keep it good and angry, but was afraid the smallest delay would be the end of him. He hurtled through the open basement door and turned right.

"Okay, mean-and-green, let's see what you can really do!" He pelted down the dark corridor of the house with the beast giving chase.

WHITNEY +39:13

Maryland heard something that sounded like a bulldozer go crashing down the hall, deeper into Château Decatur. She shuddered at the thought of that monstrosity loose in her house. Then she thought about Bryce getting eaten by it and felt another hot twinge of guilt.

Across the other side of the kitchen door, Ellis gave her and Carter the go signal.

"Get in and get out," he hissed as they hurried by. "You don't wanna be down there if that thing comes back."

"Do your job up here and we won't have to worry about it," she whispered back.

And then all thought was gone as they hurtled into the basement. Carter took the stairs three at a time, slowing only when he reached the goop near the bottom. She stayed on his ass, her heart threatening to explode. Their frenzy only served to heighten the fear.

They paused for nothing. By the time they reached the room at the far end, both were panting and blowing white clouds into the freezing cold. Carter coughed in his hand, which came away bloody. She saw his eyes bulge right out of his head before he called out, "Hernie!"

"*Heeeelp!*" The cry drifted up from the corner.

Maryland made it to the nest just ahead of Carter and leaned over the mound of debris that formed its edge. Hernie lay on the opposite side, past Bryce's body, squeezed into the corner under the PA speaker. A noise like shaken maracas issued from all around, and she realized it was coming from the eggs. Hairline fractures webbed across the surface of all five.

She held out her arms. "Come over to us Hernie, hurry!"

"I c-can't, it hurts!"

She saw it then, his right leg, the foot twisted almost backward. It made her queasy just looking at it. But he belly-flopped onto the ground and used his arms and good leg to push across to them.

"We gotta get him outta there!" Carter swung a leg over the side of the nest, and Maryland followed. They sidestepped Bryce's corpse to get to Hernie. Each got an arm under him, trying to lift him upright, but the thick layer of gunk in the bottom of the nest made it as slippery as an ice-skating rink.

From the egg closest to Maryland came a gruff *cheep*, like a baby bird with a Darth Vader voice box, and wouldn't Carter love to know she'd just made that analogy?

She turned her head while they wrestled with Hernie. The soccer-ball shell cracked in two, the top half falling over. Something stirred inside the shadowy cup and then poked its head out.

It was a miniature version of their monster in detail, that shimmery combination of dark greens and browns and purples, complete with a set of needle-like claws. It made her think of the horror movie model kits her cousin had put together years ago (the name of the company who made them popped into her head unbidden, and damned if it wasn't Aurora), tiny likenesses of Frankenstein and Wolfman and, more pertinent, the Big Bad Creature from the B.L. This one blinked at her with dismal yellow eyes and gave a hoot that would've been adorable if the thing wasn't so ugly.

The newborn launched at her.

She was still bent over, trying to help Hernie get his good leg under him. The hatchling flew through the air with the spryness of a grasshopper and clung to her arm. It buried its three-inch long muzzle in her flesh.

"Get off me!" Maryland beat at the thing as it tore skin away in strips, finally grabbing it around its spiky midsection. Its flesh was cool and slick, like holding a snake. She flung it across the nest. It bounced off the wall and landed in the muck, where it shook its head dizzily and hopped right back up.

"Go Maryland, get out!" Carter supported Hernie around the waist. Now there were cracking noises all over, and more of those tittering cries. Yellow eyes gleamed. She dodged when another baby leapt at her and went to help with Hernie.

They carried him toward the edge of the nest. Maryland's feet kept trying to slip out from under her. The monster babies followed in a circle, chittering and bouncing into the air to snap at their faces and necks. One of them scampered up Hernie's side and latched onto his shoulder. Carter issued a manly growl, then let go of Hernie to smash the thing like a mosquito. It fell away with a squeak, and Carter stomped on it until it was a crushed smear.

One of Bryce's filing cabinets was overturned against the outside of the nest. She let go of Hernie and yanked out a drawer, scattering legal files.

Pain skewered her as one of them bit her in the ass. She reached back and tore it away, then slammed its little body into the drawer. Another one streaked toward her and she flipped the drawer over on top of it before it could jump, trapping the two of them beneath. They banged and rattled against the metal sides, but it was too heavy for them to lift.

Three down. The last two were using Carter's back as a scratching post. He tumbled Hernie over the side of the nest. The poor guy screamed as he hit the floor on his twisted leg. Carter spun in a circle and tried to reach his attackers.

Maryland slapped one of them away, but the other turned and nipped the end of her index finger. It held on with the tenacity of a crocodile until she got her flailing under control, grabbed its little head, and *squeezed*. She felt bone collapse between her fingers, brains and blood squirting like a burst zit, and the baby went limp.

She spun, expecting the one she knocked away to be coming, but it had found something better. It hunched over the body of the sibling Carter killed, devouring the carcass in huge, hungry bites. Maryland grabbed another drawer and trapped it and its cannibal meal together, then stacked a heap of heavy law books on top of both makeshift cages.

All of them were bleeding from a dozen bites. They climbed out of the nest and got Hernie back on his feet. "What about the radio?" she asked.

"Just leave it for now! If Mommy comes back before we get out of here, there'll be hell to pay!"

They ran back out of the basement with Hernie dangling between them. When they made it into the pantry, the man cried out, "Hatch!"

The dog lay on the floor, under a pile of dried goods. Maryland hadn't even noticed him earlier. He lay curled on his side, with a puddle of blood under him.

Hernie struggled out of their grip before they could stop him and collapsed to his knees in front of the animal. He didn't even whimper this time, just cradled the dog's head in his lap.

"Is he gonna be okay, Mr. Carter?" They didn't answer. Hernie fixed them in a stony glare and demanded, "*Is* he?"

"I...I don't think so, Hernie."

"No, no, no, no, no." He smacked the side of his head again and again. "Not Hatch, please no, not poor Hatchy-Hatch!"

Maryland felt more tears wet her cheeks. Carter knelt beside him, caught his hand before he could hit himself any more, and wrapped an arm around his shoulders. "He was a hero, Hernie. And we'll bury him like a hero. But right now, we *have* to go."

Hernie nodded. He gave Hatch's ear one last squeeze as they helped him up and hurried toward the basement stairs.

WHITNEY +39:17

Maryland had explained the layout of the house to Lincoln before they sent him on this insane mission, but he didn't have time to actually scout it. He now saw the danger. His imagination had conjured something completely different than the reality. Even with most of the lights on, he could get lost any second. He ran through one room and then the next, coughing, hurtling over furniture and knocking over anything he could to slow the beast down. Even blind and injured, Fish-mama was keeping up with him all too well.

One of the doorways ahead on the left would be a cross hall, where he could jaunt over and take the other main corridor back to the front of the house. The question was, had he eaten up enough time? It felt like he'd been leading this fucker for hours, but he knew it couldn't be more than a few minutes, tops.

His adrenaline-pumped mind couldn't even remember where she'd said to turn. One of the last three doors. Pick the wrong one and he'd wind up in a dead-end room, where Fish-mama would have him trapped. The end of the hall was just ahead and he was running out of options…

He took the next left. Another hallway. He was so overjoyed he actually chanced a look back.

And almost paid for it with his life.

The thing was right *there*, in his face, snorting and wheezing like a mad bull, but reaching for him with webbed hands. Turning his head slowed Lincoln just enough for the claw tips to sink into his shoulders.

It yanked, pulling him off balance and into its clammy embrace. The shotgun wavered in his grasp and almost slipped from his fingers. Just as the monster reached to tear his head off, he got the barrel up, put it against the first patch of tough hide he could find, and pulled the trigger.

The blast—right next to his head—burst something deep in his right ear. But he was released. He jumped forward and, even though it'd just gotten him in trouble, paused to take a look at his handiwork.

The creature had a ragged hole in its upper chest, close to the socket of its right arm. The entire appendage jerked and flopped. She gurgled, coughed a chunk of something black on the carpet, then lurched at him.

Lincoln sprinted on, shot back into the main corridor on the north side of the house. He turned left again, completing the last leg of a circuit that would carry him back to where he'd started.

God, Ellis better be ready…

He recognized the glow from the kitchen ahead. He bounded into the room, skidding on the tile. The monster darted in behind him. Lincoln went past the island in the middle of the room, toward that huge walk-in freezer, which was now standing wide open with tendrils of fog curling out. Lincoln caught sight of Ellis hiding behind the metal slab door. He tried to pass as close as possible as he ran by.

"NOW!" he heard the cop shout. Lincoln figured he might as well stop to watch the trap get sprung; if it didn't work, they were all dead anyway.

From the opposite side of the room, Turner and four other men heaved against a heavy serving cart on rollers, driving it across the floor. It struck the beast broadside. The creature stumbled sideways, giving a few feeble slashes, but the length of the cart kept the men out of reach. Lincoln blasted it with the shotgun to keep it moving.

They kept pushing until both creature and cart were over the freezer threshold, then jumped back. Ellis and Lincoln swung the heavy door shut just as it clambered over the obstruction and charged.

The door sealed. They threw the latch.

From the other side came dull thuds. All of them stayed tense and ready to run.

Ellis grabbed Lincoln's neck. "You okay?"

"What?" His hearing on the right side was gone. Moisture dribbled down his neck. But for the moment, he thought it was a fair trade.

"Keeee-rist," Turner moaned. "I know you kept calling it a monster but…what the *hell* is that thing?"

"No idea. But it killed Lemiere. And Ellis' partner. And my best friend. Now it's payback time." Lincoln walked over to the freezer and pounded it with the bottom of one fist. "You hear me, shithead? You gonna rot in there!" The frantic banging on the other side renewed.

"Uh, Lincoln, maybe you shouldn't do that," Ellis cautioned.

Carter, Maryland and Hernie limped into the kitchen from the direction of the other entrance. All three of them bled from a dozen small wounds.

"The basement's got an infestation you would *not* believe." They eased Hernie into a kitchen chair and Carter nodded at the freezer. "It worked?"

Ellis nodded. "Yeah, but are you sure it's gonna hold? I mean, didn't that thing bash through a steel cell door at my precinct?"

"That door wasn't pressurized like this one. It's vacuum-sealed in there. Besides, it's injured now. I think it might be dying. And if it's not, it will when it runs out of air."

"Good," Lincoln spat.

They listened to its struggles from inside the freezer for a few more seconds. After it had exhausted its rage, there was a pathetic keening.

"We won," Ellis said softly. He smiled, his split lips turning the expression grotesque. "Don't you see? We beat it!"

A brief victory cry went up among the people in the kitchen.

But it was cut far too short as Garmon careened into the room.

"I don't mean to break up the tea party," he said. "But Aurora's here."

THE END OF THE LINE

"How many did you see?" Ellis asked, as he headed into the entrance foyer of Château Decatur. There was never any time to take a breath before the next disaster.

Garmon rushed ahead of him and walked backwards while talking. "It looked like one of the sweeper teams, probably five guys. I spotted them working on the gate just before they busted in."

"I thought you barricaded the gate!" Maryland said.

"Gimme a break, I didn't build a moat, I just parked your cars against it like Ellis told me to! They probably clipped the motor guide wires and forced the damn thing open!"

"Then why didn't *we* do that, genius?" Carter muttered. Lincoln snickered and gave him a high-five.

Garmon ignored them. "They made a beeline for this place, like they knew we were here. These guys were most likely the closest. But if they know, the rest won't be far behind."

Ellis stepped to the sectioned glass wall that made up the front wall of the house. His vision wasn't the best with one eye swollen closed and the pain pills Maryland gave him starting to take effect, but he could see nothing in the thirty-yard swatch of vibrant green grass between the house and the fountain. Past that, the gate was shut with five luxury automobiles parked in front of it, reminding Ellis of a joke about the redneck lottery winner's front yard. The sun shone from high on the horizon, climbing toward what was sure to be Port Allen's most blistering day since Whitney.

"Are you sure you saw—?"

He heard the odd *bomp!* before he registered the flash just inches in front of his forehead, on the other side of the glass. He flung himself away on instinct, even though it would've been far too late. "Jesus!"

"Sniper!" Garmon exclaimed, ducking.

They all hit the floor except Maryland, who said, "It's okay, that's bulletproof glass. Bryce had every base covered for the apocalypse."

Ellis eased back to the glass wall and scanned the front yard again. He thought he saw a black-clad head behind the rim of the fountain. The concrete cup was too low for more than one person to stay hidden behind it.

So where were the other four?

Garmon moved over behind a sofa in the middle of the room, keeping low. "Bulletproof glass won't hold them for long. They'll drive a tank in here if they have to."

"Tank?" Lincoln asked. "They got *tanks?*"

"The full military is at their disposal."

"But that doesn't make sense," Carter argued. "Why not just blow up the whole house, like they did with the Dome?"

Garmon shook his head. "You're asking the wrong guy, slick. I turned in my walking papers, remember? Maybe some heavy artillery is inbound, or they're keeping a low profile." He glanced around at them, and Ellis saw fear in the soldier's eyes. "Maybe Kyler is pissed and wants us alive for some reason."

From elsewhere in the house, the sound of glass breaking reached them.

Then screams and thudding automatic gunfire.

"Goddamn it, no!" Ellis limped toward the noise. He'd lost the Beretta at the precinct, but one of the new folks had an extra Smith & Wesson 9mm they'd let him use. He pulled the weapon just as a group of their people came running in the opposite direction.

Sara swam out of the crowd and grabbed at him. "Oh God, they're in the house! I can't find Doug!"

"Get upstairs!" he shouted. "Lincoln, Turner, come on! Maryland, you said your husband has weapons?"

"T-they're in a vault upstairs, I'll have to find the combination!"

He cursed under his breath. "Just get it open!" Ellis shoved against the flow of traffic down the hall. He, Lincoln, and Turner squeezed through whatever gaps they could find. The shots seemed to have quieted ahead and, as the stream of survivors thinned, they slowed to quiet their footsteps against the carpet. They could hear the trample and screams from upstairs, but the rest of the house was silent.

A doorway came up on their left. Ellis was woozy, but training took over. He waved a hand at his partners to keep them back and spun around the corner.

Inside was a den with a hunting lodge motif: high-backed leather chairs, mounted animal heads, a fireplace with a deerskin rug. Most of the people in the house had been lounging in here, sleeping or eating, and when the monster attacked he'd sent the rest in this direction. Now the tall, narrow windows—bulletproof or not—were shattered. He spotted two bodies, neither of them anyone he recognized.

Still…they were fellow survivors. The last of the Whitney refugees. *His* people.

Ellis felt his temperature skyrocket.

He went in first and Lincoln covered him. They swept the place quick and dirty, but the lounge and the adjoining library full of thick law tomes were both empty. There were several other ways in or out, so the soldiers could be anywhere. This goddamn house was a maze.

A soft tinkle came from the next room. Ellis moved toward it fast. He found a dark dining room, with a long mahogany table like something from a medieval castle. He slid along the wall toward the next doorway, then heard, *"Pssst!"*

It took him a second to realize it'd come from under the table. He bent down.

Doug peered out at him, with three or four others. "Are they gone?"

A shadow jumped into the doorway across from Ellis. From his hunched position, it would take an eternity to get his gun up. He let gravity take over and fell to the ground. Those ear-splitting bullets screeched overhead, tearing plaster from the wall.

Ellis raised his gun under the table and shot between the chair legs, taking the Aurora agent in one knee. When the man fell, Ellis shot him through the faceplate.

Lincoln rushed in and helped him stand.

"We gotta get these people upstairs." Ellis told him.

Turner's shotgun blasted from elsewhere. He came thundering into the dining room. "Got one!"

If Garmon's estimates were correct, that left three, including the one that tried to snipe him. Ellis led the group, weaving through rooms back toward the hallway. Another agent tried to ambush them, and both he and Lincoln opened fire at the same instant, taking the man in the chest.

Just before Ellis stepped into the main corridor, bullets chewed up the doorframe, missing him by inches. He pulled back. The shooter had picked his location well. From this angle, it would be nearly impossible for them to return fire.

He was about to send Lincoln and Turner around to see if they could approach from a different direction when he heard a squawk, and then a thud.

Ellis chanced a look around the corner. The Aurora agent lay on the carpet several yards away. A carving knife jutted from his back.

Garmon stepped into the hallway and stood over the agent. It took him a long time to look up from the body.

Ellis nodded at him. "Let's go," he told the others.

This time he lurched toward the front of the house, throwing caution to the wind. He would get Doug and the others upstairs and then they would figure out where they went from he—

The front door crashed open just as they reached that grand staircase.

The last Aurora agent must've gotten tired of waiting for targets. He filled the doorway, his machine gun aimed at them. Ellis saw he would never have enough time to do anything before they were mowed down by a thousand bullets.

But there was only one shot.

The last of the advance team toppled over face first, revealing his killer at the base of the wide porch steps.

An unfamiliar black man holding a hunting rifle.

But next to him was someone else that Ellis *did* recognize.

"Hey guys," Chris Sloan said. "Is my sister here?"

WHITNEY +39:33

Tangela's nightmares had enough fodder to last a lifetime. That was why, when the hand began to shake her out of an already fitful slumber, she struggled against it. She just assumed it was part of the dream.

And when she opened her eyes and saw who the hand belonged to, she was sure of it.

Her father sat on the edge of the bed she'd fallen asleep in, with Chris right next to him.

"Hey, kiddo." Daryl Sloan sounded relieved. "You were really out. I didn't think we were gonna be able to wake you up."

Tangela pulled the rebreather mask down around her neck. "Daddy?"

"Yes, baby, it's me."

She sprang up from the bed and into his arms. When she was finally convinced this wasn't her exhausted imagination playing a trick, she wept against his neck.

"I told you, Tanj." Chris stroked the back of her head. "I told you he'd find us."

"*My mommy,*" she bawled, the pain opening up in the center of her all over again. "*My mommy is dead.*"

"I know." Her daddy squeezed her tighter, tight enough to make breathing difficult, but she didn't care. That strong embrace felt like bands of iron that would keep out all the nightmares of the world from now on. "I'll take care of you. We'll be a family."

"I kept it, Chris!" She reached back and picked up the soiled rag that was once Mr. Softy and held it up for inspection. The checkered blue pattern now looked all the same shade of brown. "I didn't let anything happen to him! Well, sort of."

Chris tried to speak, but settled for hugging her. Over his shoulder, she saw Maryland across the room, watching them with shimmering lines coursing down her face. She smiled through the tears and waggled her fingers, and Tangela waved back.

She wanted to stay here, surrounded by her family, and never have to move.

But Ellis' voice suddenly came into the room through the speakers in the ceiling, reminding her of her principal at school.

"I need to see everyone downstairs," he said. "Immediately."

WHITNEY +39:35

The living room in the center of the house was just big enough to contain the entire group. Sara gave her updated roll call and came up with forty-eight people, after adding Chris and Daryl Sloan, and Burt Weaver. Everyone was here, squeezed onto couches and lining the floors in rows, except the other new guy that had arrived with them. DeWitt, that was his name; he brought the total number to forty-nine.

Ellis had met him briefly as Chris' group came in, a lean, muscular, mid-forties guy with a scar across his chin and a bruise on his forehead. He seemed a little weird. When Turner, Lincoln, Garmon and the others crowded into the entrance of Château Decatur, he'd covered his face and coughed violently until they got him an oxygen tank. Even with that on, he felt ill. Maryland took him to one of the rooms around the corner, within earshot.

Ellis stood at the front of the group, the last survivors of Hurricane Whitney and all the horrors that blew into Port Allen with it, and said, "Aurora is coming. A hundred more soldiers will be here any minute. Agent Garmon believes they don't have any plans to bomb us, so that means they're going to storm this place and either shoot us or take us."

Silence. They didn't move, didn't look at one another. "They poisoned us and shot us. Killed our friends. Ran us out of our homes and hunted us like animals from one side of this city to the other. Now they want to finish the job and sweep us all under the rug, so the world will never know what happened. An entire city eradicated, just to protect their secret. I don't know about you folks, but I'm not going to just put my hands in the air and give up."

"You're talkin about fightin 'em," Turner said.

"Yes. But I need you. Every last one of you." He stopped, shook his head. "No, that isn't right. We need each other."

He paced in front of them like Patton after the world's worst ass-kicking. Blank faces met him. Ellis looked as many in the eye as he could—Lincoln, Carter, Maryland, Turner, Chris, Sara, Hernie, Doug, Sharon, Tangela, Daryl, Justin, Burt, Garmon, those he knew by name and those he didn't—and wished he didn't have to ask. He might be doing his best to look like Patton, but he didn't have the stomach to be a general.

"Do you really think we could beat them?" Sharon's small voice barely reached him.

"Sure we can!" Chris answered from the front. "I escaped from an entire camp! Trust me, these guys are morons!"

A few laughs came at that. Ellis waited for their attention. "For everyone that doesn't know, this is Chris and Daryl Sloan. Most of you have already heard their story about the base camp Aurora set up in the hills, and how a group of mostly unarmed civilians tore the place apart. Chris is right, these people aren't gods. They're not even that organized. But they *do* have numbers on their side, and they are a trained army. So I won't lie to you. No matter what we do, I think that in a few hours…we'll all be dead. If not from them, then from the P3."

The murmur of discontent that went through them made Ellis want to sit down. One man said, "What's the point in fighting then? My whole family is already dead."

"I'm sorry for that. We've all lost people since this started, and if they were here, I'm sure they wouldn't want the same thing for us. The point in fighting is to tell Aurora 'no.' To give them a great big middle finger. To make them remember that we're human beings and…and *Americans!* And just because we can't win, doesn't mean we can't do some damage. Look at what we've got on our side! Garmon can tell us everything he knows about them. And this house is a fortress. Reinforced walls, bulletproof glass. Maryland, did you get that vault open?"

"Yes."

"How many weapons in there?"

"I didn't have a week to take inventory. It looks like Rambo's wettest dream. More than enough for everyone in this room, I'm sure."

Ellis spread his arms. "We have everything we need to take a stand."

Justin pushed at the bandages over his forehead, revealing charred flesh. "So your solution to all their brutality is lowering ourselves to their level? Well, that *is* a great way to remind them we're Americans."

The comment divided the room. Angry people like Turner shouted back and forth at the pacifists.

"*SHUT UP!*" Ellis roared. Something in his damaged throat ruptured at the strain. Blood flooded his mouth, but he swallowed it. "This isn't a town hall debate about the ethics of war. We don't have time for that. Obviously, if you don't want to fight, I can't make you. But I need every last person in this room to consider picking up a weapon for the cause."

Daryl raised a finger to get his attention. "I'm with you, Officer Wright, I'm more than willing to fight, but you can't expect my kids to—"

"No, no. They'll be in the basement, along with Hernie and the other wounded."

"*What?*" Chris was on his feet in an instant, knocking away his father's hand. "No way, I've already fought these guys by myself!"

Ellis put a hand on the boy's shoulder. "I know, and if I didn't have a more important job for you, I'd slap a gun in your hand right now. But I need you downstairs manning the radio. Get in touch with someone: the media, the police…at this point, it doesn't matter. That's our only real chance at getting help. And if Aurora breaches the house, it's up to you to lead everyone out through the emergency exit down there."

"If there's an emergency exit, maybe we should all just go through it now and hide!" someone yelled. A few others voiced agreement.

"Sure, let's go puke our guts out in the woods rather than take a nice, clean bullet through the head," Lincoln argued.

"He's right," Ellis agreed. "This is it folks. End of the line. A few of the oxygen tanks are already empty and the rest soon will be. We leave, we die. We give up, we die. If not now, then in one of their labs. I'm not going to ask who's with me. I'm just going upstairs to start handing out weapons and assignments. Follow me when—and if—you're ready."

Ellis walked out without waiting. His heart felt like a black lump inside his chest.

WHITNEY +39:41

Kyler listened from the adjoining room, stretched out on a velvet couch. He giggled through most of it (Jesus, where had the poor sap gotten that speech, from a Disney movie about an underdog sports team?), stuffed a fist in his mouth to keep the shrieky titters from leaking out, but the comments about Aurora made his jaw clench.

I'll show you gods, little man, he thought. *You'll think you just got bitch-slapped by Zeus himself when I get done with you.*

Seeing Garmon had also thrown him for a big loop. The fucking traitor was working with these assholes. Kyler didn't know if the agent would recognize him, but he feigned P3 symptoms just to get away.

He could hear movement as the toy soldiers went off to play war. He got off the couch, intent on being issued a weapon, and found his path barred by a woman whose name he thought was Sara.

"Just coming to check on you." She had a practiced, authoritative air to her voice. Kyler had her pegged as a teacher. "Why are you up?"

"Reporting for duty." He grinned, and sketched a Boy Scout salute. She flinched at the sight of his smile, so he dialed it back. "Thought I'd lend a hand to General Custer out there."

She gave him an odd smile, and the urge to jam a knife in her face struck him with the force of a lightning bolt. This was it, the straw that was finally going to crack him. He could feel his sanity coming unraveled like a loose-knit sweater.

"We appreciate that, but I counted you with the wounded. You should really go downstairs and stay on the oxygen as long as possible."

He lifted an eyebrow. "I'd *really* like to help. Sounds like you people could use every available hand."

"We could, but not at the expense of anyone's health. Tell you what, I won't make you go downstairs, but you have to lay down again and stay on the O2 tank." She touched his forearm. "Doctor's orders."

He forced himself not to jerk away from her touch. As long as he was unarmed, he couldn't break cover. He only had one shot at taking back this situation. Once he was in charge, the blood would flow.

Of course, when his men arrived, he was just as likely to be killed as the rest of them.

And, in another forty-nine minutes, it wouldn't matter what he accomplished here; he would still be a dead man in the eyes of Aurora.

Kyler gave the woman another charming smile and retreated to the couch.

WHITNEY +39:45

The gun vault was a rectangular walk-in closet with steel walls and a door like the one on the precinct armory. Black felt covered the walls behind shelves of weapons arranged in aesthetic displays with drawers of corresponding ammunition beneath. Ellis and Garmon were the first upstairs.

The soldier gave a low whistle of appreciation. "Who *was* this guy?"

"A survivalist and hunting nut with enough money to make all his fantasies come true."

"You ain't kidding. Some of these are collector pieces."

"And very illegal." Ellis looked over a row of at least twenty rifles ranging from semi to fully automatic. Besides that, there were handguns, revolvers, shotguns, large caliber hunting rifles, some choice combat knives and swords, compound bows, and, at the back of the vault mounted on pegs, two beautiful Kalashnikovs restored to a more pristine condition than when they'd rolled off the assembly line.

"No explosives though," Garmon said. "Guess you can't have everything."

"I'd settle for people to use them."

But the others *did* come, not trudging in as he expected, but marching together in one resolute group. In fact, now that the decision was made, most of them actually seemed *happy*, talking and laughing, as though a weight was off their chest. None of them even mentioned what was about to happen. Ellis had an uncle that had seen combat in Vietnam. He said the soldiers were never more at ease then right before going into combat. And the more dangerous, the higher the spirits.

Ellis distributed firearms along with whatever ammo they could carry. Some of them looked befuddled, and he gave out the quickest firearm lessons he could. He and Garmon had already worked out a bare bones defensive strategy, and Ellis shouted out assignments to the refugees that would scatter them to every corner of the mansion.

He just prayed it would be enough.

WHITNEY +39:46

"You sexist prick," Maryland growled, as she popped a clip into the semi-automatic rifle Ellis had given her. More leftover knowledge from the hay days of her marriage. She hadn't so much as looked at one of Bryce's penile compensators in years. "You put all the girls together? What's that about, so we can paint each others nails while we fight?"

"No, Maryland. I did it because there's nothing more intimidating to a man than a bunch of pissed off women. Maybe if you tell them you're all on your period, they'll turn around and leave."

"Thanks." She leaned the weapon against a nearby chair and gave him a hug. "You make a pretty good general."

She thought he might've blushed, but his dark face was so bruised it was hard to tell. "Just make sure no one gets in through the back of the house. They'll take the rest of us from behind."

Maryland gave him a thumbs up and looked at the others she'd been assigned with. Several women had already started downstairs to their assigned position. Sara and Sharon were both standing with Doug, who fought back tears. He looked so young. She tried to tell herself he was just another teenager being sent to fight someone else's war, but it didn't make it any easier to see him giving his mother a hug. Maryland turned away to give them some privacy and found Carter in front of her with a machine gun that was almost bigger than he was.

"You know," he said, hefting the weapon in the crook of one arm, "just yesterday I told myself I never wanted to hold another gun. But I figured, hey, as long as I'm breaking personal ethics, might as well do it with one big enough to hit Pluto."

"You'll never be able to fire that thing with any accuracy."

"Yeah...but it'll sure make 'em think twice."

She rolled her eyes. "Where are you stationed?"

"Front of the house, along with that Weaver guy and a few others. Ellis wants us to fire down from the windows of your solarium up here on the second floor. What is a solarium anyway?"

She ignored the question and said, "Those bullets coming at you will have germs on them, you know."

Carter lifted a shoulder. "I think the phobias are on indefinite hiatus. What about you?"

"What *about* me?"

"Scared?"

"I don't get scared, Carter. Remember?"

They stared at one another for a comfortable few seconds. Then he opened his big fat mouth and ruined it with, "This is just like in Empire, when Han is leaving Hoth, and Leia can't just admit she loves him."

"No, it isn't," she snapped. "It isn't like anything. It's like our lives, you asshole. Okay?" She leaned forward and put her hands around the back of his neck, then pressed her lips against his for the barest of heartbeats before breaking away, snatching her rifle up, and heading toward the stairs.

"Let's roll, ladies. Nobody wants to live forever."

WHITNEY +39:47

Chris sat down at the radio desk in the basement.

"You sure you know how to use that?" his father asked. Tangela stood with him, holding his hand.

"C'mon, Dad, I've *built* more complicated stuff than this."

"Boy, don't I know that. I still don't know how you managed to broadcast free cable from a Speak N' Spell." He came over, bringing Tangela with him, then knelt beside the chair. "I...I have to go upstairs now. You need to know...I love both of you so much."

"I love you too," Tangela threw herself onto him. "Don't go!"

"I have to." He pulled Chris into the embrace also, crushing them so hard Chris thought his lungs would burst.

The basement was full of the wounded and those that were too sick or refused to fight. Hernie sprawled on the floor behind them with his injured leg propped up, and Justin and a few others were outside the door of the radio room, refusing to come into the creature's den. Chris couldn't blame them; the place was creepy enough in the dark with slime on the walls, but every few minutes a rattle and an angry squall would come from the corner. Maryland told them about fifty times to stay away from over there.

Still holding them, their father whispered, "If something happens…if you think those soldiers might be in the house…" He tapped Carter's rebreather still dangling from Tangela's neck. "Just take that mask and go through the escape hatch."

"What about you?" Tangela whined.

"Don't worry about me or anyone else. I know Officer Wright told you to help get these other people out, but don't even wait for them. Just run. Head toward the hills. There's people just on the other side of the Chantilly's, people everywhere along the freeway. If you take turns with the mask, you can make it to them."

"Okay Dad," Chris said, knowing he would do no such thing.

He finally released them, but kept hold of their hands. Chris squeezed his fingers.

"You're the best thing I ever did," his father said. Then he turned and ran from the basement without looking back.

Blinking away tears, Chris turned off Maryland's recorded broadcast and began manually scanning frequencies on the radio. Tangela hung over his shoulder with the tattered remains of Mr. Softy draped over one arm. Usually that annoyed the piss out of him, but he didn't mind so much now.

"Chris," the girl said. "I'm glad you're okay."

"Thanks. I'm glad *you're* okay."

"I love you."

"I love you too, sis."

"I love both you guys!" Hernie declared from the floor.

"We love you too, Hernie!" they answered together, and laughed.

WHITNEY +39:48

Lincoln met Turner and the rest of their squad at the indoor swimming pool that ran along the south side of the house. The room had a pleasantly clean smell after the assault their noses had taken over the past two days in this swamp of a city. The wide windows let in slats of yellow sunlight that fell across the tile floor and dappled in the crystal clear water. On the other side was a view of green lawn, stretching down a shallow hillside to the brick wall at the property's boundary. The other men were undoing latches and raising the glass to give them slits to fire through.

Turner knelt, set his shotgun aside, and began checking the elephantine hunting rifle he'd taken from the vault. Lincoln had two fully loaded pistols on him and some kind of Uzi-looking machine gun. He slid into the floor next to Turner, making sure his good ear faced the big man.

"My wife," Turner said without preamble. He'd swiped a twenty-four-year-old bottle of Chivas Royal from the wine cellar earlier, and popped it open now. Lincoln expected him to drink, but he just stared at the lip. "I figure she's dead now."

Lincoln ducked his head. "Yeah, man. Prob'ly."

"And we'll most likely be joinin her before lunchtime."

"Yep." Lincoln realized he was just too weary to care about dying. Right now any variety of sleep and peace would be welcome.

He thought briefly of Mac, and Charlie, and Lemiere. And what he'd told Ellis earlier, about wanting to join the Army.

"They're gonna pay first." Turner's eyes glistened. He lifted that bottle of booze that was older than Lincoln and took three long swallows, until a liquor trail glazed down both sides of his grizzled neck. He offered the bottle to Lincoln. "I'm takin as many of those SOB's down with me as I can."

Lincoln accepted. "I'll drink to that."

WHITNEY +39:49

"I ain't doin it, man, I ain't killin *nobody!* I'm part of the solution, not the problem! War begats war! Drop acid, not bombs!"

"Burt, stop." Daryl said. "Just stop with the bumper stickers, all right? We have to do this."

"No way, don't let them tell you passive aggressiveness don't work, man! Candlelight vigils have been proven effective!"

"Oh, it'll be *effective* all right," Garmon shouted from the door of the gun vault. "It'll *affect* you when Aurora shoves the candle up your ass."

"That's not helping," Daryl told him. Then, to Burt, "I know, I understand how you feel, but this is either fight or die."

"I'd rather die."

"Okay, but that's a choice. A choice *you* made. Because you had a lifetime of experiences that let you form your opinions." Daryl put his hands on the hippie's shoulders. "But what about my kids downstairs? If these soldiers get in here, they'll never have the same opportunity. I thought the whole reason you peacenik types want to save the planet is so the generations of tomorrow will have a chance."

"Daryl, don't play mind games with me."

"Burt...*please.*"

The other man sighed. "Gimme the gun."

Daryl handed him a hunting rifle and a box of ammo. "I'll be right downstairs with that cop, guarding the front door."

"Ugh, I feel dirty just touchin this thing. You owe me, Daryl. You gotta...you gotta give five-hundred bucks to Greenpeace every year for the rest of your life! Oh, and help fund my newsletter!"

"You have a newsletter?"

"Yeah, The Truth-Behind-Fluoride Times."

Their conversation ended as the man his son had introduced as Carter drifted over to a spot at one of the windows looking down on the front lawn. He leaned against the wall with a sigh. "I'm pretty sure I'm in love, fellas."

Burt snorted. "That's what the greeting card companies want you to think, dude."

Carter smirked. "Have you met my friend Hernie? I think you two would have a lot to talk about."

WHITNEY +39:50

"That's it." It was closing in on 11:30 AM, and their army was mobilized. Ellis had tried to split everyone up with people they didn't know, so emotion wouldn't affect judgment. He took a new pistol and tucked it into his pocket, then grabbed the twin Kalashnikovs off the back wall. The pain pills were in full swing, so the action barely hurt. Of course, he also felt like laying his head against the nearest horizontal surface and sleeping for about a decade.

"I guess I'll...wait in the basement," Garmon said from outside the vault. He coughed and wiped blood from his mouth.

"Wait." Ellis held out one of the rifles. "You're with me."

The agent accepted the weapon. "Thanks."

"You earned it. The last of the oxygen tanks are downstairs; grab one and use it. If we had time, I'd find you some clothes."

"That's okay, I always wanted to die in my underwear."

Ellis hobbled to the house intercom mounted just outside the vault and pressed the TALK button. "Aurora will be here soon. From this moment on, consider anyone that tries to get into this house your enemy. Just concentrate on defending your assigned area."

He leaned in closer to the microphone slots and said, "Good luck."

WHITNEY +39:52

Mattinson jumped off the helicopter in front of the house before it touched down. One of the agents met him under the whirring blades.

"Status?"

"Most of the ground forces are here, sir. The rest are inbound. I can have choppers fully armed with a complement of Hellfires here within minutes."

"No, absolutely not! Kyler doesn't want any more mass destruction, especially this close to the outskirts of the city. Where's the advance team? I want to talk to them."

"They went radio silent just before we arrived. They have to be either dead or captured."

"Fuck! Who *are* these people?"

"I don't know, but they're probably ready for us."

The front gates of the mansion were just ahead. A yellow Hummer was parked outside, half on the sidewalk, and a group of other luxury cars sat just on the other side of the wrought iron as a rudimentary barricade. "Do we have any idea why here? Why *this* house?"

"No, sir. It's the only one still standing on the block, but they might've just ended up here." He paused, then asked, "Should we extend an offer of surrender?"

"What? *Surrender?* We're not even giving them the chance! Send in an initial wave from all sides. First priority is to destroy that radio they're using to broadcast, then I want every last person in that place taken out. No mercy, no prisoners."

WHITNEY +39:56

Maryland perched on the edge of a chair and look out the back windows at the tennis and basketball courts. The place was secure except for the back door, which looked like it had been knocked off its hinges by a wrecking ball. It didn't matter though; if they did their job, no one should even make it to this point.

She used the chance to clean some of the wounds from the baby monsters. To her right, Sara hunched forward with grim determination, slowly sweeping the back yard with a rifle. On the other side of the school teacher, Sharon wept softly. The ten or so other ladies in the room fell somewhere between 'killing machine' and 'blubbering jelly puddle' on the emotional scale.

With an army of bloodthirsty soldiers set to descend on them any minute, all Maryland could think about was Carter.

And then Sara whispered, "Here they come."

Along the back wall of the property, Aurora agents in their black suits scaled the metal spikes, repelling down the inside of the brick. Their movements synchronized as they turned toward the house and started across the lawn.

"Oh God, oh God, I can't do this," Sharon moaned. Sara put a hand on her back without taking her eyes off the advancing horde.

"Let's get this over with." Maryland slid the barrel of her gun into the gap at the bottom of the window. A numbness settled over her, one that made her sore throat, ragged nerves, and roiling stomach seem very far away.

WHITNEY +39:57

The solarium had hardwood floors, deck chairs, a marble-topped table and a low bookshelf arranged like the deck of a cruise liner behind a curving glass wall that stretched halfway overhead before it met the roof. Outside, it formed the top half of the mansion's glass front, but from in here the view gave Carter, Burt, and the others an excellent view outside the grounds, and of the choppers sitting motionless on the street that ran parallel to the brick wall. They looked like the same gunships that had blown up the Dome.

"This is gonna be bad, ain't it?" Burt asked. "I mean, shit… we're about to die." He sounded more in awe than afraid.

Carter ignored him. He was riveted to the sleek forms pouring in the front gate. Once through, they spread out around the car blockade and assembled into a strung-out line, with machine guns up and braced against their shoulders. The sunlight gleamed on their suits and glinted off those cruel, tinted faceplates. He stopped counting somewhere around thirty.

They fell into step and marched toward the house.

Carter aimed his huge weapon at those that would pass directly beneath him, held his finger against the trigger, and waited.

WHITNEY +39:58

"Just a second longer…let them get a little closer…" Garmon murmured to Ellis, Daryl, and the others kneeling in the front lobby. The bottom row of windows in the glass front wall of the house opened on a motorized track, sliding up just enough to give them a firing sight line. They stood side by side, like Civil War infantry.

"Almost…"

Ellis took aim with the Kalashnikov. Pointed it at the closest of their attackers. Next to him, a tremor went through Daryl.

Garmon said calmly, "Now."

In the war for Château Decatur, Ellis fired the first shot.

The others opened up a split second later. The mansion foyer exploded with noise and the smell of roasted cordite.

WHITNEY +39:59

The sound of gunfire from the front of the house reached the men by the pool.

"Hit 'em!" Lincoln yelled.

Everyone opened fire together, various weapons chattering and booming.

The soldiers creeping up toward them were obviously surprised to receive fire. The ones that didn't go down immediately looked around for cover that just wasn't there, or jumped to the ground.

Beside him, Turner's face turned dark scarlet as he pumped round after round from the rifle. He was a good shot, too; Lincoln saw him choose targets and hit nearly every one. The return fire from outside cracked one pane of glass and managed to get through the loophole of another, shredding the leg of one of their men.

The soldiers pressed forward, but Lincoln was thrilled to see a couple turn to retreat.

"Keep it up, they're on the run!" he cried over the gunfire.

"Don't get too excited," Turner said, snorting like a bull. Blood leaked from both corners of his mouth, and one of his eyes was a burning, red orb of burst capillaries. "It can't be this easy."

WHITNEY +40:00

The women's firearm accuracy was low. Most of them kept bracing their weapons wrong even after Maryland shouted out instructions, and ended up firing wild or, in one extreme case, breaking her own nose when the recoil bounced the weapon out of her hands. The soldiers were able to entrench themselves on the far side of the tennis courts and keep up a constant volley of shots.

"Watch the left! *The left!*"

The entire northeast corner of the house was unprotected, and a battalion of troops had made it up to the rose gardens and were creeping along the side of the house. She swung her rifle in their direction and opened up, ending at least three human lives. She forced herself to think of Tom and Imogene, of Heather and Randy, even of Kordi and Dan and Walter, who might not've been killed directly by Aurora's actions, but would probably be alive if they'd manufactured their damn population-controlling chemical somewhere else. The fury built until it tore the guilt to shreds.

"*YOU BASTARDS!*" she shrieked, unleashing that Amazon. This was where she'd gotten the willpower to leave Bryce, the strength to survive this long, and she wasn't about to let a bunch of two-bit Uncle Sam zombies in rubber pajamas take it from her now.

Tears flowed as she pulled the trigger.

WHITNEY +40:01

"Give me status!" Mattinson barked.

"These civilians are dug in deep, and seriously armed! They have resistance on both floors, all the way around the structure! This house is built like a fucking rock!" His field director listened to another report and then turned to him. "They're pushing us back!"

Mattinson felt a vein in his forehead throb. "Fine. Let's play a little rougher."

WHITNEY +40:02

Carter stopped firing as one of the helicopters parked on the street lifted off the ground. It hovered even with their bank of firing positions on the second floor, then swung in their direction. The pilot was visible under the dark canopy. The cannons mounted to either side looked big enough to shoot bullets the size of apples.

And suddenly he understood exactly what was about to happen.

"Look out!" He yelled the warning as he pushed away from the window, hitting the wooden floor of the solarium on his belly. A barrage of thunder worse than even the storm's caterwaul buffeted his ears as thousands of rounds punched through the bulletproof glass of Château Decatur. They reduced the plaster and wood of the back wall to tatters. The air was peppered with flying wood chips and heavier particles.

Burt Weaver stumbled past as Carter crawled through the wreckage. The hippie bled profusely from a wound at his shoulder. Carter reached, wanting to pull him out of the carnage, but the endless spray of bullets vaporized his torso a heartbeat later.

Carter had almost reached the door when the fire stopped. His eardrums throbbed in the sudden silence. He glanced over his shoulder.

The glass was gone, along with some of the walls and the roof, leaving a smoking crater in the side of the house. Through the chewed edges, he could see the helicopter hovering outside. The room was destroyed, covered in debris and body parts, like a terrorist bomb site. Of the six or so other people that had been in here with him, only one other had been quick enough to duck. The guy looked shell-shocked as he struggled under a sheet of wall plaster.

Something above them groaned. Carter saw the edge of suspended ceiling dip as it started to collapse, and got a queer sense of déjà vu. He clawed his way up and ran for the door. His fellow defender was buried under building material.

Carter charged into the hallway. Up and down the corridor, the other people Ellis had stationed on the second floor poked their heads out to see what was going on. He tried to shout out another warning, but his throat was full of a thick coating of dust and his own blood. He settled for motioning for them to follow and ran for the grand staircase.

WHITNEY +40:03

A shudder like an earthquake ran through the mansion after the helicopter stopped firing. Rubble and bodies rained down in chewed pieces on the lawn. The side walls of the house buckled, and Ellis saw the chopper start to move around the corner just before the window wall cracked, turning into a shimmering jigsaw puzzle.

The other defenders jumped away from their posts during the chopper's onslaught, but now they charged back and resumed firing. Targets were sparse. On the far side of the lawn, more reinforcements hustled onto the grounds. These had shoulder-mounted weapons that looked like bazookas. They took aim at the front of the house and fired rounds that left wispy tracers in the air.

Ellis heard several of them strike and bounce off the exterior, so they weren't explosive. The ones that hit the windows had enough force to shatter the stressed glass. Several canisters that looked like tin cans hit the staircase and rolled across the floor, billowing reams of white smoke.

"Gas!" Ellis yelled. He put a hand over his mouth but caught a whiff anyway; tears squirted from his eyes, even the one that was swollen closed, and he coughed so hard he could barely inhale. The cloud was too thick to see through. Panic gripped him.

"It's just tear gas!" someone shouted in his ear. He felt cold plastic press to his face. He blinked away tears and caught a glimpse of Garmon through the haze, handing him one of the almost empty oxygen tanks.

He took the mask and slipped it on, then pulled the straps of the tank over his shoulders. He could breathe, but he still could barely see through the weeping and smoke. People flooded down the stairs, and he directed them deeper into the house. He caught sight of Carter and then pushed Daryl ahead of him as the man choked and gasped. He couldn't let Chris and Tangela's one remaining parent die.

BRRRR-AAAK!

As their defenses crumbled, the Aurora agents crossed the lawn and clawed their way through the front windows. The house had been breached. All their preparation and determination had bought them maybe fifteen minutes. Why had he ever thought they would be able to make a difference?

Several other people had gotten their hands on oxygen tanks and refused to run, taking cover behind the stairwell and the first doorways of the house to return fire. Their muzzles produced ghostly flashes in the swirling tear gas, like lightning in a cloud.

Ellis pressed against the closest wall and shot at the black shapes as they floated from the smoke.

WHITNEY +40:04

"*What was that?*" Lincoln took his eye away from gun sight on his pistol. The hollow boom a few seconds ago had rocked the house, audible even over the constant concussion of their shots.

"*I don't know and I don't care!*" Turner continued firing one shell after another.

The soldiers threw themselves at their side of the house in droves. The defenders held them back admirably, but at least two of Lincoln's group had run out of ammo and another dropped his weapon and fled.

Lincoln aimed at the closest agent and squeezed off several shots. They all missed, but behind his target, he saw the property wall explode, throwing mortar and chunks of brick.

What entered the yard looked like a vehicle from a *Mad Max* movie. Five feet high, six wheels, covered with burnished steel plates, like a metallic turtle. On its front end was a spike-tipped scoop that reminded him of a bulldozer's shovel. The armored car's momentum slowed after crashing through the wall, but it picked up speed as it crossed the lawn. Aurora agents scrambled out of its path.

That wicked front end pointed right at them as it accelerated toward the house.

"*Get back!*" Lincoln screamed.

They leapt away from the windows before the vehicle rammed the wall, bashing its way through until the front four wheels rested on tile. Lincoln cried out as shrapnel hit his backside, cutting deep into his shoulders, right at his still tender gunshot wound. The man shooting to his left went down with a spear of wood jutting from his eye. Fear turned to chaos as men dove into the pool to escape, turning the water pink. The stench of diesel smothered the bitter gun smoke.

Lincoln and several others stayed to fire on the car. Bullets ricocheted off its armored hide. A hatch on the top flew open, and out popped an agent with a heavy chain gun. He sprayed bullets down at them, shredding two more of their people.

Turner had been on the opposite side, and now he gave a cough-filled roar as he unloaded on the figure. The machine-gunner toppled forward, falling over the side of the vehicle. Turner swapped out the rifle for his shotgun and hoisted himself to the hood of the car with an agility that didn't match his large size. He fired down into the open hatch again and again, cocking the shotgun mechanically. Screams of pain drifted out.

More agents on the way. Lincoln could see them regrouping to work their way across the lawn, a crowd of twenty. There were only five men left alive in here, and most of them were crawling from the far side of the pool and running inside the house.

Lincoln yelled, *"Turner, c'mon man, we're finished! We gotta go!"*

Turner, still standing astride the armored car, turned his head. Lincoln wasn't even sure the man recognized him anymore. Bloody tears poured down his face, and his mouth was stretched in a crazed, gore-caked grimace.

Then he ducked under the hole the armored car bashed through the wall, jumped off the backside, and ran to meet the soldiers all alone, waving his weapon over his head.

Lincoln turned away before he could see the big man get mowed down and took off around the pool.

WHITNEY +40:05

The end came too fast for Maryland to follow.

One second they stood at their posts, firing at the Aurora troops as they advanced, perhaps one bullet in ten striking home.

The next, the first of their enemies reached the mangled back door and hit it with his shoulder. He stood in the entry, as black as Death himself, and Ellis was wrong, the sight of so many women didn't faze him in the least. He shot the woman closest to him in the face before someone could turn a gun on him.

And then they were overrun.

Soldiers flooded the room. Bullets flew, no longer separated by glass and brick. Maryland grabbed Sharon and shoved her toward the hallway leading to the center of the house. She didn't need urging; the girl dropped her gun and fled.

Sara stood her ground, trying to jam another clip into her pistol while two of the soldiers advanced on her. Maryland fired the last burst from her rifle, hit them both in the midsection. She ran toward the woman.

"Let's go!"

Sara nodded. Together, they fled the outmatched firefight, throwing rounds over their shoulders. They headed into the main corridor, back toward the front of the house. As they passed the first cross hall, Maryland heard glass shatter, and then glanced to her right to see more bio-suited agents swarming into her home.

Nowhere to go. The Aurora agents came from all directions. They were all about to die.

WHITNEY +40:07

Kyler poked his head out of the lounge.

The noise out here was deafening. The place was a warzone. Once again, he had to give these people credit for valiant effort, but it wouldn't do any good. Mattinson must be throwing every man he had at this place.

And Kyler was trapped in the middle.

From his left came a gaggle of women screaming down the hall, the few that had guns firing blindly at the agents chasing them. To the right, he could see wisps of what smelled like tear gas, and still more people running away in panic. The groups would collide in seconds. Part of him wanted to stop and watch; the resulting bloodshed as they jammed up the hall and trampled each other would be spectacular.

But if he didn't find a way out, he would be gunned down with them.

He couldn't just wave his arms and surrender. With all this confusion, they would shoot him before they even had a chance to recognize him. No, he had to get word to Mattinson that he was in here.

He needed that radio they were using to broadcast their SOS.

Kyler slipped out of the room just before the two crowds reached him and blended into the chaos.

WHITNEY +40:09

They couldn't hold the front foyer any longer. The tear gas had thinned, to be replaced by bullets and enemy troops. They needed to regroup, start thinking about the next line of defense. If there was enough people left for one.

"*RETREAT!*" Ellis bellowed, shrugging out of the heavy 02 tank. He'd lost track of Garmon somewhere along the way. He abandoned his position and charged further into the house.

Anarchy reigned. Confused civilians scattered everywhere. Aurora agents poured into the main hallways from all directions, firing at will.

A bloodbath.

He didn't know what to do.

Carter and Daryl swam out of the chaos. Both men were bloody and wounded. They clutched at him.

"*C'mon!*" Carter shouted.

"*Where?*"

"*The middle of the house! We'll get out through the basement with the kids!*"

"*We can't leave! We can't quit!*"

Carter shook his head vehemently. "*It's over, Ellis! This is lost! Let's get out while we can!*"

Ellis nodded and followed them into the nearest cross hall, along with a contingent of other survivors. He was too stunned to tell them it wouldn't make any difference.

WHITNEY +40:10

Lincoln limped through the house. He heard more gunshots ahead. Glass breaking somewhere. Slamming doors. Screams. Booted feet behind him as the agents from the pool tore through the mansion.

He had to make it to the basement, warn Chris and the others to get moving. He was the closest, after all. He turned right, into the hallway that would take him there, and saw the way blocked by a platoon hurtling in his direction. They raised their weapons and fired.

Bee stings slapped his upper left forearm, his shoulder and chest, his right side, his thighs. He was half-thrown, half-stumbled back into the nearest wall. A flash of Mr. Kim rose in his thoughts. The lights in his head tried to go out, but somehow Lincoln remained conscious.

He threw himself through the nearest door before they could fire again. He landed on tile. The kitchen. He was in that huge kitchen. Lincoln crawled forward, dragging his numb legs behind him, leaving a snail's trail of blood across the field of gleaming white squares.

Those heavy footsteps were coming. In that moment, it seemed like they had been chasing him his whole life. He reached up, wanting to be on his feet when the end came, and grabbed the first thing his hand landed on.

A cold, slick handle.

He recognized it.

And smiled.

Lincoln flopped over on his back in the floor, then propped himself against the metal surface leading up to the handle. Blood poured down his chest, but he didn't notice. Aurora agents crowded into the room from all directions, sweeping for threats with their weapons before spotting his bloody, crumpled form.

"Hey guys," he rasped, choking on blood. "I want you...to meet a friend of mine."

He jerked the handle above him, breaking the vacuum seal and releasing a rush of cool air.

The door to the walk-in freezer swung open.

WHITNEY +40:11

Kyler navigated away from the gunshots, working his way into the interior of the house. The last of this civilian army had devolved into hysteria. They careened down hallways, slammed into one another, and ducked into doorways to hide. He was dimly aware that all this violence had given him a raging erection, and that the world had taken on a pulsing red tint behind his eyeballs.

Ahead, he saw Little Miss Nurse, the one who wouldn't let him leave the lounge, running with some of the other hens. He followed as they made a quick right turn. At least if he couldn't find the radio, he could have the satisfaction of snapping her neck after all.

Light came from another doorway on the left. The ladies passed by, then stopped to gape through it. He reached them, actually had his hands almost at her throat, when he saw what they were looking at through the open door.

Inside was a kitchen packed with at least twenty of his men. They had their guns pointed at something in the floor, blocked from Kyler's view by their bodies. As he watched, a gleaming metal door on the other side of the crowd swung open.

From the darkness within came a green tornado full of claws and teeth.

It moved so fast, he would be hard pressed to ever give a physical description. The thing hurtled through the air and landed in the midst of his men before they could react, then went into a killing frenzy that made Kyler's mouth water. It grabbed one agent around the throat and ripped the head from his shoulders, taking a length of spinal column, and then spun to disembowel another, one swipe of its claws tearing through bio-suit and flesh alike.

No, Kyler would never be able to describe its textured skin and misshapen body with any degree of accuracy, but he could tell what it was all the same.

Beautiful. Poetry in deadly motion.

Fear broke the agents' trance. Kyler watched as they opened fire from all directions, filling the air with gun smoke. Their arrangement in a rough semicircle caused a few of them to shoot each other, but they were too terrified to care. The monster raised its long arms, tilted back its head, and let loose a roar that had far more in common with a parakeet than it did a lion. The bullets that struck it drew blood, but didn't seem to do serious damage. It waded into its attackers, clawing and biting, ripping through one trained soldier after another. In fifteen seconds, it had felled at least half that many men.

And with an intuitive blink, Kyler understood. The mangled bodies in the cemetery. Those recorded screams.

These crazy Port Allen civvies had some kind of pet demon on a leash.

The rest of the troops retreated, moving toward the kitchen exit on the right. The beast stormed through their bullets. The noise felt like it was splitting his skull, but Kyler drifted after them to watch, going around the outside corner of the kitchen so as not to be in the path of fire.

More Aurora agents streamed in from all directions, drawn by the screams of their fellow soldiers. They weren't even concerned with their intended targets anymore, pushing aside the last survivors to get to the source of the commotion. The war seemed to have been called off for the moment. Civilians crept from their hiding places and followed the action along with Kyler.

The beast drove the agents all the way to the shattered front wall of the house, where glass was strewn across the floor and the last shreds of tear gas dissipated. There must be forty of them now, probably all the agents still in the house. They surrounded the beast, backing up and trying to stay ahead of it as they opened fire with clip after clip. The rounds chewed it apart, but still it lurched after them, too stubborn to go down. Finally, after the monster swept up a man in each hand and dashed their heads together hard enough to splatter brains, a few of them turned and fled, and the line broke.

The creature limped after them, crossing the long front steps of the mansion and emerging into the bright sunlight on the lawn.

Kyler and the rest of the survivors went to the window to watch.

WHITNEY +40:13

Mattinson heard the screams from inside the house, and now a flood of agents ran across the front lawn like the devil was giving chase. And maybe he was. Something that looked like a slimy, green gorilla came dragging out on their heels. The thing looked out of place ambling down the bright driveway with the sun reflecting off its wet skin, a detail that somehow made this nightmare too real. It lumbered after the men, snagged one of the stragglers, lifted him in the air, and proceeded to dismember him a limb at a time.

"Good God Almighty," Mattinson whispered. "What the hell is that?" No one had an answer, but he didn't expect one.

The creature was wounded. It loped across the grass, one arm hanging limp and almost dragging the ground, blackish fluid that could only be blood leaking from at least two dozen injuries across its broad body. It swung its head side-to-side like a wobbly radar dish, but came relentlessly toward the gate, where Mattinson and the last of the men waited.

"*Kill it, kill that thing!*" he screamed. Mattinson was struck by a sudden, blinding terror that it was actually heading for *him*.

The agents at the gate opened up fire in one united front, using the heavy-duty Rippers. The manufacturers claimed those bullets could take down a rhinoceros, but this beast just kept coming. It jerked and twitched, bits of flesh ripping away as it struggled forward.

But the hail of bullets finally hit something vital, and it staggered once before dropping to its knees.

The agents closed in all sides, still shooting. There was enough firepower concentrated on it now to level a building. It seemed to dwindle before their eyes, the bullets whittling it down to a pulpy mess.

With a final, feeble swipe at the air, it collapsed to the grass and lay still.

The men stopped firing. There was silence.

Mattinson expelled the breath he'd been holding and opened up the comm. "All agents, anyone still in the house…pull back. Nobody else goes in until we know what the fuck we're dealing with."

WHITNEY +40:14

Ellis, Carter, and Daryl were facing four Aurora agents in a back hallway when the soldiers suddenly turned tail and ran. The sounds of conflict died across the entire house. Their ears rang in the sudden silence. The trio drifted back through the wreckage, looking for survivors and trying to figure out what had happened.

They reached the broken front windows just in time to watch the monster's death throes in front of the house. Ellis spotted Maryland, Sara, and Sharon among the small crowd, along with that DeWitt guy. Doug stumbled down the stairs with a couple of other survivors and was immediately engulfed by his mother and girlfriend. When she spotted Carter, Maryland jumped into his arms, sagging against him as they stared out the window.

On the lawn, the Aurora troops treated the beast's body with caution, touching it with long poles from eight feet away and jumping back. The rest streamed from either side of Château Decatur as they abandoned the campaign. The house creaked and groaned, the silence more deafening than the gunfire.

Ellis said, "I never thought I'd have a reason to thank that monster, but…there it is."

"About time it started earning its keep," Carter muttered. "We've been feeding it for two days now."

"What…what was that thing?" DeWitt turned dreamily from the window. The look on his face creeped Ellis out. It was the glaze of someone mooning over an absent lover.

Ellis slapped an arm around his shoulders. Creepy or not, he felt like kissing the guy. He knew he was in shock—they all were—and riding high on pain pills, but right now he felt giddy. "Don't worry about it. It's dead now. Okay folks, this probably didn't buy us much time. We need to figure out who else survived and come up with a new game plan. Has anyone seen Lincoln?"

As he asked this question, Garmon pelted into the foyer from the hallway beside the staircase with a rifle over his shoulder. "What happened? The agents are pulling out of the house and—" He stopped as his gaze lit upon the man standing next to Ellis. His eyes bugged. "What the hell is *he* doing here?"

Ellis gave the man's shoulders a squeeze. "This is DeWitt, re-member? He came in with Daryl and Chris."

Garmon shook his head as forcefully as a little kid denying the monster in his closet. He jabbed a finger. "That's Kyler! *That's the guy in charge of this whole operation!*"

Ellis' sluggish brain—reluctant to give up its elation—took en-tirely too long to process this.

DeWitt threw an elbow into his stomach. He grunted and dou-bled over, and his attacker snatched the pistol still tucked into Ellis' waistband.

Everything slowed. Maryland screamed something, and across the room Garmon pulled the rifle off his shoulder.

But Kyler brought the pistol up much faster.

"Here's your discharge, fuckwad." The curved scar on his jaw stretched forward as he fired.

The bullet shredded Garmon's throat. His eyes widened. For the first time, Ellis realized how much he looked like Billy Dunham. The young soldier grabbed at the wound, blood bubbling between his fingers, and then tumbled back on the stairs.

Ellis grabbed for the arm holding the gun. Kyler tried to jerk away, but Ellis held on, pulling the man close until they snarled in each other's faces. He could hear someone else shouting now, but he was too focused on the struggle. Kyler bent his elbow, dragging the weapon down between them. Ellis fought to wrench it from his hand.

A muffled explosion sounded between their pressed bodies.

Heat blossomed deep in the center of Ellis' chest. His heart ached, seeming to fold in on itself.

Ellis let go of Kyler and fell backward as the world went black.

WHITNEY +40:15

Ellis—the officer who had saved them all countless times, the man Maryland would credit with getting them this far—fell straight backward like a cut-down tree, thudding heavily onto his back in the front foyer. She broke away from Carter and ran to him, sliding across the last few feet of tile on her knees. He had a deep, red crater in the center of his chest. His mouth hung open and his throat worked, but no sound came out, not the slightest gurgle. His one good eye pleaded.

"Get away from him." The man Garmon had called Kyler stood a few feet away with the gun he'd taken. He stared at the blood pouring out of Ellis, his words distracted.

"He's dying, you asshole!" Maryland applied pressure to the wound with her bare hands—memories of Heather and Tom flickering through the dark recesses of her head—but the blood flow was almost nonexistent. "Oh Jesus, I think it hit his heart!"

No one moved. What could they do anyway? She took Ellis' hand and held it, watched as he gasped a few more times. His movement slowed and then stopped.

"God." She looked to Carter. "He's gone."

Kyler giggled. It was such an off-putting, fingernails-on-a-chalkboard sound that at first Maryland couldn't identify it. This man standing before them looked to be in his mid-forties, but that malevolent laugh was something that would've come out of a child as it lit ants on a fire with a magnifying glass. He seemed to realize the sound was coming from him and choked it off, then swept the room with his weapon.

"You." Carter's eyes flashed. "Are you really this Kyler guy?"

"That's what it says on my secret decoder ring."

"Then this is all because of you. Everything that's happened."

"You got two in a row right! Now, let's put those guns down. Nice and slow, everybody." The few with weapons complied. Kyler backed away until he stood against the wall, next to the doorway into the rest of the house. "Okay, excellent. I have to give you goobers some credit. You're one crafty, resilient bunch of motherfuckers. I may have to add this scenario to our training exercises."

"You're despicable," Maryland spat from where she crouched next to Ellis.

He aimed the gun down at her forehead, but she realized she wasn't all that scared of it. "Save the sticks and stones for someone who gives a shit. Where's this radio you dipsticks are broadcasting from?"

"Don't tell him!" Daryl blurted.

"He can find it himself." Maryland didn't take her eyes from Kyler.

"Oh, I will." He pointed the gun at a space just over everyone's heads. "But if I don't get an answer to my next question, I'm gonna start turning skulls into bone soup: what the fuck was that thing that killed my men?"

"We don't know," Carter answered.

Kyler fired a shot that grazed past his leg close enough to send a flutter of denim into the air. He flinched. "Don't feed me that. It went after those agents like a trained pit bull."

"Only because they were stupid enough to get in its way. That thing has been hunting us almost as long as you people. We don't know what it is or where it came from. Truth is, our best guess is that it was connected to *you* somehow."

Kyler regarded him for a long moment. "Don't I wish. About twenty-five of those things dropped into an enemy camp, and I wouldn't even need agents anymore."

"What are you going to do with us?" Sara asked from behind Carter. Doug and Sharon huddled behind her.

Kyler didn't hesitate, didn't miss a beat in his answer, and the cheerfulness in his voice made Maryland hate him even more. "I'm going to round up anyone else still alive in this house and walk your happy asses out before a firing squad on the front lawn." He glanced at his watch. "And hey, look at that, if I do it in the next fifteen minutes, I might just get to keep my pension. A merry Christmas to all, and to all a good night."

From the doorway next to him, a dark hand holding a pistol eased around the corner. The tip of the barrel snuggled up against Kyler's temple. He stiffened, the smirk falling off his face.

Lincoln leaned around the corner and gasped, "I always preferred Kwanzaa, asshole."

WHITNEY +40:18

Château Decatur looked like it had been run through a cheese grater. Bullets had chewed apart everything, played connect-the-dots on walls, ceiling, and floors, and turned furniture into kindling. The carpet was covered in a layer of plaster, glass, and dirt, and littered with bodies. They lay sprawled where they died, both Aurora agents and civilians alike. Carter and the other survivors followed Lincoln as he marched Kyler at gunpoint ahead of them.

Daryl split off to check on the people in the basement, but the rest ended up back in the small den where Ellis had given his pre-battle pep talk. Lincoln prodded Kyler with the gun, then grabbed his neck and shoved him face-first into the nearest wall.

"You son of a *bitch!*" The gangbanger's voice cracked on the last syllable. He pulled the man back and then slammed him forward again. The sound of Kyler's nose breaking was like the snap of a dry twig. He slid into the floor.

"Lincoln, don't," Carter told him.

"*He killed Ellis!*"

"I know. I know he did. But you have to stop. You're hurt."

Hurt was an understatement. A single bullet had killed Ellis, but Lincoln looked like he was bleeding from at least seven or eight. Not a single inch of his clothing was unstained, and a slick, red river ran down both his muscular arms, dripping on the carpet. Only rage seemed to keep him on his feet. He turned to Carter with tears rolling down his cheeks. "He's gotta pay! For Ellis and Imogene and all the others!"

"He will. But let's figure this out first before we do anything hasty."

On the floor, Kyler rolled over. His nose was broken far worse than Mac's had been, crooked to the right and gushing blood. Carter had built the guy up in his head to epic proportions, a cross between a pro-wrestler and a vampire, but he actually looked more like a 70's era game show host. He gave them a solid-gold smile. "Don't stop now homeboy, I think you just fixed my deviated septum."

Lincoln reared back and kicked him low in the stomach. Kyler barked in pain.

"Shut your mouth," Carter told him, "Or I'll let him finish." He turned around and took stock. A total of nine people were in this room: himself and Maryland…Lincoln and Kyler in the corner… Sara, Doug and Sharon huddled just inside the door…and two men he knew by face but not by name. He pointed at them. "Go keep a watch at the front of the house. I don't know why the war got called off, but it might not last. Yell if you see those bastards make the slightest move to come back at us."

As they left, Daryl came in with three others that had been assigned to rooms along the north side of the house, and two of the people from the basement. "I don't think anyone else survived," he said. "Counting my kids and everyone else downstairs, there are seventeen of us."

Next to Carter, Maryland slumped on the edge of a ripped chair and bent over until her face was on her knees.

"*You hear that?*" Lincoln screamed. He pushed the pistol harder against Kyler's forehead, hand trembling. "*Seventeen people out of a whole fuckin* city?"

"Give me the gun, Lincoln," Carter said.

The gangbanger spun halfway around, wobbled and collapsed without warning.

They scrambled to him. Daryl snatched up the pistol and held Kyler at bay. Carter, Doug, and Sharon lifted Lincoln and laid him on the nearest intact couch.

"He's alive," Sara pronounced, leaning over him. "But just barely. We have to get this bleeding stopped."

Kyler snorted blood through his ruined nose, then coughed up even more. "Kinda pointless, wouldn't you say? You're all gonna be just as dead as him by the time this is over."

"Kill him." Maryland's voice was muffled because her head was still in her lap. She raised it to look at Carter, and he was terrified at the stark vengeance blazing in her eyes. "Kill that shit right now. At least we can do one good thing and take him out of the world before we go."

"We could do that." Carter looked down at Kyler. "But you wouldn't be any good to us dead…would you?"

The man rolled his eyes, easy and nonchalant. "You can't bargain for me. My people, the ones out there at the gate? They won't negotiate. And even if they did, once I was in charge of things, I'd put all of you—along with my second-in-command—to death on the spot."

"See? Just fucking kill the son of a bitch!" Maryland snarled.

Carter put a hand up. It was his turn to be good cop. He said to Kyler, "Get up. Sit in that chair. If you make any sudden moves, Daryl is gonna shoot you."

Kyler complied. He did so without the slightest hesitation or even a trace of fear. He was completely confident that he'd won. Now he sat in the middle of the room, legs crossed, hands clasped in his lap, nose still dribbling blood, while Sara worked on Lincoln. Carter grabbed another chair and turned it backward in front of him, then straddled it.

"Here's the deal," Carter said. "I don't want to bargain *for* you. I want to bargain *with* you."

"You have nothing I need. Except your lives."

"But *why?* Can you at least explain that to me?"

"Because you're infected with a deadly virus that cannot be allowed to spread outside the borders of this city."

"Now you're just lying."

Kyler shrugged. "Prove it."

"I don't have to. This isn't a Senate subcommittee hearing. We're just two guys talking, and both of us know the truth: you engineered some kind of biomolecular poison, accidentally let it out, and then killed an entire city just to protect yourself."

The other man snorted and shook his head in disgust. "That simple, huh? There couldn't be any more to it than that, like where this is all for the good of the nation. Where I'm working to protect this country and all it's spineless, whining liberals in ways they couldn't imagine."

"Really? And how does poisoning third word countries fit in to that resumé?"

A single muscle in Kyler's cheek twitched, then that grin came right back. "The world is only getting smaller, and this country already has far too small a slice of it."

"Oh my God. This is all just a *real estate scam?*" Carter gave tired laughter that irritated his throat and made Kyler's eyes blaze. "Didn't Superman already stop Lex Luthor from trying this?"

"Let's see if you're still laughing when we're all sardine-packaged like Japan."

Carter threw his hands up. "Whatever, we're off topic. My point was, is there any way you could ever trust us to just...keep it quiet?"

"Don't be retarded. One of you would be selling your story to *Nightline* before the week was out. Besides, a move like that isn't even my call. Even if I agreed to it, my higher-ups would just rescind the order. You would never be able to run far enough."

"Goddamn it!" Carter finally lost all the patience he'd been striving for. He jumped up from the chair and paced. It didn't help, not like it used to; that remedy had been for a phobia-ridden man who was just as dead now as any of the other corpses in this house. "We didn't ask for any of this! You and Aurora and your damn Project Mercury!"

"Boy...Garmon sure did a lot of talking, didn't he? Jesus, and you wonder why I can't let you out of here alive."

"He didn't tell us if there was a cure," Maryland said. Everyone in the room looked up, Sara stopping her work on Lincoln to wait for Kyler's response.

He pooched out his lower lip. "It's called a neutralizer. Renders P3 inert in both organic and inorganic substances. As soon as the dead are cleared out, it'll be sprayed over the entire city."

Maryland moaned, but it was an angry, exasperated noise. "Fucking Christ, you had this the whole time?" Her whole face scrunched up, so hard and fast that tears literally shot out of her slitted eyes. She balled her fists and shrieked, "*Why didn't you use it? What was the point of killing us if you could've just cured us?*"

Kyler drank up her anger; maybe he was part vampire after all. His grin turned feral. "You gotta think long term, sweetness. The lab boys that invented all this crap know what it does to the human body now, but in ten years? *Twenty?* Who knows what kind of birth defects your kids would end up with? Shit like that has a way of coming back on you. Even for upper-echelon government agencies that don't technically exist." He grunted. "So it was either kill you or cure you, and the Aurora brass thought they had a much better chance at keeping their new toy if we ghosted you all and blamed it on the hurricane."

"But why *us?*" Carter demanded. "Why Port Allen? There must be some reason you were making the stuff here in the first place!"

"Aw…you think you're special. That's cute." Kyler began to giggle again, as unsettling as a pack of hyenas. But, as mirthful as they sounded, they never touched his eyes. Those were just as reptilian as the monster's had been while they regarded Carter. "Look, you don't matter. There's no grandiose plan. This was a small, isolated, anonymous port city, where it would be easy to ship the chemical out. When you think about it, we cared about you *so little*," he held up thumb and forefinger and stared through the gap, giggling all the time, "we didn't even make sure the tanks we stored it in would hold up to a hurricane." That grin grew even wider, the laughter more shrill and choppy, just *hee hee hee*, like a cricket's chirp. "In fact—and this is a little secret between you and me—maybe I made the tanks faulty *on purpose*. Just to see what a trial run on a bunch of yokels would look like."

Carter punched him.

He'd never hit anyone in his life, and this one was in motion before he even realized. He threw his shoulder behind the swing and aimed for Kyler's broken nose. His knuckles crunched into the other man's face. He drew back his sore hand for another, but froze when he saw the smile still in place, those giggles coming harder than ever.

And suddenly he understood.

"You're crazy," Carter whispered.

WHITNEY +40:23

Chris did his best to ignore the sounds of battle filtering through the floor as he continued broadcasting. The commotion riled the infant monsters in the corner. They rattled their makeshift cages every few seconds and mewled like kittens. When his father shouted down that things were okay but to stay ready, Chris went right on working.

The desperation in his voice increased with each channel he tried. He'd reached two other people on CB radios—one a widower in Beaumont and the other a trucker just outside Lake Charles—both of whom listened to his story skeptically and promised to call the police in their areas, one cop that told him to stop playing with Daddy's radio or he would be arrested, and one Aurora agent that ordered him to stop broadcasting immediately or face 'stiff penalties.' That one almost made him laugh.

He clicked to another channel and repeated, "Mayday, mayday, this is Chris Sloan broadcasting from the city of Port Allen. I need immediate assistance. If you can hear me, please respond."

He was about to turn the dial when a voice answered, "Yeah, hey, woah, I'm here."

Chris leaned toward the mic and cut to the heart of the matter. "Who are you and where are you?"

"Uh, this is Mike Frainey." The voice was thick with accent and coming in loud and clear on the radio speaker. "I'm stuck in this godawful traffic outside. Hey, what the hell's goin on in there, pardner? We can't get a straight answer from these military boys."

"You're *outside* the city?" Chris blurted.

"That's what I said, son."

The tiniest thread of hope inched through him. "This is an absolute emergency! We're under attack!"

"Attack? What sorta attack?"

"I don't have time to explain! I'm trying to reach the authorities, or someone in the media!"

"Well…which one ya want? NBC, CBS, ABC? FOX?"

"It doesn't ma—" Chris frowned. "Wait, what?"

"I'm lookin at about a dozen news choppers on the ground twenty yards from me. Military won't let 'em in the air. Just tell me who ya want and I'll go fetch 'em. I'm sure they'd *loooove* to talk to you."

WHITNEY +40:25

"I don't think he's gonna make it much longer," Sara said, when Kyler's laughter stopped. She and Sharon hovered over Lincoln, putting pressure on every wound they could reach and looking like a bad game of Twister.

"I'm out of ideas," Carter admitted. "This guy is nuts, how am I supposed to reason with that?"

"What was that he said about his pension earlier?" Daryl asked.

"What?"

"He said if he got us out before a firing squad in the next fifteen minutes, he'd save his pension."

Carter nodded and passed the question on to Kyler. "What was that about?"

They looked to Kyler, whose lips pursed with annoyance again. The man may be insane, but he obviously hated being out of control of any given situation, even for a second. He wiped blood from his still-dripping nose and said, "My superiors gave me a time limit to finish this. If the situation isn't...*contained*...by then, I get disavowed. Hunted till the end of my days. Which won't be very long with a lungful of P3 in me."

"Dad! DAD!" They all turned to see Chris running into the room, winded and coughing.

"I told you to stay downstairs!" Daryl snapped.

Chris took in the room and frowned. "Mr. DeWitt? What's going on?"

"Don't worry about that. What do you need?"

"I got a hold of some media people downstairs! A bunch of 'em! They're all right outside the city!"

Everyone in the room glanced around at one another. No one seemed to know what this meant.

"What did you tell them?" Carter asked.

"Nothing, I asked them to wait while I got one of you."

Carter spun back to Kyler, unable to stop his own triumphant grin. "How are your bosses gonna feel if we spill the beans about your little cover-up?"

"It's bullshit." Kyler sniffled and winced. "You told him to say that. He doesn't have anyone on the radio."

"Come downstairs and see for yourself."

"You know what, it doesn't matter. No one will believe a word of it. Just be another urban legend, another unsolved mystery. Even if they did, Aurora will find a way to smoothe it over. You can tell them whatever you want. I can't help you."

Carter clenched both fists. It was like trying to play chess with a bulldozer, and every time he thought he had checkmate, the dozer just rolled over the entire board. "You can't call your people? Convince them it's in their best interest to let us go?"

"With *what?* You're coming to the bargaining table threatening to tattle! Which, if you're released you could still do at any time anyway! There's no gain in it for them to let you go, whether you tell your story or not! Aurora's just been set back months on a major biological weapon, so they're not going to be in the mood to deal!"

The words were like cold water thrown in Carter's face, bringing him fully awake. He looked at Maryland, looked at Daryl, looked at Chris. An excited buzz was building at the base of his skull.

"What if we could replace that biological weapon?"

"With what? Some home-brewed moonshine and your mother's panties?"

Carter sighed. "You know, I'm more used to hearing this than saying it, but can you be serious for five seconds?"

Kyler's eyes narrowed. "I'm listening."

"You said you could use the monster."

"The dead thing on the lawn? Thanks, but we already have it. I'm sure my people are taking the corpse in for DNA sampling as we speak."

Carter shook his head. "I'm talking about *live* specimens. Babies. Three of them. We have them trapped downstairs."

Kyler's face changed. That persistent self-confidence faded, replaced by a wistful, wall-eyed stare.

Carter continued. "You let us go, give all of us the P3 neutralizer, and we provide you with three live creatures and a promise to never talk about any of this. You said yourself no one would believe us even if we told. We live, and you get to keep your job. The alternative is, we kill the babies and burn them, then spill our guts over the radio. For whatever harm it will do to Aurora."

"Then we splatter your lunatic brains across the ceiling," Daryl added.

Kyler frowned at the plaster over their heads as though considering what his gray matter would look like up there, and rubbed the scar on his chin.

"Carter, can I speak to you over here?" Maryland asked.

"Just a sec."

"*Now.*"

Maryland grabbed his arm and led him away, to a far corner of the room. She clamped his wrist and crushed down, then spoke through clenched teeth. "No, he doesn't get this, he doesn't get off scott-free after everything that's happened."

"He does if it means our lives. There's been enough death already. Punishing him isn't gonna change that."

"*No.* He has to be stopped. So this doesn't happen again to someone else."

"Then let someone else do it. This is our only chance. If there's a way out, let's take it." Carter cupped her face in both palms. "Please be with me on this."

She closed her eyes and nodded.

"What's it gonna be Kyler?" he said, without turning from her. "Time's wasting, and if Lincoln dies, the deal is off."

"I'll...have to see the specimens first."

WHITNEY +40:29

Kyler thought they were bluffing, right up until they lifted a piece of sheet metal from the top of what looked like a filing cabinet drawer and let him peek at what was inside. He was so preprogrammed for deception that the idea someone could still tell the truth in this world was foreign and a little unnerving.

He stared at the contents of the box while the creatures tried to claw their way out to rip off his face. They were just as gorgeous as their mother. Sure, they could probably get enough of a DNA sample off her corpse, but Aurora's current cloning technologies were flawed, to say the least.

But with these three breeding *live*, in captivity...

All that potential destruction made his mouth water.

Kyler looked up at their expectant faces.

God, he *hated* making people happy.

"Can I borrow your radio?" he asked.

SURRENDER

The sky over Port Allen was full of traffic.

Lincoln could see them all from his gurney through bleary eyes, like a swarm of gnats high above: news choppers and small charter planes and air ambulances like the one on the front lawn of Château Decatur that he was about to be loaded into. Their trust in Kyler never got past a Tupac-Biggie level, so they'd insisted the air ban be lifted so help could fly to their location. Outside witnesses would be the only way for them to stay alive after surrendering the monster's babies. Of course, that also meant everyone with the means had surged into the airspace, eager for a look at the ravaged city that had been mysteriously shut down since Whitney.

It had taken ten minutes for a lone soldier to bring Kyler a secured laptop so he could contact his superiors and make arrangements, then another hour and a half for Aurora to deploy the neutralizer across the city. The army on the front lawn took their dead and cleared out, while the survivors watched Kyler warily across the sprawling basement. Lincoln regained consciousness during this, and Sara caught him up to speed. Only after the first medical helicopter touched down did they let Kyler leave through the escape hatch with the babies.

"He's as stabilized as we can get him with this equipment," one of the EMT's said. The morphine they'd given Lincoln made the voice waver in and out. It would feel so good to close his eyes and sleep, but first...

"The others," he gasped. "Where are they...?"

"We can't wait. We need to get you loaded immediately." They pushed his gurney toward the open rear doors of the red-and-white helicopter.

"Just a second." Someone strolled up behind the EMT and put a hand on his shoulder. Lincoln recognized Kyler even with the tape over his nose, and the sudden rush of fury brought him back toward consciousness. Kyler flashed a badge. "Harry Peters, FBI. I need a second alone with this young man."

"Absolutely not, he's got multiple gunshot wounds! I can't even believe he's alive!"

"I don't believe I asked for permission."

The EMT hesitated, glancing at the swelling in the middle of Kyler's face. "Fine, just for a second." They retreated a short distance.

"Well, *Harry Peters*," Lincoln wheezed. He reached over the bedrail and pawed at Kyler's shirt, but he couldn't make his fingers close to get a grip. "You get your job back, you murderer?"

"Keep your voice down, kiddo," Kyler said cheerfully, shoving his hand back down. "It's not too late to take you out of this equation, you know. And yes, I sure did, thanks to your mutant turtles."

"I hope they fuckin eat you."

"That's not very nice. Those little suckers are gonna revolutionize modern warfare. I just wish I knew what the fuck they were."

"Don't talk to me like we're friends. Between you, the hurricane, and that monster, all my friends are dead."

"All right then, straight to business. Looks like you'll be the first out of here, so I thought you might want this." Kyler pulled a tiny syringe from the breast pocket of his shirt and held it where the EMT's couldn't see.

"How do I know it ain't somethin that's gonna kill me?"

"Because I can't have you dying in a civilian hospital if there's a chance of even a single P3 molecule being in your system. But in the end, I guess you'll just have to trust me, the same way I'm trusting all of you." He grabbed Lincoln's upper arm, plunged the needle through the remains of his shirt and into his skin, then pressed the plunger. "There now, all better."

Lincoln didn't feel any different, but he was pretty numb in the first place. The world tried to swirl away, but he clung to it. "They're gonna ask us. What happened in this city, how that house got shot up. Everything. What are we supposed to say, man?"

"The simplest lies are the easiest. Just say you don't remember. We'll take care of the rest."

"Yeah, I guess that's what you assholes do best, right? Take care of things?"

Kyler smirked. "You should feel lucky. I don't know of a single civilian today that even knows Aurora exists, and you guys just got a free pass."

Lincoln gave him a shaky middle finger. "Look at me, you dumb fuck. You think I feel lucky?"

Kyler tried to turn away, but this time Lincoln sat all the way up and grabbed the man's arm. The EMT's came running.

"One more thing..." he hissed. There were two of Kyler now, then three, then a dozen. "I ever see you again...you a dead man."

"Then we better make sure that doesn't happen, Lincoln Briggs."

"I don't know, I been thinkin about joinin the army." The EMT's were at his sides now, forcing him to lay back and pushing Kyler away. "Or maybe becomin a cop..."

The last thing he remembered before slipping into haunted dreams was Kyler saying, "I'll tell you kid...I sure wouldn't mind if you were playing for my team..."

WHITNEY +42:24

Maryland stood on the driveway, looking back at the home she'd shared with Bryce. She was far enough out where she could get the big picture. The place looked like a wrecking ball had gone through the front. Rooms were exposed. Walls collapsed. The rash of bullet pockmarks across the exterior made the mansion look like it had measles.

It was unlivable, fit only to be torn down.

She couldn't be happier.

The thought had occurred to her that, since she and Bryce were technically still married, all of the money was hers, but she didn't think she wanted it. She recalled that exhilarating rush when she'd left just before Whitney hit, and the frigid fear that set in afterward. She had proof now, confirmation she could survive the absolute worst, and the thought of going back to maids and cooks and shopping made her feel sicker than the P3 ever could.

Maybe she would give it all away. To a charity to help out third-world countries.

The grounds were alive with paramedics and police, all flown in by helicopter. The reporters hadn't been allowed on the property, but they gathered outside the broken gate behind her, snapping pictures. So far, none of the seventeen people that were being dubbed the 'Port Allen Survivors' had been bothered too much with questions, but Maryland knew they were coming. They would have a lot of explaining to do in the days and weeks and months ahead, and, though the prospect sounded exhausting, and she had no idea what they would say (or what Aurora would *want* them to say; Kyler's people were debriefing them on official stories tomorrow), she was too thrilled to be alive to care.

And somewhere in the middle of it, she would have to find time to take a trip to England. The message Tom had given her was soggy and covered with grime, but she would get it to the right hands.

"Maryland!" someone called from her left. She found Tangela streaking across the lawn toward her, with Mr. Softy draped over her shoulder. Chris and Daryl tried to keep up. Maryland knelt and swept the girl up.

"Hi, baby." She buried her tears in the girl's soft braids.

"Are you coming with us to the hospital?"

"I'll be along as soon as I can. There's some things I need to take care of here." *So I never, ever have to come back.*

Chris arrived, and she gave him a hug too. "I'm glad you're all right. We were worried when we lost you."

"I'm sorry about Tom and Imogene," he whispered. "They were my friends."

"Mine too."

Daryl Sloan reached her, and she placed Tangela back on her feet to hold out a hand. He shoved it away and hugged her instead.

"They told me…they wouldn't have survived without you. I can never thank you enough. Never repay you for everything you people did."

"I'm just so sorry about your wife."

He released her and gave a short nod while he wiped at his nose with the back of his thumb. The kids leaned into him. "We have to go. They're holding one of the police helicopters for us. But we wanted to give you this back first."

He held out Carter's rebreather mask by its thick strap.

She took the device. "It's not mine, but I'll get it to the owner. If I don't see you tonight, I'll talk to you at the briefing in the morning."

They nodded. Daryl led Chris and Tangela away again, both of them looking over their shoulder just before they disappeared into the police chopper. She closed her eyes, put a hand over her mouth, and turned away.

When she opened them again, her gaze landed on Carter. He stood at one of the air ambulances over Hernie as they loaded him inside.

She suddenly found herself terrified at the prospect of talking to him.

A few hours ago, their lives had pretty much been called on account of rain. It had been easy to look past the whole leaving-Bryce-and-her-entire-life when she thought she could be dead any minute. Who could blame her for leaning on the closest nice guy in a situation like that?

Okay, maybe she'd done a little more than just lean. She could remember what it felt like to kiss him, but that could've been a dream. And a long term future with Carter Vance? Let's be realistic: he was the biggest nerd she'd ever met, they had nothing in common, and he just plain wasn't her type. He would understand that. Especially the nerd part. Surely he didn't expect the two of them to ride off into the sunset either.

Maryland took a deep breath. She couldn't put this off. If he'd gotten the wrong idea, she would set him straight. Show him that not a single damn thing about the idea of the two of them in the real world made any sense.

She sighed and started over.

WHITNEY +42:30

The EMT—a kid in his early-twenties that kept nervously glancing over at the remains of Château Decatur every few seconds—told

Carter that Hernie would probably walk again, but not well. His foot dangled from the end of his leg, the bones inside pulverized. He squeezed Carter's hand hard enough to almost do the same to while they gave him a shot for the pain and then strapped him into a gurney.

They were wheeling him out to the one of the last air ambulances when he began a rapid-fire series of questions.

"Mr. Carter, where are they taking me?"

"To the hospital, Hern-ster, remember?"

"Oh yeah. And the government won't try to get me there?"

"I'd worry more about the insurance companies."

"Will you come too?"

"I'll be there as soon as I can."

"And will you make sure they don't do anything with Hatch, so I can bury him?"

"You got it, buddy."

Hernie stopped for a second and tried to tap his temple with one finger. The drugs must be taking effect though, because he missed and poked his eyeball instead. "Do you think they'll bring me right back to Port Allen when I'm well?"

"Maybe not *right* back. The city's pretty much scrap. It'll take them years to rebuild, if they ever do." Hernie's face fell at this news. "Why do you wanna come back so bad anyway?"

"I don't know any other streets. I might get lost if I have to go somewhere else."

"Hernie..." Carter reached down and wiped a combination smear of mud and snot off the man's cheek and didn't even flinch. He was too tired to be proud. "I was kinda thinking...if you wanted...maybe you could just come live with me."

The joy that entered the Hispanic man's face could've powered the entire city. "Oh yes, Mr. Carter, oh pleasey-please, you're my best friend, and—!"

"Okay, yes, enough." Carter struggled to keep the smile off his face. "Pipe down or people are gonna think I proposed to you. But you have to drop this 'mister' business. I'm just Carter, all right?"

"Carter," Hernie said, trying it out. "And I promise not to give you hugs ever again!"

"Actually...the hugs will probably work."

They lifted the gurney up and started closing doors. Carter stepped back as the blades whipped the air around him. Hernie raised up and waved out the window at him for as long as possible before disappearing into the dazzling blue sky.

"Hey Fear Club." Maryland stood behind him. "I think this is yours."

She underhanded the rebreather at him. He caught it in midair and held the thing in front of him. The clear plastic looked yellowed and dried bits of blood still clung to the interior, his or Maryland's or Tangela's. He opened his hands and let it fall to the lawn, then stepped on it. The brittle crunch as it broke was immensely satisfying.

Maryland said, "Utensils in the garbage disposal."

He blinked. "Huh?"

"Ever since I was a kid, I've been terrified of a knife or fork falling down in the garbage disposal and then, when I turn it on, the blades hit it just right and make it fly out and stab into my eye. It got so bad I would hold up a plate as a shield before I flicked the switch."

He grinned. "Wow. That's a good one."

"I'm also not too fond of food that holds the shape of a can after it comes out."

"Great googly-moogly. You're more messed up than I am."

He took a step toward her, but she held up a hand to stop him.

"Carter, look. I just...I don't know what's gonna happen. Neither one of us does. I basically became a widow this morning so there's a lot of unresolved issues there I need to work through, and there's always the chance this between us was all just because of the situation and aw, fuck it."

She slid her arms under his and around his back. Before he knew it, her lips were back on his and, oh, look at that, her tongue was in his mouth. He pushed his own against it and didn't even wonder—*not for one second!*—how many foreign germs it might be releasing into his bloodstream.

"We'll take it as it comes," he said, when they finally surfaced for air. "I'm okay, you're okay, the universe is center."

She cocked her head. "I like that. It's pretty. What is it?"

Carter Vance shrugged and held Maryland Williams closer.

"Just something I used to say."

Like this novel?

YOUR REVIEWS HELP!

In the modern world, customer reviews are essential for any product. The artists who create the work you enjoy need your help growing their audience. Please visit Goodreads or the website of the company that sold you this novel to leave a review, or even just a star rating. Posting about the book on social media is also appreciated.

About the Author

Russell C. Connor has been writing horror since the age of five, and is the author of two short story collections, five eNovellas, and fourteen novels. His books have won two Independent Publisher Awards and a Readers' Favorite Award. He has been a member of the DFW Writers' Workshop since 2006, and served as president for two years. He lives in Fort Worth, Texas with his rabid dog, demented film collection, mistress of the dark, and demonspawn daughter.

His next novel—*The Halls of Moambati*, Volume IV of *The Dark Filament Ephemeris*—will be available 2021.